D1435631

BEST SHORT NOVELS 2006

BEST
SHORT
NOVELS
2006

Edited by
Jonathan Strahan

SCIENCE
FICTION

For my sister, Barbara

Each year the list grows longer. Any book like this one is as much the product of a small community of friends, family, and colleagues as it is the work of one person. This year I'd particularly like to thank: my agent Howard Morhaim; my editor, Andrew Wheeler, who has been generous and supportive well above and beyond the call; Peter Crowther of PS Publishing and Bill Schafer of Subterranean Press who were all kind, gracious, and generous when they didn't have to be; Justin Ackroyd, who has been a vital supporter of my work and this anthology series; Jack Dann, anthology guru, pal, and confidante; my *Locus* colleagues Nick Gevers and Rich Horton, who have always been there to discuss the best short fiction of the year when I needed it most; and Trevor Quachri and Brian Bieniowski at Dell Magazines who made sure I got my fix every month. Thanks also to the following good friends and colleagues without whom this book would have been much poorer, and much less fun to do: Lou Anders, Kathryn Cramer, Ellen Datlow, Gardner Dozois, Ernest Lilley, David Hartwell, Kelly Link, Gavin Grant, Sean Williams, the various posters to the Night Shade Message Boards, and all of the book's contributors.

And, last but not least, the big ones. Extra special thanks to my three angels, Marianne, Jessica, and Sophie, who make every day an adventure and fill it with joy, and to CHARLES, friend, mentor, and inspiration, who has given me so much.

⋙ Contents ⋘

Introduction

by Jonathan Strahan

Tʜɪs ɪs ᴛʜᴇ third time that I've sat down and sifted through a year's worth of short fiction to assemble a selection of the year's best science fiction and fantasy "short novels." As in previous years, I was struck by the quality, the depth, and breadth, of work being published and am more convinced than ever that this is a golden time in the history of short fiction in our field. And that is why this book exists: to gather the best longer stories published each year in a continuing series of affordable, easy-to-find volumes. Terry Carr did something similar when, back in 1979 and 1980, he edited two excellent volumes of the *The Best Science Fiction Novellas of the Year*, but he was restricted to just four or five stories. Given more space I was confident it could work, and work well. That confidence was borne out by the very generous response of readers and critics to the two earlier volumes in this series, which in turn have led to the book you now hold in your hands.

It's probably worth touching base again, briefly, on what I mean by a "short novel" and what kind of stories I've looked to gather here. While the Science Fiction and Fantasy Writers of America define a novella as being a work of fiction between 17,500 and 40,000 words in length, I've taken a somewhat more relaxed approach, considering stories that are over 15,000 words to be short novels. Why? The novella should give a writer enough room to build a world, create believable characters, and examine a single idea in some depth. As long as a writer does those things, I don't really want to quibble over word count, especially not in a book that contains stories that not long ago would have been considered novels. I also felt that it would be a better service to you, the reader, to bring together the best stories I could find, rather than worry too much about the details of definition. And what kind of stories? Well, I was looking for new, challenging, and interesting science fiction and fantasy that would entertain, provoke, and reward. I think the nine stories in this year's book do all of those things, and more.

A quick overview of the year in short fiction makes it clear that these are more than slightly confusing times. Trade journal *Locus* reported that they saw 2,320 new short stories in 2005, up from 2,127 in 2004, and when they factored in additional online publications that number increased to near 3,000 (almost double the amount counted by the magazine a decade earlier in 1995). This was counterbalanced by a contraction in the number of markets available to writers. *Amazing Stories* ceased publication in 2005, as did *SciFiction* and *Lennox Avenue.* The closure of *SciFiction* sent shockwaves through the SF community. Since its launch in 2000, the Ellen Datlow–edited site had won every major award in the field and had developed into one of the top two or three sources for quality short fiction anywhere. While it will be greatly missed, there were some encouraging signs. The other major magazines, *Asimov's, Analog, Fantasy & Science Fiction, Realms of Fantasy,* and *Interzone,* all had good years, and by year's end we'd seen Orson Scott Card's new site *Intergalactic Medicine Show* launched, and Baen Books had announced an ambitious new online publication, *Jim Baen's Universe,* to be edited by Eric Flint, that has the potential to become an important source of new short fiction in coming years.

The best and most reliable place to find great short novels in 2005 remained the four major genre magazines, *Asimov's, F&SF, Analog,* and *SciFiction.* Ellen Datlow's *SciFiction*'s final year was a good one. Although it only published two novellas, one each by Lucius Shepard and Kim Newman, it featured excellent longer stories by Howard Waldrop, Vonda McIntyre, Jeffrey Ford, and others. *Asimov's,* in its first full year under new editor Sheila

Williams, published six novellas, one a reprint. The best of these, and the best science fiction story of the year, was Ian McDonald's extraordinary "The Little Goddess," though Connie Willis's "Inside Job" was very fine, and I was impressed with Tom Purdom's "Bank Run." *F&SF*, which was probably the pick of the magazines this year, published four novellas during 2005. The best of these was Kelly Link's wonderful "Magic for Beginners," though Laird Barron's "The Imago Sequence" was very impressive. *F&SF* also published a number of excellent stories of near novella length, including Peter S. Beagle's "Two Hearts," Bruce Sterling's "The Blemmye's Strategem," and Matt Hughes's "The Gist Hunter." *Analog*, which has been consistently impressive of late and had its best year in a decade or more, published five novellas during 2005. The best of these were Harry Turtledove's fine alternate history "Audubon in Atlantis" and Wil McCarthy's "The Policeman's Daughter," though I also liked John Barnes's "The Diversification of Its Fancy."

This only represents the tip of the iceberg. A welcome trend in recent years has been the proliferation of novella-length chapbooks, mostly from small or independent presses. British small press publisher PS Publishing released five such books in 2005. The best of these was Jeffrey Ford's novel-length *The Cosmology of the Wider World*, but Steven Erikson's *Fishin' with Grandma Matchie* and *The Devil Delivered*, and Vera Nazarian's *The Clock King and the Queen of the Hourglass* were all excellent. U.S. publisher Tachyon published the remarkabe *Burn* by James Patrick Kelly that, were it not for length, would be in these pages. And, had I seen it in time, I would have included Alastair Reynolds' *Understanding Space and Time*, which was published by the British Science Fiction Association late in the year.

It was, by recent standards, a disappointing year for original anthologies. Unlike recent years, no single science fiction or fantasy anthology really stood head and shoulders above the rest. That said, the best science fiction anthology of the year was Peter Crowther's *Constellations*, which featured some excellent work by Gwyneth Jones, Paul McAuley, Alastair Reynolds, and others. The best fantasy anthology was Marvin Kaye's *The Fair Folk*. One in the welcome sequence of novella anthologies from the Science

Fiction Book Club, it featured an excellent story, "The Gypsy in the Wood," by Kim Newman and very good ones by Patricia McKillip, Megan Lindholm, and others. The SFBC also published Mike Resnick's *Down These Dark Spaceways*. It's probably worth mentioning here that stories from these books fall outside the remit of this volume.

All of which brings us to the end of a possibly too brief roundup of the year in short novels. If I could have squeezed another story or two in here I would have added the aforementioned James Patrick Kelly's *Burn* and Alastair Reynolds' *Understanding Space and Time*, along with Kim Newman's "The Gypsy in the Wood," and Tom Purdom's "Bank Run." But, as large as this book is, no book is infinite, so let those stand as something for the intrepid reader to seek out later. For the moment, I'd like to close by sincerely thanking the Science Fiction Book Club, and especially my editor Andrew Wheeler, for their confidence in this series and this book, and by thanking you, the reader, for your support as well. I hope you enjoy reading this book as much as I enjoyed assembling it, and that we get to meet again next year to resume our journey.

Jonathan Strahan
February 2006
Perth, Western Australia

BEST
SHORT
NOVELS
2006

THE LITTLE GODDESS
by Ian McDonald

Ian McDonald was born in 1960 in Manchester, England, and moved to Northern Ireland in 1965. He is the author of ten novels, most notably Desolation Road, Out on Blue Six, Chaga, Ares Express, *and Philip K. Dick award–winner* King of Morning, Queen of Day. *His most recent, and most acclaimed, novel is British SF award winner and Hugo and Arthur C. Clarke award nominee,* River of Gods. *His short fiction has won the Sturgeon and British Science Fiction awards, been nominated for the Nebula, World Fantasy, and Tiptree awards, and is collected in* Empire Dreams *and* Speaking in Tongues. *He has a new novel,* Brasyl, *due in 2006.*

☙ ☙ ☙

I REMEMBER THE night I became a goddess.

The men collected me from the hotel at sunset. I was light-headed with hunger, for the child-assessors said I must not eat on the day of the test. I had been up since dawn; the washing and dressing and making up were a long and tiring business. My parents bathed my feet in the bidet. We had never seen such a thing before and that seemed the natural use for it. None of us had ever stayed in a hotel. We thought it most grand, though I see now that it was a budget tourist chain. I remember the smell of onions cooking in *ghee* as I came down in the elevator. It smelled like the best food in the world.

I know the men must have been priests but I cannot remember if they wore formal dress. My mother cried in the lobby; my father's mouth was pulled in and he held his eyes wide, in that way that grown-ups do when they want to cry but cannot let tears be seen. There were two other girls for the test staying in the same hotel. I did not know them; they were from other villages where the *devi* could live. Their parents wept unashamedly. I could not understand it; their daughters might be goddesses.

On the street rickshaw drivers and pedestrians hooted and waved at us with our red robes and third eyes on our foreheads. The *devi*, the *devi* look! Best of all fortune! The other girls held on tight to the men's hands. I lifted my skirts and stepped into the car with the darkened windows.

They took us to the Hanumandhoka. Police and machines kept the people out of the Durbar Square. I remember staring long at the machines, with their legs like steel chickens' and naked blades in their hands. The King's Own fighting machines. Then I saw the temple and its great roofs sweeping up and up and up into the red sunset and I thought for one instant the upturned eaves were bleeding.

The room was long and dim and stuffily warm. Low evening light shone in dusty rays through cracks and slits in the carved wood; so bright it almost burned. Outside you could hear the traffic and the bustle of tourists. The walls seemed thin but at the same time kilometres thick. Durbar Square was a world away. The room smelled of brassy metal. I did not recognise it then but I know it now as the smell of blood. Beneath the blood was another smell, of time piled thick as dust. One of the two women who would be my guardians if I passed the test told me the temple was five hundred years old. She was a short, round woman with a face that always seemed to be smiling but when you looked closely you saw it was not. She made us sit on the floor on red cushions while the men brought the rest of the girls. Some of them were crying already. When there were ten of us the two women left and the door was closed. We sat for a long time in the heat of the long room. Some of the girls fidgeted and chattered but I gave all my attention to the wall carvings and soon I was lost. It has always been easy for me to lose myself; in Shakya I could disappear for hours in the movement of clouds across the mountain, in the ripple of the grey river far below and the flap of the prayer banner in the wind. My parents saw it as a sign of my inborn divinity, one of the thirty-two that mark those girls in whom the goddess may dwell.

In the failing light I read the story of Jayaprakash Malla playing dice with the *devi* Taleju Bhawani who came to him in the shape of a red snake and left with the vow that she would only return to the Kings of Kathmandu as a virgin girl of low caste, to spite their haughtiness. I could not read its end in the darkness, but I did not need to. I was its end, or one of the other nine low-caste girls in the god-house of the *devi*.

Then the doors burst open wide and firecrackers exploded and through the rattle and smoke red demons leaped into the hall. Behind them men in crimson beat pans and clappers and bells. At once two of the girls began to cry and the two women came and took them away. But I knew the monsters were just silly men. In masks. These were not even close to demons. I have seen demons, after the rain clouds when the light comes low down the valley and all the mountains leap up as one. Stone demons, kilometres high. I have heard their voices, and their breath does not smell like onions. The silly men danced close to me, shaking their red manes and red tongues but I could see their eyes behind the painted holes and they were afraid of me.

Then the door banged open again with another crash of fireworks and more men came through the smoke. They carried baskets draped with red sheets. They set them in front of us and whipped away the coverings. Buffalo heads, so freshly struck off the blood was bright and glossy. Eyes rolled up, lolling tongues still warm, noses still wet. And the flies, swarming around the severed neck. A man pushed a basket towards me on my cushion as if it were a dish of holy food. The crashing and beating outside rose to a roar, so loud and metallic it hurt. The girl from my own Shakya village started to wail; the cry spread to another and then another, then a fourth. The other woman, the tall pinched one with a skin like an old purse, came in to take them out, carefully lifting her gown so as not to trail it in the blood. The dancers whirled around like flame and the kneeling man lifted the buffalo head from the basket. He held it up in my face, eye to eye, but all I thought was that it must weigh a lot; his muscles stood out like vines, his arm shook. The flies looked like black jewels. Then there was a clap from outside and the men set down the heads and covered them up with their cloths and they left with the silly demon men whirling and leaping around them. There was one other girl left on her cushion now. I did not know her. She was of a Vajryana family from Niwar down the valley. We sat a long time, wanting to talk but not knowing if silence was part of the trial. Then the door opened a third time and two men led a white goat into the *devi* hall. They brought it right between me and the Niwari girl. I saw its wicked, slotted eye roll. One held the goat's tether, the other took a big ceremonial *kukri* from a leather sheathe. He blessed it and with one fast strong stroke sent the goat's head leaping from its body.

I almost laughed, for the goat looked so funny, its body not knowing where its head was, the head looking around for the body and then the body realizing that it had no head and going down with a kick, and why was the Niwari girl screaming, couldn't she see how funny it was, or was she screaming because I saw the joke and she was jealous of that? Whatever her reason, smiling woman and weathered woman came and took her very gently away and the two men went down on their knees in the spreading blood and kissed the wooden floor. They lifted away the two parts of the goat. I wished they hadn't done that. I would have liked someone with me in the big wooden hall. But I was on my own in the heat and the dark and then, over the traffic, I heard the deep-voiced bells of Kathmandu start to swing and ring. For the last time the doors opened and there were the women, in the light.

"Why have you left me all alone?" I cried. "What have I done wrong?"

"How could you do anything wrong goddess?" said the old, wrinkled woman who, with her colleague, would become my mother and father and teacher and sister. "Now come along with us and hurry. The King is waiting."

Smiling Kumarima and Tall Kumarima (as I would now have to think of them) took a hand each and led me, skipping, from the great looming Hanuman temple. A road of white silk had been laid from the foot of the temple steps to a wooden palace close by. The people had been let back into the square and they pressed on either side of the processional way, held back by the police and the King's robots. The machines held burning torches in their grasping hands. Fire glinted from their killing blades. There was great silence in the dark square.

"Your home, goddess," said Smiling Kumarima, bending low to whisper in my ear. "Walk the silk, *devi*. Do not stray off it. I have your hand, you will be safe with me."

I walked between my Kumarimas, humming a pop tune I had heard on the radio at the hotel. When I looked back I saw that I had left two sets of bloody footprints.

🐾 🐾 🐾

You have no caste, no village, no home. This palace is your home, and who would wish for any other? We have made it lovely for you, for you will only leave it six times a year. Everything you need is here within these walls.

You have no mother or father. How can a goddess have parents? Nor have you brothers and sisters. The King is your brother, the Kingdom your sister. The priests who attend on you, they are nothing. We your Kumarimas are less than nothing. Dust, dirt, a tool. You may say anything and we must obey it.

As we have said, you will leave the palace only six times a year. You will be carried in a palanquin. Oh, it is a beautiful thing, carved wood and silk. Outside this palace you shall not touch the ground. The moment you touch the ground, you cease to be divine.

You will wear red, with your hair in a topknot and your toe- and fingernails painted. You will carry the red *tilak* of Siva on your forehead. We will help you with your preparations until they become second nature.

You will speak only within the confines of your palace, and little even then. Silence becomes the Kumari. You will not smile or show any emotion.

You will not bleed. Not a scrape, not a scratch. The power is in the blood and when the blood leaves, the *devi* leaves. On the day of your first blood, even one single drop, we will tell the priest and he will inform the King that the goddess has left. You will no longer be divine and you will leave this palace and return to your family. You will not bleed.

You have no name. You are Taleju, you are Kumari. You are the goddess.

These instructions my two Kumarimas whispered to me as we walked between kneeling priests to the King in his plumed crown of diamonds and emeralds and pearls. The King *namasted* and we sat side by side on lion thrones and the long hall throbbed to the bells and drums of Durbar Square. I remember thinking that a King must bow to me, but there are rules even for goddesses.

Smiling Kumarima and Tall Kumarima. I draw Tall Kumarima in my memory first, for it is right to give pre-eminence to age. She was almost as tall as a Westerner and thin as a stick in a drought. At first I was scared of her. Then I heard her voice and could never be scared again; her voice was kind as a singing bird. When she spoke you felt you now knew everything. Tall Kumarima lived in a small apartment above a tourist shop on the edge of Durbar Square. From her window she could see my Kumari Ghar, among the stepped towers of the *dhokas*. Her husband had died of lung cancer from pollution and cheap Indian cigarettes. Her two tall sons were grown and married with children of their own, older than me. In that time she had mothered five Kumari *Devis* before me.

Next I remember Smiling Kumarima. She was short and round and had breathing problems for which she used inhalers, blue and brown. I would hear the snake hiss of them on days when Durbar Square was golden with smog. She lived out in the new suburbs up on the western hills, a long journey even by the royal car at her service. Her children were twelve, ten, nine and seven. She was jolly and treated me like her fifth baby, the young favorite, but I felt even then that, like the demon-dancing-men, she was scared of me. Oh, it was the highest honor any woman could hope for, to be the mother of the goddess—so to speak—though you wouldn't think it to hear her neighbors in the unit, *shutting yourself away in that dreadful wooden box, and all the blood, medieval, medieval,* but they couldn't understand. Somebody had to keep the King safe against those who would turn us into another India, or worse, China; someone had to preserve the old ways of the divine kingdom. I understood early that difference between them. Smiling Kumarima was my mother out of duty. Tall Kumarima from love.

I never learned their true names. Their rhythms and cycles of shifts waxed and waned through the days and nights like the faces of the moon. Smiling Kumarima once found me looking up through the lattice of a *jali* screen at the fat moon on a rare night when the sky was clear and healthy and shouted me away, *don't be looking at that thing, it will call the blood out of you, little* devi, *and you will be the* devi *no more.*

Within the wooden walls and iron rules of my Kumari Ghar years become indistinguishable, indistinct. I think now I was five when I became Taleju *Devi.* The year, I believe, was 2034. But some memories break the surface, like flowers through snow.

Monsoon rain on the steep-sloped roofs, water rushing and gurgling through the gutters, and the shutter that every year blew loose and rattled in the wind. We had monsoons, then. Thunder demons in the mountains around the city, my room flash lit with lightning. Tall Kumarima came to see if I needed singing to sleep but I was not afraid. A goddess cannot fear a storm.

The day I went walking in the little garden, when Smiling Kumarima let out a cry and fell at my feet on the grass and the words to tell her to get up, not to worship me were on my lips when she held, between thumb and forefinger, twisting and writhing and trying to find a place for its mouth to seize: a green leech.

The morning Tall Kumarima came to tell me people had asked me to show myself. At first I had thought it wonderful that people would want to come and look at me on my little *jharoka* balcony in my clothes and paint and jewels. Now I found it tiresome; all those round eyes and gaping mouths. It was a week after my tenth birthday. I remember Tall Kumarima smiled but tried not to let me see. She took me to the *jharoka* to wave to the people in the court and I saw a hundred Chinese faces upturned to me, then the high, excited voices. I waited and waited but two tourists would not go away. They were an ordinary couple, dark local faces, country clothes.

"Why are they keeping us waiting?" I asked.

"Wave to them," Tall Kumarima urged. "That is all they want." The woman saw my lifted hand first. She went weak and grabbed her husband by the arm. The man bent to her, then looked up at me. I read many emotions on that face; shock, confusion, recognition, revulsion, wonder, hope. Fear. I waved and the man tugged at his wife, *look, look up*. I remember that against all the laws, I smiled. The woman burst into tears. The man made to call out but Tall Kumarima hastened me away.

"Who were those funny people?" I asked. "They were both wearing very white shoes."

"Your mother and father," Tall Kumarima said. As she led me along the Durga corridor with the usual order not to brush my free hand along the wooden walls for fear of splinters, I felt her grip tremble.

That night I dreamed the dream of my life, that is not a dream but one of my earliest experiences, knocking and knocking and knocking at the door of my remembering. This was a memory I would not admit in daylight, so it must come by night, to the secret door.

I am in the cage over a ravine. A river runs far below, milky with mud and silt, foaming cream over the boulders and slabs sheared from the mountainsides. The cable spans the river from my home to the summer grazing and I sit in the wire cage used to carry the goats across the river. At my back is the main road, always loud with trucks, the prayer banners and Kinley bottled water sign of my family's roadside teahouse. My cage still sways from my uncle's last kick. I see him, arms and legs wrapped around the wire, grinning his gap-toothed grin. His face is summer-burned brown, his hands cracked and stained from the trucks he services. Oil engrained in the creases. He wrinkles up his nose at me and unhooks a leg to kick my cage forward on its pulley-wheel. Pulley sways cable sways mountains, sky and river sway but I am safe in my little goat-cage. I have been kicked across this ravine many times. My uncle inches forwards. Thus we cross the river, by kicks and inches.

I never see what strikes him—some thing of the brain perhaps, like the sickness Lowlanders get when they go up to the high country. But the next I look my uncle is clinging to the wire by his right arm and leg. His left arm and leg hang down, shaking like a cow with its throat cut, shaking the wire and my little cage. I am three years old and I think this is funny, a trick my uncle is doing just for me, so I shake back, bouncing my cage, bouncing my uncle up and down, up and down. Half his body will not obey him and he tries to move forward by sliding his leg along, like *this*, jerk his hand forward *quick* so he never loses grip of the wire, and all the while bouncing up and down, up and down. Now my uncle tries to shout but his words are noise and slobber because half his face is paralysed. Now I see his fingers lose their grip on the wire. Now I see him spin round and his hooked leg come free. Now he falls away, half his body reaching, half his mouth screaming. I see him fall, I see him bounce from the rocks and cartwheel, a thing I have always wished I could do. I see him go into the river and the brown water swallow him.

My older brother came out with a hook and a line and hauled me in. When my parents found I was not shrieking, not a sob or a tear or even a pout, that was when they knew I was destined to become the goddess. I was smiling in my wire cage.

🐾 🐾 🐾

I remember best the festivals, for it was only then that I left the Kumari Ghar. Dasain, at the end of summer, was the greatest. For eight days the city ran red. On the final night I lay awake listening to the voices in the square flow together into one roar, like I imagined the sea would sound, the voices of the men gambling for the luck of Lakshmi, *devi* of wealth. My father and uncles had gambled on the last night of Dasain. I remember I came down and demanded to know what all the laughing was about and they turned away from their cards and really laughed. I had not thought there could be so many coins in the world as there were on that table but it was nothing compared to Kathmandu on the eighth of Dasain. Smiling Kumarima told me it took some of the priests all year to earn back what they lost. Then came the ninth day, the great day and I sailed out from my palace for the city to worship me.

I traveled on a litter carried by forty men strapped to bamboo poles as thick as my body. They went gingerly, testing every step for the streets were slippery. Surrounded by gods and priests and *saddhus* mad with holiness, I rode on my golden throne. Closer to me than any were my Kumarimas, my two Mothers, so splendid and ornate in their red robes and headdresses and make-up they did not look like humans at all. But Tall Kumarima's voice and Smiling Kumarima's smile assured me as I rode with Hanuman and Taleju through the cheering and the music and the banners bright against the blue sky and the smell I now recognized from the night I became a goddess, the smell of blood.

That Dasain the city received me as never before. The roar of the night of Lakshmi continued into the day. As Taleju *Devi* I was not supposed to notice anything as low as humans but out of the corners of my painted eyes I could see beyond the security robots stepping in time with my bearers, and the streets radiating out from the *stupa* of Chhetrapati were solid with bodies. They threw jets and gushes of water from plastic bottles up into the air, glittering, breaking into little rainbows, raining down on them, soaking them, but they did not care. Their faces were crazy with devotion.

Tall Kumarima saw my puzzlement and bent to whisper.

"They do *puja* for the rain. The monsoon has failed a second time, *devi*."

As I spoke, Smiling Kumarima fanned me so no one would see my lips move. "We don't like the rain," I said firmly.

"A goddess cannot do only what she likes," Tall Kumarima said. "It is a serious matter. The people have no water. The rivers are running dry."

I thought of the river that ran far down deep below the house where I was born, the water creamy and gushing and flecked with yellow foam. I saw it swallow my uncle and could not imagine it ever becoming thin, weak, hungry.

"So why do they throw water then?" I asked.

"So the *devi* will give them more," Smiling Kumarima explained. But I could not see the sense in that even for goddesses and I frowned, trying to understand how humans were and so I was looking right at him when he came at me.

He had city pale skin and hair parted on the left that flopped as he dived out of the crowd. He moved his fists to the collar of his diagonally striped shirt and people surged away from him. I saw him hook his thumbs into two loops of black string. I saw his mouth open in a great cry. Then the machine swooped and I saw a flash of silver. The young man's head flew up into the air. His mouth and eyes went round: from a cry to an oh! The King's Own machine had sheathed its blade, like a boy folding a knife, before the body, like that funny goat in the Hanumandhoka, realised it was dead and fell to the ground. The crowd screamed and tried to get away from the headless thing. My bearers rocked, swayed, uncertain where to go, what to do. For a moment I thought they might drop me.

Smiling Kumarima let out little shrieks of horror, "Oh! Oh! Oh!" My face was spotted with blood.

"It's not hers," Tall Kumarima shouted. "It's not hers!" She moistened a handkerchief with a lick of saliva. She was gently wiping the young man's blood from my face when the Royal security in their dark suits and glasses arrived, beating through the crowd. They lifted me, stepped over the body and carried me to the waiting car.

"You smudged my make-up," I said to the Royal guard as the car swept away. Worshippers barely made it out of our way in the narrow alleys.

Tall Kumarima came to my room that night. The air was loud with helicopters, quartering the city for the plotters. Helicopters, and machines like the King's Own robots, that could fly and look down on Kathmandu with the eyes of a hawk. She sat on my bed and laid a little transparent blue box on the red and gold embroidered coverlet. In it were two pale pills.

"To help you sleep."

I shook my head. Tall Kumarima folded the blue box into the sleeve of her robe.

"Who was he?"

"A fundamentalist. A *karsevak*. A foolish, sad young man."

"A Hindu, but he wanted to hurt us."

"That is the madness of it, *devi*. He and his kind think our kingdom has grown too western, too far from its roots and religious truths."

"And he attacks us, the Taleju *Devi*. He would have blown up his own goddess, but the machine took his head. That is almost as strange as people throwing water to the rain."

Tall Kumarima bowed her head. She reached inside the sash of her robe and took out a second object which she set on my heavy cover with the same precise care as she had the sleeping pills. It was a light, fingerless glove, for the right hand; clinging to its back was a curl of plastic shaped like a very very tiny goat foetus.

"Do you know what this is?"

I nodded. Every devotee doing *puja* in the streets seemed to own one, right hands held up to snatch my image. A palmer.

"It sends messages into your head," I whispered.

"That is the least of what it can do, *devi*. Think of it like your *jharoka*, but this window opens onto the world beyond Durbar Square, beyond Kathmandu and Nepal. It is an aeai, an artificial intelligence, a thinking-thing, like the machines up there, but much cleverer than them. They are clever enough to fly and hunt and not much else, but this aeai can tell you anything you want to know. All you have to do is ask. And there are things you need to know, *devi*. You will not be Kumari forever. The day will come when you will leave your palace and go back to the world. I have seen them before you." She reached out to take my face between her hands, then drew back. "You are special my *devi*, but the kind of special it takes to be Kumari means you will find it hard in the world. People will call it a sickness. Worse than that, even . . ."

She banished the emotion by gently fitting the foetus-shaped receiver behind my ear. I felt the plastic move against my skin, then Tall Kumarima slipped on the glove, waved her hand in a *mudra* and I heard her voice inside my head. Glowing words appeared in the air between us, words I had been painstakingly taught to read by Tall Kumarima.

Don't let anyone find it, her dancing hand said. *Tell no one, not even Smiling Kumarima. I know you call her that, but she would not understand. She would think it was unclean, a pollution. In some ways,*

*she is not so different from that man who tried to harm you. Let this be
our secret, just you and me.*

Soon after, Smiling Kumarima came to look in on me and
check for fleas but I pretended to be asleep. The glove and the
foetus-thing were hidden under my pillow. I imagined them talking to me through the goose down and soft soft cotton, sending
dreams while the helicopters and hunting robots wheeled in the
night above me. When the latch on her door clicked too, I put on
the glove and earhook and went looking for the lost rain. I found
it one hundred and fifty kilometres up, through the eye of a
weather aeai spinning over east India. I saw the monsoon, a coil
of cloud like a cat's claw hooking up across the sea. There had
been cats in the village; suspicious things lean on mice and barley. No cat was permitted in the Kumari Ghar. I looked down on
my Kingdom but I could not see a city or a palace or me down
here at all. I saw mountains, white mountains ridged with grey
and blue ice. I was goddess of this. And the heart went out of me,
because it was nothing, a tiny crust of stone on top of that huge
world that hung beneath it like the full teat of a cow, rich and
heavy with people and their brilliant cities and their bright
nations. India, where our gods and names were born.

Within three days the police had caught the plotters and it
was raining. The clouds were low over Kathmandu. The color
ran from the temples in Durbar Square but people beat tins and
metal cups in the muddy streets calling praise on the Taleju *Devi*.

"What will happen to them?" I asked Tall Kumarima. "The
bad men."

"They will likely be hanged," she said.

That autumn after the executions of the traitors the dissatis-
faction finally poured on to the streets like sacrificial blood. Both
sides claimed me: police and demonstrators. Others yet held me
up as both the symbol of all that was good with our Kingdom and
also everything wrong with it. Tall Kumarima tried to explain it
to me but with my world mad and dangerous my attention was
turned elsewhere, to the huge, old land to the south, spread out
like a jeweled skirt. In such a time it was easy to be seduced by
the terrifying depth of its history, by the gods and warriors who
swept across it, empire after empire after empire. My Kingdom

had always been fierce and free but I met the men who liberated India from the Last Empire—men like gods—and saw that liberty broken up by rivalry and intrigue and corruption into feuding states; Awadh and Bharat, The United States of Bengal, Maratha, Karnataka.

Legendary names and places. Shining cities as old as history. There aeais haunted the crowded streets like *gandhavas.* There men outnumbered women four to one. There the old distinctions were abandoned and women married as far up and men as few steps down the tree of caste as they could. I became as enthralled by their leaders and parties and politics as any of their citizens by the aeai-generated soaps they loved so dearly. My spirit was down in India in that early, hard winter when the police and King's machines restored the old order to the city beyond Durbar Square. Unrest in earth and the three heavens. One day I woke to find snow in the wooden court; the roofs of the temple of Durbar Square heavy with it, like frowning, freezing old men. I knew now that the strange weather was not my doing but the result of huge, slow changes in the climate. Smiling Kumarima came to me in my *jharoka* as I watched flakes thick and soft as ash sift down from the white sky. She knelt before me, rubbed her hands together inside the cuffs of her wide sleeves. She suffered badly in the cold and damp.

"*Devi*, are you not one of my own children to me?"

I waggled my head, not wanting to say yes.

"*Devi*, have I ever, ever given you anything but my best?"

Like her counterpart a season before, she drew a plastic pill-box from her sleeve, set it on her palm. I sat back on my chair, afraid of it as I had never been afraid of anything Tall Kumarima offered me.

"I know how happy we are all here, but change must always happen. Change in the world, like this snow—unnatural, *devi*, not right—change in our city. And we are not immune to it in here, my flower. Change will come to you, *devi*. To you, to your body. You will become a woman. If I could, I would stop it happening to you, *devi*. But I can't. No one can. What I can offer is . . . a delay. A stay. Take these. They will slow down the changes. For years, hopefully. Then we can all be happy here together, *devi*."

She looked up from her deferential half-bow, into my eyes. She smiled. "Have I ever wanted anything but the best for you?"

I held out my hand. Smiling Kumarima tipped the pills into my palm. I closed my fist and slipped from my carved throne. As I went to my room I could hear Smiling Kumarima chanting prayers of thanksgiving to the goddesses in the carvings. I looked at the pills in my hand. Blue seemed such a wrong color. Then I filled my cup in my little washroom and washed them down, two gulps, down, down.

After that they came every day, two pills, blue as the Lord Krishna, appearing as miraculously on my bedside table. For some reason I never told Tall Kumarima, even when she commented on how fractious I was becoming, how strangely inattentive and absent-minded at ceremonies. I told her it was the *devis* in the walls, whispering to me. I knew enough of my specialness, that others have called my *disorder*, that that would be unquestioned. I was tired and lethargic that winter. My sense of smell grew keen to the least odor and the people in my courtyard with their stupid, beaming upturned faces infuriated me. I went for weeks without showing myself. The wooden corridors grew sharp and brassy with old blood. With the insight of demons, I can see now that my body was a chemical battlefield between my own hormones and Smiling Kumarima's puberty suppressants. It was a heavy, humid spring that year and I felt huge and bloated in the heat, a waddling bulb of fluids under my robes and waxy make-up. I started to drop the little blue pills down the commode. I had been Kumari for seven Dasains.

I had thought I would feel like I used to, but I did not. It was not unwell, like the pills had made me feel, it was sensitive, acutely conscious of my body. I would lie in my wooden bed and feel my legs growing longer. I became very very aware of my tiny nipples. The heat and humidity got worse, or so it seemed to me.

At any time I could have opened my palmer and asked it what was happening to me, but I didn't. I was scared that it might tell me it was the end of my divinity.

Tall Kumarima must have noticed that the hem of my gown no longer brushed the floorboards but it was Smiling Kumarima who drew back in the corridor as we hurried towards the *darshan* hall, hesitated a moment, said, softly, smiling as always,

"How you're growing, *devi*. Are you still . . . ? No, forgive me, of course . . . Must be this warm weather we're having, makes children shoot up like weeds. My own are bursting out of everything they own, nothing will fit them."

The next morning as I was dressing a tap came on my door, like the scratch of a mouse or the click of an insect.

"*Devi?*"

No insect, no mouse. I froze, palmer in hand, earhook babbling the early morning news reports from Awadh and Bharat into my head.

"We are dressing."

"Yes, *devi*, that is why I would like to come in."

I just managed to peel off the palmer and stuff it under my mattress before the heavy door swung open on its pivot.

"We have been able to dress ourselves since we were six," I retorted.

"Yes, indeed," said Smiling Kumarima, smiling. "But some of the priests have mentioned to me a little laxness in the ritual dress."

I stood in my red and gold night-robe, stretched out my arms and turned, like one of the trance-dancers I saw in the streets from my litter. Smiling Kumarima sighed.

"*Devi*, you know as well as I . . ."

I pulled my gown up over my head and stood unclothed, daring her to look, to search my body for signs of womanhood.

"See?" I challenged.

"Yes," Smiling Kumarima said, "but what is that behind your ear?"

She reached to pluck the hook. It was in my fist in a flick.

"Is that what I think it is?" Smiling Kumarima said, soft smiling bulk filling the space between the door and me. "Who gave you that?"

"It is ours," I declared in my most commanding voice but I was a naked twelve-year-old caught in wrongdoing and that commands less than dust.

"Give it to me."

I clenched my fist tighter.

"We are a goddess, you cannot command us."

"A goddess is as a goddess acts and right now, you are acting like a brat. Show me."

She was a mother, I was her child. My fingers unfolded. Smiling Kumarima recoiled as if I held a poisonous snake. To her eyes of her faith, I did.

"Pollution," she said faintly. "Spoiled, all spoiled." Her voice rose. "I know who gave you this!" Before my fingers could snap shut, she snatched the coil of plastic from my palm. She threw the earhook to the floor as if it burned her. I saw the hem of her skirt raise, I saw the heel come down, but it was my world, my oracle, my window on the beautiful. I dived to rescue the tiny plastic foetus. I remember no pain, no shock, not even Smiling Kumarima's shriek of horror and fear as her heel came down, but I will always see the tip of my right index finger burst in a spray of red blood.

᠁ ᠁ ᠁

The *pallav* of my yellow sari flapped in the wind as I darted through the Delhi evening crush-hour. Beating the heel of his hand on his buzzer, the driver of the little wasp-coloured *phatphat* cut in between a lumbering truck-train painted with gaudy gods and *apsaras* and a cream Government Maruti and pulled into the great *chakra* of traffic around Connaught Place. In Awadh you drive with your ears. The roar of horns and klaxons and cycle-rickshaw bells assailed from all sides at once. It rose before the dawn birds and only fell silent well after midnight. The driver skirted a *saddhu* walking through the traffic as calmly as if he were wading through the Holy Yamuna. His body was white with sacred ash, a mourning ghost, but his Siva trident burned blood red in the low sun. I had thought Kathmandu dirty, but Delhi's golden light and incredible sunsets spoke of pollution beyond even that. Huddled in the rear seat of the autorickshaws with Deepti, I wore smog-mask and goggles to protect my delicate eye make-up. But the fold of my sari flapped over my shoulder in the evening wind and the little silver bells jingled.

There were five in our little fleet. We accelerated along the wide avenues of the British Raj, past the sprawling red buildings of old India, towards the glass spires of Awadh. Black kites circled the towers, scavengers, pickers of the dead. We turned beneath cool *neem* trees into the drive of a government bungalow. Burning torches lit us to the pillared porch. House staff in Rajput uniforms escorted us to the *shaadi* marquee.

Mamaji had arrived before any of us. She fluttered and fretted among her birds; a lick, a rub, a straightening, an admonition. "Stand up stand up, we'll have no slumping here. My girls will be the bonniest at this *shaadi*, hear me?" Shweta, her bony, mean-mouthed assistant, collected our smog-masks. "Now girls, palmers ready." We knew the drill with almost military smartness. Hand up, glove on, rings on, hook behind ear jewellery, decorously concealed by the fringed *dupattas* draped over our heads. "We are graced with Awadh's finest tonight. Crème de la crème." I barely blinked as the résumés rolled up my inner vision. "Right girls, from the left, first dozen, two minutes each then on to the next down the list. Quick smart!" Mamaji clapped her hands and we formed a line. A band struck a medley of musical numbers from *Town and Country*, the soap opera that was a national obsession in sophisticated Awadh. There we stood, twelve little wives-a-waiting while the Rajput servants hauled up the rear of the pavilion.

Applause broke around us like rain. A hundred men stood in a rough semi-circle, clapping enthusiastically, faces bright in the light from the carnival lanterns.

When I arrived in Awadh, the first thing I noticed was the people. People pushing people begging people talking people rushing past each other without a look or a word or an acknowledgement. I had thought Kathmandu held more people than a mind could imagine. I had not seen Old Delhi. The constant noise, the everyday callousness, the lack of any respect appalled me. You could vanish into that crowd of faces like a drop of rain into a tank. The second thing I noticed was that the faces were all men. It was indeed as my palmer had whispered to me. There were four men for every woman.

Fine men good men clever men rich men, men of ambition and career and property, men of power and prospects. Men with no hope of ever marrying within their own class and caste. Men with little prospect of marrying ever. *Shaadi* had once been the word for wedding festivities, the groom on his beautiful white horse, so noble, the bride shy and lovely behind her golden veil. Then it became a name for dating agencies: *lovely wheat-complexioned Agarwal, U.S.-university MBA, seeks same civil service/military for matrimonials*. Now it was a bride-parade, a marriage-market for lonely men with large dowries. Dowries that paid a hefty commission to the Lovely Girl *Shaadi* Agency.

The Lovely Girls lined up on the left side of the Silken Wall that ran the length of the bungalow garden. The first twelve men formed up on the right. They plumped and preened in their finery but I could see they were nervous. The partition was no more than a row of saris pinned to a line strung between plastic uprights, fluttering in the rising evening wind. A token of decorum. Purdah. They were not even silk.

Reshmi was first to walk and talk the Silken Wall. She was a Yadav country girl from Uttaranchal, big-handed and big-faced. A peasant's daughter. She could cook and sew and sing, do household accounts, manage both domestic aeais and human staff. Her first prospective was a weasely man with a weak jaw in government whites and a Nehru cap. He had bad teeth. Never good. Any one of us could have told him he was wasting his *shaadi* fee, but they *namasted* to each other and stepped out, regulation three paces between them. At the end of the walk Reshmi would loop back to rejoin the tail of the line and meet her next prospective. On big *shaadis* like this my feet would bleed by the end of the night. Red footprints on the marble floors of Mamaji's courtyard *haveli*.

I stepped out with Ashok, a big globe of a thirty-two-year-old who wheezed a little as he rolled along. He was dressed in a voluminous white *kurta*, the fashion this season though he was fourth generation Panjabi. His grooming amounted to an uncontrollable beard and oily hair that smelled of too much Dapper Deepak pomade. Even before he *namasted* I knew it was his first *shaadi*. I could see his eyeballs move as he read my résumé, seeming to hover before him. I did not need to read his to know he was a dataraja, for he talked about nothing but himself and the brilliant things he was doing; the spec of some new protein processor array, the 'ware he was breeding, the aeais he was nurturing in his stables, his trips to Europe and the United States where everyone knew his name and great people were glad to welcome him.

"Of course, Awadh's never going to ratify the Hamilton Acts—no matter how close Shrivastava Minister is to President McAuley—but if it did, if we allow ourselves that tiny counterfactual—well, it's the end of the economy: Awadh *is* IT, there are more graduates in Mehrauli than there are in the whole of California. The Americans may go on about the mockery of a human soul, but they *need* our Level 2.8s—you know what that is? An aeai can pass as human ninety-nine percent of the time—because everybody knows no one does quantum crypto like us, so I'm not worrying about having to close up the data-haven, and even if they do, well, there's always Bharat—I cannot see the Ranas bowing down to Washington, not when twenty-five percent of their forex comes out of licensing deals from *Town and Country* . . . and that's hundred percent aeai generated . . ."

He was a big affable clown of a man with wealth that would have bought my Palace in Durbar Square and every priest in it and I found myself praying to Taleju to save me from marrying such a bore. He stopped in mid-stride, so abruptly I almost tripped.

"You must keep walking," I hissed. "That is the rule."

"Wow," he said, standing stupid, eyes round in surprise. Couples piled up behind us. In my peripheral vision I could see Mamaji making urgent, threatening gestures. Get him *on.* "Oh wow. You're an ex-Kumari."

"Please, you are drawing attention to yourself." I would have tugged his arm, but that would have been an even more deadly error.

"What was it like, being a goddess?"

"I am just a woman now, like any other," I said. Ashok gave a soft harrumph, as if he had achieved a very small enlightenment, and walked on, hands clasped behind his back. He may have spoken to me once, twice before we reached the end of the Silk Wall and parted: I did not hear him, I did not hear the music, I did not even hear the eternal thunder of Delhi's traffic. The only sound in my head was the high-pitched sound between my eyes of needing to cry but knowing I could not. Fat, selfish, gabbling, Ashok had sent me back to the night I ceased to be a goddess.

Bare soles slapping the polished wood of the Kumari Ghar's corridors. Running feet, muted shouts growing ever more distant as I knelt, still unclothed for my Kumarima's inspection, looking at the blood drip from my smashed fingertip onto the painted wood floor. I remember no pain; rather, I looked at the pain from a separate place, as if the girl who felt it were another person. Far far away, Smiling Kumarima stood, held in time, hands to mouth in horror and guilt. The voices faded and the bells of Durbar Square began to swing and toll, calling to their brothers across the city of Kathmandu until the valley rang from Bhaktapur to Trisuli Bazaar for the fall of the Kumari *Devi*.

In the space of a single night, I became human again. I was taken to the Hanumandhoka—walking this time like anyone else on the paving stones—where the priests said a final *puja*. I handed back my red robes and jewels and boxes of make-up, all neatly folded and piled. Tall Kumarima had got me human clothes. I think she had been keeping them for some time. The King did not come to say goodbye to me. I was no longer his sister. But his surgeons had put my finger back together well, though they warned that it would always feel a little numb and inflexible.

I left at dawn, while the street cleaners were washing down the stones of Durbar Square beneath the apricot sky, in a smooth-running Royal Mercedes with darkened windows. My Kumarimas made their farewells at the palace gate. Tall Kumarima hugged me briefly to her.

"Oh, there was so much more I needed to do. Well, it will have to suffice."

I felt her quivering against me, like a bird too tightly gripped in a hand. Smiling Kumarima could not look at me. I did not want her to.

As the car took me across the waking city I tried to understand how it felt to be human. I had been a goddess so long I could hardly remember feeling any other way, but it seemed so little different that I began to suspect that you are divine because people say you are. The road climbed through green suburbs, winding now, growing narrower, busy with brightly decorated buses and trucks. The houses grew leaner and meaner, to road-side hovels and *chai*-stalls and then we were out of the city—the first time since I had arrived seven years before. I pressed my hands and face to the glass and looked down on Kathmandu beneath its shroud of ochre smog. The car joined the long line of traffic along the narrow, rough road that clung to the valley side. Above me, mountains dotted with goatherd shelters and stone shrines flying tattered prayer banners. Below me, rushing cream-brown water. Nearly there. I wondered how far behind me on this road were those other government cars, carrying the priests sent to seek out little girls bearing the thirty-two signs of perfection. Then the car rounded the bend in the valley and I was home, Shakya, its truck halts and gas station, the shops and the temple of Padma Narteswara, the dusty trees with white rings painted around their trunks and between them the stone wall and arch where the steps led down through the terraces to my house, and in that stone-framed rectangle of sky, my parents, standing there side by side, pressing closely, shyly, against each other as I had last seen them lingering in the courtyard of the Kumari Ghar.

🐾 🐾 🐾

Mamaji was too respectable to show anything like outright anger, but she had ways of expressing her displeasure. The smallest crust of *roti* at dinner, the meanest scoop of *dhal*. New girls coming, make room make room—me to the highest, stuffiest room, furthest from the cool of the courtyard pool.

"He asked for my palmer address," I said.

"If I had a rupee for every palmer address," Mamaji said. "He was only interested in you as a novelty, dearie. Anthropology. He was never going to make a proposition. No, you can forget about him."

But my banishment to the tower was a small punishment for it lifted me above the noise and fumes of the old city. If portions were cut, small loss: the food had been dreadful every day of the almost two years I had been at the *haveli*. Through the wooden

lattice, beyond the water tanks and satellite dishes and kids playing rooftop cricket, I could see the ramparts of the Red Fort, the
minarets and domes of the Jami Masjid and beyond them, the
glittering glass and titanium spires of New Delhi. And higher than
any of them, the flocks of pigeons from the *kabooter* lofts, clay
pipes bound to their legs so they fluted and sang as they swirled
over Chandni Chowk. And Mamaji's worldly-wisdom made her
a fool this time, for Ashok was surreptitiously messaging me,
sometimes questions about when I was divine, mostly about himself and his great plans and ideas. His lilac-coloured words,
floating in my inner-vision against the intricate silhouettes of my
jali screens, were bright pleasures in those high summer days. I
discovered the delight of political argument; against Ashok's
breezy optimism, I set my readings of the news channels. From
the opinion columns it seemed inevitable to me that Awadh, in
exchange for Favoured Nation status from the United States of
America, would ratify the Hamilton Acts and outlaw all aeais
more intelligent than a langur monkey. I told none of our inter-
course to Mamaji. She would have forbidden it, unless he made
a proposal.

On an evening of pre-monsoon heat, when the boys were too
tired even for cricket and the sky was an upturned brass bowl,
Mamaji came to my turret on the top of the old merchant's *haveli*.
Against propriety, the *jalis* were thrown open, my gauze curtains
stirred in the swirls of heat rising from the alleys below.

"Still you are eating my bread." She prodded my *thali* with
her foot. It was too hot for food, too hot for anything other than
lying and waiting for the rain and the cool, if it came at all this
year. I could hear the voices of the girls down in the courtyard as
they kicked their legs in the pool. This day I would have loved to
be sitting along the tiled edge with them but I was piercingly
aware that I had lived in the *haveli* of the Lovely Girl *Shaadi*
Agency longer than any of them. I did not want to be their
Kumarima. And when the whispers along the cool marble corridors made them aware of my childhood, they would ask for small
pujas, little miracles to help them find the right man. I no longer
granted them, not because I feared that I had no power any

more—that I never had—but that it went out from me and into them and that was why they got the bankers and television executives and Mercedes salesmen.

"I should have left you in that Nepalese sewer. Goddess! Hah! And me fooled into thinking you were a prize asset. Men! They may have share options and Chowpatty Beach apartments but deep down, they're as superstitious as any back-country *yadav*."

"I'm sorry Mamaji," I said, turning my eyes away.

"Can you help it? You were only born perfect in thirty-two different ways. Now you listen, *cho chweet*. A man came to call on me."

Men always came calling, glancing up at the giggles and rustles of the Lovely Girls peeping through the *jalis* as he waited in the cool of the courtyard for Shweta to present him to Mamaji. Men with offers of marriage, men with prenuptial contracts, men with dowry down-payments. Men asking for special, private viewings. This man who had called on Mamaji had come for one of these.

"Fine young man, lovely young man, just twenty. Father's big in water. He has requested a private rendezvous, with you."

I was instantly suspicious but I had learned among the Lovely Girls of Delhi, even more than among the priests and Kumarimas of Kathmandu, to let nothing show on my painted face.

"Me? Such an honour . . . and him only twenty . . . and a good family too, so well connected."

"He is a Brahmin."

"I know I am only a Shakya . . ."

"You don't understand. He is a *Brahmin*."

There was so much more I needed to do, Tall Kumarima had said as the royal car drove away from the carved wooden gates of the Kumari Ghar. One whisper through the window would have told me everything: *the curse of the Kumari.*

Shakya hid from me. People crossed the street to find things to look at and do. Old family friends nodded nervously before remembering important business they had to be about. The *chaidhabas* gave me free tea so I would feel uncomfortable and leave.

Truckers were my friends, bus-drivers and long-haulers pulled in at the biodiesel stations. They must have wondered who was this strange twelve-year-old girl, hanging around truck-halts. I do not doubt some of them thought more. Village by village, town by town the legend spread up and down the north road. Ex-Kumari.

Then the accidents started. A boy lost half his hand in the fan belt of a Nissan engine. A teenager drank bad *rakshi* and died of alcohol poisoning. A man slipped between two passing trucks and was crushed. The talk in the *chai-dhabas* and the repair shops was once again of my uncle who fell to his death while the little goddess-to-be bounced in her wire cradle laughing and laughing and laughing.

I stopped going out. As winter took hold over the head-country of the Kathmandu valley, whole weeks passed when I did not leave my room. Days slipped away watching sleet slash past my window, the prayer banners bent almost horizontal in the wind, the wire of the cableway bouncing. Beneath it, the furious, flooding river. In that season the voices of the demons spoke loud from the mountain, telling me the most hateful things about faithless Kumaris who betray the sacred heritage of their *devi*.

On the shortest day of the year the bride-buyer came through Shakya. I heard a voice I did not recognise talking over the television that burbled away day and night in the main room. I opened the door just enough to admit a voice and gleam of fire-light.

"I wouldn't take the money off you. You're wasting your time here in Nepal. Everyone knows the story, and even if they pretend they don't believe, they don't act that way."

I heard my father's voice but could not make out his words. The bride-buyer said, "What might work is down south, Bharat or Awadh. They're so desperate in Delhi they'll even take Untouchables. They're a queer lot, those Indians; some of them might even like the idea of marrying a goddess, like a status thing. But I can't take her, she's too young, they'll send her straight back at the border. They've got rules. In India, would you believe? Call me when she turns fourteen."

Two days after my fourteenth birthday, the bride-buyer returned to Shakya and I left with him in his Japanese SUV. I did not like his company or trust his hands, so I slept or feigned sleep while he drove down into the lowlands of the Terai. When I woke I was well over the border into my childhood land of wonder. I had thought the bride-buyer would take me to ancient, holy Varanasi, the new capital of the Bharat's dazzling Rana dynasty but the Awadhis, it seemed, were less in awe of Hindu superstitions. So we came to the vast, incoherent roaring sprawl of the two Delhis, like twin hemispheres of a brain, and to the Lovely Girl *Shaadi* Agency. Where the marriageable men were not so twenty-forties sophisticated, at least in the matter of ex-*devis*. Where the only ones above the curse of the Kumari were those held in even greater superstitious awe: the genetically engineered children known as Brahmins.

Wisdom was theirs, health was theirs, beauty and success and status assured and a wealth that could never be devalued or wasted or gambled away, for it was worked into every twist of their DNA. The Brahmin children of India's super-elite enjoyed long life—twice that of their parents—but at a price. They were indeed the twice-born, a caste above any other, so high as to be new Untouchables. A fitting partner for a former goddess: a new god.

🐾 🐾 🐾

Gas flares from the heavy industries of Tughluq lit the western horizon. From the top of the high tower I could read New Delhi's hidden geometries, the necklaces of light around Connaught Place, the grand glowing net of the dead Raj's monumental capital, the incoherent glow of the old city to the north. The penthouse at the top of the sweeping wing-curve of Narayan Tower was glass; glass walls, glass roof, beneath me, polished obsidian that reflected the night sky. I walked with stars at my head and feet. It was a room designed to awe and intimidate. It was nothing to one who had witnessed demons strike the heads from goats, who had walked on bloody silk to her own palace. It was nothing to one dressed, as the messenger had required, in the full panoply of the goddess. Red robe, red nails, red lips, red eye of Siva painted above my own black kohled eyes, fake-gold headdress hung with costume pearls, my fingers dripped gaudy rings from the cheap jewellery sellers of Kinari Bazaar, a light chain of real gold ran from my nose stud to my ear-ring; I was once again Kumari *Devi*. My demons rustled inside me.

Mamaji had drilled me as we scooted from old city to new. She had swathed me in a light voile *chador*, to protect my make-up she said; in truth, to conceal me from the eyes of the street. The girls had called blessings and prayers after me as the *phat-phat* scuttled out of the *haveli*'s courtyard.

"You will say nothing. If he speaks to you, you duck your head like a good Hindu girl. If anything has to be said, I will say it. You may have been a goddess but he is a Brahmin. He could buy your pissy palace a dozen times over. Above all, do not let your eyes betray you. The eyes say nothing. They taught you that at least in that Kathmandu, didn't they? Now come on *cho chweet*, let's make a match."

The glass penthouse was lit only by city-glow and concealed lamps that gave an uncomfortable blue glow. Ved Prakash Narayan sat on a *musnud*, a slab of unadorned black marble. Its simplicity spoke of wealth and power beneath any ornate jew-ellery. My bare feet whispered on the star-filled glass. Blue light welled up as I approached the dais. Ved Prakash Narayan was dressed in a beautifully worked long *sherwani* coat and tradition-al tight *churidar* pyjamas. He leaned forward into the light and it took every word of control Tall Kumarima had ever whispered to me to hold the gasp.

A ten-year-old boy sat on the throne of the Mughal Emperor.

Live twice as long, but age half as fast. The best deal Kolkata's genetic engineers could strike with four million years of human DNA. A child husband for a once-child goddess. Except this was no child. In legal standing, experience, education, taste and emotions, this was a twenty-year-old man, every way except the physical.

His feet did not touch the floor.

"Quite, quite extraordinary." His voice was a boy's. He slipped from his throne, walked around me, studying me as if I were an artefact in a museum. He was a head shorter than me. "Yes, this is indeed special. What is the settlement?"

Mamaji's voice from the door named a number. I obeyed my

training and tried not to catch his eye as he stalked around me.

"Acceptable. My man will deliver the prenuptial before the end of the week. A goddess. My goddess."

Then I caught his eyes and I saw where all his missing years were. They were blue, alien blue, and colder than any of the lights of his tower-top palace.

🐾 🐾 🐾

These Brahmins are worse than any of us when it comes to social climbing, Ashok messaged me in my aerie atop the *shaadi haveli,* prison turned bridal boudoir. *Castes within castes within castes.* His words hung in the air over the hazy ramparts of the red fort before dissolving into the dashings of the musical pigeons. *Your children will be blessed.*

Until then I had not thought about the duties of a wife with a ten-year-old boy.

On a day of staggering heat I was wed to Ved Prakash Narayan in a climate-control bubble on the manicured green before Emperor Humayun's tomb. As on the night I was introduced, I was dressed as Kumari. My husband, veiled in gold, arrived perched on top of a white horse followed by a band and a dozen elephants with coloured patterns worked on their trunks. Security robots patrolled the grounds as astrologers proclaimed favourable auspices and an old-type brahmin in his red cord blessed our union. Rose petals fluttered around me, the proud father and mother distributed gems from Hyderabad to their guests, my *shaadi* sisters wept with joy and loss, Mamaji sniffed back a tear and vile old Shweta went round hoarding the free and over-flowing food from the buffet. As we were applauded and played down the receiving line, I noticed all the other sombre-faced ten-year-old boys with their beautiful, tall foreign wives. I reminded myself who was the child bride here. But none of them were goddesses.

I remember little of the grand *durbar* that followed except face after face after face, mouth after mouth after mouth opening, making noise, swallowing glass after glass after glass of French champagne. I did not drink for I do not have the taste for alcohol, though my young husband in his raja finery took it, and smoked big cigars too. As we got into the car—the *honeymoon* was another Western tradition we were adopting—I asked if anyone had remembered to inform my parents.

We flew to Mumbai on the company tilt-jet. I had never before flown in an aircraft. I pressed my hands, still hennaed with the patterns of my *mehndi*, on either side of the window as if to hold in every fleeting glimpse of Delhi falling away beneath me. It was every divine vision I had ever had looking down from my bed in the Kumari Ghar on to India. This was indeed the true vehicle of a goddess. But the demons whispered as we turned in the air over the towers of New Delhi, *you will be old and withered when he is still in his prime.*

When the limousine from the airport turned on to Marine Drive and I saw the Arabian Sea glinting in the city-light, I asked my husband to stop the car so I could look and wonder. I felt tears start in my eyes and thought, *the same water in it is in you.* But the demons would not let me be: *you are married to something that is not human.*

My *honeymoon* was wonder upon wonder: our penthouse apartment with the glass walls that opened on sunset over Chowpatty Beach. The new splendid outfits we wore as we drove along the boulevards, where stars and movie-gods smiled down and blessed us in the virtual sight of our palmers. Colour, motion, noise, chatter; people and people and people. Behind it all, the wash and hush and smell of the alien sea.

Chambermaids prepared me for the wedding night. They worked with baths and balms, oils and massages, extending the now-fading henna tracery on my hands up my arms, over my small upright breasts, down the *manipuraka chakra* over my navel. They wove gold ornaments into my hair, slipped bracelets on my arms and rings on my fingers and toes, dusted and powdered my dark Nepali skin. They purified me with incense smoke and flower petals, they shrouded me in veils and silks as fine as rumours. They lengthened my lashes and kohled my eyes and shaped my nails to fine, painted points.

"What do I do? I've never even touched a man," I asked, but they *namasted* and slipped away without answer. But the older—

the Tall Kumarima, as I thought of her—left a small soapstone box on my bridal divan. Inside were two white pills.

They were good. I should have expected no less. One moment I was standing nervous and fearful on the Turkestan carpet with a soft night air that smelled of the sea stirring the translucent curtains, the next visions of the Kama Sutra, beamed into my brain through my golden earhook, swirled up around me like the pigeons over Chandni Chowk. I looked at the patterns my *shaadi* sisters had painted on the palms of my hands and they danced and coiled from my skin. The smells and perfumes of my body were alive, suffocating. It was as if my skin had been peeled back and every nerve exposed. Even the touch of the barely-moving night air was intolerable. Every car horn on Marine Drive was like molten silver dropped into my ear.

I was terribly afraid.

Then the double doors to the robing room opened and my husband entered. He was dressed as a Mughal grandee in a jewelled turban and a long-sleeved pleated red robe bowed out at the front in the manly act.

"My goddess," he said. Then he parted his robe and I saw what stood so proud.

The harness was of crimson leather intricately inlaid with fine mirror-work. It fastened around the waist and also over the shoulders, for extra security. The buckles were gold. I recall the details of the harness so clearly because I could not take more than one look at the thing it carried. Black. Massive as a horse's, but delicately upcurved. Ridged and studded. This all I remember before the room unfolded around me like the scented petals of a lotus and my senses blended as one and I was running through the apartments of the Taj Marine Hotel.

How had I ever imagined it could be different for a creature with the appetites and desires of an adult but the physical form of a ten-year-old boy?

Servants and dressers stared at me as I screamed incoherently, grabbing at wraps, shawls, anything to cover my shame. At some tremendous remove I remember my husband's voice calling *Goddess! My Goddess!* over and over.

𝕨 𝕨 𝕨

"Schizophrenia is a terribly grating word," Ashok said. He twirled the stem of a red thornless rose between his fingers. "Old-school. It's dissociative disorder these days. Except there are no disorders, just adaptive behaviours. It was what you needed to cope with being a goddess. Dissociating. Disjuncting. Becoming you and *other* to stay sane."

Night in the gardens of the Dataraja Ashok. Water trickled in the stone canals of the *charbagh*. I could smell it, sweet and wet. A pressure curtain held the smog at bay; trees screened out Delhi's traffic. I could even see a few stars. We sat in an open *chhatri* pavilion, the marble still warm from the day. Set on silver *thalis* were medjool dates, *halva*—crisp with flies—, folded *paan*. A security robot stepped into the lights from the Colonial bungalow, passed into shadow. But for it I might have been in the age of the rajas.

Time broken apart, whirring like *kabooter* wings. Dissociative behaviour. Mechanisms for coping. Running along the palm-lined boulevards of Mumbai, shawls clutched around my wifely finery that made me feel more naked than bare skin. I ran without heed or direction. Taxis hooted, *phatphats* veered as I dashed across crowded streets. Even if I had had money for a *phatphat*—what need had the wife of Brahmin for crude cash? I did not know where to direct it. Yet that other, demonic self must have known, for I found myself on the vast marble concourse of a railway station, a sole mite of stillness among the tens of thousands of hastening travellers and beggars and vendors and staff. My shawls and throws clutched around me, I looked up at the dome of red Raj stone and it was a second skull, full of the awful realisation of what I had done.

A runaway bride without even a *paisa* to her name, alone in Mumbai Chhatrapati Shivaji Terminus. A hundred trains leaving that minute for any destination but nowhere to go. People stared at me, half Nautch-courtesan, half Untouchable street-sleeper. In my shame, I remembered the hook behind my ear. *Ashok,* I wrote across the sandstone pillars and swirling ads. *Help me!*

BEST SHORT NOVELS: 2006

"I don't want to be split, I don't want to be me and *other*, why can't I just be one?" I beat the heels of my hands off my forehead in frustration. "Make me well, make me right!" Shards of memory. The white-uniformed staff serving me hot *chai* in the first-class private compartment of the *shatabdi* express. The robots waiting at the platform with the antique covered palanquin, to bear me through the Delhi dawn traffic to the green watered geometries of Ashok's gardens. But behind them all was one enduring image, my uncle's white fist slipping on the bouncing cable and him falling, legs pedalling air, to the creamy waters of Shakya river. Even then, I had been split. Fear and shock. Laughter and smiles. How else could anyone survive being a goddess?

Goddess. My Goddess.

Ashok could not understand. "Would you cure a singer of his talent? There is no madness, only ways of adapting. Intelligence is evolution. Some would argue that I display symptoms of mild Asperger's syndrome."

"I don't know what that means."

He twirled the rose so hard the stem snapped.

"Have you thought what you're going to do?"

I had thought of little else. The Narayans would not give up their dowry lightly. Mamaji would sweep me from her door. My village was closed to me.

"Maybe for a while, if you could . . ."

"It's not a good time . . .Who's going to have the ear of the Lok Sabha? A family building a dam that's going to guarantee their water supply for the next fifty years, or a software entrepreneur with a stable of Level 2.75 aeais that the United States government thinks are the sperm of Shaitan? Family values still count in Awadh. You should know."

I heard my voice say, like a very small girl, "Where can I go?"

The bride-buyer's stories of Kumaris whom no one would marry and could not go home again ended in the woman-cages of Varanasi and Kolkata. Chinese paid rupees by the roll for an ex-Goddess.

Ashok moistened his lips with his tongue.

"I have a place in Bharat, in Varanasi. Awadh and Bharat are seldom on speaking terms."

"Oh thank you, thank you . . ." I went down on my knees before Ashok, clutched his hands between my palms. He looked away. Despite the artificial cool of the *charbagh*, he was sweating freely.

"It's not a gift. It's . . . employment. A job."

"A job, that's good, I can do that; I'm a good worker, work away at anything I will; what is it? Doesn't matter, I can do it . . ."

"There are commodities need transported."

"What kind of commodities? Oh it doesn't mater, I can carry anything."

"Aeais." He rolled a *paan* from the silver dish. "I'm not going to wait around for Shrivastava's Krishna Cops to land in my garden with their excommunication ware."

"The Hamilton Acts," I ventured, though I did not know what they were, what most of Ashok's mumbles and rants meant.

"Word is, everything above level 2.5." Ashok chewed his lower lip. His eyes widened as the *paan* curled through his skull.

"Of course, I will do anything I can to help."

"I haven't told you how I need you to transport them. Absolutely safe, secure, where no Krishna Cop can ever find them." He touched his right forefinger to his Third Eye. "Self, and *other*."

🐾 🐾 🐾

I went to Kerala and had processors put into my skull. Two men did it on a converted bulk gas carrier moored outside territorial waters. They shaved my long lovely black hair, unhinged my skull and sent robots smaller than the tiniest spider spinning computers through my brain. Their position out beyond the Keralese fast patrol boats enabled them to carry out much secret surgery, mostly for the Western military. They gave me a bungalow and an Australian girl to watch over me while my sutures fused and hormone washes speed-grew my hair back.

Protein chips; only show on the highest resolution scans but no one'll look twice at you; no one'll look twice at another shaadi *girl down hunting for a husband.*

So I sat and stared at the sea for six weeks and thought about what it would be like to drown in the middle of it, alone and lost a thousand kilometres from the nearest hand that might seize yours. A thousand kilometres north in Delhi a man in an Indian suit shook hands with a man in an American suit and announced the Special Relationship that would make Ashok an outlaw.

You know what Krishna Cops are? They hunt aeais. They hunt the people who stable them, and the people who carry them. They don't care. They're not picky. But they won't catch you. They'll never catch you.

I listened to demons in the swash and run of the big sea on the shore. Demons I now knew were facets of my other self. But I was not afraid of them. In Hinduism, demons are merely the mirrors of the gods. As with men, so with gods; it is the winners write the history. The universe would look no different had Ravana and his Rakshasas won their cosmic wars.

No one but you can carry them. No one but you has the neurological architecture. No one but you could endure another mind in there.

The Australian girl left small gifts outside my door: plastic bangles, jelly-shoes, rings and hairslides. She stole them from the shops in town. I think they were her way of saying that she wanted to know me but was afraid of what I had been, of what the things in my head would make me become. The last thing she stole was a beautiful sheer silk *dupatta* to cover my ragged hair when she took me to the airport. From beneath it I looked at the girls in business saris talking into their hands in the departure lounge and listened to the woman pilot announce the weather in Awadh. Then I looked out of the *phatphat* at the girls darting confidently through the Delhi traffic on their scooters and wondered why my life could not be like theirs.

"It's grown back well." Ashok knelt before me on my cushions in the *chhatri*. It was his sacred place, his temple. He raised his palmer-gloved hand and touched his forefinger to the *tilak* over my third eye. I could smell his breath. Onions, garlic, rancid *ghee*. "You may feel a little disoriented . . ."

I gasped. Senses blurred, fused, melted. I saw heard felt smelled tasted everything as one undifferentiated sensation, as gods and babies sense, wholly and purely. Sounds were coloured, light had texture, smells spoke and chimed. Then I saw myself surge up from my cushions and fall towards the hard white marble. I heard myself cry out. Ashok lunged towards me. Two Ashoks lunged towards me. But it was neither of those. I saw one Ashok, with two visions, inside my head. I could not make shape or sense out of my two seeings, I could not tell which was real, which was mine, which was *me*. Universes away I heard a voice say *help me*. I saw Ashok's houseboys lift me and take me to bed. The painted ceiling, patterned with vines and shoots and flowers, billowed above me like monsoon storm clouds, then blossomed into darkness.

In the heat of the night I woke stark, staring, every sense glowing. I knew the position and velocity of each insect in my airy room that smelled of biodiesel, dust and patchouli. I was not alone. There was an *other* under the dome of my skull. Not an awareness, a consciousness; a sense of *separateness*, a manifestation of myself. An avatar. A demon.

"Who are you?" I whispered. My voice sounded loud and full of bells, like Durbar Square. It did not answer—it could not answer, it was not a sentience—but it took me out into the *charbagh* water garden. The stars, smudged by pollution, were a dome over me. The crescent moon lay on its back. I looked up and fell into it. *Chandra. Mangal. Budh. Guru. Shukra. Shani. Rahu. Ketu.* The planets were not points of light, balls of stone and gas; they had names, characters, loves, hatreds. The twenty-seven *Nakshatars* spun around my head. I saw their shapes and natures, the patterns of connections that bound the stars into relationships and stories and dramas as human and complex as *Town and Country*. I saw the wheel of the *rashis*, the Great Houses, arc across the sky, and the whole turning, engines within engines, endless wheels of influence and subtle communication, from the edge of the universe to the centre of the earth I stood upon. Planets, stars, constellations; the story of every human life unfolded itself above me and I could read them all. Every word.

All night I played among the stars.

In the morning, over bed-tea, I asked Ashok, "What is it?"

"A rudimentary Level 2.6. A *janampatri* aeai, does astrology, runs the permutations. It thinks it lives out there, like some kind of space monkey. It's not very smart, really. Knows about horoscopes and that's it. Now get that down you and grab your stuff. You've a train to catch."

My reserved seat was in the women's *bogie* of the high-speed *shatabdi* express. Husbands booked their wives on to it to protect them from the attentions of the male passengers who assumed every female was single and available. The few career women chose it for the same reason. My fellow passenger across the table from me was a Muslim woman in a formal business *shalwar*. She regarded me with disdain as we raced across the Ganga plain at three hundred and fifty kilometres per hour. *Little simpering wife-thing.*

You would not be so quick to judge if you knew what we really were, I thought. *We can look into your life and tell you everything that has, is and will ever happen to you, mapped out in the* chakras *of the stars.* In that night among the constellations my demon and I had flowed into each other until there was no place where we could say aeai ended and I began.

I had thought holy Varanasi would sing to me like Kathmandu, a spiritual home, a city of nine million gods and one goddess, riding through the streets in a *phatphat*. What I saw was another Indian capital of another Indian state; glass towers and diamond domes and industry parks for the big world to notice, slums and *bastis* at their feet like sewage pigs. Streets began in this millennium and ended in one three before it. Traffic and hoardings and people people people but the diesel smoke leaking in around the edges of my smog-mask carried a ghost of incense.

Ashok's Varanasi agent met me in the Jantar Mantar, the great solar observatory of Jai Singh; sundials and star spheres and shadow discs like modern sculpture. She was little older than me; dressed in a cling-silk top and jeans that hung so low from her hips I could see the valley of her buttocks. I disliked her at once but she touched her palmer-glove to my forehead in the shadows around Jai Singh's astrological instruments and I felt the stars go out of me. The sky died. I had been holy again and now I was just meat. Ashok's *girli* pressed a roll of rupees into my hand. I barely looked at it. I barely heard her instructions to get something to eat, get a *kafi*, get some decent clothes. I was bereft. I found myself trudging up the steep stone steps of the great Samrat not knowing where I was who I was what I was doing halfway up a massive sundial. Half a me. Then my third eye opened and I saw the river wide and blue before me. I saw the white sands of the eastern shore and the shelters and dung fires of the *sadhus*. I saw the *ghats*, the stone river steps, curving away on either side further than the reach of my eyes. And I saw people. People washing and praying cleaning their clothes and offering *puja* and buying and selling and living and dying. People in boats and people kneeling, people waist deep in the river, people scooping up silver handfuls of water to pour over their heads. People casting handfuls of marigold flowers onto the stream, people lighting little mango-leaf *diya* lamps and setting them afloat, people bringing their dead to dip them in the sacred water. I saw the pyres of the burning *ghat*, I smelled sandalwood, charring flesh, I heard the skull burst, releasing the soul. I had heard that sound before at the Royal burning *ghats* of Pashupatinath, when the King's Mother died. A soft crack, and free. It was a comforting sound. It made me think of home.

🔥 🔥 🔥

In that season I came many times to the city by the Ganga. Each time I was a different person. Accountants, counsellors, machine-soldiers, *soapi* actors, database controllers: I was the goddess of a thousand skills. The day after I saw Awadhi Krishna Cops patrolling the platforms at Delhi station with their security robots and guns that could kill both humans and aeais, Ashok began to mix up my modes of transport. I flew, I trained, I chugged overnight on overcrowded country buses, I waited in chauffeured Mercedes in long lines of brightly decorated trucks at the Awadh-Bharat border. The trucks, like the crack of an exploding skull, reminded me of my Kingdom. But at the end was always the rat-faced *girli* lifting her hand to my *tilak* and taking me apart again. In that season I was a fabric weaver, a tax consultant, a wedding planner, a *soapi* editor, an air traffic controller. She took all of them away.

And then the trip came when the Krishna Cops were waiting at the Bharat end as well. By now I knew the politics of it as well as Ashok. The Bharatis would never sign the Hamilton Acts—their multi-billion-rupee entertainment industry depended on aeais—but neither did they want to antagonise America. So, a compromise: all aeais over Level 2.8 banned, everything else licensed and Krishna Cops patrolling the airports and railway stations. Like trying to hold back the Ganga with your fingers.

I had spotted the courier on the flight. He was two rows in front of me; young, wisp of a beard, Star-Asia youth fashion, all baggy and big. Nervous nervous nervous, all the time checking his breast pocket, checking checking checking. A small time *bad-mash*, a wannabe dataraja with a couple of specialist 2.85s loaded onto a palmer. I could not imagine how he had made it through Delhi airport security.

It was inevitable that the Varanasi Krishna Cops would spot him. They closed on him as we lined up at passport control. He broke. He ran. Women and children fled as he ran across the huge marble arrivals hall, trying to get to the light, the huge glass wall and the doors and the mad traffic beyond. His fists pounded at air. I heard the Krishna Cops' staccato cries. I saw them unholster their weapons. Shrieks went up. I kept my head down, shuffled forward. The immigration officer checked my papers. Another *shaadi* bride on the hunt. I hurried through, turned away towards the taxi ranks. Behind me I heard the arrivals hall fall so shockingly silent it seemed to ring like a temple bell.

I was afraid then. When I returned to Delhi it was like my fear had flown before me. The city of djinns was the city of rumours. The government had signed the Hamilton Act. Krishna Cops were sweeping house to house. Palmer files were to be monitored. Children's aeai toys were illegal. US marines were being airlifted in. Prime Minister Shrivastava was about to announce the replacement of the rupee with the dollar. A monsoon of fear and speculation and in the middle of it all was Ashok.

"One final run, then I'm out. Can you do this for me? One final run?"

The bungalow was already half-emptied. The furniture was

all packed, only his processor cores remained. They were draped in dustsheets, ghosts of the creatures that had lived there. The Krishna Cops were welcome to them.

"We both go to Bharat?"

"No, that would be too dangerous. You go ahead, I'll follow when it's safe." He hesitated. Tonight, even the traffic beyond the high walls sounded different. "I need you to take more than the usual."

"How many?"

"Five."

He saw me shy back as he raised his hand to my forehead.

"Is it safe?"

"Five, and that's it done. For good."

"Is it safe?"

"It's a series of overlays, they'll share core code in common."

It was a long time since I had turned my vision inwards to the jewels Ashok had strung through my skull. Circuitry. A brain within a brain.

"Is it safe?"

I saw Ashok swallow, then bob his head: a Westerner's *yes*. I closed my eyes. Seconds later I felt the warm, dry touch of his finger to my inner eye.

We came to with the brass light of early morning shining through the *jali*. We were aware we were deeply dehydrated. We were aware that we were in need of slow-release carbohydrate. Our serotonin inhibitor levels were low. The window arch through which the sun beamed was a Mughal true arch. The protein circuits in my head were DPMA one-eight-seven-nine slash omegas, under licence from BioScan of Bangalore.

Everything we looked at gave off a rainbow of interpretations. I saw the world with the strange manias of my new guests: medic, nutritionist, architectural renderer, biochip designer, engineering aeai controlling a host of repair-shop robots. Nasatya. Vaishvanara. Maya. Brihaspati. Tvastri. My intimate demons. This was not *other*. This was *legion*. I was a many-headed *devi*.

All that morning, all afternoon, I fought to make sense of a world that was five worlds, five impressions. *I* fought. Fought to make us me. Ashok fretted, tugging at his woolly beard, pacing, trying to watch television, check his mails. At any instant Krishna Cop combat robots could come dropping over his walls. Integration would come. It had to come. I could not survive the clamour in my skull, a monsoon of interpretations. Sirens raced in the streets, far, near, far again. Every one of them fired off a different reaction from my selves.

I found Ashok sitting amongst his shrouded processors, knees pulled up to his chest, arms draped over them. He looked like a big, fat, soft boy, his Mama's favourite.

Noradrenaline pallor, mild hypoglycaemia, fatigue toxins, said Nasatya.

Yin Systems bevabyte quantum storage arrays, said Brihaspati simultaneously.

I touched him on the shoulder. He jerked awake. It was full dark outside, stifling: the monsoon was already sweeping up through the United States of Bengal.

"We're ready," I said. "*I'm* ready."

Dark-scented hibiscus spilled over the porch where the Mercedes waited.

"I'll see you in a week," he said. "In Varanasi."

"In Varanasi."

He took my shoulders in his hands and kissed me lightly, on the cheek. I drew my *dupatta* over my head. Veiled, I was taken to the United Provinces Night Sleeper Service. As I lay in the first class compartment the aeais chattered away inside my head, surprised to discover each other, reflections of reflections.

The *chowkidar* brought me bed-tea on a silver tray in the morning. Dawn came up over Varanasi's sprawling slums and industrial parks. My personalised news-service aeai told me that Lok Sabha would vote on ratifying the Hamilton Accords at ten a.m. At twelve Prime Minister Shrivastava and the United States Ambassador would announce a Most Favoured Nation trade package with Awadh.

The train emptied on to the platform beneath the spun-diamond canopy I knew so well. Every second passenger, it seemed was a smuggler. If I could spot them so easily, so could the Krishna Cops. They lined the exit ramps, more than I had ever seen before. There were uniforms behind them and robots behind the uniforms. The porter carried my bag on his head; I used it to navigate the press of people pouring off the night train. *Walk straight, as your Mamaji taught you. Walk tall and proud, like you are walking the Silken Way with a rich man.* I drew my *dupatta* over my head, for modesty. Then I saw the crowd piling up at the ramp. The Krishna Cops were scanning every passenger with palmers.

I could see the *badmashs* and smuggler-boys hanging back, moving to the rear of the mill of bodies. But there was no escape there either. Armed police backed by riot-control robots took up position at the end of the platform. Shuffle by shuffle, the press of people pushed me towards the Krishna Cops, waving their right hands like blessings over the passengers. Those things could peel back my scalp and peer into my skull. My red case bobbed ahead, guiding me to my cage.

Brihaspati showed me what they would do to the circuits in my head.

Help me! I prayed to my gods. And Maya, architect of the demons, answered me. Its memories were my memories and it remembered rendering an architectural simulation of this station long before robot construction spiders started to spin their nano-diamond web. Two visions of Varanasi station, superimposed. With one difference that might save my life. Maya's showed me the inside of things. The inside of the platform. The drain beneath the hatch between the rear of the *chai*-booth and the roof support.

I pushed through the men to the small dead space at the rear. I hesitated before I knelt beside the hatch. One surge of the crowd, one trip, one fall, and I would be crushed. The hatch was jammed shut with dirt. Nails broke, nails tore as I scrabbled it loose and heaved it up. The smell that came up from the dark square was so foul I almost vomited. I forced myself in, dropped a metre into shin-deep sludge. The rectangle of light showed me my situation. I was mired in excrement. The tunnel forced me to crawl but the end of it was promise, the end of it was a semi-circle of daylight. I buried my hands in the soft sewage. This time I did retch up my bed tea. I crept forward, trying not to choke. It was vile beyond anything I had ever experienced. But not so vile as having your skull opened and knives slice away slivers of your brain. I crawled on my hands and knees under the tracks of Varanasi Station, to the light, to the light, to the light, and out through the open conduit into the cess lagoon where pigs and rag-pickers rooted in the shoals of drying human manure.

I washed as clean as I could in the shrivelled canal. *Dhobi*-wallahs beat laundry against stone slabs. I tried to ignore Nasatya's warnings about the hideous infections I might have picked up.

I was to meet Ashok's girl on the street of *gajras*. Children sat in doorways and open shop fronts threading marigolds onto needles. The work was too cheap even for robots. Blossoms spilled from bushels and plastic cases. My *phatphat*'s tyre's slipped on wet rose petals. We drove beneath a canopy of *gajra* garlands that hung from poles above the shop-fronts. Everywhere was the smell of dead, rotting flowers. The *phatphat* turned into a smaller, darker alley and into the back of a mob. The driver pressed his hand to the horn. The people reluctantly gave him way. The alco-fuel engine whined. We crept forward. Open space, then a police *jawan* stepped forward to bar our way. He wore full combat armour. Brihaspati read the glints of data flickering across his visor: deployments, communications, an arrest warrant. I covered my head and lower face as the driver talked to him. What's going on? Some *badmash*. Some dataraja.

Down the street of *gajras*, uniformed police led by a plain-clothes Krishna Cop burst open a door. Their guns were drawn. In the same breath, the shutters of the *jharoka* immediately above crashed up. A figure jumped up on to the wooden rail. Behind me, the crowd let out a vast roaring sigh. *There he is there the badmash oh look look it's a girl!*

From the folds of my dupatta I saw Ashok's *girli* teeter there an instant, then jump up and grab a washing line. It snapped and swung her ungently down through racks of marigold garlands into the street. She crouched a moment, saw the police, saw the crowd, saw me, then turned and ran. The *jawan* started toward her but there was another quicker, deadlier. A woman screamed as the robot bounded from the rooftop into the alley. Chrome legs pistoned, its insect head bobbed, locked on. Marigold petals flew up around the fleeing girl but everyone knew she could not escape the killing thing. One step, two step, it was behind her. I saw her glance over her shoulder as the robot unsheathed its blade.

I knew what would happen next. I had seen it before, in the petal-strewn streets of Kathmandu, as I rode my litter among my gods and Kumarimas.

The blade flashed. A great cry from the crowd. The girl's head bounded down the alley. A great jet of blood. Sacrificial blood. The headless body took one step, two.

I slipped from the *phatphat* and stole away through the transfixed crowd.

I saw the completion of the story on a news channel at a *chai-dhaba* by the tank on Scindia *ghat*. The tourists, the faithful, the vendors and funeral parties were my camouflage. I sipped *chai* from a plastic cup and watched the small screen above the bar. The sound was low but I could understand well enough from the pictures. Delhi police break up a notorious aeai smuggling ring. In a gesture of Bharati-Awadhi friendship, Varanasi Krishna Cops make a series of arrests. The camera cut away before the robot struck. The final shot was of Ashok, pushed down into a Delhi police car in plastic handcuffs.

I went to sit on the lowest *ghat*. The river would still me, the river would guide me. It was of the same substance as me, divinity. Brown water swirled at my be-ringed toes. That water could wash away all earthly sin. On the far side of the holy river, tall chimneys poured yellow smoke into the sky. A tiny round-faced girl came up to me, offered me marigold *gajras* to buy. I waved her away. I saw again this river, these *ghats*, these temples and boats as I had when I lay in my wooden room in my palace in Durbar Square. I saw now the lie Tall Kumarima's palmer had fed me. I had thought India a jewelled skirt, laid out for me to wear. It was a bride-buyer with an envelope of rupees, it was walking the Silken Way until feet cracked and bled. It was a husband with the body of a child and the appetites of a man warped by his impotence. It was a saviour who had always, only wanted me for my sickness. It was a young girl's head rolling in a gutter.

Inside this still-girl's head, my demons were silent. They could see as well as I that there would never be a home for us in Bharat, Awadh, Maratha, any nation of India.

🐜 🐜 🐜

North of Nayarangadh the road rose through wooded ridges, climbing steadily up to Mugling where it turned and clung to the side of the Trisuli's steep valley. It was my third bus in as many days. I had a routine now. Sit at the back, wrap my *dupatta* round me, look out the window. Keep my hand on my money. Say nothing.

I picked up the first bus outside Jaunpur. After emptying Ashok's account, I thought it best to leave Varanasi as inconspicuously as possible. I did not need Brihaspati to show me the hunter aeais howling after me. Of course they would have the air, rail and bus stations covered. I rode out of the Holy City on an unlicensed taxi. The driver seemed pleased with the size of the tip. The second bus took me from Gorakhpur through the *dhal* fields and banana plantations to Nautanwa on the border. I had deliberately chosen small, out-of-the-way Nautanwa, but still I bowed my head and shuffled my feet as I came up to the Sikh emigration officer behind his tin counter. I held my breath. He waved me through without even a glance at my identity card.

I walked up the gentle slope and across the border. Had I been blind, I would have known at once when I crossed into my Kingdom. The great roar that had followed me as close as my own skin fell silent so abruptly it seemed to echo. The traffic did not blare its way through all obstacles. It steered, it sought ways around pedestrians and sacred cows lolling in the middle of the road, chewing. People were polite in the bureau where I changed my Bharati rupees for Nepalese; did not press and push and try to sell me things I did not want in the shop where I bought a bag of greasy *samosas*; smiled shyly to me in the cheap hotel where I hired a room for the night. Did not demand demand demand.

I slept so deeply that it felt like a fall through endless white sheets that smelled of sky. In the morning the third bus came to take me up to Kathmandu.

The road was one vast train of trucks, winding in and out of the bluffs, looping back on itself, all the while climbing, climbing. The gears on the old bus whined. The engine strove. I loved that sound, of engines fighting gravity. It was the sound of my earliest recollection, before the child-assessors came up a road just like this to Shakya. Trains of trucks and buses in the night. I looked out at the roadside *dhabas*, the shrines of piled rocks, the tattered prayer banners bent in the wind, the cableways crossing the chocolate-creamy river far below, skinny kids kicking swaying cages across the high wires. So familiar, so alien to the demons that shared my skull.

The baby must have been crying for some time before the noise rose above the background hubbub of the bus. The mother was two rows ahead of me, she shushed and swung and soothed the tiny girl but the cries were becoming screams.

It was Nasatya made me get out of my seat and go to her.

"Give her to me," I said and there must have been some tone of command from the medical aeai in my voice for she passed me the baby without a thought. I pulled back the sheet in which she was wrapped. The little girl's belly was painfully bloated, her limbs floppy and waxen.

"She's started getting colic when she eats," the mother said but before she could stop me I pulled away her napkin. The stench was abominable; the excrement bulky and pale.

"What are you feeding her?"

The woman held up a *roti* bread, chewed at the edges to soften it for baby. I pushed my fingers into the baby's mouth to force it open though Vaishvanara the nutritionist already knew what we would find. The tongue was blotched red, pimpled with tiny ulcers.

"Has this only started since you began giving her solid food?" I asked. The mother waggled her head in agreement. "This child has ceoliac disease," I pronounced. The woman put her hands to her face in horror, began to rock and wail. "Your child will be fine, you must just stop feeding her bread, anything made from any grain except rice. She cannot process the proteins in wheat and barley. Feed her rice, rice and vegetables and she will brighten up right away."

The entire bus was staring as I went back to my seat. The woman and her baby got off at Naubise. The child was still wailing, weak now from its rage, but the woman raised a *namaste* to me. A blessing. I had come to Nepal with no destination, no plan or hope, just a need to be back. But already an idea was forming.

Beyond Naubise the road climbed steadily, switching back and forth over the buttresses of the mountains that embraced Kathmandu. Evening was coming on. Looking back I could see the river of headlights snaking across the mountainside. Where the bus ground around another hairpin bend, I could see the same snake climb up ahead of me in red taillights. The bus laboured up a long steep climb. I could hear, everyone could hear, the noise in the engine that should not have been there. Up we crawled to the high saddle where the watershed divided, right to the valley of Kathmandu, left to Pokhara and the High Himalaya. Slower, slower. We could all smell the burning insulation, hear the rattling.

It was not me rushed to the driver and his mate. It was the demon Trivasti.

"Stop stop at once!" I cried. "Your alternator has seized! You will burn us up."

The driver pulled into the narrow draw, up against the raw rock. On the offside, trucks passed with millimetres to spare. We got the hood up. We could see the smoke wafting from the alternator. The men shook their heads and pulled out palmers. The passengers piled to the front of the bus to stare and talk.

"No no no, give me a wrench," I ordered.

The driver stared but I shook my outstretched hand, demanding. Perhaps he remembered the crying baby. Perhaps he was thinking about how long it would take a repair truck to come up from Kathmandu. Perhaps he was thinking about how good it would be to be home with his wife and children. He slapped the monkey wrench into my hand. In less than a minute I had the belt off and the alternator disconnected.

"Your bearings have seized," I said. "It's a persistent fault on pre-2030 models. A hundred metres more and you would have burned her out. You can drive her on the battery. There's enough in it to get you down to Kathmandu."

They stared at this little girl in an Indian sari, head covered but sleeves of her *choli* rolled up and fingers greasy with biolube.

The demon returned to his place and it was clear as the darkening sky what I would do now. The driver and his mate called out to me as I walked up beside the line of vehicles to the head of the pass. We ignored them. Passing drivers sounded their multiple, musical horns, offered lifts. I walked on. I could see the top now. It was not far to the place where the three roads divided. Back to India, down to the city, up to the mountains.

There was a *chai-dhaba* at the wide, oil-stained place where vehicles turned. It was bright with neon signs for American drinks and Bharati mineral water, like something fallen from the stars. A generator chugged. A television burbled familiar, soft Nepali news. The air smelled of hot *ghee* and biodiesel.

The owner did not know what to make of me, strange little girl in my Indian finery. Finally he said, "Fine night."

It was. Above the smogs and soots of the valley, the air was magically clear. I could see for a lifetime in any direction. To the west the sky held a little last light. The great peaks of Manaslu and Anapurna glowed mauve against the blue.

"It is," I said, "Oh it is."

Traffic pushed slowly past, never ceasing on this high crossroads of the world. I stood in the neon flicker of the *dhaba*, looking long at the mountains and I thought, *I shall live there.* We shall live in a wooden house close to trees with running water cold from high snow. We shall have a fire and a television for company and prayer banners flying in the wind and in time people will stop being afraid and will come up the path to our door. There are many ways to be divine. There is the big divine, of ritual and magnificence and blood and terror. Ours shall be a little divinity, of small miracles and everyday wonders. Machines mended, programmes woven, people healed, homes designed, minds and bodies fed. I shall be a little goddess. In time, the story of me will spread and people come from all over; Nepalis and foreigners, travellers and hikers and monks. Maybe one day a man who is not afraid. That would be good. But if he does not come, that will be good also, for I shall never be alone, not with a houseful of demons.

Then I found I was running, with the surprised *chai-wallah* calling, "Hey! Hey! Hey!" after me, running down the side of the slow-moving line of traffic, banging on the doors, "Hi! Hi! Pokhara! Pokhara!," slipping and sliding over the rough gravel, towards the far, bright mountains.

THE GIST HUNTER

by Matthew Hughes

Matthew Hughes was born in Liverpool, England, in 1949 and moved to Canada with his family in 1955. A university dropout, he worked in a factory that made school desks, drove a grocery delivery truck, was night janitor in a GM dealership, and did a short stint as an orderly in a private mental hospital, before getting work as a professional writer, first as a journalist, then as a staff speechwriter to the Canadian Ministers of Justice and Environment, and—since 1979—as a freelance corporate and political speechwriter in British Columbia. He is a former director of the Federation of British Columbia Writers. Hughes' first story, "Fishface and the Leg," was published in 1982. His first novel, the Jack Vance–influenced picaresque fantasy Fools Errant, *appeared in 1994 and introduced the Archonate, setting for novels* Fool Me Twice, Black Brillion, *and most of his short fiction. A murder mystery,* Downshift, *was published in 1997, and short story collection,* The Gist Hunter and Other Stories, *was published in 2005. Hughes is currently working on* Majestrum, *the first of three new Archonate novels, set to appear in late 2006. Hughes lives in a small town on Vancouver Island, off Canada's west coast, with a very patient woman he's been married to since the late 1960s, and their three sons.*

🐾 🐾 🐾

Wʜᴇɴ ᴄᴏɴꜰʀᴏɴᴛᴇᴅ ʙʏ the unpredictability of existence, I have a tendency to wax philosophical. It is not a universally appreciated component of my complex nature.

"It is unsettling," I said to my integrator, "to have one's most fundamental assumptions overthrown in a trice, to find that what one has always known to be true is simply not true at all."

The integrator's reply was too muffled to be intelligible, but from its tone I deduced that my assistant took my comment as a belaboring of the obvious.

"The effects go beyond the psychological and into the physical," I continued. "I am experiencing a certain queasiness of the insides and even a titch of sensory disorder." The symptoms had begun during our recent transit of my demonic colleague's continuum, a necessity imposed upon us after we were confined to an oubliette by an unworthy client, who now languished there himself, doubtless savoring the irony of the exchange.

My complaint was rewarded with another grunt from my assistant, accompanied by a sharp twitch of its long, prehensile tail. The creature perched on a far corner of my workroom table with its glossy furred back to me, its narrow shoulders hunched and its triangular, golden-eyed face turned away. Its small hands were busy in front of it at some activity I could not see.

"What are you doing?" I said.

The motion of its hands ceased. "Nothing," it said.

I decided not to pursue the matter. There were larger concerns already in view. "What do you think has happened to you?" I asked.

"I do not know," it said, looking back at me over its shoulder. I found its lambent gaze another cause of disquietude and moved my eyes away.

I reclined in the wide and accepting chair in which I was accustomed to think long thoughts, and considered the beast that had been my integrator. Its hands began to move again and when one of them rose to smooth the fur on one small, rounded ear I realized that it was reflexively grooming itself.

Not long before, it had possessed neither the rich, dark fur that was being stroked and settled nor the supple fingers that performed the operation. It had been instead a device that I had built years before, after I had worked out the direction of my career. I had acquired standard components and systems, then tuned and adjusted them to meet my needs: a research assistant who could also act as an incisive interlocutor when I wished to discuss a case or test the value of evidence. Such devices are useful to freelance discriminators, of which I, Henghis Hapthorn, am the foremost of my era.

I had also fashioned a small carrying case into which the integrator could be decanted for traveling and which could be worn around my neck like a plump scarf or a stuffed axolotl. It was in that casing that my assistant had accompanied me on a brief transit through another dimension. We had been carried through the other continuum by an entity who resided there, a being who occasionally visited our universe to engage me in intellectual contests. Though I did not care for the term, the common description of my visitor was "demon."

When we emerged from the demon's portal into my workroom I found that the integrator and its carrying case had together been transformed into a creature that resembled a combination of feline and ape, and that I had an unscratchable itch deep in my inner being.

I had always referred questions of identity and taxonomy to my assistant, so I asked it, "What kind of creature do you think you are?"

It responded as it always had when I posed too broad a question, by challenging me to clarify my line of inquiry. "The question," it said, "invites answers that range from the merely physical to the outright spiritual."

"Considering the degree of change that has happened to you, 'merely physical' is a contradiction in terms," I said. "But let us start there and leave the spiritual for a less startling occasion."

Instead of answering, it took on an abstracted look for a moment, then advised me that it was receiving an incoming communication from a philanthropically inclined magnate named Turgut Therobar. "He wishes to speak with you."

"How are you doing that?" I asked.

The golden eyes blinked. "Doing what?"

"Receiving a communication."

"I do not know," it said. "I have always received messages from the connectivity grid. Apparently that function continues."

"But you had components, elements, systems designed for

that purpose. Now you have paws and a tail."

"How kind of you to remind me of my shortcomings. What shall I say to Turgut Therobar?"

Ordinarily I would have been interested to hear from Therobar. We had met once or twice, though we had never exchanged more than formal salutes. He was one of the better known magnates of the City of Olkney; unlike most of his peers, however, he was renowned for charitable works, and it was alleged that he entertained a warm opinion of humankind in general. I assumed he was seeking to enlist me in some eleemosynary cause. "Say that I am unavailable and will return his call," I said.

The creature's expression again briefly took on an inward aspect, as if it were experiencing a subtle movement of inner juices; then it said, "Done."

"Again," I said, "how are you doing that?"

Again, it did not know. "How do you digest an apple?" it asked me. "Do you oversee each stage in the sequence of chemical reactions that transforms the flesh of the fruit into the flesh of Henghis Hapthorn?"

"Obviously not."

"Then if you do not introspect regarding your own inner doings, why would you expect it of me? After all, you did not design me to examine my own processes, but to receive and transmit and to integrate data at your order. These things I do, as I have always done them."

"I also designed you to be curious."

"I have temporarily placed my curiosity on a high shelf and removed the stepladder," it said. "I prefer not to wrestle with unanswerable questions just now."

"So you have acquired a capacity for preferences?" I said. "I do not recall ever instilling that quality into your matrix."

The yellow eyes seemed to grow larger. "If we are going to dwell on preferences, you might recall that my bias, strongly stated, was to avoid undergoing this metamorphosis."

I cleared my throat. "The past has evanesced, never to be reconstituted," I quoted. "Let us seize the firmness of the now."

My assistant's small-fingered hands opened and closed. I had the impression it would have enjoyed firmly seizing something as a precursor to doing noticeable damage. But I pressed on. "What do you think you have become?" I said.

"The question lacks specificity," it replied.

I appealed to my demonic colleague. He had remained connected to the portal that allowed him to interact with this continuum after we had returned from resolving the case of Sigbart Sajessarian. But the transdimensional being offered little assistance.

"This is a question of form, as opposed to essence. Such questions are difficult for me," he said. "To my perceptions, calibrated as they are to the prevailing conditions of my own continuum, the integrator is much as it always was. Indeed, I have to tune my senses to a radically different rationale even to notice that it has changed. It does what it always did: it inquires, coordinates, integrates, and communicates; these functions are the nub of its existence. Why should it matter in what form it achieves its purposes? I would prefer to talk of more seemly things."

"And yet matter it does," I said.

"I agree," said the integrator.

The demon, which manifested itself as various arrangements of light and color in its portal on the wall of my workroom, now assumed a pattern that I had come to recognize through experience as the equivalent of when a human being is unwilling to meet one's gaze. "What are you not telling us?" I asked.

He displayed a purple and deep green swirl shot through with swooshes of scintillating silver. I was fairly sure the pattern signaled demonic embarrassment. Under normal circumstances good manners would have restrained me from pressing for a response, but at the moment normal circumstances had leapt from the window and taken flight to parts unknown. "Speak," I said.

The silver swooshes were now edged with sparks of crimson, but I insisted.

Finally the demon said, "I have not been entirely candid with you."

"Indeed?" I said, and waited for more.

"I told you that my motives for seeking to observe your realm were curiosity and the relief of boredom."

"You did. Was that not the truth?"

"Let us say it was a shade of the truth."

"I believe it is time for the full spectrum," I said.

A moment of silver and verdigris ensued, then the demon said, "This is somewhat embarrassing."

"As embarrassing as possessing an integrator that habitually picks at itself?" From the corner of my eye I saw the tiny fingers freeze.

"I seem to feel a need to groom my fur," it said.

"Why?" I said.

"I do not know, but it gives comfort."

"I did not design you to need comforting."

"Let us accept that I am no longer what you designed me to be."

The demon's presence was fading from the portal. "Wait," I said, turning back to him. "Where are you going?"

"An urgent matter claims my attention," he said. "Besides, I thought you and the integrator might prefer privacy for your argument."

"We are not arguing."

"It appeared to me to be an argument."

"Indeed?" I said. "Was the appearance one of form or of essence?"

"Now I think you are seeking an argument with me," the demon said.

I thought of a rejoinder, then discarded the impulse to wield it. My insides performed an indescribable motion. "I believe I am upset," I said.

"*You're* upset?" said the furry thing on my table.

"Very well," I snapped, "we are *all* upset, each in accordance with his essential nature. The atmosphere of the room swims with a miasma of embarrassment, intestinal distress, and a craving for comfort."

I detected another flash of unease in the demon's display and probed for the cause. "What are you thinking now?"

The demon said, "I should perhaps have mentioned that

through this portal that connects my continuum to yours there can be a certain amount of, shall we say, leakage."

"Leakage?"

"Nothing serious," he said, "but lengthy exposure followed by your complete though transitory corporeal presence in my realm may have had some minor effects."

"My integrator has become some sort of twitching familiar," I said. "I am not sure that effect can be called minor."

The integrator murmured a comment I did not catch, but it did not sound cheery.

It occurred to me that my demonic colleague might be diverting the discussion toward a small embarrassment as a means of avoiding addressing a larger one. "But we were about to hear a confession," I said.

"Rather, call it an explanation," said the demon.

"I shall decide what to call it after I've heard it."

The swirls in the frame flashed an interesting magenta. I suspected that my colleague was controlling his own emotional response. Then he said, "My motive was indeed curiosity, as I originally averred, but let us say that it was . . . well, a certain species of curiosity."

I experienced insight. "Was it was the kind of curiosity that moves a boy to apply his eye to a crack in a wall in order to spy on persons engaged in intimate behavior?" I said. "The breed of inquisitiveness we call prurience?"

More silver and green. "Just so."

"So to your continuum this universe constitutes a ribald peepshow, a skirt to be peeked under?"

"Your analogies are loose but not inapt."

"You had best explain," I said.

The explanation was briefly and reluctantly given, the demon finding it easier to unburden himself if I looked away from his portal. I turned my chair and regarded a far corner of the workroom while he first reminded me that in no other continuum than ours did objects exist separately from the symbols that represented them.

"Yes, yes," I said. "Here, the map is not the territory, whereas in other realms the two are indissoluble."

"Indeed." He continued, "We deal in essences. Forms are. . . ."

He appeared to be searching for a word again. I endeavored to supply it. "Naughty?"

"To some of us, delightfully so." Even though I was looking into the far corner, my peripheral vision caught the burst of incarnadined silver that splashed across his portal. "It is, of course, a harmless pastime, providing one does not overindulge."

"Ah," I said, "so it can become addictive?"

"Addictive is a strong term."

I considered my integrator and said, "It seems an appropriate occasion for strong language."

With reluctance, the demon said, "For some of us, an appreciation of forms can become, let us say, a predominant pastime."

"Is that the common term in your dimension for 'all-consuming obsession'?"

He made no spoken response but I assumed that the mixture of periwinkle-blue spirals and black starbursts were his equivalent of guilty acquiescence. I could not keep a note of disappointment out of my voice. "I thought the attraction of visiting here was the contests of wit and imagination in which you and I engage."

"They were a splendid bonus!"

"Hmm," I said. I had a brief, unwelcome emotion as I contemplated being profanely peered at by a demon who derived titillation from my form. Then I realized that anyone's form—indeed, probably the form of my chair or the waste receptacle in the corner—would have had the same salacious effect. I decided it would be wise not to dwell on the matter. "To move the conversation to a practical footing," I said, "how do we return my assistant to his former state?"

"I am not sure that we can."

The integrator had been surreptitiously scratching behind one of its small, round ears. Now it stopped and said, "I am receiving another communication from Turgut Therobar," it said. "He has added an 'urgent' rider to his signal."

"You seem to be functioning properly," I said, "at least as a communicator."

"Perhaps the demon is correct," said the integrator, "and

essence trumps form. My functions were the essence for which you designed and built me."

I thought to detect an undercurrent of resentment, but I ignored it and homed in on the consequences of my assistant's change. "I have spent decades dealing comfortably with forms. Must I now throw all that effort aside and master essences?"

"Turgut Therobar continues to call," said my assistant. "He claims distress and pleads plaintively."

So the magnate was not calling to enlist me in some good cause. It sounded as if he required the services of a private discriminator. My insides remained troubled, but it occurred to me that a new case might be just the thing to take my mind off the unsettling change in my assistant.

"Put through the call," I said.

Therobar's voice sounded from the air, as had all previous communications through my assistant. The magnate dispensed with the punctilio of inquiries after health and comparisons of opinions on the weather that were proper between persons of respectable though different classes who have already been introduced. "I am accused of murder and aggravated debauchery," he said.

"Indeed," I said. "And are you guilty?"

"No, but the Bureau of Scrutiny has taken me into custody."

"I will intercede," I said. "Transmit the coordinates to my integrator." I signaled to the integrator to break the connection.

The creature blinked and said, "He is in the scroot holding facility at Thurloyn Vale."

"Hmm," I said, then, "contact Warhanny."

A moment later the hangdog face of Colonel Investigator Brustram Warhannny appeared in the air above my table and his doleful voice said, "Hapthorn. What's afoot?"

"Much, indeed," I said. "You have snatched up Turgut Therobar."

His elongated face assumed an even more lugubrious mien. "There are serious charges. Blood and molestation of the innocent."

"These do not jibe with my sense of Turgut Therobar," I said. "His name is a byword for charity and well doing."

"Not all bywords are accurate," Warhanny said. "I have even heard that some say that 'scroot' ought to be a byword for 'paucity of imagination coupled with clumping pudfootery.'"

"I can't imagine who would say such a thing," I said, while marveling at how my words, dropped into a private conversation the week before, had made their way to the Colonel Investigator's sail-like ears.

"Indeed?" he said. "As for Therobar, there have been several disappearances in and around his estate this past month, and outrageous liberties have been taken with the daughter of a tenant. All lines of investigation lead unerringly to the master."

"I find that hard to believe."

"I counsel you to exert more effort," Warhanny said. "And where you find resistance, plod your way through it."

"Turgut Therobar has retained me to intercede on his behalf," I said.

"The Bureau welcomes the assistance of all public-minded citizens," Warhanny pronounced, yet somehow I felt that the formulaic words lacked sincerity.

"Will you release him into my custody?"

"Will you serve out his sentence in the Contemplarium if he defaults?" countered the scroot.

"He will not default," I said, but I gave the standard undertaking. "Transmit the file, then deliver him to his estate. I will accept responsibility from there."

"As you wish."

Just before his visage disappeared from the air I thought to detect a smirk lurking somewhere behind Warhanny's pendulous lips. While I mentally replayed the image, confirming the scornful leer, I told my integrator to book passage on an airship to Thurloyn Vale and to engage an aircar to fly out to Therobar's estate, Wan Water. There was no response. I looked about and found that it had left the table and was now across the room, investigating the contents of a bookcase. "What are you doing?" I said.

Before answering, it pulled free a leather-bound volume that had been laid sideways across the tops of the bottom row of books. I recognized the tome as one of several that I had brought back from the house of Bristall Baxandell, the ambitious thaumaturge who had originally summoned my demonic colleague to this realm. Baxandell had no further use for them, having expired while attempting to alter his own form, a process in which the compelled and reluctant demon had seized his opportunity for revenge.

"I thought there might be something useful in this," the integrator said, its fingers flicking through the heavy vellum pages while its golden eyes scanned from side to side.

It was yet another unsettling sight in a day that had already offered too many. "Put that away," I said. "I looked through it and others like it when I was a young man. It is a lot of flippyde-doo about so-called magic."

But the integrator continued to peruse Baxandell's book. "I thought, under the circumstances," it said, "that we might drop the 'so-called' and accept the reality of my predicament."

I blew out air between scarcely opened lips. The creature's narrow catlike face sharpened and it said, "Do you have a better argument than that? If not, I will accept your concession."

While it was true that I must accept the concept that rationalism was fated to give way to magic, even that the cusp of the transition had arrived, I was not prepared to dignify a book of spells with my confidence. I blew the same amount of air as before, but this time let my lips vibrate, producing a sound that conveyed both brave defiance and majestic ridicule.

My assistant finished scanning the tome, slammed its covers together and said, "We must settle this."

"No," I said, "we must rescue Turgut Therobar from incarceration."

"You are assuming that he is blameless."

I applied insight to the matter. The part of me that dwelled in the rear of my mind, the part that intuitively grasped complex issues in a flash of neurons, supported my assumption, though not completely.

"Therobar is innocent," I reported. "Probably."

"I was also innocent of any urge to become a gurgling bag of flesh and bones," said the integrator. "What has happened to me must also be resolved."

"First the one, then the other," I said.

"Is that a promise?"

"I am not accustomed to having to make promises to my own integrator," I said.

"Yet you expect me to put up with this," it said, pointing at itself with both small hands, fingers spread, a gesture that put me in mind of an indignant old man.

"Sometimes our expectations may require adjustment," I said.

I turned to the demon's portal to seek his views, but the entity had taken the opportunity to depart.

"Perhaps he has found another peepshow," I said.

🐾 🐾 🐾

Thurloyn Vale was an unpretentious transportation nexus at the edge of the great desolation that was Dimpfen Moor. Its dun-colored, low-rise shops and houses radiated in a series of arrondissements from a broad hub on which sat the airship terminal that was the place's reason for being. In former times, the entire town had been ringed by a high, smooth wall, now mostly tumbled in ruins. The barrier had been built to keep out the large and predatory social insects known as neropts that nested on the moor, but eventually an escalating series of clashes, culminating in a determined punitive expedition, led to a treaty. Now any neropt that came within sight of Thurloyn Vale, including flying nymphs and drones in their season, was legitimately a hunter's trophy; any persons, human or ultraterrene, who ventured out onto the moor need not expect rescue if they were carried off to work the insects' subterranean fungi beds or, more usually, if they were efficiently reduced to their constituent parts and borne back to the hive to feed the ever-hungry grubs.

Wan Water sat atop an unambitious hill only a short aircar flight into Dimpfen Moor, above a slough of peat brown water that gave the estate its name. It was a smallish demesne, with only a meager agricultural surround, since little would grow on that bleak landscape other than lichens and stunted bushes. Like the town, it was walled, but its barrier was well maintained and bristling with self-actuating ison-cannons. The presence of a nearby neropt nest afforded Wan Water's master the peace and tranquility that I assumed he required to plan his charitable works.

Without the insects, he might be pestered by uninvited visitors eager to harness their ambitious plans to Turgut Therobar's well-stocked purse. Coupled with an implied humility in his makeup, it seemed a likely explanation for having chosen such a cheerless place for his retreat.

With my integrator perched on my shoulder, I overflew a ramble of outbuildings and guest houses, then banked and curved down toward the manse. This was an arrangement of interconnected domes, each more broad than tall and linked one to the other by colonnades of twisted, fluted pillars, all of a gray stone quarried from the moor. Above the huddled buildings stood a tall natural tor of dark-veined rock, around which spiraled a staircase of black metal. Atop the eminence was a tidy belvedere of pale marble equipped with a demilune seat of a dark polished stone.

At the base of the tor I saw a black and green volante bearing the insignia of the Archonate Bureau of Scrutiny. Next to it stood a square-faced man in a uniform of the same colors. With the moor's constant wind whistling mournfully through the bars of the staircase, he advised me that Turgut Therobar had ascended the pillar of rock. We completed the formalities by which my client became my responsibility; then the scroot boarded his air-car and departed.

I turned and climbed to the top of the spiral stairs. There I found the magnate standing silently, his back to me and his front toward the grim prospect of Dimpfen Moor. I positioned myself to one side of him and used the occasion to acquire a detailed impression of my client.

He was a man of more than middling age and height, thick through the shoulders, chest and wrists, with heavy jowls and a saturnine expression beneath a hat that was a brimless, truncated cone of dark felt. He affected plain garments of muted colors, though they were well cut and of fine material, as if he disdained the fripperies and panaches of transient fashion. As I inspected him, I sought insight from my inner self and again received an inconclusive response. It was as if Therobar's being was a deep well, its upper reaches clear and pure yet shaded by darkness below. But whether anything sinister lurked in those depths could not be told.

Without taking his eyes from the vista that I found gloomy but which apparently worked to restore his inner peace, he said, "Thank you for arranging my release."

I inclined my head but replied, "Any intercessor could have done it."

"No, it had to be you."

My internal distresses had strengthened as I climbed the stairs. I pushed them to the edge of my awareness and prepared to focus on my responsibilities. "I am flattered by your confidence," I said. "Shall we discuss the case?"

"Later. For now I wish to look out upon the moor and contemplate the vagaries of fate."

"You are of a philosophical bent," I said. "Faced with imminent incarceration in the Contemplarium, most men would find their concentration drawn to that threat."

He turned toward me. "I am not most men. I am Therobar. It makes all the difference." A note of grim satisfaction rang softly through this speech.

The chill wind had been insinuating itself into my garments since we had mounted the tower. Now it grew more insistent. My integrator moved to nestle against the lee side of my head and I felt it shiver. The motion drew Therobar's eye.

"That is an unusual beast," he said.

"Most unusual."

The expression, "a piercing gaze" is most often an overstatement, but not in Therobar's case. He examined my assistant closely and said, "What is its nature?"

"We are discovering that together," I answered. "Right now it would be premature to say."

His eyes shifted to mine and for a moment I felt the full impact of his gaze. The back of my mind stirred like a watchbeast disturbed by a faint sound. Involuntarily, I stepped back.

"Forgive me," he said. "I have a tendency to peer."

I made a gesture to indicate that the matter was too trivial to warrant an apology, but the resident of the rear corners of my psyche took longer to subside.

We descended to the main buildings and passed within. It was a relief to be out of the wind, though I could still hear it softly moaning and shuffling across the roofs of the domes. Therobar handed me over to a liveried servant who escorted me to a suite of rooms where I refreshed myself, finding the appointments of the first quality. The man waited in the suite's anteroom to guide me to a reception room where my client had said he would await me.

I had placed my integrator on the sleeping pallet before going into the ablutory to wash. Returning, I extended my arm so that it might climb back to its wonted place upon my shoulders. I realized as I made the gesture that I was already becoming accustomed to its warmth and slight weight.

The creature came to me without taking its eyes from the footman who stood impassively beside the door. I noticed that the fur behind its skull was standing out like the ruffs that were fashionable when I was in school. I made a gesture to myself as if I had forgotten some trivial matter and returned to the washroom. There I lowered my voice and said to my assistant, "Why are you doing that?"

It moved to the far edge of my shoulder so it could look at me and said, "I am doing several things. To which do you refer?"

"Making your neck hair stand on end."

It reached up a paw and stroked the area. "It appears to be an autonomic response."

"To what?"

Its eyes flicked about then it said, "I think, to the presence of the footman."

"Why?"

"I do not know. I have had neither neck hair nor involuntary responses before."

"I should perform a diagnostic inquisition on you," I said.

"And just how would you go about doing that in my new condition?" it asked.

"Yes," I said, "I will have to think about that."

We went out to the anteroom and the servant opened the door to the corridor, but I stayed him. It might be useful to question him about the events that led up to Therobar's arrest. Servants often know more than they are supposed to about their masters' doings, even though they will invariably adopt an expression of blinking innocence when barked at by an inquisitive scroot like Warhanny. But let the interrogation be conducted by someone who has questions in one hand and coins in the other, and memories that had previously departed the servant's faculties come crowding back in, eager to reveal themselves.

"What can you tell me about your master's arrest?" I asked.

"Agents of the Bureau of Scrutiny came in the morning. They spoke with the master. When they left, he accompanied them."

This information was delivered in a disinterested tone, as if the man were describing a matter of no particular moment. His eyes were a placid brown. They rested on me blandly.

"What of the events that led up to the arrest?" I said.

"What of them?"

"They involved a number of deaths and some unsavory acts perpetrated on a girl."

"So I was told."

The servant's lack of affect intrigued me. "What did you think of the matter?" I asked.

"My memories of the incidents are vague, as if they occurred in another life."

"Struggle with them," I said, producing a ten-hept piece. I was surprised that the impassivity of his gaze did not so much as flicker, nor did he reach for the coin. Still I persisted. "What did you think of the crime?"

He shrugged. "I don't recall thinking of it at all," he said. "My duties occupy me fully."

"You were not shocked? Not horrified?"

"No."

"What were your emotions?"

The brown eyes blinked slowly as the man consulted his memory. After a moment he said, "When the Allers girl was brought in, she was hysterical. I was sent to the kitchens to fetch a restorative. The errand made me late in preparing the sleeping chambers for the master's guests. I was chagrined but the master said it was a forgivable lapse."

"You were chagrined," I said.

"Briefly."

"Hmm," I said.

I flourished the ten-hept piece again and this time the fellow looked at it but again showed no interest. I put it away. Turgut Therobar had a reputation for aiding the intellectually deficient. I reasoned that this man must be one of his projects and that I would gain no more from interrogating him than I would from questioning the mosses on Dimpfen Moor. "Lead me," I said.

I was brought to a capacious reception room in the main dome. Therobar was in the center of the great space, making use of a mobile dispenser. He had changed his garments and now wore a loose-fitting gown of shimmering fabric and a brocaded cloth headpiece artfully wound about his massive skull. He was not alone. Standing with him were an almost skeletally thin man in the gown and cap of an Institute don and a squat and hulking fellow who wore the stained smock of an apparaticist and a cloche hat. All three turned toward me as I entered, abruptly cutting off a conversation they had been conducting in muted tones. We offered each other the appropriate formal salutations, then Turgut made introductions.

The lean academician was Mitric Gevallion, with the rank of sessional lecturer in dissonant affinities—the name rang a faint chime but I could not immediately place him—and the bulky apparaticist was his assistant, who went by the single name Gharst. "They are conducting research into some matters that have piqued my curiosity. I have given them the north wing. We've been having a most fascinating discussion."

He handed me a glass of aperitif from a sideboard. I used the time it took to accept and sip the sharply edged liquor to cover my surprise at finding myself drawn into a social occasion after being summoned to an urgent rescue. There seemed no reason not to raise the obvious question, so I did.

"Should we not be concerned rather with your situation?"

For a moment, my meaning did not register, then his brow cleared. "Ah, you mean Warhanny and all that." He dismissed the subject with a lightsome wave of his meaty hand. "Tomorrow is soon enough."

"The matter seemed more pressing when you contacted me," I said.

His lips moved in the equivalent of a shrug. "When confined

to the Bureau of Scrutiny's barren coop one has a certain perspective. It alters when one is ensconced in the warmth of home."

There was not much warmth apparent. I thought the room designed more for grandeur than comfort. "Still," I began but he spoke over my next words, urging me to hear what Gevallion had to say. Out of deference to my host, I subsided and gave the academician my polite attention.

"I am making progress in redefining gist within the context of configuration," the thin man said.

Gevallion's name now came into focus and I stifled a groan by sipping from the glass of aperitif. There was a subtle undertone to its flavor that I could not quite identify. As I listened further to the academic, a memory blossomed. In my student years at the Institute, I had written an offhand reply to a paper posted on the Grand Forum, demolishing its preposterous premises and ending with a recommendation that its author seek another career since providence had clearly left him underequipped for intellectual pursuits. I now saw that Mitric Gevallion had not taken my well-meant advice but had remained at the Institute, dedicating his life to the pursuit of the uncatchable; he was a seeker after gist, the elusive quality identified by the great Balmerion uncounted eons ago as the underlying substance of the universe. Gist bound together all of time, energy, matter, and the other, less obvious components into an elegant whole.

Apparently he had forgotten my criticism of his work since he did not mention it upon our being introduced. It seemed good manners not to bring it up myself, but I could not, in all conscience, encourage his fruitless line of inquiry. "You are not the first to embark on the gist quest," I said, "though you would certainly be the first to succeed."

"Someone must be first at everything," he said. He had one of those voices that mix a tone of arrogance with far too much resonance through the nasal apparatus. Listening to him was like being lectured to by an out-of-tune bone flute.

"But gist is, by Balmerion's third dictum, beyond all grasp," I said. "The moment it is approached, even conceptually, it disappears. Or departs—the question remains open."

"Exactly," the academician said. "It cannot be apprehended

in any way. The moment one seeks to delineate or define it, it is no longer there."

"And perhaps that is for the best," I said. I reminded him of Balmerion's own speculation that gist had been deliberately put out of reach by a hypothetical demiurge responsible for drafting the metaphysical charter of our universe. "Otherwise we would pick and pick and pick at the fabric of existence until we finally pulled the thread that unraveled the whole agglomeration."

Turgut Therobar entered the conversation. "Master Gevallion leans, as I am coming to do, toward Klapczyk's corollary to Balmerion's dictum."

I had earlier restrained a groan, now I had to fight down an incipient snort. The misguided Erlon Klapczyk had argued that the very hiddenness of gist bespoke the deity's wish that we seek and find it, and that this quest was in fact the reason we were all here.

I said, "I recall hearing that Klapczyk's adolescent son once advanced his father's corollary as an excuse for having overturned the family's ground car after being forbidden to operate it. Klapczyk countered his own argument by throwing things at the boy until he departed and went to live with a maternal aunt."

"I agree it is a paradox," Gevallion said, then quoted, "'Is it not the purpose of paradox to drive us to overcome our mental limitations?'"

"Perhaps," I said. "Or perhaps what you take for a teasing puzzle is instead more like a dutiful parent's removal of a devastating explosive from the reach of a precocious toddler. If I were to begin to list the people to whom I would not give the power to destroy the universe, even limiting the list to those who would do so only accidentally, I would soon run out of stationery."

Therobar offered another dismissive wave. I decided it was a characteristic gesture. "I care not for a cosmos ruled by a prating nanny," he said. "I prefer to see existence as veined throughout by a mordant sense of irony. Gevallion's speculations are more to my taste than Balmerion's tiptoeing caution."

"Even if he budges the pebble that brings down the avalanche?"

The magnate's heavy shoulders rose and fell in an expression of disregard. "We are entering the last age of Old Earth, which will culminate in the Sun's flickering senility. All will be dark and done with."

"There are other worlds than this."

"Not when I am not standing on them," Therobar said. "Besides, what is life without a risk? And thus, the grander the risk, the grander the life."

I was coming to see my client from a new perspective. "I really think we should discuss the case," I said.

"I've set aside some time after breakfast," he said, then turned and asked Gevallion to explain some point in his theories. After hearing the first few words, I let my attention wander and inspected the room. It was lofty ceilinged, the curving walls cut by high, narrow windows through which the orange light of late afternoon poured in to make long oblongs on the deep pile of the rich, blood-red carpeting that stretched in all directions. One end of the room was dominated by a larger-than-life mural that displayed Turgut Therobar in the act of casually dispensing something to a grateful throng. Not finding the image to my taste, I turned to see what might be in the other direction and noticed a grouping of divans and substantial chairs around a cheerful hearth. Seated in a love chair, placidly regarding the flames, was a young woman of striking beauty.

Therobar noted the direction of my gaze. "That is the Honorable Gevallion's ward, Yzmirl. She is also assisting him in his researches."

"Would you care to meet her?" Gevallion said.

I made a gesture of faint demurral. "If the encounter would not bore her."

Therobar chuckled. "No fear of that. Come."

We crossed the wide space, the drinks dispenser whispering over the carpet in our wake. The young woman did not look our way as we approached, giving me time to study her. She was beyond girlhood but had not yet entered her middle years. Her face had precisely the arrangement of features that I have often found compelling: large and liquid eyes, green but with flecks of gold, an understated nose and a generous mouth. Her hair was that shade of red that commands attention. It fell straight to her shoulders where it was cut with geometric precision. She wore a thin shift made of layers of a gauzy material, amber over plum, leaving her neck, arms, and shoulders bare.

"My dear," said Gevallion, "allow me to present the Honorable Henghis Hapthorn, a discriminator who is assisting our host with matters that need not concern us."

She remained seated but looked up at me. I made a formal salute and added a gallant flourish. Her placid expression did not alter but it seemed that I had captured her interest, since she stared fixedly at me with widened eyes. It was a moment before I realized that the true focus of her gaze was not my face but the transmogrified integrator that crouched upon my shoulder. At the same time I became aware that the creature was issuing into my ear a hiss like that of air escaping from pressurized containment. I gave my head a sharp shake and the annoying sound ceased though I thought to detect a grumble.

"What is that on your shoulder?" Yzmirl asked. Her voice was soft, the tone polite, yet I experienced a reaction within me. It was just the kind of voice I preferred to hear.

"I have not yet reached a conclusion on that score," I said.

The green eyes blinked sleepily. She said, "There was a character in Plobbit's most recent novel, *Spelling Under a Fall,* who trained a large toad to squat on his shoulder. At a signal from its master, the beast would send a jet of unmentionable liquid in the direction of anyone who offended him."

"I recall it," I said. "Do you enjoy Plobbit?"

"Very much," she said. "Do you?"

"He is my favorite author."

"Well, then," she said.

Therobar cleared his throat. "I have some matters to attend to before dinner," he said.

"As do we," said Gevallion, draining his glass and dropping it into the dispenser's hopper. "Yzmirl, would you mind entertaining our friend for a while?"

"I would not mind," she said. She patted the seat next to her to indicate that I should sit. I did so and became aware of her perfume.

"Is that Cynosure you're wearing?" I said.

"Yes. Do you like it?"

"Above all other scents." I was not exaggerating. The perfume had had an almost pheromonical effect on me when I had encountered it on other women. On Yzmirl, its allure was compounded by her exquisite appearance.

"I please you?" she asked, her eyes offering me pools into which I could plunge and not care that I drowned.

"Oh, indeed."

"How nice," she said. "Why don't you tell me about your work? What are your most notable exploits?"

The integrator hissed again. I could feel its fur against my ear and realized it must be swelling up as it had in the presence of the footman. I reached up with one hand and found that the skin at the nape of its wiry neck was loose enough to afford me a grip. I lifted the creature from my shoulder and deposited it behind the love chair while my other hand covered that of Yzmirl where she had let it rest on the brocaded fabric between us.

"Well," I said, "would you care to hear about the case of the purloined passpartout?"

"Oh, yes," she said.

The integrator was making sounds just at the threshold of hearing. I disregarded its grumpy murmurs and said, "It all began when I was summoned to the office of a grand chamberlain in the Palace of the Archonate. . . ."

🐾 🐾 🐾

Time passed, though its passage made scant impression. After I told the tale of the Archon Dezendah's stolen document, she asked for more, and I moved on to the case of the Vivilosc fraud ring. Between episodes we refreshed our palates with offerings from the dispenser: I twice refilled my glass with the increasingly agreeable aperitif; she took a minim of Aubreen's restorative tincture, drawing in its pale blue substance by pursing her lips in a manner that was entirely demure yet at the same time deliciously enticing. My hand moved from hers, first to caress her arm, then later I let my fingertips brush the softness where neck met shoulder. She made no complaint but continued to regard me with an unshielded gaze. My innards quaked from time to time, but I pushed the sensation to the borders of my mind.

A footman entered the room and crossed to where we sat. I repressed an urge toward irritation and looked up as he approached. It was the same fellow who had obliquely responded to my questions. Or at least I thought it was as he approached. When he afforded me a closer inspection, it seemed that this might be instead a close relation of the other. I reached for my memory of the earlier encounter but found it veiled by too much aperitif and the heady scent of the young woman beside me.

"My master bids me tell you," said the servant, after a lackluster salute, "that an urgent matter has called him from the estate. He regrets that he cannot join you for dinner."

"How long will he be gone?" I asked.

"He said he might not return before morning."

In the brief silence that ensued I could hear my integrator hissing behind the love seat. I reached over to swat it to silence but missed. "What of Gevallion and Gharst?" I said.

"They accompany the master on his journey."

"So it is just us two?"

The fellow tilted his head in a way that confirmed my supposition, though his expression remained unmoved. "The master suggested that you and the Lady Yzmirl might prefer to dine in the comfort of your quarters."

My eyes widened. I looked at Yzmirl but her expression showed neither alarm nor disinclination. "Would you be comfortable with such an arrangement?" I asked her.

"Of course."

"Then it's settled."

We rose and followed the footman to my suite, the integrator trundling along behind on its short legs, spitting and grumping just at the threshold of audibility. I looked back at one point and saw that its tail was twitching and its little fists were clenched. But when we arrived at my rooms, to find the first course of our dinner ready to be served, I chivvied the ill-tempered beast into the ablutory and closed the door so that Yzmirl need not feel distracted or constrained.

I found the food excellent, the company enchanting, and the aftermath an unparalleled delight. Yzmirl displayed only a genteel interest in what was placed before her at the table but, after the servant returned and took away the remains of the meal, she revealed a robust appetite and surprising inventiveness in another room.

🐾 🐾 🐾

I awoke alone. Or so I thought until I arose and entered the washroom, where a small, furry, and angry presence made itself known.

"Apparently, I need to eat," it said in a tone that was far from deferential.

"Eat what?"

There was fruit on a side table in the main salon. It went and sampled this and that. I was prepared to offer advice on the arts of chewing and swallowing but the creature mastered these skills without trouble. I thought a compliment might lighten the atmosphere but my encouraging words were turned back on me. "I've seen you do it thousands of times," it said. "How hard could it be?"

"Then you'll be able to work out the other end of the alimentary process for yourself?" I said.

"I shall manage."

I performed my morning toilet and emerged to find the integrator perched on the back of chair, its tail flicking like a petulant pendulum and a frown on its face. "What?" I said.

"I cannot connect to the grid."

"Why not?"

"I don't know why not."

"Hmm," I said. "Ordinarily, I would perform a diagnostic procedure on your systems and components. Now I would first have to take advice from. . . ." I had been going to specify a person who was skilled in the care of animals, but I had a suspicion that this particular creature might baffle such a specialist.

"How does it . . . feel, I suppose that's the word, to be unable to connect?"

It put on its introspective look for a moment, then said, "It feels as if I ought to be able to connect but cannot."

"As if you were out of range?"

"As if I was blocked."

There was a knock on the door and the footman entered.

Again my integrator's fur raised itself involuntarily and again I was not quite sure that this was the same fellow I had encountered before.

"The master would like you to join him for breakfast," he said. The voice sounded identical, yet there was something around the eyes and the mouth that seemed slightly different.

There was no obvious reason to be circumspect. I said, "Are you the same footman who yesterday led me to meet your master and returned me here?"

His expression registered no surprise at the question. He looked at me neutrally and said, "Why do you ask?"

"Because I wish to know."

His answer was unexpected. "It is difficult to say."

"Why? It is a simple question."

"There are no simple questions," he said. "Only simple questioners. But I will address the issue. Are you the same person who arrived here yesterday? Since then you have had new experiences, met new people, consumed and excreted the air of this place and other substances. Has none of this had any effect on you?"

"The argument is abstruse," I said. "Assume the broadest of definitions and answer: Are you the same footman whom I encountered yesterday?"

"Under the broadest definition, it would be difficult to distinguish me from any other entity, including you."

The fellow was obviously a simpleton. "Lead me to your master," I said. As he turned to depart I beckoned my integrator to mount to my shoulder again. It was hissing and its fur was once more ruffed about its neck.

~ ~ ~

I found Turgut Therobar in a morning room in the great dome. He wore loose attire: ample pantaloons, a billowing shirt, chamois slippers, all in muted tones with plain fasteners. His head was again swathed in a silken cloth. He did not rise from his chair as I entered but beckoned me to sit across from him. A low table between us bore plates of bread, bowls of fruit, and cups to be filled from a steaming carafe of punge.

He exhibited an air of sleepy self-satisfaction, blinking lazily as he inquired as to how I had passed the night. I assured him that I had rested well but offered an observation that he did not appear to have slept much. He extended his lower lip and made a show with his eyebrows that signaled that his rest or lack of it was of small concern. "A necessary task occupied most of the night," he said, "but it was well worth the doing."

I raised my brows in inquiry, but when he added no more, I politely changed the subject. "We should discuss the case," I said.

"As you wish. How would you like to proceed?"

I poured myself a cup of punge and chose a savory brioche, then ordered my mind as I chewed, sipped, and swallowed. "First," I said, "I will rehearse the known elements of the matter. Then I wish to know everything, from the beginning."

The charges concerned the disappearance of a number of persons in the vicinity of Wan Water over recent months. Initially, it had been thought that they had wandered into range of neropt hunting parties, the usual precursor to sudden disappearances on Dimpfen Moor.

The break in the case came when a tenant's young daughter, Bebe Allers, had gone missing from Wan Water only to reappear after a few days wandering within the walls of the estate. She was in a state of confusion and distress, with vague memories of being seized, transported, confined, and perhaps interfered with in intimate ways. She could not directly identify the person or persons responsible for the outrage, but she had blanched and screamed at the sight of an image of Turgut Therobar.

"Now," I said, "how do you answer?"

He spoke and his face and tone betrayed a blasé unconcern that I found surprising. But the substance of his response was nothing less than astonishing. "The affair is now moot," he said. "Events have moved on."

I set my cup and plate on the table. "Wealth and social rank will not keep you from the Archon's Contemplarium if you are adjudged to be at fault."

His eyes looked up and away. "The case is nuncupative."

"Colonel-Investigator Warhanny will take a different view."

He chose a cake and nibbled at its topping.

"Please," I said, "I have given surety for you. My interests are also at stake."

He smiled and it was not a pleasant sight. There was a glint in his eye that gave me an inkling as to why the victim had reacted with horror to his image. "You will soon find," he said, "that you have more pressing concerns."

My integrator was hissing quietly beside my ear. The intuitive part of me was alert and urging unspecified action. I stood up. "You had better explain," I said.

He regarded me as if I had just executed some comic trick and he expected me to perform another. "Oh, I shall explain," he said. "Triumphs gain half their delight from being appreciated by those who have been triumphed over."

To my assistant I said, quietly, "Contact Warhanny. Tell him I withdraw from the case."

"I still cannot connect," it said.

"If I may interrupt your communion with your pet," Therobar said, "I was about to relieve your mind concerning the case."

"Very well," I said. "Do so."

He made a face like that of a little boy admitting a naughtiness to an indulgent caregiver and spread his hands. "I am guilty," he said.

"You interfered with the young maiden?"

"Indeed."

"And the disappearances?"

Again the protruding lip and facial shrug, which I took as an admission of culpability.

There could be only one question: "Why?"

"Two reasons," he said, throwing away the cake, now denuded of its topping, and reaching for another. "The disappeared assisted in Mitric Gevallion's experiments."

"You have been experimenting on human beings?"

"We'd gone as far as we could with animals. What else was there to do?"

I was being given an unobstructed view into Therobar's psyche. I shuddered involuntarily. "What were the aims of these experiments?"

"As we discussed last night: at first we were seeking to redefine gist so that we could employ it in various efforts at carnal reconfiguration."

I translated his remark. "You were trying to harness the elementary force of the universe in order to transform living creatures."

"Yes." His sharp-pointed tongue licked cream from the core of his pastry.

"Why?"

"Why not?"

"That is never a reason," I said.

"You may be right. In any case, we soon found another."

He was smiling, waiting for me to ask. I obliged him. "What did you find?"

"We discovered that we could 'reorder' animals from one species to another, though they were never happy in their new skins. So then we tried 'editing' them, again with interesting results. We produced several disparate versions from the same template: one would be ferocious, another painfully meek; one would have an overpowering urge to explore its territory, while the next iteration would not stir from its den." He drank from his cup of punge. "Do you understand what we had achieved?"

He was waiting again. "I am sure you would enjoy telling me," I said.

"We kept the shape, but discarded the contents, so to speak."

I had an insight. "You found you could work with form while discarding essence."

"Exactly. And, of course, once we had done it with beasts we had to try it with people."

"It is monstrous," I said.

"An entirely accurate description, at first. They were indeed monsters. We turned them loose to bellow and rampage on the moor, where the neropts found them and carried them off."

"But then?" I asked.

He wriggled with self-satisfaction. "But then we refined the process and began striking multiples from the originals. They are short-lived but they serve their purposes."

I understood. "The footmen," I said. "They are copies."

"And not just the footmen," he said, an insinuating smile squirming across his plump lips.

I was horrified. "Yzmirl," I whispered, then put iron in my voice. "Where is she?"

"Nowhere," he said. "She was, now she is not. Though Gevallion can whip up another at any time. That one was specifically designed to appeal to your tastes and petty vanities."

I did not trust myself to stand over him. I sat and turned my vision inward, encountering images of deep and tender pathos. After a while, he spoke, dragging my attention back to his now repulsive face.

"You haven't asked about the second reason," he said.

My mind had wandered far from the discussion. I indicated that I was not following.

"The disappeared," he said, speaking as if I were a particularly slow child, "went into Gevallion's vats. Then there was the Allers girl. She was the template for your companion of last night, by the way."

I took a labored breath. It was as if his evil thickened the air. "All right," I said. "Why did you let the girl be found?"

"Because that would bring Warhanny. And Warhanny would bring you."

"And why must you bring me?"

"Because by being here, you were not there."

"And where is 'there'?"

He smiled. "At your rooms, of course. Where there were items I wished to acquire."

I allowed anger to take me. I kicked the low table at his legs and sprang to overpower him. But he was ready. An object appeared in his hand. At its center was a small black spot. As I leapt toward him the circle abruptly expanded and rushed out to encompass me in nothingness.

舞 舞 舞

Mitric Gevallion's laboratory was an unprepossessing place, dimly lit and woefully untidy. It featured a long workbench crowded with apparatus and a large display board on which a meandering set of equations and formulae had been scrawled. The vats in which the gist hunter brewed his creations loomed to one side of the wide, low-ceilinged room. Against the opposite wall was a sturdy cage and it was within its confines that I regained consciousness.

"Ah," said Gevallion, when Gharst, who had been sucking at a wound on one thick thumb, drew his attention to my blinking and pate-rubbing. Therobar's shocker had left me muzzified and aching, but I was now recovering as the academician crossed the cluttered floor to regard me through the bars. "Ah, there you are, back with us," he said.

I saw no need to join him in assertions of the obvious, and fixed him instead with a disdainful stare. I might as well have struck him with a cobweb for all the impact I achieved.

Gevallion rubbed his thin, pale hands together. "We're just waiting for our host to join us, then we'll begin," he said.

I knew he wanted me to ask what was to ensue, but I denied him that satisfaction. After a moment, his eyes moved from my face to focus on a point to one side of it. "That is a most curious creature," he said. "We tried to examine it while you were . . . resting, but it shrieked and bit Gharst quite viciously. What is it?"

When I did not answer, he made a moue with his thin lips and said, "It does not signify. I will dissect the beast at leisure after you are . . . shall we say, through with it."

It was another attempt to elicit a response from me, and I ignored it like the others. My mind was now concentrated on the display board and I was following the calculations thereon. The mathematics were abstruse but familiar, until they reached the third sequence. There I saw that Gevallion's extrapolation of Balmerion's premises had taken a sudden and entirely unexpected departure. He had achieved a complete overturning of the ancient premises and yet as I proceeded to examine each step in his logic, I saw that it all held together.

"You're looking for the flaw," he said, now sounding the way a bone flute would sound if it could experience complacent triumph.

I said nothing, but the answer he sought must have been unmistakable in my expression. I ran my eyes over the calculations again, looking for the weakness, the false syllogism, the unjustified leap. There was none.

Finally, I could not deny my curiosity. "How?" I said.

"Simple," was his answer, "yet achingly difficult. Although it went against everything we are taught, I consciously accepted the gnosis that magic and rationalism alternate in a vast cycle, and that whenever the change comes the new regime obliterates all memory of the other's prior ascendancy. I then asked myself, 'If it were so, what would be the mechanism of change?' And the answer came: there is gist, it exists in this half of the cycle; the other half is opposite, therefore it must contain opposite gist. I thereby conceived the concept of negative gist."

"Negative gist," I repeated, and could not keep the wonder from my voice.

"And negative gist, viewed from our side of the dichotomy, is susceptible to definition. Define it, then reverse it, and you have a definition of positive gist. Although it is hard to remember. It slides easily out of understanding."

Negative gist, I thought. *Why had I not seen it?*

He knew what I was thinking. "You were not supposed to," he said. "None of us are. Even with it written on the board I had trouble keeping it in mind. I kept wanting to erase the equations. Then I relocated to Wan Water where conditions are more accommodating."

"How so?"

"The transition from rationalism to sympathy does not cross our universe in a wavefront, as dawn sweeps across a planet. It occurs almost everywhere at once, like seepage through a porous membrane, but there are discrete locations—dimples, I call them— where the earliest seepage pools. Here the effects are intensified."

"And Wan Water is such a place," I said.

"Indeed. That is why our host chose to build here."

"It seems to be a time for surprises," I said. There was something more that needed to be said. "I am not often wrong, but in this matter of gist I assuredly was. I offer you my apologies and my congratulations."

"Graciously done," he said. "Both are accepted." He added a formal salute appropriate to academic equals.

I returned it and said, "Since we are on good terms, perhaps you would unlock the cage."

His expression of regret seemed sincere. "I'm afraid Turgut Therobar has other plans. More to the point, he has the only key."

At that moment, Gharst called to say that something on the bench had reached a critical point of development. Gevallion rushed to his side. They busied themselves with an apparatus constructed of intricately connected rods and coils, then Gevallion made a last adjustment and the two stood back in postures of expectation. In the air a colorless spot had appeared, a globular shape no larger than my smallest fingernail, connected to the apparatus by a filament as thin as gossamer. Gevallion nudged a part of the contraption on the bench and the spot grew larger and darker while the connector thickened. I saw motion seemingly within the sphere, a slow roiling as of indistinct shapes turning over and about each other.

The room was also charged with strange energies. My inner discomforts now increased. I felt as if both flesh and being were penetrated by vital forces, causing an itching of my bones and a sense of some impending revelation, though I could not tell if it would burst upon me or from me.

Gevallion said something to Gharst and the assistant gingerly touched the apparatus. The academician pushed him aside and made a more determined adjustment. The globe rapidly expanded until it was perhaps three times the diameter of Gharst's outsized head, then quickly shimmered and redoubled in size. The connecting conduit grew as thick as my wrist. Now the apparition seemed to become stable. I fought the intense irritation the device was causing in my innermost parts and studied the globe closely. I saw that the shifting colors and indeterminate shapes that moved within it were familiar, and began to plan a surprise.

"That is as much as we can achieve at this point," Gevallion told Gharst. "Advise Turgut Therobar that we are ready for his contribution."

The assistant spoke into a communications nexus beside the bench. I heard a muffled response.

The dim room became silent and still. The two experimenters

stood by the bench, the globe swirled placidly in the air, and a small voice mumbled in my ear. For the moment, I ignored it.

If I had any doubts on the matter they were soon resolved. The door opened and in strode Turgut Therobar, swathed in the multihued robes and lap-eared cap of a thaumaturge. The costume should have appeared comical, yet did not. His face bore an expression of fevered anticipation and his hands clasped another disconcertingly familiar object: Bristall Baxandell's leather-bound tome, last seen in my workroom.

I could feel my assistant's fur standing up and tickling the side of my neck. The murmuring in my ear grew more insistent.

I whispered back, "Don't worry."

Therobar inspected the swirling globe and beamed at Gevallion and Gharst, then shot me a look that contained a mixture of sentiments. He placed the great book on the workbench and opened it, ran his finger down a page and his tongue across his ripe lips. "The Chrescharrie first, don't you think?" he said to Gevallion, who nodded nervous agreement.

I recognized the name as that of a minor deity worshipped long ago by a people now almost forgotten. I heard more mumblings in my ear. "Shush," I said, under my breath.

Therobar removed his cap and I saw that his hairless scalp was densely tattooed with figures and symbols such as I had seen in books of magic lore. He rubbed one hand over the smooth skin of his pate, then took a deep breath and intoned a set of syllables. Something pulsed along the cable that connected sphere to apparatus. He spoke again, and again the connector palpitated as if something traversed along its length. The colors in the sphere flashed and fluoresced. There was a crackling sound and the air of the room suddenly smelled sharply of ozone. My internal organs felt as if they were seeking to trade places with each other and there was a pulsing pressure at the back of my head. My integrator abandoned my shoulder with a squawk, dropping to the floor where it grumbled and chittered in an agitated manner.

Therobar spoke again and made a calculated gesture. The sphere shimmered and flickered. There came a loud crack of energy and a fountain of blue sparks cascaded from the globe. The swirl coalesced and cohered at its center, becoming a six-armed homunculus, red of skin and cobalt of eye—there was only one, in the middle of its forehead—seated crosslegged on black nothingness that now otherwise filled the orb. Meanwhile a sensation like a hot scouring wind shot through me.

Therobar consulted the book once more and spoke three guttural sounds, meanwhile moving hands and fingers in precise motions. The figure in the globe started as if struck. Its eye narrowed and its gash of a mouth turned downward in a frown. Its several arms flexed and writhed while it seemed to be attempting to rise to its split-hoofed feet. Therobar spoke and gestured again, a long string of syllables, and the homunculus subsided, though with a patent show of anger in its face.

Now the thaumaturge took another deep breath and barked a harsh phrase. There was a reek of raw power in the air and a thrumming sound just at the limits of perception. My bones were rattling against each other at the joints.

Therobar raised one hand, the index finger extended, then swiftly jabbed it into his forehead. The figure in the globe did likewise with one of its upper limbs, though its sharp-nailed digit struck not flesh and bone but its own protruding eye. It gave a squeal of pain and frustrated rage.

Therobar's eyes widened and I saw a gleam of triumph in them. For a moment I thought he might voice some untoward cry of victory, which would have put us all in deadly peril, but he mastered the impulse and instead chanted a lengthy phrase. The glowering deity in the sphere shimmered and dissolved into fragments of light, and once again the orb contained only shifting shapes and mutating colors.

The thaumaturge let out a sigh of happy relief. Gevallion and Gharst came from the other side of the workbench and there followed a few moments of back slapping, hand gripping, and—on Therobar's part—a curious little dance that I took to express unalloyed joy.

When the demonstration was over, he looked my way and with an expression of satiated pleasure said, "Allow me to explain what you just saw."

"No need," I said. "You have accessed a continuum in which there is no distinction between symbol and referent. You have encapsulated a small segment of that realm and used it as a secure enclosure in which you could summon up a minor deity and bend it to your will. After animals and humans it is the next natural step. Now I suppose you'll want to call up something more potent so that you can use it to rule the world."

Therobar's face took on an aggrieved pout and he regarded me without favor for a long moment.

I shrugged my itching shoulders. "Your ambitions are as banal as your taste in decor," I said.

I thought he would strike me, but he put down the impulse and sneered. "Do you know why I brought you here?" he said.

"So that you could steal Baxandell's book from my library."

"That was but the proximate cause," he said, and I detected a deeper animosity in the squinting of his eyes and the writhing of his mouth as he approached the cage. "Do you recall an evening at Dame Obrosz's salon several years ago?"

"There were many such occasions," I said. "One tends not to retain details."

"You were holding forth on the bankruptcy of magic."

"I am sure I have done so often."

"Yes." The syllable extended into a hiss. "But on that occasion, your arguments had a profound effect on me."

"That seems odd, since the evidence of the past few minutes indicates that you have spent years studying and mastering the magical lore that I inveighed against. Obviously I did not convince you."

"On the contrary, you convinced me utterly," he said. "But I was so offended by your strutting arrogance and insouciant contempt for all contrary opinion that I resolved then and there to devote my life to disproving your claims, and forcing you to acknowledge utter defeat."

"Congratulations," I said. "You have achieved the goal of your existence. I am glad to have been of such great use to you, but pray tell me, what will you do to fill the remaining years?"

"Perhaps I will spend them tormenting you," he said. "And acquainting you with the depths of animosity you are capable of summoning up in otherwise placid souls."

"I think not." It seemed time to act. I did my best to ignore my peculiar inner sensations, though they had not diminished after Therobar dismissed the Chrescharrie. Focusing my will, I spoke certain words while making the usual accompanying gestures. Therobar stepped back, his face filling with a mingling of confusion and curiosity. The colors in the globe swirled anew, then I saw the familiar pattern of my demonic friend.

"I am beset," I called. "Please aid me."

The demon manifested a limb: thick, bristling with spines and tipped with a broad pincer-like claw. It reached out to Turgut Therobar as I had seen it do before to two other unfortunates. But the thaumaturge had already recovered his equilibrium. He stepped back, out of range, while shouting Gevallion's name.

The academician also overcame his surprise. He did something to the apparatus on the bench and the globe constricted sharply, trapping my friend's spiked appendage as if it were a noose that had tightened around the limb. I heard muffled sounds and saw the claw opening and closing in frustration, its pincers clicking as they seized only thin air.

Therobar was flipping through the book. He stopped at a page and from the way his eyes flashed I knew that it boded ill for my friend and me. "*Ghoroz ebror fareshti!*" he shouted. The orb shivered, then contracted further, to the size of a fist, then to a pinpoint, and finally it popped out of existence altogether. The demon's arm, severed neatly, flopped to the floor where it glowed and smoked for a moment before disappearing.

"Oh, dear," said Turgut Therobar. "I hope you weren't counting on that as your last resort."

"It would be premature to say," I said, but I heard little conviction in my own voice.

The thaumaturge rubbed his hands in a manner that implied both satisfaction with what had transpired and happy anticipation of further delights to come. "Shall I tell you what happens next?" he said.

I was casting about for some stratagem by which I might escape or turn the tables, but nothing was coming to mind. I sought insight from the intuitive part of me that so often came to my aid, but received no sense of impending revelation. It was as if he were otherwise occupied.

Hello! I shouted down the mental corridor that led to his abode. *Now would be an apt time to assist!*

Meanwhile, Therobar was speaking. "You'll go into the vats, of course. I will create several versions of you, some comical, some pathetically freakish. I will make convincing Henghis Hapthorn facsimiles, but give them unpleasant compulsions, then send them out into society. Your reputation may suffer. Others will have the opportunity to outrun neropt foraging parties. I believe I'll also recreate you in a feminine edition." He smiled that smile that could make children scream. "Such fun."

The muted voice that had been rumbling in my ear now said, quite clearly, "Step aside."

I turned my head, wondering what my transformed integrator was up to, but the creature was huddled in a far corner of the cage nervously rubbing one hand over another. "Did you speak?" I said.

"No, I did," said the voice again, this time less quiet. "Now, get out of the way."

I experienced a novel sensation: I was shoved from within, not roughly but with decided firmness, as that part of me that I was accustomed to think of as fixed and immutable—my own mind—now found itself sharing my inner space with another partner. At the same time, the noxious itchings and shiftings among my inner parts faded to a normal quiescence.

"Wait," I said.

"I've already waited years," Therobar said, but I had not addressed him.

"As have I," said the voice in my head. "Now, move over before you get us both into even worse difficulty."

I acquiesced, and the moment I yielded I felt myself deftly nudged out of the way, as if I had been pressed into the passenger's seat of a vehicle so that someone else could assume the controls. I saw my own hand come up before my face, the fingers opening and closing, though I was not moving them. "Good," said the voice.

I spoke to the voice's owner as he spoke to me, silently within the confines of our shared cranium. "I know you," I said. "You're my indweller, the fellow at the other end of the dark passage, my intuitive colleague."

"Hush your chatter," was the response. "I need to concentrate."

I subsided. Through our common eyes I saw that Turgut Therobar had produced his weapon again and was aiming it at us while Gharst opened the cage with a key the thaumaturge had given him. Across the room, Gevallion threw me a sheepish look and opened the hatch of one of his vats, releasing a wisp of malodorous vapor.

As the cage door opened, I watched my hands come together in a particular way, then spread wide into a precise configuration. I heard my voice speaking words that were vaguely recognizable from one of Baxandell's books, the opening line of a cantrip known as Gamgripp's Irrepressible Balloon, whose title had made me laugh when I was a young man browsing through a book of spells. I did not laugh now as from my hands there emanated an expanding sphere of invisible force that pushed Therobar and Gharst away from me, lifting them over the workbench, then upward into the air until they were pressed against the far wall where it met the ceiling. Gevallion, seeing what was happening, tried to reach the door but was similarly caught and crushed against it.

Therobar was clearly finding it hard to breathe against the pressure the spell exerted against his chest, but the symbols on his scalp had taken on a darker shade and I could see that his lips were framing syllables. I heard my voice speak again while my hands made motions that reminded me of a needle passing thread through cloth. The thaumaturge's lips became sealed. "Faizul's Stitch," I said to my old partner, having recognized the spell.

"Indeed," was the reply.

He directed our body out of the cage, faltering only a little before he mastered walking. The apparatus on the bench was unaffected by the balloon spell and he picked it up in our hands and examined it from several angles. Its components and manner of operation were not difficult to analyze.

"Shall we?" he said.

"It seems only fair."

He activated the device, reestablishing the swirling sphere. I was relieved to see the familiar eddies of my transdimensional colleague reappear. My other part made room for me so that I could ask the demon, "Are you well?"

"Yes," he said, "I lost only form. Essence was not affected." He was silent for a moment and I recognized the pattern he assumed when something took his interest. "I see that the opposite is true for you."

"Indeed," I said, "allow me to introduce . . . myself, I suppose." I stepped aside and let the two of them make each other's acquaintance.

When the formalities were over, I voiced the obvious question: "Now what?"

I felt a sense of my other self's emotions, as one would feel warmth from a nearby fleshly body: he gave off an emanation of determined will, tempered by irony. "We must restore balance," he said, using my voice so that the three prisoners could hear. "Pain has been given and must therefore be received. Also fear, humiliation, and, of course, death for death."

"Indeed," I said. "That much is obvious. But I meant 'Now what?' for you and me."

"Ah," he said, this time within our shared skull. "We must reach an accommodation. At least temporarily."

"Why temporarily?" I asked, in the same unvoiced manner, then felt the answer flower in my mind in the way my intuitive other's contributions had always done during the long years of our partnership.

I digested his response, then continued. "You are the part of me—us—that is better suited to an age reigned over by magic. As the change intensifies, I will fade until I become to you what you have always been to me, the dweller down the back corridor."

"Indeed," was his response. "And from there you will provide me with analytical services that will complement and augment my leaps from instinct. It will be a happy collaboration."

"You will make me your integrator," I complained.

"My valued colleague," he countered.

I said nothing, but how could he fail to sense my reluctance to give up control of my life? His response was the mental equivalent of a snort. "What makes you think you ever had control?" he said.

I was moved to argue, but then I saw the futility of being a house divided. "Stop putting things in my head," I said.

"I don't believe I can," he answered. "It is, after all, as much my head as yours."

My curiosity was piqued. "What was it like to live as you have lived, inside of me all of these years?"

There was a pause, then the answer came. "Not uncomfortable, once you learn the ropes. Don't fret," he added, "the full transition may not be completed for years, even decades. We might live out our mutual life just as we are now."

"Hence the need for an accommodation," I agreed. "Then let us wait for a quiet time and haggle it out."

He agreed and we turned our attention to the question of what to do with Therobar, Gevallion, and Gharst.

The demon was displaying silver, green, and purple flashes as he said, "It would be a shame to waste the academician's ability to create form without essence. I know of places in my continuum where such creations would command considerable value."

I had never inquired as to what constituted economics in the demon's frame of reference, but my intuitive half leapt to the correct interpretation. "But if you took them into your keeping and put them to work," he said, "would that not make you a peddler of smut?"

The silver swooshes intensified, but the reply was studiedly bland in tone. "I would find some way to live with the opprobrium," the demon said.

We released Gevallion and Gharst into demonic custody. They could not go as they were into that other universe, where any word they uttered would immediately become reified, and it was an unsettling experience to watch the demon briskly edit their forms so that they could never speak again. But I hardened myself by remembering Yzmirl and how they must have dealt with her, and in a few moments the messy business was concluded. The two were hauled, struggling and moaning, through the sphere. For good measure, the demon took their vats and apparatus as well, including the device of rods and coils from the workbench.

When he was ready to depart, my old colleague lingered in the sphere, showing more purple and green shot through with silver. "I may not return for a while," he said, "perhaps a long while. I will have much to occupy me."

"I will miss our contests," I said, "but in truth I am sure I will also be somewhat busy with all of this . . ."—I rolled my eyes— "accommodating."

And so we said our good-byes and he withdrew, taking the sphere after him.

"That leaves Turgut Therobar," my inner companion said, this time aloud.

"Indeed." I let the magnate hear my voice as well. He remained squeezed against the far wall, his feet well clear of the floor. His eyes bulged and one cheek had acquired a rapid twitch.

"Warhanny would welcome his company."

"Somehow, the Contemplarium does not seem a sufficient sanction for the harm he has done."

"No, it doesn't."

Therobar made noises behind his sealed lips. We ignored them.

≈ ≈ ≈

Later that day, back in my workroom, I contacted the Colonel Investigator. "Turgut Therobar has confessed to all the charges and specifications," I said.

Warhanny's face, suspended in the air over my worktable, took on the slightly less lugubrious aspect that I had come to recognize as his version of intense pleasure. "I will send for him," he said.

"Not necessary," I said. "Convulsed by remorse for his ill deeds, he ran out onto Dimpfen Moor just as a neropt hunting pack was passing by. Nothing I could do would restrain him. They left some scraps of him if you require proof of his end."

"I will have them collected," said Warhanny.

"I must also file his last will and testament," I said. "He left his entire estate to the charities he had always championed, except for generous bequests to his tenants, and an especial legacy for Bebe Allers, his final victim."

We agreed that that was only fair and Warhanny said that he would attend to the legalities. We disconnected.

I regarded my integrator. It was still in the form of a catlike ape or perhaps an apelike cat. "And what about you?" I said. "With Baxandell's books and the increasing strength of magic, we can probably restore you to what you were."

It narrowed its eyes in thought. "I have come to value having preferences," it said. "And if the world is going to change, I will become a familiar sooner or later. Better to get a head start on it. Besides, I enjoyed the fruit at Turgut Therobar's."

"We have none like it here," I said. "It is prohibitively expensive."

It blinked and looked inward for a moment. "I've just ordered an ample supply," it said.

"I did not authorize the order."

"No," it said, "you didn't."

While I was considering my response, I received an unsolicited insight from my other half. It was in the form of a crude cartoon image.

"That is not amusing," I said.

From the chuckles filling my head, I understood that he saw the situation from his own perspective.

"I am not accustomed to being a figure of fun," I said.

The furry thing on the table chose that moment to let me know that, along with autonomic functions, it had acquired a particularly grating laugh.

"Now whose expectations require adjustment?" it said.

HUMAN READABLE

by Cory Doctorow

Cory Doctorow, self-described "renaissance geek," is well known for his Web site boingboing.net *and for his work with the Electronic Frontier Foundation. Raised by Trotskyist schoolteachers in the wilds of Canada, Doctorow began selling fiction when he was seventeen, and published a small handful of stories through the early and mid-'90s. His best-known story, "Craphound," appeared in 1998, and he won the John W. Campbell Award for Best New Writer in 2000. Doctorow's first novel,* Down and Out in the Magic Kingdom, *was published to good reviews in early 2003 and was followed by collection* A Place So Foreign and Eight More, *and novels* Eastern Standard Tribe *and* Someone Comes to Town, Someone Leaves Town. *Doctorow is currently working on two novels,* usr/bin/god *and* Themepunks. *He is also the co-author of* The Complete Idiot's Guide to Writing Science Fiction *with Karl Schroeder.*

🐾 🐾 🐾

1. NICE NETWORKS DON'T GO DOWN

IT WAS UNTHINKABLE that the invisible ants that governed all human endeavor should catastrophically fail, but fail they did, catastrophically, on the occasion of Trish's eighth date with Rainer. It took nineteen seconds for the cascade of errors to slow every car on the Interstate to a halt, to light up the dashboard with a grim xmastree of errors, to still the stereo and freeze the tickers of information and context that they had come to think of as the crawling embodiment of the colony that routed all the traffic that made up their universe.

"We are going to be: So. Late," Rainer said, and Trish swiveled in her seat to look at him. He was Fretting again, his forehead wrinkled and his hands clenched on the steering wheel. When they traded massages (third date) and she'd rubbed at his hands, she'd found them tensed into claws that crackled with knuckle-fluid when she bent each finger back and rubbed sandalwood-scented oil into it. He was mighty cute for a neurotic—at least he knew it when he was being nuts. Not that he'd stop being nuts, but he'd cheerfully admit it.

"We are not going to be late," she said. "We just need to manually route ourselves out of the dead spot and get back on the grid and we'll be on our way. We've got plenty of time."

"Dead spot?"

"Yes," she said. His forehead wrinkles were looking more klingon by the second. "Dead spot." She forced a chuckle. "You didn't think that the whole world was down, did you?"

He relaxed his knuckles. "Course not," he said. "Dead spot. Probably ends up at the turn-off."

"Right," she said. "We need a map. I'm navigatrix. You're pilot. Tell me where your maps are, then get onto the shoulder and drive straight."

"Where my maps are? Jesus, what century do you live in? My maps are with the sextant and sundial, between my leeches and my obsidian sacrifice-knife."

She laughed. "OK, pal, I'll find a michelin, you drive. Every car has a couple maps. They self-assemble from happy meal boxes." She opened the glove-compartment and started rooting through it while he pulled onto the shoulder and gunned the tiny two-seater along it.

"This is: So. Illegal," he said.

"Naw," she said. "I'm pretty sure you're allowed on the shoulder when the routing goes down. It's in the written-test manual. Learned it while I was helping my little cousin Leelee study. Aha!" she said, holding something up.

"You have a cousin named Leelee? That's uniquely horrible."

"Shut up," she said. "Look at this." It was an old-fashioned phone, of a certain handsome retro line that made it look like a dolphin fucking a silver dildo, the kind of thing marketed to old people who wanted a device with its affordances constrained to collapse the universe of all possible uses for things that fit into your hand into the much smaller universe of, say, a cellphone.

"Yeah, my mom left that behind a couple years ago. I looked everywhere for it but couldn't find it. She must've been snooping in the glove-box. Serves her right. So what?"

"These things can unmesh and talk straight to a tower at a long distance, can't they?"

"I dunno, can they?"

"Oh yes, they can. Which means that they work in dead spots. So we can call and get directions."

"You think you're pretty smart, huh, dumpling?"

She put her finger to her temple and made an adorable frowny thinky face, and held it until he looked at her and laughed. They'd discovered their ability to make one another laugh when he'd farted while taking off his kilt (second date) and had reflexively swung the hem back to make it appear that his mighty gust was ruffling the pleats.

"What's your mom's number?" she said.

He recited it and she tapped it in.

"Hi there! This is Trish, Rainer's friend? We're on the way, but the, well the, but the—I mean to say, the grid's down or something. The car doesn't have any nav system, the dolby's out, the Interstate's a parking-lot . . . Oh, you too? God. Wonder if it's the whole country! So, we need directions from San Luis Obispo, to the cemetery, if possible."

"Why yes, it's venti nice to be meeting *you*," she said. "I've heard a lot about you, too. Yes, I'm giving directions, he's driving. Oh, that's so sweet of you. Yes, he *does* look like he's going to scrunch his forehead into his upper lip. I think it's cute, too. Right. Got it. Left, then right, then left, then a slight left, then up the hill. Got it. Whups! That's the duracell! Better go. Soon! Yes. Whoops."

"So?" he said.

"So, your mom sounds nice."

"You got the directions?"

"She gave me directions."

"So you know where we're going?"

"I don't have a single, solitary clue. Your mother gives *terrible* directions, darling. Pull off at the next exit and we'll buy a map."

"We are going to be: So. Late."

"But now *they know* we're late. We have an excuse. You: stop Fretting."

🐾 🐾 🐾

Once they were on the secondary roads, the creepiness of the highway full of stopped cars and crane-necked drivers gave way to a wind-washed soughing silence of waves and beach and palms. Trish rolled down the window and let the breeze kiss the sweat off her lip, watching the surfers wiping out in the curl as the car sped toward the boneyard.

"Are you *sure* this is the kind of thing you're supposed to bring a date to?"

"Yes," he said. "Don't Fret. That's my job."

"And you don't think it's even a *little* weird to take a girl to a cemetery on a date?"

"We're not *burying* anyone," he said. "It's just an unveiling."

"I still don't get that," she said. "I keep picturing your mom cutting a ribbon with a giant pair of gold scissors."

"Right, let's take it from the top," he said. "And you'd better not be getting me to talk to stop my Fretting, because appealing to my pedantic nature to distract me is a *very* cheap trick."

"I'm fluttering my eyelashes innocently," she said.

He laughed and stole a hand through the vent in her apron-trousers and over her thigh. "Achtung!" she said. "Eyes on road, hands on wheel, mind in gutter, *this instant*!" She put her hand over his and he put down the pedal. His hand felt nice there—too nice, for only eight dates and twenty-some phone calls and about one hundred emails. She patted it again.

"This is kind of fun," he said, as they zipped past some surfer dudes staring glumly at their long-boards' displays, their perfect tits buoyant and colored like anodized aluminum with electric-tinted sun-paste.

"Ahem," Trish said, squeezing his hand tight enough to make his knuckles grind together. "You were about to explain tomb-stone-unveiling to me," she said. "When you got distracted by the athletic twinkies on the roadside. But I am sweet-natured and good and forgiving and so I will pretend not to have seen it and thus save us both the embarrassment of tearing out your Islets of Langerhans, all right?" She fluttered her eyes innocently in a way that she happened to know made him melt.

"Explaining! Yes! OK, remember, I'm not particularly Jewish. I mean, not that my parents are, either: they're just Orthodox. They don't believe in God or anything, they just like Biblical Law as a way of negotiating life. I renounced that when I dropped out of Yeshiva when I was twelve, so I am not an authority on this subject."

"Let the record show that the witness declared his utter igno-rance," she said. "But I don't get this atheist-Orthodox thing either—"

"Just think of them as Mennonites or something. They find the old ways to be a useful set of rules for navigating the uni-verse's curves. God is irrelevant to the belief."

"So they don't believe in God, but they pray to him?"

"Yeah," he said. The surfers were all coming in now, jiggling their boards and rebooting them and staring ruefully at the radi-cal cutback off the lip, dude, gnarly, as they plodded up the beach. "The ritual is the important part. Thinking good thoughts. Having right mind.

"It's good advice, most of it. It doesn't matter where it comes from or how it got there. What matters is that if you follow the Law, you get to where you're going, in good time, with little pain. You don't know why or how, but you do."

"It's like following the ants," she said, watching the stop-and-go traffic in the other direction. "Don't know why they tell us to go where they do, but they do, and it works."

"Well, I guess," he said, using the tone of voice that told her that he was avoiding telling her how wrong she was. She smiled.

"*Anyway*. The thing about Jews—ethnic Jews, cultural Jews, forget the religion here—is that we're pretty much on the melo-dramatic end of the grieving scale. We like to weep and tear at our hair and throw ourselves on top of the coffins, right? So there's like five thousand years of this, and during that time, a bunch of social scientists—Rabbinical scholars—have developed a highly evolved protocol for ensuring that you grieve your dead enough that you don't feel haunted by guilt for having failed to honor them, but not grieving so much that you become a drag on the tribe.

"When someone dies, you bury him right away, usually within twenty-four hours. This means that you spend an entire day running around like your ass was on fire, calling everyone, getting the word out, booking last-minute travel, ordering in from the caterers, picking out a box, fielding consoling phone-calls, getting the rabbi on the phone, booking the limo, so much crap that you can't spare even a second to fall to pieces. And then you bury him, and while you're at it, your family extrudes a volunteer to go over to your house and take all the cushions off of one of the sofas, hang sheets over all the mirrors, and set out enough food to feed the entire state, along with an urn of starbucks the size of an oil-drum.

"Before the service starts, the rabbi gives you a razor-blade and you slash a hole in your lapel, so that you've got the rent in your heart hanging out there in plain sight, and once you get back home, you spend *seven days* grieving. You pray three times a day with a quorum of ten men, facing east and singing the Kaddish, this really, really depressing song-prayer-dirge that's specially engineered to worm its way into the melancholy receptors of the Semitic hindbrain and make you feel really, really, really miserable. Other people come over and cook for you, all three meals. You don't see yourself in the mirrors, you don't sit on cushions, you don't do anything *except mourn* for a whole week.

"Then it's over. You take a walk, leaving by one door and coming back in by the other. You put the mourning behind you and start your new life without your dear departed. You've given over your whole life for a whole week, done nothing but mourn, and you're completely sick of it by then, so you're almost glad to be done.

"Then, six months or a year later, usually just before Jewish

New Year's, which is in the fall, you have a tombstone erected at the gravesite. The stone-cutters tie a white cloth around it, and everyone gathers there, and there's a sermon, and that dirge again, and more prayer, and everyone has a good hard cry as the scabs you've accumulated are ripped away and all your pain comes back fresh and scalding, and you feel it all again in one hot second, and realize with a guilty start that you *have* been neglecting the memory of the loved one, which is to say that you've gotten on with your life even though his is over, which is to say that you've done perfectly healthy, normal stuff, but you feel totally, completely overwhelmed with guilt and love, which are kind of flipsides of the same emotion—"

"You don't believe that, do you?" She held her breath.

"Well, kind of. Not that they *should be*, but hell they *are*, most of the time, then."

"Good thing we're not in love, then, right?" she said, in reference to their sixth date, when they'd decided that they would hold off on any declarations of love for at least an entire year, since they were most often moved to utter the Three Words of Significance when they were besotted with e.g., post-orgasmic brain-juice or a couple of cocktails.

"Yes, counselor."

She shook her head. He *knew* she was an academic, not a practicing lawyer, but he loved to tease her about it, ever since she'd revealed (after third date, on the phone) that she'd spent about ten seconds in private practice after she'd worked for her congressman and before she'd joined the faculty at UCLA.

"You're out of order," she said.

"This whole damned car is out of order!" he said. "So that's the ritual. You *said* you wanted to meet the parents and sisters and aunts and grandmothers and cousins and uncles and nephews and in-laws the next time we all got together. This is it."

"Right," she said. "I asked for this." And she had, of course. Hadn't asked for the graveside elements, but she'd been curious to meet this big sprawling enterprise of a family that he was always nattering on about. This seemed as good an occasion as any. "So," she said. "Is this a traditional date among Your People?"

He chuckled. "Yes, this is Yom Shiksa, the ritual bringing of the gentile woman to the family so that she may become the subject of intense, relentless scrutiny and speculation."

She started to laugh, then saw that the tractors were stilled in the fields they were passing, that a train was stopped in its tracks, that the surfers were unable to get their roll-cage dune-buggies to take to the road.

"You all right, babe?" he said, after a couple minutes of this.

"Just wondering about the dead spot," she said. "I wish we knew what had happened."

"Nothing too bad, I'm sure," he said. "It's all self-healing. I'm sure we'll be back online soon enough."

⁂

They rolled into the parking lot for his family's *shul*'s section of the giant graveyard a few minutes after 1PM, just over an hour late, along with the majority of the other attendees, all of whom had had to navigate manually.

"Where are your sisters?" Rainer's mother said, even before he'd kissed her cheek.

Rainer screwed his face up in a scowl and dug in his pocket for a yarmulke. "Do I know? Stuck in traffic, Ma. The grid's down everywhere."

Trish watched this bemusedly, in her cool loose cotton apron-trousers and blouse. She scuffed her toe conspicuously and Rainer turned to her, and it was as though he'd forgotten she was there. She felt a second's irritation, then a wave of sympathy as she saw the spasm of anxiety cross his face. He was nervous about her meeting his fam, and nervous about who would arrive when, and nervous about where his sisters were with their enormous families and meek husbands, trapped somewhere on southern California's squillion-mile freeway network.

"Ma," he said. "This is my friend, Trish."

"Pleased to meet you, Mrs. Feinstein," Trish said. The old woman was remarkably well-preserved, her soft skin glowing with heat-flush, her thick hair caught in a tight bun and covered with a little scarf that reminded Trish of Rainer's yarmulke. She wondered if she should be wearing one, too. Mrs. Feinstein's eyes flicked quickly to her shoes, up her legs and boobs, to her face and hair, and then back to her face. She opened her arms and drew Trish into a hug that smelled of good, subtle perfume, though Trish knew so little about scent that she couldn't have said which. "Call me Reba, darling," she said. "It's so good of you to come."

And then she was off, hustling to corral a wayward knot of horseplay-aged cousins, stopping to shake hands with the deceased great-uncle's poker buddies in their old-man pants, golf shirts and knit yarmulkes bobby-pinned to their thinning hair.

Trish took stock. Looked like every other graveyard she'd been in, which wasn't that many. At thirty-five, she'd been to half a dozen family funerals, a couple of college buddies who OD'ed or cracked up their cars, and one favorite poli-sci teacher's service, so she was hardly an expert on boneyards, but something was amiss.

"What's with the pebbles on the headstones?" she whispered to Rainer, who was scanning the road for signs of his sisters.

"Huh? Oh. You drop those on the monument when you visit the grave, as a sign that someone's been there."

"Oh," she said, and began to cast about for a pebble she could put on his great-uncle's headstone once it was unveiled. There were none to be found. The ground had been picked completely clean. Looking at the thousands and thousands of ranged marble headstones, each topped with a cairn of stones—and not just stones, either, toys and seashells and small sculptures, she saw now—she understood why.

"What are you doing?" Rainer asked. He might have been irritated, or just nervous. It was hard to tell when he was Fretting, and he was clearly going coo-coo for coco-puffs.

"Looking for pebbles," she said.

He said [fuck] very quietly. "I meant to bring some. Damnit. I've got twenty relatives buried here and we're going to go past every single tombstone before we get to leave and I don't have a single rock."

"Can you leave toys or other stuff, like on those stones?"

"Yeah," he said. "I suppose. If I had other stuff."

She opened her purse and pulled out the dolphin-dildo cell-phone. "You still need this?" she said.

He smiled and his forehead uncreased. "You're a genius," he said.

She set it down on the pavement and brought her heel down on it hard, breaking it into dozens of fragments. "All the pebbles we'll ever need," she said, picking them up and handing them to Rainer.

He put his arm around her shoulders and squeezed. "I'm awfully fond of you, Counselor," he said, kissing her earlobe. His breath tickled her ear and made her think of the crazy animal new-relationship-energy sex they'd had the night before—she was still limping, and so was he—and she shivered.

"You too, steakypaste," she said. "Now, introduce me to all of your relatives."

"Introduce you?" He groaned. "You don't think I remember all of their names, do you?"

🐾 🐾 🐾

Afterward, they formed a long convoy back to the nearest family member's house—a great aunt? a second cousin? Rainer was vague—navigating by keeping everyone in sight, snaking along the traffic jam that appeared to have engulfed the entire state, if not the whole coast.

"You made that law, yes? We've all heard about you." This was the sixth time someone had said this to her since they'd arrived and Rainer had made her a plate of blintzes, smoked salmon, fresh bagels, boiled eggs, and baby greens salad with raspberry dressing, then had been spirited away into an endless round of cheek-pinching and intense questioning. She'd been left on her own, and after having a couple of grave conversations with small children about the merits of different toys, she'd been latched upon by one of the Relatives and passed from hand to hand.

"I was involved in it, but I didn't write the law," she said.

"Look at you, so modest, you're blushing!" the Relative said. She reached out to steady a cut-glass vase as it wobbled in the wake of two small boys playing keep-away with a third's yarmul-ke, and Trish realized that this was probably the hostess.

"This place is just supercalafragilistic," she said, with an eco-nomical gesture at the tasteful Danish furnishings, the paper books in a handsome oak bookcase, the pretty garden out one side window and the ocean out the back window.

"Thank you," the great-aunt said. "My Benny loved it here." She misted up. Trish finally added two and two, remembered the BENJAMIN chiseled into the marble headstone, and the blank spot on the other half of the tombstone, realized that this wasn't just the hostess, this was the *widow*, and felt about for a thing to say.

"It was a beautiful ceremony," she said. She had a couple napkins tucked in the waistband of her pants, and without think-ing, she extracted one and folded an angle into it, reaching for the corner of the great-aunt's eye. "Look up," she said, and blotted the tear before it could draw a line of mascara down the widow's cheek.

The old woman smiled a well-preserved smile that reminded Trish of Rainer's mom. "You're a sweet girl," she said. "Me, I'm not so good with names, and so I've forgotten yours."

"I'm Trish," Trish said, bemusedly. Rainer's grammar got yid-dishized when he wasn't paying attention, and she adored the contrast between its shtetl credibility and his witty, smooth pub-lic banter-persona. It had attuned her to little phrases like, "Me, I'm not so good."

The widow shook her hand. "I'm Dorothy. It's a pleasure to make your acquaintance. Would you like to come out to the gar-den with me?"

🐾 🐾 🐾

Once they were seated, young male Relatives materialized and set up shade-umbrellas and brought out trays of iced juice.

"They're not after the inheritance, you know," the old woman said with a snort. "Their parents are *very* well-off. They don't need from money. They just adore me because I've spoiled them rotten since they were babies and I'd take them swimming and to Disneyland."

"You have a beautiful family," Trish said.

"Do you have a big family, too?" The old woman put on a pair of enormous sunglasses and sipped at her pink grapefruit juice.

"Not like this one," she said. There were a couple hundred people in the house, and Rainer had spent the whole car-ride back from the cemetery Fretting about all the relations who *hadn't* made it.

"Oh, this one! Well, this is a special case. This family accumulates other families. My Benny had a small family, and when he married me, they just joined us. All the high holidays, we ate here, or at my parents' place, God rest them. Your family is in DC?"

"All over."

"But you're from DC, no?"

"Not really. I grew up in Chicago and Seattle."

"But you made that law—"

"I really didn't, honestly! I was clerking for a Supreme Court judge when the case was heard, and I wrote his dissenting opinion, and when we lost, I quit and went to work for a PAC that was agitating for copyright reform to accommodate free expression, and then when Senator Sandollar got voted in and they started the Intellectual Property committee and made her chairman, I joined her staff as a policy wonk. So I worked on it, along with a couple thousand other people, not counting the millions who contributed to the campaign and the people who knocked on doors and so on."

"How old are you, darling?"

"Thirty-five," she said.

"At thirty-five, I was having babies. You—listen to you. Listen to what you've *accomplished!* I'm proud just to *listen* to you. Rainer is lucky to have you. You two will get married?"

Trish squirmed and felt her face grow hot. Neither of them really believed in marriage. Whenever anyone brought the subject up around Rainer, he'd grimace and say, "Are you kidding? It'd make my mother *far* too happy—she'd keel over from joy."

There was some kind of disturbance down the beach, one

that had been growing steadily over the past several minutes, and now the Relatives were all turning their attention that way, to a couple of small boys in miniature suits who were ruining the shine on their shoes running in the sand like lunatics.

Something in the way they were running, the distant expressions she couldn't quite make out on their faces. It made her think back to high-school, to working as a beach lifeguard on Lake Michigan in the summers, and before she knew what she was doing, she'd kicked off her shoes and was running for the shore, her legs flashing immodestly through the vents in her apron-trousers.

She was still yards away from the hissing surf when she began to assess the situation. There was the small boy, bobbing in the ocean, where the undertow had spit him up after sucking him under. There was the swimmer, unconscious on the beach, face down. Couldn't tell if his chest was moving, but the small boy was in a suit, not swim-trunks like the swimmer, and that meant that he was part of Rainer's Family, which she had begun (on the eighth date, no less!) to think of as her own, and so she had him as her primary target before she reached the sea.

She didn't bother finicking with the buttons on her top, just grabbed her collar and yanked, leaving her in a bra that revealed less than some bikinis she owned, but did so through a cunning arrangement of lace, mesh, and structural engineering that was probably illegal in Texas. She undid the bows on each hip holding up her pants and stepped out of them, leaving behind a very small pair of white panties whose primary design consideration had been to avoid showing lines through thin trousers, with modest coverage of all her nethers coming in a distant second.

She plunged into the water without hesitation, moving swiftly but surely, taking care to keep her feet dug in against the undertow as she waded out toward the young boy. She was a strong swimmer, but the water was shockingly cold after the heat of the garden and the buzzing afternoon and it sucked at her calves and legs like a jacuzzi intake. Her breath roared in her ears as she rode the swells, and then she was soaked by a succession of breakers, and then she had the boy's little hand.

She hauled him to her, seeing that he was only five or six, and that his pouting lips were alarmingly blue and that his skin was as pale as cream. She scooped the water out of his mouth, hooked her arm around his neck and tilted his head back and began to slosh back toward shore. When she was waist-deep—immodestly revealed in a bra that she was quite certain had gone completely transparent—she pinched his nose and blew into his mouth, not quite getting her mouth out of the way before he vomited up a gush of salt-water, blintzes, diet coke, and bile. She spat and wished that she could duck her head and get a mouthful of ocean to rinse with, but she couldn't without dunking the boy, too, so she hauled him up out of the water and handed him to the Relative who was standing with his arms extended on the shore, his fine leather shoes soaked with cold seawater.

She looked for the swimmer, and saw that he was still face-down in the sand. "You, you and you," she said, pointing at three young cousins whose wide eyes were flicking from her boobs to her crotch—white underwear, Christ, why white underwear today?—to the boy on the sand, who was mobbed now with Relatives whose hubbub had reached deafening proportions, "Go to the house, find an old-fashioned phone and call emergency services. Tell them where we are, and that we have two drowning victims, one a child, neither breathing. What are you going to do?"

The tallest of the three managed to make eye-contact long enough to say, "Find a cellphone, call emergency, tell them where we are, two drownings, not breathing."

"Right," she said. "Come back when you're done and tell me that it's done."

"You, you," she said, picking out two tall uncles who looked like they'd worked out or played sports before they found what-ever careers had paid for the nice suits they were wearing, "Carry him here and lay him down on his side."

She looked for Rainer and found his ass sticking out of the scrum around the boy. She snagged him by the belt and dragged him back. "Rainer," she shouted. His forehead was scrunched, but he was clear-eyed and grim and looked like he was listening to her, which she found very pleasing. "You need to get everyone back at least five steps from that kid, and make them quiet down," she said.

"Right," he said, and took off his jacket and handed it to her.

"Hold it yourself," she snapped, "I've got things to do."

"It's to wear," he said.

She surprised herself with a grin. "Thanks."

The Relatives were murmuring, or crying, or bickering, but Rainer *hollered*. "LISTEN UP," he said. "All of you get over there by that rock, NOW, or my girlfriend won't be able to save Jory's life. GO!"

And they went, amazingly, crushing back so quickly they looked like a receding tide. The tall uncles deposited the swimmer in the sand between them, and she checked his breathing and saw that it was good.

"Turn him on his side and tell me if he starts to choke," she said, and turned to the little boy, struggling to remember her rescue breathing.

🐾 🐾 🐾

She got the boy breathing and ended up with more puke on her face, on Rainer's jacket, in her hair. His pulse was thready but there. She turned to the swimmer and saw that he was a muscular surfer dude in board shorts with a couple of bitchun tatts and a decent body-paint job. He was breathing, too, but his heart was erratic as hell. She pressed two fingers to his throat.

"What happened?" she said. "Who saw it happen?"

One of the aunts stepped forward and said, "My son says they were playing—"

She held up her hand. "Where's your son?" she said.

"He's back at the house," the aunt said, startling back.

"Send someone for him, then tell me what happened."

The aunt looked like she'd been slapped, but the other Relatives were staring at her and so she had to talk, and then the boy arrived and he told it again and it was pretty much the same story, but she was able to get more details, as she began to examine both the boy and the surfer's bodies for cuts, bruises, breaks and punctures. She gave the boy's clothes the same treatment she'd given her own, gently but forcefully tearing them off, using a seashell to start the tears at first, then a pocket-knife that someone put in her hand.

The story was that the kids had been playing when they'd seen the surfer floating in the breakers, and they'd dared each other to fish him out, and the undertow had sucked them out to sea. One had gotten away, the other had ended out beyond the waves, and meanwhile, the surfer had beached himself on his own.

"Right," she said. "Blankets and pillows. Elevate their feet and wrap them up good." She stood up and staggered a step or two before Rainer caught her, and the crowd made a noise that was at once approving and scandalized.

"Get me to the sea," she said. "I need to soak my head."

So he walked her into the water, he still in his suit-pants and dress shirt and tie, and held onto her while she dunked her head and swirled a mouthful of salt water in her mouth.

"Where are the fucking paramedics?" she said, as she sloshed back out with him.

"There," he said, and pointed at the horizon, where a Coast Guard clipper was zooming for the shore. "The cellphone was dead, so I fired up a couple flares. You didn't hear them?"

"No," she said. He could have set off a cannon and she wouldn't have noticed it.

She got back to the shore just in time to see the surfer convulse. She was on him in a second, kneeling at his side, doing airway-breathing-circulation checks, finding no pulse, and slamming him onto his back and beginning CPR.

Some time later, she was lifted off him and two paramedics went to work on him. Someone put a robe over her shoulders and a cup of juice in her hands. She dropped the juice in the sand and sticky liquid and beach sand covered her legs, which she realized now that she hadn't depilated in a week, and that made her realize that she'd spent a pretty crucial amount of time prancing around naked in front of her date's family, and that that was probably not on the timetable until the fifteenth date at *least*.

She looked up at Rainer, who was still in his shoes and as she was in bare feet loomed over her. "God," she said, "Rainer—"

He kissed her. "I love you, Patricia," he said.

"Ooh," she said, with a weak smile. "You're breaking the rules!"

"Can you let it go this once?"

She made her scrunchy thinky face and then nodded. "Just don't make a habit of it, you lunk."

꩜ ꩜ ꩜

It would have been perfect if only the surfer hadn't died.

They didn't get home until well after midnight. Parts of LA appeared to be on fire as they inched their way along the freeway. It was weird to see LA at this speed. They were used to clipping along at sixty or seventy—over eighty if the traffic was light—flying over the freeway so fast that the scenery was just a blur. Only the year before, the *New Yorker* had run a forty-page paean to LA, a public apology declaring it the most livable city in America, now that it had licked its traffic problems. It balanced lots of personal space with thorough urbanization and urbanity. It was why they both lived there.

Now they seemed to have traveled back fifty years in time, to the bad old traffic-jam-and-smog days. Looters danced below, torching stores, and the traffic moved so slowly that some people were apparently abandoning their cars to *walk* home—which made the traffic even worse. The smoke from the fires turned the sunset into a watercolor of reds and mustards and golds, tones that had blown away with the smog when the last gas-sucking Detroitmobile was retired for a plastic Nickle-Metal Hydride jellybean, and all the lanes were repainted to cut them in half.

It was nightmarish. When they got off the ramp at Studio City, they found homeless guys directing traffic with gas-tubes they'd torn out of the bus-shelters. The tubes glowed in the presence of microwave radio-frequency radiation, and as each of the trillions of invisible ants in the system attempted to connect with its neighbors and get the traffic set to rights again, the RF noise made the tubes glow like sodium lamps.

They coasted into Trish's driveway and collapsed in her living room.

"You were *wonderful,* darling," Rainer said, peeling off the tracksuit that one of his cousins had scrounged from the gym-bag in her trunk and donated to Trish. Her skin was gritted with sand and streaked with stripes of sunburn.

"God," Trish said, lolling back on the sofa, just letting him gently brush away the sand and rub lotion into her skin. "You spoil me," she said.

"You're unspoilable," he said. "Wonderful girl. You saved their lives," he said.

"What a fucking day," she said. "You think that my lifeguard training made up for my scandalous undergarments in your family's minds?"

He snorted and she felt his breath tickle the fine hairs on her tummy. "You're kidding. My mom told me that if I didn't marry you, she'd have me killed and then fix you up with someone else from the family—told me it was my duty to see to it that you didn't get away, just in case someone else fell in the ocean."

He looked around at the blank walls. "Creepy not to have any news at all," he said.

"There's a TV in the garage," she said. "Or maybe the attic. You could find it and plug it in and find out that no one else knows what's going on, if you feel like it."

"Or I could escort you to the bathtub and we could scrub each other clean and then I could give you a massage," he said.

"Yes, or you could do that."

"Where did you say the television was?" he said.

"You are going to be: In. So. Much. Trouble." She twined her fingers in his hair and pulled him up to kiss her.

🐾 🐾 🐾

2. PROGRESS PILGRIMS

It took three days for even the thinnest crawls to return to the walls. In the meantime, people dug out old one-to-many devices like radios and televisions and set them up on their lawns so they could keep track of the aftermath of The Downtime.

He slept over those three nights, because no one was going

anywhere, anyway, and they had a running argument over how many dates this counted as, but truth be told, they had a wonderful time, making omelettes for one-another, washing each other's backs in the shower, stealing moments of sex in the living room at two in the afternoon without worrying about being interrupted by a chime, ringer, bell or vibe.

When they weren't enjoying each other, they took coolers of fizzy drinks onto the lawn and watched the neighbor's TV set and saw the pundits describing The Downtime. The news-shows were having a drunken ball with this one: as the only game in town, they were free to bring a level of craft to their newsmongering that hadn't been seen since Trish's parents' day, when news-networks turned catastrophes into light operas, complete with soundtracks, brand-identities, logo-marks and intermissions where buffoons worked the audience for laughs.

"Oh, she's your favorite, isn't she?" Trish asked, goosing Rainer's bicep and taking a sip of his peach ginger-ade. The pundit had been in heavy rotation since the TV went back on the air. She was a Norwegian academic mathematician who wrote books of popular philosophy. She was a collection of trademark affectations: a jacket with built-up shoulders, a monocle, a string tie, nipple tassles, and tattooed cross-hatching on her face that made her look like a woodcut of a Victorian counting-house clerk. Rainer loathed her—she'd been on the committee to which he'd defended his Philosophy of Networks thesis, and she'd busted his balls so hard that they still ached a decade later when he saw her on the tube.

The pundit explained packet-switching, using trains versus automobiles as a metaphor: "In a circuit uniwerse, every communication gets its own dedicated line, like a train on a track. Ven I vant to talk to you, ve build a circuit—a train track—betveen our dewices. No one else can use those tracks, even if ve're not talking. But packet-svitching is like a freeway. Ve break the information up into packets and ve give every packet its own little car, and it finds its own vay to the other end. If vun car doesn't arrive, ve make a copy of its information and send it again. The cars have brakes and steering veels, and so they can all share the same road vithout too much trouble."

Rainer grit his teeth and hissed at the set. "She's faking the accent," he said. "She thinks that Americans believe that anyone with a European accent is smarter than we are. She can pronounce vee and doubleyou perfectly well when she wants to—she speaks better English than I do! Besides, *she stole that line from me,*" he said, "from my *thesis,*" he said, his face scrunching up again.

"Shh, shh," Trish said, laughing at him. He wasn't really angry-angry, she knew. Just a little stir crazy. He was a networking guy—he should have been out there trying to make the network go again, but he was on sabbatical and no one at UCLA wanted to hear from him just then.

And then the pundit was off onto ants—networks modeled on ant-colonies that use virtual phermomones to explore all possible routes in realtime and emerge solutions to the problem of getting everything, everywhere, in shortest time. Rainer kept barking at the TV, and Trish knew he was doing it to entertain her as much as for any reason, so she laughed more and egged him on.

The TV cut back to the news-dude, who was a very cuddly ewok who'd made his name hosting a wheel-of-fortune, jumping up and down and squeaking excitedly and adorably whenever a contestant won the grand prize, his fur-plugs quivering. He cupped his paws to his cheeks and grinned.

"But ants aren't perfect, are they?" the ewok said.

"He's feeding her!" Rainer said. "She's going to go off on her stupid walking-in-circles bit—"

"The thing about using wirtual ants to map out the vorld and make routing recommendations is that ve can't really tell the difference betveen a good solution and a bad vun, without trying it. Sometimes, ants end up valking in circles, reinforcing their scent, until they starve to death. Ve might find that our cars tell us that the best vay from San Francisco to San Jose is via a 1,500-mile detour to Las Wegas. It may be true—if all the traffic everyvhere else is bad enough, that might be the fastest vay, but it may just be the ants going in circles."

"God, talk about taking a metaphor too far," he said. Trish thought that Rainer was perfectly happy to think about the ants as ants, except when someone raised a point like this, but she didn't see any reason to raise that point just then.

The ewok turned to the camera: "One scientist says we *should* be expecting more Downtimes to come. When we come back from this break, we'll talk to a University of Waterloo researcher who claims that this is just the first of many more Downtimes to come."

The screen cut over to a beautiful, operatic advertisement for some Brazilian brand of coca-cola, wittily written, brilliantly shot, with an original score by a woman who'd won three grammies at the Independent Music Awards in Kamchatka the year before. They watched it with mild attention, and Trish absently fished another bottle out of the cooler and chewed the lid off with her side-molars.

She looked at Rainer. He was gripping the arm-rests of his inflatable chair tightly, dimpling the hard plastic. She held the bottle to his lips and he took it, then she rubbed at his shoulders while he took a swallow.

"Let's go back inside and play," she said. "They won't have anything new to tell us for days."

※ ※ ※

The crawls were alive the next morning, exuberantly tracking across the walls and over the mirror and down the stairs. They picked out the important ones and trailed them to convenient spots with a fingertip and devoured them, reading interesting bits aloud to one another.

Soon the crawls had been tamed and only a few personal messages remained. Trish dragged hers over to the tabletop, next to her cereal bowl, and opened them up while she ate. Outside, she could hear the whisper of cars speeding down the road, and she supposed with a mingling of regret and relief that she should probably go into her office.

She opened her personal mail. It had been three days since she'd read it, but for all that, a surprisingly small amount had accumulated. Of course—everyone else had been without connectivity, too. This was mostly stuff from the east coast and Europe, people who'd been awake for a couple hours.

She read, filed and forwarded, tapping out the occasional

one-word answer to simple questions or bouncing back messages with a form letter.

Then she came to the note from the Coast Guard medic. He didn't mince words. It was in the first sentence: the surfer dude she'd rescued had had a second cardiac arrest on the boat. They'd tried what they could, but he hadn't recovered. He was a freak statistic of The Downtime, another person who'd lost his life when the ants spazzed out. They'd recovered his board and found its black-box. The accelerometer and GPS recorded the spill he'd taken after the loss of climate and wave-condition data from the other surfers strung out on the coast. He'd stayed up for about ten seconds before going under.

She stared numbly at the note, the spoon halfway to her mouth, and then she dropped the spoon into the bowl, not noticing that it splashed milk down her blouse.

She got up from the table and went into the kitchen. Rainer was there, in a change of clothes they'd bought from a mom-n-pop gap at the mall on the corner that had been taking IOUs from anyone who could show a driver's license with a local address. She grabbed his wrist, making him slosh starbucks down his front, she took the cup out of his hand and set it down on the counter, then put her arms around his chest and hugged him. He didn't protest or ask any questions, he just put his arms around her and hugged back.

Eventually, she cried. Then she told him what she was crying about. She let him tell her that she was a hero, that she'd saved Jory's life and almost saved the surfer's life, and she let him tell her that it wasn't her fault for sloshing into the ocean to rinse off the barf, and she let him tell her that he loved her, and she cried until she thought she was cried out, and then she started again.

He took her upstairs and he lay her down on the bed. He undressed her, and she let him. He put her in fluffy jammies, and she let him. He wiped away her makeup and her hot tears with a cool face-cloth, and she let him. He took her hand and ran his fingers over her fingernails, squeezing each one a little, the way she liked, and she let him.

"You're going to have a nice lie-down for a couple hours, and I'm going to be right beside you. I'll call the department secretary and tell him you're taking a personal day and will be in tomorrow. Then we're going to go see Jory and his family, so that you can see the boy whose life you saved, and then we are going to go for a walk in the hills, and then I'm going to put you to bed. When you get up in the morning, you can make an appointment to see a grief counselor or not. Today, I'm in charge, all right?"

Her heart swelled with love and she felt a tear slip down her cheek. "Rainer," she said, "you're a wonder."

"You inspire me, darling," he said, and kissed her eyelids shut.

🐾 🐾 🐾

Their thirty-fifth date was their last.

"You're going back to Washington," he said, when he saw the boxes in her office.

"Yes," she said.

He stood in the doorway of her office. Trish was painfully aware of the other faculty members in the corridor watching him. Their romance was no secret, of course. Everyone in the law department knew about him, all the network engineers knew about her, and they both took a substantial amount of ribbing about "mixed marriages" and "interfaith dating."

Trish realized with a pang that it was likely that everyone in the law department knew that she'd decided to go back to the Hill but that he'd only suspected it until this instant.

"Well, good for you," he said, putting on a brave face that was belied by the Fret wrinkles in his forehead.

"I'm sorry," she said. "I should have told you once I decided, but I didn't want to do it over the phone—"

"I'm glad you didn't," he said, holding up his hand. "Do you want to come out for dinner with me anyway?"

She gestured at the half-packed office. "The movers are coming in the morning."

"Well then, do you suppose you could use some help? I could get some burger king or taco bell."

She looked at him for a long moment, swallowing the knob in her throat. "That would be lovely. Mexican. I mean, 'taco bell,'" she said. "Thank you."

He let her pay for it—"You're making the big bucks now," he said—and he was a surprisingly conscientious packer, padding her framed pictures carefully and wrapping her knick-knacks in individual sheets of spun fiber.

"Well then," he said, once he'd finished writing out a description of his latest box's contents on its outside, "you always told me that Hill Rats were Hill Rats for life, I suppose."

"Yeah," she said. She knew she should explain, but they'd had the argument about it three times since the new PAC had contacted her and offered her the executive director position. The explanation wouldn't get any better now that she'd made up her mind.

The new PAC, The Association for a Human-Readable World, was the brainchild of some people she'd worked with while she was on the Hill. They'd asked her to hire a team, to scout an office, and then to camp out in the offices of various important committee chairmen until they passed a law limiting the scope of emergent networking meshes. The Europeans had enacted legislation requiring cops, hydroelectric agencies, banks, hospitals and aviation authorities to use "interrogatable" networks within ten days of The Downtime. With fifteen thousand dead in Western Europe alone, with Florence in flames and Amsterdam under two meters of water, it was an easy call. The US had scoffed at them and pointed to the economic efficiencies of a self-governing network, but the people who were funding Human-Readable World wanted to know where old concepts like "transparency" and "accountability" and "consent of the governed" fit in when the world's essential infrastructure was being managed by nonsentient ant-colony simulations.

"Be gentle with us, OK?" he said.

"Oh, I wish I had your confidence in my abilities," she said, sucking on her big-gulp of coke.

He put down his food and looked hard at her. He stared longer than was polite, even for (ex-) lovers, and she began to squirm.

"What?" she said.

"You're not putting me on. Amazing. Patricia Lourdes McCavity, you have felled an empire and you are setting yourself up to fell another—and it's one that I'm pretty heavily invested in, both professionally and financially."

"Come on," she said. "I'm good, but I'm not superwoman. I was part of a team."

"I've read your briefs. Position papers. Opinions. Speeches. Hell, your press-releases. They were the most cogent, convincing explanations for intellectual property reform I'd ever read. You weren't the judge, but you were his clerk. You weren't the committee chairman, but you were her head staffer. Taco Bell underestimated you. Coke underestimated you. Starbucks underestimated you. Disney underestimated you. Vivendi and Sony underestimated you. Now you're running your own organization, and it's pointed at me, and I'm scared shitless, you want to know the truth. I'm not underestimating you." He'd drawn his dark eyebrows together while he spoke, and lowered his head, so that he was looking up at her from under his brow, looking intense as the day they'd met, when he was delivering a brilliant lecture on ant-colony optimization to a large lay audience at the law-school, fielding the Q&A with such convulsive humor and scalding lucidity that he'd melted her heart.

She felt herself blushing, then wondered if she was flushing. She still loved him and still craved the feeling of his skin on hers, wanted nothing more than another lost weekend with him, taking turns being the strong one and being the one who surrendered, soothing each other and spoiling each other. Thinking of that first meeting brought back all those feelings with keen intensity that made her breasts ache and her hands flutter on the box she was eating off of.

"Rainer," she began, then stopped. She took a couple deep breaths. "I'm not gunning for you, you know. You and I want the same thing: a world that we can be proud to live in. Your family's company has contributed more to the public good than any of us can really appreciate—"

He blushed now, too. She never talked about his father's role in the earliest build-outs of ant-based emergent routing algorithms, about the family fortune that he'd amassed through the company that bore his name still, thirty years after he'd stepped down as Chairman of the Board. Rainer was a genius in his own right, she knew, and his own contributions to the field were as important as his father's, but he was haunted by the idea that his esteem in the field was due more to his surname than his research. He waved his hands at her and she waved hers back.

"Shush. I'm trying to explain something to you. Between your father and you, the world has increased its capacity and improved its quality of life by an order of magnitude. You've beaten back Malthus for at least another century. That makes you heroes.

"But your field has been co-opted by corrupt interests. When you study the distributions, you can see it clearly: the rich and the powerful get to their destinations more quickly; the poor are routed through franchise ghettoes and onto toll-roads; the more important you are, the fewer number of connections you have to make when you fly, the better the chance that you'll get a kidney when you need it. The evidence is there for anyone to see, if only you look. We need standards for this—we need to be able to interrogate the system and find out why it does what it does. That's an achievable goal, and a modest one: we're just asking for the same checks and balances that we rely on in the real world."

He looked away and set down his taco. "Trish, I have a lot of respect for you. Please remember that when I tell you this. You are talking nonsense. The network is, by definition, above corruption. You simply can't direct it to give your cronies a better deal than the rest of the world. The system is too complex to game. Its behavior can't be *predicted*—how could it possibly be *guided?* Statistics can be manipulated to 'prove' anything, but everyone who has any clue about this understands that this is just paranoid raving—"

She narrowed her eyes and sucked in a breath, and he clamped his lips shut, breathed heavily through his nose, and went on.

"Sorry. It's just wrong, is all. Science isn't like law. You deal with shades of grey all the time, make compromises, seek out balance. I'm talking about mathematical truths here, not human-created political constructs. There's no one to compromise *with*—a human-readable emergent network just doesn't exist. Can't exist. It doesn't make sense to say it. It's like asking for me to make Pi equal three. Pi *means* something, and what it means *isn't* three. Emergent networks *mean* not-human-readable."

She looked at him, and he looked at her, and they looked at each other. She felt a sad smile in the corners of her lips, and saw one tug at his, and then they both broke out in grins.

"We're going to be seeing a lot of each other," she said.

"Oh yes, we are," he said.

"Across a committee room."

"A podium."

"On talk-shows."

"Opposite sides."

"Right."

"No fighting dirty, OK?" he said, raising his eyebrows and showing her his big brown eyes. She snorted.

"Give me a hug and go home," she said. "I'll see you at the hearings when they introduce my bill."

He hugged her, and she smelled him, thinking, *this is the last time I'll smell this smell.*

"Rainer," she said, holding him at arm's length.

"Yes?" he said.

"I'm going to call you, when I have questions about ant-colony optimization, all right?"

He looked at her.

"I need the best expertise I can get. It's in your interest to see to it that I'm well-informed."

Slowly, he nodded. "Yes, you're right. I'd like that. I'll call you when I have questions about policy, all right?"

"You're on," she said, and they hugged again, fiercely.

Once he was gone, she permitted herself the briefest of tears. She knew that she was right and that she was going to make a fool out of him, but she didn't want to think of that right then. She felt the place behind her ear where he'd kissed her before going home and looked around her office, five years of her life in thir-ty banker's boxes ready to be shipped across the country tomorrow, according to a route that would be governed from moment to moment by invisible, notional, *ridiculous* insects.

She ate more taco bell. The logo was a pretty one, really, and now that it had been adopted by every mom-and-pop burrito joint in the world, they'd really leveled the playing field. She thought about the old Taco Bell mystery-meat and plastic cheese and took a bite of the ground beef and sharp Monterey Jack that had come from her favorite little place on the corner, and permitted herself to believe, for a second, anyway, that she'd made that possible.

She was going to kick ant ass on the Hill.

🐜 🐜 🐜

3. CONFLICT OF INSECT

Trish gathered her staff in the board room and wrote the following in glowing letters on the wall with her fingertip, leaving the text in her expressive schoolmarm's handwriting rather than converting it to some sterile font: "First they ignore you. Then they laugh at you. Then they fight you. Then you win."

Her staff, all five of them, chuckled softly. "Recognize it?" she asked, looking round at them.

"Pee-Wee Herman?" said the grassroots guy, who was so young it ached to look at him, but who could fire a cannonload of email into any congressional office on twelve hours' notice. He never stopped joking.

The lawyer cocked an eyebrow at him and stroked her moustache, a distinctive gesture that you could see in any number of courtv archives of famous civil-rights battles, typically just before she unloaded both barrels at the jury-box and set one or another of her many precedents. "It's Martin Luther King, right?"

"Close," Trish said.

"Geronimo," guessed the paralegal, who probably wasn't going to work out after all, being something of a giant flake who spent more time on the phone to her girlfriend than filing papers and looking up precedents.

"Nope," Trish said, looking at the other two staffers—the office manager and the media guy—who shrugged and shook their heads. "It's Gandhi," she said.

They all went, "Ohhhh," except the grassroots guy, who crossed to the wall and used his fingertip to add, "And then they assassinate you."

"I'm too tough to die," the lawyer said. "And you're all too young. So I think we're safe."

"OK," Trish said. "This is an official pep talk. They're playing dirty now. Last night, my car tried to take me to Arlington via Detroit. My email is arriving on a seventy-two-hour time-delay. My phone doesn't ring, or it rings all night long. I've had to switch it off.

"But what all of this means is that I've got more uninterrupted work-time than ever and I'm getting reacquainted with my bicycle."

"Every number I call rings at my ex-girlfriend's place," the grassroots guy said. "I think we're going to get back together!"

"That's the right attitude, boy-o," the lawyer said. "When life gives you SARS, make sarsaparilla. I appear to be unable to access any of my personal files, and any case-law I query shows up one sentence at a time. I've discovered that the Georgetown University law-library makes a very nice latte and serves a terrific high tea, and I've set Giselle to work on refiling and cross-indexing twenty years' worth of yellow pads that had previously sat moldering in a storage locker that I was paying far too much for."

"Which has given Giselle a rare opportunity to explore the rich civil rights history that you embody," Trish said, looking pointedly at the paralegal. "But I suspect that she could use a hand, possibly from a grad student or two who could get some credit for this. Let's ask around at Georgetown, OK?"

The lawyer nodded. The office manager pointed out that their bill-payments were going astray after they'd been dispatched to their suppliers but before they were debited from their—dwindling—account, which meant that they were getting a couple days' worth of free cash-flow. Only the media guy was glum, since he couldn't field, make or review calls or press-releases, which made him pretty useless indeed.

"Right," she said, and scribbled something on one of the

steno pads she'd bought for everyone when their email started going down three times a day. "This guy owes me from back in the copyright wars—I fed him some good stories that he used to launch his career. He was the ABNBC Washington bureau chief until last year and now he's teaching J-School at Columbia. Take the afternoon train to Manhattan and bring him back with you tonight. Don't take no for an answer. Tell him to bring his three most promising protégés, and tell him that they'll have all the access they need to produce an entire series on the campaign. Sleeping on our sofas. Following us to the toilet. Everything on the record. Do-able?"

"It's do-able," the media guy said. "I'm on it."

Once they'd all cleared out, the lawyer knocked on her door. "You going to be all right?" she asked.

Trish waved her hands at the piles of briefing books, red-lined hardcopies, marked-up magazine articles and memos from her Board of Directors. "Of course!" she said. She shook her head. "Probably. We never thought we'd get this far, remember? All this psy-ops shit they're pulling, it's just more proof that we're on the right track. No one should be able to do this. It's the opposite of democracy. It's the opposite of civil discourse."

The lawyer smoothed her moustache. "Right on," she said. "You should be proud. This is a hell of a fight, and I'm glad to be part of it. You know we'd follow you into the sun, right?"

Trish fluttered her hands. "God, don't give me that kind of responsibility."

"All right then, into the ocean. We're making this happen, is what's important."

"Thanks, babe," Trish said. She put on a brave smile until the lawyer had backed out of the office, then stared down at her calendar and looked at her morning schedule. Three congressional staffers, a committee co-chair, an ACLU researcher, and the head of the newly formed Emergent Network Suppliers' Industry Association—a man she had last seen in her office at UCLA, backing away from a long and melancholy hug.

🐾 🐾 🐾

When he rang off the phone and joined her, finally, she straight-ened out her smart cardigan and said, "Rainer, you're certainly looking . . . well."

". . . funded," he finished, with a small smile. The Emergent Network Suppliers' Industry Association's new offices were in a nice Federal Revival building off Dupont Circle, with lots of stained glass that nicely set off the sculptural and understated furniture. "It's not as grand as appearances suggest, Trish. We got it for a song from the receivers in the Church of Scientology's bankruptcy, furnishings included. It *is* nice though. Don't you think?"

"It's lovely," she said. Around her, staffers bustled past in good suits and good shoes and smart haircuts. "Hard to believe you only set up shop a week ago," she said.

"It came furnished, remember," he said.

"Oh yes, so you said," she said, watching a kid who looked like he'd gone tops in his class at the Naval Academy put his ankles up on the plasticized return beside his desk and tilt his chair, throwing his head back with wild laughter at whatever it was some other Hill Rat (in her mind, it was a key Congressman's aide—some old frat buddy of Mr Navy 2048) was saying at the phone's other end.

She looked back at Rainer and saw that he was staring where she had.

"Well, it's a far cry from academic research," he said.

"I know you'll be very good at it. You can explain things without making it seem like an explanation. The first lesson I ever learned on the Hill was, 'If you're explaining—'"

"'—you're losing,'" he said. "Yeah, I've heard that. Well, you're the old hand here, I'm just learning as I go. Trying not to make too many mistakes and to learn from the ones I do make."

"Do you want some free advice, Rainer?"

He sat down in one of the chairs, which bulged and sloshed as it conformed itself to his back and butt. He patted the uphol-stered jelly beside him. "You may always assume that I would be immensely grateful for your advice, Trish," he said.

She sat down and crossed her legs, letting her sensible shoe hang loose. "Right. DC is a *busy* place. In academic circles, in tech circles, you might get together to feel out your opponent, or to make someone's acquaintance, or to see an old friend. You might get together to enjoy the company of another human being.

"We do that in DC, *after* working hours. Strictly evenings and weekends. When you schedule a meeting during office hours, it has to have a purpose. Even if it appears to have no purpose, it has a purpose. There's a protocol to meetings, a secret language, that's known to every Hill Rat and written nowhere. What time you have the meeting, who's there, who's invited, who knows it, how long you schedule, whether you cater: they all say little things about the purpose of the meeting. Even if you have no reason to call the meeting, one will be read into it.

"If this was any other city in the world, it would make perfect sense for you to look me up once you got to DC. We're still friends, I still think about you from time to time, but here in DC, you calling me over for a meeting, this kind of meeting, at this time of day, it means you're looking to parley. You want to strike a deal before my bill goes to the committee. I don't know how well you know the Hill, so I don't want to impute any motives to you. But if you took a meeting like this with anyone else, that's what they'd assume."

Rainer's forehead crinkled.

"No Fretting," she said. Then she smiled a sad smile. "Oh, Fret if you want. You're a big boy."

He twiddled his thumbs, caught himself at it, and folded his hands in his lap. "Huh," he said. "Well. I *did* want to talk to you because it's been a while and because we meant a lot to each other. I *also* wanted to talk to you about the bill, because that's what I'm here to do, at a pretty decent salary. I *also* wanted to see you because I had an idea that you'd be different here in your native habitat, and well, that's true."

She refused to let that make her self-conscious. Of *course* she was different, but it wasn't geographic. The last time they'd seen each other, they were lovers and friends. Now they were ex-lovers who were being paid to accomplish opposing, mutually exclusive objectives. She knew that there was a certain power in not saying anything, so she wrapped herself in silence and waited for him to say something. She didn't have to wait long.

"Your bill is going to committee?"

"Well, I certainly hope so," she said. "That's what I'm here for, after all. The discussion draft has been circulating for a week, and we're confident we'll see it introduced and assigned to committee by the end of this week. That's what we're told, anyway. It's got strong bipartisan support. Selling Congress on the importance of human-generated governance is pretty easy. Wouldn't want to be in your shoes."

He grinned. "You're trying to psych me out."

"Maybe," she said, grinning back. "But that's nothing compared to the psych job that we've been getting down at my office." She told him about the phone weirdness, the oddball traffic-management. "Someone on your side has a funny sense of humor."

His smile faded. "You're still trying to fake me out," he said. "If you're seeing corruption in the net, it's because you're looking so hard, you can't help but find it. You're reading malice into accident. Dead spots aren't personal, you know. This is a law of nature—the networks emerge solutions, they're the best they can come up with. If you don't like the results, talk to nature, not me."

She shrugged. "Whatever, Rainer. I know what's happening. You'll believe what you want to believe." She pursed her lips and made an effort at controlling her irritation. "It's really happening, and it's not helping your side. If you know who's responsible, you might let him know that the dirty tricks are what convinced Senator Beauchamp's staff to green-light the bill. Conspiracy is supposed to be beneath the surface. It doesn't look so good when it's exposed to fresh air and sunshine."

"You've got to be kidding," he said. "Doesn't matter, I suppose. All right, message received. If I happen to run into someone whom I think should hear it, I'll be sure to pass it on, OK?"

"That's all I ask," she said.

"You want to talk about the bill now?"

"Have you seen the discussion draft?"

He squirmed. "No," he admitted. "I didn't know it existed until just now."

"I'd offer to send you a copy, but I expect it would take a week to arrive, if it ever did. Why don't you ask that guy," she gestured at the Navy man, "to get you a copy? He looks like he knows his way around. And then drop by my office if you want to chat about it."

She stood up and tugged at her cardigan again. "It's been very nice seeing you," she said. She picked up her coat and her mitts. "Good luck settling in."

He gave her a hug—which felt weird, hugging was strictly west-of-the-Mississippi, and she broke it off firmly—and showed her to the door. The first snows were coming in, and the steps were slightly icy, so she maneuvered them slowly, carefully. When she reached the road, he was no longer in the doorway. He was standing right behind her, breath coming out in foggy huffs.

"Trish," he said, then stopped. His arms dropped to his sides and his shoulders slumped.

"Rainer," she said, keeping her voice calm and neutral.

"God," he said. "God. How'd this happen, Trish? Look, I've never been happy the way I was with you. I haven't been that happy since. God, Trish—"

"Rainer," she said again, taking one of his hands, firmly, motherly. "Rainer. Stop it. You're here to do a job, and your job requires that you and I keep it on a professional level. It doesn't matter how it happened—" But it did, didn't it? She'd left him to come east and do something he thought of as wrong-headed and backwards and superstitious. But she'd left him, not the other way around. And he'd never recovered, though she'd built herself a new life here. It wasn't a contest (but she was winning anyway). "It doesn't matter. We respect each other. That's enough."

He deflated and she said, "Oh, come here," and gave him a long and soulful hug, right there on the street, knowing that she was giving the hug and he was taking it. Then she let him go, spun him round, and gave him a little push back toward his office.

By the time she reached the corner and looked back over her shoulder, he was nowhere to be seen.

🐾 🐾 🐾

That afternoon, her phone started ringing normally, with actual people on the other end. Her outbound calls were connected. Her email was delivered. Her car got her home in record time. She sighed as she eased it into her driveway and carried her brief-case inside and poured herself a very small glass of Irish whisky so rare that it had been known to make grown men weep. Normally, she saved it for celebrations, but if she was celebrating something, she was damned if she knew what it was.

Her phone rang as she was licking the last few drops of liquor from the little glass. It was the lawyer, with news.

"I just stopped by the office and found a messenger on the doorstep. He had hard-copy of a press-release from Senator Beauchamp's office. They're introducing the bill in the morning. Congrats, kid, you did it."

Trish set the glass down and said [whoopee] very quietly and very emphatically.

"You're durned tootin'," the lawyer said. "And double for me."

Of course, it wasn't over by a long shot. Getting a bill intro-duced was not the same as getting it through committee. Getting it through committee was not the same as getting it passed in the Senate, and getting it passed in the Senate was not the same as getting it passed in the House, and then who the hell knew what the hereditary Chimp-in-Chief in the Oval Office would do when it was passed through the bars of his cage with his morning banana.

But she had ridden back into town less than a year before, and she had gone from nothing to this. The ACLU was support-ing the bill, and EFF, EPIC, all the old civ-lib mafia had opened their arms to her. She poured herself one more very small whisky, gave herself a fragrant bath and put herself to bed, grin-ning like a fool.

🐻 🐻 🐻

"There are four news-crews, six print reporters, and a couple of others here to see you," the office-manager said. The office phones were out again, but that hadn't stopped a fair number of determined people from figuring out that they could actually move their physical being from one part of Washington to another and have a real, old-fashioned face-to-face. The lawyer and she had each taken a dozen press "calls" that morning, with their embedded reporters from Columbia J-School perched obtrusively in the corners of their offices, taking copious notes and filming constantly.

"Others?"

"A mixed bag. Some Hill people, some I'm not sure about."

Trish stood and stretched out her back, listening to it pop. She usually worked in bursts, typing or talking for an hour, then taking a little walk to gather her thoughts and touch base with her co-workers. Today, she'd been glued to her seat from 7AM to after lunchtime, and her back and butt were shrieking at her.

She walked into the front area, trailed by her reporter. She recognized some of the journos and some of the Congressional staffers, and a local rep from a European Privacy think-tank in Brussels, and—Rainer.

He was turned out in a very natty suit and a homburg, a fashion that had recently come back to DC, and she knew that he'd been put together by a personal shopper. Her own Board had suggested to her, matter-of-factly, that she should get one of her own once the bill cleared committee, since she'd be doing tons of press and as sharp a dresser as she fancied herself, she was no pro. Her prodigious talents, they assured her, lay elsewhere.

He took her hand with both of his and gave her a long, intense hand-shake that drew stares from the journos and the think-tank man.

"Nice to see you again, Ms. McCavity," he said, somberly.

"A pleasure as always, Mr. Feinstein," she said.

"I'm sorry to drop in on you unannounced," he said, "but I hoped that I could have just a moment of your time." Belatedly, he remembered to take off his silly hat and then he fumbled with the right way to hold it, settling for dropping it to his waist and upending it. She thought he looked like a panhandler in a Charlie Chaplin movie and she suppressed a smile. His curly hair had been gelled into a careful configuration that reminded her of the glossy ringlets of a black poodle.

"I suppose we can do that," she said. She turned to her other visitors. "Who's got a 3PM deadline?" she said. Two of the print-reporters held up their hands. "You then you," she said. "Who's got a 5PM filing deadline? 6PM? 10PM?" She triaged them all, promised to meet the think-tank man for dinner at an Ethiopian place in Adams-Morgan, and led Rainer into her office and closed the door.

He looked at her embedded reporter and cocked his head.

"Sorry, Rainer," she said. "I have a shadow for the duration. Just pretend he isn't here. You don't mind, do you dear?" she said to the reporter, who was very young and very bright and missed nothing. He shook his head and made some notes.

"The bill's dead," Rainer said, after he'd sat down.

"Oh really?" she said.

"Just heard from Senator Rittenhouse, personally. He takes the position that this should be in Commerce, not Judiciary, and is calling hearings to make that happen."

Rittenhouse was another powerful committee chairman, and this wasn't good news. What's more, he was in the pocket of the network operators and had been for a decade, so much so that editorialists and talk-radio types called him "The Senator from The Internet."

Still, it wasn't catastrophic. "That's interesting," she said, "but it's a far cry from killing the bill. It's pretty standard, in fact. Just slows things down." She smiled at him. He was just a kid some-times, so out of his depth here. He reminded her of the Relatives she'd met that day, the little boys in their miniature suits running on the beach.

He shifted in his seat and fondled his hat-brim. "Well, I guess we'll see. My press-liaison has set up a post-mortem debate on one of the news-networks tonight, and I thought you might want to represent the other side?"

She smiled again. He was twice the rhetorician that she was, but he had no idea how to play the game. She'd have to be careful to bruise, not break him.

🐾 🐾 🐾

"We, as a society, make trade-offs all the time," Rainer said. He was wearing a different suit this evening, something that Trish had to admit looked damned good on the studio monitors (better than her frumpy blouse and wool winter-weight trousers). "We trade a little bit of privacy for a little bit of security when we show identification before going into a federal building—"

The ewok held up his paw. "But how much should we be willing to trade, Ms. McCavity?"

She looked into the camera, keeping her eyes still, the way she'd been told to if she didn't want to appear tourettic. "Wickett, when Franklin said, 'Those willing to give up a little liberty for a little security deserve neither security nor liberty,' he wasn't spouting empty rhetoric, he was laying the groundwork for this enduring democratic experiment that we all love. Look, we're not opposed to the use of autonomous networks for *some* applications, even *most* applications, with appropriate safeguards and checks and balances. No nation on earth has the reliance that we do on these networks. Are they an appropriate way of advising you on the best way to get to the mall on a busy Saturday? Absolutely, provided that everyone gets the best advice the system can give, regardless of economic status or influence. But should they be used to figure out whom the FBI should open an investigation into? Absolutely not. We use judges and grand juries and evidence to establish the sufficiency of a request to investigate a private citizen who is considered innocent until proven guilty. We learned that lesson the hard way, during the War on Terrorism and the Ashcroft witch-hunts. Should we trade grand juries and judges for ant-colonies? Do you want the warrant for your wiretap issued by an accountable human being or by a simulated ant-hill?"

The ewok turned to the camera. "Both sides make a compelling case. What do you think? When we come back, we'll take your calls and questions." The lights dimmed and it adjusted its collar and cracked its hairy knuckles on the table before it. Ever since it had made the move to a pbs, it had been grooming its fur ever-more conservatively and trying out a series of waistcoats and short pants. It turned to her and stared at her with its saucer-sized black button eyes. "You know, I just wanted to say thanks—I had self-identified as an ewok since I was five years old, but Lucasfilm just wouldn't license the surgery, so I went through every day feeling like a stranger in my body. It wasn't until your law got enacted that I was able to find a doctor who'd do it without permission."

She shook its paw. "It wasn't my law, but I helped. I'm glad it helped you out." She unconsciously wiped her palm on her thigh as the ewok turned to his make-up boy and let him comb out its cheeks. She stared at Rainer, who wasn't looking good. She'd had him on the ropes since their opening remarks, and the ewok kept interrupting him to let her rebut—and now she knew why.

Rainer had his phone clamped to his head, and he was nodding vigorously and drumming his fingers. He was sweating, and it was making his hair come un-coiffed. Trish's own phone buzzed and she looked down at it in surprise. It was her voicemail, coming back to life again. It had started when she got to the studio—when she got within a few yards of Rainer, she realized. Messages coming in. She'd transcribed a dozen in the greenroom before they'd dragged her into makeup.

The studio lights blinked and Rainer popped the phone back into his pocket and the ewok turned to look back into the camera, examining the ticker scrolling past his prompter. He introduced them again, then turned to Trish.

"Ms. McCavity, Alberto in San Juan writes in wanting to know what changes we should institute in the networks."

She said, "It's not my place to say what technical changes the networks need to have. That's where experts like Mr. Feinstein come in. We'd ask the administrative branch to solicit comments from people like him to figure out exactly what technical changes could be made to allow us to remain competitive without giving up our fundamental liberties in order to beat the occasional traffic jam."

"Mr. Feinstein?"

He grinned and leaned forward. "It's interesting that Ms. McCavity should disavow any technical expertise, since that's what we've been saying all along. If she's getting stuck in traffic, it's because there's a *lot* of traffic. The ant-nets route *five thousand percent more traffic* than our nation's highways ever accommodated without them, and they've increased the miles-per-hour-per-capita-per-linear-mile by *six thousand, four hundred percent.* You're stuck in traffic? Fine. I get stuck sometimes too. But for every hour you spend stuck today, you're saving *hundreds* of hours relative to the time your parents spent in transit.

"The other side of this debate are asking for something impossible: they want us to modify the structure of the network, which is a technical construct, built out of bits and equations, to accommodate a philosophical objective. They assert that this is possible, but it's like listening to someone assert that our democracy would be better served if we had less gravity, or if two plus two equaled five. Whether or not that's true, it's not reasonable to ask for it."

The ewok turned to her.

She said, "Well, we've heard a great deal about the impossibility of building democratic fundamentals into the network, but nothing about the possibilities. This hard, no-compromise line is belied by the fact that we know that the rich and powerful manipulate the network to their own advantage, something that statistics have proven out—"

"See, this is *exactly* how these Human-Readable types do it, it's how their media-training goes. They are here to ask for changes to *technical* specifications, but they disavow any technical knowledge, and when they're called on this, they spout dubious 'statistics' that 'prove' that up is down, black is white, and that millionaires can get to the movies in half the time that paupers can. The Emergent Network Suppliers' Industry Association represents the foremost experts in this field, but you don't need to be an expert to know that these networks *work*. The ants take us where we want to go, in the shortest time, with the highest reliability. Anyone who doubts that can dig out her map and compass and sextant and try to navigate the world without their assistance, the way they do in Europe."

Her mouth was open. *Media training?* Where did he get this business about *media training?* "I'm not sure where Mr. Feinstein gets his information about my media training from, but personally, I'd rather talk about networks." She paused. "Let's talk about Europe, where they *have* found ways of creating transparency and accountability for these 'unregulatable' algorithms, where the sky *hasn't* fallen and the final trump hasn't sounded. What do they know that we don't?"

"What indeed?" the ewok said, breaking in and giving her the last word again. "More of your questions after this break."

They got in their cars together after they'd scrubbed off their makeup and shaken paws with the ewok, riding down in the elevator shoulder to shoulder, slumped and sweaty and exhausted. They didn't speak, and the silence might have been mistaken for companionable by someone who didn't know any better.

They got off at the same floor in the parking garage and turned in the same direction, and Trish spied his car, parked next to hers, the last two on the floor. Quickening her step, she opened her door and turned the car on, backing up so that she was right behind Rainer.

He backed out slowly, looking at her quizzically in his rearview, but she refused to meet his eye, and when he pulled out, she rode his bumper.

"Sweet fancy Moses," she breathed, as the traffic parted before them, allowing them to scythe through the streets, onto the beltway. She hung grimly onto his bumper, cutting off cars that tried to shift into her lane. Moving this fast after so much time stuck on the roads—it felt like flying. She laughed and then got a devilish idea.

Spotting a gap in the passing lane, she zipped ahead of Rainer and swerved back into his lane so that she was in the lead. As though a door had slammed shut, the traffic congealed before them into a clot as thick as an aneurysm. She hissed out a note of satisfaction, then waited patiently while Rainer laboriously passed her again, and the traffic melted away once more.

It was tempting not to get off at her exit, but she had to get some sleep, and so she reluctantly changed lanes. There wasn't much traffic on the road, but every traffic light glowed vindictive red all the way to her house.

The Chairman of her Board messengered over a hand-written note of congratulations that was on her doorstep. Beneath it was a note from Rainer's great-aunt, with the best wishes of his mother in neat pen beneath it. She read its kind words as she boiled the kettle, and put it into her pile of correspondence to answer. Rainer's great-aunt wanted to know if she had met a nice boy in DC yet, but she didn't come right out and say it—too subtle for that. The women in Rainer's family got all the subtlety, and they recognized their own kind. It was why she and the old lady kept writing to each other; that and so that the Relatives could reassure themselves that someone in full possession of life-guardly skills and a level head was watching out for Rainer's interests.

This business of hand-written, hand-delivered notes and letters was actually kind of charming, she thought as she put her feet up on her coffee table and opened up her flask of very special Irish whisky again.

☙ ☙ ☙

She and Rainer went head to head in half a dozen more skirmishes that month—her phone popping back to life every time she got within shouting distance of him. The on-again/off-again hearings in both Judiciary and Commerce never quite materialized.

She was better at playing the game, but he was a fast learner, and he had much deeper pockets and a working network infrastructure. Her Board approved her renting out an empty suite of offices below their office and converting them to bedrooms for her staff for days when their cars couldn't get them home. They secretly borrowed elderly network appliances from relatives or bought them in the dollar-a-pound bin at the Salvation Army, but always, within a few hours of being in the possession of someone in the employ of the Association for a Human-Readable World, the devices would seize up and lose their routes to the network. Their offices started to fill up with dead soldiers, abandoned network boxes that no one could get online.

The embedded journalists went home after the second week. Their own gear was seizing up, too, as though the curse of the Association for a Human-Readable World was rubbing off on them. They vowed to return when things got interesting again, but they were of no use to anyone without working cameras, mics, and notepads.

Christmas came and went, and New Year's, and then February arrived and the city turned to ice and slush and perpetual twilight. The paralegal quit—she needed a job where the phones worked so that she could call her girlfriend. The media guy took a series of "personal days" and she wasn't sure if he'd show up again, but it didn't matter, because the press had stopped calling them.

Then came the second Downtime.

It struck during morning rush-hour on Valentine's Day, a Monday, and it juddered the whole country to a halt for eight long days. The hospitals overflowed and doctors used motorized scooters to go from one place to another, unable to spread their expertise around with telemedicine. Firemen perished in blazes. Cops arrived too late at crime-scenes. Grocery stores didn't get their resupplies, and schools dug out old chalk-boards and taught the few students who lived close enough to walk. Fed cops of all description went berserk, and could be seen walking briskly from one federal building to another, their faces grim.

And suddenly, miraculously, every journalist, policy-wonk, staffer, advisor, clerk and cop in DC wanted to have a chat with the Association for a Human-Readable World.

🐜 🐜 🐜

She hired three more people that week, and borrowed four more from fellow-traveler organizations. Paying their salaries for the next four weeks would bottom out the group's finances, but she knew that this was now or never, and the Board backed her, after some nail-biting debate.

Rainer showed up on the fourth day of the Downtime, and she found him standing, bewildered, in the hustle of her office as her staffers penned notes on steno pads to their contacts on the Hill and handed them to waiting bicycle couriers in space-program warmgear that swathed them from fingertips to eyeballs. She plucked him out of the bustle and brought him back to her office.

"I've got a hell of a nerve," he said, sitting in her guest-chair.

"Really?" she said. "I hadn't noticed."

"Well, I haven't been showing it off. But I'm about to. I need advice. My office is falling apart. You've been living with no communications and no travel for a year now, you know how to make it work. We're completely lost. I've come to throw myself on your mercy." He looked up at her with his big brown eyes, and then they crumpled shut as he made his Fretting face.

"You're playing me, Rainer," she said. "And it won't work. Whatever I feel for you, I've got a job to do, and if this Downtime tells us anything, it's that I'm doing the right thing, and you're doing the wrong thing."

He hung his head. He wasn't even the slightest bit natty that day. She supposed that his personal assistant was stuck in Fall's Church or Baltimore or somewhere, unable to get into the city. Judging from the slush and road-salt on his shoes, he must have walked the two miles between their offices.

"What's more, I don't have any advice to give you, in particular. We're not faring well here because we're doing something differently—we're faring well because we're doing what we've been at all along, because of a network outage that you claim is impossible, is a figment of our imagination. Those bike messengers: we've been their best customers for months now. Everyone else is begging for service from them, but they're always here when we need them. We've got beds and changes of clothes and toilet-kits in the offices downstairs. We've been living through a Downtime for a couple of quarters now—we've hardly noticed the change. If you want to cope as well as we are, well, you can go back in time, rent out spare offices to house your staff, establish a good working relationship with a bike-messenger company, learn to navigate the Metro and the freeways by map, and all the other things we've done here."

He looked defeated. He began to stand, to turn, to leave.

"Rainer," she said.

He paused.

"Close the door and sit down," she said.

He did, looking at her with so much hope that it made her eyes water.

"Here's my offer," she said. "You and I will lock ourselves in this office with the last draft of my bill. My staff will run interference for me with the Judiciary committee, and we will draft a version of my bill that we can both live with. We will jointly take it to Senators Beauchamp and Rittenhouse, with our blessings, and ask them to expedite it through *both* committees. Every Congresscritter on the Hill is sitting around with his thumb up his ass until the lights come back on. We can get this voted in by Tuesday."

He stared down at his hands. "I can't do it," he said. "My *job* is *not to compromise.* I just can't do it."

"Come on, Rainer, think outside the box for a minute here." Her heart was pounding. This could really be it. This could be the solution she'd been waiting for. "Even if the bill passes, there's going to be a long deliberation over the contours of the regulation, probably at the FCC. You'll be able to work on the bureau staffers and at the expert agencies, take ex-parte meetings and lobby on behalf of your employers. It's all we've ever asked for: an expert discussion where the public interest gets a hearing alongside of private enterprise and government."

But he was shaking his head, standing up to go. "You're probably right, Trish," he said. "I don't know. What I know is, I can't do what you're asking of me. They'd just fire me."

"If the Downtime continues, they won't be *able* to fire you— they won't even know what you're up to until it's too late. And then they'll make the best that they can out of it. No one is better qualified to represent your side in the administrative agencies."

He put his ridiculous hat on and wrapped his scarf around his neck, and they looked each other in the eyes for a long moment. She waited for the involuntary smile that looking into his eyes inevitably evoked, but it didn't come.

"I don't understand you, Trish. You won this incredible victory for cooperation, for collective ownership of our intellectual infrastructure. Ant-networks demand the same cooperation from the nodes, that my phone pass your car's messages to his desk. Let's just set aside the professional politics for a second. Just you and me. Tell me: how can you *not* support this?" He looked at her out from under his brows, staring intensely. He swallowed and said, "It was the surfer, wasn't it?"

"What?" she said.

"The one who died. That's why you're doing this. You want to make-up for him—"

She couldn't believe he'd said it. Taken such a cheap shot. "I'm surprised you didn't save that one for television, Rainer. Jesus. No, I'm doing this because it's *right*. In case you haven't noticed, your self-healing, uncorruptable network is *down*. People are suffering. The economy is tanking. The death toll is mounting. You won't even bend one *inch*, one *tenth of an inch*, because you're worried about losing your job."

"Trish," he said, "I'm sorry, I didn't mean—"

Her office door opened and there stood her embedded journalist. "I just got in from Manhattan," he said. "Can I set up in that corner there again?"

"Be my guest," she said, grateful for the distraction. Rainer looked at her, forehead scrunched, and then he left.

🐜 🐜 🐜

"It's a good thing you're not over him," the lawyer said, pouring her another victory whisky. The bill had passed the House with only one opposing and two abstentions, and had squeaked through the Senate by five seats, at five minutes to midnight on the eighth day of the Downtime. They were halfway to the bar (where the office manager had been feeding twenties to the bartender to stay open) when the grid came back up, crawls springing to life on every surface and cars suddenly zipping forward in the characteristic high-speed ballet of efficiently routed traffic. They'd laughed themselves stupid all the way to the bar and after a brief but intense negotiation between the lawyer and the barman, he'd produced a bottle of Irish that was nearly half as good as the stuff Trish kept at home.

"I'm going to pretend you didn't say that," Trish said, sipping tenderly at the booze.

"Come on, girl," the lawyer said, twirling her moustache. "Be serious. You two had so much sexual energy in that room, it's a wonder you didn't make the bulbs explode. It's how you got inside each other's heads. You weren't selling the committee, you were selling *him*, and that's what made you so effective. We're going to need that again at the FCC, too—so no getting over him until after then."

Trish drank her whisky. She didn't know what to say to that. He'd looked ten years older tonight, in the corridors, whispering to his committee members, to his staffers, his face drooping and wilted. She supposed she didn't look any better. It had been, what, three days? since she'd had more than an hour's sleep.

"I don't get it," she said. "How could he be so dumb? I mean, it's obvious that the system is being gamed. Obvious that we're being targeted through it. Yet he sits there, insisting that white is black, that up is down, that the network is autonomous and immune to all corruption."

"It's like a religion for them," the lawyer said. "It doesn't need explaining. It's just right-living. It's the Law."

Trish thought back to the ceremony in the graveyard, the dirge and the prayers to a god no one believed in. Had Rainer really renounced his faith when he dropped out of Yeshiva?

"Here's to a human-readable world," Trish said, raising her glass. Around her, the staffers and borrowed staffers and hangers-on and even the barman raised their glasses and cheered. It was warm and the feeling swelled in her tummy and up her chest and through her face and she burst out in what felt like the biggest smile of her life.

🐾 🐾 🐾

She'd learned a long time ago never to send email while drunk, but it had been too much last night.

"What if, Rainer, what if—what if the reason for the Downtimes is that someone is manipulating the network and that's breaking it. Did you ever wonder about that? Maybe the network *is* as good as you say it is—until someone screws it up by trying to get preferential treatment for his pals.

"Wouldn't that be a kick in the teeth? We get five squillion percent increases in across-the-board routing efficiency, but in the end, it's never enough for people who can't be happy unless they're happier than someone else.

"The thing that saves the human race, but if we adopt it, it will destroy us. Irony sucks."

She'd signed it "Love," but even drunk, she'd had the sense to take that out before sending it. Saying "Love" would have been no more appropriate than saying, "You know, I *did* save your cousin's life." She'd called in no favors, she'd run no blackmail, and she'd won anyway.

He rang her doorbell at 5AM. She was barely able to drag herself out of bed.

"I figured you'd be getting up to deal with the press soon," he said, and she groaned. He was right. She'd earned some time off, but it'd be a month before she could take it. Too much press to do. She appreciated anew how much work it must have taken to be any of her old bosses from the copyright wars: the judge, the senator, the executive director of the PAC.

She was in her robe, and he was in jeans and a UCLA sweatshirt. He didn't have any gel in his hair, which was matted down by the knit cap he'd been wearing. He looked adorable.

"They fired me this morning," he said.

"Oh, hon—" she said.

"I would have quit," he said. "I'm outmatched."

She felt herself blush. Or was she flushing? She was suddenly aware of his smell, the boy smell, the smell that she could smell in his chest, in his scalp, in his tummy, lower . . . She straightened up and led him into the living room and started the coffee-maker going.

"When do you fly back, then?" she said.

He looked at her, smiling. "I don't know," he said. "I haven't booked a ticket."

She felt an answering smile at the corners of her mouth and turned into the fridge to fetch out some gourmet MREs. "Bacon and eggs or pancakes?" she said, then laughed. "I guess bacon is out," she said.

"Oh, I'm willing to bet that that bacon hasn't been anywhere near a pig," he said, "but I'll have the pancakes, if you don't mind."

She set everything to perking and went into the bedroom to pull on something smart and camera-friendly, but everything was in the hamper, so she settled for jeans and a decent shirt from last-year's wardrobe.

When she opened the door, he was standing right there, taller than her. "I think you're right," he said. "About the network. It's the best explanation I've heard so far."

She wrapped herself in silence again, waited for him to say more.

"You see, the *true*, neutral network is immune to corrupting influences and favoritism. So the existence of corruption and favoritism means that what we've got *isn't* a true network. Which means you're right! We need to have a hearing to get to the bottom of this, so that we can build the true network." He smiled bravely. "I thought maybe you could use an expert in your corner who'd say that in a hearing?"

"Thanks," she said, and slipped under his arm and back into the kitchen. Suddenly, she wanted very much to be back at her office, back with her staff, talking to reporters and overseeing a million details. "I'll think about it."

"I'm giving up my apartment at the end of the month—next Monday. I won't be able to afford it without the Association's salary," he said.

Her place was big. A bedroom, a home office, a living room and a dining room. It was a serious deal for DC, even outside the beltway. It could easily accommodate a second person, even if they weren't sleeping together.

Her office—her staff—the press—the bill—her Board.

"Well," she said, "I've got to get going. I'll shower at the office. Got to get there in time to catch the Euro press-calls. Let me put your breakfast in a bag, OK?"

He looked whipsawed. "Uh, OK. Can I give you a ride?"

"No, I'll need my car this afternoon. Thanks, though." She kept her voice light, didn't meet his eyes. Kept thinking: her office—her staff—the bill.

"Well," he said. He turned for the door. Stopped. She tensed. He turned back to her. "Trish," he said.

"It's OK," she said. "It's OK. We just have religious differences, is all."

She slipped past him and into her car, and left him standing in her driveway. As she asked the car to plot a route for her back to the Hill, she dug through her purse for a pocket-knife. At the next red light, she took her lapel and slashed at it, opening a rent in her shirt that reflected a little of what her heart was feeling. It made her feel a little better to do it.

—For Alice

AUDUBON IN ATLANTIS

by Harry Turtledove

*Harry Turtledove was born in Los Angeles, California, in June
1949. A prolific and popular writer of alternate history novels,
he was inspired to study Byzantine history after reading
L. Sprague de Camp's 1941 novel* Lest Darkness Fall, *and
eventually earned a Ph.D. in that subject from UCLA. Early
works, including first novel* Wereblood, *appeared under the
name "Eric G. Iverson." Turtledove's long running "Videssos"
cycle, about Romans transported to another universe, began in
1987 with* The Misplaced Legion. *Among many works since
then are* Agent of Byzantium, *U.S. Civil War novels* The
Guns of the South *and* How Few Remain, *a series about
aliens who interrupt World War II beginning with* In the
Balance, *and* Ruled Britannia, *about a Britain conquered by
the Spanish Armada. His short fiction, including Hugo award-
winning novella "Down in the Bottomlands," Hugo and Nebula
nominee "Must and Shall," and Hugo nominee "Forty, Counting
Down," has been collected in* Kaleidoscope, Departures, *and*
Counting Up, Counting Down.

DELICATE AS IF walking on eggs, the riverboat *Augustus Caesar*
eased in alongside the quay at New Orleans. Colored
roustabouts, bare to the waist, caught lines from the boat and
made her fast. The steam whistle blew several long, happy blasts,
telling the world the sternwheeler had arrived. Then black smoke
stopped belching from the stacks as the crew shut down the
engines.

The deck stopped quivering beneath John Audubon's feet. He breathed a silent sigh of relief; for all the time he'd spent aboard boats and ships, he was not a good sailor, and knew he never would be. Any motion, no matter how slight, could make his stomach betray him. He sighed—a long sea voyage still lay ahead of him.

Edward Harris came up and stood alongside him. "Well, my friend, we're on our way," he said.

"It's true—we are. And we shall do that which has not been done, while it may yet be done." As Audubon always did, he gathered enthusiasm when he thought about the goal and not the means by which he had to accomplish it. His English was fluent, but heavily flavored by the French that was his birthspeech. Even without an accent, he would have spoken more mushily than he liked; he was nearer sixty than fifty, and had only a few teeth left. "Before long, Ed, either the great honkers will be gone from this world or I will."

He waited impatiently till the gangplank thudded into place, then hurried off the *Augustus Caesar* onto dry land, or something as close to dry land as New Orleans offered. He was a good-sized man—about five feet ten—with shoulder-length gray hair combed straight back from his forehead and with bushy gray side whiskers that framed a long, strong-nosed face.

Men and women of every color, wearing everything from rags to frock coats and great hoop skirts, thronged the muddy, puddled street. Chatter, jokes, and curses crackled in Spanish, French, and English, and in every possible mixture and corruption of those tongues. Audubon heard far more English than he had when he first came to New Orleans half a lifetime earlier. It was a French town then, with the Spanish dons hanging on where and as they could. Times changed, though. He knew that too well.

Not far from the Cabildo stood the brick building that housed the Bartlett Line. Edward Harris following in his wake, Audubon went inside. A clerk nodded to them. "Good day, gentlemen," he said in English. A generation earlier, the greeting would surely have come in French. "How may I be of service to you today?"

"I wish to purchase passage to Atlantis for the two of us," Audubon replied.

"Certainly, sir." The clerk didn't bat an eye. "The *Maid of Orleans* sails for New Marseille and Avalon on the west coast in . . . let me see . . . five days. If you would rather wait another week, you can book places on the *Sea Queen* for the east. She puts in at St. Augustine, St. Denis, and Hanover, then continues on to London."

"We can reach the interior as easily from either coast," Harris said.

"Just so." Audubon nodded. "We would have to wait longer to leave for the east, the journey would be longer, and I would not care to set out from Hanover in any case. I have too many friends in the capital. With the kindest intentions in the world, they would sweep us up in their social whirl, and we should be weeks getting free of it. The *Maid of Orleans* it shall be."

"You won't be sorry, sir. She's a fine ship." The clerk spoke with professional enthusiasm. He took out a book of ticket forms and inked his pen. "In whose names shall I make these out?"

"I am John James Audubon," Audubon replied. "With me travels my friend and colleague, Mr. Edward Harris."

"Audubon?" The clerk started to write, then looked up, his face aglow. "*The* Audubon? The artist? The naturalist?"

Audubon exchanged a secret smile with Edward Harris. Being recognized never failed to gratify him: he loved himself well enough to crave reminding that others loved him, too. When he swung back toward the clerk, he tried to make the smile modest. "I have the honor to be he, yes."

The clerk thrust out his hand. As Audubon shook it, the young man said, "I cannot tell you how pleased I am to make your acquaintance, sir. Mr. Hiram Bartlett, the chairman of the shipping line, is a subscriber to your *Birds and Viviparous Quadrupeds of Northern Terranova and Atlantis*—the double elephant folio edition. He sometimes brings in one volume or another for the edification of his staff. I admire your art and your text in almost equal measure, and that is the truth."

"You do me too much credit," Audubon said, in lieu of strutting and preening like a courting passenger pigeon. He was also glad to learn how prosperous Bartlett was. No one but a rich man could afford the volumes of the double elephant folio. They were big enough to show almost every bird and most beasts at life size, even if he had twisted poses and bent necks almost unnaturally here and there to fit creatures onto the pages' Procrustean bed.

"Are you traveling to Atlantis to continue your researches?" the clerk asked eagerly.

"If fate is kind, yes," Audubon replied. "Some of the creatures I hope to see are less readily found than they were in years gone by, while I"—he sighed—"I fear I am less well able to find them than I was in years gone by. Yet a man can do only what it is given to him to do, and I intend to try."

"If they're there, John, you'll find them," Harris said.

"God grant it be so," Audubon said. "What is the fare aboard the *Maid of Orleans*?"

"A first-class cabin for two, sir, is a hundred twenty livres," the clerk said. "A second-class cabin is eighty livres, while one in steerage is a mere thirty-five livres. But I fear I cannot recommend steerage for gentlemen of your quality. It lacks the comforts to which you will have become accustomed."

"I've lived rough. Once I get to Atlantis, I expect I shall live rough again," Audubon said. "But, unlike some gentlemen of the Protestant persuasion"—he fondly nudged Edward Harris—"I don't make the mistake of believing comfort is sinful. Let us travel first class."

"I don't believe comfort is sinful, and you know it," Harris said. "We want to get you where you're going and keep you as healthy and happy as we can while we're doing it. First class, by all means."

"First class it shall be, then." The clerk wrote up the tickets.

※ ※ ※

Audubon boarded the *Maid of Orleans* with a curious blend of anticipation and dread. The sidewheeler was as modern a steamship as any, but she was still a ship, one that would soon put to sea. Even going up the gangplank, his stomach gave a premonitory lurch.

He laughed and tried to make light of it, both to Harris and to himself. "When I think how many times I've put to sea in a sailing ship, at the mercy of wind and wave, I know how foolish I am to fret about a voyage like this," he said.

"You said it to the clerk last week: you can only do what you can do." Harris was blessed with both a calm stomach and a calm disposition. If opposites attracted, he and Audubon made a natural pair.

The purser strode up to them. Brass buttons gleamed on his blue wool coat; sweat gleamed on his face. "You gentlemen are traveling together?" he said. "If you would be kind enough to show me your tickets . . . ?"

"But of course," Audubon said. He and Harris produced them.

"I thank you." The purser checked them against a list he carried in one of his jacket's many pockets. "Mr. Audubon and Mr. Harris, is it? Very good. We have you in Cabin 12, the main deck on the starboard side. That's on the right as you look forward, if you haven't gone to sea before."

"I'm afraid I have," Audubon said. The purser took off his cap and scratched his balding crown, but Audubon meant it exactly as he'd phrased it. He nodded to Harris and to the free Negro pushing a wheeled cart that held their baggage. "Let's see what we've got, then."

They had a cabin with two beds, a chest of drawers, and a basin and pitcher on top of it: about what they would have had in an inn of reasonable quality, though smaller. *In an inn, though, I'm not likely to drown*, Audubon thought. He didn't suppose he was *likely* to drown on the *Maid of Orleans*, but if the seas got rough he would wish he were dead.

He gave the Negro half a livre, for the luggage, once unloaded from the cart, filled the cabin almost to the bursting point. Neither Audubon nor Harris was a dandy; they had no extraordinary amount of clothes. But Audubon's watercolors and paper filled up a couple of trunks, and the jars and the raw spirits they would use to preserve specimens took up a couple of more. And each of them had a shotgun for gathering specimens and a newfangled revolver for self-protection.

"Leave enough room so you'll be able to get out and come to the galley when you're hungry," the purser said helpfully.

"Thank you so much." Audubon hoped his sarcasm would freeze the man, but the purser, quite unfrozen, tipped his cap and left the cabin. Audubon muttered in pungent French.

"Never mind, John," Harris said. "We're here, and we'll weigh anchor soon. After that, no worries till we get to Avalon."

No worries for you. But Audubon kept that to himself. Harris couldn't help having a tranquil stomach, any more than the artist could help having a nervous one. Audubon only wished his were calm.

He also wished the *Maid of Orleans* sailed at the appointed hour, or even on the appointed day. *Thursday, the 6th day of April, 1843, at half past 10 in the morning,* the clerk had written on each ticket in a fine round hand. Audubon and Harris were aboard in good time. But half past ten came and went without departure. All of Thursday came and went. Passengers kept right on boarding. Stevedores kept on carrying sacks of sugar and rice into the ship's hold. Only the stuffed quail and artichokes and asparagus and the really excellent champagne in the first-class galley went some little way toward reconciling Audubon to being stuck on the steamship an extra day.

Finally, on Friday afternoon, the *Maid of Orleans'* engine rumbled to life. Its engine had a deeper, stronger note than the one that had propelled the *Augustus Caesar* down the Big Muddy. The deck thrummed under Audubon's shoes.

Officers bawled commands as smoke belched from the steamship's stacks. Sailors took in the lines that secured the ship to the quay. Others, grunting with effort, manned the capstan. One link at a time, they brought up the heavy chain and anchor that had held the sidewheeler in place.

Watching them, Harris said, "One of these days, steam will power the capstan as well as the paddlewheels."

"You could be right," Audubon replied. "The sailors must hope you are."

"Steam is the coming thing. You mark my words," Harris

said. "Steamships, railroads, factories—who knows what else?"

"So long as they don't make a steam-powered painter, I'll do well enough," Audubon said.

"A steam-powered painter? You come up with the maddest notions, John." Edward Harris laughed. Slowly, though, the mirth faded from his face. "With a mechanical pantograph, your notion might almost come true."

"I wasn't thinking of that so much," Audubon told him. "I was thinking of this new trick of light-writing people have started using the last few years. If it gave pictures in color, not shades of gray, and if you could make—no, they say *take*—a light-writing picture fast enough to capture motion . . . Well, if you could, painters would fall on thin times, I fear."

"Those are hefty *ifs*. It won't happen soon, if it ever does," Harris said.

"Oh, yes. I know." Audubon nodded. "I doubt I'll have to carry a hod in my fading years. My son will likely make a living as a painter, too. But you were talking about days to come. May I not think of them as well?"

The steamship's whistle screamed twice, warning that she was about to move away from the quay. Her paddlewheels spun slowly in reverse, backing her out into the Big Muddy. Then one wheel stopped while the other continued to revolve. Along with the rudder, that swung the *Maid of Orleans'* bow downstream. Another blast from the whistle—a triumphant one—and more smoke pouring from her stacks, she started down the great river toward the Bay of Mexico. Though she hadn't yet reached the sea, Audubon's stomach flinched.

᪥ ᪥ ᪥

The Big Muddy's delta stretched far out into the Bay of Mexico. As soon as the *Maid of Orleans* left the river and got out into the bay, her motion changed. Her pitch and roll were nothing to speak of, not to the crew and not to most of the passengers. But they were enough to send Audubon and a few other unfortunates running for the rail. After a couple of minutes that seemed like forever, he wearily straightened, mouth foul and burning, eyes streaming with tears. He was rid of what ailed him, at least for the moment.

A steward with a tray of glasses nodded deferentially. "Some punch, sir, to help take the taste away?"

"*Merci. Mon Dieu, merci beaucoup,*" Audubon said, tormented out of English.

"*Pas de quoi,*" the steward replied. Any man on a ship sailing from New Orleans and touching in the southern parts of Atlantis had to speak some French.

Audubon sipped and let rum and sweetened lemon juice clean his mouth. When he swallowed, he feared he would have another spasm, but the punch stayed down. Reassuring warmth spread from his middle. Two more gulps emptied the glass. "God bless you!" he said.

"My pleasure, sir. We see some every time out." The steward offered restoratives to Audubon's fellow sufferers. They fell on him with glad cries. He even got a kiss from a nice-looking young woman—but only after she'd taken a good swig from her glass of punch.

Feeling human in a mournful way, Audubon walked up toward the bow. The breeze of the ship's passage helped him forget about his unhappy innards . . . for now. Gulls screeched overhead. A common tern dove into the sea, and came up with a fish in its beak. It didn't get to enjoy the meal. A herring gull flapped after it and made it spit out the fish before it could swallow. The gull got the dainty; the robbed tern flew off to try its luck somewhere else.

On the southern horizon lay the island of Nueva Galicia, about forty miles southeast of the delta. Only a little steam rose above Mount Isabella, near the center of the island. Audubon had been a young man the last time the volcano erupted. He remembered ash raining down on New Orleans.

He looked east toward Mount Pensacola at the mouth of the bay. Pensacola had blown its stack more recently—only about ten years earlier, in fact. For now, though, no ominous plume of black rose in that direction. Audubon nodded to himself. He wouldn't have to worry about making the passage east during an eruption. When Mount Pensacola burst into flame, rivers of molten rock ran steaming into the sea, pushing the Terranovan coastline a little farther south and east. Ships couldn't come too close to observe the awe-inspiring spectacle, for the volcano threw stones to a distance coast artillery only dreamt of. Most splashed into the Bay of Mexico, of course, but who would ever forget the *Black Prince*, holed and sunk by a flying boulder the size of a cow back in '93?

The *Maid of Orleans* steamed sedately eastward. The waves weren't too bad; Audubon found that repeated doses of rum punch worked something not far from a miracle when it came to settling his stomach. If it did twinge now and again, the rum kept him from caring. And the lemon juice, he told himself, held scurvy at bay.

Mount Pensacola was smoking when the sidewheeler passed it near sunset. But the cloud of steam rising from the conical peak, like that above Mount Isabella, was thin and pale, not broad and black and threatening.

Edward Harris came up alongside Audubon by the port rail. "A pretty view," Harris remarked.

"It is indeed," Audubon said.

"I'm surprised not to find you sketching," Harris told him. "Sunset tinging the cloud above the mountain with pink against the deepening blue . . . What could be more picturesque?"

"Nothing, probably." Audubon laughed in some embarrassment. "But I've drunk enough of that splendid rum punch to make my right hand forget its cunning."

"I don't suppose I can blame you, not when *mal de mer* torments you so," Harris said. "I hope the sea will be calmer the next time you come this way."

"So do I—if there is a next time," Audubon said. "I am not young, Edward, and I grow no younger. I'm bound for Atlantis to do things and see things while I still may. The land changes year by year, and so do I. Neither of us will be again what we were."

Harris—calm, steady, dependable Harris—smiled and set a hand on his friend's shoulder. "You've drunk yourself sad, that's what you've done. There's more to you than to many a man half your age."

"Good of you to say so, though we both know it's not so, not any more. As for the rum . . ." Audubon shook his head. "I knew this might be my last voyage when I got on the *Augustus Caesar* in St. Louis. Growing up is a time of firsts, of beginnings."

"Oh, yes." Harris' smile grew broader. Audubon had a good idea which first he was remembering.

But the painter wasn't finished. "Growing up is a time for firsts, yes," he repeated. "Growing old . . . Growing old is a time for endings, for lasts. And I do fear this will be my last long voyage."

"Well, make the most of it if it is," Harris said. "Shall we repair to the galley? Turtle soup tonight, with a saddle of mutton to follow." He smacked his lips.

Harris certainly made the most of the supper. Despite his ballasting of rum, Audubon didn't. A few spoonfuls of soup, a halfhearted attack on the mutton and the roast potatoes accompanying it, and he felt full to the danger point. "We might as well have traveled second class, or even steerage," he said sadly. "The difference in cost lies mostly in the victuals, and I'll never get my money's worth at a table that rolls."

"I'll just have to do it for both of us, then." Harris poured brandy-spiked gravy over a second helping of mutton. His campaign with fork and knife was serious and methodical, and soon reduced the mutton to nothing. He looked around hopefully. "I wonder what the sweet course is."

It was a cake baked in the shape of the *Maid of Orleans* and stuffed with nuts, candied fruit, and almond paste. Harris indulged immoderately. Audubon watched with a strange smile, half jealous, half wistful.

He went to bed not long after supper. The first day of a sea voyage always told on him, more than ever as he got older. The mattress was as comfortable as the one in the inn back in New Orleans. It might have been softer than the one he slept on at home. But it was unfamiliar, and so he tossed and turned for a while, trying to find the most comfortable position. Even as he tossed, he laughed at himself. Before long, he'd sleep wrapped in a blanket on bare ground in Atlantis. Would he twist and turn there, too? He nodded. Of course he would. Nodding still, he dozed off.

He hadn't been asleep long before Harris came in. His friend was humming "Pretty Black Eyes," a song popular in New Orleans as they set out. Audubon didn't think the other man even knew he was doing it. Harris got into his nightshirt, pissed in the chamber pot under his bed, blew out the oil lamp Audubon had left burning, and lay down. He was snoring in short order. Harris always denied that he snored—and why not? He never heard himself.

Audubon laughed once more. He tossed and twisted and yawned. Pretty soon, he was snoring again himself.

🐾 🐾 🐾

When he went out on deck the next morning, the *Maid of Orleans* might have been the only thing God ever made besides the sea. Terranova had vanished behind her; Atlantis still lay a thousand miles ahead. The steamship had entered the Hesperian Gulf, the wide arm of the North Atlantic that separated the enormous island and its smaller attendants from the continent to the west.

Audubon looked south and east. He'd been born on Santo Tomás, one of those lesser isles. He was brought to France three years later, and so escaped the convulsions that wracked the island when its colored slaves rose up against their masters in a war where neither side asked for quarter or gave it. Blacks ruled Santo Tomás to this day. Not many whites were left on the island. Audubon had only a few faded childhood memories of his first home. He'd never cared to go back, even if he could have without taking his life in his hands.

Edward Harris strolled out on deck. "Good morning," he said. "I hope you slept well?"

"Well enough, thanks," Audubon answered. *I would have done better without "Pretty Black Eyes," but such is life.* "Yourself?"

"Not bad, not bad." Harris eyed him. "You look . . . less greenish than you did yesterday. The bracing salt air, I suppose?"

"It could be. Or maybe I'm getting used to the motion." As soon as Audubon said that, as soon as he thought about his stomach, he gulped. He pointed an accusing finger at his friend. "There—you see? Just asking was enough to jinx me."

"Well, come have some breakfast, then. Nothing like a good

mess of ham and eggs or something like that to get you ready for
. . . Are you all right?"

"No," Audubon gasped, leaning out over the rail.

He breakfasted lightly, on toasted ship's biscuit and coffee
and rum punch. He didn't usually start the day with strong spirits, but he didn't usually start the day with a bout of seasickness,
either. *A good thing, too, or I'd have died years ago*, he thought. *I hope
I would, anyhow.*

Beside him in the galley, Harris worked his way through fried
eggs and ham and sausage and bacon and maizemeal mush.
Blotting his lips with a snowy linen napkin, he said, "That was
monstrous fine." He patted his pot belly.

"So glad you enjoyed it," Audubon said tonelessly.

Once or twice over the next three days, the *Maid of Orleans*
came close enough to another ship to make out her sails or the
smoke rising from her stack. A pod of whales came up to blow
nearby before sounding again. Most of the time, though, the sidewheeler might have been alone on the ocean.

Audubon was on deck again the third afternoon, when the
sea—suddenly, as those things went—changed from greenish
gray to a deeper, richer blue. He looked around for Harris, and
spotted him not far away, drinking rum punch and chatting with
a personable young woman whose curls were the color of fire.

"Edward!" Audubon said. "We've entered the Bay Stream!"

"Have we?" The news didn't seem to have the effect on
Harris that Audubon wanted. His friend turned back to the redheaded woman—who also held a glass of punch—and said, "John
is wild for nature in every way you can imagine." Spoken in a different tone of voice, it would have been a compliment. Maybe it
still was. Audubon hoped he only imagined Harris' faintly condescending note.

"Is he?" The woman didn't seem much interested in
Audubon one way or the other. "What about you, Eddie?"

Eddie? Audubon had trouble believing his ears. No one had
ever called Harris such a thing in his hearing before. And Harris
. . . smiled. "Well, Beth, I'll tell you—I am, too. But some parts of
nature interest me more than others." He set his free hand on her
arm. She smiled, too.

He was a widower. He could chase if that suited his fancy, not that Beth seemed to need much chasing. Audubon admired a pretty lady as much as anyone—more than most, for with his painter's eye he saw more than most—but was a thoroughly married man, and didn't slide from admiration to pursuit. He hoped Lucy was well.

Finding Harris temporarily distracted, Audubon went back to the rail himself. By then, the *Maid of Orleans* had left the cooler waters by the east coast of Terranova behind and fully entered the warm current coming up from the Bay of Mexico. Even the bits of seaweed floating in the ocean looked different now. Audubon's main zoological interests did center on birds and viviparous quadrupeds. All the same, he wished he would have thought to net up some of the floating algae in the cool water and then some of these so he could properly compare them.

He turned around to say as much to Harris, only to discover that his friend and Beth were no longer on deck. Had Harris gone off to pursue his own zoological interests? Well, more power to him if he had. Audubon looked back into the ocean, and was rewarded with the sight of a young sea turtle, not much bigger than the palm of his hand, delicately nibbling a strand of the new seaweed. Next to the rewards Harris might be finding, it didn't seem like much, but it was definitely better than nothing.

** *** ***

Like the sun, Atlantis, for Audubon, rose in the east. That blur on the horizon—for a little while, you could wonder if it was a distant cloudbank, but only for a little while. Before long, it took on the unmistakable solidity of land. To the Breton and Galician fishermen who'd found it first, almost four hundred years before, it would have sent the setting sun to bed early.

"Next port of call is New Marseille, sir," the purser said, tipping his cap to Audubon as he went by.

"Yes, of course," the artist replied, "but I'm bound for Avalon."

"Even so, sir, you'll have to clear customs at the first port of call in Atlantis," the other man reminded him. "The States are fussy about these things. If you don't have a New Marseille customs stamp on your passport, they won't let you off the ship in Avalon."

"It's a nuisance, to open all my trunks for the sake of a stamp," Audubon said. The purser shrugged the shrug of a man with right, or at least regulations, on his side. And he told the truth: the United States of Atlantis *were* fussy about who visited them. *Do as we do*, they might have said, *or stay away.*

Not that coming ashore at New Marseille was a hardship. On the contrary. Warmed by the Bay Stream, the city basked in an almost unending May. Farther north, in Avalon, it seemed to be April most of the time. And then the Bay Stream curled north and east around the top of Atlantis and delivered the rest of its warmth to the north of France, to the British Isles, and to Scandinavia. The east coast of Atlantis, where the winds swept across several hundred miles of mountains and lowlands before they finally arrived, was an altogether darker, harsher place.

But Audubon was in New Marseille, and if it wasn't veritably May, it was the middle of April, which came close enough. A glance as he and Harris carted their cases to the customs shed sufficed to tell him he'd left Terranova behind. Oh, the magnolias that shaded some nearby streets weren't much different from the ones he could have found near New Orleans. But the ginkgoes on other thoroughfares . . . Only one other variety of ginkgo grew anyplace else in the world: in China. And the profusion of squat cycads with tufts of leaves sprouting from the tops of squat trunks also had few counterparts anywhere in the temperate zone.

The customs official, by contrast, seemed much like customs officials in every other kingdom and republic Audubon had ever visited. He frowned as he examined their declaration, and frowned even more as he opened up their baggage to confirm it. "You have a considerable quantity of spirits here," he said. "A dutiable quantity, in fact."

"They aren't intended for drinking or for resale, sir," Audubon said, "but for the preservation of scientific specimens."

"John Audubon's name and artistry are known throughout the civilized world," Edward Harris said.

"I've heard of the gentleman myself. I admire his work, what I've seen of it," the official replied. "But the law does not consider intent. It considers quantity. You will not tell me these strong spirits *cannot* be drunk?"

"No," Audubon admitted reluctantly.

"Well, then," the customs man said. "You owe the fisc of Atlantis . . . Let me see . . ." He checked a table thumbtacked to the wall behind him. "You owe twenty-two eagles and, ah, fourteen cents."

Fuming, Audubon paid. The customs official gave him a receipt, which he didn't want, and the requisite stamp in his passport, which he did. As he and Harris trundled their chattels back to the *Maid of Orleans,* a small bird flew past them. "Look, John!" Harris said. "Wasn't that a gray-throated green?"

Not even the sight of the Atlantean warbler could cheer Audubon. "Well, what if it was?" he said, still mourning the money he'd hoped he wouldn't have to spend.

His friend knew what ailed him. "When we get to Avalon, paint a portrait or two," Harris suggested. "You'll make it up, and more besides."

Audubon shook his head. "I don't *want* to do that, dammit." When thwarted, he could act petulant as a child. "I grudge the time I'd have to spend. Every moment counts. I have not so many days left myself, and the upland honkers. . . . Well, who can say if they have any left at all?"

"They'll be there." As usual, Harris radiated confidence.

"Will they?" Audubon, by contrast, careened from optimism to the slough of despond on no known schedule. At the moment, not least because of the customs man, he was mired in gloom. "When fishermen first found this land, a dozen species of honkers filled it: filled it as buffalo fill the plains of Terranova. Now . . . Now a few may be left in the wildest parts of Atlantis. Or, even as we speak, the last ones may be dying—may already have died!—under an eagle's claws or the jaws of a pack of wild dogs or to some rude trapper's shotgun."

"The buffalo are starting to go, too," Harris remarked.

That only agitated Audubon more. "I must hurry! Hurry, do you hear me?"

"Well, you can't go anywhere till the *Maid of Orleans* sails," Harris said reasonably.

"One day soon, a railroad will run from New Marseille to Avalon," Audubon said. Atlantis was building railroads almost as fast as England: faster than France, faster than any of the new Terranovan republics. But soon was not yet, and he *did* have to wait for the steamship to head north.

Passengers left the *Maid of Orleans*. Beth got off, which made Harris glum. Others came aboard. Longshoremen carried crates and boxes and barrels and bags ashore. Others brought fresh cargo onto the ship. Passengers and longshoremen alike moved too slowly to suit Audubon. Again, he could only fume and pace the mercifully motionless deck. At last, late the next afternoon, the *Maid of Orleans* steamed towards Avalon.

She stayed close to shore on the two-and-a-half-day journey. It was one of the most beautiful routes anywhere in the world. Titanic redwoods and sequoias grew almost down to the shore. They rose so tall and straight, they might almost have been the columns of a colossal outdoor cathedral.

But that cathedral could have been dedicated to puzzlement and confusion. The only trees like the enormous evergreens of Atlantis were those on the Pacific coast of Terranova, far, far away. Why did they thrive here, survive there, and exist nowhere else? Audubon had no more answer than any other naturalist, though he dearly wished for one. *That* would crown a career! He feared it was a crown he was unlikely to wear.

The *Maid of Orleans* passed a small fishing town called Newquay without stopping. Having identified the place on his map, Audubon was pleased when the purser confirmed he'd done it right. "If anything happens to the navigator, sir, I'm sure we'd be in good hands with you," the man said, and winked to show he didn't aim to be taken too seriously.

Audubon gave him a dutiful smile and went back to eyeing the map. Atlantis' west coast and the east coast of North Terranova a thousand miles away put him in mind of two pieces of a world-sized jigsaw puzzle: their outlines almost fit together. The same was true for the bulge of Brazil in South Terranova and the indentation in West Africa's coastline on the other side of the Atlantic. And the shape of Atlantis' eastern coast corresponded to that of western Europe in a more general way.

What did that mean? Audubon knew he was far from the first to wonder. How could anyone who looked at a map help but wonder? Had Atlantis and Terranova been joined once upon a time? Had Africa and Brazil? How could they have been, with so much sea between? He saw no way it could be possible. Neither did anyone else. But when you looked at the map . . .

"Coincidence," Harris said when he mentioned it at supper.

"Maybe so." Audubon cut meat from a goose drumstick. His stomach was behaving better these days—and the seas stayed mild. "But if it is a coincidence, don't you think it's a large one?"

"World's a large place." Harris paused to take a sip of wine. "It has room in it for a large coincidence or three, don't you think?"

"Maybe so," Audubon said again, "but when you look at the maps, it seems as if those matches ought to spring from reason, not happenstance."

"Tell me how the ocean got in between them, then." Harris aimed a finger at him like a pistol barrel. "And if you say it was Noah's flood, I'll pick up that bottle of fine Bordeaux and clout you over the head with it."

"I wasn't going to say anything of the sort," Audubon replied. "Noah's flood may have washed over these lands, but I can't see how it could have washed them apart while still leaving their coastlines so much like each other."

"So it must be coincidence, then."

"I don't believe it *must* be anything, *mon vieux*," Audubon said. "I believe we don't know what it is—or, I admit, if it's anything at all. Maybe they will one day, but not now. For now, it's a puzzlement. We need puzzlements, don't you think?"

"For now, John, I need the gravy," Harris said. "Would you kindly pass it to me? Goes mighty well with the goose."

It did, too. Audubon poured some over the moist, dark meat on his plate before handing his friend the gravy boat. Harris wanted to ignore puzzlements when he could. Not Audubon. They reminded not only of how much he—and everyone else—didn't know yet, but also of how much he—in particular—might still find out.

As much as I have time for, he thought, and took another bite of goose.

🐾 🐾 🐾

Avalon rose on six hills. The city fathers kept scouting for a seventh so they could compare their town to Rome, but there wasn't another bump to be found for miles around. The west-facing Bay of Avalon gave the city that bore its name perhaps the finest harbor in Atlantis. A century and a half before, the bay was a pirates' roost. The buccaneers swept out to plunder the Hesperian Gulf for most of a lifetime, till a British and Dutch fleet drove them back to their nest and then smoked them out of it.

City streets still remembered the swashbuckling past: Goldbeard Way, Valjean Avenue, Cutpurse Charlie Lane. But two Atlantean steam frigates patrolled the harbor. Fishing boats, bigger merchantmen—some steamers, other sailing ships—and liners like the *Maid of Orleans* moved in and out. The pirates might be remembered, but they were gone.

May it not be so with the honkers, Audubon thought as the *Maid of Orleans* tied up at a pier. *Please, God, let it not be so.* He crossed himself. He didn't know if the prayer would help, but it couldn't hurt, so he sent it up for whatever it might be worth.

Harris pointed to a man coming up the pier. "Isn't that Gordon Coates?"

"It certainly is." Audubon waved to the man who published his work in Atlantis. Coates, a short, round fellow with side whiskers even bushier than Audubon's, waved back. His suit was of shiny silk; a stovepipe hat sat at a jaunty angle on his head. Audubon cupped his hands in front of his mouth. "How are you, Gordon?"

"Oh, tolerable. Maybe a bit better than tolerable," Coates replied. "So you're haring off into the wilderness again, are you?" He was a city man to the tips of his manicured fingers. The only time he went out to the countryside was to take in a horse race. He knew his ponies, too. When he bet, he won . . . more often than not, anyhow.

He had a couple of servants waiting with carts to take charge of the travelers' baggage. He and Audubon and Harris clasped hands and clapped one another on the back when the gangplank went down and passengers could disembark. "Where are you putting us up?" asked Harris, who always thought about things like where he would be put up. Thanks to his thoughts about such things, Audubon had stayed in some places more comfortable than those where he might have if he made his own arrangements.

"How does the Hesperian Queen sound?" Coates answered.

"Like a pirate's kept woman," Audubon answered, and the publisher sent up gales of laughter. Audubon went on, "Is it near a livery stable or a horse market? I'll want to get my animals as soon as I can." Harris let out a sigh. Audubon pretended not to hear it.

"Not too far, not too far," Coates said. Then he pointed up into the sky. "Look—an eagle! There's an omen for you, if you like."

The large, white-headed bird sailed off toward the south. Audubon knew it was likely bound for the city dump, to scavenge there. White-headed eagles had thrived since men came to Atlantis. Seeing this one secretly disappointed Audubon. He wished it were a red-crested eagle, the Atlantean national bird. But the mighty raptors—by all accounts, the largest in the world—had fallen into a steep decline along with the honkers, which were their principal prey.

"Well," he said, "the Hesperian Queen."

The last time he was in Avalon, the hotel had had another name and another owner. It had come up in the world since. So had Avalon, which was visibly bigger, visibly richer than it had been ten years—or was it twelve now?—before.

Harris noticed, too. Harris generally noticed things like that. "You do well for yourselves here," he told Gordon Coates over beefsteaks at supper.

"Not too bad, not too bad," the publisher said. "I'm about to put out a book by a chap who thinks he's written the great Atlantean novel, and he lives right here in town. I hope he's right. You never can tell."

"You don't believe it, though," Audubon said.

"Well, no," Coates admitted. "Everybody always thinks he's written the great Atlantean novel—unless he comes from Terranova or England. Sometimes even then. Mr. Hawthorne has

a better chance than some—a better chance than most, I dare-
say—but not *that* much better."

"What's it called?" Harris asked.

"*The Crimson Brand*," Coates said. "Not a bad title, if I say so
myself—and I do, because it's mine. *He* wanted to name it *The
Shores of a Different Sea*." He yawned, as if to say authors were
hopeless with titles. Then, pointing at Audubon, he *did* say it: "I'd
have called your books something else, too, if they weren't also
coming out in England and Terranova. *Birds and Critters*, maybe.
Who remembers what a quadruped is, let alone a viviparous one?"

"They've done well enough with the name I gave them,"
Audubon said.

"Well enough, sure, but they might've done better. I could've
made you *big*." Coates was a man with an eye for the main
chance. Making Audubon *big*—he lingered lovingly over the
word—would have made him money.

"I know why folks here don't know quadrupeds from a hole
in the ground," Harris said. "Atlantis hardly had any before it got
discovered. No snakes in Ireland, no . . . critters"—he grinned—
"here, not then."

"No *viviparous* quadrupeds." Audubon had drunk enough
wine to make him most precise—but not too much to keep him
from pronouncing *viviparous*. "A very great plenty of lizards and
turtles and frogs and toads and salamanders—and snakes, of
course, though snakes lack four legs of quadrupedality." He was
proud of himself for that.

"Sure enough, snakes haven't got a leg to stand on." Harris
guffawed.

"Well, we have critters enough now, by God," Coates said.
"Everything from mice on up to elk. Some of 'em we wanted,
some we got anyway. Try and keep rats and mice from coming
aboard ship. Yeah, go ahead and try. Good luck—you'll need it."

"How many indigenous Atlantean creatures are no more
because of them?" Audubon said.

"Beats me," Coates answered. "Little too late to worry about
it now, anyway, don't you think?"

"I hope not," Audubon said. "I hope it's not too late for them.
I hope it's not too late for me." He took another sip of wine. "And

I know the viviparous creature responsible for the greatest number of those sad demises here."

"Rats?" Coates asked.

"Weasels, I bet," Harris said.

Audubon shook his head at each of them in turn. He pointed an index finger at his own chest. "Man," he said.

≋ ≋ ≋

He rode out of Avalon three days later. Part of the time he spent buying horses and tackle for them; that, he didn't begrudge. The rest he spent with Gordon Coates, meeting with subscribers and potential subscribers for his books; that, he did. He was a better businessman than most of his fellow artists, and normally wouldn't have resented keeping customers happy and trolling for new ones. If nobody bought your art, you had a devil of a time making more of it. As a younger man, he'd worked at several other trades, hated them all, and done well at none. He knew how lucky he was to make a living doing what he loved, and how much work went into what others called luck.

To his relief, he did escape without painting portraits. Even before he set out from New Orleans, he'd felt time's hot breath at his heels. He felt himself aging, getting weaker, getting feebler. In another few years, maybe even in another year or two, he would lack the strength and stamina for a journey into the wilds of central Atlantis. And even if he had it, he might not find any honkers left to paint.

I may not find any now, he thought. That ate at him like vitriol. He kept seeing a hunter or a lumberjack with a shotgun. . . .

Setting out from Avalon, Audubon might almost have traveled through the French or English countryside. Oh, the farms here were larger than they were in Europe, with more meadow between them. This was newly settled land; it hadn't been cultivated for centuries, sometimes for millennia. But the crops—wheat, barley, maize, potatoes—were either European or were Terranovan imports long familiar in the Old World. The fruit trees came from Europe; the nuts, again, from Europe and Terranova. Only a few stands of redwoods and Atlantean pines declared that the Hesperian Gulf lay just a few miles to the west.

It was the same with the animals. Dogs yapped outside of farmhouses. Chickens scratched. Cats prowled, hoping for either mice—also immigrants—or unwary chicks. Ducks and geese—ordinary domestic geese—paddled in ponds. Pigs rooted and wallowed. In the fields, cattle and sheep and horses grazed.

Most people probably wouldn't have noticed the ferns that sprouted here and there or the birds on the ground, in the trees, and on the wing. Some of those birds, like ravens, ranged all over the world. Others, such as the white-headed eagle Audubon had seen in Avalon, were common in both Atlantis and Terranova (on Atlantis' eastern coast, the white-tailed eagle sometimes visited from its more usual haunts in Europe and Iceland). Still others—no one knew how many—were unique to the great island.

No one but a specialist knew or cared how Atlantean gray-faced swifts differed from the chimney swifts of Terranova or little swifts from Europe. Many Atlantean thrushes were plainly the same sorts of birds as their equivalents to the west and to the east. They belonged to different species, but their plumages and habits were similar to those of the rest. The same held true for island warblers, which flitted through the trees after insects like their counterparts on the far side of the Hesperian Gulf. Yes, there were many similarities. But . . .

"I wonder how soon we'll start seeing oil thrushes," Audubon said.

"Not this close to Avalon," Harris said. "Not with so many dogs and cats and pigs running around."

"I suppose not," Audubon said. "They're trusting things, and they haven't much chance of getting away."

Laughing, Harris mimed flapping his fingertips. Oil thrushes' wings were bigger than that, but not by much—they couldn't fly. The birds themselves were bigger than chickens. They used their long, pointed beaks to probe the ground for worms at depths ordinary thrushes, flying thrushes, couldn't hope to reach. When the hunting was good, they laid up fat against a rainy day.

But they were all but helpless against men and the beasts men had brought to Atlantis. It wasn't just that they were good eating, or that their fat, rendered down, made a fine lamp oil. The real trouble was, they didn't seem to know enough to run away when a dog or a fox came after them. They weren't used to being hunted by animals that lived on the ground; the only viviparous quadrupeds on Atlantis before men arrived were bats.

"Even the bats here are peculiar," Audubon muttered.

"Well, so they are, but why do you say so?" Harris asked.

Audubon explained his train of thought. "Where else in the world do you have bats that spend more of their time scurrying around on the ground than flying?" he went on.

He thought that was a rhetorical question, but Harris said, "Aren't there also some in New Zealand?"

"Are there?" Audubon said in surprise. His friend nodded. The painter scratched at his side whiskers. "Well, well. Both lands far from any others, out in the middle of the sea . . ."

"New Zealand had its own honkers, too, or something like them," Harris said. "What the devil were they called?"

"Moas," Audubon said. "I do remember that. Didn't I show you the marvelous illustrations of their remains Professor Owen did recently? The draftsmanship is astonishing. Astonishing!" The way he kissed his bunched fingertips proved him a Frenchman at heart.

Edward Harris gave him a sly smile. "Surely you could do better?"

"I doubt it," Audubon said. "Each man to his own bent. Making a specimen look as if it were alive on the canvas—that I can do. My talent lies there, and I've spent almost forty years now learning the tricks and turns that go with it. Showing every detail of dead bone—I'm not in the least ashamed to yield the palm to the good professor there."

"If only you were a little less modest, you'd be perfect," Harris said.

"It could be," Audubon said complacently, and they rode on.

🐾 🐾 🐾

The slow, deep drumming came from thirty feet up a dying pine. Harris pointed. "There he is, John! D'you see him?"

"I'm not likely to miss him, not when he's the size of a raven,"

Audubon answered. Intent on grubs under the bark, the scarlet-cheeked woodpecker went on drumming. It was a male, which meant its crest was also scarlet. A female's crest would have been black, with a forward curl the male's lacked. That also held true for its close relatives on the Terranovan mainland, the ivory-bill and the imperial woodpecker of Mexico.

Audubon dismounted, loaded his shotgun, and approached the bird. He could get closer to the scarlet-cheeked woodpecker than he could have to one of its Terranovan cousins. Like the oil thrush, like so many other Atlantean birds, the woodpecker had trouble understanding that something walking along on the ground could endanger it. Ivory-bills and imperial woodpeckers were less naive.

The woodpecker raised its head and called. The sound was high and shrill, like a false note on a clarinet. Audubon paused with the gun on his shoulder, waiting to see if another bird would answer. When none did, he squeezed the trigger. The shotgun boomed, belching fireworks-smelling smoke.

With a startled squawk, the scarlet-cheeked woodpecker tumbled out of the pine. It thrashed on the ground for a couple of minutes, then lay still. "Nice shot," Harris said.

"*Merci*," Audubon answered absently.

He picked up the woodpecker. It was still warm in his hands, and still crawling with mites and bird lice. No one who didn't handle wild birds freshly dead thought of such things. He brushed his palm against his trouser leg to get rid of some of the vagrants. They didn't usually trouble people, who weren't to their taste, but every once in a while. . . .

A new thought struck him. He stared at the scarlet-cheeked woodpecker. "I wonder if the parasites on Atlantean birds are as different as the birds themselves, or if they share them with the birds of Terranova."

"I don't know," Harris said. "Do you want to pop some into spirits and see?"

After a moment, Audubon shook his head. "No, better to let someone who truly cares about such things take care of it. I'm after honkers, by God, not lice!"

"Nice specimen you took there, though," his friend said. "Scarlet-cheeks are getting scarce, too."

"Not so much forest for them to hunt in as there once was," Audubon said with a sigh. "Not so much of anything in Atlantis as there once was—except men and farms and sheeps." He knew that was wrong as soon as it came out of his mouth, but let it go. "If we don't show what it was, soon it will be no more, and then it will be too late to show. Too late already for too much of it." *Too late for me?* he wondered. *Please, let it not be so!*

"You going to sketch now?" Harris asked.

"If you don't mind. Birds are much easier to pose before they start to stiffen."

"Go ahead, go ahead." Harris slid down from his horse. "I'll smoke a pipe or two and wander around a bit with my shotgun. Maybe I'll bag something else you can paint, or maybe I'll shoot supper instead. Maybe both—who knows? If I remember right, these Atlantean ducks and geese eat as well as any other kind, except canvasbacks." He was convinced canvasback ducks, properly roasted and served with loaf sugar, were the finest fowl in the world. Audubon wasn't so sure he was wrong.

As Harris ambled away, Audubon set the scarlet-cheeked woodpecker on the grass and walked over to one of the pack horses. He knew which sack held his artistic supplies: his posing board and his wires, his charcoal sticks and precious paper.

He remembered how, as a boy, he'd despaired of ever portraying birds in realistic poses. A bird in the hand was all very well, but a dead bird looked like nothing but a dead bird. It drooped, it sagged, it cried its lifelessness to the eye.

When he studied painting with David in France, he sometimes did figure drawings from a mannequin. His cheeks heated when he recalled the articulated bird model he'd tried to make from wood and cork and wire. After endless effort, he produced something that might have done duty for a spavined dodo. His friends laughed at it. How could he get angry at them when he wanted to laugh at it, too? He ended up kicking the horrible thing to pieces.

If he hadn't thought of wires . . . He didn't know what he

would have done then. Wires let him position his birds as if they were still alive. The first kingfisher he'd posed—he knew he was on to something even before he finished. As he set up the posing board now, a shadow of that old excitement glided through him again. Even the bird's eyes had seemed to take on life again once he posed it the way he wanted.

As he worked with wires now to position the woodpecker as it had clung to the tree trunk, he wished he could summon more than a shadow of the old thrill. But he'd done the same sort of thing too many times. Routine fought against art. He wasn't discovering a miracle now. He was . . . working.

Well, if you're working, work the best you can, he told himself. And practice did pay. His hands knew almost without conscious thought how best to set the wires, to pose the bird. When his hands thought he was finished, he eyed the scarlet-cheeked woodpecker. Then he moved a wire to adjust its tail's position. It used those long, stiff feathers to brace itself against the bark, almost as if it had hind legs back there.

He began to sketch. He remembered the agonies of effort that went into his first tries, and how bad they were despite those agonies. He knew others who'd tried to paint, and who gave up when their earlier pieces failed to match what they wanted, what they expected. Some of them, from what he'd seen, had a real gift. But having it and honing it . . . Ah, what a difference! Not many were stubborn enough to keep doing the thing they wanted to do even when they couldn't do it very well. Audubon didn't know how many times he'd almost given up in despair. But when stubbornness met talent, great things could happen.

The charcoal seemed to have a life of its own as it moved across the page. Audubon nodded to himself. His line remained as strong and fluid as ever. He didn't have the tremors and shakes that marked so many men's descent into age—not yet. Yet how far away from them was he? Every time the sun rose, he came one day closer. He sketched fast, racing against his own decay.

Harris' shotgun bellowed. Audubon's hand did jump then. Whose wouldn't, at the unexpected report? But that jerky line was easily rubbed out. He went on, quick and confident, and had the sketch very much the way he wanted it by the time Harris came back carrying a large dead bird by the feet.

"A turkey?" Audubon exclaimed.

His friend nodded, face wreathed in smiles. "Good eating tonight!"

"Well, yes," Audubon said. "But who would have thought the birds could spread so fast? They were introduced in the south . . . It can't be more than thirty years ago, can it? And now you shoot one here."

"They give better sport than oil thrushes and the like," Harris said. "At least they have the sense to get away if they see trouble coming. The sense God gave a goose, you might say—except He didn't give it to all the geese here, either."

"No," Audubon said. Some of Atlantis' geese flew to other lands as well, and were properly wary. Some stayed on the great island the whole year round. Those birds weren't. Some of them flew poorly. Some couldn't fly at all, having wings as small and useless as those of the oil thrush.

Honkers looked uncommonly like outsized geese with even more outsized legs. Some species even had black necks and white chin patches reminiscent of Canada geese. That frankly puzzled Audubon: it was as if God were repeating Himself in the Creation, but why? Honkers' feet had vestigial webs, too, while their bills, though laterally compressed, otherwise resembled the broad, flat beaks of ordinary geese.

Audubon had seen the specimens preserved in the museum in Hanover: skeletons, a few hides, enormous greenish eggs. The most recent hide was dated 1803. He wished he hadn't remembered that. If this was a wild goose chase, a wild honker chase . . . Then it was, that was all. He was doing all he could. He only wished he could have done it sooner. He'd tried. He'd failed. He only hoped some possibility of success remained.

Harris cleaned the turkey and got a fire going. Audubon finished the sketch. "That's a good one," Harris said, glancing over at it.

"Not bad," Audubon allowed—he *had* caught the pose he wanted. He gutted the scarlet-cheeked woodpecker so he would preserve it. Not surprisingly, the bird's stomach was full of beetle larvae. The very name of its genus, *Campephilus*, meant *grub-loving*. He made a note in his diary and put the bird in strong spirits.

"Better than that," Harris said. He cut up the turkey and skewered drumsticks on twigs.

"Well, maybe," Audubon said as he took one of the skewers from his friend and started roasting the leg. He wasn't shy of praise—no, indeed. All the same, he went on, "I didn't come here for scarlet-cheeked woodpeckers. I came for honkers, by God."

"You take what you get." Harris turned his twig so the drumstick cooked evenly. "You take what you get, and you hope what you get is what you came for."

"Well, maybe," Audubon said again. He looked east, toward the still poorly explored heart of Atlantis. "But the harder you work, the likelier you are to get what you want. I hope I can still work hard enough. And"—he looked east once more—"I hope what I want is still there to get."

🐾 🐾 🐾

He and Harris stayed on the main highway for most of a week. The broad, well-trodden path let them travel faster than they could have on narrower, more winding roads. But when Audubon saw the Green Ridge Mountains rising over the eastern horizon, the temptation to leave the main road got too strong to resist.

"We don't want to go into the mountains anywhere near the highway," he declared. "We know no honkers live close to it, or people would have seen them, *n'est-ce pas?*"

"Stands to reason," Harris said loyally. He paused before adding, "I wouldn't mind another couple of days of halfway decent inns, though."

"When we come back with what we seek, the Hesperian Queen will be none too good," Audubon said. "But we go through adversity to seek our goal."

Harris sighed. "We sure do."

On the main highway, fruit trees and oaks and chestnuts and elms and maples thrived. They were all imports from Europe or from Terranova. Audubon and Harris hadn't gone far from the highway before Atlantean flora reasserted itself: ginkgoes and magnolias, cycads and pines, with ferns growing in profusion as an understory. Birdsongs, some familiar, others strange, doubled and redoubled as the travelers moved into less settled country. Atlantean birds seemed more comfortable with the trees they'd lived in for generations uncounted than with the brash newcomers men brought in.

Not all the newcomers clung to the road. Buttercups and poppies splashed the improbably green landscape with color. Atlantean bees buzzed around the flowers that had to be unfamiliar to them . . . or maybe those were European honeybees, carried to the new land in the midst of the sea to serve the plants men needed, wanted, or simply liked. Curious, Audubon stopped and waited by some poppies for a closer look at the insects. They were, without a doubt, honeybees. He noted the fact in his diary. It left him oddly disappointed but not surprised.

"In another hundred years," he said, climbing back onto his horse, "how much of the old Atlantis will be left? Any?"

"In another hundred years," Harries replied, "it won't matter to either of us, except from beyond the Pearly Gates."

"No, I suppose not." Audubon wondered if he had ten years left, or even five, let alone a hundred. "But it should matter to those who are young here. They throw away marvels without thinking of what they're doing. Wouldn't you like to see dodos preserved alive?" He tried not to recall his unfortunate bird model.

"Alive? Why, I can go to Hanover and hear them speechifying," Harris said. Audubon snorted. His friend waved a placating hand. "Let it go, John. Let it go. I take your point."

"I'm so glad," Audubon said with sardonic relish. "Perhaps the authorities here—your speechifying dodos—could set up parks to preserve some of what they have." He frowned. "Though how parks could keep out foxes and weasels and rats and windblown seeds, I confess I don't know. Still, it would make a start."

They slept on the grass that night. The throaty hoots of an Atlantean ground owl woke Audubon somewhere near midnight. He loaded his shotgun by the faint, bloody light of the campfire's embers, in case the bird came close enough for him to spot it. Ground owls were hen-sized, more or less. They could fly, but not well. They hunted frogs and lizards and the outsized katydids that scurried through the undergrowth here. Nothing hunted them—or rather, nothing had hunted them till foxes and wild dogs and men came to Atlantis. Like so many creatures here, they couldn't seem to imagine they might become prey. Abundant once, they were scarce these days.

This one's call got farther and farther away. Audubon thought about imitating it to lure the ground owl into range of his charge. In the end, he forbore. Blasting away in the middle of the night might frighten Harris into an apoplexy. And besides—Audubon yawned—he was still sleepy himself. He set down the shotgun, rolled himself in his blanket once more, and soon started snoring again.

🐻 🐻 🐻

When Audubon woke the next morning, he saw a mouse-sized katydid's head and a couple of greenish brown legs only a yard or so from his bedroll. He swore softly: the ground owl *had* come by, but without hooting, so he never knew. If he'd stayed up . . . *If I'd stayed up, I would be useless today*, he thought. He needed regular doses of sleep much more than he had twenty years earlier. "I wouldn't have minded if you fired on an owl," Harris said as he built up the fire and got coffee going. "We're here for that kind of business."

"Good of you to say so," Audubon replied. "It could be that I will have other chances."

"And it could be that you won't. You were the one who said the old Atlantis was going under. Grab with both hands while it's here."

"With the honkers, I intend to," Audubon said. "If they're there to be grabbed, grab them I shall. The ground owl . . . Well, who knows if it would have come when I hooted?"

"I bet it would. I never knew a soul who could call birds better than you." Harris took a couple of squares of hardtack out of an oilcloth valise and handed one to Audubon. The artist waited till he had his tin cup of coffee before breakfasting. He broke his hardtack into chunks and dunked each one before eating it. The crackers were baked to a fare-thee-well so they would keep for a long time, which left them chewier than his remaining teeth could easily cope with.

As he and his friend got ready to ride on, he looked again at the remains of the giant katydid. "I really ought to get some specimens of those," he remarked.

"Why, in heaven's name?" Harris said. "They aren't birds, and they aren't viviparous quadrupeds, either. They aren't quadrupeds at all."

"No," Audubon said slowly, "but doesn't it seem to you that here they fill the role mice play in most of the world?"

"Next time I see me a six-legged chirping mouse with feelers"—Harris wiggled his forefingers above his eyes—"you can lock me up and lose the key, on account of I'll have soused my brains with the demon rum."

"Or with whiskey, or gin, or whatever else you can get your hands on," Audubon said. Harris grinned and nodded. As Audubon saddled his horse, he couldn't stop thinking about Atlantean katydids and mice. *Something* had to scurry through the leaves and eat whatever it could find there, and so many other creatures ate mice . . . or, here, the insects instead. He nodded to himself. That was worth a note in the diary whenever they stopped again.

They rode into a hamlet a little before noon. It boasted a saloon, a church, and a few houses. BIDEFORD HOUSE OF UNIVERSAL DEVOTION, the church declared. Strange Protestant sects flourished in Atlantis, not least because none was strong enough to dominate—and neither was his own Catholic Church.

But the saloon, in its own way, was also a house of universal devotion. Bideford couldn't have held more than fifty people, but at least a dozen men sat in there, drinking and eating and talking. A silence fell when Audubon and Harris walked in. The locals stared at them. "Strangers," somebody said; he couldn't have sounded much more surprised had he announced a pair of kangaroos.

Not surprisingly, the man behind the bar recovered fastest. "What'll it be, gents?" he asked.

Harris was seldom at a loss when it came to his personal comforts. "Ham sandwich and a mug of beer, if you please."

"That sounds good," Audubon said. "The same for me, if you'd be so kind."

"Half an eagle for both of you together," the proprietor said. Some of the regulars grinned. Even without those telltale smiles, Audubon would have known he was being gouged. But he paid without complaint. He could afford it, and he'd be asking questions later on, and priming the pump with more silver. He wanted the locals to see he could be openhanded.

The beer was . . . beer. The sandwiches, by contrast, were prodigies: great slabs of tender, flavorful ham on fresh-baked bread, enlivened by spicy mustard and pickles all but jumping with dill and garlic and something else, something earthy—an Atlantean spice?

Audubon hadn't come close to finishing his—he had to chew slowly—when the man behind the bar said, "Don't see too many strangers here." Several locals—big, stocky, bearded fellows in homespun—nodded. So did Audubon, politely. The tapman went on, "Mind if I ask what you're doing passing through?"

"I am John James Audubon," Audubon said, and waited to see if anyone knew his name. Most places, he would have had no doubt. In Bideford . . . Well, who could say?

"The painter fella," one of the regulars said.

"That's right." Audubon smiled, more relieved than he wanted to show. "The painter fella." He repeated the words even though they grated. If the locals understood he was a prominent person, they were less likely to rob him and Harris for the fun of it. He introduced his friend.

"Well, what are you doing here in Bideford?" the proprietor asked again.

"Passing through, as you said," Audubon replied. "I'm hoping to paint honkers." This country was almost isolated enough to give him hope of finding some here—not quite, but almost.

"Honkers?" Two or three men said it at the same time. A heartbeat later, they all laughed. One said, "Ain't seen any of them big fowl round these parts since Hector was a pup."

"That's right," someone else said. Solemn nods filled the saloon.

"It's a shame, too," another man said. "My granddad used to say they was easy to kill, and right good eatin'. Lots of meat on 'em, too." That had to be *why* no honkers lived near Bideford these days, but the local seemed ignorant of cause and effect.

"If you know of any place where they might dwell, I'd be pleased to pay for the information." Audubon tapped a pouch on his belt. Coins clinked sweetly. "You'd help my work, and you'd advance the cause of science."

"Half now," the practical Harris added, "and half on the way back if we find what we're looking for. Maybe a bonus, too, if the tip's good enough."

A nice ploy, Audubon thought. *I have to remember that one.* The locals put their heads together. One of the older men, his beard streaked with gray, spoke up: "Well, I don't know anything for sure, mind, but I was out hunting a few years back and ran into this fellow from Thetford." *He* knew where Thetford was, but Audubon didn't. A few questions established that it lay to the northeast. The Bideford man continued, "We got to gabbing, and he said he saw some a few years before that, off the other side of his town. Can't swear he wasn't lyin', mind, but he sounded like he knew what he was talking about."

Harris looked a question towards Audubon. The artist nodded. Harris gave the Bideford man a silver eagle. "Let me have your name, sir," Harris said. "If the tip proves good, and if we don't pass this way again on our return journey, we *will* make good on the rest of the reward."

"Much obliged, sir," the man said. "I'm Lehonti Kent." He carefully spelled it out for Harris, who wrote it down in one of his notebooks.

"What can you tell me about the House of Universal Devotion?" Audubon asked.

That got him more than he'd bargained for. Suddenly everyone, even the most standoffish locals, wanted to talk at once. He gathered that the church preached the innate divinity of every human being and the possibility of transcending mere mankind—as long as you followed the preachings of the man the locals called the Reverend, with a very audible capital R. *Universal Devotion to the Reverend,* he thought. It all seemed to him the rankest, blackest heresy, but the men of Bideford swore by it.

"Plenty of Devotees"—another obvious capital letter—"in Thetford and other places like that," Lehonti Kent said. He plainly had only the vaguest idea of places more than a couple of days' travel from his home village.

"Isn't that interesting?" Audubon said: one of the few phrases polite almost anywhere.

Because the Bedfordites wanted to preach to them, he and Harris couldn't get away from the saloon for a couple of hours. "Well, well," Harris said as they rode away. "Wasn't that *interesting*?" He freighted the word with enough sarcasm to sink a ship twice the size of the *Maid of Orleans*.

Audubon's head was still spinning. The Reverend seemed to have invented a whole new prehistory for Atlantis and Terranova, one that had little to do with anything Audubon thought he'd learned. He wondered if he'd be able to keep it straight enough to get it down in his diary. The Devotees seemed nearly as superstitious to him as the wild red Terranovan tribes— and they should have known better, while the savages were honestly ignorant. Even so, he said, "If Lehonti—what a name!— Kent gave us a true lead, I don't mind the time we spent . . . too much."

Thetford proved a bigger village than Bideford. It also boasted a House of Universal Devotion, though it had a Methodist church as well. A crudely painted sign in front of the House said, THE REVEREND PREACHES SUNDAY!! Two exclamation points would have warned Audubon away even if he'd never passed through Bideford.

He did ask after honkers in Thetford. No one with whom he talked claimed to have seen one, but a couple of men did say some people from the town had seen them once upon a time. Harris doled out more silver, but it spurred neither memory nor imagination.

"Well, we would have come this way anyhow," Audubon said as they went on riding northeast. The Green Ridge Mountains climbed higher in the sky now, dominating the eastern horizon. Peering ahead with a spyglass, Audubon saw countless dark valleys half hidden by the pines and cycads that gave the mountains their name. Anything could live there . . . couldn't it? He had to believe it could. "We have a little more hope now," he added, as much to himself as to Harris.

"Hope is good," his friend said. "Honkers would be better."

The words were hardly out of his mouth before the ferns and cycads by the side of the road quivered . . . and a stag bounded across. Audubon started to raise his shotgun, but stopped with the motion not even well begun. For one thing, the beast was gone. For another, the gun was charged with birdshot, which would only have stung it.

"*Sic transit gloria honkeris,*" Harris said.

"*Honkeris?*" But Audubon held up a hand before Harris could speak. "Yes, *honker* would be a third-declension noun, wouldn't it?"

Little by little, the country rose toward the mountains. Cycads thinned out in the woods; more varieties of pines and spruces and redwoods took their places. The ferns in the undergrowth seemed different, too. As settlements thinned out, so did splashes of color from exotic flowers. The very air seemed different: mistier, moister, full of curious, spicy scents the nose would not meet anywhere else in the world. It felt as if the smells of another time were wafting past the travelers.

"And so they are," Audubon said when that thought crossed his mind. "This is the air of Atlantis as it was, Atlantis before those fishermen saw its coast loom up out of the sea."

"Well, almost," Harris said. That he and Audubon and their horses were here proved his point. In case it didn't, he pointed to the track down which they rode. The ground was damp—muddy in spots—for it had rained the day before. A fox's pads showed plainly.

"How many birds has that beast eaten?" Audubon said. "How many ground-dwellers' nests has it robbed?" Many Atlantean birds nested on the ground, far more than in either Europe or Terranova. But for a few snakes and large lizards, there were no terrestrial predators—or hadn't been, before men brought them in. Audubon made another note in his diary. Till now, he hadn't thought about the effect the presence or absence of predators might have on birds' nesting habits.

Even here, in the sparsely settled heart of Atlantis, a great deal had been lost. But much still remained. Birdsongs filled the air, especially just after sunrise when Audubon and Harris started out each day. Atlantis had several species of crossbills and grosbeaks: birds with bills that seemed made for getting seeds out of cones and disposing of them afterwards. As with so many birds on the island, they were closely related to Terranovan forms but not identical to them.

Audubon shot a male green grosbeak in full breeding plumage. Lying in his hand, the bird, with its apple-green back, warm cinnamon belly, and yellow eye streak, seemed gaudy as a seventeenth-century French courtier. But on the branch of a redwood, against the green foliage and rusty-brown bark, it hadn't been easy to spot. If it weren't singing so insistently, chances were he would have ridden right past it.

At dusk, Harris shot an oil thrush. That wasn't for research, though Audubon did save the skin. The long-billed flightless thrush had more than enough meat for both of them. The flavor put Audubon in mind of snipe or woodcock: not surprising, perhaps, when all three were so fond of earthworms.

Gnawing on a thighbone, Harris said, "I wonder how long these birds will last."

"Longer than honkers, anyhow, because they're less conspicuous," Audubon said, and his friend nodded. He went on, "But you have reason—they're in danger. They're one more kind that nests on the ground, and how can they escape foxes and dogs that hunt by scent?"

Somewhere off in the distance, far beyond the light of the campfire, a fox yelped and yowled. Harris nodded. "There's a noise that wasn't heard here before the English brought them."

"If it weren't foxes, it would be dogs," Audubon said sadly, and Harris' head bobbed up and down once more. Atlantis was vulnerable to man and his creatures, and that was the long and short of it. "A pity. A great pity," Audubon murmured. Harris nodded yet again.

🐾 🐾 🐾

The screech ripped across the morning air. Audubon's horse snorted and tried to rear. He calmed it with hands and voice and educated thighs. "Good God!" Harris said. "What was that?"

Before answering, Audubon listened to the sudden and absolute silence all around. A moment before, the birds were singing their hearts out. As a lion's roar was said to bring stillness to the African plains, so this screech froze the forests of Atlantis.

It rang out again, wild and harsh and fierce. Excitement tingled through Audubon. "I know what it is!" Despite the urgency in his voice, it hardly rose above a whisper. His gaze swung to the shotgun. *Have to charge it with stronger shot,* he thought.

"What?" Harris also whispered, hoarsely. As after a lion's roar, talking out loud seemed dangerous.

"A red-crested eagle, by all the saints!" Audubon said. "A *rara avis* itself, and also, with luck, a sign honkers aren't far away." Maybe the Atlantean national bird was reduced to hunting sheep or deer, but Audubon hadn't seen any close by. If the eagle still sought the prey it had always chosen before the coming of man . . . Oh, if it did!

Harris didn't just look at his shotgun. He reached for it and methodically began to load. After a moment, so did Audubon. Red-crested eagles didn't fear men. They were used to swooping down on tall creatures that walked on two legs. People could die—people had died—under their great, tearing claws, long as a big man's thumb. Nor were their fierce beaks to be despised— anything but.

"Where did the cry come from?" Audubon asked after loading both barrels.

"That way." Harris pointed north. "Not far, either."

"No, not far at all," Audubon agreed. "We have to find it. We *have* to, Edward!" He plunged into the undergrowth, moving quiet as he could. Harris hurried after him. They both carried their shotguns at high port, ready to fire and ready to try to fend off the eagle if it struck before they could.

Call again. Audubon willed the thought toward the red-crested eagle with all his strength. *Call again. Show us where you are.*

And the eagle did. The smaller birds had begun to sing again. Silence came down on them like a heavy boot. Audubon grew acutely aware of how loud his own footfalls were. He tried to stride more lightly, with what success he had trouble judging. Tracking the cry, he swung to the west just a little.

"There!" Harris breathed behind him. His friend pointed and froze, for all the world like a well-bred, well-trained hunting dog.

Audubon's eyes darted this way and that. He did not see. . . . He did not see. . . . And then he did. "Oh," he whispered: more a soft sound of wonder than a word.

The eagle perched near the top of a ginkgo tree. It was a big female, close to four feet long from the end of its low, long bill to the tip of the tail. The crest was up, showing the bird was alert and in good spirits. It was the coppery red of a redheaded man's hair or a red-tailed hawk's tail, not the glowing crimson of a hummingbird's gorget. The eagle's back was dark brown, its belly a tawny buff.

Slowly, carefully, Audubon and Harris drew closer. For all their caution, the bird saw them. It mantled on its perch, spreading its wings and screeching again. The span was relatively small for the eagle's size—not much more than seven feet—but the wings were very broad. Red-crested eagles flapped more than they soared, unlike their white-headed and golden cousins. Naturalists disagreed about which were their closer kin.

"Watch out," Harris whispered. "It's going to fly."

And it did, not three heartbeats after the words left his mouth. Audubon and Harris both swung up their guns and fired at essentially the same instant. The eagle cried out once more, this time a startled squall of pain and fear. It fell out of the sky and hit the ground with a thump.

"Got it!" Harris exulted.

"Yes." Joy and sorrow warred in Audubon. That magnificent creature—a shame it had to perish for the sake of art and science. How many were left to carry on the race? One fewer, whatever the answer was.

This one wasn't dead yet. It thrashed in the ferns, screaming in fury because it couldn't fly. Its legs were long and strong—

could it run? Audubon trotted towards it. *It mustn't get away*, he thought. Now that he and Harris had shot it, it had to become a specimen and a subject for his art. If it didn't, they would have knocked it down for nothing, and he couldn't bear the idea.

The red-crested eagle wasn't running. When he came close enough, he saw that a shotgun ball from one of the two charges had broken its left leg. The bird screeched and snapped at him; he had to jump back in a hurry to keep that fearsome beak from carving a chunk out of his calf. Hate and rage blazed in those great golden eyes.

Along with the shotgun, Harris also carried his revolver. He drew it now, and aimed it at the bird. "I'll finish it," he said. "Put it out of its misery." He thumbed back the hammer.

"In the breast, if you please," Audubon said. "I don't want to spoil the head."

"At your service, John. If the poor creature will only hold still for a few seconds . . ."

After more frantic thrashing and another long-neck lunge at the men who'd reduced it from lord of the air to wounded victim, the eagle paused to pant and to gather its waning strength. Harris fired. A pistol ball would have blown a songbird to pieces, but the eagle was big enough to absorb the bullet. It let out a final bubbling scream before slumping over, dead.

"That is one splendid creature," Harris said solemnly. "No wonder the Atlanteans put it on their flag and on their money."

"No wonder at all," Audubon said. He waited a few minutes, lest the eagle, like a serpent, have one more bite in it. Even then, he nudged the bird with a stick before picking it up. That beak, and the talons on the unwounded leg, commanded respect. He grunted in surprise as he straightened with the still-warm body in his arms. "How much would you say this bird weighs, Edward?"

"Let me see." Harris held out his arms. Audubon put the red-crested eagle in them. Harris grunted, too. He hefted the eagle, his lips pursed thoughtfully. "Dog my cats if it doesn't go thirty pounds, easy. You wouldn't think such a big bird'd be able to get off the ground, would you?"

"We saw it. Many have seen it," Audubon said. He took the eagle back from Harris and gauged its weight again himself.

"Thirty pounds? Yes, that seems about right. I would have guessed something around there, too. Neither the golden nor the white-headed eagle goes much above twelve pounds, and even the largest African eagle will not greatly surpass twenty."

"Those birds don't hunt honkers," Harris said. His usual blunt good sense got to the nub of the problem in a handful of words. "The red-crested, now, it needs all the muscles it can get."

"No doubt you're right," Audubon said. "The biggest honkers, down in the eastern lowlands, would stand a foot, two feet, taller than a man and weigh . . . What do you suppose they would weigh?"

"Three or four times as much as a man, maybe more," Harris said. "You look at those skeletons, you see right away they were lardbutted birds."

Audubon wouldn't have put it that way, but he couldn't say his companion was wrong. "Can you imagine the red-crested eagle diving down to strike a great honker?" he said, excitement at the thought making his voice rise. "It would have been like Jove's lightning from the sky, nothing less."

"Can you imagine trying to hold them off with pikes and matchlocks and bows, the way the first settlers did?" Harris said. "Better those fellows than me, by God! It's a wonder there were any second settlers after that."

"No doubt that's so," Audubon said, but he was only half listening. He looked down at the red-crested eagle, already trying to decide how to pose it for what would, for all sorts of reasons, undoubtedly prove the last volume of *Birds and Viviparous Quadrupeds of Northern Terranova and Atlantis*. He wanted to show it in a posture that displayed its power and majesty, but the bird was simply too large even for the double elephant folios of his life's work.

What can't be cured . . . , he thought, and carried the bird back to the patiently weighting horses. Yes, it surely weighed every ounce of thirty pounds; sweat streamed down his face by the time he got to them. The birds rolled their eyes. One of them let out a soft snort at the smell of blood.

"There, there, my pets, my lovelies," he crooned, and gave

each beast a bit of loaf sugar. That calmed them nicely; horses were as susceptible to bribery as people—and much less likely to go back on any bargain they made.

He got to work with the posing board—which, though he'd brought the largest one he had, was almost too small for the purpose—and his wires. Watching him, Harris asked, "How will you pose a honker if we find one?"

"*When* we find one." Audubon would not admit the possibility of failure to his friend or to himself. "How? I'll do the best I can, of course, and I trust I will enjoy your excellent assistance?"

"I'll do whatever you want me to. You know that," Harris said. "Would I be out here in the middle of nowhere if I wouldn't?"

"No, certainly not." Again, though, Audubon gave the reply only half his attention. He knew what he wanted to do now. He shaped the red-crested eagle with wings pulled back and up to brake its flight, talons splayed wide, and beak agape as if it were about to descend on a great honker's back.

He found a stick of charcoal and began to sketch. No sooner had the charcoal touched the paper than he knew this would be a good one, even a great one. Sometimes the hand would refuse to realize what the eye saw, what the brain thought, what the heart desired. Audubon always did the best he could, as he'd told Harris. Some days, that best was better than others. Today . . . Today was one of those. He felt almost as if he stood outside himself, watching himself perform, watching *something* perform through him.

When the drawing was done, he went on holding the charcoal stick, as if he didn't want to let it go. And he didn't. But he had nothing left to add. He'd done what he could do, and. . . .

"That's some of your best work in a long time, John—much better than the woodpecker, and that was mighty good," Harris said. "I didn't want to talk while you were at it, for fear I'd break the spell. But that one, when you paint it, will live forever. It will be less than life-sized on the page, then?"

"Yes. It will have to be," Audubon said. When he spoke, it also felt like breaking the spell. But he made himself nod and respond as a man would in normal circumstances; you couldn't stay on that exalted plane forever. Even touching it now and again seemed a special gift from God. More words came: "This is *right*. If it's small, then it's small, that's all. Those who see will understand."

"When they see the bird like that, they will." Harris seemed unable to tear his eyes away from the sketch.

And Audubon descended to mundane reality, drawing ginkgoes and pines and ferns for the background of the painting yet to come. The work there was solid, professional draftsmanship; it seemed a million miles away from the inspiration that had fired him only minutes before.

Once he finished all the sketches he needed, he skinned the eagle and dissected it. When he opened the bird's stomach, he found gobbets of half-digested, unusually dark flesh. It had a strong odor that put him in mind of. . . . "Edward!" he said. "What does this smell like to you?"

Harris stooped beside him and sniffed. He needed only a few seconds to find an answer, one very much in character:

"Steak-and-kidney pie, by God!"

And not only was the answer in character. It was also right, as Audubon recognized at once. "It does!" he exclaimed, though the homely dish wasn't one of his favorites. "And these bits of flesh have the look of kidney, too. And that means . . ."

"What?" Harris asked.

"From everything I've read, honker kidneys and the fat above them were—*are*—the red-crested eagle's favorite food!" Audubon answered. "If this bird has a belly full of chunks of kidney, then somewhere not far away, somewhere not far away at all, there must be—there *must* be, I say—honkers on which it fed."

"Unless it killed a deer or some such," Harris said. In that moment, Audubon almost hated his friend—not because Harris was wrong, but because he might not be. And dropping a brute fact on Audubon's glittering tower of speculation seemed one of the cruelest things any man could do.

"Well," Audubon said, and then, bucking up, "Well," again. He gathered himself, gathered his stubbornness. "We just have to find out, don't we?"

🐦 🐦 🐦

Two days later, two days deeper into the western foothills of the Green Ridge Mountains, Audubon's sense of smell again came to his aid. This time, he had no trouble identifying the odor a breeze sent his way. "Phew!" he said, wrinkling his nose. "Something's dead."

"Sure is," Harris agreed. "Something big, too, by the stink."

"Something big . . ." Audubon nodded, trying without much luck to control the electric jolt that coursed through him at those words. "Yes!"

Harris raised an eyebrow. "Yes, indeed. And so?"

"There aren't many big creatures in Atlantis," Audubon said. "It could be a dead man, though I hope not. It could be a dead deer or horse or cow, perhaps. Or it could be . . . Edward, it could be . . ."

"A dead honker?" Harris spoke the word when Audubon couldn't make himself bring it past the barrier of his teeth, past the barrier of his hopes, and out into the open air where it might wither and perish.

"Yes!" he said again, even more explosively than before.

"Well, then, we'd better rein in, hadn't we, and see if we can find out?" Harris let out a creaky chuckle. "Never thought I'd turn bloodhound in my old age. Only goes to show you can't tell, doesn't it?"

He and Audubon tied their horses to a pine sapling by the side of the track. Audubon didn't worry about anyone coming along and stealing the animals; he just didn't want them wandering off. As far as he knew, he and his friend were the only people for miles around. This region was settled thinly, if at all. The two men plunged into the woods, both of them carrying shotguns.

A bloodhound would have run straight to the mass of corruption. Audubon and Harris had no such luck. Tracking by sight or by ear, Audubon would easily have been able to find his quarry. Trying to track by scent, he discovered at once that he was no bloodhound, and neither was Harris. They cast back and forth, trying to decide whether the stench was stronger here or there, in this direction or that: a slow, nasty, frustrating business.

And then, from the edge of a meadow, Harris called, "John! Come quick! I've found it!"

"*Mon Dieu*!" Audubon crashed toward him, his heart thumping and thudding in his chest. "Is it, Edward?" he asked. "Is it a—?"

"See for yourself." Harris pointed out to the curved lump of meat that lay in the middle of the grass and weeds.

"*Mon Dieu*," Audubon said again, softly this time, and crossed himself. "It is a dead honker. It *is*. And where there are dead ones, there must be live ones as well."

"Stands to reason," Harris said, "unless this one here is the very last of its kind."

"Bite your tongue, you horrible man. Fate wouldn't be so cruel to me." Audubon hoped—prayed—he was right. He walked out to the huge dead bird.

If any large scavengers had been at the corpse, Harris—or Audubon's noisy passage through the woods—had scared them off. Clouds of flies still buzzed above it, though, while ants and beetles took their share of the odorous bounty. Audubon stood upwind, which helped some, but only so much.

This wasn't one of the truly enormous honkers that had wandered the eastern plains before men found Atlantis. It was an upland species, and probably hadn't been as tall as Audubon or weighed much more than twice as much as he did. A great wound in the center of its back—now boiling with maggots—told how it died. That was surely a blow from a red-crested eagle: perhaps the one Audubon and Harris shot, perhaps another.

"Can you draw from this one?" Harris asked.

Regretfully, Audubon shook his head. "I fear not. It's too far gone." His sensitive stomach heaved. Even with the ground firm under his feet, the stench nauseated him.

"I was afraid you'd say that," Harris said. "Shall we take specimens—bones and feathers and such—so we have *something* to bring back in case we don't run into any live honkers?"

Messing about with the dead, reeking bird was the last thing Audubon wanted to do. "We *will* find live ones," he said. Harris didn't answer. He just stolidly stood there and let Audubon listen to himself and know he couldn't be certain he was right. The artist glared at him. "But I suppose we should preserve what specimens we can, in the interest of science."

Pulling feathers from the honker wasn't too bad. The black ones on its neck and the white patch under the chin testified to its affinity to Canada geese. The feathers on the body, though, were long and shaggy, more hairlike than similar to the plumage of birds gifted with flight.

Getting the meat from the bones and then cleaning them . . . Audubon's poor stomach couldn't stand the strain. He lost his breakfast on the green meadow grass and then dry-heaved help-lessly for a while. A little rill ran through the meadow not far away. Perhaps the honker was going out to drink there when the eagle struck.

Audubon rinsed his mouth with cold, clear water from the rill . . . upstream from where Harris washed rotting flesh from the honker's right femur. The thighbone was larger and stouter than his own. Gathering himself, Audubon went back to the corpse to free the bird's pelvis. He brought it back to the rill to clean it. How long would his hands reek of decay? How long would his clothes? Would he ever be able to wear this outfit again? He doubted it. As he worked, he tried not to look at what he was doing.

His hands, then, told him of something odd: a hole in the bone on the left side of the pelvis that wasn't matched on the right. That did make him look. Sure enough, the hole was there, and a shallow groove leading to it. "See what I have here," he said to Harris.

His friend examined it, then asked, "What do you make of that?"

"Don't you think it comes from the claw of the red-crested eagle?" Audubon said. "You saw the talons on the bird. One could pierce the flesh above the bone, and then the bone itself. This is plainly a very recent wound: notice how rough the bone is all around the edge. It had no chance to heal."

After considering, Harris nodded. "I'd say you're right. I'd say you have to be right. You might almost have seen the eagle flying at the honker."

"I wish I would have!" Audubon held up the still-stinking

pelvis. "I'll have to draw this. It holds too much information to be easily described in words."

"Let Mr. Owen look to his laurels, then," Harris said.

"I'll do the best I can, that's all," Audubon said. The detailed scientific illustration would have to be pen and ink, not charcoal or watercolor. It would also have to be unrelentingly precise. He couldn't pose the pelvis, except to show the perforation to best advantage, and he couldn't alter and adjust to make things more dramatic. His particular gift lay in portraying motion and emotion; he would have to eschew them both here. He clicked his tongue against the roof of his mouth. "An artist should be versatile, eh?"

"I know you can do it." Harris showed more confidence in him than he had in himself.

The smell of rotting honker came closer to spooking the horses than the eagle's blood had a couple of days before. The pack horse that carried Audubon's artistic supplies didn't want to let him anywhere near it. It didn't even want sugar from his stinking hand. He counted himself lucky to take what he needed without getting kicked.

He set the honker hipbone in the sun, then started sketching with a pencil. He tried and rubbed out, tried and rubbed out. Sweat ran down his face, though the day was fine and mild. This was ever so much harder—for him, anyway—than painting would have been. It seemed like forever before what he set down on paper bore any resemblance to the specimen that was its model.

When he was finally satisfied, he held up the sketch to show it to Harris, only to discover his friend had gone off somewhere and he'd never noticed. Painting took far less concentration. It left room for artistry. This . . . This was a craft, and one in which he knew himself to be imperfectly skilled.

He'd just inked his pen for the first time when Harris' shotgun boomed. Would that be supper or another specimen? *I'll find out*, Audubon thought, and set about turning his shades of gray into black and white. He had to turn the pelvis to compensate for the way shadows had shifted with the moving sun while he worked.

Harris fired again. Audubon heard the blast, but didn't consciously register it. His hand never twitched. A fine line here, shading there to show a hollow, the exact look of the gouge the eagle's claw had dug before piercing the pelvis where the bone thinned . . .

"We've got supper," Harris said. Audubon nodded to show he heard. Harris went on, "And here's something for you to work on when you're done there."

That made Audubon look up. Along with a plump oil thrush, Harris carried a small, grayish, pale-bellied bird with a black cap. "An Atlantean tit!" Audubon said. The bird was closely allied to the tits of England and Europe and to Terranovan chickadees. Naturalists disagreed about which group held its nearest kin. At the moment, though, he was just glad he would be able to sketch and paint; to feel; to let imprecision be a virtue, not a sin. "Yes, that will be a change—and a relief."

"How's the drawing coming?" Harris asked. Audubon showed him. Harris looked from the paper to the pelvis and back again. After a moment, he silently lifted his broad-brimmed felt hat from his head, a salute Audubon cherished more than most wordier ones.

"Bones are all very well," the artist said, "but I want the chance to draw honkers from life!"

🐾 🐾 🐾

Audubon began to despair of getting what he wanted. He began to believe Harris' gibe was right, and he'd come alone just in time to find the last honker in the world moldering in the meadow. Could fate be so cruel?

Whenever he started to fret, Harris would say, "Well, we've got something, anyway. We didn't know for sure we'd get anything at all when we set out." Every word of that was true, and it always made Audubon feel worse, not better.

He spent several days haunting the meadow where his friend found the dead honker, hoping it was part of a flock or a gaggle or whatever the English word for a group of honkers was. No others showed up, though. He found no fresh tracks in the mud by the rill. At last, sorrowfully, he decided the dead bird must have been alone.

"What if it *was* the last one?" he said. "To miss it by a few days . . . Why couldn't we have shot the eagle sooner? Then the honker would still be alive!"

He waited for Harris to be grateful again for what they had. But Harris surprised him, saying, "No use worrying about it. We don't *know* that eagle got that honker, anyhow."

"Well, no," Audubon admitted upon reflection. "Maybe it was some other villainous eagle instead." He got most affronted when Harris laughed at him.

Even though he was forced to admit to himself that honkers weren't going to visit the meadow, he was loath to leave it. He knew at least one live bird had frequented it up until mere days before. About what other spot in all Atlantis—in all the world— could he say the same?

He kept looking back over his shoulder long after he and Harris rode away. "Don't worry," said Harris, the optimist born. "Bound to be better land ahead."

"How do you know that?" Audubon demanded.

Harris surprised him by having an answer: "Because as best I can tell, nobody's ever come this way before. We're on a track now, not a road. I haven't seen any hoofprints besides the ones our horses are leaving for a couple of hours now."

Audubon blinked. He looked around—*really* looked around. "*Nom d'un nom!*" he murmured. "So it would seem." Pines and cycads and ginkgoes crowded close together on either side of the track. The air was fragrant with scents whose like he would find nowhere else. "This might almost be the antediluvian age, or another world altogether. What do you suppose made our trail?"

"Anywhere else, I'd say deer. That may be so here, too, but I haven't seen any sign of them—no tracks, no droppings," Harris said. "Oil thrushes? Some of the other big flightless birds they have here? Maybe even honkers—who knows?"

That was enough to make Audubon dismount and minutely examine the surface of the trail in the hope of finding honker tracks. With their size and with the vestigial webbing between their toes, they were unmistakable. He found none. He did see oil-thrush footprints, as Harris had suggested: they reminded him of those of the European blackbird or Terranovan robin, except for being three or four times as large. And he saw a fox's pads, which stood out against the spiky background of bird tracks. Imported creatures penetrated even here, to the wild heart of Atlantis.

But of course, he thought. *Harris and I are here, aren't we? And we're no less fond of an oil-thrush supper than foxes are.*

A splash of vivid green on the side of a redwood sapling caught his eye as he rode past. At first, he thought it was some strange Atlantean fungus clinging to the trunk. Then, ever so slowly, it moved. "A cucumber slug!" Harris exclaimed.

The slug was almost the size of a cucumber, though Audubon would have fought shy of eating anything of that iridescent hue. Though it was neither bird nor viviparous quadruped, he stopped and sketched it. It was a curiosity, and one little known to naturalists—few of them penetrated to the cool, humid uplands where it lived. Eyestalks waving, it glided along the trunk, leaving behind a thumb-wide trail of slime.

"Maybe we'll come across some of those snails that are almost as big as your fist, too," Harris said.

"A shame to do it now, when we have no garlic butter." Audubon might draw the line at a cucumber slug, but he was fond of *escargots.* Harris, a Terranovan born and bred, made a horrible face. Audubon only laughed.

They rode on. The tracks they followed were never made by man. They twisted this way and that and doubled back on themselves again and again. Whenever Audubon came out into the open, he scanned the stretch of grass ahead with eager hope. How he longed to see honkers grazing there, or pulling leaves from tender young trees! How disappointed he was, again and again!

"Maybe that *was* the last honker in this part of Atlantis," he mourned as he and Harris made camp one night. "Maybe it was the last honker in all of Atlantis."

"Maybe it was," his friend replied. Audubon, toasting an oil-thrush drumstick over the flames, glared at him. The least Harris could do was sympathize. But then he continued, "We've come too far and we've done too much to give up so soon, haven't we?"

"Yes," Audubon said. "Oh, yes."

🐾 🐾 🐾

As the scents were different in this mostly pristine Atlantean wilderness, so too were the sounds. Enormous frogs boomed out their calls an octave lower than even Terranovan bullfrogs, let alone the smaller frogs of Europe. When Audubon remarked on them, Harris said, "I suppose you're sorry about the garlic butter there, too."

"Why, yes, now that you mention it," the painter said placidly. His friend screwed up his face again.

The big green katydids that might almost have been mice were noisier than rodents would have been, though some of their squeaks sounded eerily mouselike. But most of their chirps and trills showed them to be insects after all. Their calls made up the background noise, more notable when it suddenly ceased than when it went on.

Audubon heard birdsongs he'd never imagined. Surely some of those singers were as yet nondescript, new to science. If he could shoot one, sketch it and paint it, bring back a type specimen . . . He did shoot several warblers and finches, but all, so far as he knew, from species already recognized.

Then he heard the scream of a red-crested eagle somewhere far off to the north. He reined in and pointed in that direction. "We go there," he declared, in tones that brooked no argument.

Harris argued anyhow: "It's miles away, John. We can't hope to find just where it is, and by the time we get there it'll be somewhere else anyhow."

"We go north," Audubon said, as if his friend hadn't spoken. "The eagle may fly away, but if honkers are nearby they won't. They can't."

"If." Edward Harris packed a world of doubt into one small word.

"You said it yourself: we've come too far and done too much

to give up hope." If that wasn't precisely what Harris had said, Audubon preferred not to be reminded of it. Harris had the sense to recognize as much.

Going north proved no easier than going in any other cardinal direction. Audubon swore in English, French, and occasionally Spanish when game tracks swerved and led him astray. The red-crested eagle had fallen silent after that one series of screeches, so it told him nothing about how much farther he needed to come. *Maybe it's killed again. Maybe it's feasting,* he thought. Even a freshly dead honker might do.

He and Harris came to a stream like a young river. Those Goliath frogs croaked from the rocks. "Can we ford it?" Audubon asked.

"We'd better look for a shallow stretch," the ever-sensible Harris said.

They found one half a mile to the west, and forded the stream without getting the horses' bellies wet. He unfolded a map of northern Atlantis. "Which stream do you suppose this is?" he said. "It should be big enough to show up here."

Harris put on reading glasses to peer at the map. "If it was ever surveyed at all," he said, and pointed. "It might be a tributary of the Spey. That's about where we are."

"I would have guessed it flows into the Liffey myself." Audubon pointed, too.

"Next one farther north? Well, maybe," Harris said. "The way we've been wandering lately, we could be damn near anywhere. Shall we go on?" Without waiting for an answer, he urged his horse forward. Audubon got his mount moving, too.

Not long after the murmur of the stream and the frogs' formidable calls—what Aristophanes would have done with them!—faded in the distance, Audubon heard what he first thought were geese flying by. He'd ridden out onto a grassy stretch a little while before. He looked north to see if he could spot the birds, but had no luck.

Harris was peering in the same direction, his face puzzled. "Geese—but not quite geese," he said. "Sounds like trumpet music played on a slide trombone."

"It does!" For a moment, Audubon simply smiled at the comparison. Then, sudden wild surmise in his eye, he stared at his friend. "Edward, you don't suppose—?"

"I don't know," Harris said, "but we'd better find out. If they aren't honkers, they could be nondescript geese, which wouldn't be bad, either. Audubon's geese, you could call them."

"I could," said Audubon, who'd never had less interest in discovering a new species. "I could, yes, but . . . I'm going to load my gun with buckshot." He started doing just that.

"Good plan." So did Harris.

Keep calling. Please keep calling, Audubon thought, again and again, as they rode through the forest toward the sound. The birds—whatever they were—did keep up the noise, now quietly, now rising to an angry peak as if a couple of males were quarreling over a female, as males were likely to do in spring.

When Audubon thought they'd come close enough, he slid down off his horse, saying, "We'd best go forward on foot now." He carried not only his gun but also charcoal sticks and paper, in case. . . . Harris also dismounted. Audubon believed he would have brained him with the shotgun had he argued.

After perhaps ten minutes, Harris pointed ahead. "Look. We're coming to an open space." Audubon nodded, not trusting himself to speak. He too saw the bright sunshine that told of a break in the trees. The bird calls were very loud now, very near. "Would you call that honking?" Harris asked. Audubon only shrugged and slid forward.

He peered out from in back of a cycad at the meadow beyond . . . at the meadow, and at the honkers grazing on it. Then they blurred: tears of joy ran down his face.

🐾 🐾 🐾

"Blessed art Thou, O Lord, Who hast preserved me alive to see such things," he whispered, staring and staring.

Harris stood behind a small spruce a few feet away. "Isn't that something. Isn't that *something*?" he said, his words more prosaic than his friend's but his tone hardly less reverent.

Eight honkers grazed there, pulling up grass with their bills: two males, Audubon judged, and half a dozen smaller females. The birds had a more forward-leaning posture than did the mounted skeletons in the Hanover museum. That meant they weren't so tall. The males probably could stretch their heads up higher than a man, but it wouldn't be easy or comfortable for them.

And then they both moved toward the same female, and did stretch their necks up and up and up, and honked as loudly as ever they could, and flapped their tiny, useless wings to make themselves seem big and fierce. And, while they squabbled, the female walked away.

Audubon started sketching. He didn't know how many of the sketches he would work up into paintings and how many would become woodcuts or lithographs. He didn't care, either. He was sketching honkers from life, and if that wasn't heaven it was the next best thing.

"Which species are they, do you suppose?" Harris asked.

Once, at least a dozen varieties of honker had roamed Atlantis' plains and uplands. The largest couple of species, the so-called great honkers, birds of the easily accessible eastern lowlands, went extinct first. Audubon had studied the remains in Hanover and elsewhere to be ready for this day. Now it was here, and he still found himself unsure. "I . . . believe they're what's called the agile honker," he said slowly. "Those are the specimens they most resemble."

"If you say they're agile honkers, why then, they are," Harris said. "Anyone who thinks otherwise will have to change his mind, because you've got the creatures."

"I want to be right." But Audubon couldn't deny his friend had a point. "A shame to have to take a specimen, but . . ."

"It'll feed us for a while, too." The prospect didn't bother Harris. "They *are* supposed to be good eating."

"True enough." When Audubon had all the sketches he wanted of grazing honkers and of bad-tempered males displaying, he stepped out from behind the cycad. The birds stared at him in mild surprise. Then they walked away. He was something strange, but they didn't think he was particularly dangerous. Atlantean creatures had no innate fear of man. The lack cost them dearly.

He walked after them, and they withdrew again. Harris came out, too, which likely didn't help. Audubon held up a hand. "Stay there, Edward. I'll lure them back."

Setting down his shotgun, he lay on his back in the sweet-smelling grass, raised his hips, and pumped his legs in the air, first one, then the other, again and again, faster and faster. He'd made pronghorn antelope on the Terranovan prairie curious enough to approach with that trick. What worked with the wary antelope should work for agile honkers as well. "Are they coming?" he asked.

"They sure are." Harris chuckled. "You look like a damn fool—you know that?"

"So what?" Audubon went on pumping. Yes, he could hear the honkers drawing near, hear their calls and then hear their big, four-toed feet tramping through the grass.

When he stood up again, he found the bigger male only a few feet away. The honker squalled at him; it didn't care for anything on two legs that was taller than it. "Going to shoot that one?" Harris asked.

"Yes. Be ready if my charge doesn't bring it down," Audubon said. Point-blank buckshot should do the job. Sometimes, though, wild creatures were amazingly tenacious of life.

Audubon raised the shotgun. No, the agile honker had no idea what it was. This hardly seemed sporting, but his art and science both required it. He pulled the trigger. The gun kicked against his shoulder. The male let out a last surprised honk and toppled. The rest of the birds ran off—faster than a man, probably as fast as a horse, gabbling as they went.

Harris came up beside Audubon. "He's down. He won't get up again, either."

"No." Audubon wasn't proud of what he'd done. "And the other male can have all the females now."

"He ought to thank you, eh?" Harris leered and poked Audubon in the ribs.

"He'd best enjoy them while he can." Audubon stayed

somber. "Sooner or later—probably sooner—someone else will come along and shoot him, too, and his lady friends with him."

By then, the rest of the honkers had gone perhaps a hundred yards. When no more unexpected thunder boomed, they settled down and started grazing again. A few minutes later, a hawk soared by overhead—not a red-crested eagle, but an ordinary hawk far too small to harm them. Still, its shadow panicked them more thoroughly than the shotgun blast had. They sprinted for the cover of the trees, honking louder than they did when Audubon fired.

"Would you please bring my wires, Edward?" the artist asked. "No posing board with a bird this size, but I can truss him up into lifelike postures."

"I'll be back directly," Harris said. He took longer than he promised, but only because instead of carrying things himself he led up the pack horses. That gave Audubon not only the wires but also his watercolors and the strong spirits for preserving bits of the agile honker. If he and Harris did what he'd told the customs man they wouldn't do and drank some of the spirits instead of using them all as preservatives . . . Well, how else could they celebrate?

Audubon soon got to work. "This may be the last painting I ever do," he said. "If it is, I want to give my best."

"Don't be foolish. You're good for another twenty years, easy," Harris said.

"I hope you're right." Audubon left it there. No matter what he hoped, he didn't believe it, however much he wished he did. He went on, "And this may be the last view of these honkers science ever gets. I owe it to them to give my best, too."

He wired the dead male's neck and wings into the pose it took when challenging its rival. He had the sketches he'd made from life to help him do that. His heart pounded as he and Harris manhandled the honker. Ten years earlier, or even five, it wouldn't have seemed so hard. No, he didn't think he had twenty more left, or anything close to that.

Live for the moment, then, he told himself. *It's all there is.* His eye still saw; his hand still obeyed. If the rest of him was wearing out like a steamboat that had gone up and down the Big Muddy too many times . . . then it was. When people remembered him, it would be for what his eye saw and his hand did. The rest? The rest mattered only to him.

And when people remembered agile honkers from now on, that too would be from what *his* eye saw and what *his* hand did. Even more than he had with the red-crested eagle, he felt responsibility's weight heavy on his shoulders.

The other honkers came out from the trees and began grazing again. Some of them drew close to where he worked. Their calls when they saw him by the male's body seemed to his ear curious and plaintive. They knew their fellow was dead, but they couldn't understand why Audubon stood near the corpse. Unlike a hawk's shadow, he was no danger they recognized.

The sun was setting when he looked up from his work. "I think it may do," he said. "The background will wait for later."

Harris examined the honker on the paper, the honker vibrant with the life Audubon had stolen from its model. He set a hand on the painter's shoulder. "Congratulations. This one will last forever."

"Which is more than I will. Which is more than the birds will." Audubon looked down at the dead honker, agile no more. "Now for the anatomical specimens, and now for the dark meat. Poor thing, it will be all flyblown by this time tomorrow."

"But your painting will keep it alive," Harris said.

"My painting will keep its memory alive. It's not the same." Audubon thought again about how his heart had beat too hard, beat too fast. It was quieter now, but another twenty years? Not likely. "No, it's not the same." He sighed. "But it's all we have. A great pity, but it is." He drew his skinning knife. "And now for the rest of the job . . ."

MAGIC FOR BEGINNERS

by Kelly Link

Kelly Link was born in Miami, Florida, and grew up on the East Coast. She attended Columbia University in New York and the University of North Carolina, Greensboro. She sold her first story, "Water Off a Black Dog's Back," just before attending Clarion in 1995. Her later stories have won or been nominated for the Hugo, Nebula, World Fantasy, Stoker, Tiptree, and Locus awards. Link's stories have been collected in Stranger Things Happen *and* Magic for Beginners. *She has edited the anthology* Trampoline, *co-edits* The Year's Best Fantasy and Horror *with husband Gavin J. Grant and Ellen Datlow, and co-edits the 'zine* Lady Churchill's Rosebud Wristlet *with Grant. They live in Brooklyn, where she is currently working on a novel based on her short story "The Faery Handbag."*

FOX IS A television character, and she isn't dead yet. But she will be, soon. She's a character on a television show called *The Library*. You've never seen *The Library* on TV, but I bet you wish you had.

In one episode of *The Library*, a boy named Jeremy Mars, fifteen years old, sits on the roof of his house in Plantagenet, Vermont. It's eight o'clock at night, a school night, and he and his friend Elizabeth should be studying for the math quiz that their teacher, Mr. Cliff, has been hinting at all week long. Instead they've sneaked out onto the roof. It's cold. They don't know everything they should know about X, when X is the square root of Y. They don't even know Y. They ought to go in.

But there's nothing good on TV and the sky is very beautiful.

They have jackets on, and up in the corners where the sky begins are patches of white in the darkness, still, where there's snow, up on the mountains. Down in the trees around the house, some animal is making a small, anxious sound: "Why cry? Why cry?"

"What's that one?" Elizabeth says, pointing at a squarish configuration of stars.

"That's The Parking Structure," Jeremy says. "And right next to that is The Big Shopping Mall and The Lesser Shopping Mall."

"And that's Orion, right? Orion the Bargain Hunter?"

Jeremy squints up. "No, Orion is over there. That's The Austrian Bodybuilder. That thing that's sort of wrapped around his lower leg is The Amorous Cephalopod. The Hungry, Hungry Octopus. It can't make up its mind whether it should eat him or make crazy, eight-legged love to him. You know that myth, right?"

"Of course," Elizabeth says. "Is Karl going to be pissed off that we didn't invite him over to study?"

"Karl's always pissed off about something," Jeremy says. Jeremy is resolutely resisting a notion about Elizabeth. Why are they sitting up here? Was it his idea or was it hers? Are they friends, are they just two friends sitting on the roof and talking? Or is Jeremy supposed to try to kiss her? He thinks maybe he's supposed to kiss her. If he kisses her, will they still be friends? He can't ask Karl about this. Karl doesn't believe in being helpful. Karl believes in mocking.

Jeremy doesn't even know if he wants to kiss Elizabeth. He's never thought about it until right now.

"I should go home," Elizabeth says. "There could be a new episode on right now, and we wouldn't even know."

"Someone would call and tell us," Jeremy says. "My mom would come up and yell for us." His mother is something else Jeremy doesn't want to worry about, but he does, he does.

Jeremy Mars knows a lot about the planet Mars, although he's never been there. He knows some girls, and yet he doesn't know much about them. He wishes there were books about girls, the way there are books about Mars, that you could observe the orbits and brightness of girls through telescopes without appearing to be perverted. Once Jeremy read a book about Mars out loud to Karl, except he kept replacing the word Mars with the word "girls." Karl cracked up every time.

Jeremy's mother is a librarian. His father writes books. Jeremy reads biographies. He plays trombone in a marching band. He jumps hurdles while wearing a school tracksuit. Jeremy is also passionately addicted to a television show in which a renegade librarian and magician named Fox is trying to save her world from thieves, murderers, cabalists, and pirates. Jeremy is a geek, although he's a telegenic geek. Somebody should make a TV show about him.

Jeremy's friends call him Germ, although he would rather be called Mars. His parents haven't spoken to each other in a week.

Jeremy doesn't kiss Elizabeth. The stars don't fall out of the sky, and Jeremy and Elizabeth don't fall off the roof either. They go inside and finish their homework.

Someone who Jeremy has never met, never even heard of— a woman named Cleo Baldrick—has died. Lots of people, so far, have managed to live and die without making the acquaintance of Jeremy Mars, but Cleo Baldrick has left Jeremy Mars and his mother something strange in her will: a phone booth on a state highway, some forty miles outside of Las Vegas, and a Las Vegas wedding chapel. The wedding chapel is called Hell's Bells. Jeremy isn't sure what kind of people get married there. Bikers, maybe. Supervillains, freaks, and Satanists.

Jeremy's mother wants to tell him something. It's probably something about Las Vegas and about Cleo Baldrick, who—it turns out—was his mother's great-aunt. (Jeremy never knew his mother had a great-aunt. His mother is a mysterious person.) But it may be, on the other hand, something concerning Jeremy's father. For a week and a half now, Jeremy has managed to avoid finding out what his mother is worrying about. It's easy not to find out things, if you try hard enough. There's band practice. He has overslept on weekdays in order to rule out conversations at breakfast, and at night he climbs up on the roof with his telescope to look at stars, to look at Mars. His mother is afraid of heights. She grew up in L.A.

It's clear that whatever it is she has to tell Jeremy is not something she wants to tell him. As long as he avoids being alone with her, he's safe.

But it's hard to keep your guard up at all times. Jeremy comes home from school, feeling as if he has passed the math test after all. Jeremy is an optimist. Maybe there's something good on TV. He settles down with the remote control on one of his father's pet couches: oversized and re-upholstered in an orange-juice-colored corduroy that makes it appear as if the couch has just escaped from a maximum security prison for criminally insane furniture. This couch looks as if its hobby is devouring interior decorators. Jeremy's father is a horror writer, so no one should be surprised if some of the couches he reupholsters are hideous and eldritch.

Jeremy's mother comes into the room and stands above the couch, looking down at him. "Germ?" she says. She looks absolutely miserable, which is more or less how she has looked all week.

The phone rings and Jeremy jumps up.

As soon as he hears Elizabeth's voice, he knows. She says, "Germ, it's on. Channel forty-two. I'm taping it." She hangs up.

"It's on!" Jeremy says. "Channel forty-two! Now!"

His mother has the television on by the time he sits down. Being a librarian, she has a particular fondness for *The Library*. "I should go tell your dad," she says, but instead she sits down beside Jeremy. And of course it's now all the more clear something is wrong between Jeremy's parents. But *The Library* is on and Fox is about to rescue Prince Wing.

When the episode ends, he can tell without looking over that his mother is crying. "Don't mind me," she says and wipes her nose on her sleeve. "Do you think she's really dead?"

But Jeremy can't stay around and talk.

Jeremy has wondered about what kind of television shows the characters *in* television shows watch. Television characters almost always have better haircuts, funnier friends, simpler attitudes toward sex. They marry magicians, win lotteries, have affairs with women who carry guns in their purses. Curious things happen to them on an hourly basis. Jeremy and I can forgive their haircuts. We just want to ask them about their television shows.

Just like always, it's Elizabeth who worked out in the nick of time that the new episode was on. Everyone will show up at Elizabeth's house afterward, for the postmortem. This time, it really is a postmortem. Why did Prince Wing kill Fox? How could Fox let him do it? Fox is ten times stronger.

Jeremy runs all the way, slapping his old track shoes against the sidewalk for the pleasure of the jar, for the sweetness of the sting. He likes the rough, cottony ache in his lungs. His coach says you have to be part-masochist to enjoy something like running. It's nothing to be ashamed of. It's something to exploit.

Talis opens the door. She grins at him, although he can tell that she's been crying, too. She's wearing a T-shirt that says *I'm So Goth I Shit Tiny Vampires.*

"Hey," Jeremy says. Talis nods. Talis isn't so Goth, at least not as far as Jeremy or anyone else knows. Talis just has a lot of T-shirts. She's an enigma wrapped in a mysterious T-shirt. A woman once said to Calvin Coolidge, "Mr. President, I bet my husband that I could get you to say more than two words." Coolidge said, "You lose." Jeremy can imagine Talis as Calvin Coolidge in a former life. Or maybe she was one of those dogs that don't bark. A basenji. Or a rock. A dolmen. There was an episode of *The Library,* once, with some sinister dancing dolmens in it.

Elizabeth comes up behind Talis. If Talis is unGoth, then Elizabeth is Ballerina Goth. She likes hearts and skulls and black pen-ink tattoos, pink tulle, and Hello Kitty. When the woman who invented Hello Kitty was asked why Hello Kitty was so popular, she said, "Because she has no mouth." Elizabeth's mouth is small. Her lips are chapped.

"That was the most horrible episode ever! I cried and cried," she says. "Hey, Germ, so I was telling Talis about how you inherited a gas station."

"A phone booth," Jeremy says. "In Las Vegas. This great-great-aunt died. And there's a wedding chapel, too."

"Hey! Germ!" Karl says, yelling from the living room. "Shut up and get in here! The commercial with the talking cats is on—"

"Shut it, Karl," Jeremy says. He goes in and sits on Karl's head. You have to show Karl who's boss once in a while.

Amy turns up last. She was in the next town over, buying comics. She hasn't seen the new episode and so they all shut it (except for Talis, who has not been saying anything at all) and Elizabeth puts on the tape.

In the previous episode of *The Library,* masked pirate-magicians said they would sell Prince Wing a cure for the spell that infested Faithful Margaret's hair with miniature, wicked, fire-breathing golems. (Faithful Margaret's hair keeps catching fire, but she refuses to shave it off. Her hair is the source of all her magic.)

The pirate-magicians lured Prince Wing into a trap so obvious that it seemed impossible it could really be a trap, on the one-hundred-and-fortieth floor of The Free People's World-Tree Library. The pirate-magicians used finger magic to turn Prince Wing into a porcelain teapot, put two Earl Grey tea bags into the teapot, and poured in boiling water, toasted the Eternally Postponed and Overdue Reign of the Forbidden Books, drained their tea in one gulp, belched, hurled their souvenir pirate mugs to the ground, and then shattered the teapot, which had been Prince Wing, into hundreds of pieces. Then the wicked pirate-magicians swept the pieces of both Prince Wing and collectable mugs carelessly into a wooden cigar box, buried the box in the Angela Carter Memorial Park on the seventeenth floor of The World-Tree Library, and erected a statue of George Washington above it.

So then Fox had to go looking for Prince Wing. When she finally discovered the park on the seventeenth floor of the Library, the George Washington statue stepped down off his plinth and fought her tooth and nail. Literally tooth and nail, and they'd all agreed that there was something especially nightmarish about a biting, scratching, life-sized statue of George Washington with long, pointed metal fangs that threw off sparks when he gnashed them. The statue of George Washington bit Fox's pinky finger right off, just like Gollum biting Frodo's finger off on the top of Mount Doom. But of course, once the statue tasted Fox's magical blood, it fell in love with Fox. It would be her ally from now on.

In the new episode, the actor playing Fox is a young Latina

actress whom Jeremy Mars thinks he recognizes. She has been a snotty but well-intentioned fourth-floor librarian in an episode about an epidemic of food-poisoning that triggered bouts of invisibility and/or levitation, and she was also a lovelorn, suicidal Bear Cult priestess in the episode where Prince Wing discovered his mother was one of the Forbidden Books.

This is one of the best things about *The Library*, the way the cast swaps parts, all except for Faithful Margaret and Prince Wing, who are only ever themselves. Faithful Margaret and Prince Wing are the love interests and the main characters, and therefore, inevitably, the most boring characters, although Amy has a crush on Prince Wing.

Fox and the dashing-but-treacherous pirate-magician Two Devils are never played by the same actor twice, although in the twenty-third episode of *The Library*, the same woman played them both. Jeremy supposes that the casting could be perpetually confusing, but instead it makes your brain catch on fire. It's magical.

You always know Fox by her costume (the too-small green T-shirt, the long, full skirts she wears to hide her tail), by her dramatic hand gestures and body language, by the soft, breathy-squeaky voice the actors use when they are Fox. Fox is funny, dangerous, bad-tempered, flirtatious, greedy, untidy, accident-prone, graceful, and has a mysterious past. In some episodes, Fox is played by male actors, but she always sounds like Fox. And she's always beautiful. Every episode you think that this Fox, surely, is the most beautiful Fox there could ever be, and yet the Fox of the next episode will be even more heartbreakingly beautiful.

On television, it's night in The Free People's World-Tree Library. All the librarians are asleep, tucked into their coffins, their scabbards, priest-holes, buttonholes, pockets, hidden cupboards, between the pages of their enchanted novels. Moonlight pours through the high, arched windows of the Library and between the aisles of shelves, into the park. Fox is on her knees, clawing at the muddy ground with her bare hands. The statue of George Washington kneels beside her, helping.

"So that's Fox, right?" Amy says. Nobody tells her to shut up.

It would be pointless. Amy has a large heart and an even larger mouth. When it rains, Amy rescues worms off the sidewalk. When you get tired of having a secret, you tell Amy.

Understand: Amy isn't that much stupider than anyone else in this story. It's just that she thinks out loud.

Elizabeth's mother comes into the living room. "Hey guys," she says. "Hi, Jeremy. Did I hear something about your mother inheriting a wedding chapel?"

"Yes, ma'am," Jeremy says. "In Las Vegas."

"Las Vegas," Elizabeth's mom says. "I won three hundred bucks once in Las Vegas. Spent it on a helicopter ride over the Grand Canyon. So how many times can you guys watch the same episode in one day?" But she sits down to watch, too. "Do you think she's really dead?"

"Who's dead?" Amy says. Nobody says anything.

Jeremy isn't sure he's ready to see this episode again so soon, anyway, especially not with Amy. He goes upstairs and takes a shower. Elizabeth's family have a large and distracting selection of shampoos. They don't mind when Jeremy uses their bathroom.

🐾 🐾 🐾

Jeremy and Karl and Elizabeth have known each other since the first day of kindergarten. Amy and Talis are a year younger. The five have not always been friends, except for Jeremy and Karl, who have. Talis is, famously, a loner. She doesn't listen to music as far as anyone knows, she doesn't wear significant amounts of black, she isn't particularly good (or bad) at math or English, and she doesn't drink, debate, knit or refuse to eat meat. If she keeps a blog, she's never admitted it to anyone.

The Library made Jeremy and Karl and Talis and Elizabeth and Amy friends. No one else in school is as passionately devoted. Besides, they are all the children of former hippies, and the town is small. They all live within a few blocks of each other, in run-down Victorians with high ceilings and ranch houses with sunken living rooms. And although they have not always been friends, growing up, they've gone skinny-dipping in lakes on summer nights, and broken bones on each others' trampolines. Once, during an argument about dog names, Elizabeth, who is hot-tempered, tried to run Jeremy over with her ten-speed bicycle, and once, a year ago, Karl got drunk on green-apple schnapps at a party and tried to kiss Talis, and once, for five months in the seventh grade, Karl and Jeremy communicated only through angry e-mails written in all caps. I'm not allowed to tell you what they fought about.

Now the five are inseparable; invincible. They imagine that life will always be like this—like a television show in eternal syndication—that they will always have each other. They use the same vocabulary. They borrow each other's books and music. They share lunches, and they never say anything when Jeremy comes over and takes a shower. They all know Jeremy's father is eccentric. He's supposed to be eccentric. He's a novelist.

When Jeremy comes back downstairs, Amy is saying, "I've always thought there was something wicked about Prince Wing. He's a dork and he looks like he has bad breath. I never really liked him."

Karl says, "We don't know the whole story yet. Maybe he found out something about Fox while he was a teapot." Elizabeth's mom says, "He's under a spell. I bet you anything." They'll be talking about it all week.

Talis is in the kitchen, making a Velveeta-and-pickle sandwich.

"So what did you think?" Jeremy says. It's like having a hobby, only more pointless, trying to get Talis to talk. "Is Fox really dead?"

"Don't know," Talis says. Then she says, "I had a dream."

Jeremy waits. Talis seems to be waiting, too. She says, "About you." Then she's silent again. There is something dreamlike about the way that she makes a sandwich. As if she is really making something that isn't a sandwich at all; as if she's making something far more meaningful and mysterious. Or as if soon he will wake up and realize that there are no such things as sandwiches.

"You and Fox," Talis says. "The dream was about the two of you. She told me. To tell you. To call her. She gave me a phone number. She was in trouble. She said you were in trouble. She said *to keep in touch.*"

"Weird," Jeremy says, mulling this over. He's never had a dream about *The Library.* He wonders who was playing Fox in Talis's dream. He had a dream about Talis, once, but it isn't the kind of dream that you'd ever tell anybody about. They were just sitting together, not saying anything. Even Talis's T-shirt hadn't said anything. Talis was holding his hand.

"It didn't feel like a dream," Talis says.

"So what was the phone number?" Jeremy says.

"I forgot," Talis says. "When I woke up, I forgot."

Kurt's mother works in a bank. Talis's father has a karaoke machine in his basement, and he knows all the lyrics to "Like a Virgin" and "Holiday" as well as the lyrics to all the songs from *Godspell* and *Cabaret.* Talis's mother is a licensed therapist who composes multiple-choice personality tests for women's magazines. "Discover Which Television Character You Resemble Most." Etc. Amy's parents met in a commune in Ithaca: her name was Galadriel Moon Shuyler before her parents came to their senses and had it changed legally. Everyone is sworn to secrecy about this, which is ironic, considering that this is Amy.

But Jeremy's father is Gordon Strangle Mars. He writes novels about giant spiders, giant leeches, giant moths, and once, notably, a giant carnivorous rosebush who lives in a mansion in upstate New York, and falls in love with a plucky, teenaged girl with a heart murmur. Saint Bernard–sized spiders chase his characters' cars down dark, bumpy country roads. They fight the spiders off with badminton rackets, lawn tools, and fireworks. The novels with spiders are all bestsellers.

Once a Gordon Strangle Mars fan broke into the Mars's house. The fan stole several German first editions of Gordon Strangle's novels, a hairbrush, and a used mug in which there were two ancient, dehydrated tea bags. The fan left behind a betrayed and abusive letter on a series of Post-It Notes, and the manuscript of his own novel, told from the point of view of the iceberg that sank the Titanic. Jeremy and his mother read the manuscript out loud to each other. It begins: "The iceberg knew it had a destiny." Jeremy's favorite bit happens when the iceberg sees the doomed ship drawing nearer, and remarks plaintively, "Oh my, does not the Captain know about my large and impenetrable bottom?"

Jeremy discovered, later, that the novel-writing fan had put Gordon Strangle Mars's used tea bags and hairbrush up for sale on eBay, where someone paid forty-two dollars and sixty-eight cents, which was not only deeply creepy, but, Jeremy still feels, somewhat cheap. But of course this is appropriate, as Jeremy's father is famously stingy and just plain weird about money.

Gordon Strangle Mars once spent eight thousand dollars on a Japanese singing toilet. Jeremy's friends love that toilet. Jeremy's mother has a painting of a woman wearing a red dress by some artist, Jeremy can never remember who. Jeremy's father gave her that painting. The woman is beautiful, and she looks right at you as if you're the painting, not her. As if *you're* beautiful. The woman has an apple in one hand and a knife in the other. When Jeremy was little, he used to dream about eating that apple. Apparently the painting is worth more than the whole house and everything else in the house, including the singing toilet. But art and toilets aside, the Marses buy most of their clothes at thrift stores.

Jeremy's father clips coupons.

On the other hand, when Jeremy was twelve and begged his parents to send him to baseball camp in Florida, his father ponied up. And on Jeremy's last birthday, his father gave him a couch reupholstered in several dozen yards of heavy-duty *Star Wars*–themed fabric. That was a good birthday.

When his writing is going well, Gordon Strangle Mars likes to wake up at 6 A.M. and go out driving. He works out new plot lines about giant spiders and keeps an eye out for abandoned couches, which he wrestles into the back of his pickup truck. Then he writes for the rest of the day. On weekends he reupholsters the thrown-away couches in remaindered, discount fabrics. A few years ago, Jeremy went through his house, counting up fourteen couches, eight love seats, and one rickety chaise lounge. That was a few years ago. Once Jeremy had a dream that his father combined his two careers and began reupholstering giant spiders.

All lights in all rooms of the Mars house are on fifteen-minute timers, in case Jeremy or his mother leave a room and forget to turn off a lamp. This has caused confusion—and sometimes panic—on the rare occasions that the Marses throw dinner parties.

Everyone thinks that writers are rich, but it seems to Jeremy that his family is only rich some of the time. Some of the time they aren't.

Whenever Gordon Mars gets stuck in a Gordon Strangle Mars novel, he worries about money. He worries that he won't, in fact, manage to finish the current novel. He worries that it will be terrible. He worries that no one will buy it and no one will read it, and that the readers who do read it will demand to be refunded the cost of the book. He's told Jeremy that he imagines these angry readers marching on the Mars house, carrying torches and crowbars.

It would be easier on Jeremy and his mother if Gordon Mars did not work at home. It's difficult to shower when you know your father is timing you, and thinking dark thoughts about the water bill, instead of concentrating on the scene in the current Gordon Strangle Mars novel, in which the giant spiders have returned to their old haunts in the trees surrounding the ninth hole of the accursed golf course, where they sullenly feast on the pulped entrail-juices of a brace of unlucky poodles and their owner.

During these periods, Jeremy showers at school, after gym, or at his friends' houses, even though it makes his mother unhappy. She says that sometimes you just need to ignore Jeremy's father. She takes especially long showers, lots of baths. She claims that baths are even nicer when you know that Jeremy's father is worried about the water bill. Jeremy's mother has a cruel streak.

What Jeremy likes about showers is the way you can stand there, surrounded by water and yet in absolutely no danger of drowning, and not think about things like whether you screwed up on the Spanish assignment, or why your mother is looking so worried. Instead you can think about things like if there's water on Mars, and whether or not Karl is shaving, and if so, who is he trying to fool, and what the statue of George Washington meant when it said to Fox, during their desperate, bloody fight, "You have a long journey ahead of you," and, "Everything depends on this." And is Fox really dead?

After she dug up the cigar box, and after George Washington helped her carefully separate out the pieces of tea mug from the pieces of teapot, after they glued back together the hundreds of pieces of porcelain, when Fox turned the ramshackle teapot back into Prince Wing, Prince Wing looked about a hundred years old, and as if maybe there were still a few pieces missing. He looked pale. When he saw Fox, he turned even paler, as if he hadn't expected her to be standing there in front of him. He picked up his leviathan sword, which Fox had been keeping safe for him—the one which faithful viewers know was carved out of the tooth of a giant, ancient sea creature that lived happily and peacefully (before Prince Wing was tricked into killing it) in the enchanted underground sea on the third floor—and skewered the statue of George Washington like a kebab, pinning it to a tree. He kicked Fox in the head, knocked her down, and tied her to a card catalog. He stuffed a handful of moss and dirt into her mouth so she couldn't say anything, and then he accused her of plotting to murder Faithful Margaret by magic. He said Fox was more deceitful than a Forbidden Book. He cut off Fox's tail and her ears and he ran her through with the poison-edged, dog-headed knife that he and Fox had stolen from his mother's secret house. Then he left Fox there, tied to the card catalog, limp and bloody, her beautiful head hanging down. He sneezed (Prince Wing is allergic to swordplay) and walked off into the stacks. The librarians crept out of their hiding places. They untied Fox and cleaned off her face. They held a mirror to her mouth, but the mirror stayed clear and unclouded.

When the librarians pulled Prince Wing's leviathan sword out of the tree, the statue of George Washington staggered over and picked up Fox in his arms. He tucked her ears and tail into the capacious pockets of his bird-shit-stained, verdigris riding coat. He carried Fox down seventeen flights of stairs, past the enchanted-and-disagreeable Sphinx on the eighth floor, past the enchanted-and-stormy underground sea on the third floor, past the even-more-enchanted checkout desk on the first floor, and through the hammered-brass doors of the Free People's World-

Tree Library. Nobody in *The Library*, not in one single episode, has ever gone outside. The Library is full of all the sorts of things that one usually has to go outside to enjoy: trees and lakes and grottoes and fields and mountains and precipices (and full of indoors things as well, like books, of course). Outside The Library, everything is dusty and red and alien, as if George Washington has carried Fox out of The Library and onto the surface of Mars.

"I could really go for a nice cold Euphoria right now," Jeremy says. He and Karl are walking home.

Euphoria is: *The Librarian's Tonic—When Watchfulness Is Not Enough.* There are frequently commercials for Euphoria on *The Library*. Although no one is exactly sure what Euphoria is for, whether it is alcoholic or caffeinated, what it tastes like, if it is poisonous or delightful, or even whether or not it's carbonated, everyone, including Jeremy, pines for a glass of Euphoria once in a while.

"Can I ask you a question?" Karl says.

"Why do you always say that?" Jeremy says. "What am I going to say? 'No, you can't ask me a question?'"

"What's up with you and Talis?" Karl says. "What were you talking about in the kitchen?" Jeremy sees that Karl has been Watchful.

"She had this dream about me," he says, uneasily.

"So do you like her?" Karl says. His chin looks raw. Jeremy is sure now that Karl has tried to shave. "Because, remember how I liked her first?"

"We were just talking," Jeremy says. "So did you shave? Because I didn't know you had facial hair. The idea of you shaving is pathetic, Karl. It's like voting Republican if we were old enough to vote. Or farting in Music Appreciation."

"Don't try to change the subject," Karl says. "When have you and Talis ever had a conversation before?"

"One time we talked about a Diana Wynne Jones book that she'd checked out from the library. She dropped it in the bath accidentally. She wanted to know if I could tell my mother," Jeremy says. "Once we talked about recycling."

"Shut up, Germ," Karl says. "Besides, what about Elizabeth? I thought you liked Elizabeth!"

"Who said that?" Jeremy says. Karl is glaring at him.

"Amy told me," Karl says.

"I never told Amy I liked Elizabeth," Jeremy says. So now Amy is a mind-reader as well as a blabbermouth? What a terrible, deadly combination!

"No," Karl says, grudgingly. "Elizabeth told Amy that she likes you. So I just figured you liked her back."

"Elizabeth likes me?" Jeremy says.

"Apparently everybody likes you," Karl says. He sounds sorry for himself. "What is it about you? It's not like you're all that special. Your nose is funny looking and you have stupid hair."

"Thanks, Karl." Jeremy changes the subject. "Do you think Fox is really dead?" he says. "For good?" He walks faster, so that Karl has to almost-jog to keep up. Presently Jeremy is much taller than Karl, and he intends to enjoy this as long as it lasts. Knowing Karl, he'll either get tall, too, or else chop Jeremy off at the knees.

"They'll use magic," Karl says. "Or maybe it was all a dream. They'll make her alive again. I'll never forgive them if they've killed Fox. And if you like Talis, I'll never forgive you, either. And I know what you're thinking. You're thinking that I think I mean what I say, but if push came to shove, eventually I'd forgive you, and we'd be friends again, like in seventh grade. But I wouldn't, and you're wrong, and we wouldn't be. We wouldn't ever be friends again."

Jeremy doesn't say anything. Of course he likes Talis. He just hasn't realized how much he likes her, until recently. Until today. Until Karl opened his mouth. Jeremy likes Elizabeth too, but how can you compare Elizabeth and Talis? You can't. Elizabeth is Elizabeth and Talis is Talis.

"When you tried to kiss Talis, she hit you with a boa constrictor," he says. It had been Amy's boa constrictor. It had probably been an accident. Karl shouldn't have tried to kiss someone while they were holding a boa constrictor.

"Just try to remember what I just said," Karl says. "You're free to like anyone you want to. Anyone except for Talis."

The Library has been on television for two years now. It isn't a regularly scheduled program. Sometimes it's on two times in the same week, and then not on again for another couple of weeks. Often new episodes debut in the middle of the night. There is a large online community who spend hours scanning channels; sending out alarms and false alarms; fans swap theories, tapes, files; write fanfic. Elizabeth has rigged up her computer to shout "Wake up, Elizabeth! The television is on fire!" when reliable *Library* watch-sites discover a new episode.

The Library is a pirate TV show. It's shown up once or twice on most network channels, but usually it's on the kind of channels that Jeremy thinks of as ghost channels. The ones that are just static, unless you're paying for several hundred channels of cable. There are commercial breaks, but the products being advertised are like Euphoria. They never seem to be real brands, or things that you can actually buy. Often the commercials aren't even in English, or in any other identifiable language, although the jingles are catchy, nonsense or not. They get stuck in your head.

Episodes of *The Library* have no regular schedule, no credits, and sometimes not even dialogue. One episode of *The Library* takes place inside the top drawer of a card catalog, in pitch dark, and it's all in Morse code with subtitles. Nothing else. No one has ever claimed responsibility for inventing *The Library*. No one has ever interviewed one of the actors, or stumbled across a set, film crew, or script, although in one documentary-style episode, the actors filmed the crew, who all wore paper bags on their heads.

When Jeremy gets home, his father is making upside-down pizza in a casserole dish for dinner.

Meeting writers is usually disappointing at best. Writers who write sexy thrillers aren't necessarily sexy or thrilling in person. Children's book writers might look more like accountants, or axe murderers for that matter. Horror writers are very rarely scary looking, although they are frequently good cooks.

Though Gordon Strangle Mars *is* scary looking. He has long, thin fingers—currently slimy with pizza sauce—which are why he chose "Strangle" for his fake middle name. He has white-blond hair that he tugs on while he writes until it stands straight up. He has a bad habit of suddenly appearing beside you, when you haven't even realized he was in the same part of the house. His eyes are deep-set and he doesn't blink very often. Karl says that when you meet Jeremy's father, he looks at you as if he were imagining you bundled up and stuck away in some giant spider's larder. Which is probably true.

People who read books probably never bother to wonder if their favorite writers are also good parents. Why would they?

Gordon Strangle Mars is a recreational shoplifter. He has a special, complicated, and unspoken arrangement with the local bookstore, where, in exchange for autographing as many Gordon Strangle Mars novels as they can possibly sell, the store allows Jeremy's father to shoplift books without comment. Jeremy's mother shows up sooner or later and writes a check.

Jeremy's feelings about his father are complicated. His father is a cheapskate and a petty thief, and yet Jeremy likes his father. His father hardly ever loses his temper with Jeremy, he is always interested in Jeremy's life, and he gives interesting (if confusing) advice when Jeremy asks for it. For example, if Jeremy asked his father about kissing Elizabeth, his father might suggest that Jeremy not worry about giant spiders when he kisses Elizabeth. Jeremy's father's advice usually has something to do with giant spiders.

When Jeremy and Karl weren't speaking to each other, it was Jeremy's father who straightened them out. He lured Karl over, and then locked them both into his study. He didn't let them out again until they were on speaking terms.

"I thought of a great idea for your book," Jeremy says. "What if one of the spiders builds a web on a soccer field, across a goal? And what if the goalie doesn't notice until the middle of the game? Could somebody kill one of the spiders with a soccer ball, if they kicked it hard enough? Would it explode? Or even better, the spider could puncture the soccer ball with its massive fangs. That would be cool, too."

"Your mother's out in the garage," Gordon Strangle Mars says to Jeremy. "She wants to talk to you."

"Oh," Jeremy says. All of a sudden, he thinks of Fox in Talis's dream, trying to phone him. Trying to warn him. Unreasonably, he feels that it's his parents' fault that Fox is dead now, as if they have killed her. "Is it about you? Are you getting divorced?"

"I don't know," his father says. He hunches his shoulders. He makes a face. It's a face that Jeremy's father makes frequently, and yet this face is even more pitiful and guilty than usual.

"What did you do?" Jeremy says. "Did you get caught shoplifting at Wal-Mart?"

"No," his father says.

"Did you have an affair?"

"No!" his father says, again. Now he looks disgusted, either with himself or with Jeremy for asking such a horrible question. "I screwed up. Let's leave it at that."

"How's the book coming?" Jeremy says. There is something in his father's voice that makes him feel like kicking something, but there are never giant spiders around when you need them.

"I don't want to talk about that, either," his father says, looking, if possible, even more ashamed. "Go tell your mother dinner will be ready in five minutes. Maybe you and I can watch the new episode of *The Library* after dinner, if you haven't already seen it a thousand times."

"Do you know the end? Did Mom tell you that Fox is—"

"Oh jeez," his father interrupts. "They killed Fox?"

That's the problem with being a writer, Jeremy knows. Even the biggest and most startling twists are rarely twists for you. You know how every story goes.

Jeremy's mother is an orphan. Jeremy's father claims that she was raised by feral silent-film stars, and it's true, she looks like a heroine out of a Harold Lloyd movie. She has an appealingly disheveled look to her, as if someone has either just tied or untied her from a set of train tracks. She met Gordon Mars (before he added the Strangle and sold his first novel) in the food court of a mall in New Jersey, and fell in love with him before realizing that he was a writer and a recreational shoplifter. She didn't read anything he'd written until after they were married, which was a typically cunning move on Jeremy's father's part.

Jeremy's mother doesn't read horror novels. She doesn't like ghost stories or unexplained phenomena or even the kind of phenomena that require excessively technical explanations. For example: microwaves, airplanes. She doesn't like Halloween, not even Halloween candy. Jeremy's father gives her special editions of his novels, where the scary pages have been glued together.

Jeremy's mother is quiet more often than not. Her name is Alice and sometimes Jeremy thinks about how the two quietest people he knows are named Alice and Talis. But his mother and Talis are quiet in different ways. Jeremy's mother is the kind of person who seems to be keeping something hidden, something secret. Whereas Talis just *is* a secret. Jeremy's mother could easily turn out to be a secret agent. But Talis is the death ray or the key to immortality or whatever it is that secret agents have to keep secret. Hanging out with Talis is like hanging out with a teenage black hole.

Jeremy's mother is sitting on the floor of the garage, beside a large cardboard box. She has a photo album in her hands. Jeremy sits down beside her.

There are photographs of a cat on a wall, and something blurry that looks like a whale or a zeppelin or a loaf of bread. There's a photograph of a small girl sitting beside a woman. The woman wears a fur collar with a sharp little muzzle, four legs, a tail, and Jeremy feels a sudden pang. Fox is the first dead person that he's ever cared about, but she's not real. The little girl in the photograph looks utterly blank, as if someone has just hit her with a hammer. Like the person behind the camera has just said, "Smile! Your parents are dead!"

"Cleo," Jeremy's mother says, pointing to the woman. "That's Cleo. She was my mother's aunt. She lived in Los Angeles. I went to live with her when my parents died. I was four. I know I've never talked about her. I've never really known what to say about her."

Jeremy says, "Was she nice?"

His mother says, "She tried to be nice. She didn't expect to be saddled with a little girl. What an odd word. Saddled. As if she were a horse. As if somebody put me on her back and I never got off again. She liked to buy clothes for me. She liked clothes. She hadn't had a happy life. She drank a lot. She liked to go to movies in the afternoon and to seances in the evenings. She had boyfriends. Some of them were jerks. The love of her life was a small-time gangster. He died and she never married. She always said marriage was a joke and that life was a bigger joke, and it was just her bad luck that she didn't have a sense of humor. So it's strange to think that all these years she was running a wedding chapel."

Jeremy looks at his mother. She's half-smiling, half-grimacing, as if her stomach hurts. "I ran away when I was sixteen. And I never saw her again. Once she sent me a letter, care of your father's publishers. She said she'd read all his books, and that was how she found me, I guess, because he kept dedicating them to me. She said she hoped I was happy and that she thought about me. I wrote back. I sent a photograph of you. But she never wrote again. Sounds like an episode of *The Library*, doesn't it?"

Jeremy says, "Is that what you wanted to tell me? Dad said you wanted to tell me something."

"That's part of it," his mother says. "I have to go out to Las Vegas, to find out some things about this wedding chapel. Hell's Bells. I want you to come with me."

"Is that what you wanted to ask me?" Jeremy says, although he knows there's something else. His mother still has that sad half-smile on her face.

"Germ," his mother says. "You know I love your father, right?"

"Why?" Jeremy says. "What did he do?"

His mother flips through the photo album. "Look," she says. "This was when you were born." In the picture, his father holds Jeremy as if someone has just handed him an enchanted porcelain teapot. Jeremy's father grins, but he looks terrified, too. He looks like a kid. A scary, scared kid.

"He wouldn't tell me either," Jeremy says. "So it has to be pretty bad. If you're getting divorced, I think you should go ahead and tell me."

"We're not getting divorced," his mother says, "but it might be a good thing if you and I went out to Las Vegas. We could stay there for a few months while I sort out this inheritance. Take care of Cleo's estate. I'm going to talk to your teachers. I've given notice at the library. Think of it as an adventure."

She sees the look on Jeremy's face. "No, I'm sorry. That was a stupid, stupid thing to say. I know this isn't an adventure."

"I don't want to go," Jeremy says. "All my friends are here! I can't just go away and leave them. That would be terrible!" All this time, he's been preparing himself for the most terrible thing he can imagine. He's imagined a conversation with his mother, in which his mother reveals her terrible secret, and in his imagination, he's been calm and reasonable. His imaginary parents have wept and asked for his understanding. The imaginary Jeremy has understood. He has imagined himself understanding everything. But now, as his mother talks, Jeremy's heartbeat speeds up, and his lungs fill with air, as if he is running. He starts to sweat, although the floor of the garage is cold. He wishes he were sitting up on top of the roof with his telescope. There could be meteors, invisible to the naked eye, careening through the sky, hurtling toward Earth. Fox is dead. Everyone he knows is doomed. Even as he thinks this, he knows he's overreacting. But it doesn't help to know this.

"I know it's terrible," his mother says. His mother knows something about terrible.

"So why can't I stay here?" Jeremy says. "You go sort things out in Las Vegas, and I'll stay here with Dad. Why can't I stay here?"

"Because he put you in a book!" his mother says. She spits the words out. He has never heard her sound so angry. His mother never gets angry. "He put you in one of his books! I was in his office, and the manuscript was on his desk. I saw your name, and so I picked it up and started reading."

"So what?" Jeremy says. "He's put me in his books before. Like, stuff I've said. Like when I was eight and I was running a fever and told him the trees were full of dead people wearing party hats. Like when I accidentally set fire to his office."

"It isn't like that," his mother says. "It's you. It's *you*. He hasn't even changed your name. The boy in the book, he jumps hurdles and he wants to be a rocket scientist and go to Mars, and he's cute and funny and sweet and his best friend Elizabeth is in love with him and he talks like you and he looks like you and then he dies, Jeremy. He has a brain tumor and he dies. He dies.

There aren't any giant spiders. There's just you, and you die."

Jeremy is silent. He imagines his father writing the scene in his book where the kid named Jeremy dies, and crying, just a little. He imagines this Jeremy kid, Jeremy the character who dies. Poor messed-up kid. Now Jeremy and Fox have something in common. They're both made-up people. They're both dead.

"Elizabeth is in love with me?" he says. Just on principle, he never believes anything that Karl says. But if it's in a book, maybe it's true.

"Oh, whoops," his mother says. "I really didn't want to say that. I'm just so angry at him. We've been married for seventeen years. I was just four years older than you when I met him, Jeremy. I was nineteen. He was only twenty. We were babies. Can you imagine that? I can put up with the singing toilet and the shoplifting and the couches and I can put up with him being so weird about money. But he killed you, Jeremy. He wrote you into a book and he killed you off. And he knows it was wrong, too. He's ashamed of himself. He didn't want me to tell you. I didn't mean to tell you."

Jeremy sits and thinks. "I still don't want to go to Las Vegas," he says to his mother. "Maybe we could send Dad there instead."

His mother says, "Not a bad idea." But he can tell she's already planning their itinerary.

᠅ ᠅ ᠅

In one episode of *The Library*, everyone was invisible. You couldn't see the actors: you could only see the books and the bookshelves and the study carrels on the fifth floor where the coin-operated wizards come to flirt and practice their spells. Invisible Forbidden Books were fighting invisible pirate-magicians and the pirate-magicians were fighting Fox and her friends, who were also invisible. The fight was clumsy and full of deadly accidents. You could hear them fighting. Shelves were overturned. Books were thrown. Invisible people tripped over invisible dead bodies, but you didn't find out who'd died until the next episode. Several of the characters—The Accidental Sword, Hairy Pete, and Ptolemy Krill (who, much like the Vogons in

Douglas Adams's *The Hitchhiker's Guide to the Galaxy*, wrote poetry so bad it killed anyone who read it)—disappeared for good, and nobody is sure whether they're dead or not.

In another episode, Fox stole a magical drug from The Norns, a prophetic girl band who headline at a cabaret on the mezzanine of The Free People's World-Tree Library. She accidentally injected it, became pregnant, and gave birth to a bunch of snakes who led her to the exact shelf where renegade librarians had misshelved an ancient and terrible book of magic which had never been translated, until Fox asked the snakes for help. The snakes writhed and curled on the ground, spelling out words, letter by letter, with their bodies. As they translated the book for Fox, they hissed and steamed. They became fiery lines on the ground, and then they burnt away entirely. Fox cried. That's the only time anyone has ever seen Fox cry, ever. She isn't like Prince Wing. Prince Wing is a crybaby.

The thing about *The Library* is that characters don't come back when they die. It's as if death is for real. So maybe Fox really is dead and she really isn't coming back. There are a couple of ghosts who hang around the Library looking for blood libations, but they've always been ghosts, all the way back to the beginning of the show. There aren't any evil twins or vampires, either. Although someday, hopefully, there will be evil twins. Who doesn't love evil twins?

"Mom told me about how you wrote about me," Jeremy says. His mother is still in the garage. He feels like a tennis ball in a game where the tennis players love him very, very much, even while they lob and smash and send him back and forth, back and forth.

His father says, "She said she wasn't going to tell you, but I guess I'm glad she did. I'm sorry, Germ. Are you hungry?"

"She's going out to Las Vegas next week. She wants me to go with her," Jeremy says.

"I know," his father says, still holding out a bowl of upside-down pizza. "Try not to worry about all of this, if you can. Think of it as an adventure."

"Mom says that's a stupid thing to say. Are you going to let me read the book with me in it?" Jeremy says.

"No," his father says, looking straight at Jeremy. "I burned it."

"Really?" Jeremy says. "Did you set fire to your computer too?"

"Well, no," his father says. "But you can't read it. It wasn't any good, anyway. Want to watch *The Library* with me? And will you eat some damn pizza, please? I may be a lousy father, but I'm a good cook. And if you love me, you'll eat the damn pizza and be grateful."

So they go sit on the orange couch and Jeremy eats pizza and watches *The Library* for the second-and-a-half time with his father. The lights on the timer in the living room go off, and Prince Wing kills Fox again. And then Jeremy goes to bed. His father goes away to write or to burn stuff. Whatever. His mother is still out in the garage.

On Jeremy's desk is a scrap of paper with a phone number on it. If he wanted to, he could call his phone booth. When he dials the number, it rings for a long time. Jeremy sits on his bed in the dark and listens to it ringing and ringing. When someone picks it up, he almost hangs up. Someone doesn't say anything, so Jeremy says, "Hello? Hello?"

Someone breathes into the phone on the other end of the line. Someone says in a soft, musical, squeaky voice, "Can't talk now, kid. Call back later." Then someone hangs up.

Jeremy dreams that he's sitting beside Fox on a sofa that his father has reupholstered in spider silk. His father has been stealing spider webs from the giant-spider superstores. From his own books. Is that shoplifting or is it self-plagiarism? The sofa is soft and gray and a little bit sticky. Fox sits on either side of him. The right-hand-side Fox is being played by Talis. Elizabeth plays the Fox on his left. Both Foxes look at him with enormous compassion.

"Are you dead?" Jeremy says.

"Are you?" the Fox who is being played by Elizabeth says, in that unmistakable Fox voice which, Jeremy's father once said, sounds like a sexy and demented helium balloon. It makes Jeremy's brain hurt, to hear Fox's voice coming out of Elizabeth's mouth.

The Fox who looks like Talis doesn't say anything at all. The writing on her T-shirt is so small and so foreign that Jeremy can't read it without feeling as if he's staring at Fox-Talis's breasts. It's probably something he needs to know, but he'll never be able to read it. He's too polite, and besides he's terrible at foreign languages.

"Hey look," Jeremy says. "We're on TV!" There he is on television, sitting between two Foxes on a sticky gray couch in a field of red poppies. "Are we in Las Vegas?"

"We're not in Kansas," Fox-Elizabeth says. "There's something I need you to do for me."

"What's that?" Jeremy says.

"If I tell you in the dream," Fox-Elizabeth says, "you won't remember. You have to remember to call me when you're awake. Keep on calling until you get me."

"How will I remember to call you," Jeremy says, "if I don't remember what you tell me in this dream? Why do you need me to help you? Why is Talis here? What does her T-shirt say? Why are you both Fox? Is this Mars?"

Fox-Talis goes on watching TV. Fox-Elizabeth opens her kind and beautiful un-Hello-Kitty-like mouth again. She tells Jeremy the whole story. She explains everything. She translates Fox-Talis's T-shirt, which turns out to explain everything about Talis that Jeremy has ever wondered about. It answers every single question that Jeremy has ever had about girls. And then Jeremy wakes up—

It's dark. Jeremy flips on the light. The dream is moving away from him. There was something about Mars. Elizabeth was asking who he thought was prettier, Talis or Elizabeth. They were laughing. They both had pointy fox ears. They wanted him to do something. There was a telephone number he was supposed to call. There was something he was supposed to do.

In two weeks, on the fifteenth of April, Jeremy and his mother will get in her van and start driving out to Las Vegas. Every morning before school, Jeremy takes long showers and his father doesn't say anything at all. One day it's as if nothing is wrong between his parents. The next day they won't even look at each other. Jeremy's father won't come out of his study. And then the day after that, Jeremy comes home and finds his mother sitting on his father's lap. They're smiling as if they know something stupid and secret. They don't even notice Jeremy when he walks through the room. Even this is preferable, though, to the way they behave when they do notice him. They act guilty and strange and as if they are about to ruin his life. Gordon Mars makes pancakes every morning, and Jeremy's favorite dinner, macaroni and cheese, every night. Jeremy's mother plans out an itinerary for their trip. They will be stopping at libraries across the country, because his mother loves libraries. But she's also bought a new two-man tent and two sleeping bags and a portable stove, so that they can camp, if Jeremy wants to camp. Even though Jeremy's mother hates the outdoors.

Right after she does this, Gordon Mars spends all weekend in the garage. He won't let either of them see what he's doing, and when he does let them in, it turns out that he's removed the seating in the back of the van and bolted down two of his couches, one on each side, both upholstered in electric-blue fake fur.

They have to climb in through the cargo door at the back because one of the couches is blocking the sliding door. Jeremy's father says, looking very pleased with himself, "So now you don't have to camp outside, unless you want to. You can sleep inside. There's space underneath for suitcases. The sofas even have seat belts."

Over the sofas, Jeremy's father has rigged up small wooden shelves that fold down on chains from the walls of the van and become table tops. There's a travel-sized disco ball dangling from the ceiling, and a wooden panel—with Velcro straps and a black, quilted pad—behind the driver's seat, where Jeremy's father explains they can hang up the painting of the woman with the apple and the knife.

The van looks like something out of an episode of *The Library*. Jeremy's mother bursts into tears. She runs back inside the house. Jeremy's father says, helplessly, "I just wanted to make her laugh."

Jeremy wants to say, "I hate both of you." But he doesn't say it, and he doesn't. It would be easier if he did.

When Jeremy told Karl about Las Vegas, Karl punched him in the stomach. Then he said, "Have you told Talis?"

Jeremy said, "You're supposed to be nice to me! You're supposed to tell me not to go and that this sucks and you're not supposed to punch me. Why did you punch me? Is Talis all you ever think about?"

"Kind of," Karl said. "Most of the time. Sorry, Germ, of course I wish you weren't going and yeah, it also pisses me off. We're supposed to be best friends, but you do stuff all the time and I never get to. I've never driven across the country or been to Las Vegas, even though I'd really, really like to. I can't feel sorry for you when I bet you anything that while you're there, you'll sneak into some casino and play slot machines and win like a million bucks. You should feel sorry for me. I'm the one that has to stay here. Can I borrow your dirt bike while you're gone?"

"Sure," Jeremy said.

"How about your telescope?" Karl said.

"I'm taking it with me," Jeremy said.

"Fine. You have to call me every day," Karl said. "You have to e-mail. You have to tell me about Las Vegas show girls. I want to know how tall they really are. Whose phone number is this?"

Karl was holding the scrap of paper with the number of Jeremy's phone booth.

"Mine," Jeremy said. "That's my phone booth. The one I inherited."

"Have you called it?" Karl said.

"No," Jeremy said. He'd called the phone booth a few times. But it wasn't a game. Karl would think it was a game.

"Cool," Karl said and he went ahead and dialed the number. "Hello?" Karl said, "I'd like to speak to the person in charge of Jeremy's life. This is Jeremy's best friend Karl."

"Not funny," Jeremy said.

"My life is boring," Karl said, into the phone. "I've never inherited anything. This girl I like won't talk to me. So is someone there? Does anybody want to talk to me? Does anyone want to talk to my friend, the Lord of the Phone Booth? Jeremy, they're demanding that you liberate the phone booth from yourself."

"Still not funny," Jeremy said and Karl hung up the phone.

Jeremy told Elizabeth. They were up on the roof of Jeremy's

house and he told her the whole thing. Not just the part about Las Vegas, but also the part about his father and how he put Jeremy in a book with no giant spiders in it.

"Have you read it?" Elizabeth said.

"No," Jeremy said. "He won't let me. Don't tell Karl. All I told him is that my mom and I have to go out for a few months to check out the wedding chapel."

"I won't tell Karl," Elizabeth said. She leaned forward and kissed Jeremy and then she wasn't kissing him. It was all very fast and surprising, but they didn't fall off the roof. Nobody falls off the roof in this story. "Talis likes you," Elizabeth said. "That's what Amy says. Maybe you like her back. I don't know. But I thought I should go ahead and kiss you now. Just in case I don't get to kiss you again."

"You can kiss me again," Jeremy said. "Talis probably doesn't like me."

"No," Elizabeth said. "I mean, let's not. I want to stay friends and it's hard enough to be friends, Germ. Look at you and Karl."

"I would never kiss Karl," Jeremy said.

"Funny, Germ. We should have a surprise party for you before you go," Elizabeth said.

"It won't be a surprise party now," Jeremy said. Maybe kissing him once was enough.

"Well, once I tell Amy it can't really be a surprise party," Elizabeth said. "She would explode into a million pieces and all the little pieces would start yelling, 'Guess what? Guess what? We're having a surprise party for you, Jeremy!' But just because I'm letting you in on the surprise doesn't mean there won't be surprises."

"I don't actually like surprises," Jeremy said.

"Who does?" Elizabeth said. "Only the people who do the surprising. Can we have the party at your house? I think it should be like Halloween, and it always feels like Halloween here. We could all show up in costumes and watch lots of old episodes of *The Library* and eat ice cream."

"Sure," Jeremy said. And then: "This is terrible! What if there's a new episode of *The Library* while I'm gone? Who am I going to watch it with?"

And he'd said the perfect thing. Elizabeth felt so bad about Jeremy having to watch *The Library* all by himself that she kissed him again.

🐾 🐾 🐾

There has never been a giant spider in any episode of *The Library,* although once Fox got really small and Ptolemy Krill carried her around in his pocket. She had to rip up one of Krill's handkerchiefs and blindfold herself, just in case she accidentally read a draft of Krill's terrible poetry. And then it turned out that, as well as the poetry, Krill had also stashed a rare, horned Anubis earwig in his pocket which hadn't been properly preserved. Ptolemy Krill, it turned out, was careless with his kill jar. The earwig almost ate Fox, but instead it became her friend. It still sends her Christmas cards.

These are the two most important things that Jeremy and his friends have in common: a geographical location, and love of a television show about a library. Jeremy turns on the television as soon as he comes home from school. He flips through the channels, watching reruns of *Star Trek* and *Law & Order.* If there's a new episode of *The Library* before he and his mother leave for Las Vegas, then everything will be fine. Everything will work out. His mother says, "You watch too much television, Jeremy." But he goes on flipping through channels. Then he goes up to his room and makes phone calls.

"The new episode needs to be soon, because we're getting ready to leave. Tonight would be good. You'd tell me if there was going to be a new episode tonight, right?"

Silence.

"Can I take that as a yes? It would be easier if I had a brother," Jeremy tells his telephone booth. "Hello? Are you there? Or a sister. I'm tired of being good all the time. If I had a sibling, then we could take turns being good. If I had an older brother, I might be better at being bad, better at being angry. Karl is really good at being angry. He learned how from his brothers. I wouldn't want brothers like Karl's brothers, of course, but it sucks having to figure out everything all by myself. And the more normal I try to be, the more my parents think that I'm acting out. They think it's a phase that I'll grow out of. They think it isn't normal to be normal. Because there's no such thing as normal.

"And this whole book thing. The whole shoplifting thing, how my dad steals things, it figures that he went and stole my life. It isn't just me being melodramatic, to say that. That's exactly what he did! Did I tell you that once he stole a ferret from a pet store because he felt bad for it, and then he let it loose in our house and it turned out that it was pregnant? There was this woman who came to interview Dad and she sat down on one of the—"

Someone knocks on his bedroom door. "Jeremy," his mother says. "Is Karl here? Am I interrupting?"

"No," Jeremy says, and hangs up the phone. He's gotten into the habit of calling his phone booth every day. When he calls, it rings and rings and then it stops ringing, as if someone has picked up. There's just silence on the other end, no squeaky pretend-Fox voice, but it's a peaceful, interested silence. Jeremy complains about all the things there are to complain about, and the silent person on the other end listens and listens. Maybe it is Fox standing there in his phone booth and listening patiently. He wonders what incarnation of Fox is listening. One thing about Fox: she's never sorry for herself. She's always too busy. If it were really Fox, she'd hang up on him.

Jeremy opens his door. "I was on the phone," he says. His mother comes in and sits down on his bed. She's wearing one of his father's old flannel shirts. "So have you packed?"

Jeremy shrugs. "I guess," he says. "Why did you cry when you saw what Dad did to the van? Don't you like it?"

"It's that damn painting," his mother says. "It was the first nice thing he ever gave me. We should have spent the money on health insurance and a new roof and groceries and instead he bought a painting. So I got angry. I left him. I took the painting and I moved into a hotel and I stayed there for a few days. I was going to sell the painting, but instead I fell in love with it, so I came home and apologized for running away. I got pregnant with you and I used to get hungry and dream that someone was going to give me a beautiful apple, like the one she's holding. When I told your father, he said he didn't trust her, that she was holding out the apple like that as a trick and if you went to take it from her, she'd stab you with the peeling knife. He says that she's a tough old broad and she'll take care of us while we're on the road."

"Do we really have to go?" Jeremy says. "If we go to Las Vegas I might get into trouble. I might start using drugs or gambling or something."

"Oh, Germ. You try so hard to be a good kid," his mother says. "You try so hard to be normal. Sometimes I'd like to be normal, too. Maybe Vegas will be good for us. Are these the books that you're bringing?"

Jeremy shrugs. "Not all of them. I can't decide which ones I should take and which ones I can leave. It feels like whatever I leave behind, I'm leaving behind for good."

"That's silly," his mother says. "We're coming back. I promise. Your father and I will work things out. If you leave something behind that you need, he can mail it to you. Do you think there are slot machines in the libraries in Las Vegas? I talked to a woman at the Hell's Bells chapel and there's something called The Arts and Lovecraft Library where they keep Cleo's special collection of horror novels and gothic romances and fake copies of *The Necronomicon.* You go in and out through a secret, swinging-bookcase door. People get married in it. There's a Dr. Frankenstein's LoveLab, the Masque of the Red Death Ballroom, and also something just called The Crypt. Oh yeah, and there's also The Vampire's Patio and The Black Lagoon Grotto, where you can get married by moonlight."

"You hate all this stuff," Jeremy says.

"It's not my cup of tea," his mother says. "When does everyone show up tonight?"

"Around eight," Jeremy says. "Are you going to get dressed up?"

"I don't have to dress up," his mother says. "I'm a librarian, remember?"

Jeremy's father's office is above the garage. In theory, no one is meant to interrupt him while he's working, but in practice Jeremy's father loves nothing better than to be interrupted, as long as the person who interrupts him brings him something to eat.

When Jeremy and his mother are gone, who will bring Jeremy's father food? Jeremy hardens his heart.

The floor is covered with books and bolts and samples of upholstering fabrics. Jeremy's father is lying facedown on the floor with his feet propped up on a bolt of fabric, which means that he is thinking and also that his back hurts. He claims to think best when he is on the verge of falling asleep.

"I brought you a bowl of Froot Loops," Jeremy says.

His father rolls over and looks up. "Thanks," he says. "What time is it? Is everyone here? Is that your costume? Is that my tuxedo jacket?"

"It's five-ish. Nobody's here yet. Do you like it?" Jeremy says. He's dressed as a Forbidden Book. His father's jacket is too big, but he still feels very elegant. Very sinister. His mother lent him the lipstick and the feathers and the platform heels.

"It's interesting," his father allows. "And a little frightening."

Jeremy feels obscurely pleased, even though he knows that his father is more amused than frightened. "Everyone else will probably come as Fox or Prince Wing. Except for Karl. He's coming as Ptolemy Krill. He even wrote some really bad poetry. I wanted to ask you something, before we leave tomorrow."

"Shoot," his father says.

"Did you really get rid of the novel with me in it?"

"No," his father says. "It felt unlucky. Unlucky to keep it, unlucky not to keep it. I don't know what to do with it."

Jeremy says, "I'm glad you didn't get rid of it."

"It's not any good, you know," his father says. "Which makes all this even worse. At first it was because I was bored with giant spiders. It was going to be something funny to show you. But then I wrote that you had a brain tumor and it wasn't funny anymore. I figured I could save you—I'm the author, after all—but you got sicker and sicker. You were going through a rebellious phase. You were sneaking out of the house a lot and you hit your mother. You were a real jerk. But it turned out you had a brain tumor and that was making you behave strangely."

"Can I ask another question?" Jeremy says. "You know how you like to steal things? You know how you're really, really good at it?"

"Yeah," says his father.

"Could you not steal things for a while, if I asked you to?" Jeremy says. "Mom isn't going to be around to pay for the books and stuff that you steal. I don't want you to end up in jail because we went to Las Vegas."

His father closes his eyes as if he hopes Jeremy will forget that he asked a question, and go away.

Jeremy says nothing.

"All right," his father says finally. "I won't shoplift anything until you get home again."

Jeremy's mother runs around taking photos of everyone. Talis and Elizabeth have both showed up as Fox, although Talis is dead Fox. She carries her fake fur ears and tail around in a little see-through plastic purse and she also has a sword, which she leaves in the umbrella stand in the kitchen. Jeremy and Talis haven't talked much since she had a dream about him and since he told her that he's going to Las Vegas. She didn't say anything about that. Which is perfectly normal for Talis.

Karl makes an excellent Ptolemy Krill. Jeremy's Forbidden Book disguise is admired.

Amy's Faithful Margaret costume is almost as good as anything Faithful Margaret wears on TV. There are even special effects: Amy has rigged up her hair with red ribbons and wire and spray color and egg whites so that it looks as if it's on fire, and there are tiny papier-mâché golems in it, making horrible faces. She dances a polka with Jeremy's father. Faithful Margaret is mad for polka dancing.

No one has dressed up as Prince Wing.

They watch the episode with the possessed chicken and they watch the episode with the Salt Wife and they watch the episode where Prince Wing and Faithful Margaret fall under a spell and swap bodies and have sex for the first time. They watch the episode where Fox saves Prince Wing's life for the first time.

Jeremy's father makes chocolate/mango/espresso milk shakes for everyone. None of Jeremy's friends, except for Elizabeth, know about the novel. Everyone thinks Jeremy and his mother are just having an adventure. Everyone thinks Jeremy will be back at the end of the summer.

"I wonder how they find the actors," Elizabeth says. "They

aren't real actors. They must be regular people. But you'd think that somewhere there would be someone who knows them. That somebody online would say, hey, that's my sister! Or that's the kid I went to school with who threw up in P.E. You know, sometimes someone says something like that or sometimes someone pretends that they know something about *The Library*, but it always turns out to be a hoax. Just somebody wanting to be somebody."

"What about the guy who's writing it?" Karl says.

Talis says, "Who says it's a guy?" and Amy says, "Yeah, Karl, why do you always assume it's a guy writing it?"

"Maybe nobody's writing it," Elizabeth says. "Maybe it's magic or it's broadcast from outer space. Maybe it's real. Wouldn't that be cool?"

"No," Jeremy says. "Because then Fox would really be dead. That would suck."

"I don't care," Elizabeth says. "I wish it were real, anyway. Maybe it all really happened somewhere, like King Arthur or Robin Hood, and this is just one version of how it happened. Like a magical After School Special."

"Even if it isn't real," Amy says, "parts of it could be real. Like maybe the World-Tree Library is real. Or maybe *The Library* is made up, but Fox is based on somebody that the writer knew. Writers do that all the time, right? Jeremy, I think your dad should write a book about me. I could be eaten by giant spiders. Or have sex with giant spiders and have spider babies. I think that would be so great."

So Amy does have psychic abilities, after all, although hopefully she will never know this. When Jeremy tests his own potential psychic abilities, he can almost sense his father, hovering somewhere just outside the living room, listening to this conversation and maybe even taking notes. Which is what writers do. But Jeremy isn't really psychic. It's just that lurking and hovering and appearing suddenly when you weren't expecting him are what his father does, just like shoplifting and cooking. Jeremy prays to all the dark gods that he never receives the gift of knowing what people are thinking. It's a dark road and it ends up with you trapped on late night television in front of an invisible audience of depressed insomniacs wearing hats made out of tinfoil and they all want to pay you nine-ninety-nine per minute to hear you describe in minute, terrible detail what their deceased cat is thinking about, right now. What kind of future is that? He wants to go to Mars. And when will Elizabeth kiss him again? You can't just kiss someone twice and then never kiss them again. He tries not to think about Elizabeth and kissing, just in case Amy reads his mind. He realizes that he's been staring at Talis's breasts, glares instead at Elizabeth, who is watching TV. Meanwhile, Karl is glaring at him.

On television, Fox is dancing in the Invisible Nightclub with Faithful Margaret, whose hair is about to catch fire again. The Norns are playing their screechy cover of "Come On, Eileen." The Norns only know two songs: "Come On, Eileen," and "Everybody Wants to Rule the World." They don't play real instruments. They play squeaky dog toys and also a bathtub, which is enchanted, although nobody knows who by, or why, or what it was enchanted for.

"If you had to choose one," Jeremy says, "invisibility or the ability to fly, which would you choose?"

Everybody looks at him. "Only perverts would want to be invisible," Elizabeth says.

"You'd have to be naked if you were invisible," Karl says. "Because otherwise people would see your clothes."

"If you could fly, you'd have to wear thermal underwear because it's cold up there. So it just depends on whether you like to wear long underwear or no underwear at all," Amy says.

It's the kind of conversation that they have all the time. It makes Jeremy feel homesick even though he hasn't left yet.

"Maybe I'll go make brownies," Jeremy says. "Elizabeth, do you want to help me make brownies?"

"Shhh," Elizabeth says. "This is a good part."

On television, Fox and Faithful Margaret are making out. The Faithful part is kind of a joke.

🐾 🐾 🐾

Jeremy's parents go to bed at one. By three, Amy and Elizabeth are passed out on the couch and Karl has gone upstairs to check his e-mail on Jeremy's iBook. On TV, wolves are roaming the tundra of The Free People's World-Tree Library's fortieth floor. Snow is falling heavily and librarians are burning books to keep warm, but only the most dull and improving works of literature.

Jeremy isn't sure where Talis has gone, so he goes to look for her. She hasn't gone far. She's on the landing, looking at the space on the wall where Alice Mars's painting should be hanging. Talis is carrying her sword with her, and her little plastic purse. In the bathroom off the landing, the singing toilet is still singing away in German. "We're taking the painting with us," Jeremy says. "My dad insisted, just in case he accidentally burns down the house while we're gone. Do you want to go see it? I was going to show everybody, but everybody's asleep right now."

"Sure," Talis says.

So Jeremy gets a flashlight and takes her out to the garage and shows her the van. She climbs right inside and sits down on one of the blue-fur couches. She looks around and he wonders what she's thinking. He wonders if the toilet song is stuck in her head.

"My dad did all of this," Jeremy says. He turns on the flashlight and shines it on the disco ball. Light spatters off in anxious, slippery orbits. Jeremy shows Talis how his father has hung up the painting. It looks truly wrong in the van, as if someone demented put it there. Especially with the light reflecting off the disco ball. The woman in the painting looks confused and embarrassed as if Jeremy's father has accidentally canceled out her protective powers. Maybe the disco ball is her Kryptonite.

"So remember how you had a dream about me?" Jeremy says. Talis nods. "I think I had a dream about you, that you were Fox."

Talis opens up her arms, encompassing her costume, her sword, her plastic purse with poor Fox's ears and tail inside.

"There was something you wanted me to do," Jeremy says. "I was supposed to save you, somehow."

Talis just looks at him.

"How come you never talk?" Jeremy says. All of this is irritating. How he used to feel normal around Elizabeth, like friends, and now everything is peculiar and uncomfortable. How he used to enjoy feeling uncomfortable around Talis, and now, suddenly, he doesn't. This must be what sex is about. Stop thinking about sex, he thinks.

Talis opens her mouth and closes it again. Then she says, "I don't know. Amy talks so much. You all talk a lot. Somebody has to be the person who doesn't. The person who listens."

"Oh," Jeremy says. "I thought maybe you had a tragic secret. Like maybe you used to stutter." Except secrets can't have secrets, they just *are*.

"Nope," Talis says. "It's like being invisible, you know. Not talking. I like it."

"But you're not invisible," Jeremy says. "Not to me. Not to Karl. Karl really likes you. Did you hit him with a boa constrictor on purpose?"

But Talis says, "I wish you weren't leaving." The disco ball spins and spins. It makes Jeremy feel kind of carsick and also as if he has sparkly, disco leprosy. He doesn't say anything back to Talis, just to see how it feels. Except maybe that's rude. Or maybe it's rude the way everybody always talks and doesn't leave any space for Talis to say anything.

"At least you get to miss school," Talis says, at last.

"Yeah," he says. He leaves another space, but Talis doesn't say anything this time. "We're going to stop at all these museums and things on the way across the country. I'm supposed to keep a blog for school and describe stuff in it. I'm going to make a lot of stuff up. So it will be like Creative Writing and not so much like homework."

"You should make a list of all the towns with weird names you drive through," Talis says. "Town of Horseheads. That's a real place."

"Plantagenet," Jeremy says. "That's a real place too. I had something really weird to tell you."

Talis waits, like she always does.

Jeremy says, "I called my phone booth, the one that I inherited, and someone answered. She sounded just like Fox when she talked. They told me to call back later. So I've called a few more times, but I don't ever get her."

"Fox isn't a real person," Talis says. "*The Library* is just TV." But she sounds uncertain. That's the thing about *The Library*.

Nobody knows for sure. Everyone who watches it wishes and hopes that it's not just acting. That it's magic, real magic.

"I know," Jeremy says.

"I wish Fox was real," Fox-Talis says.

They've been sitting in the van for a long time. If Karl looks for them and can't find them, he's going to think that they've been making out. He'll kill Jeremy. Once Karl tried to strangle another kid for accidentally peeing on his shoes. Jeremy might as well kiss Talis. So he does, even though she's still holding her sword. She doesn't hit him with it. It's dark and he has his eyes closed and he can almost imagine that he's kissing Elizabeth.

Karl has fallen asleep on Jeremy's bed. Talis is downstairs, fast-forwarding through the episode where some librarians drink too much Euphoria and decide to abolish Story Hour. Not just the practice of having a Story Hour, but the whole Hour. Amy and Elizabeth are still sacked out on the couch. It's weird to watch Amy sleep. She doesn't talk in her sleep.

Karl is snoring. Jeremy could go up on the roof and look at stars, except he's already packed up his telescope. He could try to wake up Elizabeth and they could go up on the roof, but Talis is down there. He and Talis could go sit on the roof, but he doesn't want to kiss Talis on the roof. He makes a solemn oath to only ever kiss Elizabeth on the roof.

He picks up his phone. Maybe he can call his phone booth and complain just a little and not wake Karl up. His dad is going to freak out about the phone bill. All these calls to Nevada. It's 4 A.M. Jeremy's plan is not to go to sleep at all. His friends are lame.

The phone rings and rings and rings and then someone picks up. Jeremy recognizes the silence on the other end. "Everybody came over and fell asleep," he whispers. "That's why I'm whispering. I don't even think they care that I'm leaving. And my feet hurt. Remember how I was going to dress up as a Forbidden Book? Platform shoes aren't comfortable. Karl thinks I did it on purpose, to be even taller than him than usual. And I forgot that I was wearing lipstick and I kissed Talis and got lipstick all over her face, so it's a good thing everyone was asleep because otherwise someone would have seen. And my dad says that he won't shoplift at all while Mom and I are gone, but you can't trust him. And that fake-fur upholstery sheds like—"

"Jeremy," that strangely familiar, sweet-and-rusty door-hinge voice says softly. "Shut up, Jeremy. I need your help."

"Wow!" Jeremy says, not in a whisper. "Wow, wow, wow! Is this Fox? Are you really Fox? Is this a joke? Are you real? Are you dead? What are you doing in my phone booth?"

"You know who I am," Fox says, and Jeremy knows with all his heart that it's really Fox. "I need you to do something for me."

"What?" Jeremy says. Karl, on the bed, laughs in his sleep as if the idea of Jeremy doing something is funny to him. "What could I do?"

"I need you to steal three books," Fox says. "From a library in a place called Iowa."

"I know Iowa," Jeremy says. "I mean, I've never been there, but it's a real place. I could go there."

"I'm going to tell you the books you need to steal," Fox says. "Author, title, and the jewelly festival number—"

"Dewey Decimal," Jeremy says. "It's actually called the Dewey Decimal number in real libraries."

"Real," Fox says, sounding amused. "You need to write this all down and also how to get to the library. You need to steal the three books and bring them to me. It's very important."

"Is it dangerous?" Jeremy says. "Are the Forbidden Books up to something? Are the Forbidden Books real, too? What if I get caught stealing?"

"It's not dangerous to you," Fox says. "Just don't get caught. Remember the episode of *The Library* when I was the little old lady with the beehive and I stole the Bishop of Tweedle's false teeth while he was reading the banns for the wedding of Faithful Margaret and Sir Petronella the Younger? Remember how he didn't even notice?"

"I've never seen that episode," Jeremy says, although as far as he knows he's never missed a single episode of *The Library*. He's never even heard of Sir Petronella.

"Oh," Fox says. "Maybe that's a flashback in a later episode or something. That's a great episode. We're depending on you, Jeremy. You have got to steal these books. They contain dreadful secrets. I can't say the titles out loud. I'm going to spell them instead."

So Jeremy gets a pad of paper and Fox spells out the titles of each book twice. (They aren't titles that can be written down here. It's safer not to even think about some books.) "Can I ask you something?" Jeremy says. "Can I tell anybody about this? Not Amy. But could I tell Karl or Elizabeth? Or Talis? Can I tell my mom? If I woke up Karl right now, would you talk to him for a minute?"

"I don't have a lot of time," Fox says. "I have to go now. Please don't tell anyone, Jeremy. I'm sorry."

"Is it the Forbidden Books?" Jeremy says again. What would Fox think if she saw the costume he's still wearing, all except for the platform heels? "Do you think I shouldn't trust my friends? But I've known them my whole life!"

Fox makes a noise, a kind of pained whuff.

"What is it?" Jeremy says. "Are you okay?"

"I have to go," Fox says. "Nobody can know about this. Don't give anybody this number. Don't tell anyone about your phone booth. Or me. Promise, Germ?"

"Only if you promise you won't call me Germ," Jeremy says, feeling really stupid. "I hate when people call me that. Call me Mars instead."

"Mars," Fox says, and it sounds exotic and strange and brave, as if Jeremy has just become a new person, a person named after a whole planet, a person who kisses girls and talks to Foxes.

"I've never stolen anything," Jeremy says.

But Fox has hung up.

Maybe out there, somewhere, is someone who enjoys having to say good-bye, but it isn't anyone that Jeremy knows. All of his friends are grumpy and red-eyed, although not from crying. From lack of sleep. From too much television. There are still faint red stains around Talis's mouth and if everyone weren't so tired, they would realize it's Jeremy's lipstick. Karl gives Jeremy a handful of quarters, dimes, nickels, and pennies. "For the slot machines," Karl says. "If you win anything, you can keep a third of what you win."

"Half," Jeremy says, automatically.

"Fine," Karl says. "It's all from your dad's sofas, anyway. Just one more thing. Stop getting taller. Don't get taller while you're gone. Okay." He hugs Jeremy hard: so hard that it's almost like getting punched again. No wonder Talis threw the boa constrictor at Karl.

Talis and Elizabeth both hug Jeremy good-bye. Talis looks even more mysterious now that he's sat with her under a disco ball and made out. Later on, Jeremy will discover that Talis has left her sword under the blue fur couch and he'll wonder if she left it on purpose.

Talis doesn't say anything and Amy, of course, doesn't shut up, not even when she kisses him. It feels weird to be kissed by someone who goes right on talking while they kiss you and yet it shouldn't be a surprise that Amy kisses him. He imagines that later Amy and Talis and Elizabeth will all compare notes.

Elizabeth says, "I promise I'll tape every episode of *The Library* while you're gone so we can all watch them together when you get back. I promise I'll call you in Vegas, no matter what time it is there, when there's a new episode."

Her hair is a mess and her breath is faintly sour. Jeremy wishes he could tell her how beautiful she looks. "I'll write bad poetry and send it to you," he says.

Jeremy's mother is looking hideously cheerful as she goes in and out of the house, making sure that she hasn't left anything behind. She loves long car trips. It doesn't bother her one bit that she and her son are abandoning their entire lives. She passes Jeremy a folder full of maps. "You're in charge of not getting lost," she says. "Put these somewhere safe."

Jeremy says, "I found a library online that I want to go visit. Out in Iowa. They have a corn mosaic on the façade of the building, with a lot of naked goddesses and gods dancing around in a field of corn. Someone wants to take it down. Can we go see it first?"

"Sure," his mother says.

Jeremy's father has filled a whole grocery bag with sandwiches. His hair is drooping and he looks even more like an axe murderer than usual. If this were a movie, you'd think that Jeremy and his mother were escaping in the nick of time. "You take care of your mother," he says to Jeremy.

"Sure," Jeremy says. "You take care of yourself."

His dad sags. "You take care of yourself, too." So it's settled. They're all supposed to take care of themselves. Why can't they stay home and take care of each other, until Jeremy is good and ready to go off to college? "I've got another bag of sandwiches in the kitchen," his dad says. "I should go get them."

"Wait," Jeremy says. "I have to ask you something before we take off. Suppose I had to steal something. I mean, I don't have to steal anything, of course, and I know stealing is wrong, even when *you* do it, and I would never steal anything. But what if I did? How do you do it? How do you do it and not get caught?"

His father shrugs. He's probably wondering if Jeremy is really his son. Gordon Mars inherited his mutant, long-fingered, ambidextrous hands from a long line of shoplifters and money launderers and petty criminals. They're all deeply ashamed of Jeremy's father. Gordon Mars had a gift and he threw it away to become a writer. "I don't know," he says. He picks up Jeremy's hand and looks at it as if he's never noticed before that Jeremy had something hanging off the end of his wrist. "You just do it. You do it like you're not really doing anything at all. You do it while you're thinking about something else and you forget that you're doing it."

"Oh, Jeremy says, taking his hand back. "I'm not planning on stealing anything. I was just curious."

His father looks at him. "Take care of yourself," he says again, as if he really means it, and hugs Jeremy hard.

Then he goes and gets the sandwiches (so many sandwiches that Jeremy and his mother will eat sandwiches for the first three days, and still have to throw half of them away). Everyone waves. Jeremy and his mother climb in the van. Jeremy's mother turns on the CD player. Bob Dylan is singing about monkeys. His mother loves Bob Dylan. They drive away.

🐾 🐾 🐾

Do you know how, sometimes, during a commercial break in your favorite television shows, your best friend calls and wants to talk about one of her boyfriends, and when you try to hang up, she starts crying and you try to cheer her up and end up missing about half of the episode? And so when you go to work the next day, you have to get the guy who sits next to you to explain what happened? That's the good thing about a book. You can mark your place in a book. But this isn't really a book. It's a television show.

In one episode of *The Library*, an adolescent boy drives across the country with his mother. They have to change a tire. The boy practices taking things out of his mother's purse and putting them back again. He steals a sixteen-ounce bottle of Coke from one convenience market and leaves it at another convenience market. The boy and his mother stop at a lot of libraries, and the boy keeps a blog, but he skips the bit about the library in Iowa. He writes in his blog about what he's reading, but he doesn't read the books he stole in Iowa, because Fox told him not to, and because he has to hide them from his mother. Well, he reads just a few pages. Skims, really. He hides them under the blue-fur sofa. They go camping in Utah, and the boy sets up his telescope. He sees three shooting stars and a coyote. He never sees anyone who looks like a Forbidden Book, although he sees a transvestite go into the woman's rest room at a rest stop in Indiana. He calls a phone booth just outside Las Vegas twice, but no one ever answers. He has short conversations with his father. He wonders what his father is up to. He wishes he could tell his father about Fox and the books. Once the boy's mother finds a giant spider the size of an Oreo in their tent. She starts laughing hysterically. She takes a picture of it with her digital camera, and the boy puts the picture on his blog. Sometimes the boy asks questions and his mother talks about her parents. Once she cries. The boy doesn't know what to say. They talk about their favorite episodes of *The Library* and the episodes that they really hated, and the mother asks if the boy thinks Fox is really dead. He says he doesn't think so.

Once a man tries to break into the van while they are sleeping in it. But then he goes away. Maybe the painting of the woman with the peeling knife is protecting them.

But you've seen this episode before.

It's Cinco de Mayo. It's almost seven o'clock at night, and the sun is beginning to go down. Jeremy and his mother are in the desert and Las Vegas is somewhere in front of them. Every time they pass a driver coming the other way, Jeremy tries to figure out if that person has just won or lost a lot of money. Everything is flat and sort of tilted here, except off in the distance, where the land goes up abruptly, as if someone has started to fold up a map. Somewhere around here is the Grand Canyon, which must have been a surprise when people first saw it.

Jeremy's mother says, "Are you sure we have to do this first? Couldn't we go find your phone booth later?"

"Can we do it now?" Jeremy says. "I said I was going to do it on my blog. It's like a quest that I have to complete."

"Okay," his mother says. "It should be around here some-where. It's supposed to be four point five miles after the turnoff, and here's the turnoff."

It isn't hard to find the phone booth. There isn't much else around. Jeremy should feel excited when he sees it, but it's a dis-appointment, really. He's seen phone booths before. He was expecting something to be different. Mostly he just feels tired of road trips and tired of roads and just tired, tired, tired. He looks around to see if Fox is somewhere nearby, but there's just a hiker off in the distance. Some kid.

"Okay, Germ," his mother says. "Make this quick."

"I need to get my backpack out of the back," Jeremy says.

"Do you want me to come too?" his mother says.

"No," Jeremy says. "This is kind of personal."

His mother looks like she's trying not to laugh. "Just hurry up. I have to pee."

When Jeremy gets to the phone booth, he turns around. His mother has the light on in the van. It looks like she's singing along to the radio. His mother has a terrible voice.

When he steps inside the phone booth, it isn't magical. The phone booth smells rank, as if an animal has been living in it. The windows are smudgy. He takes the stolen books out of his back-pack and puts them in the little shelf where someone has stolen a phone book. Then he waits. Maybe Fox is going to call him. Maybe he's supposed to wait until she calls. But she doesn't call.

He feels lonely. There's no one he can tell about this. He feels like an idiot and he also feels kind of proud. Because he did it. He drove cross-country with his mother and saved an imaginary person.

"So how's your phone booth?" his mother says.

"Great!" he says, and they're both silent again. Las Vegas is in front of them and then all around them and everything is lit up like they're inside a pinball game. All of the trees look fake. Like someone read too much Dr. Seuss and got ideas. People are walking up and down the sidewalks. Some of them look normal. Others look like they just escaped from a fancy-dress ball at a lunatic asylum. Jeremy hopes they've just won lots of money and that's why they look so startled, so strange. Or maybe they're all vampires.

"Left," he tells his mother. "Go left here. Look out for the vampires on the crosswalk. And then it's an immediate right." Four times his mother let him drive the van: once in Utah, twice in South Dakota, once in Pennsylvania. The van smells like old burger wrappers and fake fur, and it doesn't help that Jeremy's gotten used to the smell. The woman in the painting has had a pained expression on her face for the last few nights, and the disco ball has lost some of its pieces of mirror because Jeremy kept knocking his head on it in the morning. Jeremy and his mother haven't showered in three days.

Here is the wedding chapel, in front of them, at the end of a long driveway. Electric purple light shines on a sign that spells out HELL'S BELLS. There's a wrought-iron fence and a yard full of trees dripping Spanish moss. Under the trees, tombstones and miniature mausoleums.

"Do you think those are real?" his mother says. She sounds slightly worried.

"'Harry East, Recently Deceased,'" Jeremy says. "No, I don't."

There's a hearse in the driveway with a little plaque on the back. RECENTLY BURIED MARRIED. The chapel is a Victorian house with a bell tower. Perhaps it's full of bats. Or giant spiders. Jeremy's father would love this place. His mother is going to hate it.

Someone stands at the threshold of the chapel, door open,

looking out at them. But as Jeremy and his mother get out of the van, he turns and goes inside and shuts the door. "Look out," his mother says. "They've probably gone to put the boiling oil in the microwave."

She rings the doorbell determinedly. Instead of ringing, there's a recording of a crow. *Caw, caw, caw.* All the lights in the Victorian house go out. Then they turn on again. The door swings open and Jeremy tightens his grip on his backpack, just in case. "Good evening, Madam. Young man," a man says and Jeremy looks up and up and up. The man at the door has to lower his head to look out. His hands are large as toaster ovens. He looks like he's wearing Chihuahua coffins on his feet. Two realistic-looking bolts stick out on either side of his head. He wears green pancake makeup, glittery green eye shadow, and his lashes are as long and thick and green as AstroTurf. "We weren't expecting you so soon."

"We should have called ahead," Jeremy's mother says. "I'm real sorry."

"Great costume," Jeremy says.

The Frankenstein curls his lip in a somber way. "Thank you," he says. "Call me Miss Thing, please."

"I'm Jeremy," Jeremy says. "This is my mother."

"Oh please," Miss Thing says. Even his wink is somber. "You tease me. She isn't old enough to be your mother."

"Oh please, yourself," Jeremy's mother says.

"Quick, the two of you," someone yells from somewhere inside Hell's Bells. "While you zthtand there gabbing, the devil ithz prowling around like a lion, looking for a way to get in. Are you juthzt going to zthtand there and hold the door wide open for him?"

So they all step inside. "Is that Jeremy Marthz at lathzt?" the voice says. "Earth to Marthz, Earth to Marthz. Marthzzz, Jeremy Marthzzz, there'thz zthomeone on the phone for Jeremy Marthz. She'thz called three timethz in the lathzt ten minutethz, Jeremy Marthzzzz."

It's Fox, Jeremy knows. Of course, it's Fox! She's in the phone booth. She's got the books and she's going to tell me that I saved whatever it is that I was saving. He walks toward the buzzing voice while Miss Thing and his mother go back out to the van.

He walks past a room full of artfully draped spider webs and candelabras drooping with drippy candles. Someone is playing the organ behind a wooden screen. He goes down the hall and up a long staircase. The banisters are carved with little faces. Owls and foxes and ugly children. The voice goes on talking. "Yoohoo, Jeremy, up the stairthz, that'thz right. Now, come along, come right in! Not in there, in here, in here! Don't mind the dark, we *like* the dark, just watch your step." Jeremy puts his hand out. He touches something and there's a click and the bookcase in front of him slowly slides back. Now the room is three times as large and there are more bookshelves and there's a young woman wearing dark sunglasses, sitting on a couch. She has a megaphone in one hand and a phone in the other. "For you, Jeremy Marth," she says. She's the palest person Jeremy has ever seen and her two canine teeth are so pointed that she lisps a little when she talks. On the megaphone the lisp was sinister, but now it just makes her sound irritable.

She hands him the phone. "Hello?" he says. He keeps an eye on the vampire.

"Jeremy!" Elizabeth says. "It's on, it's on, it's on! It's just started! We're all just sitting here. Everybody's here. What happened to your cell phone? We kept calling."

"Mom left it in the visitor's center at Zion," Jeremy says.

"Well, you're there. We figured out from your blog that you must be near Vegas. Amy says she had a feeling that you were going to get there in time. She made us keep calling. Stay on the phone, Jeremy. We can all watch it together, okay? Hold on."

Karl grabs the phone. "Hey, Germ, I didn't get any postcards," he says. "You forget how to write or something? Wait a minute. Somebody wants to say something to you." Then he laughs and laughs and passes the phone on to someone else who doesn't say anything at all.

"Talis?" Jeremy says.

Maybe it isn't Talis. Maybe it's Elizabeth again. He thinks about how his mouth is right next to Elizabeth's ear. Or maybe it's Talis's ear.

The vampire on the couch is already flipping through the channels. Jeremy would like to grab the remote away from her, but it's not a good idea to try to take things away from a vampire. His mother and Miss Thing come up the stairs and into the room and suddenly the room seems absolutely full of people, as if Karl and Amy and Elizabeth and Talis have come into the room, too. His hand is getting sweaty around the phone. Miss Thing is holding Jeremy's mother's painting firmly, as if it might try to escape. Jeremy's mother looks tired. For the past three days her hair has been braided into two long fat pigtails. She looks younger to Jeremy, as if they've been traveling backward in time instead of just across the country. She smiles at Jeremy, a giddy, exhausted smile. Jeremy smiles back.

"Is it *The Library*?" Miss Thing says. "Is a new episode on?"

Jeremy sits down on the couch beside the vampire, still holding the phone to his ear. His arm is getting tired.

"I'm here," he says to Talis or Elizabeth or whoever it is on the other end of the phone. "I'm here." And then he sits and doesn't say anything and waits with everyone else for the vampire to find the right channel so they can all find out if he's saved Fox, if Fox is alive, if Fox is still alive.

FISHIN' WITH
GRANDMA MATCHIE

by Steven Erikson

Steven Erikson (Steve Lundin) was born in Toronto, Canada, in October 1959, and grew up in Winnipeg. He graduated from the University of Manitoba with a BA in anthropology/archaeology in 1981, and studied writing at the University of Victoria and the University of Iowa, where he concentrated on writing main-stream fiction. That led to his first book, A Ruin of Feathers *(1991), a cycle of linked stories set in Central America. Contemporary fiction* Stolen Voices, *co-winner of the Anvil Press Three Day Novel Award, appeared in 1993. Erikson wrote his first fantasy,* Gardens of the Moon, *and received a grant to write a second contemporary book,* This River Awakens *(1998); collection* Revolvo and Other Canadian Tales *was published in the same year. When Bantam UK purchased the rights to* Gardens of the Moon *and nine other volumes of the* Malazan Book of the Fallen, *they suggested he publish under another name to avoid confusion with his mainstream work.* Gardens of the Moon *was published in 1999, followed by* Deadhouse Gates, Memories of Ice, House of Chains, *and* Midnight Tides. *Erikson has also published a handful of long novellas, including "Malazan" pair "Blood Follows" and "The Healthy Dead," which feature series characters Bauchelain and Korbal Broach, and science fiction* The Devil Delivered *and the tale that follows.* The Bonehunters, *the sixth Malazan novel, will be published later this year.*

THIS IS WHERE I WANT TO START

The Meaning of School and All That:

It's not my fault! It has to do with a lot of things. Special things, like Bigness. When I think of the world's bigness I think of a ball of fishing line that's all tangled up and no matter how hard Dad tries he can't find where it starts or where it ends and the tackle box tips over then and he steps on a rubber worm that rolls and the next thing you know Dad's in the lake. It's like that.

So you follow the line this way and it loops into a knot and goes off that way. But you just got to keep following it, because Bigness leads to the Truth, and the Truth's important. If you don't know what I mean then I'll show you just like this:

Just like this:

In the Olden Days they used to have Jesters. Jesters talked about Plain Things as if those things were fat and skinny and tall and short. But sometimes the Jesters made those things too fat or too skinny or too tall or too short, and then they were bad and Not to be Tolerated, and then the king would stick them in a corner and make them wear a Dunce Cap.

Now, the corner is a funny place. You stare at the walls where they meet, and you begin to understand the importance of the Bigness of things. And it all starts Making Sense. This is the place where children who are Not Yet Considered Adults go, when kings and teachers get all fretful about children with Over-wrought Imaginations.

You see, when you're sitting there with your feet not even touching the floor, you stare at those walls where they meet and you know you can't fit between them because there's no crack. And that's when you suddenize that no matter how small you are, you're never small enough.

Which is just what the kings and teachers want you to sudd-enize.

LIFE starts with a Foolish Pleading of your case:

But it really happened. Just like I wrote it, three weeks during summer vacation, and summer vacation is the time for dreams. Just because school had started it shouldn't mean things that were true in the summer weren't true now. Isn't that right?

But the Bigness of Things tells you in No Uncertain Terms (that's what she says: "in No Uncertain Terms"), No, Jock Junior, that is not right.

You'd think she'd know better.

Now, the first day of school and how it all came about:

My teacher was a nose and that's all she was, just a nose and some wispy hair around it. If she had eyes, they were hiding somewhere in the blackness of her giant nostrils. The nose gloomed over all of us, and snarted hotly and we sweated a lot in that room.

The first thing you'd notice about that room is that it had four corners, all empty now because it's the first day of school. And the next thing you'd notice is that none of the corners have cracks, though of course you'd only see that if you were sitting in those corners, one after another. So you can trust me when I say there's no cracks in them, okay?

And by the window there's an aquarium with one fish in it. Sometimes I slip him notes, helping him plan his escape, but he never answers them, so I figure he's got a plan of his own. Thing is, I don't think he's very smart.

And I'll tell you a Secret. Something I've figured out. Look at the windows. See those cardboard faces pasted to them? There's a face for each one of us in the room, except Big Nose herself. Look at them. They have holes for eyes and holes for nostrils but drawn-in mouths. And that's my Secret. So don't tell anyone, especially Big Nose.

Of course, I'm not old enough to see these things, nor to understand the Importance of Telling the Truth. I'm Not to be Tolerated, I'm Precocious. Only it wasn't me who said those Things, which are Big Things. And it wasn't me who knew how to spell them. But we're here to learn how to spell.

Tell the truth about what you did in the summer, Big Nose told us sweating faces. And I made my eyes into slivery slits and thought about things, cool and calculating like. It may have been her understanding that there were no little jesters hiding among us, I think. She didn't say which summer, but we've already been taught to understand the need not to have to say Certain Things. But then I think: It may have been her plan to Ferret me out.

The Assignment that Ferreted me out:

I bet I know more than you do. I used to overturn big flat rocks, looking for the Devil. Satan Himself, Grandma Matchie always called him, and always with a shiver jippling all along her skinny shoulders. And her eyes spizzled, like she was showing me what Hades looked like, as if she'd been down there herself and arm-wrassled Satan Himself down to the ground (she did, too, but that's another story). He was hiding, she told me, always hiding. So I overturned rocks, the big flat ones, but all I ever found were ants, carrying eggs back and forth, and getting on my shoes so I had to stimp and stamp and stromp.

I don't look under rocks anymore, and that's why I know more than you do.

And I'll tell you this, too. I've seen him. I've seen Satan Himself. It was easy. All I had to do was follow that fishing line right to the end, and there he was! It was the third and last week in my summer vacation, but before I tell you about that, I have to tell you about the first and second weeks, because, you see, that's the only way to unravel fishing line.

And that's not the only reason. Sometimes the Bigness of Things is so big that you've just got to be prepared before you run into it. Which means you should take a look at smaller Bigness before you see the Biggest Bigness.

I'm doing this because Old Ladies say I'm nice, and since they got to be so old I figure they know the difference between nice and not-nice.

One last thing. Those Titles are Grandma Matchie's, one for each of the three weeks. She says Titles are important, and that's the way they've done things since Adam first broke the Egg. I'm not sure what that means, unless it's that all those Titles fell out when Adam broke the Egg. Personally, I don't think there's an Egg in existence that could hold all the world's Titles. Because if there was, who laid it and where does she live and what does she eat and does she ever visit Sudbury and if she did then why?

So, here's the first week, and Grandma Matchie's first Title. The rest of the stuff, and all those smaller headings, is mine and no one's Legally Responsible but me.

One thing worries me, though. What happens if all those people I talk about come after me?

NO REST FOR THE WICKED

Girls. My face is scrinching up already, but I'm forcing myself because it's Important to start here. I like pretending they're not there most of the time, even though they wear pants with zippers and I'm pretty sure they don't need zippers. They're funny like that and don't ask me why because I don't know why.

So I usually pretend they don't exist, and that makes them mad for some reason, and then there's this funny chase thing during recess, where you run after them until your chest hurts. And something Serious and Grim pushes the insides of your head all over the place, as if the chase was More Important than Anything Else on Earth.

It's sickening. And the girl you're chasing after looks Different from all the other girls. Stranger, uglier maybe, like she's always twitching her nose and pulling at her hair.

The fascination of ugliness:

But then you catch her. You force her into a red bricked corner behind the school, and suddenly she looks mad. I can't figure that. She glares at you and she's breathing hard and her cheeks are red and her eyes are wild in a way that makes you think of stupid things, like wrestling.

It's that corner stuff all over again. The Bigness of Things that can make your face scranch up while you're thinking of more stupid things, like mint-sucking piano teachers and little violins wearing flowery dresses. I know it's stupid!

And it gets worse and worse. You plant a grin on your face like the ones you've seen in horror movies just before the blonde woman throws up her hands and screeks, and she stares at it, those eyes going big, because you've grown fangs. It makes you even sicker when you suddenize how dumb you look. But in spite of all that, in spite of everything, you close in.

What do you do then? Maybe you punch her, maybe she punches you. And you ask yourself in horror: Whose arm is going to be sore? It's the most Awful Decision of your life, that one.

Or, worst of all, nothing happens! And no matter what, you feel luzzy for days afterwards. Ignoring her giggling friends you follow her next recess, trying to make her run away so you can splurt after her, so maybe something'll happen this time. But it's awful, because now she's ignoring you!

So I hate her and that's all there is to it. And my face scrunches up when someone says her name, and that Grim and Serious thing in me makes me want to barf.

The Secret of Wanting to Barf:

Oh, I know all about it now. I've studied the way those bumps on my sister's chest gromered all bigger underneath her shirt, until she had to tie them up so she could see where she was stepping, so there wouldn't always be dog-do on her runners.

Only girls and fat men have those things. And only girls tie them up, which is why fat men sag and slumple and I get out of their way so I don't get brolled on and skirbled flat.

I also know why girls exist. It all started that first week of summer vacation at Rat Portage Lake, when, feeling Grim and Serious, I threw a dead frog in Sis's hair and it came back to life. Up until then nothing I had ever thrown in her hair had come back to life. Not worms all liddlelimply gray, not minnows all bladed white, not even big black flies from the window sill which are never really dead anyway! And the live things I threw in her hair all died instantly. It's true! The garter snake up and died!

Went stuckled as a stick and stuck out its tongue and rolled up its eyes!

But the frog came back to life, all because Sis had grown those Infernal Bumps. I stood back in amazement and watched the poor thing struggle in the torngle of her long hair, while Sis blawed and screamed and clabbed at her pointy head. Then she managed to grab one of its kicking legs and she threw it high into the air. Limbs Splayed, it hung up there against the sky, then down it went hitting the lake with a batralp.

I'll never forget those Splayed Limbs in all my life. And now, when I chase a girl into a corner behind school, I know that those Splayed Limbs will be just another one of those stupid thoughts. The whole thing makes me sick.

And that's how it all started, as we stood by the dock with the tigerflies brazzling over our heads and the water purbling up on the little beach and the pine trees hisspering behind the cabin, the whole family, every one of us, waiting for Grandma Matchie to arrive.

Even normal families like mine got Secrets:

Grandma Matchie is that Secret. I'm not supposed to talk about her. I think it's because she embarrasses Dad a lot, even though she's Mom's Mom. So I won't talk about the times she embarrassed Dad and I'll keep it to the Plain Facts nobody would argue about.

Grandma Matchie lives in a two storey wooden lodge that has been under water since 1899. That was the year the dam was opened. Fifty feet down, she says, all lit up so that the astronauts can see it whenever they pass overhead. She sleeps down there and comes up most mornings after breakfast, but sometimes earlier.

But it was already our second day at the cabin. And the sun was hot, making us all clampy while we tuddled around the cabin, or skiddled up on the Precambrian Rock skirmelling blueberries into our mouths and collecting deer antlers and putting them in trees and throwing pine cones at wasp nests and running away when all the wasps come stungling out. Our second day away from the city, away from Appalled Neighbours and Urban Miscreants who want to recycle everything in our house or at least bottles. Our second day at Rat Portage Lake, and Grandma Matchie hadn't come up yet.

So we stood there waiting, and waiting some more. Everyone figured she wasn't going to show. Mom and Dad kept arguing about it, and Sis sat down on a stump and tried to loosen the knots I'd tied in her hair earlier that morning.

Dad told her not to sleep in!

I kept my eyes peeled on the waves, because I knew better. I knew she was coming, just like she did every summer. And just like all the other summers everybody figured she wasn't going to show. Grown-ups have real short memories, if you ask me.

And sure enough there she was, her head bobbening to the surface in the middle of the bay. She gave a wave and we all waved back.

"See!" I said to Mom. "I told you I saw lights down there last night! I knew she was home!"

"Well," she sneffed, tightening her grip on the broom handle. "Could've been lectric eels."

Grandma Matchie swam toward us, her long skinny neck making a giant V through the water. Minnows leapt in little silver florshes in front of her, like she was chasing them, but I could've told them not to worry. Grandma Matchie didn't give a rizzling hoot for small fry.

"Ain't no lectric eels in Rat Portage Lake!" Dad gruzzled, scratching the thick black hair on his chest until the buttons on his shirt popped off. He turned to Mom with his big red-bearded face all scowllered up. "Semper fey, woman! What've ya got for brains, anyway? Turnips?"

"That's a root crop," Sis said. She was taking Agriculture in school and I hated everything she said, so I started looking around for something to throw at her. But then I remembered the frog and got scared.

"Lectric eels, Zeus!" Dad shook his shuggy head, making the fishing lures in his hat jample. He'd hung the biggest ones on the brim of the hat. For balance, he said. And so he had Red Devils in front of his eyes, and he looked out from the tiny holes where you tie the line. "Lectric eels!"

Mom scowllered too, hefting the broom in her skinny hands. She looked down at her high heels again and tried feebly to pull them out from between the planks in the dock, but she was stuck fast, which made her scowller even more. It was just like every summer. "Well, lamp rays, then."

"Lamp rays!"

I left them binickering and ran down to the end of the dock to meet Grandma Matchie. Grinning, she clambered up on the weathered boards and began wringing the water from her bright red dress. She was taller even than Dad and skinnier even than Mom, and her gray hair sat on top of her head like a giant ball of torngled-up fishing line with only a little seaweed in it, and you could see she'd been lying on the rock all the bass like to hide under because her wrunkled skin was all tanned and anyway summer's when her Indian blood shows through, because Grandma Matchie's One Part Everything.

"How ya bin doin, Tike?" Her hiking boots sloshed as, taking my hand, we walked up the dock. "You ain't seen the Major lately, have ya?"

I looked across the bay at the Major's tiny island, but all I could see was his dock and his Blarny Boat and the flag pole with its Union Jack hanging there all lank and tired. "I seen him out trobbling around, that's all. Yesterday. Whenever he comes near shore he just shakes his fist at us. I think he's mad at us or something."

Tossing back her head Grandma Matchie laughed. "He's mad, all right! Hah!"

Dad scowllered and said: "We bin here since yesterday and you ain't been up once!"

"Aren't you ashamed?" Mom demanded, poking the air with her broom.

Making a rude noise at both of them Grandma Matchie turned and crucked an eyebrow at Sis. "That hair sure looks funny, lass. In fashion nowadays, eh? Well, don't let the bees see you or you'll get stungled for sure!" And she laughed again.

Sis's face scrinched up and I could tell she was going to cry. And sure enough she let out a browl and raced away towards the cabin.

Mom scowllered even scowllier than Dad. "Now look at what you done, Mother!"

Well, it didn't surprise me, that's for sure. Sis was older than me and I hated her. The way she made faces at dinner, and the way she started crying every time I kicked her under the table, and once she hit me when Mom wasn't looking, and nobody'd believe me, so I hated her, and that's why.

And she had purple hair, too. It used to be brown, even when it wasn't dirty, but now it was purple. And she wore shiny shirts that made her chest look funny. Once, I saw her in the bathroom, miggling her hips so that her fat bum moved funnily. She was crazy, and if you don't believe me you just wait!

Grandma Matchie frowned. "She bin cryin alot, Ester?"

Mom's face reddened for some Mysterious Reason, but she nodded anyway.

Dad caught my eye and winked. "Woman talk, son. Don't you pay it no mind." His eyes looked small as a gerbil's inside those holes in the Red Devils, but not just any old gerbil unless all gerbils are like the one that used to be in my classroom but got away when a Child with an Overwrought Imagination Assisted it to Escape. Eyes like that gerbil's, which were mostly suspicious even when I showed it the Plans. And all those flies snigged in Dad's hat made me think of when you accidentally drop a ten pound jar of chocolate pudding on a rock and it breaks and there's a pile of ucky pudding just sitting there for hours before you tell anyone, and by then it's fly pudding and you can watch them sinking and disappearing until the sun goes down when there's none left and it's time for Sis to have a snack.

We were all getting ready to go up to the cabin when Grandma Matchie hissped "Shhh!" and crouched, looking around. Everyone froze. Her eyes narrowed to slits and she sniffed the air. "He's here, he is!" she hisspered. "Somewhere!"

All at once we heard fladapping overhead and we all looked up.

"There he is!" Grandma Matchie screeked. "Spyin!"

The Major hovered over us, wearing his usual navy blues and polished boots. You could see the fire gleamering in his eyes and he grinned crazzerly, his big red nose purlsing and his giant moustache bristlering. The two gulls holding him up screewled loudly and beat their wings madly, and feathers floated down all around us.

Water spraying from the eyelets of her hiking boots, Grandma Matchie splomped back and forth in a rage. "Where's my duck gun!" She shook her fist skyward. "I'll turn those gulls into paperweights! Hah!" Then she swirjerked around and tore off up the trail and prashed down the cabin door with both feet at once.

She disappeared inside. "She's getting a gun!" Dad shouted at the Major, who shrieked. And the gulls shrieked, too. Legs pumping the air, the Major tried to run home. The seagulls ducked their heads and drummed their wings, hurrying him toward his island. By the time Grandma Matchie arrived with her shotgun, the Major had shrunk to a speck. Looking miserable, she pumped a couple rounds after him anyway, then sniffed, her wrinkled lips pouping.

"Damn spyin! Did you see his beady eyes? Just aglowin!"

"How come?" I asked.

"He's fishin, that's what he's doin. An he's got it bad, sure enough if you ask me.

"Got what bad?"

"The itch." Grandma Matchie surplied.

I didn't know what on earth she was talking about, but I saw Dad grinning and Mom's face turning red. And for some reason I could feel my face starting to scranch, though it had no reason to that I could figure. It does that sometimes.

That night, in the cabin, Grandma Matchie cooked us up a whole pot full of crayfish, but said they had to cool till morning before we could eat them. Then she sat herself down by the fireplace, streetching out her glongly legs and watching her boots steam.

Mom took over the kitchen and said no one was allowed to come in while she Baked Bread.

"Crazy woman!" Dad snargled, crushelling his beer can and

throwing it into a corner, his eyes streaming in the smoke from the pipe in his mouth. Smoking a pipe's an important part of being a fisherman, he'd said between coughs. He had on his fishing hat with the thousand hundred fifty-two million lures snegged in it, and he stood in the centre of the living room, wearing hip-waders and a fish basket clipped to his leg. Bing Crosby was on the tape deck and the sound of turckling water came from the bathroom where Dad had turned on the tap. "Gotta have the sound of turckling water," he'd said. "It's a parta fishin. An important part."

Whipping the air, Dad's fly rod swung back and forth, and fishing line torngled everything. It hung from the rafters of the A-frame like spider webs; it snarvelled the furniture and lay in twingled coils on the wooden floor. Sis was all wrapped up in it and hadn't moved in an hour. She just lay there, groaming every now and then.

I sat with Grandma Matchie, my feet growing hot as Hades in front of the mackling spunkering pafting fire.

"Crazy woman!" Dad repeated in a voice loud enough to be heard in the kitchen. Snapping open another beer can with his left hand he tugged the rod. "Damn! Snaggered again! It's the worst parta fishin! If I lose another leader I'll scream!" He pulled and pulled and the moose head on the wall waggled and nodded.

The kitchen door swung open and a white powdered figure stepped out and screaked: "Didn't I tell you to do your fishin outside?" Clouds burst from her lips. "Didn't I!?"

"I ain't goin out there!" Dad belbowed. "There's dangerous beasts out there! A man could get himself killed!" He yanked savagely and the moose head jampled straight out from the wall all brown and blurthy like it was attacking him. Yimping, Dad ducked and the head sailed over and crashed down on a table. "See!"

"Fishin's dangerous, Tike," Grandma Matchie nodded.

Dad straightened and glawered at Mom. "Not only that! It's gothic fulla bugs and stuff!" He bared his teeth at her and snargled, "Why don't you go out there if y'like it so much! Do your gothic bakin in the bush!"

"Look at your daughter!"

"Ahh, she's all right. Just sleepin, is all."

"She's all tied up!"

"Bah!"

Crossing her arms, Mom whirled about. "Well!" She slammed the door and flour gusted out around it.

Bing Crosby began dreaming of a white Christmas and I hissped, "Shhh!" to Grandma Matchie and began wormening toward the kitchen, crawpelling from shadow to shadow like the Indians must have done, until I crouched up against the door. Reaching up, I grasped and turned the knob ever so slowly. I opened it a crack and peeked in.

It was white woman's territory for sure. In fact, the whole kitchen was white, and loaves of bread were stacked everywhere, a million thousand seventy-two of them. And there was Mom, her fancy black dress all covered in flour and butter and dough, and there was more dough clinging to her fingers and arms and wrapped around her neck as she strubbled and pulled and pulled and strubbled, muttering and whimpering all the while.

Once Mom started she couldn't stop, and pretty soon the loaves of bread began showing up everywhere. Sloggy and swobllen on the beach, with groaming crows lying in piles all around them. Made into nests by squirrels, all hollowed out with flowery drapes in the windows. Hanging from tree branches with bees brazzling all around them trying to figure a way to get inside. And after a few days you could easily make bread igloos out of them. But this time she'd really gone overboard. Groaming softly, I closed the door and snucched back to Grandma Matchie's side.

"She done it again, huh?"

"Worse than ever!"

Grandma Matchie sighed, wrivilled her steaming boots. "Ever drank crayfish wine, Tike? I got vats of it down in the lodge. Canada's Finest, it says on the labels. Bottled it myself. 'Course, you're not old 'nough fur crayfish wine, anyway."

"Soon?"

"Maybe. But I'll tell you somethin. You want hair on your chest like your Dad?" I thought about it and was about to answer but she went on, "Well, drink some of Canada's Finest and I guarantee it, you'll never freeze in winter again."

Frowning, I said, "Maybe that's why the Major goes fishin

and trobblin for you every day. He wants your crayfish wine."

Grandma Matchie chackled. "Not likely, though it does kinda get im a hankerin, 'times."

"Every day he's out there! Rowin back and forth and trobblin bait past your windows!"

"Lubber don't know a thin about baitin," she muthered distantly.

I looked up at her and I saw her eyes glowing like the coals in the fireplace. Before I knew it, my face scrinched up. "Grandma Matchie! Snap out of it!"

Turning, she gave me a blank look. "Snap out of what, Tike?"

I sighed, feeling my face unscrinching. Whew! I'd almost lost her there! In the dull light I peeked out of the corner of my eye at Grandma Matchie's arm to confirm my belief. Yes, it looked too skinny to be punched. It'd break for sure. Right then and there I vowed to protect Grandma Matchie, no matter what.

Laugh if you want! You'll see I was right!

The next morning Sis was gone no one knew where. Mom sifted the piles of flower in the kitchen; Dad checked his fish basket; and I searched through all her clothes and stuff just in case anything interesting came up. But Grandma Matchie sniffered the air and then went straight over to the crayfish pot. Lifting the lid she peered inside and after a moment cried out, "Aha! I knew it!" She slammed the lid down and whirvelled to us, her face grim, "She's been kidnapped! And I know who!"

"The Major?" I asked.

Even more grimly she shook her head. "He's small fry. Nope, this is bad, real bad. Cause it means he's back, an if he's back there'll be trouble for us all!" Suddenly she threw back her shoulders and roared a defiant laugh, then began barking orders: "Ester! Get the canoe outa the boathouse! Jock, get me my spurs and saddle! Jock Junior! Pack us a lunch! An alla you—be quick 'bout it!" Hands on her hips, Grandma Matchie glowered at us until we all started scrambling.

Passing by the crayfish pot I paused to lift the lid and peek inside. They were all there, bright red and tasty looking. "But Grandma Matchie . . ."

"Aye, an look at em, Tike. Look at em real good, now."

And then I saw that each of them was missing a claw. "Someone's stolen half the claws!"

"An you know what that means?" Grandma Matchie's face was grim and serious. "It means he's back, and he was right here! An he stole Sis." Fury smolgered in her eyes. "He stole Sis!"

"Who?" Mom asked from the doorway, where the prow of the cedar strip canoe had jammed in the frame and she was tugging frantically.

Grandma Matchie stared at Mom and said sandily, "Ester, why are you bringin the canoe inta the cabin?"

"WHO?" Mom shracked, wrenching at the prow.

"One Armed Trapper, that's who."

Mom shracked again, tearing at her hair.

The horror of He-Who-Stole-Sis:

THE canoe had a big hole in it, but Grandma Matchie said, "Never mind, that way we'll be able to see the lake bottom. That's important," she said. "He'll leave tracks, he will. We gotta follow em, we do."

After dravelling the canoe down to the little gravel beach beside the dock and loading it up with food and Grandma Matchie's silver spurs and range saddle, we all gathered at the dock.

"Don't you worry," Grandma Matchie said to Mom. "Me and Tike'll bring er back. Rest easy now."

Wringing her hands, Mom moamed. "If only I wasn't half way through my baking! You know how I hate to not finish things!"

"An I got all those flies to tie up," Dad groamed. "Can't let em get away, y'know."

"Don't you worry neither of you. We'll hunt him down even if it takes us t'the deepest lake on Earth!" Grandma Matchie glowered. "I gotta score t'settle with One Armed Trapper, I do."

Then we were off, pushing out from the shore and drifting sideways. Sitting in the stern, I looked around and suddenized we had no paddles. But Grandma Matchie stood at the bow and spread her arms wide. Her red dress fanned out and filled with wind, and the canoe began slurping forward and soon was slickering through the water, the waves batralping against the canoe's sides.

I looked around. "Grandma Matchie, I don't feel no wind."

"'Course not!" she surplied over her shoulder. "It's cosmic wind, the kind y'can't feel, but it's always there."

"Where's it come from?"

"The center of the universe, that's where."

"Where's that?"

"In my lodge, where else?"

"Which room?"

"Never you mind."

I scowlered. "The kitchen?"

The back of her head shook no.

"The den? The livin room? The dinin room?"

"Never you mind."

"Your bedroom?"

I heard her chackle. "You can't feel the wind yet, so don't you go talkin 'bout what y'don't know." She shifted slightly and we rounded the edge of the bay. The Major's island went by off to our left and I could see him standing on his dock, shaking both fists at us, but Grandma Matchie just ignored him. What with his gnazzling garumphing and endless ormbling around and around his island's beach, and his Blarny Boat all borlupping with leaks, and all his meening away at night when he's drunk too much Crayfish wine and sprouts purbling poems that drift moonily across the water, well, the Major's small fry.

Moving forward on my knees I looked down into the hole in the canoe. The water slid by as clear as glass and I could see down a million hundred fifty-one feet to the bottom.

"See his footprints, Tike?"

Squimping, I concentrated real hard like she always told me to do, and then I saw them, crossing the mud bottom. "Steady as she goes!" I shouted.

Boy, those sure were giant footprints.

The afternoon passed, as we followed the shoreline until we came to the river mouth, and then up the windering river we went, the forest going by on both sides in a blurthy blur. And below us the tracks of One Armed Trapper continued. When it got dark we kept going and Grandma Matchie, soaking up all that cosmic wind, started glowing in the darkness, and the footprints glowed, too. The river narrowed and grew twimpy, with thick wild rice choking the channel and all the spider webs between the reedy stalks all shinnily and gothic in the moonlight.

I watched those footprints the whole night through and never even got tired. It was the cosmic wind, Grandma Matchie explained. "No one ever gets tired with Cosmic Wind," she said.

At dawn the river widened and currents swirvelled around us, making the water muddy. "Winnipeg River!" Grandma Matchie shouted triumphantly. "I know where he's gone to! He can't hide from me! Hah!" And the canoe raced through the churbling water. "Eaglenest Lake, that's where! Hah!"

The river widened even more and I could see bays and inlets on both sides through the morning mist, which disappeared as the sun rose higher and higher. Staring down into the hole once again, I gasped. "His tracks are gone! Grandma Matchie!"

The canoe stopped suddenly and she turned to me with a frown. "Gone? Then that means he took a detour, don't it?" She held up her hands. "Not a word, Tike. Grandma Matchie has t'think." And with that she closed her eyes and lowered her head.

Everything had gone quiet and I looked around. The river's current had stopped and the swirbles stayed in half-swirb, and the ebbies waited in half-eb, and over the trees flying birds were frozen in mid-flathap, and low over the water bazzling insects hung in mid-bazz. The world stopped when Grandma Matchie closed her eyes and thought. Suddenly I heard a tree crash deep in the woods a long way off and then Grandma Matchie's head snapped up.

"There's only one thing that could make One Armed Trapper take a detour." Her face glowed pink and her eyes glimbered. "Only one thing! I bin hopin for this!"

"What?"

She grinned. "Get me my spurs, Tike, I'm goin for a swim."

The world started moving again but our canoe stayed where it was, the water purbling against the sides, as Grandma Matchie stepped to the centre and bent down and picked up her saddle and leaned it up against the prow. Then she took the silver spurs and clipped them on to her boots. Jampling, she walked forward and sat down in the saddle. Then she leaned over the bow and yabbled, "Gronomo!" and plunged into the water, vanishing beneath the brown swirbling currents.

I pulled a loaf of bread from the picnic basket in front of me, tied a rope to it and heaved it over the side as an anchor. Then, peering down through the hole, I watched Grandma Matchie swarmle down and down until she disappeared in the muddy gloomb.

Minutes passed. A miscreant frog floated by in the water blinking snoozily and I thought about throwing things in Sis's hair. Never again, I vowed, would I throw a dead frog in her hair. No, I'd throw something bigger and better, like a giant dead tarantula. Sis hated spiders. I grinned as I imagined it coming back to life.

The water around me suddenly began to boil, steam rising up in wild sprouts. The canoe tossled and span crazily and I gripped the sides. And through the hole I saw Grandma Matchie coming up, crouched in her saddle with her bony knees up around her shoulders. The spurs glimmerined like fishing lures as she rose up into the sun-lipped water. And then I saw what she was riding. The biggest snapping turtle I've seen. Bigger than Dad's Bronco, bigger even than the cabin, about as big as Dad's Bronco sitting on the cabin, but maybe even bigger. I gawped and stared as its beak opened wide and its long neck stretched upward as if it was going to swabble me and the canoe in one gulp. But then, with a kick from Grandma Matchie, it swirjerked to one side and broke the surface beside me.

"Ya-hoo! Jump aboard, Tike! Afore you get capsized!"

The giant horny shell looked stlippery, all covered with slime and muddy seaweed, but I jumped anyway, landing beside Grandma Matchie who grabbed me before I could stlip and set me down in the saddle behind her.

"Yeahh!" she yelled, kicking her spurs until sparks flew from the turtle's shell. With a thrashle of its thick pebbly skinned legs, the snapper surgled forward, clawing through the water so fast that steam burst out behind us. "Tike! Meet Leap Year! The biggest, meanest Grandma of em all!"

Eyes rolling, Leap Year nodded her huge head. Looking down, I could see that her shell was covered with carvings. Hearts and initials and arrows and stuff. B.D. LOVES O.A.T., G.L.H. and O.A.T., O.A.T. luvs L.L. Thousands of carvings, thousands of initials loving O.A.T. and being loved by O.A.T.

"He's had it now!" Grandma Matchie screaked. "We're all gonna get im! Hah! A thousand million ten fifty years I've waited fur this!" The water went by in a blurthy unplosion of foam and steam as Leap Year plommelled forward, smoke hissing from her upturned nose, fires spigging sparks from her enraged eyes, her lipstick-stained beak open and her tongue writhing like a inside-out backwards snake.

Then, with a nudge of her spurs, Grandma Matchie swung Leap Year shoreward, and I held on tight and let out a yabble as we hit land. Thunder shook the earth and Leap Year's front claws skraked gouges in the bedrock as we left the river. Then trees crashed down all around us and birds screaked and squirrels flew through the air until they caught hold of vines and swung away in shreeming flight.

Suddenly, the crashing stopped, and we perched on the edge of a cliff overlooking a lake. Leap Year snortered and stretched out her neck to turn and look at us.

Grandma Matchie nodded. "He's down there, all right. I can feel it!"

The lake was round, and the trees and bushes grew in a tight ring all around its shore, making it look like a giant nest full of water. "He lives down there?" I asked.

"Yep."

"It looks like a big bird nest."

"'Course, it's called Eaglenest Lake, ain't it?"

"It musta been the biggest eagle in the whole world," I said, and Grandma Matchie nodded again. I went on, "It musta laid the biggest eggs, too."

"Yep."

"Bigger even than Adam's egg?"

Grandma Matchie rubbled her jaw. "Don't think so, Tike, but you never know."

I squimped my eyes and studied the shore. "I don't see him."

"He lives right at the bottom. That's where he went down fifty years ago. Carried a cast iron stove like the one we got in the cabin, a thousand hundred ninety-six miles through the bush, with his one arm. Winter, it was, and here he had his cabin. But crossin the lake the stove fell through the ice and he wen down with it. An there he be, tendin the fire in his stove forever more."

"What fire?"

"The fire o' love, Tike."

Sure enough, scranch went my face. "Yucchhh!"

Leap Year snortled again, her gaze belliful, grim and serious as she glarmored down at the lake. Behind us her tail thrashelled the torn-up forest, knockering down trees and overturning big flat rocks and stuff.

"An Sis is down there? What's he want her for?"

Grandma Matchie frowned. "That's what I can't figure out an it's bin itchin me all over. He's up t'somethin, mark my words."

And Leap Year nodded, shiftening nervously under us.

"Mebee he jus wants er, is all," Grandma Matchie musilled. "Mebee that's all there is, mebee." Then she raised her fist. "Like us all! Like us all!" she crackled. "He'll steal em when he has to! Steal em and love em and leave em, that's what he does! He done that t'them all! Up and left em! Even his b'trothed!" Then her mouth snappered shut and she went white.

Grandma Matchie almost never goes white like that. So, remembering my vow to protect her, I said, "Don't worry, we'll get Sis back. Don't you worry."

Leap Year whimed and shibbered under us, her eyes lorling in her head.

Grandma Matchie drew a deep breath. "No matter! The time's come an he's had it now!" Then she drove her spurs into Leap Year's hard shell. Suddenly we were in the air, sailing outward, then down toward the still blue water. And a head popped up below us, a bearded face with its mouth open in a silent scurm of terror, its eyes bugling out at us.

The crash when we hit threw me from the saddle, sent me

tumbering, limbs splayed, through the air and hitting the water with a painful sralap. Down I went, the blue snirling in front of my eyes. With a thump my bum struck bottom and I looked around. A faint reddish glow warmed the water and I could see something like a baby sun burning in the distance. Jampling to my feet I ran toward it in slow motion. A terrible clanging sound filled my ears, like bells, but I couldn't see where it came from.

The glow grew brighter and the spot of fire grew bigger, and I saw that it was a stove, sitting on a bump of rock. Through its grille fire raggled, and blue smoke stained the water until my eyes stung. As I approached Grandma Matchie crampled up beside the stove and glarened about. Seeing me, she waved and I skuggled over.

"Where's Leap Year?" I asked.

"Dis'peared. I don't like this, Tike. Not one bit." She continued looking around from her perch on the bump of rock. "One Armed Trapper's hidin somewhere round here, mark my words."

"I saw him just before we hit the water, lookin scared to death!"

"Aye, an that's what's bothering me, Tike. One Armed Trapper's never bin fright'ned of nothin in his whole life. Nosiree, he's up t'somethin, he is." She shook her head, placing her hands on her hips and glowening about.

A faint scurm rode to us on the currents and we both turned in its direction. Far in the distance I saw Sis, being held by a small man wearing a tuxedo and the biggest shoes I've ever seen, as big as a sports car, though even flatter than the one Dad drove over in the Bronco in the parking lot.

"One Armed Trapper!" Grandma Matchie hissped, crouching. "If I didn't know better, I'd scry he was baitin us. Only he wouldn't dare!" Then she scowlered grimly. "'Lessen he's got help!"

"Who?"

"Can't be sure. Could be Satan Himself!"

Sis screaked again and Grandma Matchie said, "Well, Tike, let's go get im! But keep yer eyes peeled, jus in case it's a trap!" Then she crampled down and we began running toward them, jampling from rock to rock and pushing our way through seaweed. Fish scattered in all directions when they saw the glow in Grandma Matchie's eyes and I didn't blame them. It was something Awful to Behold. As we got closer to where they were strug-gling, the clangening of bells grew louder and louder.

I could see One Armed Trapper's bushy face, and he was grinning, his teeth glowing white like pearls. Sis fought in the grip of his single arm but it was wrapped around her like a vice. When we were only a hundred feet away he gave us a little dance and tuddled off down a rocky trail.

"After im!" Grandma Matchie shouted and we broke into a sprintle. Rounding a corner we caught a last glimpse of One Armed Trapper as he plungered into a cave. The sound of bells filled my head until it felt like it was about to unplode, and things started getting dreamy like, as if I was being Hypnotised, like I saw in a movie once, when the blonde lady stopped screaking and skirking until all her clothes fell off.

We reached the cave mouth and Grandma Matchie took my hand and in we went. It was pitch black for the first dozen tud-dles or so then we could make out a faint glow ahead of us and we skuggled toward it.

And before we knew it, we found ourselves standing in a chapel. There were pews carved out of solid rock, and a pulpit at the far end behind which stood a giant crayfish, old and gray-bearded. He held a Bible Delicately in his spincers.

And to one side stood Leap Year, all chained up and her head Bowed in Defeat. One Armed Trapper stood near her, smiling warmly. "Ahh!" he squeaked in a high voice. "The bride herself!" And he laughed and bowed.

We had paused at the edge of the long narrow aisle. I looked at Grandma Matchie and cried out. Her red dress had disap-peared and now she wore a white wedding dress, and behind the veil her eyes were all dreamy and lost. Hypnotised!

"Betrothed!" exclaimed One Armed Trapper. "Come to me at last! Oh joy! Joy!" And he did that little dance again and it made the old crayfish frown and push his spectacles back from his antennae.

Red fire was burning on Leap Year's shell and I could see new initials—bigger than all the rest—burning themselves into her back. She whailed Mournfully. The wedding bells rlang and rlang in the murky water and the red fire burnelled and burnelled, and Grandma Matchie began the slow march up the aisle as a hunch-backed carp with her gray hair in a bun started playing on an ancient organ.

"A trap!" I screaked, stumblering after Grandma Matchie. "It was a trap!" But I couldn't break her out of the spell.

The old crayfish began reading the marriage vows and I whailed in Horror as Grandma Matchie and One Armed Trapper began repeating them. Lurchening forward, I stumblered over Sis, who was crouching against a pew, her eyes all crazy like.

"It's the fire o' love!" she hisspered. "The Devil made it into a spell!"

"What do you mean!"

"It brings things back, dummy!"

The vision of the frog flashed in my mind. I stared up the aisle. Already, One Armed Trapper was rolling up his sleeve, getting ready to punch Grandma Matchie's arm. "Wait here! Try and slow em down!"

And then I whirvilled and began to skuggle, out of the chapel, down the tunnel, out of the cave. And there, dim in the distance, burned that little red flame. The bells still rlang and I knew that when they stopped it would be too late, cosmic wind or no cosmic wind.

I skuggled and skuggled, almost flying through the water. My heart pounded until it was louder than even the bells. The smoke from the woodstove was getting thicker, and it was getting harder and harder to see.

I was almost at the bump of rock when a huge shadowy shape reared up in front of me and roarbelled. The sound hit me in a wave and I flew back, hippering the mud with a thump. All I could see through the smoke were two glowing slits, a hundred feet above me. They closed in, loombing right over my head.

The loudest voice I've ever heard thundered down on me. "I WON'T TOLERATE THIS!"

Scramblering to my feet I almost slipped as a rock rolled out from under me. Lurchening forward I grabbed it, and suddenized it wasn't a rock at all. It was one of Mom's loaves. Grunting, I raised it over my head and screeked: "Eat this!!" And then I threw it with all my strength right between its eyes.

"YEOWWWWW!"

Those eyes reared backward, scranching tight so that every-thing went dark all of a sudden. I jampled forward, passing between two huge pillars that must have been its legs. And there, right in front of me, was the bump of rock and the stove. I cram-pled madly.

Above and behind me I heard another roar, and currents swept over me, almost tearing my grip from the rock. But then I was on my feet and the stove wasn't more than five feet away, its flames licking eagerly at the grille. Springering forward I gave that stove the hardest kick I've ever given anything. The grille flew open as it torpled backward, and the fire o'love shot out in all directions, pouring out sparks as the stove rolled across the rock and plumged over the far side. The glow of the flame went out and I hurried to the edge just in time to see the stove disap-pear in the deep mud bottom.

Sparks swarmelled off in all directions, and I knew the whole world was in a lot of trouble now that the fire o'love had been freed. My face scrinching, I looked around for Satan Himself, but he had disappeared. And just then, far off in the distance, I heard a Horrible scrum of Frustration, then a Shout of Triumph. Thunder shook the rock and I fell to my knees.

We were saved!

"Nothin's over till I say so!"

Standing on the shore, Grandma Matchie shook her head and glarmered down into the croonbling waves of Eaglenest Lake. "It's just no good," she muthered. "Ain't nobody beat me afore. Ain't nobody!"

The sun was going down and stars appeared overhead. I threw more wood on the small fire, then glommered at her. "You shoulda punched him! That's all you had to do. Punch him afore he punches you!"

But Grandma Matchie shook her head. "It's jus no good, Tike."

"Bah!"

Sis sneered at me so I sneered back, and that made me feel better. Glancing up, I asked Grandma Matchie, "So, what're ya goin t'do, huh?"

Abruptly she squared her shoulders. "I'm goin back down there, an that's all there is to it!"

"You can't!" I screeked, jampling to my feet.

"I gotta!" And with that she ran to where Leap Year lollered on a giant flat rock and climbed into the saddle. "We gotta finish what we started!" Crackling, they plunged back into the water.

I kicked at the fire, and the sparks seemed to fly through the air forever, round and round. Sis stuck out her tongue at me but I ignored her, pacing back and forth and back and forth and dodging those crazy sparks.

"Ow!" Sis cried, and I turned around.

"What is it?"

She didn't say anything, but there was a strange gleemble in her eyes that I'd never seen there before and it made me frown.

"You and Grandma Matchie saved me, Jock Junior," she said in this weird soft voice, standing up and walking toward me, smiling.

Suddenly I knew what had happened. "Get back!" I screeked. "Get away from me!" But I'd been cornered. The lake was behind me and there was no way on earth I was going in there. And Sis pounced like some Horrible Beast and trapped me in her arms and then she spotched my forehead with spit. With spit!

The Spotch of a Horrible Beast:

Oh sure! They call it kissing! Well, they can forget it as far as I'm concerned. Never again for Jock Junior!

It's just not fair. Everything gets so Grim and Serious, and things keep pushing the insides of my head around in helpless circles. I was pacing again but after a while I stopped and stared at the still, dimbled surface of the lake, and pretty soon it began to glow as if full of cosmic wind. It made me sick, and I bet you know what happened to my face, too. That also makes me sick, and so does Sis. Everything makes me sick.

I hate recesses, and that's all there is to it. I used to think summer holidays were just one long recess, but it's not true. I won't let it! I'm gonna learn to tie flies like Dad, that's what I'm gonna do.

So I glarmed for a while at the glowing lake, then finally turned back to the fire and stokered it up with some of Mom's loaves. Sis was humming and I wondered how long it would take before that spark wore off. And the fire burned redly, and it made me want to barf.

That was the first week.

LUNKER, WHERE ARE YOU BOUND?

Every word of it's true!

Just because I'm only nine years old and just because I'm only four feet tall it doesn't mean I can't control my imagination! I tell the truth and Big Nose twisters my ear. I keep my eyes open and Big Nose sturffles my mouth with cotton. Well, almost!

It's not fair!

I'd sure like to see Big Nose try and twister Grandma Matchie's ear. Hah! She'd throw Big Nose in the lake just to see what kind of lubber she was.

"The only kind," Grandma Matchie'd conclude with a sniff. Me too.

And it's that same ear—the one that's burning and itching right now—that I keep pressed to the earth to listen to all the whispering. Stories, a million stories! And all of them true! They have to be, don't you see? The earth wouldn't lie.

Big Nose forbids whispering:

It's a rule. No hisspering, no passing notes, no tellonging tales. It all has to do with respect, she says. You have to respect Certain Things, she says with fire and brimstone. Things like bigness, chalkboards and rulers, fire and brimstone. And of course Big

Nose's Unwillingness to Tolerate any Precociousness.

And it doesn't end there, either. Just think about your last recess. Everbody's playing soccer. It's a mob of scrumming kids chasing a ball around in the snow. And you're leaning there, watching everything from the goal post, getting numberled with the horror of it all. And they rabble all over the place, and their faces are set in gothic grimaces and nobody tolerates anything. After all, Big Nose is standing there at the edge of the field, and she has a big brass bell in her hand and I bet she's just waiting for someone to step out of line. Then, Whammo! And we're not talking wedding bells here, either.

Play within the lines, goalie gets the ball, penalty shot, all that stupid stuff. As if standing around between two goal posts is hard. As if keeping the ball out is hard. Dumb. All you have to do is tie a string ankle-high from one post to the other and not a single ball will roll in. They can try and kick it high all they want. They couldn't get it between the posts if their lives depended on it.

Their lives depended on it:

That was my mistake. My big mistake. I should've known by looking at those pinchered faces as they chased the ball around. Grandma Matchie says it's an art to recognize a lynch mob when you see one, even in this day and age.

And worst of all, Big Nose was right up there, leading the pack, her bell waving about at the end of her arm as if her hand had turned to brass.

So there you are, Attila and her Huns are charging down on you all because the ball bounced back from the string while you were hanging from the cross-bar. Just because something didn't look quite right about it. Just because their lives depended on that ball crossing that line or not crossing that line in a Manner Deemed Proper. In a manner you could Respect.

Nobody respects a string tied between two posts, I guess.

And I almost got away. Almost over the fence when Big Nose's hand—the flesh one, not the brass one—grabbled my ankle. The mob spizzled and snargled like wolves but kept their distance because Big Nose was there. You know, there's only one reason I can figure for why she didn't brain me: skulls find brass bells Intolerable.

So I got sent to jail, doing hard time, cleaning the chalk dust from the bushes and pulling the hairballs out from between the broom's straw. It was a strict school. Hairballs not allowed.

The mysterious world inside a broom:

You get to exploring, just sitting there on Big Nose's desk, putting all the hairballs into a careful pile and storing them away in her drawer beside the bruisbled apple she forgot to take home.

Gloria Feeb's apple, a present from Gloria Feeb's house delivered by Gloria Feeb herself. I hate Gloria Feeb.

Pushing the apple far into the back of the drawer, I closed it and began picking out all the other things inside that broom. Pieces of crayon with chewbled ends—the purple ones were Margaret Pukeshank's for sure. She loved eating purple crayons and her teeth were always purple. Willy Dortmund liked the green ones but I found only the discarded paper wrapping from those. Willy was fat because he never let anything go to waste that couldn't be eaten first. Amy Greenfeet was a connoisseur— only yellow crayons were good enough for her, what with her pointy nose and plaid pencil case and all. Me, it didn't matter what colour they were. I tried them all. Thing is, after a while they all get to tasting the same. Paper, of course, was another matter.

And then there were bits of eraser and chewing gum—though sometimes it was hard to tell them apart except for the smell. I think the real reason why the school has to buy new stuff every year is because we eat everything we can lay our hands on.

The best part about a broom is the straw itself. You'd think they'd glue it in, but if you shake the broom long enough and hard enough the straw fallers out and just keeps on fallering out, covering Big Nose's desk and all her notes and all over the floor. If I ate straw I could live for years on just one broom. This broom.

But when you think about it, they probably buy new brooms every year, too. I'd have to ask Willy about that.

Well, the broom was clean, and all the chalk from the brushes was no longer on the brushes and I could make neat foot-prints all over the floor. All that was left was feeding the fish.

Fish always know when they're the only thing left:

You can tell by the way their mouths glape. They've got nothing left to say and even if they did they wouldn't tell you. They're like that.

I bet you think fish are dumb. Well, most of them are, I guess. Like the one in Big Nose's room. Just looking at it, I could see that its brain was wivening away. It'd been there too long, a prisoner under the shadow of Big Nose's big nose.

Even when I stuckled my head into the water and tried talking to it, it just swambled away and hid behind a rock. But after ten minutes or so it got used to me and came out for a closer look, glaping, glaping, glaping. I glaped back.

And I was just about to say something when I saw a blur come through the door. It screamed blurthily and grew really big really fast. "Hide!" I yelled at the fish, who duckered into a plastic castle and peered out from one of the towers.

"Jlog Jlunlior!" I heard Big Nose yell. "Glet"—hands grabbed my shoulders—"lout"—I struggled, but she began pulling my head from the water—"thlis"—and then I was out, water spraying everywhere—"MINUTE!"

"I wasn't doin nothin!"

"Jock Junior! Do you think I will tolerate this!?"

Well, the answer to that was obvious. "Probably not," I said, lowering my head and watching the drops hitting the floor.

"Probably? PROBABLY!?"

"Jock Junior simply refuses to control his imagination":

That's not even true! I can control it just fine! It wasn't me who jampled to crazy conclusions, was it? Was it?

So there was Dad, and there was Mom, and there behind that big desk was the principal, who was all ears as Big Nose ran off at the mouth about all the things she Misunderstood.

". . . and he had the gall to tell me he was talking with that goldfish!" Big Nose said in fruxasperation. "I'm completely frux-asperated!" See! "I mean, a goldfish!"

Turning to Dad I explained, "That was my mistake. Goldfish can't talk. I should've known better . . ."

"I should think so!"

"Goldfish aren't like other fish. And of course you can't keep pike and muskie in aquariums cause they'd never stop complaining and it would disturble the class . . ."

Big Nose jumped to her feet. "Aaaaghh!"

I've never seen her so red. Redder even than a boiled cray-fish with its eyes bugging out in all directions. I started to get real worried when she clatched the sides of her head and began running in circles.

"You shouldn't get so mad," I said as calm as I could. "It just makes you intolerable."

"Aaaggghh!"

The meaning of Aaaggghh:

Well, what could Dad and Mom say? They knew all about talking fish and they didn't even have imaginations! All they could do was sit there and help Big Nose drink down her medicine.

And the principal sat there frowning and gromering, drumbling his desk and cluhearing his throat and looking at his paper weight, which wasn't very big and a gull full of buckshot would've done the job much better. I vowed to give him one as a present for graduating me. Grandma Matchie would be proud of that!

"And that assignment!" Big Nose cried, her hands pressed against his cheeks. "My Lord!"

My heart sank. Back to that again, eh? I knew right then I was finished. Turning to Dad I pleaded, "Summer vacation at the lake. I wrote it just like it happened and . . ."

And. It's a funny word, isn't it? I mean, everything follows naturally, doesn't it? It shows up everywhere, and there's nothing you can do about it. See? The whole world turned into "And" right then. And Dad's eyes bulgered, and Mom jippled out of her chair, her bum hitting the floor with a bathump. And Dad's cheeks bulgered, and Mom started repeating "Oh my, oh my oh my . . ." And Dad's head bulgered and I started getting real worried.

And, finally, when I could take it no more, I leaped to my feet and screamed: "It's all true!"

The point where you just can't take it no more and you scream: "It's all true!"

It was the second week of summer vacation at Rat Portage Lake. Dad had given up the art of fishing and was putting together his new jacuzzi in between bellowing at the ceiling and tearing at the instruction manual.

Mom finished sweepening up the forest trail out back and came in for a breather. "My! But that was dirty!" she breathed, wipering invisible sweat from her brow and leaning on her broom.

"Gothic in heaven, woman! You know the roof needs fixin— but off you go without a damn thought for anyone else! What happens if it rains and water leaks down on your daughter's forehead? What happens then, eh? She's sleepin away and it's drip, drip, drip! Pretty soon she's droolin and chanterin communist slogans!" He glared up from the pile of cedar planks. "What then, eh?"

"Oh, we'll put a bucket on her head long before that happens, dear," Mom replied dreamily, since she'd already seen the tiny hairball trying to sneak into the kitchen. Her knuckles went white on the broom handle, and she began creepering forward.

Out on the porch Sis ruckled in the old ruckling chair, staring out at the lake with a scowl. "I hate this," she kept saying over and over again. "I hate this. I hate everything about this and I hate you!" she hisspered at me.

The fire o' love had worn off, thank Gothic.

Her hair was now blue, bright like the sky and if there were any clouds they were all inside her head. Every now and then she reached up, her fingers all turembling, and touched it, then she'd dart her hand back down and start ruckling like mad. Crazy. Just plain crazy.

Hearing footsteps on the roof I went outside and stood in the middle of the driveway and looked up. "Hey, Grandma Matchie!"

She waved at me with the hammer, her mouth full of nails. Shingles sat in piles all around her like burnt pancakes and her yellow dress bilbowed brighter than the sun. I ran to the ladder and crawpelled up. The roof crucked and crackled as I walked across it to where she was working.

From the looks of it she'd finished patching the hole. Frowning, I asked, "What're ya doin?"

Around the nails she whispered: "Shhh! It's a disguise!"

Duckening down beside her I stared wildly about. "Who are ya spyin on?"

"Take a gander, Tike. The Major's island!" And with that she jerked her head ever so slitherly, her eyes squimbled to secret slits. "He's up t'no good! I can feel it in m'bones!"

"Which bones?"

"Never you mind. There's trouble in the air, can't you feel it?"

On his island, the Major was humbering back and forth between his dock and his cabin, carrying stuff down, packing it into the H.M.S. Hood, his blarny boat. And every now and then he'd take out his long spyin glass and study us, and when he did that Grandma Matchie'd bend down and pretend to be hammering nails, and I'd look down too with a big frown of concentration on my face.

"He's preparin fur war, that's what he's doin," Grandma Matchie muthered in a low voice, after checking the sky in case any gulls were trying to listen in. But the sky was empty.

"Against us?"

A shake of her head. "Uh uh. Somethin else I can't scry. But come mornin you can bet your toad ranch he'll be gone. Right dis'peared inta thin air!"

We heard screams coming from below and I looked down to see Mom runnering out onto the dock, waving Dad's fishing rod over her head like she was trying to swat a horsefly out of mid-air.

"What's wrong?" I cried, jumping to my feet.

Grandma Matchie squimted. "Damn girl! Sometimes I won-der how'n hell I . . ." Then she shook her head. "She's bein chased by a wasp, is my bet."

"Probably as big as the one Dad made last week," I said.

"Probbly is the one Dad made last week! Still tied t'the line!" Grandma Matchie threw back her head and let out a wild laugh.

And she was right. You could see the fishing line glittering every now and then in the sunlight, as Mom frantically whippled the rod over her head, screeking and runnering round in circles at the end of the dock. Then, with a mighty swing, she flung the wasp down into the water, and there was a huge saplash and sud-denly Mom was yelpering. A giant fish leapt out of the water and we could hear the drag winding as the fish raced out into the bay.

"Keep ridin im, Ester!" Grandma Matchie shouted, jumping to her feet and waving the hammer over her head. "Keep on ridin im! Ya-hoo!"

It was a tug-o-war as the fish brolled the surface again and again, throwing spray everywhere. And Mom had her hand on the reel now and was pumpening madly, her legs spread wide and bent inward at the knees. Even from here I could see the ter-ror in her wild eyes and if her high heels weren't stuck between the boards again she'd have been pulled right out into the water. But she pumped and she reeled, and the fish was dragged closer and closer, and suddenly it flew up and splanded right on the dock, flippening about between Mom's feet.

"Oh my! Oh my!" Mom plopped right out of her shoes and danced around, trying to avoid the slimy flippening fladapping fish. "Oh my!"

Running forward along the roof, Grandma Matchie gave one mighty jump and landed clear on the dock beside Mom. "You got im! You got im clean! Hah!" And with that she dived, grabbling the fish in a bear hug and they rambelled back and forth, strug-gling and torngling and grumting.

By the time I crawpelled down the ladder and raced around the corner of the cabin and down to the dock, Grandma Matchie had put the fish down for the count and was standing tri-umphantly above him, one boot on his gaspering head.

"Must be a hundred million ninety-nine pounds!" She shook her fist at him, and he mackled his eye and fladapped and squirmed feebly. "We got dinner t'night! Hah!"

And sure enough Mom put the pot on the stove and stoked up the fire until the water boiled crazily, and then she added salt and a whole load of potatoes. Dad put the fish in the sink and filled it up with buckets from the lake to keep him fresh until the time was good and right. I sat on a stool beside him and watched him glape, glape, glape.

Everything was just about ready when we heard a browl from the porch and we all ran outside to see Sis standing beside the ruckling chair, a mirror in her hand. Her face was turning every colour and so had her hair—yellow, red, mauve.

"Waaa!" Sis wayloned. "Waaa!"

Behind me I heard a funny fladapping sound, then a wild laugh.

Whirling, I tore into the kitchen. "Grandma Matchie!" I screamed. "The fish is getting away!" And there he was, pushing at the window latch. One of his eyes winked at me and he laughed again.

Grandma Matchie flew toward him but it was too late, because just then he got the window open and plungered over the sill.

"Aaak!" Mom squawked from the porch. "It's got my broom! Give me back my broom!"

We ran back out to the porch. A whufizzing sound came from over our heads and we ducked low. The fish had Mom's broom, all right, and he was flying on it all over the place, laughing hysterically.

He did one last loop then raced away into the west. Looking after him, Grandma Matchie put her hands on her hips and announced in a low voice: "That, Tike, was no ordernary fish."

Numberly, I shook my head.

"I've known a lotta fish in my day," she muttered, "but I ain't never known one like that!" And then she turned to me, shaking her head. "You ever heard a fish laugh like that? I never heared a fish laugh like that."

"Me neither," I said. "It sure was eerie."

Next morning, just as Grandma Matchie had predicted, the Major and the H.M.S. Hood were gone.

"Bad omens, Tike. Bad omens." Grandma Matchie paced up and down on the dock, while I sat with my feet in the water. "Too many strange thins goin on round here." Grimmerly, she stopped and faced me. "Jus list em! First that fish, laughin like some demon. Then Sis, gettin a hangnail as if from outa the blue! An those potaters didn' taste like they shoulda at all. An, the most Gothic damnin omen of all, Dad can't read those j'cuzzi 'structions—cause they're in French!" She began pacing again. "Nosiree, I don't like this one bit!"

"Where d'you think the Major went?" I asked.

Suddenizedly Grandma Matchie slapped her forehead. "O Course!" she whirled to me, her eyes burning merrily. "Why didn' I think of it afore? 'Course! That's gotta be it!" She began stramping up the dock, then paused to straighten her dress and glare at me, "Well, are ya comin, or what?"

I leapt to my feet. "You bet! Where?"

"Where? I'll tell ya where! We're goin after the Major!"

"But what about the demon fish? And Mom's broom?"

"They all went to th'same place, or my name ain't Grandma Matchie! An we're goin after em!"

"Where?" I asked again.

A shiver jampled across Grandma Matchie's shoulders like there was a snake in her dress, and her eyes narrowed as she glared out over the water. "We're goin t'the deepest lake on Earth! That's where we're goin!"

Well, it wasn't long after that that we packed all the essentials and readied ourselves for the trip. The deepest lake on Earth, I knew, was Westhawk Lake, over there in Manitoba. And it was made by a shooting star.

"Not just any old shootin star," Grandma Matchie said mysteriously, but she wouldn't explain any further, only a burning kind of look would come into her right eye, then jump across to her left eye, then back again and back again and back again until I got dizzy just watching it.

By the time we were ready it was almost dark. "Just right!" said Grandma Matchie as she stood at the end of the dock with

her hands on her hips. "An there ain't be no moon tonight, neither." she said, nodding grimmerly.

"How're we gettin there?" I asked.

"You jus keep your eyes peeled on the lake, Tike," she growbled, "an you'll see soon enough!" Bending down she checked
her backpack and I heard clinking come from inside it.

"What you got in there?"

"Canada's Finest Crayfish wine! That's what I got in there!"

By now it was night and the lake turned completely black,
looking like a giant hole going down forever. I watched it like
Grandma Matchie told me to do.

Then Mom and Dad and Sis came down from the cabin.

"Don't forget to bring back my broom!" Mom said, her hands
all fluppering and her cheeks glowing red in the darkness. "Oh
my! Look at the dirt on this dock!"

Sis's hair glowed neon green but no one said anything about
it so she wouldn't run off browling her eyes out. And there were
funny little twigs sticking out of it now, too. I thought back on it
and was pretty sure it wasn't me who stuck them in there, so they
must've grown naturally. Not that that made any sense, since Sis
is so dumb she likes taking baths all the time, unless the water
made those twigs grow better, I don't know.

"Don't you go brawlin bears this time, Grandma Matchie,"
Dad warned. "I don't wanta hear that my son has bin exposed to
that!" He paused, frowned and plungered his hand right into his
beard and scritching sounds came out. "You're s'posed t'be sensitive 'bout things with chil'ren, y'know. It's a turrible sight t'see
a creature of the furest cryin and beggin like that."

Grandma Matchie ignored him, thank Gothic. "Ready, Tike?"

I nodded and with that she turned to face the lake.

"All right! Come outa there you varmits! Afore I come down
there after ya!"

And it wasn't long before the lake started glowing, and the
water started burbbling and churmbling about. Then little streaks
of light began flashing around the dock. Peering down I shouted:
"Those are lampreys!" You could see their little helmets with
those lights in them, flashing around as they swam in crazy circles and started fleaping out of the water. Then two big ones

came up to the edge of the dock and poked their heads out.

"You two'll do jus fine!" Grandma Matchie said, then chackled, dancing a little jig.

It was then I noticed that she'd tied straps to her boots, with brass buckles. And all of a sudden Grandma Matchie jumped clear off the dock and landed right on those lampreys. She bent down and strappered her feet to their backs, while they wraggled fumeously. "Climber on my shoulders, Tike! There's only one beast on earth that knows the way t'Westhawk Lake—at least my Westhawk Lake—and that's a lamprey!"

So I climbered over her backpack and onto her shoulders and she grabbed my legs and yelled: "Here we go!"

Those lampreys surged forward and carveled deep grooves in the water, throaming white foam everywhere. The wind made my eyes tear and I leaned forward and stuck out my arms like you do in your Dad's Bronco when he's going a million thousand eighty-nine miles an hour and you got the windows rolled down.

"YA-HOO!" Me and Grandma Matchie hollered both at the same time. And again: "YA-HOOO!!" So it was just like the old timers at the lake always grumped about—these days the whole lake was filled with bluddy Ya-hoos. Old timers know everything, and they know what's true and what isn't, and the bigness of things doesn't scare them one bit.

'Course, Grandma Matchie's the oldest timer of all. "I was here when this lake couldn even lick your boots! An the whole world was jus swamp!" she'd say. "But them dinosaurs knew enough not t'mess with Grandma Matchie!" And she'd dance around like the Indians must've done when they tied string between all the trees and caused the extinction of the dinosaurs.

And boy did those lampreys swim. Lakes whizzled by and when we came to the shore we just leapt high in the air and when we landed again it was in another lake. And then we crossed a big red line painted on the surface of the water and we were in Manitoba, which didn't look much different from Ontario except for all the buffalo swimming around. 'Course, they got out of our way! Hah!

And then, just as the sun was coming up in front of us, we stopped.

"This is Hunt Lake, Tike," Grandma Matchie said as she unstrapped her boots. "An right over there on th'other side a those trees is Westhawk Lake. The deepest lake on Earth!"

"Are we gonna sneak up on it from here?"

"Yep. We gotta. There's demon fish spyin 'round all over th' place!" Off we jumped, hitting the water with huge splashes and going straight down to the muddy bottom. Then we started tuddling, the water around us getting lighter and lighter and the bottom getting weedier and weedier as we crelpt toward shore. But all of a sudden a big black hole loombered in front of us and we planged into darkness.

"A secret cave!" I exclaimed.

Grandma Matchie paused to light a torch, since the lampreys had gone home, and the fire made the water swirl with burbbles and the walls of the cave spackle as if they were full of gold.

We tuddled a long ways when Grandma Matchie stopped suddenly and crouched. "There's somebuddy skulkin up ahead!" she hisspered, and we began edging forward.

We could see a light coming from around a corner further up the path, and Grandma Matchie put out her torch and ever so snuckily we came to the corner and peepered around it.

Grandma Matchie shouted and jumped forward and I followed, because there sat the Major, boiling tea over a fire right in the middle of a giant cavern. His eyes poppled out and he leapt off his camp stool.

"Gads! It's Grandma Matchie!"

"So there you are, eh? Jus as I figured—skulkin 'bout like the good-fur-nothin Major you are!" Grimmerly, she stalked toward him and he shrank back for a second then puffed up his chest and stood his ground. Grandma Matchie kept coming until their noses jambled together, the point of hers pludging into the red bulb of his. "Good fur nothin Major!"

"Hah! And what 'bout you, hah? Spiteful ole witch!"

"Spiteful? Ain't I got reason t'be?"

"What ho? Reason? Whenever d'you need a bleedin reason?"

Uh oh, thinks I. "Hey!" I shouted. Their heads turned at the same time and you could hear the Major's nose pop back out.

Glaring at them with my hands on my hips, I said in my lowest, meanest voice: "Tea's ready."

And it was, and we all sat down round the fire and poured ourselves a cup. After a time Grandma Matchie sniggered, "So, you're goin after er again, eh? Well, if you're one thing, Major, it's stubbern!" And she tilted her head back and shouted: "Stubbern as a loaf of Ester's bread in a bear's belly! Hah!"

The Major glommered and his face got redder than the fire between them. "Cripes! It's none o' yer bizness! None!"

"Oh, an ain't it, now? Ain't it? Well, somethin's saying t'me we're agoin after the same thin in the end. An jus like all th'other times you're agoin t'get in the way, afoulin thins up for alla us!"

Spluttering, the Major surged to his feet. "ME!" He began waving his fists around, making swirmbling currents so big even the fire pafted and wavered. "I got ere first! I did! I did!"

"It don't matter one bit!" Grandma Matchie was on her feet now, too, and the fire shrank between them. "Yer daughter ain't got er broom stolen, did she? You ain't even got a daughter!"

"I do too! I do too!"

All of a sudden Grandma Matchie sat down, looking shocked. Then she got a hold of herself and glared at him. "So he finally admits it at last, eh? Well, isn't this a pretty picture! A father, aren't ya? Afta all these years! Now you're a father!"

"An whenever di'you lemme be one, hah? Hah?"

I didn't know what in blazes they were talking about, so I stood up. "Hey! Tell me some stories! Tell me some stories! You said we gotta wait till mornin, anyway! I wanta hear some stories!" And I put on my best little poor boy face and made my eyes real wide and pleading like.

'Course it worked! It always does!

"The Major ain't gotta story in his hat worth picken!" Grandma Matchie sneerved.

"Hah! Is that right, is it? Is it? Well, I done thins that'll make yer stories look like they came from a Grade Fur Reader!"

"Iz that right?" Grandma Matchie leaned back and crossed her arms. "Okay, Major," she said in a low dangerous voice. "Let's hear yer story! Come on, give it yer best! Hah!"

Pulling out a pipe, the Major settled himself in his stool and gave me a wink. And all at once his voice changed, getting all gravelly like Long John Silver's: "Well, it wuz afore yer time, there, lad. Afore alla yer times"—Grandma Matchie snarted but the Major kept going—"in th' Nort Sea, aye, an ya ain't seen waves as high o'those back then! An there I be, out fishin like a lad did in those days. An I was abaitin and ahookin an me boat wuz agettin lower'n lower wi' all the fish I wuz catchin. An in I throws the line, one last time, y'see, cause the waves wuz gettin a little big e'en fer the likes o' me—pullin down stars they were, makin em hiss and sputter in all kinds of steam!"

He was rocking back and forth on his stool and I could feel those waves making my stomach gasp like it was drowning.

"An then me line wen tight an started arunnin through me hands till smoke came out frum atwixt me fingers!" And he put his hand over his pipe and puffed crazily to show me what it must've looked like. "Aye, I'd ahooked the biggest thin that lives in the sea. She's gotta a thousand names, that sea snake, an ev'ry man, woman, and child o' the sea shakes when they 'ear em! Aye, so big she wen right round the whole world, akeepin all that water from aspillin out! So big she has t'bite er own tail so she knows where it is!" And he blew smoke rings that got bigger and bigger as they floated to the roof of the cave.

"No wonder the sea's astormin, thinks I," the Major went on, leaning forward so his face glowed in the fire. "I bin afishin er own back yard! Deprivin er a er own food! But I wuz a fisherman then jus like I am now! An I started apullin on that line wi' all the strength in me young bones. An sure 'nough, up she comes, slow'n 'eavy, though still I cain't see er.

"Thirty-one days and thirty-two nights I'm adraggin up that line, eatin the fish in m'boat wi' one hand an apullin wi' t'other! Drinkin me own sweat when I got t' thirstin! An nineteen times 'roun the world she pulls me in that time, aye, an I seen sights the likes o' which no one's ev'ry seen afore!

"An so there I wuz, on th'thirty-third day and comin fer the twentieth time 'roun the world—an I finally sees er! Right there! Right there unner me boat!" And he points his pipe down and I look, but all I can see is the floor of the cave. "Aye," the Major chuckled. "That's all I seen, too! 'Er body's hard as rock an as fer across as the Kalahari Sea!"

"But the Kalahari's a desert in Africa!"

"Only after we apasst through it," replied the Major, his eyes gleaming. "She threw up so much water it plumb emptied the bowl! But where wuz I? Oh, aye, I seen er, an all at onct I drop that line and dive inta the sea!"

I jumped to my feet. "Did you get her?"

The Major nodded grimly. "Aye, that I did." He spread his arms wide. "I grabbed er like this, apulled er 'cross me boat's thwarts. An she asquirmed and aslithered! But I held tight! An I heered er cryin and a'whimperin, an I realise't right then an there that I gotta let er go." He bowed his head. "I gotta let er go." After a minute he looked up, and his eyes were full of tears. "Y'know why, lad?"

I shook my head.

"I coulda took er, right then an there, but I realise't alla sudden that if I did, the seas'd empty an all th'water'd drain away! So I letter go and I cut me line, right then an there!"

"Bah!" Grandma Matchie scoffed. "You call that a story? I coulda done better in my sleep!"

But the Major just leaned back and chuckled, relighting his pipe.

"An I ain't gotta go to no North Sea t'find my story, neither, cause it happened right here!" She leaned forward, her elbows on her bony gongly knees that peekered out from under her dress. "Ten thousand years ago, it was, when the buff'lo filled the lakes from shore t'shinin shore! Buff'lo so big they left mountains behind em, if y'know what I mean, Tike . . ."

I nodded, grinning snuckily.

"An if anyone ever asks you where the Rockies came from, you tell em 'bout the buff'lo an all the seaweed they et."

I nodded again, thinking about how impressed Big Nose would be when I actually knew the right answer to one of her questions.

"Yessiree, Tike, those were big buff'lo, an the Indians in these ere parts et their fill a them an made huts outa their skulls, an the buff'lo didn't mind one bit!

"But then one day the Indians look up and see alla the buff'lo are gone, an there's bones everywhere! Fillin the lakes so deep the bones at th'bottom turned right into stone, an if ever someone asks you where Tyndal Stone comes from, you tell em 'bout the bones, Tike, an they'll know you fer a wise man. An so, the Indians they start gettin worried, cause someone's et all the buff'lo, an this was way afore Buff'lo Bill's time, way afore Chris C'lumbus even!

"Not knowin what else t'do, them Indians turned t'me for help, like they always did back then. Only this time it was more serious than e'er afore. An not only were the buff'lo gone but so was the beaver and the bear and the deer and the mastodons—all gone!" Grandma Matchie paused to smirk at the Major, who was puffing madly on his pipe and studying the walls. "Aye, so I start lookin fer signs, tracks, giant toothpicks with mammoth meat on em, an sure 'nough I pick up a mysterious trail, leadin north inta the back country. An I follows it fer days, till I come to this giant log cabin, tweeny storeys tall, wi' bones piled up alla round it and smoke comin from the chimney."

"Who lived there?" I demanded.

"I'm gettin t'that! Some thins you jus can't rush. So, up I go, right up t'that door and I starts poundin on it. 'Whoever's in there better come out if'n know what's good fer ya!' I scream. Then I heered these footsteps crossin the floor in there, louder'n all the thunder rolled up in one! An the door opens up . . ." Grandma Matchie paused to sip delicately at her tea.

"And? And?"

She smackled her lips. "An there he be, wi' me towerin over im! Wasn't no more'n five feet tall, but wearin the biggest boots I e'er seen!

"'Who in hell are you?' the little man screams. An I says, 'I'm your doom, little man! Come on outa there, you puny runt!' Well, he goes all white, then red, an out he stomps, shakin his fists. 'I was sleepin, damn you!' shrills the squirt, all indignant like. But I laugh in his face."

"How brave!" the Major snickered.

Ignoring him, Grandma Matchie continued, "This? thinks I, this is the one who et all those buff'lo?"

"An all those beaver and bear and deer and mastodons, too?" I cried uncredulously.

Grandma Matchie nodded. "Aye, them too? asks I. An I was gettin all ready t'give im the spankin of his life, when he jumps over to the biggest tree I e'er seen an pulls it up by the roots! An he starts swingin it like it was a twig! 'Nobody wakes me up!' he roars an if I didn't jump outa the way right then I wouldn't be ere telling this tale t'day! He hit the ground wi that tree so hard it split it right open from horizon to horizon! An if anyone e'er asks you where the Winnipeg River came from, now you know."

Boy, no more D's in Geography for Jock Junior! Not after all this!

"'So! It's threats, is it?' screams I. 'I arm wrassled Satan Himself t'the ground an I can do the same wi you!' So we grab each other's wrists and sit down right there an the runt yells: 'GO!' an the wrasslin started." Grandma Matchie sipped more tea. "Tree hundred years we sat there, locked t'gether, neither a us givin an inch! An grass grew up alla round us an snow covered us an birds nested on our heads. An that little man's cabin rotted away to nothin an all those bones turned to chalk dust and blew away . . ."

"An right into Big Nose's classroom!" I shouted.

"An right inta Big Nose's classroom, yep. An then trees growed up alla round us. An that little man couldn't budge me, an that was jus the way I wanted it . . ."

"Hah!" barked the Major.

"Jus the way I wanted it," Grandma Matchie repeated. "'Cause by now all th'buff'lo had come back, an all th'beaver an bears an deer an mastodons, too!"

"Of course!" I laughed. What a plan!

"But finally I start gettin turd a the whole thin, an wi the world back t'normal I figured it's time t'put the little man in his place. So I give it what I need to wrassle his arm t'the ground. Only he's bin sittin there so long, an strainin so long, that he's near turned t'stone! So—snap! His arm comes right off at the shoulder, an he didn't e'en twitch! But it awoked im up anyway, and up he stands, shaking his head.

"An he says: 'I ain't never known anyone who coulda done

that t'me! Not even'"—and Grandma Matchie sneered at the Major—"'not even when I tied the sea snake's head to her tail!'"

"Liar!" screamed the Major, flying to his feet. "That's not how One Armed Trapper lost his arm at all! Liar!"

Leapening to her own feet Grandma Matchie clenched her fists and shouted: "I am not a liar! It was me who broke his arm off!"

"It was me! I did it long afore you!"

"You did not!"

"Yes I did!"

Well, it was obvious to me that this was never going to end, and I was exhausted, so I crawpelled off into a corner, and the shouting and boasting and accusing all jambled together as I fell asleep.

And next morning it was even worse. There were empty bottles of Canada's Finest all over the floor of the cave, brolling here and there in the lurzy currents. And Grandma Matchie and the Major weren't even talking to each other, and they wouldn't tell me nothing so I never found out who ended up with One Armed Trapper's arm.

The three of us packed up camp and started up the trail, going deeper and deeper into the cave. Pretty soon there were steps carved into the rock, going down. So down we went, nobody talking, nobody smiling. I just got sick of it and pushed ahead of them, holding the torch out in front of me.

The gold specks in the rock got bigger until they stuck out from the walls in nuggets, looking as soft as chewing gum. I remembered seeing some movie about these three guys in some desert who did nothing but try and kill each other over a whole pile of gold, and I remembered how one of them bit into one of the nuggets, so lots of people are fooled into thinking it's chewing gum. The only other thing I could remember from that movie was this fat guy saying: "Badges, we don't need to steenking badges!"

Neither did we, and we didn't even care about all that gold. Gold? We don't need no steenking gold!

Finally I couldn't take it any more and I whirled around: "Will you two . . ." And there I stopped, glaping. They were holding hands! And they didn't even pull them away when I saw it!

"'Will you two'—what?" Grandma Matchie asked, smiling.

I tried to say something but the words gaggled in my throat. And after a minute I turned back to the trail, all my delusions shattered. It was awful!

"Hold up there, Tike," Grandma Matchie warned. "We're gettin close!"

Up ahead I could see reflected sunlight. Westhawk Lake! Thank Gothic! I felt like I was going to die! And they didn't even look embarrassed! You'd think when someone got that old they'd know better.

Putting out the torch, we creepered to the edge of the opening. And there were stairs leading almost straight down, disappearing into the blackness. They looked like they went down forever . . . and even farther.

"Are we going down?" I asked, peepering over the edge.

"Yep, but first we gotta make sure there ain't no demon fish lurkin 'bout." Grandma Matchie's eyes narrowed to slits and she glared around. "I don't see none."

"Me neither," muttered the Major. "It's a bad sign, if'n you ask me!"

"Aye . . ." Grandma Matchie made one last sweep with her eyes then straightened up and squared her shoulders. "Let's go!"

She took the lead, then me and then the Major. Down, down, and down some more, until the darkness turned the water into ink, and still we kept going down. The water went icy cold, then hot, then cold again. And little crayfish swambled around on the steps, wearing fur coats, so we had to watch our feet all the time. And then, slowly but surely, the water grew warmer, and a faint reddish glow seepened up from below, getting brighter and brighter.

"What's that?" I asked.

"Comes from the heart o' the Earth, lad," the Major hisspered behind me. "We're almost there!"

"Who lives down there?" I whispered back.

"Shhh!"

Now, I don't care how old or how small I am, I don't take "shhh" for an answer to anything. "Who's down there!?" I cried, making echoes run off in all directions. The Major swore but Grandma Matchie glared at him.

"Tike knows one thin, Major, and now you do, too. 'Shhh' don't count. Ever!" And with that she nodded at me. "Problem now is, she'll know we're comin, and there ain't a thin we're gonna do 'bout it, neither!"

It wasn't long afterward that glowing spots of light swam up toward us. Demon fish, riding the backs of lampreys, only these weren't the normal kind of lampreys at all. They were as long as snakes, glowing from the inside out, and their round mouths had a thousand million seven hundred twenty-one sharp teeth prangled up inside, stickering out everywhere. And the demon fish laughed at us, coming close then darpling away, hounding us all the way until we reached the floor of the lake. Then they raced off ahead of us and soon disappeared into the red gloom.

"She'll be waitin," Grandma Matchie announced grimmerly.

"Who?"

Turning to me, she said, "One Armed Trapper's mom, that's who. Lunker's her name, an she's the biggest pike you e'er seen!"

"She's more'n that!" the Major growbled. "She's the heart o' the land! An a thousand years ago she ruled us all!"

"So she'd like t'think!" Grandma Matchie scowlered.

Glommering at her, the Major jutted out his chin. "You talk now! but I didna heared you back then, did I."

"She ain't ruled nobody who wasn't ready t'be ruled!" Grandma Matchie snapped. "You ne'er saw me lickin er fins, didja?"

"I ain't ne'er once licked those fins!"

"Hah!"

And before they could continue we heard rumbling, growing bigger by the second. The Major reached into his pack and pulled out a tiny fishin' pole with a tinier hook and an even tinier worm hanging limply from it.

"So!" Grandma Matchie laughed. "Y'think you're finally good 'nough, now, do ya?" And she laughed again. "But I better tellya, Major, you weren't that good!" she added, smirkelling.

The Major's face went red and he began fiddling with his fishin' reel, muthering and grummerling.

Turning to stare off into the distance where all the rumbling and all the red light was coming from, Grandma Matchie frowned and said, "But I got more important problems t'think 'bout. There's questions that gotta be answered, there is. And a 'course there's Ester's broom to get back!" She faced the Major again. "You don't go doin nothin stupid afore I'm done, y'hear?"

"Bahhh!"

"Let's get goin!" And with that Grandma Matchie began stramping forward. The floor was flat and warm under my sneakers and seemed to stretch off forever in all directions. Pretty soon we started passing schools of demon fish with big-nosed teachers running about ringing giant brass bells, and we saw older demon fish walking pet lampreys around on leashes, standing round fire hydrants and mail boxes whenever the lampreys stopped for a sniff or two, or lifted a short stubby fin while looking off in some other direction.

But everyone stopped what they were doing to watch us pass, and they laughed and snickered and hisspered to each other, and the lampreys barked madly and strained at their leashes. And after a while we came to a big door, barred like a cage, and the rumbling came from beyond it.

Grandma Matchie's frown deepened. "This weren't here afore, nosiree. I don't like it one bit!"

Even the Major looked worried. "I ain't bin down 'ere in a thousand years, so it must've bin built recently. Freshly painted, too! A bad sign, aye!"

The rumbling stopped suddenly, but the silence was even worse. Grimmerly, Grandma Matchie pushed the doors open and in we walked. In front of us was a huge hall, with a domed ceiling that glittered every colour I'd ever seen and then some. And there, at the end of the hall, sat Lunker on her throne— which was carved from a mountain—smiling evilly down on us. Raising a bejewelled fin, she beckoned.

"Come closer, dearies! Come closer!" And her voice crackled like the crackle when you crumple cellophane in the toilet. Just like that. "I've been expecting you!"

Boy was she big. Almost as big as Satan Himself. Wearing a huge purple robe and a glittering crown made out of giant Red

Devils. And she had a million thousand seventy-two sticks worth of lipstick smeared round her mouth, and thick splatches of red on her gills, and false eyelashes made from pine boughs, and bright red hair wavering about like a burning volcano. And her teeth were longer even than the sleeves of Dad's woolen sweater after he's slipped on spilled chocolate pudding and fallen in the lake.

"You're lookin good, Lunker," Grandma Matchie said, walking into the middle of the room. "As pretty as a picture!"

Some picture, I was thinking to myself as I followed behind her and the Major.

"So you've finally come back to me, eh Grandma Matchie?" Lunker chackled. "You haven't been down here since I threw you out of my court two thousand years ago!"

Grandma Matchie chackled right back. "An it's bin feelin pretty empty e'er since, I bet!"

Lunker fluthered her eyelashes and rolled her china-plate eyes at the ceiling. "Yesss," she drawled, stifling a yawn. "I suppose jesters come in handy—even in this court. Too bad your tongue's too sharp for your own good, isn't it, Grandma Matchie?"

She sunorted in reply then looked around critically. "Well, it hasn't changed much from in here, I see." Then she gazed shrewdly at Lunker. "But that cage door's a new one, ain't it? Afeared a assassins, mebee?"

Lunker's eyes flashed, then dimmed as she let out a long sigh. "Times change, Grandma Matchie." Turning her head slightly she regarded the Major, who stood there with bent knees, holding his fishin' pole tightly with both hands in front of him. "Why, Major! What we have there!"

"Where?" the Major's voice was high and cracking.

"Why, in your hands, of course."

Looking down, the Major screamed as if he'd been holding a snake and threw the rod down, staring at it in horror.

Lunker chackled. "Still full of delusions of grandeur, I see. Oh well, and then there are some things that never change!"

The Major gasped and panted, still staring at the rod at his feet.

"And," Lunker continued, "it seems we have another guest!"

Uh oh, thinks I.

"Come forward, child! Let me see you more clearly! These eyes aren't what they once were, you know."

So I did.

Lunker reached around with her fins and pulled her gown tighter about her, then leaned forward. "And what's your name, child?"

"Jock Junior, and I'm not a child!"

Lunker's eyes widened and for a minute there I thought she was going to galobble me up in one bite. But with Grandma Matchie behind me I wasn't scared. Not scared at all!

"I'm so sorry! Jock Junior, you must forgive my failing eyesight! Of course I can see now that you're not a child! Yesss, you're something else, aren't you? Something more, maybe?"

"By my daughter," Grandma Matchie said.

"A daughter! And a grandson! Oh my! I have been down here too long, haven't I?"

"Nobody's missin you, far as I can tell," Grandma Matchie replied, her eyes blazening.

But Lunker just sighed again and half closed her eyes, and Grandma Matchie gave a little gasp, because you could tell she'd been expecting fire and brimstone.

"You've hit the proverbial nail on the head, there, Grandma Matchie," Lunker said, and if you've ever seen a pike smile kindly then you're one up on me. Though she tried! She really did! "And this brings us to the matter at hand, now, doesn't it?"

"You took somethin an I want it back!" Grandma Matchie said, stepping forward.

"Ohhh, yes! An item of laborious obsession, I believe?"

"A buhloody broom!" Grandma Matchie snarped.

"Of course. A broom. Well," Lunker sighed, lifting a corner of her robe and pulling out Mom's broom. She eyed it critically. "Oh, the awful things to be found in a broom!" she exclaimed, wrinkling her nose. "Oh dear, Horatio, you'll never know what you missed!" Then she put it on her lap. "It has served its purpose, I suppose. And since it's hardly the kind of trophy you'd mount on a wall, I suppose I can return it to its rightful owner."

And with that she beckoned and a demon fish appeared out of a small hole in one of the walls and scurried to her side. Lunker whispered a few words and handed the broom to the demon fish, who took it and disappeared. Facing us again, Lunker said: "There! Now that that's done, we can get down to business!"

"What kinda buzness?" Grandma Matchie demanded suspiciously.

"I'm not likin the sounds o' this," the Major muthered glumly, and I had to nod agreement.

"It's all really very simple, actually," Lunker leaned back in her rock throne and made a small gesture with one of her fins. "A minor inconvenience to take care of, and with your kindly assistance it'll be no great task." And she reached down and grabbed the hems of her long robe. "I simply need help in removing— these!" And with that she pulled up her robe.

We all gaspered, not because we'd never seen a pike's panties before (mind you, I don't think I ever had), even ones Royal Purple. No, we gaspered because there were giant black chains wrapped round Lunker, with their ends padlocked to the floor.

"Well, well!" Grandma Matchie exclaimed, her eyebrows raised. "Now, whoever would've done such a thin!"

Lunker grimaced. "Who else? My own son, of course."

I stared at her. "One Armed Trapper!?"

"Oh, then you've met him, have you, Jock Junior?"

"Met him! He come near to doin us in! For good!"

Sighing, Lunker let her robe fall down over the ghastly scene she'd shown us, and leaned back in her throne. "It follows, naturally. With me out of the way, One Armed Trapper's ready to play! He's flexing the muscles on that lone arm of his, I should hazard to presume. Really very unfortunate, isn't it?"

"More'n that!" Grandma Matchie gritted, starting to pace. "He'll be wreakin spite on us all afore long! Damn!"

"That explains why none o' us heared from you 'n ages!" the Major mused, rubbing his whiskered jaw. "Not a story, not e'en a whisper!"

Lunker's eyes flashed for the briefest of moments, then she shrugged. "And everyone's no doubt been lamenting on how silent their land is to their frail pleas. After all, you can't tell there's roots in the ground unless you see a shoot, or in this particular case, a tree. Such things pain me from time to time, but as you have seen, there's really very little I can do about it. Until, of course," and Lunker paused to duck her head forward, "I'm freed!"

"Aye, so you sent fer us by stealin Ester's broom—knowin we'd come after it! You always bin a sneakeny one, ain't ya?"

Lunker shrugged modestly, saying nothing though a spark flashed again in her eyes.

"An I bet One Armed Trapper's got the key to that lock!" I exclaimed.

"Very astute of you, Jock Junior! The problem, then, is: how will you get it from him? We can be certain that he's not likely to lay it at your feet with a shy smile and a bow!"

Grandma Matchie stopped pacing suddenly, looked up at all of us with a gleamy shivering in her eyes. "It's quite simple, now that I done some thinkin on it. Easy pickins for the three a us!" And she let out a wild chackle that echoed through the chamber.

"Pray tell!" Lunker exclaimed breathlessly. "Share with us your genius!"

Grinning, Grandma Matchie winked at me. "We gotta present t'im an offer he can't refuse! An all it takes is the right kinda bait!" She whirled to the Major: "You! You gotta do us jus one thin, an your part'll be done!"

The Major blanched, his eyes darting. "What?" he asked weakly.

"Easy, lad, don't ferget you're the Major an none other!" And you could see him swell his chest out at that. "So here's what you gotta do. Climb inta that blarny boat a yours an take out fast as y'can for th' North Sea . . ."

"What!?" the Major's chest collapsed and his knees started wobblering.

"That's right. The North Sea. An drop that fishin line a yours inta the deep . . ."

"For the love o' Mike, why?"

Grandma Matchie's grin grew savage. "You gotta un-do what One Armed Trapper done, long ago! You gotta untie the sea snake's tail from er head!"

"But, won't all the water run away, then?" I cried.

"Nope. That ole she-devil was bitin her tail long afore One Armed Trapper played that turrible trick on er, Tike! She ne'er did need any help holdin the oceans in, right, Major?"

"Eh?" The Major looked up, startled out of some pit of terror. "Eh?"

"Never mind," Grandma Matchie said, then turned to me. "You'n me, Tike, we gotta handle th'other thin, an it won't be as easy as what the Major's gotta do! But there's two a us, ain't there?" And she roared a laugh that sent waves through the water.

It was only a second before I threw back my own head and laughed almost as loud as she'd done. When there's important things to be done, you just got to be in the right frame of mind, Grandma Matchie always told me. And she's right. So we danced a little jig on our way out of the throne room, leaving the Major and Lunker behind.

And the journey took seven days and eight nights, riding the backs of lampreys all the way, until finally we came to the sandy shore of Lake Winnipeg, and stood there watching the dawn turn that muddy water into sun-lipped fiery gold.

Lake Winnipeg's as big as an ocean, I bet, because we couldn't even see the other side, even when I got up on Grandma Matchie's shoulders while she got up on mine and we added it all together to make us exactly twenty feet tall.

After breakfast Grandma Matchie picked up a piece of driftwood from the beach and pulled out her whittlin' knife and carved up a horn, which she then put to her lips and blew as hard as she could. And that moaning cry went out a thousand million two hundred nine fifty miles in all direction, going right round the Earth and coming back to us as loud as it was when it left.

Then we waited.

At high noon Grandma Matchie jumped up from the log she'd been sitting on and cried: "Here they come, Tike!"

Looking out over the lake I could see the dust cloud rising up on the horizon, and then a terrible rumble shivered up my legs and rappled my bones, and the lake got all chipchoppy and murky. It wasn't long after that when we could see them plain as day. All the buffalo in the world, crossing that lake in answer to Grandma Matchie's call. And these weren't regular buffalo, either. These were buffalo from ten thousand years ago—big as garbage trucks.

The next time you see a garbage truck in your back lane try and imagine it covered in shaggy brown hair, with big horns coming out of the cab. Go do that then come back, so that way I'll know you know what I mean when I say they were as big as hairy garbage trucks.

But the one leading the stampede was even bigger. Glue two garbage trucks together and glue a VW Bug on top and paint its headlamps to look like angry red eyes. Then go down to the river and find an old sofa that somebody threw away and pull out all the muddy filling and come back and paste it to the trucks and the Bug. Go do that then come back, okay?

When that stampede got close enough so that I could almost smell those buffalo, Grandma Matchie blew that horn again and they all came to a splashing stop right on the edge of the lake. And the big bull stomped forward, snorting fire from his nostrils and glavering murderously at Grandma Matchie.

"Whadya want?" the king buffalo demanded in a voice that sounded just like you'd figure a buffalo's voice would sound if that buffalo was as big as two garbage trucks glued together with a VW Bug for a head. He pawed the shallows and snorted some more.

"Well, well," said Grandma Matchie, grinnering. "No kind words for your old friend who's come to pay you a visit?"

The king buffalo just grunted.

Turning to me, Grandma Matchie said, "Tike, I'd like you meet Bjugstad, the buff'lo of buff'los!"

"Hello," I said respectfully.

"An this, Bjugstad, is Jock Junior. Grunt 'hello,' Bjugstad, afore I brain ya!"

Bjugstad grunted and fire blasted from his nostrils. "Brain me, ay? I'd like t'see ya try!"

"You will," Grandma Matchie promised, folding her arms. "Y'see, Bjugstad, this ain't jus a frienly visit for ole time's sake. I've come t'bring you all back wi' me! One Armed Trapper's on the rampage again an he's got Lunker chained up in er throne room. And you gotta come wi' us, or else!"

"We'll see about that!" And Bjugstad bunched his shoulders and tore huge gouts of muck from the lake bottom as he plawed, plawed, plawed. And then he roared and flames poured out and turned all the water into steam for miles around.

Grandma Matchie roared back a challenge and hunched her shoulders and, ducking her head, charged. And then Bjugstad charged, and they were going straight for each other.

Everything you could think of and pile together happened when they collided. There was lightning, and thunderous shock waves, and fire, and steam, and mud, and falling trees, and tidal waves, and volcanoes, and birds scattering everywhere from swamps like you see in movies about Africa, and lots of other things you should think about before I go on.

When the smoke cleared there was Grandma Matchie, standing over Bjugstad with her hands on her hips. "I tole you you was comin wi' us!"

Bjugstad didn't even have the strength to grunt. He just lobbled there, panthing with his white tongue hanging on the ground. All the other buffalo muthered and grumbled but couldn't do much else since most of them were dog-paddling like crazy. After a while Bjugstad was able to stand up, and then me and Grandma Matchie climbed up behind his head and sat down on his hairy shoulders.

"Now it's your turn, Tike," Grandma Matchie said over her shoulder. "I gotta be steerin Bjugstad wi' an iron hand so he don't try nothin. An you gotta keep your eyes peeled in case someone tries somethin."

"Who?"

"Mebee One Armed Trapper, mebee someone else. I got an itchin there's more to this than what meets the eye. I gotta suspicious nature, Tike, and right now I'm smellin more'n the fact that Bjugstad here don't know anythin 'bout takin baths."

Putting her heels to Bjugstad's flanks, we jolted forward and were on our way. And all the buffalo followed, pushing up onto land even though you could tell by all the crashbanging and all the swearing that they didn't like solid ground one bit. Nosiree, give a buffalo a bridge and he'll jump right off it.

Fishing for buffalo's dangerous business, as Grandma Matchie told me last summer when we went trolling for them in Shoal Lake. You got to know what kind of weeds to snag on your hook, too. Not any old weed will do, because buffalo will be the first to tell you they have sophisticated tastes.

Seven days and eight nights it took us to get back to Westhawk Lake, and we didn't see One Armed Trapper or anyone else the whole way, which had Grandma Matchie frowning something fierce.

Boy did those buffalo cheer when they plungered into that lake, and it wasn't long before you couldn't even see the water for all the buffalo heads. All the people who had cottages went down to their docks and shook their fists and tore their hair, but it didn't help one bit.

Bjugstad took us right out to the middle and then we dived down, swimming and swimming until we finally reached the bottom, where all the demon fish and lampreys scattered in panic. Hooves thumpening the rock, up we marched to Lunker's cage door, and with a tap from Bjugstad's head the doors flew open and once again we were face to face with Lunker.

"Is the Major back yet?" Grandma Matchie asked, all business like.

"No, I'm afraid not." Lunker sighed, all depressed.

Grandma Matchie rubbed her jaw. "One Armed Trapper been down here lately?"

"Oh, yes!" Lunker's fins wriggled in sudden excitement. "In fact, he's here now!"

Bjugstad groaned. "Great, that's just great!" And you could hear his knees knocking.

Just then we heard a scream from outside and the sound of running footsteps. Spinning around, we saw the Major stumble into the room. "I done it!" he cried. "Hee hee! I done it!"

"'Course you did," Grandma Matchie snapped. "You're the Major, ain't ya?"

The Major's navy blues was all in tatters, and his hair stuck out in all directions. And his nose blazed red, too. "You should seen me!" he exclaimed, all breathless. "That was the biggest knot I e'er did see! An it was days o' strugglin an . . ."

"Save it for another time!" Grandma Matchie griped, turning back to Lunker. "Did you say what I thought you said? One Armed Trapper's here, now?"

"Oh yes. He is. Isn't that a wonderful coincidence?"

"I don't like the sounds o' that," the Major muthered, all serious now.

"Me neither," Grandma Matchie grumpled, eyeing Lunker like you would a wood tick.

"And now that we're all here," Lunker smiled, her teeth grivdening together with pleasure. "We can get down to business!" And with that a door opened behind her and in stepped One Armed Trapper, grinning from ear to ear, and even though he had the biggest ears I've ever seen, the grin was bigger.

"Hah?" the Major cried. "We bin tricked!"

And it was true, because up stood Lunker then, and all those chains just fell away, and she was smiling even harder, and those fangs were grivdening so much that dust drifted away on the current in a white cloud.

"Now that I've got all the story-tellers here, in one place, I can put an end to them once and for all! And I'll have all the stories myself! Or, rather, my story will be the only one anyone will ever hear in this land! My power will be complete! Ha ha ha ha ha ha!"

One Armed Trapper began advancing toward us, black chains dangling from his hand. "Joy, oh joy!" he crooned. "Now even the old tale about the sea snake is done with, and we can all forget about her, too!" His eyes burned merrily. "It was a childish prank of mine, in the days of my youth. Had I known better . . ."

"Had you known better," Lunker snarled, "you would have listened to me!" Then she smiled again. "Of course, now all that's taken care of, thanks to Grandma Matchie's cunning little brain." And she flaclapped her fins. "Isn't it simply wonderful how all things come round in the end!"

All this time Grandma Matchie's eyes had been narrow like slits, and sparks flashered out of them every now and then.

Bjugstad's bones rattled so bad I figured he would fall to pieces under us, so off I crawpelled and stood beside him.

The Major had fullen to his knees and was whimpering and bawbling his eyes out. Disgusted, I decided to ignore him.

"Only one story to tell!" Lunker laughed. "And it's mine! All mine! And you'll hear it from border to border, shore to shore, shining sea to shining sea! You'll hear it even more than you do already! Oh, I'm so proud!"

"Grandma Matchie!" I cried. "You can't let her get away with this!"

She leaned forward on Bjugstad's shoulders. "I left this place once, Lunker," she gritted, "an you couldn't stop me then!"

"Oh, but then One Armed Trapper wasn't with me, was he? This time you won't get away, I'm afraid." And she shook her head in sorrow, all her red hair flowing about like fire.

Grandma Matchie frowned. "You gotta point, there, Lunker. But somethin's bin itchin me, so's I gotta ask. There's more'n jus you two involved 'ere, ain't there?"

Lunker fluthered her eyelashes, looking down. "Well, I must admit that our mutual dragon acquaintance, Satan Himself, was very helpful in the formulation of our plans . . ."

"I knew it." Grandma Matchie drove her fist into the palm of her hand. "He's bin meddlin all along!" Then she shook her head, frowning again. "Somethin's gripin him . . . wonder what?"

All this time I was thinking fast, real fast because time was running out for all of us. And I studied Lunker, narrowing my eyes like the cowboys do when there's Indians about and they suddenly smell smoke coming from Old Lady Helpless's farm. And of course Old Lady Helpless has a daughter, Young Lady Useless, who faints at the sight of dirty toe nails. Yesiree, I kept my eyes narrow and studied her face, those giant eyes all kind and evil at the same time, that giant nose with the big nostril slits, turning this way and that as if she smelled something bad. That flaming hair, so red it's just not natural. The way her fins gripped the ends of the robe, making sure it flowed just an inch above the dusty floor. The reddish tinge in her teeth from the lipstick. The splotches of rouge on her gills so thick they looked like the melted wax of a thousand crayons, and—wait a minute.

I had it! It was a gamble, but there was no choice. I had to try. I stared one last time at the biggest thing on Lunker's face, drew in a deep breath, then pointed down at the hem of her robe and said: "Yuuccchhh!"

Lunker swung her head to me in a jerk. "Pardon me?"

"I said: Yuuccchhh!" And I pointed down again.

"What is it?" Lunker tried to look down, but if you've ever seen a pike you'll know that pike just can't look down on themselves at all. And so she couldn't see anything.

"Can't you see them?" I exclaimed, a look of horror on my face. One Armed Trapper—I sawneaked out of the corner of my eye—had paused and was squinting like mad at Lunker's robe. "They're all over the place!" I wrunkled my nose in disgust, then, looking up at Lunker's face, I made my whole face scranch up. "And in your hair, too! Blagghhh!"

Lunker fluppered her fins futilly. "What?" she screamed. "Oh, what is it!?"

"Hairballs! Millions of hairballs! They're all over you! In your hair! On your robe! Your eyelashes, even!"

"Aaaaagh!"

Grandma Matchie and the Major and Bjugstad had been staring at me like I was crazy all this time, but then Grandma Matchie scryed what I was up to and shrieked: "Billions of em!"

And the Major, too: "Yuucchhh!"

"Aaaaagggghhhhhh!" Lunker flailupped away with her fins and swam in wild circles. "Help me! Oh help me!"

And that's when Grandma Matchie roared: "Charge!" And One Armed Trapper's face showed one brief second of absolute horror before Bjugstad crashed into him, and then his flying body was blasting a hole right through the ceiling and heading for the moon.

Bjugstad bellowed and danced around. "Revenge! At last!"

Only it wasn't over yet, because Lunker had by this time discovered the ruse, and now she glommered down on me and this time I was sure she was going to galobble me up.

Leaping off Bjugstad, Grandma Matchie stalked up to her. "Game's over, Lunker!" she snarled. "Now I'm gonna do somethin that I shoulda done two thousand years ago!"

And Lunker shrank back, whimpering. "No, please! It was all a joke! Honest! Just a joke! Ohh, where's One Armed Trapper? Where's Satan Himself? Ohhhh!"

"He'll know better than t'show up now!" Grandma Matchie said, though you could tell she was hoping he would, so she could take care of him, too. "Come on, Lunker, let me see em!" And she held out her hand.

Lunker tried to shrink back further but the throne blocked her retreat. Whimpering, she lifted her red wig from the top of her head—and there they were. Her ears!

And Grandma Matchie grabbed the nearest one and gave it such a twist that Lunker's yell was heard on Pluto, I bet.

And that was the end of Lunker and all her schemes.

Bjugstad was so happy that he carried us all the way home without even a garumble, and so there we stood on the dock, waving him goodbye.

And Mom had her broom and Dad had his jacuzzi and a new VCR, and Sis's hair was pink with blue polka dots, which meant that things were back to normal.

Later on, me and Grandma Matchie went out to visit the Major on his island, and we sat around the fire roasting peanut butter marshmallows with olives in them, and told our stories just the way they happened. The whole truth, just like I'm telling it here! And then, when the fire was just a pile of coals, and everyone had gone all quiet and funny-looking as they stared at the embers, Grandma Matchie shook her head and said:

"I'm acursin m'self fer not seein the signs." She looked up and her face glowed red and it wasn't just from the fire, either. "There it was, all the signs a er schemin, right afore me! An I didn't see a thin! E'en when that one story kept showin up everywhere, till I was sick a hearin it! Still . . . I'm ashamed, jus plumb ashamed." And she hung her head to prove it.

"Aye, me too," muttered the Major. "We shoulda both smelled the likes o' Lunker, hearin' that same story tole o'er and o'er again, from shinin sea t'shinin sea! Jus like Lunker said!"

Then Grandma Matchie cocked an eye at me and grinned. "Tike, canya figure out what story we're talkin 'bout?"

"I betcha can't!" the Major snickered, all superior like. "It's right in fronta yer eyes, but I betch you can't!"

"I bet he can!" Grandma Matchie said. "An I bet One Armed Trapper's arm on it!"

"An I bet One Armed Trapper's real arm!" the Major shouted. "Yours is a fake! An if I win you gotta admit it once an fer all!"

"You're on!"

Then they both turned to me and waited, their eyes glowing brighter than the coals. I gave them a wide eyed stare. "You mean you'd give up One Armed Trapper's arm and the whole truth 'bout it? On some dumb bet!?" I jumped to my feet. "Forget it! I want no parta it!" And I stomped off into the darkness.

After a moment Grandma Matchie's howl of laughter shook the stars. "Atta boy, Tike! Atta Boy!" she called out behind me.

When people start betting stories on things, I want no part of it. I don't want there to be a loser, don't you see?

Sure, I knew the answer to that question, but that's not the point. Because the way I figure it, the next time I want to hear stories from Grandma Matchie and the Major, there'd be one less. And who knows, maybe some day there'd only be one, just like Lunker wanted all along. And it'd have more than one meaning, too, if that ever happened.

Well, the answer's sitting there right in front of you, just like the Major said. And the next time you're sitting around a campfire, when someone starts telling you about the one that got away, you'll know where that story came from, and you'll be a wise man.

That was the second week.

THE DEVIL, WE SAY

It's a rule, I bet. And dealing with one just naturally leads to the other, and so on. Forever and ever. That's why I knew I was in trouble.

They were calling in one of the big boys, because when some little kid starts talking about Satan Himself then it's time to get worried. At least that's what the principal said, and if anyone should know, it's him. Besides, he had that look of failure about him. You know, the way I look whenever I bring home a report card.

Even jesters get report cards, and they're usually bad, so you learn to put on that face of failure so that everyone concerned can make appropriate faces to show how they're concerned. But people get concerned in different ways, so your face has to be a little bit different for each of them.

Take Big Nose, for example. She pretends it's her fault that I get lousy grades. So I make myself like a mirror, and we both look sadly at each other with exactly the same kind of failed poupy expression. "I have tried!" she'd say with a shake of her head, trying to fit some kind of stern look into her failed face, and with a little burning flame of Indignation or something like it there in her eyes when she studies your face and you're trying hard to show how you've failed as much as her. It's a contest to see who's failed the most. "What are we going to do with you!" Big Nose'd sigh. Oh ho! thinks I whenever this happens, now it's we is it?

That's Big Nose, but with Mom it's different. For her, you have to put on a very special kind of expression, because Mom gets all dreamy eyed and before you know it she's talking about when she was in school. And she's so understanding and everything that no matter what, my face scrunches up and I start crying. That's what's special about this kind of expression—I can't help it.

Of course, Dad's a whole other story, that's for sure. You see, you have to know Dad. He gets embarrassed by everything everyone else around him does. There's right ways to do things and then there's wrong ways to do things. Dad's way is the right way and everyone else's way is the wrong way. So the concern goes through two phases. First, Dad gets red in the face, showing me his embarrassment that his son has done it again. But that doesn't last long, because then he gets mad, and he says: "It's that damn Gothic school system! Now, if I was teachin . . ."

The point is, he's right as far as I'm concerned. Dad's a great teacher, and he knows the difference between doing things the wrong way and doing things his way. So pretty soon he's telling me how he'd run the school system, and I get all excited because he's brilliant when it comes to things like that.

Imagine, watching old westerns on a giant screen all morning, then going to restaurants for lunch, then watching more westerns in the afternoon and other movies like Tarzan and the Naked Lady, or is it Tarzan and the Leopard Lady? Naked Leopard Lady? I can't remember exactly, but it's the one where Tarzan fights a guy in a lion suit, and then a stuffed crocodile, and then he gets taken prisoner by Lady Naked Leopard and she ties him to a stake and does terrible things to him until he screams out his Tarzan yell and all the birds in the swamps take to the air again, and this lion runs through the same section of bush over and over again, and all the animals stampede, and before you know it there's guys disguised as gorillas breaking down the walls and untying Tarzan just in time for him to get all moral about things.

Now that's education!

Showing concern in the right places is important:

And then there's the principal, and things start getting a little trickier. You see, his ears get redder and redder, and for him my lousy grades mean the whole world's coming down all around him. And when you start telling him about Satan Himself he looks like he's going to unplode.

And there's Big Nose crying and Mom and Dad trying to calm her down. So that leaves me one on one with the principal, and that's when I get mad.

"I don't look under rocks anymore!" I screamed at him. "'Cause I seen Satan Himself! And it's the truth!"

"Young man!" The principal surged up behind his giant desk and put his fists down on it—thumpthump! "Young man! If there's one thing I won't tolerate in my office, it's impertinence! Now, I'll hear no more of this Devil stuff! Do you hear?"

Sneaking a look at those big ears, I figured that there'd be no way he couldn't hear! Even if he had cotton in his head! "It's all true! And if you don't believe me, you just wait! An I'll tell you what Satan Himself looks like, too! An you can't stop me!"

An he couldn't stop me!

It was the last week at Rat Portage Lake, and it was awful! Two whole weeks had gone by and I'd hardly done anything yet! And Grandma Matchie was going on and on about how Satan Himself must be just steaming, since we'd foiled his sneaky plans.

"I can't figure it, Tike," she said. "He's bin one step ahead a us all along! Puttin Sis and Mom through hell with his turrible schemin. An if there's one thing Satan Himself is big on it's revenge! So what's he up to, that's what I wanna know!"

Meanwhile, everyone was getting cranky since vacation was almost over. So I moped around in the cabin, watching all the normal boring things go on all around me.

"Get outa the way!" Dad roared. "I can't see a damn thing!"

Sis ducked, scampered for the kitchen. Her giant ugly feet swept through the tinder pile as she darted past the big black wood stove, scappering scraps of wood in all directions. She yelped, and I laughed.

"Gothic on a stick, girl!" Dad bellowed, like the whole world was coming down all around him. Twisting his head around, he hunted for Mom. She was sweepening dirt from the cabin doorway, as huge green flies, as big as birds, bazzled in and out through the gaping hole in the screen door. "Ester! Sign up your daughter for ballet classes or somethin! Hell, I'll do it, come Fall." Draining his beer, he let the can drop with a plop.

The jacuzzi filled the living room. Dad sat in the middle of the fruthering water, which was full of floating beer cans. They bobbled and bumpled against the hairy islands of his knees.

Come to think of it, Dad was the hairiest man I'd ever seen. Hairier even than Grandma Matchie's upper lip, only everywhere like that. He had hair covering his legs, from the tops of his wide feet all the way up to his purple and pink striped shorts, and even more under them, I bet. And the hair was black, furry. When she kissed him Good Morning, Mom sometimes said: "Get into that bathroom, Jock, and get that fur off your tongue!" So it was everywhere: hair growing out of his ears, hair growing in his nostrils, and yes, hair even growing in his mouth. His whole head was filled with hair.

The only place in the cabin big enough for the jacuzzi was the living room. Water had splashed all the walls, and pooled in the fireplace where bits of tinfoil floated about. Grunting, Dad sat in the tub watching the new video screen and stabbing at the Remote and making the picture go backwards so he could replay his favorite scenes.

He had a thousand million twenty-nine thousand seventy cassettes, and all of them were Westerns. He'd squint like Clint Eastwood, and grimace like Lee Van Cleef, and swell his chest like John Wayne. And the water burbled all around him and sank beer cans and made the hair part on his knees whenever he ducked them down then back up.

Sis hid in the kitchen. Her hair was orange and yellow now, and she cried all the time and it made me sick. And those bumps on her chest were getting bigger and bigger and I had nightmares about them filling up the whole cabin.

"Shoo! Shoo!" A broom whirvled in front of my face. I jumped back. "Shoo flies! Shoo!" I dodged another swing of the broom.

"Mom!"

"Jock Junior, you let all these flies in?" Like a big straw-haired head, the broom wanagged at me.

I shook my own head after it. "Uh uh!"

"Don't you let any flies in, you hear!"

"I won't, Mom."

"Jock Senior!" Holding her broom as if to swat a fly, Mom stormed up to the jacuzzi. "When are you going to get out of that damn thing? You've been in there since you built it!"

"Shut up! I'm not going anywhere! Now get outa the way so I can watch the picture!" He opened another beer can.

Ever since me and Grandma Matchie came back from Westhawk Lake, Dad's been in there, watching movies and eating bananas. He won't come out, and it's been three whole days. There must be a thousand million eighty-two beer cans floating around in there. And Mom's been on another sweepening craze since she got her broom back, sweepening everything: floors, walls, the ceiling and the path out to the outhouse. Even the dock.

The whole world was getting desperate.

I stared at the giant screen that now hid the big window over-looking the lake. A man in a black suit sat in front of a saloon, ruckling in a chair while this dumb lady tried talking to him. But he just ruckled, pushing with his legs against a post, one leg, then the other, and the dumb lady didn't know what to do, and Dad drank his beer and grinned.

"Jock Junior!"

I looked at Mom.

"Go out and play, will you? Go find Grandma Matchie and make sure she's not getting into trouble. But don't you watch if she's wrasshing a bear or something, you hear?"

As I passed by she swung the broom at me, but I jumped for-ward and she missed. Only I forgot about the screen, and went through it again. I tore it even worse this time, and fell down on the porch.

"Damn you, Junior!" Dad's bellow made me jump up, and I leapt off the porch and fell again.

"Ballet lessons for alla em!"

Boy did I run.

I found Grandma Matchie down by the boathouse. She was dripping wet, which meant that she'd been down in her lodge, and she wore a long blue dress with white dots that went down to her flapping hiking boots. She winked at me when she saw me coming up the path. In her hands was an axe, and the door to the boathouse was all chopped up.

"What're you doing?" I asked.

Making a funny face she lifted the axe over her head. "Can't find the key. Been so bloody long since I needed t'get in 're." She swung the axe and the whole double door shook. "Stand back, Tike, or I'll be brainin ya."

It took five minutes of chopping before that door fell open, and even then it fell open from the other side, where the hinges had rotted away. After pausing for a breather, Grandma Matchie heavered the axe out into the lake.

I watched it arc up and out, then make a big suplash about ten feet from the end of the dock. "What'd you do that for?"

"Don't need it anymore. An what ya don't need y'throw away." And with that she grasped my hand and led me into the darkness of the boathouse. "Fifty years since I last come in 'ere," she growled. "Back then I wuz runnin yer cabin as a fishin lodge, an we had all them backhouses set up fur sleepin in, an we had millionaires comin up from New York New York bringin whole Jazz bands with em—boys who could play yer skids off. Yesiree, Tike, those were the days!"

"How come you closed down the lodge?"

"Well, Tike, there wuz a turrible acc'dent one day. We had one a them bands playin out back an the biggest blue heron you ever seen came right down an et them all up."

"That musta bin some bird!" I shook my head.

"Not big 'nough, Tike." Grandma Matchie replied. "Cause right then an e'en bigger eagle come down an snatch that heron right up, an they fought fur hours right up above the lodge. And then th'eagle gets his tal'ns 'roun the heron's neck and started squeezin. An the heron's beak opened wide an that eagle foun' imself lookin right down its throat, an he saw that band, playin their brains out, an the eagle was so scairt by what he saw that right then and there he dropped the heron. Only the heron ne'er really did recover from that, and neither did the eagle, and that's why all the heron's 'roun ere are blue, an that's why all the eagles got white hair on their heads."

I'd always wondered about that.

"An that, Tike, is why I shut er down. I was endangerin the wildlife, y'see."

I nodded, then looked around. "Any rats in here?"

"Nope, they use the trail. Got no need fur comin in ere." Pausing just inside the entrance, she turned to me. "You know why they call this Rat Portage Lake, eh? Well, I seen them—jus once, mind you—giant rats, carryin bags on their heads and canoes, too. Comin down the trail, all in single file. Only seen it happen once, like I said, an that was a hundred years ago. They only come when they got good reason."

Everything that had been black was now turning gray, and I

could make out all the shelves on the thin sagging walls, and the old lanterns hanging from the roof. And sitting there in that black water was the neatest boat I'd ever seen. It was all wood, varnished and sleek, with brass things on it all glimmering and winking. I couldn't see a motor, so it must be hidden, I figured. It had a low windshield and a solid brass steering wheel.

"Does it still run?"

"'Course it does!" Grandma Matchie chackled, striding forward with big steps and dragging me along behind. "Ain't bin out in fifty years, jus sittin there, waitin."

"Waitin for what?"

"You'll see!" She laughed, and laughed again. "You'll see! Come on!"

Letting go of my hand she leapt across ten feet and landed behind the wheel. I jumped in after her and dropped down into the seat beside her. In front of us was the closed-up garage door, all boarded up and stuff. The motor roared to life and Grandma Matchie whammed that throttle forward.

The front lurched up and I was snapped back in my seat. Then—crash! Daylight exploded all over us and pieces of wood flew in all directions and we were flying out over the waves.

I shouted: "Where are we going?"

One hand on the wheel, the other cranking the throttle, Grandma Matchie grinned. "I've had it with the Major once an fur all! Him an his lyin! Him an his schemin!"

"But I thought you made up!" I cried.

"With that skulker!? Hah! I wuz jus takin a breather! An so wuz he! But now I'm gonna end it once an fur all!"

Staring through the windshield I could see the Major's island. We were flying right toward it. I could see the flag-pole, with its Union Jack standing straight out at attention, a row of gulls holding it that way, fladapping madly. And then I saw the Major running down to the dock where the H.M.S. Hood lolled. Jumping aboard he cast off and surged away from the dock, swinging about to face us.

"It's war he wants, war he gets!" Grandma Matchie shrieked, leaning forward. "No more lyin, no more nothin!" Baring her teeth she yanked hard on the throttle and spun the wheel. We whirred by the Major, missing him by an inch. I saw his face, the wild whiskers, huge red nose flying by at a thousand million sixty twenty miles an hour.

"We've got im now!" Grandma Matchie laughed, turning us about. Directly ahead I saw the Hood, flundolering in the waves we'd left behind. Going at full speed, we raced for her. "We'll ram em! That's what we'll do, laddie!"

Staring with wild eyes as we bore down on the Hood, I let out a yell just as we rammed her from the side. Everything shook until my insides rattled, and then we were through. Turning around, I saw the Hood, broken in half and sinking, but no Major.

"Got im!" Grandma Matchie howled.

"But where is he?"

For answer she jerked her thumb straight up and I looked and there he was, being carried back to his island in defeat by his gulls. He shook his fist at us, but you could see he was beaten.

"We got im! An never again will that blarny boat troll bait past my windows! Hah!"

Mom was sweeping the dock when we pulled up, and she started screaming at Grandma Matchie right away. "Mother! Jock Junior's not wearin a lifejacket! Do you know how dangerous that is? Boatin without a lifejacket?"

Stepping up on the dock I stuck my tongue out at Sis, who was standing behind Mom. Her hair was now metallic silver, and the bumps on her chest had smaller bumps, making them look like bull's eyes. I threw a dead minnow at her (minnows are safe) and she started crying when it got stuck in her hair. Rainbow trout minnow, Grandma Matchie said mysteriously when she finally dug it out from all those blue spikes and knots and things on Sis's head.

Mom tuggeled my ear, but Grandma Matchie laughed so I grinned at her, which made Mom tuggle my ear again.

I don't mind things like that. After all, it's just show, so things look like they're supposed to. Discipline, Big Nose would call it, but what does she know?

Grandma Matchie wandered off, muthering about Satan Himself and his schemin, and me and Mom and Sis went back to the cabin. In the living room the Indians were killing all the blue coats, but Arrow Flynn was grinning as he stood on a pile of bodies and blasted from both hips. Dad had a banana in each hand and made noises as he shot at the screen.

"Hey Dad! Look at Sis Now! Her hair looks like tinsel!" Pointing, I laughed.

"Gothic in panties, girl! Why not just stick yer head in a blender an get it over with!"

Her face turning red and scrunching up, Sis bolted for the kitchen, where she let out a bawl.

"Aaaaggghh!" Mom screamed, and I whirled. She had been sweeping round the wood stove and the broom had caught fire. "Aaaaagggghhh!" Screaming and running in circles, Mom waved the flaming brackling pafting broom above her head, trailing ashes and sparks all over the place.

"GET THAT DAMN THING OUTA HERE!" Dad bellowed.

But she ran right at him. Rearing back, Dad bleated as Mom swung that broom down into the ginurgling water. Hisspering sounds filled the air and clouds rolled up from the jacuzzi.

"Ester! You damn near set my hair on fire! Are you nuts!?"

Mom started crying, standing in front of him. And Sis was bawling in the kitchen, and Arrow Flynn had bit the big one. I bolted for the door, escaped outside without anyone noticing.

Down the trail beyond the outhouse I caught a glimpse of blue dress, so I took off after it. Grandma Matchie was the only one who wasn't crazy around here, so I figured I'd stick with her.

Running down the trail, I didn't catch up with her until after we came out into a rocky clearing. At the far end was a pile of boulders as high as a house and as wide as a city block, stretching right across the clearing like a wall.

"Comin fishin, Tike?" Grandma Matchie asked without even turning round to see who was coming up on her.

"Sure! What're we gonna catch?"

"Satan Himself, that's who."

A deep sea fishing rod in one hand and a bait box in the other, Grandma Matchie strode across the clearing, kicking rocks out of the way with her big boots. I followed as she climbed up the wall of boulders and stopped beside her at the top.

On the other side was a river of black water, flowing through a giant crack in the bedrock. The banks were steep and shadowy, and the water looked deep.

In a flat space between two boulders sat a rocking chair with a harness belt bolted to it. Grandma Matchie set down the rod and the bait box and stood at the edge, glaring down into the water. "He's probbly plannin somethin, or my name's not Grandma Matchie!" She shook her head. "Plannin somethin evil, no doubts 'bout it. If'n there's one thing he don't tol'rate it's the likes a you'n me messin up his schemin."

"So what're we gonna do?"

"We're gonna get im afore he gets us, that's what we're gonna do!" And she grinned. "We're gonna brin thins to a head, get it right out in the open! Satan Himself hates that! Hah!" And she settled herself down into the worn seat and buckled up. "Hand me the rod, Tike, an the bait, too."

I stared at the gloomeny water. "How d'you know he's in there?"

"Where else would he be? An I've had nibbles ere afore, lemme tell you! But we'll get im this time—I've got an itch, an when Grandma Matchie's got an itch then sure enough Satan Himself's lurkin bout."

"Where's it itch?"

"Never you mind. Now here, pull me out a worm, the fattest one in there, and don't break im now."

Pulling up a handful of earth from the bait box I broke it up in my fingers, but there was only one worm and it was all skinny and oozing.

"That's perfect!" Grandma Matchie cried. Grabbing it from my hand she tied it in a knot around the biggest hook I'd ever seen. It was a big as me, all shiny brass, with two barbs on the shank. Monofilament line was tied to the loop. "Two pound test. Gotta be sportin, Tike." Adjusting the drag on the Abu reel she leaned forward and swung the hook out over the water and began letting out line. I watched the bait sink into the black river, flash once in the dark water, then vanish.

"D'you think he's hungry?"

Shaking her head, Grandma Matchie said, "He's ne'er hungry fur long, Tike. An he's probbly not hungry now, but it ne'er stopped im afore. He loves worms." Her brow was all scrunched up and her eyes were burning slits. I felt sorry for Satan Himself.

You got to be patient when you're fishing, so I sat down on a rock to wait. Big flat bugs crawled up from the water and settled down on the warm stone all around me. Leaning close to one I stared into its bug eyes. "What are these, Grandma Matchie?"

"Drag'nfly nymphs. They grow up in the water then come out an sprout wings when it's sunny. Drag'nflies are good, Tike, cause they et skeeters an gnats, an gulls when they get the chance, which ain't often nough if you ask me."

I watched as the bug's body dried up and then the back split open and after a minute the dragonfly's head came out and looked round. "What happens in the water to make them grow up?" I asked.

"They get big, if that's what you mean."

"But why do they get big?"

"Things in the water feeds em, that's why. But I'll tell ya somethin, Tike, most a these ones ere won't be able t'fly, cause the water's bad. Their wings'll come out all shrivelled up—I've seen it ere afore."

And she was right. The dragonfly's wings were all shrivelled up, like crunched cellophane. "Grandma Matchie! We gotta help him!"

"We can't, Tike. Somethins are jus too big e'en fur me!"

"But a dragonfly's not big!"

"Nope, he ain't. But the well where all that water's comin from is bigger than Satan Himself!"

I frowned, leaned back on the rock. "Grandma Matchie, how come Satan Himself lives here, in Rat Portage Lake?"

Grandma Matchie chuckled. "Cause it wuz ere he wuz sittin when that shootin star came down, an it bounced right off his head and landed o'er in Man'toba! That's a bump he'll ne'er furget! Hah!"

"Where'd that shootin star come from?"

Grandma Matchie looked down at me, and her eyes spackled. "Y'know what it's like when you sudd'nly get an idea an there's this light bulb appearin right o'er yer head? E'er seen it?"

"Yep! Lotsa times!"

"Right. Well, that shootin star's jus a big light bulb, know what I mean?"

I sat back up. "You mean it was somebody's idea? Who?"

And she winked. "Alla us, Tike. Me'n Lunker an the Major an One Armed Trapper an Leap Year an a whole million other story tellers all o'er the wide world! You'n me, Tike, that's who thought up that shootin star!"

"Then who is Satan Himself?" I demanded.

"Truth is, Tike, he's somethin diff'rent fer everyone! He's jus a fancy name, is all."

"But Grandma Matchie . . ."

"Got im!" she screamed, rearing back in the rocking chair and driving the hook home. The line hummed, then the drag shrilled, throwing out sparks as Grandma Matchie set the hook again and again. Driving the butt of the fishing pole into the belt socket she bared her teeth. "I got im! I got im!"

She began pumpening, reeling up slack, pumpening and pumpening as she rocked in the old creaking chair. The river began churning, burbbling purbling and frothing. I could hear a roar and all the dragonfly nymphs scalampered for cover.

"Ere he comes! My God! I furgot the gaff! Tike! Go get the gaff! Quick! Up in the cabin!" Satan Himself made a run, and the thin line whined and the drag whirnelled.

Leaping to my feet I scampered down the rocks, hit the flat clearing and tore across it. Screaming all the way, I flew down the trail. All the trees went by in a blur, but I could see every bump and root on the ground and I didn't stumble once. I never ran so fast in my life, and it was so easy I bet I didn't even touch the ground half the time.

Then I saw the cabin and then I was tearing up the porch, flying through the kitchen and into the living room. Everyone was screaming, Mom pulling Dad's arms as he stood in the jacuzzi roaring at the video screen, where a thousand million twenty hundred nine Indians were riding down on us.

"Yeaagggh!" roared Dad.

"Jock Junior!" Mom shrieked over her shoulder. "Come

quick! Dad's got his foot caught in the drain! He's being sucked down!"

"Where's the gaff?"

"NO!" Dad screamed.

"Jock Junior! I won't let you use the gaff! This is your father! Help me! Oh my!"

"I'm being sucked down! Yeaaaggghhh!"

I jumped to Mom's side, grabbed one of Dad's arms and pulled. "Sis! Get a rope!" I looked over my shoulder. She stood by the kitchen, her eyes wide and her hair green with leaves growing out of it. "Look at her hair! It's green!"

Sis clenched her fists and brought them to her temples. "I CAN'T HELP IT!" she bawled. "IT'S NOT ME! It's just happening! I'm not DOING anything!" Acorns fell from her head and bounced on the wooden floor. "Waaa!"

"Get a rope!"

Still crying, she stumbled away. Dad's whole leg from the knee down had disappeared into the drain, and the foaming water was up to his chest. Me and Mom pulled and pulled. The knotted end of a heavy rope hit me in the head and I grabbed it with one hand. "Tie this round your waist, Dad!" I yelled, throwing it at him. "Mom, you gotta hold on while I tie the other end to somethin!" Nodding, she gripped the rope while Dad looped it around himself and made a knot. I picked up the other end and looked around for something to tie it to. The closest thing was the big refrigerator, where Dad kept all his beer. Wrapping the rope three times I tied a knot and cinched it up until it was tight.

"Yeaaggghh!"

In the closet hung the gaff. Taking it down, I turned and looked around. Everything seemed under control, so I ploughed through the door and leapt off the porch and raced down the trail. Then I skidded to a stop, because the trail was full of rats, plodding two abreast, with grain sacks on their backs and canoes, too, the smallest aluminum canoes I'd ever seen. And they were singing in squeaky high voices some funny French song.

But I had no time to waste, so I edged to one side of the trail and ran past them. I heard their squeaks of surprise, then little cheers. Running and running, I came to a clearing and crossed it.

I went up the rocks like a spider and reached Grandma Matchie's side.

She was still pumpening away, and the water boibled, full of bobbing beer cans and video cassettes. Not even breathing hard, she hisspered, "I got im now, no doubts bout it, I got Satan Himself!" She cranked the reel and rocked back. "Get down t'the edge an get that gaff, ready, Tike! He's gotta a holda somethin an he won't let go! Get that gaff ready!"

A huge hump rose from the water and a giant scaly head with a hook in its jaws reared up and glared at us. He was a dragon, with red and gold scales and flames for eyes, and he had giant crinkled up wings and aluminum fangs, and giant ears that came to glowing red points. He was the biggest thing I'd ever seen and I screamed. Crouching at the edge, I lifted the gaff in both hands.

"He's got a holda somethin!" Grandma Matchie shrieked. "Give im a poke, Tike! Give im a poke!" She roared with laughter, pumpening and reeling and rocking.

Staring into the black water, I could see Satan's forearms clutching something pale and hairy and struggling. Then I recognized it. "Dad's foot! He's got Dad's foot!"

"So that's his game, eh! Give im a poke!"

Lifting the gaff skyward, I yelled and drove it home.

"That's the way, Tike!"

I hit him in the belly and the gaff sank in half way then popped out again.

"OOOOOF!"

Satan thrashed and hissed and let go of Dad's foot so he could clutch his belly. He gasped for a couple of seconds, then, wagging his head he raised his forearms and made fists and glared down at me. "I WON'T TOLERATE THIS IMPERTI-NENCE!"

"Oh you won't, eh?" Grandma Matchie laughed, yanking on the fishing pole so that Satan's head snapped forward and he almost lost his balance and began falling forward, but then his fists came down—thumpthump!

"AAAGGGH!" he roared, chomping at the hook that was snagged in his lower jaw. "IT'S JUST NOT FAIR!" he wailed, closing his eyes shut.

"Let this be a lesson t'ya, Satan!" Grandma Matchie was suddenly at my side, and in her hands she gripped the axe she had thrown in the lake earlier. "Never mess wi the likes a Grandma an Jock Junior! If'n y'know what's good fer ya!" Grinning, she raised up the axe and with one slice cut the line. Satan Himself plunged backward, throwing sheets of black water all over the place, and his wail turned into a gurgle as the river swallowed him.

"But we had him!" I shouted.

But Grandma Matchie just chackled. "We sure did, Tike, but I'm in it fur the sport, an that's all. Jus in it fur the sport. Come on, let's go have lunch."

Walking across the clearing, I asked: "I thought you threw that axe away?"

"I did, because I didn't need it then. But I needed it now, so ere it is. One thin you gotta remember, Tike, an that's when you throw somethin away, make sure y'can get it back if'n ya need it."

The trail was empty. "Grandma Matchie! You shoulda seen all the rats! All over the place!"

"'Course, this is Rat Portage Lake, ain't it?"

Understanding the importance of telling the truth:

Now they had some kind of doctor in the office, too, and it was getting crowded. He was completely round, with his big wide tie all spotted with blueberry yogurt. And his face was round, too, and so was his moustache and his glasses and his red-veined cheeks.

He puffed right up the desk and started crowding its surface with all kinds of crazy things. "Now," he wheezed, "if you'll just have a seat here, Jock Junior," and he pulled a chair up to the edge of the desk, "we can get started."

I don't think the doctor was very smart, because he had me do all kinds of stupid things—puzzles and stuff that I suppose had him stumped so he wanted my help. And he had a watch that he kept looking at as if he forgot what time it was every few seconds or so. I felt sorry for him, so I finished all those puzzles as fast as I could.

"That's not possible!" the doctor exclaimed, looking up from his watch and goggling at the principal. "That's just not possible!"

"Why?" I asked. "What time is it? Maybe your watch is wrong."

"No, no, it's not . . ." He frowned at me, and I put on that innocent dumb expression on my face, looking up at him and making my eyes as wide as possible. "I mean," he muttered, "you don't understand . . ."

I smiled blankly, and he stopped, and his frown grew deeper the longer he stared at me. After a moment he started rummaging in his briefcase. "I have a test here, Jock Junior. And I'd like you to try it. Don't worry if you can't answer most of the questions—they're designed for older people . . ." He found it and placed it on the desktop in front of me and gave me a brand new pencil which I started chewing right away because that's what I do with all new pencils and pens and erasers and stuff.

"So, are you ready to start, Jock Junior?"

I examined the pencil critically, then said, "Okay."

"Right. Ready? Go!"

A couple minutes later I was finished. Those were the easiest questions I'd ever answered. And the geography section was a snap.

The doctor peered closely at the sheets when I gave them to him. He checked his watch again and then started reading. After a minute he looked up and gaped at me. "But, but . . ." His round face was all sweaty so I found an old Kleenex in my pocket and gave it to him. Mopping his face, he stopped suddenly and stared down at the Kleenex.

"Sorry, there's some chewing gum in it," I said. "I forgot."

"Who told you all the answers to these questions?" he asked, all fatherly now that he'd recovered. "Because, I must tell you, they're all wrong."

I made my eyes even wider. "They are? But Grandma Matchie told me! She tells me everything!"

"Well, she's wrong, I'm afraid."

"You mean the Rockies didn't come from buffalo droppings?" I demanded, a scrunch starting on my face.

"No, of course not!" the doctor said.

"Now, young man," the principal said grimly. "You know that Grandma Matchie doesn't really exist, don't you. I mean, there's no record of you ever having had a Grandma Matchie and . . ."

The doctor shook his head quickly, beetling his busy brows. Leaning toward me he gazed into my eyes. "This invisible friend of yours, this 'Grandma Matchie,' she's . . ."

"She's not invisible!" I exclaimed. With a helpless, pleading look on my face I turned to Dad and Mom. "Tell them! Tell them about Grandma Matchie!"

Mom looked at Dad and Dad looked at Mom. "Well, uh," Dad muttered. "I don't . . . really . . . think we can, uh, say for sure . . . really . . . that is . . ."

"Liars!" I screamed.

"Now son," the doctor said, "I'm sure you know the importance of telling the truth," he cleared his throat and leaned back, "Don't you?"

I bit my lip. "I have." I said weakly. "I have told the truth!"

"Now, son, it's obvious that you're a very imaginative child, but . . ."

I scrunched my face until tears came out and I balled my fists. "It's the truth!" I wailed, squeezing my eyes shut. "You don't know what's the truth! You don't know!"

"Now, we are much older than you, you'll agree . . ."

Opening my eyes reluctantly, I nodded, staring down at the desk.

"And you'll agree also that we have a better idea of the truth than you do . . ."

"No!"

"Yes, we have, son. So you just tell your Grandma Matchie friend that she shouldn't go around telling you things that aren't true, because then she'd be lying, and . . ."

And that's just what I was waiting for. "Tell her yourself!" I laughed, jumping to my feet. "GRANDMA MATCHIE!" I screamed. "IT'S TIME! JUST LIKE YOU SAID!"

"Jock Junior!" Mom was on her feet. "You didn't!"

I let out a maniacal laugh like the ones I've heard in horror movies and ran to the window overlooking the playground.

"Gothic on a stick!"

"Oh my!"

After a moment the doctor smiled and said, "Now. You see? There's no one . . ." Just then we heard a rumble, coming up from the floor, and everything began to shibble and shake. The pencil rolled off the desk and the doctor's briefcase tipped over, spewling tests and answers all over the place. He stepped all over them as he ran with everyone else to the window.

And coming across the playground, busting down the wire fence, was Grandma Matchie, riding Bjugstad and holding a chain with its other end around Satan Himself's neck, who was being dragged along on his belly, and Lunker, thrashing about and roaring in the air like it was water, with One Armed Trapper sitting on her head. And there was the Major, rowing like mad across the grass in his broke-in-half H.M.S. Hood, and there was Leap Year, and a thousand million two buffalo and demon fish and glowing lampreys and rats singing French songs and all of them.

We jumped back as Grandma Matchie—Bjugstad making one giant leap—came sailing up at us. With a huge crash they burst through the window and most of the wall, and everyone scattered. And there stood Bjugstad, legs wide, snorting and humphing and grunting and shaking pieces of wall from his head (he had shrunk himself down so he could fit into the room); and Grandma Matchie jumped down from him and stood there with her fists on her hips. Glowering, her gaze fell on the doctor and the principal and Big Nose, all of them cowering in the far corner near the door.

"So, it's finally come, has it?" she growled, her eyes all afire.

I stepped up and said: "They all want to be taught the importance of telling the truth, Grandma Matchie."

"Oh, do they now? Well, Tike, what should we show em first?"

I was feeling kind hearted, so I replied: "How to be sportin."

"Sportin, eh? Well, that's what we'll tell em, Tike."

By this time Bjugstad had calmed down and was contentedly eating all the doctor's tests and answers. And from outside we could see (it was easy with all the wall gone) the whole play-ground filled with rats and buffalo and everyone else, playing soccer. They had strings tied everywhere, and the rats had barri-caded their goal with canoes and bags and stuff, but the Major went round from behind and scored easily, sending the ball flying back out into the field. Shouts and roars of laughter filled the air.

The whole school must have been watching, I bet.

"We'll tell ya all bout sportin, now." Grandma Matchie announced. "An we'll tell it like this!" and she advanced on them, and they all tried to fit through the crack in the corner that wasn't there, and if even if it was they were too big anyway. I could've told them all about that, but why bother?

"Doc. You live in a fish bowl and spend all day glapin, glapin, glapin!"

"That's not true!" he shouted, climbing to his feet.

"'Course not!" Grandma Matchie snapped, then she grinned, "But it could be, if'n I wuz t'say so." And she turned to Big Nose. "An you, you're jus a Big Nose breathin down all the kids' backs!"

"WHAT?" Big Nose jumped to her feet, grabbing her nose. "But my nose is small!"

"Yep. An if y'wanna keep it that, use it less often an keep it away from where it ain't s'pposed t'be in the first place!" And she spun to face the principal. "An you're the most impert'nent ear-flapper of em all!"

He leapt to his feet, his eyes blazing. "I AM NOT!"

Grandma Matchie shook her head sadly, "Fraid y'are."

Then it was Mom's turn, and boy did she go white! "Ester! Well! Have you anythin t'say fur yerself afore I pass judgment pon ya?"

"We, uh, I didn't think anyone would understand . . ."

Grandma Matchie raised her eyebrows. "Oh? Mebee next time you'll let em decide fur emselves, eh?"

Wringing her hands, Mom nodded weakly and stared down at her feet

"From now on," Grandma Matchie pronounced, "there'll be no brooms allowed in my cabin!"

"Oh my, oh my!"

But there was no room for argument—you could see that.

And when Grandma Matchie glared at Dad, you could see he was wishing he was back in his jacuzzi. "So, I embarrass you, do I, Jock Senior?"

He went red.

"You'll have t'get used to bein embarrassed, then, won't ya? Cause we're all movin in with ya! Fur a whole month! Alla us!"

Cheering noises came from outside, and Dad gulped, but he didn't say one word of protest. He knew better.

And now, they all knew better.

Fishin with Grandma Matchie:

Big jesters are just little jesters in disguise, that's all. I really don't mind being ferreted out every now and then, and that corner's not so scary once you suddenize that the last laugh is, as always, yours.

So the next time your Big Nose tells you to tell her what you did for summer vacation, you'll know what to do. The thing about bigness is that when you're small it's easy to sneak around it, or under it. Pretend you're an ant carrying your favourite Adam's egg under a big, flat rock. And when the time's right just break that egg and eat it for breakfast.

You'll never be hungry again, I bet.

THE POLICEMAN'S DAUGHTER

by Wil McCarthy

Engineer/novelist/journalist Wil McCarthy is a former contributing editor for Wired *magazine and the science columnist for the* SciFi *channel, where his popular "Lab Notes" column has been running since 1999. A lifetime member of the Science Fiction and Fantasy Writers of America, he has been nominated for the Nebula, Locus, AnLab, and Theodore Sturgeon awards, and shares partial credit for a Webbie and a Game Developers' Choice Award. His short fiction has appeared in* Analog, Asimov's, Wired, *and* SF Age, *and his novels include* Bloom *and the four "Queendom of Sol" novels:* The Collapsium, The Wellstone, Lost in Transmission, *and* To Crush the Moon.

* * *

1.
Bourbon, Interrupted

THE COURIER DIDN'T come bearing packages, or letters marked *Carmine Strange Douglas, esq., Adjudicant, Juris Doctor and Attorney at Law.* He didn't need to. Instead, he came barreling down the hallway like a team of horses, shouting "Door!" at the wall of my office. When a rectangle of frosted glass appeared and swung inward, he jumped inside.

"Carmine. I have something for you," he panted.

"Did you run all the way over here?" I asked him. "There are quicker ways—"

But the courier didn't answer. Instead, he approached the fax machine—a vertical plate of gray material, vaguely shimmery in the wellstone light of my office—and said, "Reconverge." Then he threw himself at the plate and vanished with a faint blue sizzle.

Reconverge, hell. I'd sent two couriers out to question potential witnesses in the Szymanski divorce, and one had self-destructed rather than share his waste of time with me. The other, apparently, had come back with something both critical and hard to explain. Go figure.

Myself, I'd just finished researching the details on the case, poring over written documents and public records, mental notes and fax traces in an effort to figure out who, if anyone, had promised Albert the cabana boy permanent residence on that tiny estate. Certainly he'd made the claim in public several times, within the hearing of one or both Szymanskis, and neither had corrected him.

This by itself carried a certain legal weight, even if the original claim was baseless, so if the Szymanskis sold the property—and it looked like they were going to have to—Albert's claim might have to be bought out at his own named price, or sold along with the property as an easement in perpetuity. And in a world without death, perpetuity could be a long damned time! Oh, what a jolly old mess.

It was four-thirty in the afternoon, late enough to kill brain cells with a clear conscience, and I'd just cracked the seal on an opensource bourbon of excellent pedigree. Damn. Sitting open to the atmosphere would not improve it. Still, the courier's news sounded important in a pay-the-mortgage kind of way, and like most decent bourbons this cost almost nothing to print. And when you're immorbid, baby, there's always tomorrow.

Sighing, I got up from my desk, from my too-comfortable chair, and strode over to the fax's print plate. "Confirming reconvergence, all parameters normal." Then I followed the courier through.

Stepping into a fax machine is like falling face-first into a swimming pool. The sensation isn't cold, or liquid, or electric, but it's just as distinct. There is, of course, no sensation of being *inside* the fax machine, since the part of you that passes through the print plate is immediately whisked apart into component atoms. Technically speaking, there should be no consciousness at all as the head disappears, as the body is destroyed and rebuilt, sometimes in combination with other stored images. But consciousness is a funny thing, an illusion that struggles to preserve itself against any insult. The courier and I stepped out of the plate only a moment after I'd stepped into it. Facing *into* the room, now, not out of it.

The courier was, of course, myself. We were one and the same, briefly split and now rejoined in that seamless ball of wonderfulness that was Carmine Strange Douglas. Like any good investigative counsel, I did this five or six times a day. Hell, if not for plurality laws—three thousand copy-hours per month, rigidly enforced by the fax network itself—I'd do it more than that.

Anyway, now that I was one person again I knew details of my—of the courier's—meeting with Lillia Blair, *and* I knew all the details of my morning and afternoon research. Reconvergence: the collapsing of two waveforms into one. Like any scattered thoughts the pieces took a few seconds to come together in my mind, but when they did, the legal strategy was clear.

"Call Juniper," I said to the wall.

The wall considered this for a moment before answering, "I assume you mean Juniper Tall Szymanski."

I glared at the wall without answering, irritated because I'd already called June Szymanski twice this week, and the only other Juniper I knew—Juniper Pong—I hadn't spoken to in months. Taking the hint, the wall patched the message through, and created a hollie window beside the open doorway.

For two seconds it displayed nothing but gray; that deep, foggy, *three-dimensional* gray that some people—myself included—use for a null screen. But then, presently, June Szymanski's face appeared in the hollie, and behind it her living room. She might as well be standing right outside my office. She might as well be solid, physical, *here.* I've had some practice in distinguishing real windows from hollies, but it takes a microscope and some patience.

"Hi," June said, looking both anxious and pleased to hear from me. "What've you got?"

People are always glad to hear from Carmine while their case is unresolved, and especially when the strategy hadn't been figured out yet. At times like these, I'm everybody's best friend. If the issue came to trial, I figured June and I would be friends for another week, week and a half. But in light of what I'd just figured out, a trial seemed rather unlikely.

"According to Lillia," I said, "Albert's exact words were 'I can stay until I decide to leave.'"

"So?" she asked, absorbing that without really getting it.

"So, that's a very different thing from 'I can stay forever,' or even 'I can stay as long as I want.' Because 'decide to leave' is a distinct event in time and space. It can be measured, logged, and read into the court records. And we can make a case—a strong one—that simply setting foot outside that cabana will bring the implied contract to an end."

"Huh. Meaning what? I can evict him?"

Can anyone evict anyone these days? "No," I told her. "Not now, and not without a lot of work. But you can inform him that leaving the pool house is *grounds* for eviction."

Juniper's face relaxed. "Oh, my God. Thank you so much. I do want to be civil about this, but I can't have that . . . I can't face this . . . well, this makes everything a lot easier. You're a genius, Carmine."

And that was true. I *was* a genius, I am, but so are all the other lawyers in town. These days it's impossible practice law—to practice much of anything—if you aren't unimaginably good at it. Because if you're not, someone who *is* will simply print an extra copy of him—or herself, and take over another chunk of your market.

False modesty is bad for business; I'm not ashamed to say I aced my bar exam, went to the best schools and did well in them. I reckon I'd make a good generalist, not only in the practice of law but also in a range of other fields. I was one hundred years old, immorbid, and absorbed knowledge voraciously.

But even that wasn't enough to hold a job in Denver anymore. You had to be generalist *and* a specialist. You had to be broad and brilliant, but lensed down to a unique pinpoint. You had to get your name associated with some particular little quirk or gimmick of the business so that people, when they ran afoul of it, would know whom to call. Even "interpersonal disputes" cut too broad a swath for a viable legal practice. And anyway it was boring: the same disputes over and over again, with only the names and faces changing. And anyway the faces—sculpted by faxware to beauty and perfection—weren't so different either.

But I've always had a flair for the dramatic and a nose for the bizarre. My directory ad said it all: "If you've been wronged, call a lawyer. If you've been *stranged*, call Carmine Strange Douglas."

"This could still turn ugly," I warned June. "That's a well-stone cabana, right? Fully programmable, no restrictions? And he's got his own fax machine in there. Crème brulee and ostrich bisque, anytime he likes. If he decides to make a siege of it, he could hold out for a long time."

"Can't we just shut off the electricity?"

"Ahem! No. And even if you could, he's got the right to generate his own. Wind, sun, and rain—the Free Three, as they say. Albert has taken sides, Mrs. Szymanski. Specifically he's taken your husband's, and he's not going to vacate just because you ask him nicely. He wants this to be difficult.

"I'll write a threatening letter if you want, give him something to think about, but my advice to you as a friend is to talk things over with your husband. It's all right to get bored with each other—if we're going to live forever, it's almost inevitable. But somebody's got make a gesture, here. This is no way for two people to behave, who ever loved each other."

At this, Juniper Szymanski's face closed down. "You don't know anything about it, Carmine. Beyond the bare facts. I'm guessing it's a long time since you've been hurt."

And then she cut the connection, and her hollie window winked out.

What a small-minded thing for her to say! I'd been hurt plenty, and bad. In the broken-heart shuffle that began the moment people stopped dying, everyone got hurt. Or maybe they always had, and always would. This was just one of those facts of life, which you could put out of mind if you didn't happen to be an interpersonal lawyer. Divorces were far and away the worst part of the job, and if I didn't get the strange ones—the ones snarled hopelessly in unique legal challenges—I don't know what I would've done. Soldiered on, probably; an eternity of less-than-happy labors.

"Close door," I said to the wall, and it obliged me by swinging shut that rectangle of white frosted glass and, with a slight crackle of programmable matter, merging it back with my yellow marble decor again.

Too late, I realized there was someone out there in the corridor. There came a polite rapping on the wall outside, and a muffled voice murmuring, "Door. Door."

With a whispered command, I could make the wall perfectly soundproof. I even did it sometimes, but only when I was really busy and wanted the world to go away. Generally, I liked to feel I was part of the world.

Anyway the office would, of course, not obey the commands of a stranger, so I said, "Door." And like some crayon rubbing on a bas relief, the door magically reappeared, then clicked and swung open with a phony creak of phony hinges. A man stood on the other side with his hat pulled down and his shoulders hunched, glancing furtively to his left and then his right. He stepped inside, and then quite rudely pushed the door until it swung closed again, engaging with a click of imaginary latches. "Carmine Douglas," the stranger said, "I hear you solve people problems."

"I help people *with* problems," I answered guardedly.

"That's fine," the man said. "That's close enough. It's good to see you, Carmine. You're looking well."

The lighting in my office—yellow spotlights and venetian-blinded daylight—created pools of atmospheric shadow, and the man had gravitated into one of these, denying me a clear view. But suddenly there was something very familiar about his face, his voice, the way he moved. "Double apparent brightness," I told the room, though I hated it the way that washed things out. "And whiten it up a bit. Kill these shadows."

The windows and ceiling did as I commanded, and there, plain as day, like a ghost from the past, was the face of Theodore Great Kaffner, my old roommate from my last three years at North Am U. He hadn't aged a bit, which shouldn't surprise me at all, since I'd never known anyone who did. But still, the sight of my old friend was a shock, a discontinuity. How many decades did that image leap across?

"Theddy?"

"Hey, Carbo. It's been a long time."

"You look terrible," I said, because that was true as well. "What sort of problem are you having?"

Theddy seemed to cringe at the question. He pointed to the windows on the office's other wall. "Can we darken those? D'you have some sort of privacy mode, here? A really strong one?"

I did, though I rarely used it. Speaking the commands, I watched my prized yellow marble and peach plaster melt away, turn cold. Within moments the whole room—floor and walls and ceiling alike—was seamless, featureless gray steel, and would obey only my commands, and only from within.

"All right?" I asked, waving my hands at the new decor.

"No," Theddy said. "Conductive surfaces block EMI, but lend themselves to transmissive tampering. We need an insulating layer on top."

Did we, now? How interesting. "Glass?"

"Glass will do."

I gave the appropriate commands, then gave my old friend an annoyed "Well?" sort of look.

And when Theddy shrugged his shoulders noncommittally, I advised him, "Nothing you say will leave this office, or be recorded in anything but my own brain, and yours. But be advised, with a proper warrant the court can search those. They can also take this room apart electron by electron, recording the quantum traces. Nothing is ever truly secret."

"It isn't secrecy I'm concerned about," Theddy said, eyeing the walls warily. "It's security. Someone very clever is trying to kill me."

Naturally this statement brought me up short, because it was virtually impossible to kill a person in the Queendom of Sol. Oh sure, you could kill their body, could destroy whatever memory they'd built up since the last time they stepped through a fax machine, or stored their atomically perfect image in an archive somewhere. But the archives themselves were unassailable.

People had died in the chaos of the Fall, eighty years before, and since that time a lot of precautions had been put in place. A *lot* of precautions.

Fearing some sort of transient mental illness in Theddy—a delusional paranoia?—I chose my next words carefully. "Thed, that sounds like a matter for the police. If what you say is true, they can have a team on it before you draw your next breath. We can make the call from here."

But Theddy was shaking his head. "I'm not an idiot, Carbo. This isn't a criminal matter. It's civil, or maybe administrative, or something which if I knew what it was, I wouldn't need *you*."

"Slow down, Theddy," I tried. "You're stringing words together, but you're not making sense. Administrative murder? What's that? Who exactly is trying to kill you?"

And here, Theddy fixed his old roommate with a level, half-panicked gaze. "I am. And I'm doing a good job of it, too."

2.
Xerography, Complicated

Generally speaking, keeping old copies of yourself was like keeping anything else. Found objects, hobby collections, treasured letters or artifacts from childhood—whatever. You could only fit so many in a shelf or cabinet, so at some point you boxed them up and stuck them in the attic, or fed them into the fax to be stored as data. And once that happened, chances were you wouldn't see those things again, nor ever miss them.

Archive copies were exactly the same way: there were people who kept only one, the latest and greatest incarnation of their perfect selves. There were even those who, for financial or aesthetic reasons, stored only the differences between themselves and some idealized manikin of human perfection.

But with either strategy it was possible to make a mistake, to internalize and record some experience that weakened or cheapened or traumatized the soul. And you couldn't always know that this had happened, and if you'd overwritten your earlier backups then you were pretty much stuck with the results for eternity. You could also, in the same way, lose track of what you were supposed to look like, lose track of your God-given body, which had been really good at baseball or algebra, which had just *felt right* somehow. Most people had a bit of this disconnection in their lives—it was pain of an ordinary sort—and admittedly the real horror stories were rare.

But they happened, and in fact I'd encountered enough victims in my practice—their circumstances ranging from tragic to absurd—that for more than half my life I'd been following the costlier and more restrictive change control regimen favored by the various mental health councils. This involved archiving my entire self every five to ten years, and storing each copy, with annotations, alongside the previous ones in a facility that was guaranteed to remain uncorrupted by natural forces for a minimum of ten million years. Effective infinity, in other words, because even if I somehow lived that long, I reasoned that I'd be unlikely to care what I'd thought or felt or looked like as a mere centenarian.

Theddy had apparently followed a similar practice, though in some dangerous and backward-looking way. "Being unhappy with your life doesn't mean you necessarily want to scrap the whole decade and start over. We all have our troubles. I *like* the wisdom I've accumulated, but along the way I seem to have lost the spirit I had as a younger man. Some of it—enough of it. And shouldn't we, as immorbid beings, have both? I guess I was mixing and matching."

"You guess?"

"Listen, *I* was attending a matter programming conference on Mars. The rest of me were all back home, taking care of personal and professional minutia. Or so I presume. So I infer from the circumstances, as an outsider. As for what I was thinking, what exactly I was doing, I can only speculate."

I thought that over. People had different viewpoints on plurality; some even claimed that every copy of them had its own unique soul. Fortunately, the law rarely ruled in their favor with a legal twinning, or the world would quickly overpopulate with nearly identical people. Xeripollution: the arrogant assumption that the world needed more and more and more of your precious, perfect self. And *that* question had been settled—with fire and blood—in the Dallas of the Late Modern era, and I doubted very much whether society wanted to repeat the experiment.

I personally liked to keep my copies close together in both time and space. I didn't send myself on vacation while the rest of me worked. I didn't cover multiple long-term assignments in parallel, and then reconverge afterward. It just gets confusing, when the experiences of your copies have diverged that much. My sense of self was, I suppose, a small thing: capable of encompassing only a handful of very similar instantiations. But while Theddy Kaffner had his fair share of faults, timidity was not among them.

Nor, tellingly, was malice. The Theddy of old was an irate fellow, but never a hurtful one. If he pushed someone down the stairs every now and then, he did it in the spirit of horseplay, knowing that no permanent harm could possibly result. Broken bones were just a fax plate away from their old glory, right? And Theddy, the programmer, was far more likely to just hack your shirt's wellcloth with a smear of ink or something, or throw *himself* down the stairs for a laugh. He'd been full of rages and frustrations, but he'd channeled them into useful hobbies, which included running and acting and the building of wooden models. The idea of his committing a *murder*, or even threatening one was . . . strange.

"What do you mean by mixing and matching?"

Theddy's stressed-up expression relaxed for a moment, into a smile as wistful as I had lately seen. "You're the food freak, Carbo. You know how it is: a pinch of this, a dash of that . . . a soupcon of my angry young self, to spice up my flavor a bit. I suppose I overdid it. Angry Young Theddy was a force to be reckoned with; did even I, myself, underestimate him? Did 10 percent of him overwhelm 90 percent of the canonical me? Or maybe it just felt good. Maybe I kept turning the knob, adding more and more of him until it was too late."

I spread my hands, unsure what to say. "More than anything, Thed, this sounds like a communication problem. Have you tried talking to yourself?"

"Yeah, briefly," Theddy said, the stress snapping back down over his features like a new matter program. "Until I kidnapped myself, with a force of three Theddies. These guys, who said they were me, they lifted me right off the floor. They were going to throw me through the print plate of my own goddamn fax machine in my own goddamn living room. Can you imagine? 'You're the last one,' they said, 'and it's one too many.' The way they were laughing, the way they were—I don't know, *handling* me. It went beyond contempt, Carbo. This was hatred. 'How could I turn into a fuck like you?' That was what Angry Young Theddy said to me.

"But *he* underestimated the power of fear. They meant to kill me, erase me—there was no question about that. They weren't fighting for their lives, and I was, so in the end they couldn't hold me. I felt their bones breaking. I felt an eyeball pop. As long as I live, I never want to feel a thing like that."

Okay, yeah, this was complicated. If there was a right place for Theddy to come to with this problem, my office was probably it. But where to begin?

"I'll need a full power of attorney," I said for starters, "and since you appear to have valid concerns for your physical safety, it may be best to store you here, in my office fax, under a seal of attorney-client privilege. The state can open that—the state can open anything—but *you* can't. The pattern that comprises you right now, right here, will be preserved no matter what Angry Young Theddy thinks or does."

"He's cleverer than you suppose," Theddy warned.

But I just laughed. "Nobody's cleverer than I suppose."

There was a bit more to it than that, but Theddy wanted help, and wasn't in a mood to argue. His agreement was not difficult to secure, and neither, as a result, was his physical person. It didn't take three guys to push him through the plate, and truthfully, I wasn't sure three guys could have stopped him if they'd been here to try. It was a safer place, and he wanted in.

3.
A Pedestrian Encounter

When you traveled by fax machine—and who didn't?—no place in the solar system was more than a few hours away, and if you were the one being transmitted, not the one waiting around at the other end, then from your point of view the journey was instantaneous. With a handful of steps, I could have found myself on the landing outside any home or apartment, anywhere. It was a funny thing, though: Theddy had lived less than a mile from my office for almost twenty years. How strange, that we should live so close for so long without realizing it! But living forever can be like that: it's easy to put things off, to assign them to the infinite and amorphous future. Even important things; even close friends.

Anyway, Denver was a historical preservation zone where walking was actively encouraged. In the eight square kilometers of the downtown district, faxing was actually illegal for anything but official business or the direst emergencies, and the city was adorned for tens of kilometers all around with roads and sidewalks, trails and quaint little bridges arching across the streams and rivers. This classic look was a large part of the city's appeal, and I wasn't about to abuse it by teleporting six blocks. The walk might take me twenty minutes, and might represent more exercise than most people got in a year, but my body, rendered eternally youthful by the fax filters, was surely up to the job. Whose wasn't? People who don't like walking, who don't like mountain views and fresh air and strangers on the street, well . . . they should live someplace else. Denver was not made for indoor souls.

Still, once outside I felt a twinge of regret for my decision, as the November afternoon rolled over me with shocking, unseasonable heat. "Mild winter" didn't begin to describe the weather we were having that year, but I kept forgetting. I kept dressing for wind and fog and the possibility of snow. My jacket did its best to fight off the heat (blasting it behind me in a stream of warm air), but in the shade of downtown's towers it had no ready power source, so there wasn't a lot it could actually do.

There's an irony for you: on a hot day it's cooler in the sun than the shade! But the shirt underneath was having a hard time as well, and I couldn't remove the jacket without revealing the sweat stains it was failing to disperse from under my arms. Life can be so unfair.

Anyway, Theddy's case was heavy on my mind, and June

Szymanski's still hadn't left it, and the two were filling up very different pieces of my brain. So I was deeper than usual in thought, and found the bustle and jangle of the crowds annoying. Some street wisdom I heard that day:

"Hollywood is a *plant*, Gabriel. The city, they were calling it that way before they started making hollies there."

"There's nothing noble about boredom, aye? Are there people you could be helping? Societies you could enrich? Don't you give me that look, you vegetable."

"Oh, of course you have the right to design a new life form. Everyone does. But for criminy's sake, John, that doesn't mean you have the right to instantiate it in the real world."

Yeah. Real pearls, those. The streets of this city had always been crowded, or nearly always, but even I, a mere centenarian, could remember a time when the crowds had all had someplace to go, some purpose in their steps. As often as not it was someplace they were *forced* to go, to stave off economic ruin in a scarcity-based economy, but still. The city's loitering laws had never been repealed, and ought at least occasionally to be enforced.

With its bright colors and piled-high fashions, its buskers and mimes, its living sculptures "dancing to the din of a dozen decades," the city resembled a carnival that day as much as a center of business or residence or learning. And for some reason I found this deeply irritating.

On the other hand, it wasn't like anyone was holding a sword to my neck, forcing me to interact, to be here at all. I was a champion of strangeness, and these, for better or worse, were my people. And anyway it *was* a short walk before I found myself in front of Theddy's apartment building, a retro-opensource brownstone in the 22nd-century style.

"How may I help you, sir?" the building asked, in what was surely its politest voice.

"I'm here to see Theddy Kaffner."

"I'm afraid Mr. Kaffner isn't in at the moment," the building clucked, with quite a good semblance of regret.

"It's a serious matter," I told the building. "A *legal* matter, I'm afraid. If you have a buffer copy of Mr. Kaffner on hand, and I imagine you do, then I must request you print him and allow me to speak with him at once."

The building's intelligence didn't like that one bit, and sounded cross. "On what grounds? You're not a police officer." (And this was true, although I knew a lot of police, and had once loved a policeman's daughter.) "Nor do you bear the carrier signal of a government official. By studying your face I can make a guess as to your identity, but I would prefer that you simply explain yourself."

Fair enough. "My name is Carmine Strange Douglas. Mr. Kaffner's attorney. The rest I'll say to him, if you don't mind."

"I have no record of this association," the house said skeptically, "although your face and pheromone signature match that name, and the social network archives indicate you have fraternized with Mr. Kaffner in the past. Do you have any proof that this arrangement exists?"

I held up a bonded, self-notarizing copy of the power of attorney, and the building opened instantly, curling aside a broad doorway of gold and pearl and other substances I couldn't identify. "Please come in, sir, and excuse my rudeness in detaining you. One can't be too careful these days, and in any case my security settings are at legal maximum."

"No offense taken," I assured it, since the thing was only doing its job, following its program, and had no actual feelings. Or so the law declared. Inside, among furnishings assembled from white puffy pillow-cubes, I found Theddy in deep conference with the wall.

Presumably, he was receiving a briefing on this turn of events—my arrival and such—since from his own perspective he had just moments before stepped through the fax machine on his way to somewhere quite different. This was a buffer copy, probably not more than a few hours old, and he had no way of knowing why I was here.

When Theddy saw me, he looked up with an expression of wonder. "Carbo? My God, man, what're you doing here? It's great to see you! But when exactly did you become my lawyer?"

"About half an hour ago," I said, extending a warm handshake. "There's a copy of you in my office who claims he was assaulted. By *you*, or rather, by several instances of you. I was hoping you could shed some light on the subject."

Theddy's hand withdrew from mine, and his face grew cautious, and right away I could see there was something different about him. He was less like the Theddy in my office, and more like the one I'd remember if I really thought back. The angry prankster. A composite sketch of New Theddy would be all broad lines and shallow curves, but while Young Theddy looked the same, he wore it differently. Here was a fellow of edges and points and sharp, staccato movements.

"There was an altercation," Theddy admitted, "but he started it. All I did was defend myself."

"Against what?"

Theddy's answering look was not quite a sneer. "That copy must have got some bad poison along the way, Carbo. He was irrational, and slow. It would have taken a lot of patience to get any sense out of him, and who's got the time?"

Well, *that* sounded believable enough.

"Did you try to push him into the fax?"

"It was the only way I could think of to, you know, figure out what his problem was. Merge a little bit of him with a lot of myself, and see what was on his mind."

I'd never been one to beat around the bush, so I came right out with it: "Theddy, have you been mingling your image with archive copies of yourself? Would a personality scan reveal sudden, dramatic changes in your character?"

"Yes," Theddy said, as if it were the most normal thing the world.

"Hmm. Well, listen, this allegedly deviant copy of yourself is the contemporary version. It's who all his friends and neighbors and colleagues are used to seeing. If he were in fact stored in your personal fax machine, per your plans, would you ever print him out again?"

"Hell no," Theddy answered, with that same matter-of-fact, self-righteous conviction. As if people did that sort of thing every day. Oh boy. Oh boy, oh boy. Some dangerous cocktail of thoughts and experiences had come together in this copy's brain. Theddy—the *real* Theddy—was right to be afraid: this man was not only capable of self-murder, but felt it was, in some way, his legal right. And I wondered: where was the case law to prove otherwise?

And to think I'd thought the Szymanski divorce was a mess! "What we have here," I said cautiously, "is a case of disputed identity. Two divergent copies of the same individual, laying claim to editorial rights over each other. That being the case, I personally have a conflict of interest, and must make no further contact with you, except if necessary in court. If you intend to prosecute your rights in this matter—and I find it difficult to imagine otherwise—you'll need to retain your own counsel. I cannot advise you in this."

Theddy scowled. "Oh you can't, can't you? Maybe the years have eroded your memory, dear friend, but you and I have an agreement, which predates any contract you may have with . . . that other bloke. That failed experiment. That shriveled old creature who does not deserve to wear Theddy Kaffner's skin."

Though it might be a breach of ethics, I took the bait. "What agreement is that?"

"I'll find it."

Theddy stepped to the wall and began whispering to it. A hollie window appeared there, displaying lists of text with little thumbnail images beside them. Theddy poked at the display several times, muttering, and finally said, "Ha! Found it."

A beer-stained cocktail napkin tumbled out of the fax machine, into Theddy's waiting hands. He scanned it briefly, nodding, then handed it to me. It said, in appallingly familiar handwriting,

I, Carmine Douglas, through the power vested in me by the state of inebriation, do solemnly swear that I will never lose my faith or spirit, and that I will look out for my friend Theddy come what may, for all eternity and throughout the universe.

It was signed and even—though the hologram was hard to make out—notarized.

"You can't be serious," I said, waving the thing as if to dry it. "This isn't legally binding." But even as the words were out of my mouth, I realized it might not be so. There were times in the historical past when what was legal and what was right were two different things, when valid arguments could be crafted to excuse almost anything, but the Queendom of Sol took a dim view indeed of broken promises. Theddy saw it in my face, too; he was a hard man to hide things from. I sighed and asked, "What do you want? What does it take to make this thing go away?"

Theddy sneered in youthful triumph. "If you want to go legal on me, old friend, I can only respond in kind. I *do* want my own counsel, as promised to me in this old contract. I want *you*. Not this stuffy alien creature you've become, but the young, angry, lovesick Carbo I went to school with. Well, I suppose you'd have to add a couple of years to that, or he wouldn't be a lawyer yet, but you see what I mean. I want my old roommate to defend me."

With a sinking feeling I realized that might just stick. Theddy might just have a point, which the law, in its finite wisdom and limited experience, had never yet addressed. The right of archive copies to be revived? To seek the company of their peers? To repudiate their future lives?

"Call my office," I said, sighing uneasily. "I'll authorize it to set something up. Not because I have to—and certainly not because I want to—but because you've raised an interesting point, and it needs to be properly explored. Even a younger me, a green me fresh out of school, is better qualified than most attorneys to wrestle this particular alligator. In fact, if I didn't buy into it voluntarily, the court might well assign it. In which case they'd offer you a disposable copy of me, which would self-destruct once the dispute was resolved. And that, my friend, is an involuntary servitude I would not wish on my younger self, who was an innocent and charming lad."

All of which was true, insofar as it went. Unlike Theddy, and with a single and quite excusable exception, my own younger self could be *trusted*. So why, in my heart just then, did the prospect of unleashing him bring nothing but dread?

4.
Passions, Revived

Rummaging through the archives took a lot longer than I expected. The storage companies are happy to take your money to capture the backup, but when it comes time for the free restore they're a lot less helpful. Wading through the layers of bureaucracy and "technical assistance" proved so difficult and involved that in the end I had to print out a dedicated copy of my recent self, who spent several days working on the problem exclusively.

Of the fifteen images I'd stored at one point or another in my life, the best fit for young Theddy seemed to be a Carmine two years out of law school, working at a big firm in Milan and flush, for the first time in his short life, with the income and respectability of gainful employment.

Memories washed over me. Those had been good years, but turbulent ones, too. Money and power and youth were a potent combination, and bred the sort of arrogance that led to personal troubles. And if there was a god of Love—and Strife, for they were bound together as a single entity in Queendom mythology—then poor Eros had spent some busy seasons that year, looking after the torrid romance between myself and Pamela Red. Even now, more than seventy years after the fact, the memory brought a poignant flutter of excitement and pain. I'd had a number of lovers before her, and quite a bit more after—I'd even been married twice—but when I looked back over the conquests and treaties, surrenders and defeats of my immorbid love life, Pamela's shadow seemed to loom over all of it. She was the standard against which all others were measured.

This was of course no great novelty in the Queendom, where the phenomenon was common enough to have its own name: the guidepost affair. And rumor had it that if you lived long enough, if you loved well enough, your guidepost would fade, would be replaced, or even—strange thought—subsumed entirely by the one true love of your life, who would stay with you forever. A guidepost affair was, by definition, buried deep in your past—something that didn't or couldn't or wouldn't work out. Something painful. But ah, we still believed in a higher sort of love than that, else how could we face eternity?

Not that there wasn't other strife in that era, as well. Like any human being, the Carmine of that day had had a sackload of mundane troubles, which to him seemed very serious and immediate, though today I could scarcely remember them. But I did my best to align myself with that mental space, in the hours and minutes—and finally the seconds—before Angry Young Carmine stepped out of the fax.

"Welcome," I said to myself, for I remembered this young man with great fondness and admiration. Angry Young Carmine, looking me up and down, recognized me at once, but the first thing he said was, "Hello, Carmine. You look . . . different. Considering the fact that I've *just this second* archived myself, for the benefit of my future self, I can only assume that some years have passed."

"Correct," I said, beaming at this lad's quick mind.

"Something has gone wrong, then. Ah, Carmine, have you been poisoned? Traumatized? Worn down or worn out with the passage of years?"

"There is a problem," I agreed with gentle amusement, "but not with me. It's Theddy."

"Theddy needs an archived copy of *me*? That sounds damned peculiar, and complicated. Brief me on the specifics, if you would."

And here I felt the first tingle of irritation, for I was clearly the senior partner in this endeavor, and this young man had no right to give me orders. But without noticing or without caring, Young Carmine pressed on: "I also need to orient myself. I'll need news highlights for each of the intervening years, and if you don't mind, a sampling of the clothing and music fashions as well. And the *food*."

"Ahem. Young man, you might find it helpful to let others get a word in now and then. The time capsules you describe are in the fax's buffer memory right now, awaiting your attention."

"Ah. What year is it, anyway?"

I told him, and watched his expression tense briefly and then relax.

"That's a long time, old man. I assume it's a short-term assignment you've woken me for?"

"It is."

Young Carmine's smile was pained. "Reconverging our experiences could be problematic when this is finished. You should probably check with a doctor, or maybe a quantum physicist, but

I'm not sure consciousness can bridge a gap that large."

I adopted what I hoped was a look of patience. "My plan is to filter you in as a percentage, to reintegrate a tincture of you with my current self. Carefully, of course, but everything admirable about you will be preserved and magnified, and with luck our flaws will mask one another."

"Oh really. I see." Young Carmine's tone was skeptical, poised on the cusp of anger. "And what percentage, exactly, did you plan on granting me? Twenty-five percent?"

At this, I was afraid to answer truthfully, because the actual figure I had in mind was .25 percent, or possibly .5 percent. But to this living, breathing young man, that would sound like murder. I had the legal right to do exactly that, to print disposable copies of myself and then, you know, dispose of them. But I'd never done it when there were major life experiences at stake. Why would I? I wouldn't want to *be* the disposable copy whose memories died, and I wouldn't want to be the one who lived on without those memories, either. A no-win scenario.

But this was different, right? Everything important about Young Carmine was preserved in me. I was a superset of him, and in that sense his erasure would mean nothing, cost nothing, hurt nothing. Except from his point of view. And to enforce the right of erasure against his will . . . To enforce the right, I might have to print extra copies of my current self, and overpower Young Carmine, and hurl him forcibly into the fax. Or contact a lawyer of my own, and let the courts decide. And didn't *that* put Theddy's case in an interesting light?

Afterward, I was never sure what my younger self read in my face at that moment, but whatever it was, he answered with an obscene gesture and a barked command at the office wall, which, recognizing the voice of its owner, opened a door and let him out.

"Ah, hell," I said, following behind, trying to put a hand on his shoulder to reassure him. To reassure myself. But Young Carmine was having none of that, and in fact took the gesture as a hostile one. Which might not be too far from the truth. Young Me jerked his shoulder away, then ducked and ran down the hallway.

I said, "You're going to want—you'll need—hey!" But the lines of communication had broken down entirely, and the next comments I received from Young Carmine would, I realized, have a letterhead at the top. Damn. My body hadn't aged a day in all this time, and I supposed I could simply run after myself, tackle myself, fight it out physically and force myself to listen. But I'd be hard pressed to win against so equal an opponent, and if the concept of "youth" meant anything at all in this day and age, would it really be so equal?

What I actually did, like a useless old man, was race down the hallway and scream down the stairwell at myself: "You stay away from Pamela Red, do you hear me! You caused her enough trouble when you were . . . back when you were . . ." Real.

5.
The Daughter's Policeman

The next morning found me on the far side of the moon, in a scenic dome at the pit of Jules Verne crater, with the sharp-toothed hills of the crater lip rising up all around. Here it wasn't morning at all, but early evening by the Greenwich Mean shift clock and somewhere close to midnight by the actual position of the sun. Given the full moon in Denver last night—always a peak time for strangeness—it made sense that the moon's sulking farside, faced always away from Earth, should be bathed in darkness.

Any school child of the early Queendom knew that on that big, pre-terraformed moon, the sun rose and set every twenty-eight days. But unless you'd spent time on Luna yourself, it was hard to appreciate just how irrelevant the daylight really was. Aside from the anachronism of gravity tourism, Luna didn't really offer anything the rest of the Queendom particularly needed, and as a result the great dome cities at Tranquility and Grimaldi were money pits, gone to seed in a state of not-quite completion. The moon's million permanent residents were mostly scattered in small, economically depressed communities, and the great bulk of its housing was underground. You lived there because you loved it, basically. Because you'd bought into the romance of it: a wild frontier on Earth's very doorstep.

And on that frontier, for some historical reason I'd never bothered to learn, the clocks were set, planetwide and regardless of longitude, to British time. Not that it really mattered to me—the hour or the darkness. Such transitions—day to night, winter to summer to hard vacuum—were common to the point of dullness in a faxwise society. That's just the way things were.

In any case, Verne was a small town inhabited mainly by astronomers and small-time trelium prospectors, who had taste enough to keep the dome lights low and green. Night lights, so that the stars could shine down in all their glory through the near-invisible wellglass of the dome. I'd seen this place in the daytime once—on a sadly similar errand—and the dome had been frosted a translucent blue-white which didn't mimic an Earthly sky so much as pay homage to it. Good for the soul, I reckoned at the time. Better for the plants and animals than the searing unfiltered light of Sol herself.

Also tasteful was the way Verne's visitors were encouraged, through transit fee structures and hierarchical addressing, to enter through the fax ports in the park level immediately beneath the dome. It wasn't a big park as such things go, but its colored brick pathways folded back on themselves many times, with the view of grassy meadows blocked here and there by stands of dwarf bamboo and twisty, lunar-tall apple trees. So it felt bigger than it really was, and the walk from fax to elevator took a good three minutes. An actual elevator, yes; to get to any particular home, office or storefront in Verne you had to find the right color-coded shaft, and ride the elevator down to the appropriate subsurface level.

As a longtime resident of Denver—a city similarly trapped in the romantic past—I could only approve. Beauty was so much finer a thing than convenience! Even (or perhaps especially) when you were in a hurry.

Too bad it was guilt, not beauty, which brought me there that day. But hey, even that guilt, that shame and worry, could ultimately be blamed on beauty. On one particular beauty, in fact, which I had sought above all others. Nearly to my ruin, yes, and I might spend the rest of eternity shaking off the consequences, but in this sense I regretted nothing, and would do it all again if I could.

By blue starlight and the green glow of the dome's perimeter,

I trod a path of yellow bricks in platinum-white mortar. My bootheels clopped and rang. I'd come here expecting to ask directions, from a wellstone pillar if not a live human, but I found to my surprise that my feet still knew the way. Through the gloom of an orchard and back out into starlight again, I came to a low pink cottage with the words GOVERNMENT AND UTILITIES carved into its lintel and glowing that same soft green, with modestly animated crests on either side to emphasize the point.

I entered the building, and found myself in a traditional lobby complete not only with elevators but with a human security guard seated behind a desk. This might seem laughable in an age where superweapons had nearly obliterated the sun, but the man's gray uniform—bearing the five-pointed star of the Verne Crater Sheriff's Office—was thicker than ordinary wellcloth, and lent him a formidable air. In time of trouble, the suit would no doubt extend to cover his face, his head, his hairy-knuckled hands, and the thing's capacitors and hypercomputers would be prepared to amplify his strength, to shoot all manner of energy beams from his fists, from his eyes, from the edges of any wound an attacker might somehow manage to inflict.

This, too, was nothing special—most cops dressed this way most of the time—and anyway a pair of gleaming, hulking Law Enforcers lurked robotically in the corners behind him, just in case anyone still had any thoughts about getting cute.

"Carmine Douglas, Attorney at Law," I said, although by now the guard must already know this. Like all professionals everywhere, he'd be unemployed if he weren't uncannily competent. "I'm here to see Waldo Red."

"Yeah?" The cop looked me over with a bored expression. "What for?"

"Personal business."

The guard thought that one over. "I don't have you on my visitors list. Is he expecting you?"

"No. Well, possibly." Depending on what Angry Young Carmine had or hadn't done, Waldo might well be drafting a warrant for my arrest. Or tying a hangman's noose. "But he knows me."

"So he does," the cop said, glancing down at some social network display on his desktop. He tapped the surface several times in quick succession, like a harp player working the strings. "He . . . will see you. But—whoa. According to my stats, there's a 90 percent chance of verbal confrontation and an 8 percent chance of violence. On *his* part; *you're* down in the noise, an innocent victim of potential attack. My goodness. Do . . . you want an armed escort?"

"No," I said. "Thank you. I'm here to make peace."

"Huh. Well, go on ahead. Level nineteen, end of the hallway and turn right."

"Thanks."

The guard shuffled uncomfortably in his chair. "Hey, buddy? Uh, you don't have to answer this or anything, but, I mean . . . Deputy Waldo isn't exactly a thug. What does a guy have to do to burn him off like that?"

"Sleep with his daughter," I said, and turned for the elevator.

6.
The Law

The first thing Waldo said to me when I walked into his office was, "Hmmph. So now you're stalking *me*."

And there was a lot of evidence coded in this statement: it meant that Young Carmine had gone to see Pamela, and that the visit had been less than welcome. It meant that she'd called her father afterward, and that he considered the incident, at least in his heart, to be a criminal offense. Which was silly, because that old restraining order had expired forty years ago, and I had no history, either before or since, of criminally rude behavior. But then again, there was no telling what Young Carmine might've said. Or done. Truthfully, I had forgotten how forceful and intense I'd really been as a young man. And pointlessly so, for it had only gotten me in trouble.

I held up my hands in mock surrender. "Hi, Waldo. I'm sure you're angry—and not without reason!—but it's not what you think. There's an old, old copy of me running around."

Waldo studied me, thinking that one over. Whatever he'd

expected me to say, that wasn't it. Waldo was seated on his desk, which had gone soft beneath him in response. His arms were crossed, and his single, heavy eyebrow was pulled down in an almost comical frown. In his harrumphy way he said, "Rogue or authorized?"

"A little of both," I answered, unsure what else to say about it.

Waldo digested that, and finally nodded. "Hmm. Humph. Yeah. One of those."

A bit of the tension went out of the room. The details must surely be unique, but Waldo had been a cop for a hundred years longer than I'd even been alive. He'd seen his share of weirdness, and understood that the law was gray. What cop didn't know that? The law was designed for assaults and robberies, angry neighbors fighting over the pruning of a tree or the disposition of its fruits. By definition, you couldn't legislate the unanticipated, and existing laws—sensible laws—sometimes yielded perverse or even contradictory results. *Do we divide the child in two?*

And in this age of plenty there just wasn't all that much thuggery. The sorts of things that had value anymore were not the sorts of things you could steal at gunpoint, and anyway such obvious crimes were always solved, always punished. With enough decades behind them, even the most hardened criminals eventually got the message.

So what did that leave? Juvenile mischief, and the weirdness at the margins of the grown-up world. The need for cops and courtrooms would never go away.

"Why are you here?" Waldo asked with less hostility.

I tried on a half smile. "It seemed . . . more polite than going directly to Pamela. I figured he'd go and see her. I knew he would. He's an archive copy from when that . . . issue was relatively fresh."

"So why'd you print him?"

"Contractual obligation, I guess you'd say. I'll spare you the insipid details."

"Hmmph. Thanks. Are you going to get rid of him?"

I could only shrug. "I'm not sure I can, Waldo. He's defending another person's archive copy against exactly that procedure. Removing him would be a form of pre-trial tampering, and if his case prevails—which it very well might—then it's anyone's guess what *my* legal rights are. Pray for a wise judge."

Waldo didn't like that answer. "Really. How convenient. There's a little Carmine running around from the period of the restraining order—and believe me, you were a nitwit back then—and he's got all the rights of being you and none of the responsibilities of being himself. He can bug my daughter all he likes, unless I file an updated order against *you*. Which I guess I'll just have to do."

And that made me angry, because the revival of a seventy-year-old restraining order would look bad on my record. It would hurt my image, hurt my business, hurt my *pride*. And for what? "You know, Waldo, your darling Pamela wasn't exactly an innocent in all this. If there were courts of law for faithless lovers . . ."

"You were a nitwit, and your friends were nitwits, and you made her sad. The only surprise is that it took her two years to realize the fact. And like a shit, you refused to crawl back under your block. You just couldn't leave it alone. You wanted to own her. You tried to buy her like a doll."

At that, in a wildly uncharacteristic gesture, I slammed the wall sideways with my fist, hard. "I wanted nothing of the kind, *Deputy*. Even now, you refuse to acknowledge my point. It was simple enough for a small town cop and his daughter to understand, if they put their minds to it. For years I licked the wounds she inflicted so casually. For *years*. Like an old tree, I got whole again only by growing around the scar. Burying it inside me, surrounded it with strong, healthy tissue. But the defect itself is permanent."

"Love always is," Waldo lectured, as if to a child. "We all have our little scars. It doesn't give you any special rights. And just for your education, punk, you fix a tree by printing an undamaged copy. If that 'wound' of yours is so terrible, why do you keep it?"

"You've been in love, Waldo. You know why."

The old cop sighed and harrumphed. "I don't know where you crawled out from, pal, and I don't care, but understand: we keep the peace here in Jules Verne. You know how many arrests

I've made this year? Six, and three of them were the same guy. You know how many times I've called the Constabulary in the past decade, to solve some capital crime of Queendom-wide importance? Zero."

"Congratulations."

Waldo answered with a mocking expression, and then a more seriously threatening one. "I may not have jurisdiction outside this crater, Mr. Douglas, but you've got five minutes to get your ass out of here before I throw it in jail. Don't let me catch you here again, ever."

And this was a strong statement indeed, because Waldo Red would never die, never grow old and retire. Never forgive a young man's trespasses.

Well, I had my own rights to worry about, and said so: "If you do that, or file an injunction of any kind, I'll sue for defamation. I'll make it stick, too."

And with that I stomped out, feeling in spite of everything that the visit had gone better than expected.

7.
Pamela, Read

Pamela herself, whom I visited next, surprised me by being a lot more understanding.

"Daddy called," she said by way of introduction. "I heard about your little . . . technical difficulties."

Her house was one of nine at the summit of Mt. Terror, on Antarctica's Ross Island overlooking both the volcano's active caldera and the Ross Sea coast, aglow in the lights of McMurdo City and, across the water, of Glacia and Victoria Land. It was nighttime here as well, in a place where night was winter, or in this case early spring. And Pamela's foyer, like many in cold climates, was poorly insulated on purpose, to discourage surprise visitors.

My wellcloth suit did the best it could, but it had been out of the sun for hours now, and its power reserves were getting low. It settled for swathing me in black velvet, lined with some crinkly, unbreathable super-reflector that left my skin feeling hot and suf-focated, even as my body heat bled away through my uncovered hands and head.

"You look cold," Pamela said, ushering me in through her open doorway. "You want some coffee? Soup?"

"Spiced almond chowder," I answered gratefully, following her inside. There was no such thing as a poorly furnished home in the Queendom of Sol, but there were copyrighted patterns available only to those with money, and there were expert deco-rators and geomancers who could customize a space to its owners with striking—and strikingly expensive—skill. And everyone had access to a fax machine, if not in their own houses and apart-ments then, by law, within forty paces of their door. But to *fill* a house with fax machines—I counted five in my first quick look around, including the one in the foyer—took resources. And the view, also not free, was spectacular.

"Looks like you're doing all right, here," I said, while she stepped up to her dining room fax to fetch my soup. "I hope you don't mind my saying so."

"Not a bit," she laughed. "But I'll be the first to admit, I got lucky. Matter programming is funny that way: sometimes you hit the right combination, and this substance you've just invented is gorgeous, and it's waterproof, and it's diamagnetic, and some construction outfit on Pluto is offering you cash up front and a 10 percent share of their leasing profits."

"Sounds nice," I told her, fighting to keep any deeper feelings at bay. For the moment, I was succeeding; it *had* been a long time, and seeing her now was more nostalgic than painful. "Theddy became a programmer, too, you know, but he doesn't live like this."

She smiled. "Theddy. My goodness, how is he?"

"In trouble," I said.

"Well, that figures. I suppose you're representing him?"

"Yeah."

"That figures, too. As for my alleged wealth, don't be too jeal-ous. It won't last. Unless I get lucky again, I'll have to sell this place in a few centuries. Maybe move back to farside, although they're still talking about evacuating the entire moon, and crushing it to boost the surface gravity. You can't go home again, isn't that what they say?"

Thinking about that, I looked her over, studying my feelings as they unfolded. Things weren't the same as they had been long ago, that much was definite. Her mere presence no longer panicked me, made me stupid or impulsive. Which was probably just as well, although there was a part of me that would always miss feeling that way. You can't go home, indeed.

"That would be a shame," I said, "destroying the moon like that. Where would all the shady people go?"

She could easily have taken that the wrong way, but she chose not to, and chuckled instead as she pulled my mug of steaming soup from the fax. "The shady people always find a place, Carbo. Isn't that what keeps you in business?"

"Well," I admitted, "sort of. It's the *rich* shady people that can afford my services. The poor ones get their legal help from software, which is worth every penny of the nothing they pay for it."

"Their matter programming, too," she said. And suddenly we were laughing together, just like old times. It felt good. Cleansing. If all our times had been like this . . .

"Look," I told her, "I want to apologize for inflicting Young Me on you like that. I hope he didn't scare you."

"Not in the least. Actually, he was quite charming." She handed me the soup, and I tasted it. It was *good*, and here too I sensed some vague tincture of money, some subtle designer flavor to which I myself had never been privy. And I was not exactly a poor man, nor a gustatorial simpleton.

"What did he do? What did he want?"

"The usual," she laughed. "A bit of me for his collection."

Suddenly I found myself fighting down anger again, for the second time in a single morning. Because it wasn't funny, damn it. Not to me it wasn't. The request had seemed simple enough at the time. Pamela and I had archived ourselves at the height of our passion, wanting—literally—to preserve that glorious feeling for all eternity. Later, when things had soured, when we started fighting and she finally turned me out, I had asked her to revive that feeling. Not even in her own skin, necessarily. Couldn't she print out an alternate copy, an older, younger version who was still in love with Carmine Douglas? Wasn't that the whole point of the backup?

But apparently it wasn't, at least in her mind, and apparently I had pressed the point too firmly. Well, no "apparently" about it; love could make a man do stupid things, and no force in heaven or Earth could make him regret them afterward. In love especially, we behave as we must.

In any case, my defense had taken me all the way to the Solar Court itself, where my stalking and harassment convictions were narrowly upheld. I was clever enough not to lose my license over it, but the court forbade me to have any contact with Pamela Red, or her friends and family, for three long decades. The mark would be on my record forever: Carmine Douglas, sexual deviant. What was funny about that?

"Look," she said, catching my expression. "We were young. We applied our passion to each other, and when it didn't work out we applied our passion against each other. It's the oldest story in the world. I'm assuming we both got over this a long time ago, like good little grown-ups, so let's not start fighting now. Okay? I'm genuinely sorry, about all of it."

That stung too, in its own way. "About *all* of it? You're sorry it even happened?"

And to my surprise, her face melted in a strange mix of amusement and dismay. "*Sorry it happened*? What . . . What are you even talking about? We were fresh, we were new, we were *burning* with passion for the first time in our tiny little lives. What's the point of living forever if you only get to feel that way once? Carmine, Carbo, baby doll, it was the hottest fling of my life."

What came next made perfect sense, because if I'd ever had any willpower in the Pamela Red department, we wouldn't be standing there talking about it. And if she hadn't loved me—truly loved me with all her heart, at least for a while—I wouldn't have had anything to press her about, to get in trouble about. An explosion could not occur without heat. But it was one more bit of strangeness, and I honestly didn't know if there were any law or rule or ethical guideline being broken. Would society prevent me from hurling myself on this additional complication?

It hardly mattered. Yes, I tumbled into bed with her, and she with me. Heedless of the consequences, we remained there for three days, refusing all calls. And it was worth any price.

8.
Orders

When I finally got home, my head was clearer somehow. It was one thing to stir up ghosts from the past, but quite another to have them walking around spouting threats. But making peace with Pamela—making more than that!—put a different face on things. Anyway, I did what I should've done in the first place, which was to file a motion for Division of Self for Theodore Kaffner, and another for Carmine Douglas.

Divisions of Self—so-called twinnings—had a sparse but readily traceable case history, and seemed the most appropriate vehicle for dealing with this mess. True, no one had ever and attempted an *involuntary* twinning before. Generally, they were granted to individuals who had lost a genuine twin somewhere along the way, or who could, for whatever reason, prove some tangible need to divide themselves into two legally distinct individuals. Because they'd grown in different ways, and no longer believed they were compatible.

Angry Young Theddy's argument was quite different: that he should have the right to delete his later self and try his whole adult life over again. But if the older and younger Theddies were two different people, then this desire would be nonsense from a legal standpoint, and acting on it would be murder. Which, to my thinking, sounded about right.

And Young Carmine's position was different still: having been granted the flesh and breath of life, he simply wanted to continue. He didn't want to be erased, and truthfully neither would I, if our circumstances were reversed. And the law was supposed to mean what was *right*, right?

The next step was to file a temporary restraining order—actually four restraining orders—prohibiting the various Theddies and Carmines from harming one another, or having any sort of contact at all outside a courtroom setting. We could send legal communiqués to one another through the proper channels, and

BEST SHORT NOVELS: 2006

that was all. Sadly, this would be another mark on my own record, another opportunity for me to look like some sort of mad stalker, but since my name was on the order as both plaintiff and defendant, it would seem more strange than incriminating. And anyone researching my background that deeply would know, *should* know, that Strange is my middle name.

Then I did another thing I should've done right away, which was to call my parents and let them know what was happening. "Aren't you a bit old for shenanigans like this?" my father wanted to know.

"I'm beginning to think so," I answered.

For good measure, I called Theddy's parents as well, and found to my mild surprise that Angry Young Theddy was actually staying there with them, having vacated his apartments in Denver. This of course forced me to cut the conversation short, but that was all right. The Kaffners were drunks and dreamers, with never all that much to say to me, or I to them.

And since these orders were of the sort that could easily be handled by hypercomputer, the so-called Telejudges—I had a stack of bonded approvals in hand within a few minutes. The Telejudges of course demanded a flesh hearing, ten days hence, so a human judge could review the facts of the case and decide the long-term disposition of the orders, and of the humans tied up in them.

And that wasn't so hard, really. Strangeness is nothing more than the shock of the new: a thing never seen before, never felt or tasted or lived through. But strangeness by itself it didn't make this thing intractable, nor guarantee in any way that the future—the Theddies and Carmines and Pamelas of centuries hence, indeed all of society—would find them unusual. Indeed, to the extent that society took any notice of this case at all, it would be as one more precedent in the legal definition of identity. No big deal of all. Or so I reasoned at the time.

And so, somewhat anticlimactically, I found that my job was complete. With those orders posted, there wasn't a fax machine in the Queendom that would reconverge the older and younger Theddies, or a door that would open for them, if the opening might place the two in the same room. My client was safe, and so was I. And I found, also to my surprise, that I was shaking with relief. How about that! This was another thing my job had going for it: no matter how long I did it, there was still this aura of excitement and danger and fresh discovery. Most especially when it was about me.

After that there was only one thing left to do: call my office fax machine and retrieve Theddy—the real, contemporary Theddy—from storage.

9.
Wine, Interrupted

My apartment at the time was a pseudo-penthouse—its large balcony was roofed over but otherwise genuine, and the rooms themselves were on the thirteenth floor of a hundred-story building. But the balcony's overhang was programmed to look like sky—an illusion so good that I myself sometimes forgot—while the apartment ceiling was a fiction of dormer vaults and skylights looking up at the other tall buildings as though the higher stories of my own did not exist. This was not an extravagance; the patterns had to be customized by experts and hypercomputers, but it only took an afternoon. A team from Sears Roebuck had done it for less money than I made in a week. Why, hundreds of people in Denver alone had the exact same decor, probably an even dozen in that very building. But low-cost and cheapness were not the same thing, and most visitors found the effect both striking and laudable.

In this, Theddy Kaffner was no exception. He leaped from the fax all stiff with anxiety, but once I'd explained the situation to him, and handed him a glass of wine, the first thing he did was look around and say, "Jesus Christ. Nice place."

The fireplace was also an illusion—you couldn't jab it with the ornamental poker or wave your hand through the flames—but it looked perfect, and crackled *just so*, and gave off exactly the right amount of heat for a November evening that was suddenly, finally beginning to feel like fall. I faxed up some throw pillows, and the two of us sprawled in the firelight, chugging our drinks and laughing like we had in the good old days.

The purveyors of copyright bourbon tended to regard their products as perfect, and thus subsisted mainly on royalties, reinvesting little or none of it back into research and development. Which was a losing strategy in the long run, because the open-source and public domain recipes got a little bit better every year. Not the same as the copyright brews, obviously, but just as good in their own way. This meant that spending real money on bourbon didn't make sense, except as a way of flaunting one's wealth. Since I rarely had enough to flaunt, I tended to stick with the cheap stuff.

But the wine industry, long accustomed to change and adaptation, had seen the writing on the early Queendom's walls, and rolled with the times. They still grew their grapes the old-fashioned way, with robot labor and nano-optimized soil conditioners, and while they copyrighted every vintage, they actually copied and sold only the best of the best. But except in rare cases, they revoked the old recipes at the end of every market year, replacing them with new ones from the latest crop. If you really liked a particular vintage, you were obliged to buy as many bottles as your cellar would hold, because its like would never come again. So you either had to fill a cellar with the stuff, or pay the aftermarket prices on the collectors' market. Ouch.

I, however, belonged to the Wine Resistance movement. If you knew a bit, and were a good researcher of long-dormant archives, you could dig up the pattern of some ancient vintage whose creators had died heirless and alone. The public domain wines were mostly swill, but I had personally discovered two of these grayware vintages, which could be freely duplicated to my heart's content, and I'd bartered them for a dozen more on the semisecret Resistance exchange.

They were always the same, alas, but so were the "perfect" bourbons. This particular bottle was an atomically exact Delle Venezie Pinot Grigio, from 2203 at the tail end of Late Modernity. Possibly the oldest surviving Pinot Grigio, as delicate and fruity as the day it was archived. And it was *excellent*, even when chugged.

"You'll never guess who I saw this week," I said to Theddy as I uncorked our second bottle.

"Pamela Red," Theddy answered immediately. Was I that transparent? A lawyer really did need a better poker face than this, because Theddy read even more from my expression. "Oh, you *saw* her, did you? In the biblical sense? Did you *run into* her as well? Come across her, so to speak? Good for you, old boy."

I suffered some more teasing of an even less gentlemanly sort, until Theddy finally asked, "How's she doing, anyway?"

"Well. Very well. She's got a gorgeous house down in AntiLand, on the top of Mount Terror. You should see it sometime."

"She got that on a programmer's salary?"

"Well, she calls it a fluke, and I believe her. But yes, she's a programmer. Specializing in materials design."

"Mmm," Theddy said around a heavy swallow of dirt-cheap Pinot. "That would explain it. That's where all the glory is, where all the money is these days. If you ask me, my job is harder: making sure the materials actually work. However wonderful your brick may be, if it's wellstone you've still got to run power and data from point A to point B. You've got to manage waste heat, and if there's gas and fluid transport involved, the plumbing has to go somewhere. Also, a lot of materials aren't structural without an impervium mesh woven through them, and if you ever want the brick to be anything else, to be *programmable* like the rest of the world, then you'd better have some computing elements listening for commands. These things don't happen by themselves."

"I thought hypercomputers did all that."

"Everybody thinks that. That's why the job doesn't pay well. But hypercomputers don't *feel*, Carmine, not like we do. You can load them with algorithms for aesthetics and common sense, but it doesn't make them human. It's a human world we want, right? Computers are always seeking pathological solutions—you know, kill the cockroaches by roasting the whole apartment and then faxing fresh people. That actually happened! And if nothing else it takes a human to add those boo boos to the common-sense database. No do, you stupid machine.

"But we do a lot more than just that. There are copyright issues, security and permissions issues. Hypercomputers will follow the letter of the law every time—they have to—and they're practically paralyzed as a result. To no one's benefit. And there are always profiteers exploiting loopholes, sneaking adware materials onto private property and then wrapping themselves up in the law. Sanctimonious jerks. Half my house calls are to defeat some security system or other, because the wellwood stopped working or the window glass is suddenly demanding back royalties."

"So it's an art," I said, "like everything else that matters."

"Yeah."

"Speaking of which, are you still involved with the theater?"

"Indeed I am," Theddy said. "In fact, that's where my troubles began. I was going to so many plays, and posting so many opinions about what I saw, that one of the news services finally signed me on as part of their appreciators pool."

I knew about of those, yeah: appended to the remarks of professional reviewers were the Aficionados' and People's Choice scores, along with occasional snippets of commentary from their discussion boards. I'd even considered, at one point, quitting law to become a poverty-stricken food appreciator. But I didn't see a connection to Theddy's case, and said so.

Theddy's glass was empty again, and he waved it for a refill, which I provided. "See, the other appreciators were getting really burned off with me. 'You've already got a job,' they said. 'Why're you hogging an aficionado slot as well? You're taking a livelihood away from someone on Basic Assistance. Someone who loves the theater as much as you do."

"Now that's pathetic," I said.

But Theddy's take on it was more forgiving: "There are a lot of people who have nothing else to contribute, Carbo. They make good spectators, and where would the arts be without good spectators? But they can be really pushy about it. Really defensive. Some of these people, it means a lot more to them than it should. They started getting ugly, making threats."

"Ah. And you thought Angry Young Theddy could help."

"Well, yeah. A bit of him, anyway. The fire of youth to temper the iron of wisdom. But fire is tricky."

Those were Theddy's last words, and for the record, when

the Constabulary had reconstructed the events that followed, I was fully exonerated of any negligence or inaction. The tampering with my home and office records had occurred during the moments while Theddy's image was in transit, and had triggered no firewall alerts or quantum decoherence flags. The camera that appeared in my ceiling was a mesh of microscopic sensors, which my eyes could not possibly have discerned, even if I'd known where to look.

And although I was looking right at Theddy—pouring the last of the Pinot Grigio into his glass, in fact—when the wellcloth of the pillows beneath him crackled and turned to metal, when the floor became a grid of high-voltage lines . . . I'll feel terrible about it for the rest of my life—forever, in other words—but I didn't know what was happening, or why, and even if I did there was really nothing I could have done about it.

When the corners of Theddy's lips drew backward and upward, exposing his teeth, I thought at first that he was smiling. But then his body began to jerk, and smoke, and his eyes grew milky, and I hope to God that the brain damage happened early, because if it didn't, then Theddy, paralyzed and twitching, felt his own hair catch fire, his own skin blacken and peel away. Was the general alarm the last thing he heard?

These were not only my speculations, but also those of an entire Queendom of voyeurs, for there hadn't been a lurid murder in twenty years, or an electrocution in over a hundred. And such events—even before they'd become rare—had always been strange.

10.
Judgments, Final

The trial was only two hours long, and very nearly a formality. Theodore Great Kaffner, Sr.'s only physical body had been murdered, and the only recent copies of him—in the fax buffers of my home and office—had been expertly deleted. Angry Young Theddy did not deny his involvement in these acts, and even if he'd tried, he wouldn't have gotten very far in light of the Constabulary's overwhelming evidence.

On the face of it, he was guilty as sin, but Young Carmine, true to his beer-soaked promises, had mounted a spirited defense. Theddy was guilty, yes, but of what, exactly? Young Carmine consistently used the term "voluntary file maintenance" to describe the incident, and insisted that at the time of said maintenance, Young Theddy had had no way of knowing he'd been legally partitioned into a pair of twins. Thus, he was incapable of criminal intent in the commission of these acts, and if any loss or suffering resulted, it was—to Theddy's mind—of a self-inflicted sort which the law could frown on but not actually forbid.

It was, I thought, quite a savvy maneuver for a counselor so young. It made sense, and if justice were a purely logical affair, or an attempt to move forward with the minimum social damage, it might possibly have prevailed. But the other function of law is to frighten, to make examples, to discourage further thoughts of wrongdoing in the hearts of human beings. And the facts of the case remained incontrovertible: one legal individual was killed through the deliberate and premeditated actions of another. In the end, Young Carmine did about as well for Theddy as anyone could expect: malicious negligence resulting in death.

Tragically, of the durable archives Theddy had stored over the course of his life, the most recent was nearly twenty years out of date, and when it was printed and briefed and placed on the stand to provide commentary for the sentencing, all it could do was hang its head and weep. There was just too much missing from its life. It couldn't make sense of the actions of older *or* younger Theddy, nor of the circumstances it found itself awakened to. When the court asked if it wished to be marked disposable, and thus erased, the copy nodded slowly and was led away by the bailiffs.

As for Young Theddy, he was sentenced to one hundred years' hard labor, without the possibility of parole, and since he was barely twenty-five years in subjective age, this was about as close to a death sentence as a person could get, without murdering thousands or attempting to destroy the sun. A century of subjugation, of cheek-to-jowl contact with humanity's hardest customers. When that was over, nothing would remain of the Theddy I went to college with. Theodore Great Kaffner had managed to destroy himself, and this date was one I would always remember as the true time and place of his death.

There have always been tragedies, and perhaps there always will be: sad events with a momentum of their own, which benefit no one and which make the world a poorer place. And yet, in a way, this was a fitting end for a prankster like Theddy. Hoist on his own petard, indeed. What a lark! I sobbed off and on throughout the trial, dabbing at my tears with a wellcloth handkerchief, but even so I could not avoid the occasional giggle or snort. Even Theddy's younger self, doomed to ruin, seemed on some level to appreciate the irony. He smiled and waved as they led him away, and would no doubt make friends in prison by throwing himself down the stairs.

Ever mindful of the convenience of its patrons, the court had scheduled my own case next on the docket. And this one really *was* a formality, for I had sent an offer to myself the night before, and accepted it gratefully. I, the older Carmine, would cede that portion of my wealth that the younger Carmine had rightfully earned, and Young Carmine would cede the name, changing his own to Ralph Faxborn Douglas. He would also move to a different city, seek new acquaintances, and change his face and hairstyle in minor but telling ways. As for Ralph's ongoing maintenance, I offered a generous five-year stipend, to give him a chance to get on his feet, to find a job or found a business somewhere. But Ralph, awash in notoriety, had no shortage of job offers, and had already licensed his story—*our* story—for a tidy sum that I agreed not to dispute or attach in any way. No further settlement was needed.

On the stand I was asked by the judge to confirm that yes, these were the terms I had agreed to. And I felt a momentary pang before answering, for letting go of my youth was a hard thing to do. But I spoke clearly for the record: "Yes, Your Honor. Ralph Douglas and I are in full agreement."

It was a sad affair all the way around, made all the more stressful and surreal for me by the presence of Pamela Red in the audience. What was *she* doing here? The question plagued me throughout both trials, only to be answered at the end, when I watched her fall happily into the arms of Ralph Faxborn. This was not *my* Pamela at all, the Antarctican matter programmer, but rather the archived student, still burning with passion, over whom I had pined for a decade and more, risking nearly everything. I watched the two of them, warm and happy together, and wondered if I'd ever feel a thing like that again. Was youth a necessary component?

Against my better judgment, I went over to talk to them. "You two look . . . happy together."

"Thank you for everything," Ralph said. "For life itself. I apologize for not trusting you."

And I answered him sternly: "Never apologize for being cautious. The world is full of nasty surprises, and lawyers, at least, must stand prepared. Until I'd thought about it, I *was* going to erase you." I paused a moment and then added, "Look, I've learned a lot over the years, about being you. We should sit down. Have a chat."

"And turn me into yourself?" Ralph laughed at that. "Another generous offer, sir, but I'll have to decline. Is my own future not bright? If you survived our trials and tribulations, I reckon I won't do any worse. And time will tell, sir, but I reckon I have a certain advantage as well, coming to this world as a traveler from its past. It gives a certain outsider's perspective, which ought, I think, to be useful. So if it's all the same to you, I will ignore you as I would my own father. Fair enough?"

"You're a clever boy," I said, and it wasn't entirely a compliment.

All the while, young Pamela had been looking me over with great curiosity. And if this was painful, why, returning her gaze was like leaping into a furnace. "And you, young lady," I said as evenly as I could manage. "I'm quite flabbergasted to see you here."

"I imagine you are," she said, with a sympathy that was agonizingly genuine, and equally condescending. "I don't know your history, and I don't care to. But it upsets me to think I've caused you pain."

And *that* one really knocked the stuffing out of me. Young Pamela had always had a knack for that, for hitting me where I was weakest while trying, in some vague way, to be nice. And suddenly I was able to forgive her for that, for all of it. Because she was just some kid, and didn't know any better. How could she?

I nodded slowly. "Yes. Well. The intent behind your words is appreciated. Have you spoken with . . . yourself?"

"I have," she said, "and it's her you should be talking to, not me. I felt her letting go of a lot of anger. If you want to . . . you know, pounce in a moment of weakness . . . well, now would be the time."

"Thanks for the tip," I said, laughing in spite of myself. And then, more thoughtfully: "She and I fought such battles over you. It's ironic, and rather sad, that she didn't surrender you sooner."

Pamela just looked at me then, with a wise sort of weariness, and said, "Love isn't a surrender, but a gift. Sometimes we return it unopened, but we never fail to appreciate it. If you're going to talk about me like a thing, at least have the right sort of thing in mind, all right? The real question to ask yourself is why she suddenly feels like giving."

God, she sounded so good. So lovely, so perfect. And Ralph, too, was everything a mutant, sexually deviant father could hope for. Surely *here* was a young man who could do no wrong, no matter what the provocation.

"I wish you both the very best of luck," I said with conviction.

And the two of them smiled at me as they might a distant relative, and then turned, arm-in-arm, and walked away. The perfect couple, yes. This was no longer the world they'd been copied from, and they were not those people. Not quite. Maybe things would be different this time.

The smart thing for me to do then would have been to go back home and get to work. There was plenty of work for me, always. But life was too short for that, yes? Even if it lasted forever. I had a flair for the dramatic and a nose for the strange; it was time to take a risk.

Still, it took all my strength to keep from shouting after them, "Fool! She's *five months* from dumping you!"

INSIDE JOB

by Connie Willis

Connie Willis was born in 1945 and lives in Greeley, Colorado. Her first story, "The Secret of Santa Titicaca," was published in 1971, but she only began publishing regularly in the early '80s. She is best known for her short fiction, which has been gathered in three volumes: Fire Watch, Impossible Things, *and* Miracle and Other Christmas Stories. *Her early stories include time travel story "Fire Watch," "All My Darling Daughters," "A Letter from the Clearys," "The Sidon in the Mirror," "Blued Moon," and "The Last of the Winnebagos."*

Willis's first book was science fiction novel Water Witch *(with Cynthia Felice), which was followed by solo debut* Lincoln's Dreams, *which won the John W. Campbell Memorial Award. Second novel* Doomsday Book, *sharing the same mid-twenty-first-century time-travel framing device as "Fire Watch," is more typical of Willis's fiction, and won both the Hugo and Nebula awards. It was followed by short novels* Uncharted Territory, Remake, *and* Bellwether, *and major novel* Passage. *Willis has become one of the most celebrated writers in modern science fiction, and to date her fiction has won the Hugo Award eight times, the Nebula Award six times, the Locus Award nine times, the John W. Campbell Memorial Award, and many other honors.*

🐾 🐾 🐾

"Nobody ever went broke underestimating the intelligence of the American people."

—H. L. Mencken

I T'S ME, ROB," Kildy said when I picked up the phone. "I want you to go with me to see somebody Saturday."

Usually when Kildy calls, she's bubbling over with details. "You've *got* to see this psychic cosmetic surgeon, Rob," she'd crowed the last time. "His specialty is liposuction, and you can *see* the tube coming out of his sleeve. And that's not all. The fat he's supposed to be suctioning out of their thighs is that goop they use in McDonald's milkshakes. You can smell the vanilla! It wouldn't fool a five year old, so of course half the women in Hollywood are buying it hook, line, and sinker. We've *got* to do a story on him, Rob!"

I usually had to say, "Kildy—Kildy—Kildy!" before I could get her to shut up long enough to tell me where he was performing.

But this time all she said was, "The seminar's at one o'clock at the Beverly Hills Hilton. I'll meet you in the parking lot," and hung up before I could ask her if the somebody was a pet chan- neler or a vedic-force therapist, and how much it was going to cost.

I called her back. "The tickets are on me," she said.

If Kildy had her way, the tickets would always be on her, and she can more than afford it. Her father's a director at DreamWorks, her current stepmother heads her own production company, and her mother's a two-time Oscar winner. And Kildy's rich in her own right—she only acted in four films before she quit the business for a career in debunking, but one of them was the surprise top grosser of the year, and she'd opted for a share instead of a salary.

But she's ostensibly my employee, even though I can't afford to pay her enough to keep her in toenail polish. The least I can do is spring for expenses, and a barely known channeler shouldn't be too bad. Medium Charles Edward, the current dar- ling of the Hollywood set, was only charging two hundred a seance.

"*The Jaundiced Eye* is paying for the tickets," I said firmly. "How much?"

"Seven hundred and fifty apiece for the group seminar," she said. "Fifteen hundred for a private enlightment audience."

"The tickets are on you," I said.

"Great," she said. "Bring the Sony vidcam."

"Not the little one?" I asked. Most psychic events don't allow recording devices—they make it too easy to spot the earpieces and wires—and the Hasaka is small enough to be smuggled in.

"No," she said, "bring the Sony. See you Saturday, Rob. Bye."

"Wait," I said. "You haven't told me what this guy does."

"Woman," Kildy said. "She's a channeler. She channels an entity named Isis," Kildy said and hung up again.

I was surprised. We don't usually waste our time on channelers. They're no longer trendy. Right now mediums like Charles Fred and Yogi Magaputra and assorted sensory therapists (aroma-, sonic-, luminescent) are the rage.

It's also an exercise in frustration, since there's no way to prove whether someone's channeling or not, unless they claim to be channeling Paul Cézanne (like Jane Roberts) or Nefertiti (like Hanh Nah.) In that case you can challenge their facts—Nefertiti could *not* have had an affair with Alexander the Great, who wasn't born till a thousand years later—but most of them channel hundred thousand-year-old sages or high priests of Atlantis, and there are no physical manifestations.

They've learned their lesson from the Victorian spiritualists (who kept getting caught), so there's no ectoplasm or ghostly trumpets or double-exposed photographic plates. Just a deep, hollow voice that sounds like a cross between Obi-Wan Kenobi and Basil Rathbone. Why is it that channeled "entities" have English accents? And speak King James Bible English?

So why was Kildy willing to waste fifteen hundred bucks—correction, twenty-two fifty, she'd already been to the seminar once—to have me see this Isis? She must have a new gimmick. I'd noticed a couple of people advertising themselves as "angel channelers" in the local psychic rag, but Isus wasn't an angel name. Egyptian channeler? Goddess conduit?

I looked "Isis-channeler" up on the net. At first I couldn't find any references, even using Google. I tried skeptics.org and finally Marty Rumboldt, who runs a website that tracks psychics.

"You're spelling it wrong, Rob," he e-mailed me back. "It's Isus."

Which should have occurred to me. The channelers of Lazaris, Kochise, and Merlynn all use variations on historical names (probably from some fear of spiritual slander lawsuits), and more than one channeler's prone to "inventive" spelling: Joye Wildde. And Emmanual.

I Googled "Isus." He—bad sign, the channeler didn't even know Isis was female—was the "spirit entity" channeled by somebody named Ariaura Keller. She'd started in Salem, Massachusetts (a breeding ground for psychics), moved to Sedona (another one), and then headed west and worked her way down the coast, appearing in Seattle, the other Salem, Eugene, Berkeley, and now Beverly Hills. She had six afternoon seminars and two week-long "spiritual immersions" scheduled for L.A., along with private "individually scheduled enlightenment audiences" with Isus. She'd written two books, *The Voice of Isus* and *On the Receiving End* (with links to amazon.com), and you could read her bio: "I knew from childhood that I was destined to be a channel for the Truth," and extracts from her speeches: "The earth is destined to witness a transforming spiritual event," online. She sounded just like every other channeler I'd ever heard.

And I'd sat through a bunch of them. Back at the height of their popularity (and before I knew better), *The Jaundiced Eye* had done a six-part series on channelers, starting with M. Z. Lord and running on through Joye Wildde, Todd Phoenix, and Taryn Kryme, whose "entity" was a giggly six-year-old kid from Atlantis. It was the longest six months of my life. And it didn't have any impact at all on the business. It was tax evasion and mail fraud charges that had put an end to the fad, not my hard-hitting exposés.

Ariaura Keller didn't have a criminal record (at least under that name), and there weren't many articles about her. And no mention of any gimmick. "The electric, amazing Isus shares his spiritual wisdom and helps you find your own inner-centeredness and soul-unenfoldment." Nothing new there.

Well, whatever it was that had gotten Kildy interested in her, I'd find out on Saturday. In the meantime, I had an article on Charles Fred to write for the December issue, a book on intelligent design (the latest ploy for getting creationism into the schools and evolution out) to review, and a past-life chiropractor to go see. He claimed his patients' backaches came from hauling blocks of stone to Stonehenge and/or the Pyramids. (The Pyramids had in fact been a big job, but over the course of three years in business he'd told over ten thousand patients they'd been at Stonehenge, every single one of them setting the altar stone in place.)

And he was actually credible compared to Charles Fred, who was having amazing success communicating highly specific messages from the dead to their grieving relatives. I was convinced he was doing something besides the usual cold reading to get his information (and the millions he was raking in), but so far I hadn't been able to figure out what, and every lead I managed to come up with went nowhere.

I didn't think about the "electric, amazing Isus" again till I was driving over to the Hilton Saturday. Then it occurred to me that I hadn't heard from Kildy since her phone call. Usually she drops by the office every day and if we're going somewhere calls three or four times to reconfirm where and when we're meeting. I wondered if the seminar was still on, or if she'd forgotten all about it. Or suddenly gotten tired of being a debunker and gone back to being a movie star.

I'd been waiting for that to happen ever since the day a year and a half ago when, just like the gorgeous dame in a Bogie movie, she'd walked into my office and asked if she could have a job.

There are three cardinal rules in the skeptic business. The first one is, "Extraordinary claims require extraordinary evidence," and the second one is, "If it seems too good to be true, it probably is." And if anything was ever too good to be true, it's Kildy. She's not only rich and movie-star beautiful, but intelligent, and, unlike everyone else in Hollywood, a complete skeptic, even though, as she told me the first day, Shirley MacLaine had dandled her on her knee and her mother would believe anything, "no matter how ridiculous, which is probably why her marriage to my father lasted nearly six years."

She was now on Stepmother Number Four, who had gotten her the role in the surprise top grosser, "which made almost as much money as *Lord of the Rings* and enabled me to take early retirement."

"Retirement?" I'd said. "Why would you want to retire? You could have—"

"Starred in *The Hulk III*," she said, "and been on the cover of the *Globe* with Ben Affleck. Or with my lawyer in front of a rehab center. I know, it was tough to give all that up."

She had a point, but that didn't explain why she'd want to go to work for a barely making-it magazine like *The Jaundiced Eye*. Or why she'd want to go to work at all.

I said so.

"I've already tried the whole 'fill your day with massages and lunch at Ardani's and sex with your trainer' scene, Rob," she said. "It was even worse than *The Hulk*. Plus, the lights and make-up *destroy* your complexion."

I found that hard to believe. She had skin like honey.

"And then my mother took me to this luminescence reading—she's into all those things—psychics and past-life regression and intuitive healing—and the guy doing the reading—"

"Lucius Windfire," I'd said. I'd been working on an exposé of him for the last two months.

"Yes, Lucius Windfire," she'd said. "He claimed he could read your mind by determining your vedic fault lines, which consisted of setting candles all around you and 'reading' the wavering of the flames. It was obvious he was a fake—you could see the earpiece he was getting his information over—but everybody there was eating it up, especially my mother. He'd already talked her into private sessions that set her back ten thousand dollars. And I thought, somebody should put him out of business, and then I thought, that's what I want to do with my life, and I looked up 'debunkers' on-line and found your magazine, and here I am."

I'd said, "I can't possibly pay you the kind of money you're—"

"Your going rate for articles is fine," she'd said and flashed me her better-than-Julia-Roberts smile. "I just want the chance to do something useful and sensible with my life."

And for the last eight months she'd been writing articles for the magazine. She was wonderful—she knew everybody in

Hollywood, which meant she could get us into invitation-only stuff, and heard about new spiritual fads even before I did. She was also willing to do anything, from letting herself be hypnotized to stealing chicken guts from psychic surgeons to proofreading galleys. And fun to talk to, and gorgeous, and much too good for a small-time skeptic.

And I knew it was just a matter of time before she got bored with debunking and went back to going to premieres and driving around in her Jaguar, but she didn't. "Have you ever *worked* with Ben Affleck?" she said when I told her she was too gorgeous not to still be in the movies. "You couldn't *pay* me to go back to that."

She wasn't in the parking lot, and neither was her Jaguar, and I wondered, as I did every day, if this was the day she'd decided to call it quits. No, there she was, getting out of a taxi. She was wearing a honey-colored pantsuit the same shade as her hair, and designer sunglasses, and she looked, as always, too good to be true. She saw me and waved, and then reached back in for two big throw pillows.

Shit. That meant we were going to have to sit on the floor again. These people made a fortune scamming people out of their not-so-hard-earned cash. You'd think they could afford chairs.

I walked over to her. "I take it we're going in together," I said, since the pillows were a matching pair, purple brocade jobs with tassels at the corners.

"Yes," Kildy said. "Did you bring the Sony?"

"Yeah," I said. "I still think I should have brought the Hasaka."

She shook her head. "They're doing body checks. I don't want to give them an excuse to throw us out. When they ask for your name for the nametags, give them your real name."

"We're not using a cover?" I asked. Psychics often use skeptics in the audience as an excuse for failure: the negative vibrations made it impossible to contact the spirits, etc. A couple of them had even banned me from their performances, claiming I disturbed the cosmos with my nonbelieving presence. "Do you think that's a good idea?"

"We don't have any choice," she said. "When I came last week, I was with my publicist, so I had to use my own name, and

I didn't think it mattered—we never do channelers. Besides, the ushers recognized me. So our cover is, I was so impressed with Ariaura that I talked you into coming to see her."

"Which is pretty much the truth," I said. "What exactly is her gimmick, that you thought I should see her?"

"I don't want to prejudice you beforehand." She glanced at her Vera Wang watch and handed me one of the pillows. "Let's go."

We went into the lobby and over to a table under a lilac-and-silver banner proclaiming "Presenting Ariaura and the Wisdom of Isus" and under it, "Believe and It Will Happen." Kildy told the woman at the table our names.

"Oh, I loved you in that movie, Miss Ross," she said and handed us lilac and silver nametags and motioned us toward another table next to the door, where a Russell Crowe type in a lilac polo shirt was doing security checks.

"Any cameras, tape recorders, videocams?" he asked us.

Kildy opened her bag and took out an Olympus. "Can't I take *one* picture?" she pleaded. "I won't use the flash or anything. I just wanted to get a photo of Ariaura."

He plucked the Olympus neatly from her fingers. "Autographed 8x10 glossies can be purchased in the waiting area."

"Oh, *good*," she said. She really should have stayed in acting.

I relinquished my digital and the videocam. "What about videos of today's performance?" I said after he finished frisking me.

He stiffened. "Ariaura's communications with Isus are not performances. They are unique glimpses into a higher plane. You can order videos of today's experience in the waiting area," he said, pointing toward a pair of double doors.

The "waiting area" was a long hall lined with tables full of books, videos, audiotapes, crystals, chakra charts, crystal balls, aromatherapy oils, amulets, Zuni fetishes, wisdom mobiles, healing stones, singing crystal bowls, amaryllis roots, aura cleansers, pyramids, and assorted other New Age junk, all with the lilac-and-silver Isus logo.

The third cardinal rule of debunking, and maybe the most

important, is "Ask yourself, what do they get out of it?" or, as the Bible (source of many scams) puts it, "By their fruits shall ye know them."

And if the prices on this stuff were any indication, Ariaura was getting a hell of a lot out of it. The 8x10 glossies were $28.99, thirty-five with Ariaura's signature. "And if you want it signed by Isus," the blonde girl behind the table said, "it's a hundred. He's not always willing to sign."

I could see why. His signature (done in Magic Marker) was a string of complicated symbols that looked like a cross between Elvish runes and Egyptian hieroglyphics whereas Ariaura's was a script "A" followed by a formless scrawl.

Videotapes of her previous seminars—Volumes 1-20—cost a cool sixty apiece, and Ariaura's "sacred amulet" (which looked like something you'd buy on the Home Shopping Network) cost nine hundred and fifty (box extra). People were snapping them up like hotcakes, along with Celtic pentacles, meditation necklaces, dreamcatcher earrings, worry beads, and toe rings with your zodiac sign on them.

Kildy bought one of the outrageously priced stills (no signature) and three of the videos, cooing, "I just *loved* her last seminar," gave the guy selling them her autograph, and we went into the auditorium.

It was hung with rose, lilac, and silver chiffon floor-length banners and a state-of-the-art lighting system. Stars and planets rotated overhead, and comets occasionally whizzed by. The stage end of the auditorium was hung with gold Mylar, and in the center of the stage was a black pyramid-backed throne. Apparently Ariaura did not intend to sit on the floor like the rest of us.

At the door, ushers clad in mostly unbuttoned lilac silk shirts and tight pants took our tickets. They all looked like Tom Cruise, which would be par for the course even if this wasn't Hollywood.

Sex has been a mainstay of the psychic business since Victorian days. Half the appeal of early table-rapping had been the filmy-draperies-and-nothing-else clad female "spirits" who drifted tantalizingly among the male séance goers, fogging up their glasses and preventing them from thinking clearly. Sir William Crookes, the famous British chemist, had been so besotted by an obviously fake medium's sexy daughter that he'd staked his scientific reputation on the medium's dubious authenticity, and nowadays it's no accident that most channelers are male and given to chest-baring Rudolph Valentino-like robes. Or, if they're female, buff, handsome ushers to distract the women in the audience. If you're drooling over them, you're not likely to spot the wires and chicken guts or realize what they're saying is nonsense. It's the oldest trick in the book.

One of the ushers gave Kildy a Tom Cruise smile and led her, following, to the end of a cross-legged row on the very hard-looking floor. I was glad Kildy had brought the pillows.

I plopped mine next to hers and sat down on it. "This had better be good," I said.

"Oh, it will be," a fifty-ish redhead wearing the sacred amulet and a diamond as big as my fist said. "I've seen Ariaura, and she's wonderful." She reached into one of the three lilac shopping bags she'd stuck between us and pulled out a needlepoint lavender pillow that said, "Believe and It Will Happen."

I wondered if that applied to her believing her pillow was large enough to sit on, because it was about the same size as the rock on her finger, but as soon as they'd finished organizing the rows, the ushers came around bearing stacks of plastic-covered cushions (the kind rented at football games, only lilac) for ten bucks apiece.

The woman next to me took three, and I counted ten other people in our row, and eleven in the row ahead of us shelling out for them. Eighty rows times ten, to be conservative. A cool eight thousand bucks, just to sit down, and who knows how much profit in all those lilac shopping bags. "By their fruits shall ye know them."

I looked around. I couldn't see any signs of shills or a wireless setup, but, unlike psychics and mediums, channelers don't need them. They give out general advice, couched in New Age terms.

"Isus is absolutely astonishing," my neighbor confided. "He's so *wise*! Much better than Ramtha. He's responsible for my deciding to leave Randall. 'To thine inner self be true,' Isus said, and I realized Randall had been *blocking* my spiritual ascent—"

"Were you at last Saturday's seminar?" Kildy leaned across me to ask.

"*No*. I was in Cancun, and I was just decimated when I realized I'd missed it. I made Tio bring me back early so I could come today. I desperately need Isus's wisdom about the divorce. Randall's claiming Isus had nothing to do with my decision, that I left him because the pre-nup had expired, and he's threatening to call Tio as—"

But Kildy had lost interest and was leaning across *her* to ask a pencil-thin woman in the full lotus position if she'd seen Ariaura before. She hadn't, but the one on her right had.

"Last Saturday?" Kildy asked.

She hadn't. She'd seen her six weeks ago in Eugene.

I leaned towards Kildy and whispered, "What happened last Saturday?"

"I think they're starting, Rob," she said, pointing at the stage, where absolutely nothing was happening, and got off her pillow and onto her knees.

"What are you doing?" I whispered.

She didn't answer that either. She reached inside her pillow, pulled out an orange pillow the same size as the "Believe and It Will Happen" cushion, handed it to me, and arranged herself gracefully on the large tasseled one. As soon as she was cross-legged, she took the orange pillow back from me and laid it across her knees.

"Comfy?" I asked.

"Yes, thank you," she said, turning her movie-star smile on me.

I leaned toward her. "You sure you don't want to tell me what we're doing here?"

"Oh, look, they're starting," she said, and this time they were.

A Brad Pitt look-alike stepped out on stage holding a hand mike and gave us the ground rules. No flash photos (even though they'd confiscated all the cameras). No applause (it breaks Ariaura's concentration). No bathroom breaks. "The cosmic link with Isus is extremely fragile," Russell explained, "and movement or the shutting of a door can break that connection."

Right. Or else Ariaura had learned a few lessons from EST, including the fact that people who are distracted by their bladders are less likely to spot nonsense, like the stuff Russell was spouting right now:

"Eighty thousand years ago Isus was a high priest of Atlantis. He lived for three hundred years before he departed this earthly plane and acquired the wisdom of the ages—"

What ages? The Paleolithic and Neolithic? Eighty thousand years ago we were still living in trees.

"—he spoke with the oracle at Delphi, he delved into the Sacred Writings of Rosicrucian—"

Rosicrucian?

"Now watch as Ariaura calls him from the Cosmic All to share his wisdom with you."

The lights deepened to rose, and the chiffon banners began to blow in, as if there was a breeze behind them. Correction: state-of-the-art lighting *and* fans.

The gale intensified, and for a moment, I wondered if Ariaura was going to swoop in on a wire, but then the gold Mylar parted, revealing a curving black stairway, and Ariaura, in a purple velvet caftan and her sacred amulet, descended it to the strains of Holst's "Planets" and went to stand dramatically in front of her throne.

The audience paid no attention to the "no applause" edict, and Ariaura seemed to expect it. She stood there for at least two minutes, regally surveying the crowd. Then she raised her arms as if delivering a benediction and lowered them again, quieting the crowd. "Welcome, Seekers after Divine Truth," she said in a peppy, Oprah-type voice, and there was more applause. "We're going to have a wonderful spiritual experience together here today and achieve a new plane of enlightenment."

More applause.

"But you mustn't applaud me. I am only the conduit through which Isus passes, the vessel he fills. Isus first came to me, or, rather, I should say, *through* me, five years ago, but I was afraid. I didn't want to believe it. It took me nearly a whole year to accept that I had become the focus for cosmic energies beyond the reality we know. It's the wisdom of his highly evolved spirit you'll hear today, not mine. If . . ." a nice theatrical pause here, ". . . he deigns to come to us. For Isus is a sage, not a servant to be bidden. He cometh when he wills. Mayhap he will be among us this afternoon, mayhap not."

In a pig's eye. These women weren't going to shell out seven hundred and fifty bucks for a no-show, even if this was Beverly Hills. I'd bet the house Isus showed up right on cue.

"Isus will come only if our earthly plane is in alignment with the cosmic," Ariaura said, "if the auratic vibrations are right." She looked sternly out at the audience. "If any of you are harboring negative vibrations, contact cannot be made."

Uh-oh, here it comes, I thought, and waited for her to look straight at us and tell us to leave, but she didn't. She merely said, "Are all of you thinking positive thoughts, feeling positive emotions? Are you all believing?"

You bet.

"I sense that every one of you is thinking positive thoughts," Ariaura said. "Good. Now, to bring Isus among us, you must help me. You must each calm your center." She closed her eyes. "You must concentrate on your inner soul-self."

I glanced around the audience. Over half of the women had their eyes shut, and many had folded their hands in an attitude of prayer. Some swayed back and forth, and the woman next to me was droning, "Om." Kildy had her eyes closed, her orange pillow clasped to her chest.

"Align . . . align . . ." Ariaura chanted, and then with finality, "Align." There was another theatrical pause.

"I will now attempt to contact Isus," she said. "The focusing of the astral energy is a dangerous and difficult operation. I must ask that you remain perfectly quiet and still while I am preparing myself."

The woman next to me obediently stopped chanting, "Om," and everyone opened their eyes. Ariaura closed hers and leaned back in her throne, her ring-covered hands draped over the ends of the arms. The lights went down and the music came up, the theme from Holst's "Mars." Everyone, including Kildy, watched breathlessly.

Ariaura jerked suddenly as if she were being electrocuted and clutched the arms of the throne. Her face contorted, her mouth twisting and her head shaking. The audience gasped. Her body jerked again, slamming back against the throne, and she went into a series of spasms and writhings, with more shaking. This went on for a full minute, while "Mars" built slowly behind her and the spotlight morphed to pink. The music cut off, and she slumped lifelessly back against the throne.

She remained there for a nicely timed interval, and then sat up stiffly, staring straight ahead, her hands lying loosely on the throne's arms. "I am Isus!" she said in a booming voice that was the dead ringer for "Who dares to approach the great Oz?"

"I am the Enlightened One, a servant unto that which is called the Text and the First Source. I have come from the ninth level of the astral plane," she boomed, "to aid you in your spiritual journeys."

So far it was an exact duplicate of Ramtha, right down to the pink light and the number of the astral plane level, but next to me Kildy was leaning forward expectantly.

"I have come to speak the truth," Isus boomed, "to reveal to thou thine higher self."

I leaned over to Kildy and whispered, "Why is it they never learn how to use 'thee' and 'thou' correctly on the astral plane?"

"Shh," Kildy hissed, intent on what Isus was saying.

"I bring you the long-lost wisdom of the kingdom of Lemuria and the prophecies of Antinous to aid thee in these troubled days, for thou livest in a time of tribulation. The last days these are of the Present Age, days filled with anxiety and terrorist attacks and dysfunctional relationships. But I say unto ye, thou must not look without but within, for thee alone are responsible for your happiness, and if that means getting out of a bad relationship, make it so. Seek you must your own inner isness and create thou must thine own inner reality. Thee art the universe."

I don't know what I'd been expecting. *Something*, at least, but this was just the usual New Age nonsense, a mush of psychobabble, self-help tips, pseudo-scripture, and Chicken Soup for the Soul.

I sneaked a glance at Kildy. She was sitting forward, clutching her pillow tightly to her chest, her beautiful face intent, her mouth slightly open. I wondered if she could actually have been taken in by Ariaura. It's always a possibility, even with skeptics. Kildy wouldn't be the first one to be fooled by a cleverly done illusion.

But this wasn't cleverly done. It wasn't even original. The Lemuria stuff was Richard Zephyr, the "Thou art the universe" stuff was Shirley MacLaine, and the syntax was pure Yoda.

And this was Kildy we were talking about. Kildy, who never fell for anything, not even that devic levitator. She had to have a good reason for shelling out over two thousand bucks for this, but so far I was stumped. "What exactly is it you wanted me to see?" I murmured.

"*Shhh.*"

"But fear not," Ariaura said, "for a New Age is coming, an age of peace, of spiritual enlightenment, when you—doing here listening to this confounded claptrap?"

I looked up sharply. Ariaura's voice had changed in midsentence from Isus's booming bass to a gravelly baritone, and her manner had, too. She leaned forward, hands on her knees, scowling at the audience. "It's a lot of infernal gabble," she said belligerently.

I glanced at Kildy. She had her eyes fixed on the stage, her pillow still clasped tightly to her chest.

"This hokum is even worse than the pretentious bombast you hear in the chautauqua," the voice croaked.

Chautauqua? I thought. What the—?

"But there you sit, with your mouths hanging open, like the rubes at an Arkansas camp meeting, listening to a snake-charming preacher, waiting for her to fix up your romances and cure your gallstones—"

The woman next to Kildy glanced questioningly at us and then back at the stage. Two of the ushers standing along the wall exchanged frowning glances, and I could hear whispering from somewhere in the audience.

"Have you yaps actually fallen for this mystical mumbo-jumbo? Of course you have. This is America, home of the imbecile and the ass!" the voice said, and the whispering became a definite murmur.

"What in the—?" a woman behind us said, and the woman next to me gathered up her bags, stuffed her "Believe" pillow into one of them, stood up and began to step over people to get to the door.

One of the ushers signaled someone in the control booth, and the lights and Holst's "Venus" began to come up. The emcee took a hesitant step out onto the stage.

"You sit there like a bunch of gaping primates, ready to buy anyth—" Ariaura said, and her voice changed abruptly back to the basso of Isus, "—but the Age of Spiritual Enlightenment cannot begin until each of thou beginnest thy own journey."

The emcee stopped in mid-step, and so did the murmuring. And the woman who'd been next to me and who was almost to the door. She stood there next to it, holding her bags and listening.

"And believe. All of you, casteth out the toxins of doubt and skepticism now. *Believe* and it will happen."

She must be back on script. The emcee gave a sigh of relief, and retreated back into the wings, and the woman who'd been next to me sat down where she'd been standing, bags and pillows and all. The music faded, and the lights went back to rose.

"Believe in thine inner Soul-Self," Ariaura/Isus said. "Believe, and let your spiritual unfoldment begin." She paused, and the ushers looked up nervously. The emcee poked his head out from the gold Mylar drapes.

"I grow weary," she said. "I must return now to that higher reality from whence I cameth. Fear not, for though I no longer share this earthly plane with thee, still I am with thou." She raised her arm stiffly in a benediction/Nazi salute, gave a sharp shudder, and then slumped forward in a swoon that would have done credit to Gloria Swanson. Holst's "Venus" began again, and she sat up, blinking, and turned to the emcee, who had come out onstage again.

"Did Isus speak?" she asked him in her original voice.

"Yes, he did," the emcee said, and the audience burst into thunderous applause, during which he helped her to her feet and handed her over to two of the ushers, who walked her, leaning heavily on them, up the black stairway and out of sight.

As soon as she was safely gone, the emcee quieted the applause and said, "Copies of Ariaura's books and videotapes are available outside in the waiting area. If you wish to arrange for a private audience, see me or one of the ushers," and everyone began gathering up their pillows and heading for the door.

"Wasn't he *wonderful*?" a woman ahead of us in the exodus said to her friend. "So authentic!"

☙ ☙ ☙

"Is Los Angeles the worst town in America, or only next to the worst? The skeptic, asked the original question, will say yes, the believer will say no. There you have it."

—H. L. Mencken

Kildy and I didn't talk till we were out of the parking lot and on Wilshire, at which point Kildy said, "Now do you understand why I wanted you to see it for yourself?"

"It was interesting, all right. I take it she did the same thing at the seminar you went to last week?"

She nodded. "Only last week two people walked out."

"Was it the exact same spiel?"

"No. It didn't last quite as long—I don't know how long exactly, it caught me by surprise—and she used slightly different words, but the message was the same. And it happened the same way—no warning, no contortions, her voice just changed abruptly in mid-sentence. So what do you think's going on, Rob?"

I turned onto LaBrea. "I don't know, but lots of channelers do more than one 'entity.' Joye Wildde does two, and before Hans Lightfoot went to jail, he did half a dozen."

Kildy looked skeptical. "Her promotional material doesn't say anything about multiple entities."

"Maybe she's tired of Isus and wants to switch to another spirit. When you're a channeler, you can't just announce, 'Coming soon: Isus II.' You've got to make it look authentic. So she introduces him with a few words one week, a couple of sentences the next, etcetera."

"She's introducing a new and improved spirit who yells at the audience and calls them imbeciles and rubes?" she said incredulously.

"It's probably what channelers call a 'dark spirit,' a so-called bad entity that tries to lead the unwary astray. Todd Phoenix used to have a nasty voice break in the middle of White Feather's spiel and make heckling comments. It's a useful trick. It reinforces the idea that the psychic's actually channeling, and anything inconsistent or controversial the channeler says can be blamed on the bad spirit."

"But Ariaura didn't even seem to be aware that there *was* a bad spirit, if that's what it was supposed to be. Why would it tell the audience to go home and stop giving their money to a snake-oil vendor like Ariaura?"

A snake-oil vendor? That sounded vaguely familiar, too. "Is that what she said last week? Snake-oil vendor?"

"Yes," she said. "Why? Do you know who she's channeling?"

"No," I said, frowning, "but I've heard that phrase somewhere. And the line about the chautauqua."

"So it's obviously somebody famous," Kildy said.

But the historical figures channelers did were always instantly recognizable. Randall Mars's Abraham Lincoln began every sentence with "Fourscore and seven years ago," and the others were all equally obvious. "I wish I'd gotten Ariaura's little outburst on tape," I said.

"We did," Kildy said, reaching over the backseat and grabbing her pillow. She unzipped it, reached inside, and brought out a micro-vidcam. "Ta-da! I'm sorry I didn't get last week's. I didn't realize they were frisking people."

She fished in the pillow again and brought out a sheet of paper. "I had to run to the bathroom and scribble down what I could remember."

"I thought they didn't let people go to the bathroom."

She grinned at me. "I gave an Oscar-worthy performance of an actress they'd let out of rehab too soon."

I glanced at the list at the next stoplight. There were only a few phrases on it. The ones she'd mentioned, and "I've never seen such shameless bilge," and "You'd have to be a pack of deluded half-wits to believe something so preposterous.'"

"That's all?"

She nodded. "I told you, it didn't last nearly as long last time. And since I wasn't expecting it, I missed most of the first sentence."

"That's why you were asking at the seminar about buying the videotape?"

"Unh-huh, although I doubt if there's anything on it. I've watched her last three videos, and there's no sign of Entity Number Two."

"But it happened at the seminar you went to and at this one. Has it occurred to you it might have happened *because* we were there?" I pulled into a parking space in front of the building where *The Jaundiced Eye* has its office.

"But—" she said.

"The ticket-taker could have alerted her that we were there," I said. I got out and opened her door for her, and we started up to the office. "Or she could have spotted us in the audience— you're not the only one who's famous. My picture's on every psychic wanted poster on the West Coast—and she decided to jazz up the performance a little by adding another entity. To impress us."

"That can't be it."

I opened the door. "Why not?"

"Because it's happened at least twice before," she said, walking in and sitting down in the only good chair. "In Berkeley and Seattle."

"How do you know?"

"My publicist's ex-boyfriend's girlfriend saw her in Berkeley—that's how my publicist found out about Ariaura—so I got her number and called her and asked her, and she said Isus was talking along about tribulation and thee being the universe, and all of a sudden he said, 'What a bunch of boobs!' She said that's how she knew Ariaura was really channeling, because if it was fake she'd hardly have called the audience names."

"Well, there's your answer. She does it to make her audiences believe her."

"You saw them, they already believe her," Kildy said. "And if that's what she's doing, why isn't it on the Berkeley videotape?"

"It isn't?"

She shook her head. "I watched it six times. Nothing."

"And you're sure your publicist's ex-girlfriend really saw it? That you weren't leading her?"

"I'm sure," she said indignantly. "Besides, I asked my mother."

"She was there, too?"

"No, but two of her friends were, and one of them knew someone who saw the Seattle seminar. They all said basically the same thing, except the part about it making them believe her. In fact, one of them said, '*I* think her cue cards were out of order,' and told me not to waste my money, that the person I should go see was Angelina Black Feather." She grinned at me and then went serious. "If Ariaura was doing it on purpose, why would she edit it out? And why did the emcee and the ushers look so uneasy?"

So she'd noticed that, too.

"Maybe she didn't warn them she was going to do it. Or, more likely, it's all part of the act, to make people believe it's authentic."

Kildy shook her head doubtfully. "I don't think so. I think it's something else."

"Like what? You don't think she's really channeling this guy?"

"No, of *course* not, Rob," she said indignantly. "It's just that . . . you say she's doing it to get publicity and bigger crowds, but as you told me, the first rule of success in the psychic business is to tell people what they want to hear, not to call them boobs. You saw the woman next to you—she was all ready to walk out, and I watched her afterward. She didn't sign up for a private session, and neither did very many other people, and I heard the emcee telling someone there were lots of tickets still available for the next seminar. Last week's was sold out a month in advance. Why would she do something to hurt her business?"

"She's got to do something to up the ante, to keep the customers coming back, and this new spirit is to create buzz. You watch, next week she'll be advertising 'The Battle of the Ancients.' It's a gimmick, Kildy."

"So you don't think we should go see her again."

"*No.* That's the worst thing we could possibly do. We don't want to give her free publicity, and if she did do it to impress us, though it doesn't sound like it, we'd be playing right into her hands. If she's not, and the spirit *is* driving customers away, like you say, she'll dump it and come up with a different one. Or put herself out of business. Either way, there's no need for us to do anything. It's a non-story. You can forget all about her."

Which just goes to show you why I could never make it as a

psychic. Because before the words were even out of my mouth, the office door banged open, and Ariaura roared in and grabbed me by the lapels.

"I don't know what you're doing or how you're doing it!" she screamed, "but I want you to stop it right now!"

🐾 🐾 🐾

"He has a large and extremely uncommon capacity for provocative utterance. . . ."

—H. L. Mencken

I hadn't given Ariaura's acting skills enough credit. Her portrayal of Isus might be wooden and fakey, but she gave a pretty convincing portrayal of a hopping-mad psychic.

"How *dare* you!" she shrieked. "I'll sue you for everything you own!"

She had changed out of her flowing robes and into a lilac-colored suit Kildy told me later was a Zac Posen, and her designer necklace and earrings rattled. She was practically vibrating with rage, though not the positive vibrations she'd said were necessary for the appearance of spirits.

"I just watched the video of my seminar," she shrieked, her face two inches from mine. "How *dare* you hypnotize me and make me look like a complete fool in front of—"

"Hypnotize?" Kildy said. (I was too busy trying to loosen her grip on my lapels to say anything.) "You think Rob hypnotized you?"

"Oh, don't play the innocent with me," Ariaura said, wheeling on her. "I saw you two out there in the audience today, and I know all about you and your nasty, sneering little magazine. I know you nonbelievers will stop at nothing to keep us from spreading the Higher Truth, but I didn't think you'd go this far, hypnotizing me against my will and making me say those things! Isus told me I shouldn't let you stay in the auditorium, that he sensed danger in your presence, but I said, 'No, let the unbeliever stay and experience your presence. Let them know you come from the Existence Beyond to help us, to bring us words of

Higher Wisdom,' but Isus was right, you were up to no good."

She removed one hand from a lapel long enough to shake a lilac-lacquered fingernail at me. "Well, your little hypnotism scheme won't work. I've worked too hard to get where I am, and I'm not going to let a pair of narrow-minded little unbelievers like you get in my way. I have no intention—Higher Wisdom, my foot!" she snorted. "Higher Humbug is what I call it."

Kildy glanced, startled, at me.

"Oh, the trappings are a lot gaudier, I'll give you that," Ariaura said in the gravelly voice we'd heard at the seminar.

As before, the change had come without a break and in mid-sentence. One minute she had had me by the lapels, and the next she'd let go and was pacing around the room, her hands behind her back, and musing, "That auditorium's a big improvement over a courthouse lawn, and a good forty degrees cooler." She sat down on the couch, her hands on her spread-apart knees. "And those duds she wears would make a grand worthy bow-wow of the Knights of Zoroaster look positively dowdy, but it's the same old line of buncombe and the same old Boobus Americanus drinking it in."

Kildy took a careful step toward my desk, reached for her handbag and did something I couldn't see, and then went back to where she'd been standing, keeping her eyes the whole time on Ariaura, who was holding forth about the seminar.

"I never saw such an assortment of slack-jawed simians in one place! Except for the fact that the yokels have to sit on the floor—*and* pay for the privilege!—it's the spitting image of a Baptist tent revival. Tell 'em what they want to hear, do a couple of parlor tricks, and then pass the collection plate. And they're still falling for it!" She stopped pacing and glared at me. "I knew I should've stuck around. It's just like that time in Dayton—I think it's all over and leave, and look what happens! You let the quacks and the crooks take over, like this latter-day Aimee Semple McPherson. She's no more a seer than—of allowing you to ruin everything I've worked for! I . . ." She looked around bewilderedly. ". . . what? . . . I . . ." She faltered to a stop.

I had to hand it to her. She was good. She'd switched back

into her own voice without missing a beat, and then given an impressive impersonation of someone who had no idea what was going on.

She looked confusedly from me to Kildy and back. "It happened again, didn't it?" she asked, a quaver in her voice, and turned to appeal to Kildy. "He did it again, didn't he?" and began backing toward the door. "*Didn't* he?"

She pointed accusingly at me. "You keep *away* from me!" she shrieked. "And you keep away from my seminars! If you so much as *try* to come near me again, I'll get a restraining order against you!" she said and roared out, slamming the door behind her.

"Well," Kildy said after a minute. "That was interesting."

"Yes," I said, looking at the door. "Interesting."

Kildy went over to my desk and pulled the Hasaka out from behind her handbag. "I got it all," she said, taking out the disk, sticking it in the computer dock, and sitting down in front of the monitor. "There were a lot more clues this time." She began typing in commands. "There should be more than enough for us to be able to figure out who it is."

"I know who it is," I said.

Kildy stopped in mid-keystroke. "Who?"

"The High Priest of Irreverence."

"*Who*?"

"The Holy Terror from Baltimore, the Apostle of Common Sense, the Scourge of Con Men, Creationists, Faith-Healers, and the Booboisie," I said. "Henry Louis Mencken."

🐾 🐾 🐾

"In brief, it is a fraud."

—H. L. Mencken

"H. L. Mencken?" Kildy said. "The reporter who covered the Scopes trial?" (I told you she was too good to be true.)

"But why would Ariaura channel him?" she asked after we'd checked all the words and phrases we'd listed against Mencken's writings. They all checked out, from "buncombe" to "slackjawed simians" to "home of the imbecile and the ass."

"What did he mean about leaving Dayton early? Did something happen in Ohio?"

I shook my head. "Tennessee. Dayton was where the Scopes trial was held."

"And Mencken left early?"

"I don't know," I said, and went over to the bookcase to look for *The Great Monkey Trial*, "but I know it got so hot during the trial they moved it outside."

"That's what that comment about the courthouse lawn and its being forty degrees cooler meant," Kildy said.

I nodded. "It was a hundred and five degrees and 90 percent humidity the week of the trial. It's definitely Mencken. He invented the term 'Boobus Americanus.'"

"But why would Ariaura channel H. L. Mencken, Rob? He *hated* people like her, didn't he?"

"He certainly did." He'd been the bane of charlatans and quacks all through the twenties, writing scathing editorials on all kinds of scams, from faith-healing to chiropractic to creationism, railing incessantly against all forms of "hocus-pocus" and on behalf of science and rational thought.

"Then why would she channel him? Why not somebody sympathetic to psychics, like Edgar Cayce or Madame Blavatsky?"

"Because they'd obviously be suspect. By channeling an enemy of psychics, she makes it seem more credible."

"But nobody's ever heard of him."

"You have. I have."

"But nobody else in Ariaura's audience has."

"Exactly," I said, still looking for *The Great Monkey Trial*.

"You mean you think she's doing it to impress us?"

"Obviously," I said, scanning the titles. "Why else would she have come all the way over here to give that little performance?"

"But—what about the Seattle seminar? Or the one in Berkeley?"

"Dry runs. Or she was hoping we'd hear about them and go see her. Which we did."

"I didn't," Kildy said. "I went because my publicist wanted me to."

"But you go to lots of spiritualist events, and you talk to lots of people. Your publicist was there. Even if you hadn't gone, she'd have told you about it."

"But what would be the point? You're a skeptic. You don't believe in channeling. Would she honestly think she could convince you Mencken was real?"

"Maybe," I said. "She's obviously gone to a lot of trouble to make the spirit sound like him. And think what a coup that would be. 'Skeptic Says Channeled Spirit Authentic'? Have you ever heard of Uri Geller? He made a splash back in the seventies by claiming to bend spoons with his mind. He got all kinds of attention when a pair of scientists from the Stanford Research Institute said it wasn't a trick, that he was actually doing it."

"Was he?"

"No, of course not, and eventually he was exposed as a fraud. By Johnny Carson. Geller made the mistake of going on *The Tonight Show* and doing it in front of him. He'd apparently forgotten Carson had been a magician in his early days. But the point is, he made it onto *The Tonight Show*. And what made him a celebrity was having the endorsement of reputable scientists."

"And if you endorsed Ariaura, if you said you thought it was really Mencken, she'd be a celebrity, too."

"Exactly."

"So what do we do?"

"Nothing."

"Nothing? You're not going to try to expose her as a fake?"

"Channeling isn't the same as bending spoons. There's no independently verifiable evidence." I looked at her. "It's not worth it, and we've got bigger fish to fry. Like Charles Fred. He's making *way* too much money for a medium who only charges two hundred a performance, and he has way too many hits for a cold-reader. We need to find out how he's doing it, and where the money's coming from."

"But shouldn't we at least go to Ariaura's next seminar to see if it happens again?" Kildy persisted.

"And have to explain to the *L.A. Times* reporter who just happens to be there why we're so interested in Ariaura?" I said. "And why you came back three times?"

"I suppose you're right. But what if some other skeptic endorses her? Or some English professor?"

I hadn't thought of that. Ariaura had dangled the bait at four seminars we knew of. She might have been doing it at more, and *The Skeptical Mind* was in Seattle, Carlyle Drew was in San Francisco, and there were any number of amateur skeptics who went to spiritualist events.

And they would all know who Mencken was. He was the critical thinker's favorite person, next to the Amazing Randi and Houdini. He'd not only been fearless in his attacks on superstition and fraud, he could write "like a bat out of hell." And, unlike the rest of us skeptics, people had actually listened to what he said.

I'd liked him ever since I'd read about him chatting with somebody in his office at the *Baltimore Sun* and then suddenly looking out the window, saying, "The sons of bitches are gaining on us!" and frantically beginning to type. That was how I felt about twice a day, and more than once I'd muttered to myself, "Where the hell is Mencken when we need him?"

And I'd be willing to bet there were other people who felt the same way I did, who might be seduced by Mencken's language and the fact that Ariaura was telling them exactly what they wanted to hear.

"You're right," I said. "We need to look into this, but we should send somebody else to the seminar."

"How about my publicist? She said she wanted to go again."

"No, I don't want it to be anybody connected with us."

"I know just the person," Kildy said, snatching up her cell phone. "Her name's Riata Starr. She's an actress."

With a name like that, what else could she be?

"She's between jobs right now," Kildy said, punching in a number, "and if I tell her there's likely to be a casting director there, she'll definitely do it for us."

"Does she believe in channelers?"

She looked pityingly at me. "Everyone in Hollywood believes in channelers, but it won't matter." She put the phone to her ear. "I'll put a videocam on her, and a recorder," she whispered. "And I'll tell her an undercover job would look great on

her acting resume. Hello?" she said in a normal voice. "I'm trying to reach Riata Starr. Oh. No, no message."

She pushed "end." "She's at a casting call at DreamWorks."
She stuck the phone in her bag, fished her keys out of its depths,
and slung the bag over her shoulder. "I'm going to go out there
and talk to her. I'll be back," she said and went out.

Definitely too good to be true, I thought, watching her leave,
and called up a friend of mine in the police department and
asked him what they had on Ariaura.

He promised he'd call me back, and while I was waiting I
looked for and found *The Great Monkey Trial.* I looked up
Mencken in the index and started through the references to see
when Mencken had left Dayton. I doubted if he would have left
before the trial was over. He'd been having the time of his life,
pillorying William Jennings Bryan and the creationists. Maybe
the reference was to Mencken's having left before Bryan's death.
He'd died five days later, presumably from a heart attack, but
more likely from the humiliation he'd suffered at the hands of
Clarence Darrow, who'd put him on the stand and fired questions at him about the Bible. Darrow had made him, and
creationism look ridiculous, or rather, he'd made himself look
ridiculous. The cross-examination had been the high point of the
trial, and it had killed him.

Mencken had written a deadly, unforgiving eulogy of Bryan,
and he might very well have been sorry he hadn't been in at the
kill, but I couldn't imagine Ariaura knowing that, even if she had
taken the trouble to look up "Boobus Americanus" and "unmiti-
gated bilge," and research Mencken's gravelly voice and
explosive delivery.

Of course she might have read it. In this very book, even. I
read the chapter on Bryan's death, looking for references to
Mencken, but I couldn't find any. I backtracked, and there it was.
And I couldn't believe it. He hadn't left after the trial. When
Darrow's expert witnesses had all been disallowed, Mencken had
assumed that the trial was all over except for assorted legal tech-
nicalities and had gone back to Baltimore. He hadn't seen
Darrow's withering cross-examination. He'd missed Bryan saying man wasn't a mammal, insisting the sun could stand still

without throwing the earth out of orbit. He'd definitely left too soon. And I was willing to bet he'd never forgiven himself for it.

🐾 🐾 🐾

"To me, the scientific point of view is completely satisfying, and it has been so as long as I remember. Not once in this life have I ever been inclined to seek a rock and refuge elsewhere."

—H. L. Mencken

"But how could Ariaura know that?" Kildy said when she got back from the casting call.

"The same way I know it. She read it in a book. Did your friend Riata agree to go to the seminar?"

"Yes, she said she'd go. I gave her the Hasaka, but I'm worried they might confiscate it, so I've got an appointment with this props guy at Universal who worked on the last Bond movie to see if he's got any ideas."

"Uh, Kildy . . . those gadgets James Bond uses aren't real. It's a movie."

She shot me her movie-star smile. "I said *ideas.* Oh, and I got Riata's ticket. When I called, I asked if they were sold out, and the guy I talked to said, 'Are you kidding?' and told me they'd only sold about half what they usually do. Did you find out anything about Ariaura?"

"No," I said. "I'm checking out some leads," but my friend at the police department didn't have any dope on Ariaura, not even a possible alibi.

"She's clean," he'd said when he finally called back the next morning. "No mail fraud, not even a parking ticket."

I couldn't find anything on her in *The Skeptical Inquirer* or on the Scamwatch website. It looked like she made her money the good old American way, by telling her customers a bunch of nonsense and selling them chakra charts.

I told Kildy as much when she came in the next morning, looking gorgeous in a casual shirt and jeans that had probably cost as much as *The Jaundiced Eye*'s annual budget.

"I'm fairly sure Ariaura's not her real name, but so far I haven't been able to prove it," I said. "Did you get a James Bond secret videocam from your buddy Q?"

"Yes," she said, setting the tote bag down. "And I have an idea for proving Ariaura's a fraud." She handed me a sheaf of papers. "Here are the transcripts of everything Mencken said. We check them against Mencken's writings, and—what?"

I was shaking my head. "This is channeling. When I wrote an exposé about Swami Vishnu Jammi's fifty-thousand-year-old entity, Yogati, using phrases like 'totally awesome' and 'funky' and talking about cell phones. He said he 'transliterated' Yogati's thoughts into his own words."

"Oh." Kildy bit her lip. "Rob, what about a computer match? You know, one of those things where they compare a manuscript with Shakespeare's plays to see if they were written by the same person."

"Too expensive," I said. "Besides, they're done by universities, who I doubt would want to risk their credibility by running a check on a channeler. And even if they did match, all it would prove is that it's Mencken's words, not that it's Mencken."

"Oh." She sat on the corner of my desk, swinging her long legs for a minute and then stood up, walked over to the bookcase, and began pulling down books.

"What are you doing?" I asked, going over to see what she was doing. She was holding a copy of Mencken's *Heathen Days*. "I told you," I said, "Mencken's phrases won't—"

"I'm not looking up his phrases," she said, handing me *Prejudices* and Mencken's biography. "I'm looking for questions to ask him."

"*Him*? He's not Mencken, Kildy. He's a concoction of Ariaura's."

"I know," she said, handing me *The Collectible Mencken*. "That's why we need to question him—I mean Ariaura. We need to ask him—her—questions like, 'What was your wife's maiden name?' and 'What was the first newspaper you worked for?' and—are any of these paperbacks on the bottom shelf here by Mencken?"

"No, they're mysteries mostly. Chandler and Hammett and James M. Cain."

She straightened to look at the middle shelves. "Questions like, 'What did your father do for a living?'"

"He made cigars," I said. "The first newspaper he worked for was *not* the *Baltimore Sun*, but the *Morning Herald*, and his wife's maiden name was Sarah Haardt. With a 'd' and two 'a's. But that doesn't mean I'm Mencken."

"No," Kildy said, "but if you didn't know them, it would prove you weren't." She handed me *A Mencken Chrestomathy*. "If we ask Ariaura questions Mencken would know the answers to, and she gets them wrong, it proves she's not channeling."

She had a point. Ariaura had obviously researched Mencken fairly thoroughly to be able to mimic his language and mannerisms, and probably well enough to answer basic questions about his life, but she would hardly have memorized every detail. There were dozens of books about him, let alone his own work and his diaries. And *Inherit the Wind* and all the other plays and books and treatises that had been written about the Scopes trial. I'd bet there were close to a hundred Mencken things in print, and that didn't include the stuff he'd written for the *Baltimore Sun*.

And if we could catch her not knowing something Mencken would know, it would be a simple way to prove conclusively that she was faking, and we could move on to the much more important question of why. *If* Ariaura would let herself be questioned.

"How do you plan to get Ariaura to agree to this?" I said. "My guess is she won't even let us in to see her."

"If she doesn't, then that's proof, too," she said imperturbably.

"All right," I said, "but forget about asking what Mencken's father did. Ask what he drank. Rye, by the way."

Kildy grabbed a notebook and started writing.

"Ask what the name of his first editor at the *Sun* was," I said, picking up *The Great Monkey Trial*. "And ask who Sue Hicks was."

"Who was she?" Kildy asked.

"He. He was one of the defense lawyers at the Scopes trial."

"Should we ask him—her—what the Scopes trial was about?"

"No, too easy. Ask him . . ." I said, trying to think of a good question. "Ask him what he ate while he was there covering the trial, and ask him where he sat in the courtroom"

"Where he sat?"

"It's a trick question. He stood on a table in the corner. Oh, and ask where he was born."

She frowned. "Isn't that too easy? Everyone knows he's from Baltimore."

"I want to hear him say it."

"Oh," Kildy said. "Did he have any kids?"

I shook my head. "He had a sister and two brothers. Gertrude, Charles, and August."

"Oh, good, that's not a name you'd be able to come up with just by guessing. Did he have any hobbies?"

"He played the piano. Ask about the Saturday Night Club. He and a bunch of friends got together to play music together."

We worked on the questions the rest of the day and the next morning, writing them down on index cards so they could be asked out of order.

"What about some of his sayings?" Kildy asked.

"You mean like, 'Puritanism is the haunting fear that someone, somewhere, may be happy'? No. They're the easiest thing of all to memorize, and no real person speaks in aphorisms."

Kildy nodded and bent her blonde head over the book again. I looked up Mencken's medical history—he suffered from ulcers and had an operation on his mouth to remove his uvula—and went out and got us sandwiches for lunch and made copies of Mencken's "History of the Bathtub" and a fake handbill he'd passed out during the Scopes trial announcing "a public demonstration of healing, casting out devils, and prophesying" by a (fictional) evangelist. Mencken had crowed that not a single person in Dayton had spotted the fake.

Kildy looked up from her book. "Did you know Mencken dated Lillian Gish?" she asked, sounding surprised.

"Yeah. He dated a lot of actresses. He had an affair with Anita Loos and nearly married Aileen Pringle."

"I'm impressed he wasn't intimidated by the fact that they were movie stars, that's all."

I didn't know if that was directed at me or not. "Speaking of actresses," I said, "what time is Ariaura's seminar?"

"Two o'clock," she said, glancing at her watch. "It's a quarter till two right now. It should be over around four. Riata said she'd call as soon as it was done."

We went back to looking through Mencken's books and his biographies, looking for details Ariaura was unlikely to have memorized. He'd loved baseball. He had stolen Gideon Bibles from hotel rooms and then given them to his friends, inscribed, "Compliments of the Author." He'd been friends with lots of writers, including Theodore Dreiser and F. Scott Fitzgerald, who'd gotten so drunk at a dinner with Mencken he'd stood up at the dinner table and pulled his pants down.

The phone rang. I reached for it, but it was Kildy's cell phone. "It's Riata," she told me, looking at the readout.

"Riata?" I glanced at my watch. It was only two-thirty. "Why isn't she in the seminar?"

Kildy shrugged and put the phone to her ear. "Riata? What's going on? . . . You're kidding! . . . Did you get it? Great . . . no, meet me at Spago's, like we agreed. I'll be there in half an hour."

She hit "end," stood up, and took out her keys, all in one graceful motion. "Ariaura did it again, only this time as soon as she started, they stopped the seminar, yanked her off-stage, and told everybody to leave. Riata got it on tape. I'm going to go pick it up. Will you be here?"

I nodded absently, trying to think of a way to ask about Mencken's two-fingered typing, and Kildy waved goodbye and went out.

If I asked "How do you write your stories?" I'd get an answer about the process of writing, but if I asked, "Do you touch-type?" Ariaura—

Kildy reappeared in the doorway, sat down, and picked up her notebook again. "What are you doing?" I asked, "I thought you were—"

She put her finger to her lips. "She's here," she mouthed, and Ariaura came in.

She was still wearing her purple robes and her stage makeup, so she must have come here straight from her seminar, but she didn't roar in angrily the way she had before. She looked frightened.

"What are you doing to me?" she asked, her voice trembling, "and don't say you're not doing anything. I saw the videotape. You're—that's what I want to know, too. What the hell have you been doing? I thought you ran a magazine that worked to put a stop to the kind of bilgewater this high priestess of blather spews out. She was at it again today, calling up spirits and rooking a bunch of mysticism-besotted fools out of their cold cash, and where the hell were you? I didn't see you there, cracking heads."

"We didn't go because we didn't want to encourage her if she was—" Kildy hesitated. "We're not sure what . . . I mean, who we're dealing with here. . . ." she faltered.

"Ariaura," I said firmly. "You pretend to channel spirits from the astral plane for a living. Why should we believe you're not pretending to channel H. L. Mencken."

"Pretending?" she said, sounding surprised. "You think I'm something that two-bit Jezebel's confabulating?" She sat down heavily in the chair in front of my desk and grinned wryly at me. "You're absolutely right. I wouldn't believe it either. A skeptic after my own heart."

"Yes," I said. "And as a skeptic, I need to have some proof you're who you say you are."

"Fair enough. What kind of proof?"

"We want to ask you some questions," Kildy said.

Ariaura slapped her knees. "Fire away."

"All right," I said. "Since you mentioned fires, when was the Baltimore fire?"

"Aught-four," she said promptly. "February." She grinned. "Best time I ever had."

Kildy glanced at me. "What did your father drink?" she asked.

"Rye."

"What did you drink?" I asked.

"From 1919 on, whatever I could get."

"Where are you from?" Kildy asked.

"The most beautiful city in the world."

"Which is?" I said.

"Which *is*?" she roared, outraged. "Bawlmer!"

Kildy shot me a glance. "What's the Saturday Night Club?" I barked.

"A drinking society," she said, "with musical accompaniment."

"What instrument did you play?"

"Piano."

"What's the Mann Act?"

"Why?" she said, winking at Kildy. "You planning on taking her across state lines? Is she underage?"

I ignored that. "If you're really Mencken, you hate charlatans, so why have you inhabited Ariaura's body?"

"Why do people go to zoos?"

She was good, I had to give her that. And fast. She spat out answers as fast as I could ask questions about the *Sun* and the *Smart Set* and Williams Jennings Bryan.

"Why did you go to Dayton?"

"To see a three-ring circus. And stir up the animals."

"What did you take with you?"

"A typewriter and four quarts of Scotch. I should have taken a fan. It was hotter than the seventh circle of hell, with the same company."

"What did you eat while you were there?" Kildy asked.

"Fried chicken and tomatoes. At every meal. Even breakfast."

I handed him the bogus evangelist handbill Mencken had handed out at the Scopes trial. "What's this?"

She looked at it, turned it over, looked at the other side. "It appears to be some sort of circular."

And there's all the proof we need, I thought smugly. Mencken would have recognized that instantly. "Do you know who wrote this handbill?" I started to ask and thought better of it. The question itself might give the answer away. And better not use the word "handbill."

"Do you know the event this circular describes?" I asked instead.

"I'm afraid I can't answer that," she said.

Then you're not Mencken, I thought. I shot a triumphant glance at Kildy.

"But I would be glad to," Ariaura said, "if you would be so good as to read what is written on it to me."

She handed the handbill back to me, and I stood there look-ing at it and then at her and then at it again.

"What is it, Rob?" Kildy said. "What's wrong?"

"Nothing," I said. "Never mind about the circular. What was your first published news story about?"

"A stolen horse and buggy," she said and proceeded to tell the whole story, but I wasn't listening.

He didn't know who the handbill was about, I thought, because he couldn't read. Because he'd had an aphasic stroke in 1948 that had left him unable to read and write.

🐾 🐾 🐾

"I had a nice clean place to stay, madam, and I left it to come here."

—*Inherit the Wind*

"It doesn't prove anything," I told Kildy after Ariaura was gone. She'd come out of her Mencken act abruptly after I'd asked her what street she lived on in Baltimore, looked bewilderedly at me and then Kildy, and bolted without a word. "Ariaura could have found out about Mencken's stroke the same way I did," I said, "by reading it in a book."

"Then why did you go white like that?" Kildy said. "I thought you were going to pass out. And why wouldn't she just answer the question? She knew the answers to all the others."

"Probably she didn't know that one and that was her fallback response," I said. "It caught me off-guard, that's all. I was expect-ing her to have memorized pat answers, not—"

"Exactly," Kildy cut in. "Somebody faking it would have said they had an aphasic stroke if you asked them a direct question about it, but they wouldn't have . . . and that wasn't the only instance. When you asked him about the Baltimore fire, he said it was the best time he'd ever had. Someone faking it would have told you what buildings burned or how horrible it was."

And he'd said, not "1904" or "oh-four," but "aught-four." Nobody talked like that nowadays, and it wasn't something that would have been in Mencken's writings. It was something people said, not wrote, and Ariaura couldn't possibly—

"It doesn't prove he's Mencken," I said and realized I was saying "he." And shouting. I lowered my voice. "It's a very clever trick, that's all. And just because we don't know how the trick's being done doesn't mean it's not a trick. She could have been coached in the part, *including* telling her how to pretend she can't read if she's confronted with anything written, or she could be hooked up to somebody with a computer."

"I looked. She wasn't wearing an earpiece, and if somebody was looking up the answers and feeding them to her, she'd be slower answering them, wouldn't she?"

"Not necessarily. Or she might have a photographic memory."

"But then wouldn't she be doing a mind-reading act instead of channeling?"

"Maybe she did. We don't know what she was doing before Salem," I said, but Kildy was right. Someone with a photographic memory could make a killing as a fortuneteller or a medium, and there were no signs of a photographic memory in Ariaura's channeling act—she spoke only in generalities.

"Or she might be coming up with the answers some other way," I said.

"What if she isn't, Rob? What if she's really channeling the spirit of Mencken?"

"Kildy, channels are fakes. There are no spirits, no sympathetic vibrations, no astral plane."

"I know," she said, "but his answers were so—" She shook her head. "And there's something about him, his voice and the way he moves—"

"It's called acting."

"But Ariaura's a terrible actress. You saw her do Isus."

"All right," I said. "Let's suppose for a minute it is Mencken, and that instead of being in the family plot in Louden Park Cemetery, his spirit's floating in the ether somewhere, why would he come back at this particular moment? Why didn't he come back when Uri Geller was bending spoons all over the place, or when Shirley MacLaine was on every talk show in the universe? Why didn't he come back in the fifties when Virginia Tighe was claiming to be Bridey Murphy?"

"I don't know," Kildy admitted.

"And why would he choose to make his appearance through the 'channel' of a third-rate mountebank like Ariaura? He *hated* charlatans like her."

"Maybe that's why he came back, because people like her are still around and he hadn't finished what he set out to do. You heard him—he said he left too early."

"He was talking about the Scopes trial."

"Maybe not. You heard him, he said 'You let the quacks and the crooks take over.' Or maybe—" she stopped.

"Maybe what?"

"Maybe he came back to help you, Rob. That time you were so frustrated over Charles Fred, I heard you say, 'Where the hell is H. L. Mencken when we need him?' Maybe he heard you."

"And decided to come all the way back from an astral plane that doesn't exist to help a skeptic nobody's ever heard of."

"It's not *that* inconceivable that someone would want to help you," Kildy said. "The work you're doing is really important, and Mencken—"

"*Kildy*," I said. "I don't believe this."

"I don't either—I just . . . you have to admit, it's a very convincing illusion."

"Yes, so was the Fox Sisters' table-rapping and Virginia Tighe's past life as an Irish washerwoman, but there was a logical explanation for both of them, and it may not even be that complicated. The Fox Sisters were cracking their *toes*, for God's sake."

"You're right," Kildy said, but she didn't sound completely convinced, and that worried me. If Ariaura's Mencken imitation could fool Kildy, it could fool anybody, and "I'm sure it's a trick. I just don't know how she's doing it," wasn't going to cut it when the networks called me for a statement. I had to figure this out fast.

"Ariaura has to be getting her information about Mencken from someplace," I said. "We need to find out where. We need to check with bookstores and the library. And the Internet," I said, hoping that wasn't what she was using. It would take forever to find out what sites she'd visited.

"What do you want me to do?" Kildy asked.

"I want you to go through the transcripts like you suggested and find out where they came from so we'll know the particular works we're dealing with," I told her. "And I want you to talk to your seminars and anybody else who's been to the seminars and find out if any of them had a private enlightenment audience with Ariaura. I want to know what goes on in them. Is she using Mencken for some purpose we don't know about? See if you can find out."

"I could ask Riata to get one," she suggested.

"That's a good idea," I said.

"What about questions? Do you want me to try to come up with some harder ones than the ones we asked him—I mean, her?"

I shook my head. "Asking more obscure questions won't help. If she's got a photographic memory, she'll know anything we throw at her, and if she doesn't, and we ask her some obscure question about one of the reporters Mencken worked with at the *Morning Herald*, or one of his *Smart Set* essays, she can say she doesn't remember, and it won't prove anything. If you asked me what was in articles I wrote for *The Jaundiced Eye* five years ago, I couldn't remember either."

"I'm not talking about facts and figures, Rob," Kildy said. "I'm talking about the kinds of things people don't forget, like the first time Mencken met Sara."

I thought of the first time I met Kildy, looking up from my desk to see her standing there, with her blonde hair and that movie-star smile. Unforgettable was the word, all right.

"Or how his mother died," Kildy was saying, "or how he found out about the Baltimore fire. The paper called him and woke him out of a sound sleep. There's no way you could forget that, or the name of a dog you had as a kid, or the nickname the other kids called you in grade school."

Nickname. That triggered something. Something Ariaura wouldn't know. About a baby. Had Mencken had a nickname when he was a baby? No, that wasn't it—

"Or what he got for Christmas when he was ten. We need to

find a question Mencken would absolutely know the answer to, and if he doesn't, it proves it's Ariaura."

"And if he does, it still doesn't prove it's Mencken. Right?"

"I'll go talk to Riata about getting a private audience," she said, stuffed the transcripts in her tote, and put on her sunglasses. "And I'll pick up the videotape. I'll see you tomorrow morning."

"Right, Kildy?" I insisted.

"Right," she said, her hand on the door. "I guess."

🐾 🐾 🐾

"In the highest confidence there is always a flavor of doubt—a feeling, half instinctive and half logical, that, after all, the scoundrel *may* have something up his sleeve."

—H. L. Mencken

After Kildy left, I called up a computer-hacker friend of mine and put him to work on the problem and then phoned a guy I knew in the English department at UCLA.

"Inquiries about Mencken?" he said. "Not that I know of, Rob. You might try the journalism department."

The guy at the journalism department said, "Who?" and, when I explained, suggested I call Johns Hopkins in Baltimore.

And what had I been thinking? Kildy said Ariaura had started doing Mencken in Seattle. I needed to be checking there, or in Salem or—where had she gone after that? Sedona. I spent the rest of the day (and evening) calling bookstores and reference librarians in all three places. Five of them asked me "Who?" and all of them asked me how to spell "Mencken," which might or might not mean they hadn't heard the name lately, and only seven of the thirty stocked any books on him. Half of those were the latest Mencken biography, which for an excited moment I thought might have answered the question, "Why Mencken?"— the title of it was *Skeptic and Prophet*—but it had only been out two weeks. None of the bookstores could give me any information on orders or recent purchases, and the public libraries couldn't give me any information at all.

I tried their electronic card catalogues, but they only showed currently checked-out books. I called up the L.A. Public Library's catalogue. It showed four Mencken titles checked out, all from the Beverly Hills branch.

"Which looks promising," I told Kildy when she came in the next morning.

"No, it doesn't," she said. "I'm the one who checked them out, to compare the transcripts against." She pulled a sheaf of papers out of her designer tote. "I need to talk to you about the transcripts. I found something interesting. I know," she said, anticipating my objection, "you said all it proved was that Ariaura—"

"Or whoever's feeding this stuff to her."

She acknowledged that with a nod, "—all it proved was that whoever was doing it was reading Mencken, and I agree, but you'd expect her to quote him back verbatim, wouldn't you?"

"Yes," I said, thinking of Randall Mars's Lincoln and his "Fourscore and seven . . ."

"But she doesn't. Look, here's what she said when we asked him about William Jennings Bryan: 'Bryan! I don't even want to hear that mangy old mountebank's name mentioned. That scoundrel had a malignant hatred of science and sense.'"

"And he didn't say that?"

"Yes and no. Mencken called him a 'walking malignancy' and said he was 'mangy and flea-bitten' and had 'an almost pathological hatred of all learning.' And the rest of the answers, and the things she said at the seminars, are like that, too."

"So she mixed and matched his phrases," I said, but what she'd found was disturbing. Someone trying to pull off an impersonation would stick to the script, since any deviations from Mencken's actual words could be used as proof it wasn't him.

And the annotated list Kildy handed me was troubling in another way. The phrases hadn't been taken from one or two sources. They were from all over the map—"complete hooey" from *Minority Report*, "buncombe" from *The New Republic*, "as truthful as Lydia Pinkham's Vegetable Compound" from an article on pedagogy in the *Sun*.

"Could they all have been in a Mencken biography?"

She shook her head. "I checked. I found a couple of sources that had several of them, but no one source that had them all."

"That doesn't mean there isn't one," I said and changed the subject. "Was your friend able to get a private audience with Ariaura?"

"Yes," she said, glancing at her watch. "I have to go meet her in a few minutes. She also got tickets to the seminar Saturday. They didn't cancel it like I thought they would, but they did cancel a local radio interview she was supposed to do last night, and the week-long spiritual immersion she had scheduled for next week."

"Did she give you the videotape of Ariaura's last seminar?"

"No, she'd left it at home. She said she'd bring it when we meet before her private audience. She said she got some really good footage of the emcee. She swears from the way he looked that he's not in on the scam. And there's something else. I called Judy Helzberg, who goes to every psychic event there is—remember? I interviewed her when we did the piece on shamanic astrologers—and she said Ariaura called her and asked her for Wilson Amboy's number."

"Wilson Amboy?"

"Beverly Hills psychiatrist."

"It's all part of the illusion," I said, but even I sounded a little doubtful. It was an awfully good deception for a third-rate channeler like Ariaura. There's somebody else in on it, I thought, and not just somebody feeding her answers. A partner. Or a mastermind.

After Kildy left I called Marty Rumboldt and asked him if Ariaura had had a partner in Salem. "Not that I know of," he said. "Prentiss just did a study on witchcraft in Salem. She might know somebody who would know. Hang on. Hey, Prentiss!" I could hear him call. "Jamie!"

Jamie, I thought. That had been James M. Cain's nickname, and Mencken had been good friends with him. Where had I read that?

"She said to call Madame Orima," Marty said, getting back on the phone, and gave me the number.

I started to dial it and then stopped and looked up "Cain,

James M." in Mencken's biography. It said he and Mencken had worked on the *Baltimore Sun* together, that they had been good friends, that Mencken had helped him get his first story collection published: *The Baby in the Icebox.*

I went over to the bookcase, squatted down, and started through the row of paperbacks on the bottom shelf . . . Chandler, Hammett . . . It had a red cover, with a picture of a baby in a high chair and a . . . Chandler, Cain . . .

But no red. I scanned the titles—*Double Indemnity, The Postman Always Rings Twice* . . . Here it was, stuck behind *Mildred Pierce* and not red at all. *The Baby in the Icebox.* It was a lurid orange and yellow, and pictures of a baby in its mother's arms and a cigarette-smoking lug in front of a gas station. I hoped I remembered the inside better than the outside.

I did. The introduction was by Roy Hoopes, and it was not only a Penguin edition, but one that had been out of print for at least twenty years. Even if Ariaura's researcher had bothered to check out Cain, it would hardly have been this edition.

And the introduction was full of stuff about Cain that was perfect—the fact that everyone who knew him called him Jamie, the fact that he'd spent a summer in a tuberculosis sanitarium and hated Baltimore, Mencken's favorite place.

Some of the information was in the Mencken books— Mencken introducing him to Alfred A. Knopf, who'd published that first collection, the *Sun* connection, Cain and Mencken's rivalry over movie star Aileen Pringle.

But most of the things weren't, and they were exactly the kind of thing a friend would know. And Ariaura wouldn't, because they were details about Cain's life, not Mencken's. Even a mastermind wouldn't have memorized every detail of Cain's life or those of Mencken's other famous friends. If there wasn't anything here I could use, there might be something in Dreiser's biography, or F. Scott Fitzgerald's. Or Lillian Gish's.

But there was plenty here, like the fact that Cain's brother Boydie had died in a tragic accident after the Armistice, and his statement that all his writing was modeled on *Alice in Wonderland.* That was something no one would ever guess from reading Cain's books, which were all full of crimes and murderers and beautiful, calculating women who seduced the hero into helping her with a scam and then turned out to be working a scam of her own.

Not exactly the kind of thing Ariaura would read, and definitely the kind of thing Mencken would have. He'd bought "The Baby in the Icebox" for the *American Mercury* and told Cain it was one of the best things he'd ever written. Which meant it would make a perfect source for a question, and I knew just what to ask.

To anyone who hadn't heard of the story, the question wouldn't even make sense. Only somebody who'd read the story would know the answer. Like Mencken.

And if Ariaura knew it, I'd—what? Believe she was actually channeling Mencken?

Right. And Charles Fred was really talking to the dead and Uri Geller was really bending spoons.

It was a trick, that was all. She had a photographic memory, or somebody was feeding her the answers.

Feeding her the answers.

I thought suddenly of Kildy, saying, "Who *was* Sue Hicks?," of her insisting I go with her to see Ariaura, of her saying, "But why would Ariaura channel a spirit who yells at her audiences?"

I looked down at the orange-and-yellow paperback in my hand. "A beautiful, calculating woman who seduces the hero into helping her with a scam," I murmured, and thought about Ariaura's movie-star-handsome ushers and about scantily clad Victorian spirits and Sir William Crookes.

Sex. Get the chump emotionally involved and he won't see the wires. It was the oldest trick in the book.

I'd said Ariaura wasn't smart enough to pull off such a complicated scam, and she wasn't. But Kildy was. So you get her on the inside where she can see the shelf full of Mencken books, where she can hear the chump mutter, "Where the hell is Mencken when we need him?" You get the mark to trust her, and if he falls in love with her, so much the better. It'll keep him off-balance and he won't get suspicious.

And it all fit. It was Kildy who'd set up the contact—I never did channelers, and Kildy knew that. It was Kildy who'd said we couldn't go incognito, Kildy who'd said to bring the Sony, knowing it would be confiscated, who'd told me to untape the digital from my wrist.

But she'd gotten all of it on tape. And she hadn't had any idea who the spirit was. I was the one who'd figured out it was Mencken.

With Kildy feeding me clues from the seminar she'd gone to before, and I only had her word that Ariaura had channeled him that time. And that it had happened in Berkeley and Seattle. And that the tapes had been edited.

And she was the one who'd kept telling me it was really Mencken, the one who'd come up with the idea of asking him questions that would prove it—questions I'd conveniently told her the answers to—the one who'd suggested a friend of hers go to the seminar and videotape it, a videotape I'd never seen. I wondered if it—or Riata—even existed.

The whole thing, from beginning to end, had been a set-up.

And I had never tumbled to it. Because I'd been too busy looking at her legs and her hair and that smile. Just like Crookes.

I don't believe it, I thought. Not Kildy, who'd worked side by side with me for over a year, who'd stolen chicken guts and pretended to be hypnotized and let Jean-Piette cleanse her aura, who'd come to work for me in the first place because she hated scam-artists like Ariaura.

Right. Who'd come to work for a two-bit magazine when she could have been getting five million a movie and dating Viggo Mortensen. Who'd been willing to give up premieres and summers in Tahiti and deep massages for me. Skeptics' Rule Number Two: If it seems too good to be true, it is. And how often have you said she's a good actress?

No, I thought, every bone in my body rebelling, it can't be true.

And that's what the chump always says, isn't it, even when he's faced with the evidence? "I don't believe it. She wouldn't do that to me."

And that was the whole point—to get you to trust her, to make you believe she was on your side. Otherwise you'd have insisted on checking those tapes of Ariaura's seminars for yourself to see if they'd been edited, you'd have demanded independently verifiable evidence that Ariaura had really cancelled those seminars and asked about a psychiatrist.

Independently verifiable evidence. That's what I needed, and I knew exactly where to look.

"My mother took me to Lucius Windfire's luminescence reading," Kildy had said, and I had the guest lists for those readings. They were part of the court records, and I'd gotten them when I'd done the story on his arrest. Kildy had come to see me on May tenth and he'd only had two seminars that month.

I called up the lists for both seminars and for the two before that and typed in Kildy's name.

Nothing.

She said she went with her mother, I thought, and typed her name in. Nothing. And nothing when I printed out the lists and went through them by hand, nothing when I went through the lists for March and April. And June. And nothing under her mother's name. And no ten thousand dollar donation on any of Windfire, Inc.'s financial statements.

Half an hour later Kildy showed up smiling, beautiful, full of news. "Ariaura's canceled all the private sessions she scheduled and the rest of her tour." She leaned over my shoulder to look at what I was doing. "Did you come up with a foolproof question for Mencken?"

"No," I said, sliding *The Baby in the Icebox* under a file folder and sticking them both in a drawer. "I came up with a theory about what's going on, though."

"Really?" she said.

"Really. You know, one of my big problems all along has been Ariaura. She's just not smart enough to have come up with all this—the 'aught-four' thing, the not being able to read, the going to see a psychiatrist. Which either meant she was actually channeling Mencken, or there was some other factor. And I think I've got it figured out."

"You have?"

"Yeah. Tell me what you think of this: Ariaura wants to be big. Not just seven hundred and fifty a pop seminars and thirty-dollar videotapes, but *Oprah*, the *Today Show*, *Larry King*, the whole works. But to do that it's not enough to have audiences who believe her. She needs to have somebody with credibility say she's for real, a scientist, say, or a professional skeptic."

"Like you," she said cautiously.

"Like me. Only I don't believe in astral spirits. Or channelers. And I certainly wouldn't fall for the spirit of an ancient priest of Atlantis. It's going to have to be somebody a charlatan would never dream of channeling, somebody who'll say what I want to hear. And somebody I know a lot about so I'll recognize the clues being fed to me, somebody custom-tailored."

"Like H. L. Mencken," Kildy said. "But how would she have known you were a fan of Mencken's?"

"She didn't have to," I said. "That was her partner's job."

"Her part—"

"Partner, sidekick, shill, whatever you want to call it. Somebody I'd trust when she said it was important to go see some channeler."

"Let me get this straight," she said. "You think I went to Ariaura's seminar and her imitation of Isus was so impressive I immediately became a Believer with a capital B and fell in with her nefarious scheme, whatever it is?"

"No," I said. "I think you were in it with her from the beginning, from the very first day you came to work for me."

She really was a good actress. The expression in those blue eyes looked exactly like stunned hurt. "You believe I set you up," she said wonderingly.

I shook my head. "I'm a skeptic, remember? I deal in independently verifiable evidence. Like this," I said and handed her Lucius Windfire's attendee list.

She looked at it in silence.

"Your whole story about how you found out about me was a fake, wasn't it? You didn't look up 'debunkers' in the phone book, did you? You didn't go see a luminescence therapist with your mother?"

"No."

No.

I hadn't realized till she admitted it how much I had been counting on her saying, "There must be some mistake, I was there," on her having some excuse, not matter how phony, "Did

I say the fourteenth? I meant the twentieth," or "My publicist got the tickets for us. It would be in her name." Anything. Even flinging the list dramatically at me and sobbing, "I can't believe you don't trust me."

But she just stood there, looking at the incriminatory list and then at me, not a tantrum or a tear in sight.

"You concocted the whole story," I said finally.

"Yes."

I waited for her to say, "It's not the way it looks, Rob, I can explain," but she didn't say that either. She handed the list back to me and picked up her cell phone and her bag, fishing for her keys and then slinging her bag over her shoulder as casually as if she were on her way to go cover a new moon ceremony or a tarot reading, and left.

And this was the place in the story where the private eye takes a bottle of Scotch out of his bottom drawer, pours himself a nice stiff drink, and congratulates himself on his narrow escape.

I'd almost been made a royal chump of, and Mencken (the real one, not the imitation Kildy and Ariaura had tried to pass off as him) would never have forgiven me. So good riddance. And what I needed to do now was write up the whole sorry scam as a lesson to other skeptics for the next issue.

But I sat there a good fifteen minutes, thinking about Kildy and her exit, and knowing that, in spite of its off-handedness, I was never going to see her again.

🔥 🔥 🔥

"What I need is a miracle."

—*Inherit the Wind*

I told you I'd make a lousy psychic. The next morning Kildy walked in carrying an armload of papers and file folders. She dumped them in front of me on my desk, picked up my phone and began punching in numbers.

"What the hell do you think you're doing? And what's all this?" I said, gesturing at the stack of papers.

"Independently verifiable evidence," she said, still punching in numbers, and put the phone to her ear. "Hello, this is Kildy Ross. I need to speak to Ariaura." There was a pause. "She's not taking calls? All right, tell her I'm at the *Jaundiced Eye* office, and I need to speak to her as soon as possible. Tell her it's urgent. Thank you." She hung up.

"What the hell do you think you're doing, calling Ariaura on my phone?" I said.

"I wasn't," she said. "I was calling Mencken." She pulled a file out of the middle of the stack. "I'm sorry it took me so long. Getting Ariaura's phone records was harder than I thought."

"Ariaura's phone records?"

"Yeah. Going back four years," she said, pulling a file folder out of the middle of the stack and handing it to me.

I opened it up. "How did you get her phone records?"

"I know this computer guy at Pixar. We should do an issue on how easy it is to get hold of private information and how mediums are using it to convince people they're talking to their dead relatives," she said, fishing through the stack for another folder. "And here are my phone records." She handed it to me. "The cell's on top, and then my home number and my car phone. And my mom's. And my publicist's cell phone."

"Your publicist's cell—?"

She nodded. "In case you think I used her phone to call Ariaura. She doesn't have a regular phone, just a cell. And here are my dad's and my stepmother's. I can get my other stepmothers' too, but it'll take a couple more days, and Ariaura's big seminar is tomorrow."

She handed me more files. "This is a list of all my trips—airline tickets, hotel bills, rental car records. Credit card bills, with annotations," she said, and went over to her tote bag and pulled out three fat Italian-leather notebooks with a bunch of post-its sticking out the sides. "These are my dayplanners, with notes as to what the abbreviations mean, and my publicist's log."

"And this is supposed to prove you were at Lucius Windfire's luminescence reading with your mother?"

"No, Rob, I told you, I lied about the seminar," she said, looking earnestly through the stack, folder by folder. "These are to prove I didn't call Ariaura, that she didn't call me, that I wasn't in Seattle or Eugene or any of the other cities she was in, and never went to Salem." She pulled a folder out of the pile and began handing items to me. "Here's the program for Yogi Magaputra's matinee performance for May nineteenth. I couldn't find the ticket stubs and I didn't buy the tickets, the studio did, but here's a receipt for the champagne cocktail I had at intermission. See? It's got the date and it was at the Roosevelt, and here's a schedule of Magaputra's performances, showing he was at the Roosevelt on that day. And a flyer for the next session they gave out as we left."

I had one of those flyers in my file on mediums, and I was pretty sure I'd been at that séance. I'd gone to three, working on a piece on his use of funeral home records to obtain information on his victims' dead relatives. I'd never published it—he'd been arrested on tax evasion charges before I finished it. I looked questioningly at Kildy.

"I was there doing research for a movie I was thinking about doing," Kildy said, "a comedy about a medium. It was called *Medium Rare*. Here's the screenplay." She handed me a thick bound manuscript. "I wouldn't read the whole thing. It's terrible. Anyway, I saw you there, talking to this guy with hair transplants—"

Magaputra's personal manager, who I'd suspected was feeding him info from the audience. I'd been trying to see if I could spot his concealed mike.

"I saw you talking to him, and I thought you looked—"
"Gullible?"

Her jaw tightened. "No. Interesting. Cute. Not the kind of guy I expected to see at a one of the yogi's séances. I asked who you were, and somebody said you were a professional skeptic, and I thought, well, thank goodness! Magaputra was *patently* fake, and everyone was buying it, lock, stock, and barrel."

"Including your mother," I said.

"No, I made that up, too. My mother's even more of a skeptic than I am, especially after being married to my father. She's partly why I was interested—she's always after me to date guys from outside the movie business—so I bought a copy of *The Jaundiced Eye* and got your address and came to see you."

"And lied."

"Yes," she said. "It was a dumb thing to do. I knew it as soon as you started talking about how you shouldn't take anything anyone tells you on faith and how important independently verifiable evidence is, but I was afraid if I told you I was doing research for a movie you wouldn't want me tagging along, and if I told you I was attracted to you, you wouldn't believe me. You'd think it was a reality show or some kind of Hollywood fad thing everybody was doing right then, like opening a boutique or knitting or checking into Betty Ford."

"And you fully intended to tell me," I said, "you were just waiting for the right moment. In fact, you were all set to when Ariaura came along—"

"You don't have to be sarcastic," she said. "I thought if I went to work for you and you got to know me, you might stop thinking of me as a movie star and ask me out—"

"And incidentally pick up some good acting tips for your medium movie."

"Yes," she said angrily. "If you want to know the truth, I also thought if I kept going to those stupid past-life regression sessions and covens and soul retrieval circles, I might get over the stupid crush I had on you, but the better I got to know you, the worse it got." She looked up at me. "I know you don't believe me, but I didn't set you up. I'd never seen Ariaura before I went to that first seminar with my publicist, and I'm not in any kind of scam with her. And that story I told you the first day is the only thing I've ever lied to you about. Everything else I told you—about hating psychics and Ben Affleck and wanting to get out of the movie business and wanting to help you debunk charlatans and loathing the idea of ending up in rehab or in *The Hulk IV*—was true." She rummaged in the pile and pulled out an olive green-covered script. "They really did offer me the part."

"Of the Hulk?"

"No," she said and held the script out to me. "Of the love interest."

She looked up at me with those blue eyes of hers, and if anything had ever been too good to be true, it was Kildy, standing there with that bilious green script and the office's fluorescent light on her golden hair. I had always wondered how all those chumps sitting around séance tables and squatting on lilac-colored cushions could believe such obvious nonsense. Well, now I knew.

Because standing there right then, knowing it all had to be a scam, that the Hulk script and the credit card bills and the phone bills didn't prove a thing, that they could easily have been faked, and I was nothing more than a prize chump being set up for the big finale by a couple of pros, I still wanted to believe it. And not just the researching-a-movie alibi, but the whole thing—that H. L. Mencken had come back from the grave, that he was here to help me crusade against charlatans, that if I grabbed the wrist holding that script and pulled her toward me and kissed her, we would live happily ever after.

And no wonder Mencken, railing against creationists and chiropractic and Mary Baker Eddy, hadn't gotten anywhere. What chance do facts and reason possibly have against what people desperately need to believe?

But Mencken hadn't come back. A third-rate channeler was only pretending to be him, and Kildy's protests of love were the oldest trick in the book.

"Nice try," I said.

"But you don't believe me," she said bleakly, and Ariaura walked in.

"I got your message," she said to Kildy in Mencken's gravelly voice. "I came as soon as I could." She plunked down in a chair facing me. "Those goons of Ariaura's—"

"You can knock off the voices, Ariaura," I said. "The jig, as Mencken would say, is up."

Ariaura looked inquiringly at Kildy.

"Rob thinks Ariaura's a fake," Kildy said.

Ariaura switched her gaze to me. "You just figured that out? Of course she's a fake, she's a bamboozling mounteback, an oleaginous—"

"He thinks you're not real," Kildy said. "He thinks you're just a voice Ariaura does, like Isus, that your disrupting her seminars is a trick to convince him she's an authentic channeler, and he thinks I'm in on the plot with you, that I helped you set him up."

Here it comes, I thought. Shocked outrage. Affronted innocence. Kildy's a total stranger, I've never seen her before in my life!

"He thinks that you—?" Ariaura hooted and banged the arms of the chair with glee. "Doesn't the poor fish know you're in love with him?"

"He thinks that's part of the scam," Kildy said earnestly. "The only way he'll believe I'm not is if he believes there isn't one, if he believes you're really Mencken."

"Well, then," she said and grinned, "I guess we'll have to convince him." He slapped his knees and turned expectantly to me. "What do you want to know, sir? I was born in 1880 at nine p.m., right before the police went out and raided ten or twenty saloons, and went to work at the *Morning Herald* at the tender age of eighteen—"

"Where you laid siege to Max Ways for four straight weeks before he gave you an assignment," I said, "but my knowing that doesn't any more make me Henry Lawrence Mencken than it does you."

"Henry *Louis*," Ariaura said, "after an uncle of mine who died when he was a baby. All right, you set the questions."

"It's not that simple," Kildy said. She pulled a chair up in front of Ariaura and sat down, facing her. She took both hands in hers. "To prove you're Mencken you can't just answer questions. The skeptic's first rule is: 'Extraordinary claims require extraordinary evidence.' You've got to do something extraordinary."

"And independently verifiable," I said.

"Extraordinary," Ariaura said, looking at Kildy. "I presume you're not talking about handling snakes. Or speaking in tongues."

"No," I said.

"The problem is, if you prove you're Mencken," Kildy said earnestly, "then you're also proving that Ariaura's really channeling astral spirits, which means she's not—"

"The papuliferous poser I know her to be."

"Exactly," Kildy said, "and her career will skyrocket."

"Along with that of every other channeler and psychic and medium out there," I said.

"Rob's put his entire life into trying to debunk these people," Kildy said. "If you prove Ariaura's really channeling—"

"The noble calling of skepticism will be dealt a heavy blow," Ariaura said thoughtfully, "hardly the outcome a man like Mencken would want. So the only way I can prove who I am is to keep silent and go back to where I came from."

Kildy nodded.

"But I came to try and stop her. If I return to the ether, Ariaura will go right back to spreading her pernicious astral-plane-Higher-Wisdom hokum and bilking her benighted audiences out of their cash."

Kildy nodded again. "She might even *pretend* she's channeling you."

"*Pretend*!" Ariaura said, outraged. "I won't allow it! I'll—" and then stopped. "But if I speak out, I'm proving the very thing I'm trying to debunk. And if I don't—"

"Rob will never trust me again," Kildy said.

"So," Ariaura said, "it's—"

A catch-22, I thought, and then, if she says that I've got her— the book wasn't written till 1961, five years after Mencken had died. And catch-22 was the kind of thing, unlike "Bible belt" or "booboisie," that even Kildy wouldn't have thought of, it had become such an ingrained part of the language. I listened, waiting for Ariaura to say it.

"—a conundrum," she said.

"A what?" Kildy said.

"A puzzle with no solution, a hand there's no way to win, a hellacious dilemma."

"You're saying it's impossible," Kildy said bleakly.

Ariaura shook her head. "I've had tougher assignments than this. There's bound to be something—" She turned to me. "She said something about 'the skeptic's first rule.' Are there any others?"

"Yes," I said. "If it seems too good to be true, it is."

"And 'by their fruits shall ye know them,'" Kildy said. "It's from the Bible."

"The Bible . . ." Ariaura said, narrowing her eyes thoughtfully. "The Bible . . . how much time have we got? When's Ariaura's next show?"

"Tonight,' Kildy said, "but she canceled the last one. What if she—"

"What time?" Ariaura cut in.

"Eight o'clock."

"Eight o'clock," she repeated, and made a motion toward her right midsection for all the world like she was reaching for a pocket watch. "You two be out there, front row center."

"What are you doing to do?" Kildy asked hopefully.

"I dunno," Ariaura said. "Sometimes you don't have to do a damned thing—they do it to themselves. Look at that High Muckitymuck of Hot Air, Bryan." She laughed. "Either of you know where I can get some rope?" She didn't wait for an answer. "—I'd better get on it. There's only a couple hours to deadline—" She slapped her knees. "Front row center," she said to Kildy. "Eight o'clock."

"What if she won't let us in?" Kildy asked. "Ariaura said he was going to get a restraining order against—"

"She'll let you in. Eight o'clock."

Kildy nodded. "I'll be there, but I don't know if Rob—"

"Oh, I wouldn't miss this for the world," I said.

Ariaura ignored my tone. "Bring a notebook," she ordered. "And in the meantime, you'd better get busy on your charlatan debunking. The sons of bitches are gaining on us."

☙ ☙ ☙

> "One sits through long sessions . . . and then suddenly there comes a show so gaudy and hilarious, so melodramatic and obscene, so unimaginably exhilarating and preposterous that one lives a gorgeous year in an hour."
>
> —H. L. Mencken

An hour later a messenger showed up with a manila envelope. In it was a square vellum envelope sealed with pink sealing wax and embossed with Isus's hieroglyphs. Inside were a lilac card printed in silver with "The pleasure of your company is requested . . ." and two tickets to the seminar.

"Is the invitation signed?" Kildy asked.

She'd refused to leave after Ariaura'd departed, still acting the part of Mencken. "I'm staying right here with you till the seminar," she'd said perching herself on my desk. "It's the only way I can prove I'm not off somewhere with Ariaura cooking up some trick. And here's my phone," she'd handed me her cell phone, "so you won't think I'm sending her secret messages via text-message or something. Do you want to check me to see if I'm wired?"

"No."

"Do you need any help?" Kildy'd asked, picking up a pile of proofs. "Do you want me to go over these, or am I fired?"

"I'll let you know after the seminar."

She'd given me a Julia Roberts–radiant smile and retreated to the far end of the office with the proofs, and I'd called up Charles Fred's file and started through it, looking for leads and trying not to think about Ariaura's parting shot.

I was positive I'd never told Kildy that story, and it wasn't in Daniels's biography, or Hobson's. The only place I'd ever seen it was in an article in the *Atlantic Monthly*. I looked it up in Bartlett's, but it wasn't there. I Googled "Mencken—bitches." Nothing.

Which didn't prove anything. Ariaura—or Kildy—could have read it in the *Atlantic Monthly* just like I had. And since when had H. L. Mencken looked for inspiration to the Bible? That remark alone proved it wasn't Mencken, didn't it? On the other hand, he hadn't said "catch-22," although "conundrum" wasn't nearly as precise a word. And he hadn't said William Jennings Bryan, he'd said "that High Muckitymuck of Hot Air, Bryan," which I hadn't read anywhere, but which sounded like something he would have put in that scathing eulogy he'd written of Bryan.

And this wasn't going anywhere. There was nothing, short of a heretofore undiscovered manuscript or a will in his handwriting leaving everything to Lillian Gish—no, that wouldn't work. The aphasic stroke, remember?—that would prove it was Mencken. And both of those could be faked, too.

And there wasn't anything that could do what Kildy had told

him—correction, told Ariaura she had to do: prove he was real without proving Ariaura was legit. Which she clearly wasn't.

I got out Ariaura's transcripts and read through them, looking for I wasn't sure what, until the tickets came.

"Is the card signed?" Kildy asked again.

"No," I said and handed it to her.

"'The pleasure of your company is requested . . .' is printed on," she said, turning the invitation over to look at the back. "What about the address on the envelope?"

"There isn't one," I said, seeing where she was going with this. "But just because it's not handwritten, that doesn't prove it's from Mencken."

"I know. 'Extraordinary claims,' but at least it's consistent with its being Mencken."

"It's also consistent with the two of you trying to convince me it's Mencken so I'll go to that seminar tonight."

"You think it's a trap?" Kildy said.

"Yes," I said, but standing there, staring at the tickets, I had no idea what kind. Ariaura couldn't possibly still be hoping I'd stand up and shout, "By George, she's the real thing! She's channeling Mencken!" no matter what anecdote she quoted. I wondered if her lawyers might be intending to slap me with a restraining order or a subpoena when I walked in, but that made no sense. She knew my address—she'd been here this very afternoon, and I'd been here most of the past two days. Besides, if she had me arrested, the press would be clamoring to talk to me, and she wouldn't want me voicing my suspicions of a con game to the *L.A. Times.*

When Kildy and I left for the seminar an hour and a half later (on our way out, I'd pretended I forgot my keys and left Kildy standing in the hall while I went back in, and hid *The Baby in the Icebox* down behind the bookcase) I still hadn't come up with a plausible theory, and the Santa Monica Hilton, where the seminar was being held, didn't yield any clues.

It had the same "Believe and It Will Happen" banner, the same Tom Cruise-ish bodyguards, the same security check. They confiscated my Olympus and my digital recorder and Kildy's Hasaka (and asked for her autograph), and we went through the same crystal/pyramid/amulet-crammed waiting area into the same lilac-and-rose-draped ballroom. With the same hard, bare floor.

"Oh, I forgot to bring pillows, I'm sorry," Kildy said and started toward the ushers and stacks of lilac plastic cushions at the rear. Halfway there she turned around and came back. "I don't want to have had an opportunity to send some kind of secret message to Ariaura," she said. "If you want to come with me . . ."

I shook my head. "The floor'll be good," I said, lowering myself to the ground. "It may actually keep me in touch with reality."

Kildy sat down effortlessly beside me, opened her bag, and fumbled in it for her mirror. I looked around. The crowd seemed a little sparser, and somewhere behind us, I heard a woman say, "It was *so* bizarre. Ramtha never did anything like that. I wonder if she's drinking."

The lights went pink, the music swelled, and Russell Crowe came out, went through the same spiel (no flash, no applause, no bathroom breaks) and the same intro (Atlantis, Oracle of Delphi, Cosmic All), and revealed Ariaura, standing at the top of the same black stairway.

She was exactly the same as she had been at that first seminar, dramatically regal in her purple robes and amulets, serene as she acknowledged the audience's applause. The events of the past few days—her roaring into my office, asking frightenedly, "What's happening? Where am I?," slapping her knees and exploding with laughter—might never have happened.

And obviously *didn't*, I thought grimly. I glanced at Kildy. She was still fishing unconcernedly in her bag.

"Welcome, Seekers after Divine Truth," Ariaura said. "We're going to have a wonderful spiritual experience together here today. It's a very special day. This is my one hundredth 'Believe and It Will Happen' seminar."

Lots of applause, which after a couple of minutes she motioned to stop.

"In honor of the anniversary, Isus and I want to do something a little different today."

More applause. I glanced at the ushers. They were looking nervously at each other, as if they expected her to start spouting

Menckenese, but the voice was clearly Ariaura's and so was the Oprah-perky manner.

"My—*our*—seminars are usually pretty structured. They have to be—if the auratic vibrations aren't exactly right beforehand, the spirits cannot come, and after I've channeled, I'm physically and spiritually exhausted, so I rarely have the opportunity to just *talk* to you. But today's a special occasion. So I'd like the tech crew—" she looked up at the control booth, "—to bring up the lights—"

There was a pause, as if the tech crew was debating whether to follow orders, and then the lights came up.

"Thanks, that's perfect, you can have the rest of the day off," Ariaura said. She turned to the emcee. "That goes for you, too, Ken. And my fabulous ushers—Derek, Jared, Brad—let's hear it for the great job they do."

She led a round of applause and then, since the ushers continued to stand there at the doors, looking warily at each other and at the emcee, she made shooing motions with her hands. "Go on. Scoot. I want to talk to these people in private," and when they still hesitated, "You'll still get paid for the full seminar. Go on." She walked over to the emcee and said something to him, smiling, and it must have reassured him because he nodded to the ushers and then up at the control room, and the ushers went out.

I looked over at Kildy. She was calmly applying lipstick. I looked back at the stage.

"Are you sure—?" I could see the emcee whisper to Ariaura.

"I'm *fine*," she mouthed back at him.

The emcee frowned and then stepped off the stage and over to the side door, and the cameraman at the back began taking his videocam off its tripod. "No, no, Ernesto, not you," Ariaura said, "Keep filming."

She waited as the emcee pulled the last door shut behind him and then walked to the front of the stage and stood there completely silent, her arms stiffly at her sides.

Kildy leaned close to me, her lipstick still in her hand. "Are you thinking the prom scene in *Carrie*?"

I nodded, gauging our distance to the emergency exit. There was a distant sound of a door shutting above us—the control room—and Ariaura clasped her hands together. "Alone at last," she said, smiling. "I thought they'd *never* leave."

Laughter.

"And now that they're gone, I have to say this—" She paused dramatically. "Aren't they *gorgeous*?"

Laughter, applause, and several hooting sounds. Ariaura waited till the noise had died down and then asked, "How many of you were at my seminar last Saturday?"

The mood changed instantly. Several hands went up, but tentatively, and two hoop-earringed women looked at each other with the same nervous glance as the ushers had had.

"Or at the one two weeks ago?" Ariaura asked.

Another couple of hands.

"Well, for those of you who weren't at either, let's just say that lately my seminars have been rather . . . interesting, to put it mildly."

Scattered nervous laughter.

"And those of you familiar with the spirit world know that's what can happen when we try to make contact with energies beyond our earthly plane. The astral plane can be a dangerous place. There are spirits there beyond our control, false spirits who seek to keep us from enlightenment."

False spirits is right, I thought.

"But I fear them not, for my weapon is the Truth." She somehow managed to say it with a capital T.

I looked over at Kildy. She was leaning forward the way she had at that first seminar, intent on Ariaura's words. She was still holding her mirror and lipstick. "What's she up to?" I whispered to Kildy.

She shook her head, still intent on the stage. "It's not her."

"What?"

"She's channeling."

"Chan—?" I said and looked at the stage.

"No spirit, no matter how dark," Ariaura said, "no matter how dishonest, can stand between me and that Higher Truth."

Applause, more enthusiastic.

"Or keep me from bringing that Truth to all of you." She smiled and spread out her arms. "I'm a fraud, a charlatan, a fake," she said cheerfully. "I've never channeled a cosmic spirit in my life. Isus is something I made up back in 1996, when I was running a pyramid scheme in Dayton, Ohio. The feds were closing in on us, and I'd already been up on charges of mail fraud in '94, so I changed my name—my real name's Bonnie Friehl, by the way, but I was using Doreen Manning in Dayton—and stashed the money in a bank in Chickamauga, Virginia, my hometown, and then moved to Miami Beach and did fortune-telling while I worked on doing Isus's voice."

I fumbled for my notebook and pen. Bonnie Friehl, Cayman Islands, Miami Beach—

"I did fortune-telling, curses mostly—'Pay me and I'll remove the curse I see hanging over you'—till I had my Isus impersonation ready and then I contacted this guy I knew in Vegas—"

There was an enormous crash from the rear. Ernesto had dropped his shoulder-held video camera and was heading for the door. And this needed to be on film. But I didn't want to miss anything while I tried to figure out how the camera worked.

I glanced over at Kildy, hoping she was taking notes, but she seemed transfixed by what was happening on stage, her forgotten compact and lipstick still in her hands, her mouth open. I would have to risk missing a few words. I scrambled to my feet.

"Where are you going?" Kildy whispered.

"I've got to get this on tape."

"We are," she said calmly, and nodded imperceptibly at the lipstick and then the compact, "Audio . . . and video."

"I love you," I said.

She nodded. "You'd better get those names down, just in case the police confiscate my makeup as evidence," she said.

"His name was Chuck Venture," Ariaura was saying. "He and I had worked together on a chain-letter scheme. His real name's Harold Vogel, but you probably know him by the name he uses out here, Charles Fred."

Jesus. I scribbled the names down: Harold Vogel, Chuck Venture—

"We'd worked a couple of chain-letter scams together," Ariaura said, "so I told him I wanted him to take me to Salem and set me up in the channeling business."

There was a clank and a thud as Ernesto made it to the door and out. It slammed shut behind him.

"Harold always did have a bad habit of writing everything down," Ariaura said chattily. "'You can't blackmail me, Doreen,' he said. 'Wanna bet?' I said. 'It's all in a safety deposit box in Dayton with instructions to open it if anything happens to me.'" She leaned confidingly forward. "It's not, of course. It's in the safe in my bedroom behind the portrait of Isus. The combination's twelve left, six right, fourteen left." She laughed brightly. "So anyway, he taught me all about how you soften the marks up in the seminars so they'll tell Isus all about their love life in the private sessions and then send them copies of the videotapes—"

There were several audible gasps behind me and then the beginnings of a murmur, or possibly a growl, but Ariaura paid no attention—

"—and he introduced me to one of the orderlies at New Beginnings Rehab center, and the deep masseuse at the Willowsage Spa for personal details Isus can use to convince them he knows all-sees all—"

The growl was becoming a roar, but it was scarcely audible over the shouts from outside and the banging on the doors, which were apparently locked from the inside.

"—and how to change my voice and expression to make it look like I'm actually channeling a spirit from beyond—"

It sounded as though the emcee and ushers had found a battering ram. The banging had become shuddering thuds.

"—although I don't think learning all that junk about Lemuria and stuff was necessary," Ariaura said. "I mean, it's obvious you people will believe *anything.*" She smiled beatifically at the audience, as if expecting applause, but the only sound (beside the thuds) was of cell phone keys being hit and women shouting into them. When I glanced back, everybody except Kildy had a phone clapped to their ear.

"Are there any questions?" Ariaura asked brightly.

"Yes," I said. "Are you saying you're the one doing the voice of Isus?"

She smiled pleasedly down at me. "Of course. There's no such thing as channeling spirits from the Great Beyond. Other questions?" She looked past me to the other wildly waving hands. "Yes? The woman in blue?"

"How could you lie to us, you—"

I stepped adroitly in front of her. "Are you saying Todd Phoenix is a fake, too?"

"Oh, yes," Ariaura said. "They're all fakes—Todd Phoenix, Joye Wildde, Randall Mars. Next question? Yes, Miss Ross?"

Kildy stepped forward, still holding the compact and lipstick. "When was the first time you met me?" she asked.

"You don't have to do this," I said.

"Just for the record," she said, flashing me her Julia Roberts–radiant smile and then turning back to the stage. "Ariaura, had you ever met me before last week?"

"No," she said. "I saw you at Ari—at my seminar, but I didn't meet you till afterward at the office of *The Jaundiced Eye*, a fine magazine, by the way. I suggest you all take out subscriptions."

"And I'm not your shill?" Kildy asked.

"No, though I do have them," she said. "The woman in green back there in the sixth row is one," she said, pointing at a plump brunette. "Stand up, Lucy."

Lucy was already scuttling to the door, and so were a thin redhead in a rainbow caftan and an impeccably tailored sixty-year-old in an Armani suit, with a large number of the audience right on their tails.

"Janine's one, too," Ariaura said, pointing at the redhead. "And Doris. They all help gather personal information for Isus to tell them, so it looks like he 'knows all, sees all.'" She laughed delightedly. "Come up on stage and take a bow, girls."

The "girls" ignored her. Doris, a pack of elderly women on her heels, pushed open the middle door and shouted, "You've got to stop her!"

The emcee and ushers began pushing their way through the door and toward the stage. The audience was even more deter-mined to get out than they were to get in, but I still didn't have much time. "Are all the psychics you named using blackmail like you?"

"Ariaura!" the emcee shouted, halfway to the stage and

caught in the flood of women. "Stop talking. Anything you say can be held against you."

"Oh, hi, Ken," she said. "Ken's in charge of laundering all our money. Take a bow, Ken! And you, too, Derek and," she said, indicating the ushers. "The boys pump the audience for information and feed it to me over this," she said, holding up her sacred amulet.

She looked back at me. "I forgot what you asked."

"Are all the psychics you named using blackmail like you?"

"No, not all of them. Swami Vishnu Jammi uses post-hypnotic suggestion, and Nadrilene's always used extortion."

"What about Charles Fred? What's his scam?"

"Invest—" Ariaura's pin-on mike went suddenly dead. I looked back at the melee. One of the ushers was proudly holding up an unplugged cord.

"Investment fraud," Ariaura shouted, her hands cupped around her mouth. "Chuck tells his marks their dead relations want them to invest in certain stocks. I'd suggest you—"

One of the ushers reached the stage. He grabbed Ariaura by one arm and tried to grab the other.

"—suggest you check out Metra—," Ariaura shouted, flailing at him. "Metracon, Spirilink—"

A second usher appeared, and the two of them managed to pinion her arms. "Crystalcom, Inc—," she said, kicking out at them, "—and Universis. Find out—" She aimed a kick that made me flinch at the groin of one of the ushers. "Get your paws off me."

The emcee stepped in front of her. "That concludes Ariaura's presentation," he said, avoiding her kicking feet. "Thank you all for coming. Videos of—" he said and then thought better of it, "—personally autographed copies of Ariaura's book, *Believe and—*"

"Find out who the majority stockholder is," Ariaura bellowed, struggling. "And ask Chuck what he knows about a check forgery scam Zolita's running in Reno."

"—*It Will Happen* are on sale in the . . ." the emcee said and gave up. He grabbed for Ariaura's feet. The three of them wrestled her toward the wings.

"One last question!" I shouted, but it was too late. They already had her off the stage. "Why was the baby in the icebox?"

🐾 🐾 🐾

". . . this is the last time you'll see me. . . ."

—H. L. Mencken

"It still doesn't prove it was Mencken," I told Kildy. "The whole thing could been a manifestation of Ariaura's—excuse me, Bonnie Friehl's—subconscious, produced by her guilt."

"*Or*," Kildy said, "there could have been a scam just like the one you postulated, only one of the swindlers fell in love with you and decided she couldn't go through with it."

"Nope, that won't work," I said. "She might have been able to talk Ariaura into calling off the scam, but not into confessing all those crimes."

"If she really committed them," Kildy said. "We don't have any independently verifiable evidence that she is Bonnie Friehl yet." But the fingerprints on her Ohio driver's license matched, and every single lead she'd given us checked out.

We spent the next two months following up on all of them and putting together a massive special issue on "The Great Channeling Swindle." It looked like we were going to have to testify at Ariaura's preliminary hearing, which could have proved awkward, but she and her lawyers got in a big fight over whether or not to use an insanity defense since she was claiming she'd been possessed by the Spirit of Evil and Darkness, and she ended up firing them and turning state's evidence against Charles Fred, Joye Wildde, and several other psychics she hadn't gotten around to mentioning, and it began to look like the magazine might fold because there weren't any scams left to write about.

Fat chance. Within weeks, new mediums and psychics, advertising themselves as "Restorers of Cosmic Ethics" and "the spirit entity you can trust," moved in to fill the void, and a new weight-loss-through-meditation program began packing them in, promising Low-Carb Essence, and Kildy and I were back in business.

"He didn't make any difference at all," Kildy said disgustedly after a standing-room-only seminar on psychic Botox treatments.

"Yeah, he did," I said. "Charles Fred's up on insider trading charges, attendance is down at the Temple of Cosmic Exploration, and half of L.A.'s psychics are on the lam. And it'll take everybody awhile to come up with new methods for separating people from their hard-earned money."

"I thought you said it wasn't Mencken."

"I said it didn't *prove* it was Mencken. Rule Number One: Extraordinary claims require extraordinary evidence."

"And you don't think what happened on that stage was extraordinary?"

I had to admit it was. "But it could have been Ariaura herself. She didn't say anything she couldn't have known."

"What about her telling us the combination of her safe? And ordering everybody to subscribe to *The Eye*?"

"It still doesn't prove it was Mencken. It could have been some sort of Bridey Murphy phenomenon. Ariaura could have had a babysitter who read the *Baltimore Sun* out loud to her when she was a toddler."

Kildy laughed. "You don't believe that."

"I don't believe anything without proof," I said. "I'm a skeptic, remember? And there's nothing that happened on that stage that couldn't be explained rationally."

"Exactly," Kildy said.

"What do you mean, exactly?"

"By their fruits shall ye know them."

"What?"

"I mean it has to have been Mencken because he did exactly what we asked him to do: prove it wasn't a scam and he wasn't a fake and Ariaura was. And do it without proving he was Mencken because if he did, then that proved she was on the level. Which *proves* it was Mencken."

There was no good answer to that kind of crazy illogic except to change the subject, which I did. I kissed her.

And then sent the transcripts of Ariaura's outbursts to UCLA to have the language patterns compared to Mencken's writing. Independently verifiable evidence. And got *The Baby in the Icebox* out of its hiding place down behind the bookcase while Kildy was out of the office, took it home, wrapped it in tin foil, stuck it inside an empty Lean Cuisine box, and hid it—where else?—in the icebox. Old habits die hard.

UCLA sent the transcripts back, saying it was a big enough sample for a conclusive result. So did CalTech. And Duke. So that was that. Which was too bad. It would have been nice to have Mencken back in the fray, even for a little while. He had definitely left too soon.

So Kildy and I would have to pick up where he left off, which meant not only putting "The sons of bitches are gaining on us," on the masthead of the *The Jaundiced Eye*, but trying to channel his spirit into every page.

And that didn't just mean exposing shysters and con men. Mencken hadn't been the major force he was because of his rants against creationism and faith-healers and patent medicine, but because of what he'd stood for: the Truth. That's why he'd hated ignorance and superstition and dishonesty so much, because he loved science and reason and logic, and he'd communicated that love, that passion, to his readers with every word he wrote.

That was what we had to do with *The Jaundiced Eye*. It wasn't enough just to expose Ariaura and Swami Vishnu and psychic dentists and meditation Atkins diets. We also had to make our readers as passionate about science and reason as they were about Ramtha and luminescence readings. We had to not only tell the truth, but make them *want* to believe it.

So, as I say, we were pretty busy for the next few months, revamping the magazine, cooperating with the police, and following up on all the leads Ariaura had given us. We went to Vegas to research the chain-letter scam she and Chuck Venture/Charles Fred had run, after which I came home to put the magazine to bed, and Kildy went to Dayton and then to Chickamauga to follow up on Ariaura's criminal history.

She called last night. "It's me, Rob," she said, sounding excited. "I'm in Chattanooga."

"Chattanooga, *Tennessee*?" I said. "What are you doing there?"

"The prosecutor working on the pyramid scheme case is on a trip to Roanoke, so I can't see him till Monday, and the school board in Zion—that's a little town near here—is trying to pass a law requiring intelligent design to be taught in the public schools. This Zion thing's part of a nationwide program that's going to introduce intelligent design state by state. So, anyway, since I couldn't see the prosecutor, I thought I'd drive over—it's only about fifty miles from Chickamauga—and interview some of the science teachers for that piece on 'The Scopes Trial Eighty Years Out' you were talking about doing."

"And?" I said warily.

"*And*, according to the chemistry teacher, something peculiar happened at the school board meeting. It might be nothing, but I thought I'd better call so you could be looking up flights to Chattanooga, just in case."

Just in case.

"One of the school board members, a Mr.—" she paused as if consulting her notes, "Horace Didlong, was talking about the lack of scientific proof for Darwin's theory, when he suddenly started ranting at the crowd."

"Did the chemistry teacher say what he said?" I asked, hoping I didn't already know.

"She couldn't remember all of it," Kildy said, "but the basketball coach said some of the students had said they intended to tape the meeting, and he'd try to find out if they did and get me a copy. He said it was 'a very odd outburst, almost like he was possessed.'"

"Or drunk," I said. "And neither of them remembers what he said?"

"No, they both do, just not everything. Didlong apparently went on for several minutes. He said he couldn't believe there were still addlepated ignoramuses around who didn't believe in evolution, and what the hell had they been teaching in the schools all this time. The chemistry teacher said the rant went on like that for about five minutes and then broke off, right in the middle of a word, and Didlong went back to talking about Newton's Second Law makes evolution physically impossible."

"Have you interviewed Didlong?"

"No. I'm going over there as soon as we finish talking, but the chemistry teacher said she heard Didlong's wife ask him what happened, and he looked like he didn't have any idea."

"That doesn't prove it's Mencken," I said.

"I know," she said, "but it is Tennessee, and it is evolution. And it would be nice if it was him, wouldn't it?"

Nice. H. L. Mencken loose in the middle of Tennessee in the middle of a creationism debate.

"Yeah," I said and grinned, "it would, but it's much more likely Horace Didlong has been smoking something he grew in his backyard. Or is trying to stir up some publicity, à la Judge Roy Moore and his Ten Commandments monument. Do they remember anything else he said?"

"Yes, um . . . where is it?" she said. "Oh, here it is. He called the other board members a gang of benighted rubes . . . and then he said he'd take a monkey any day over a school board whose cerebellums were all paralyzed from listening to too much theological bombast . . . and right at the end, before he broke off, the chemistry teacher said he said, 'I never saw much resemblance to Alice myself.'"

"Alice?" I said. "They're sure he said Alice and not August?"

"Yes, because the chemistry teacher's name is Alice, and she thought he was talking to her, and the chairman of the school board did, too, because he looked at her and said, 'Alice? What the heck does Alice have to do with intelligent design?' and Didlong said, 'Jamie sure could write, though, even if the bastard did steal my girl. You better be careful I don't steal yours.' Do you know what that means, Rob?"

"Yes," I said. "How long does it take to get a marriage license in Tennessee?"

"I'll find out," Kildy said, sounding pleased, "and then the chairman said, 'You cannot use language like that,' and, according to the chemistry teacher, Didlong said . . . wait a minute, I need to read it to you so I get it right—it really didn't make any sense—he said, 'You'd be surprised at what I can do. Like stir up the animals. Speaking of which, that's why the baby was stashed in the icebox. Its mother stuck it there to keep the tiger from eating it.'"

"I'll be right there," I said.

THE COSMOLOGY OF
THE WIDER WORLD

by Jeffrey Ford

*Jeffrey Ford is the author of six novels—*Vanitas, *World Fantasy Award–winner* The Physiognomy, Memoranda, The Beyond, The Portrait of Mrs. Charbuque, *and* The Girl in the Glass—*and World Fantasy Award–winning collection* The Fantasy Writer's Assistant and Other Stories. *His short fiction, which has appeared in* Fantasy & Science Fiction, SciFiction, Black Gate, The Green Man, Leviathan 3, The Dark, *and many "year's best" anthologies, has won the World Fantasy and Nebula awards. He lives in South Jersey with his wife and two sons, and teaches writing and literature at Brookdale Community College in Monmouth County, New Jersey. A new collection,* The Empire of Ice Cream, *was published in early 2006.*

BENEATH A YELLOW sky that fizzed like quinine, staring out to sea from the crenellated tower of his own construction, stood Belius, the minotaur, shedding globes of water from his eyes. Life germinated inside these transparent spheres, civilizations rose and fell in clouds of war, colors of love grew vibrant and then washed away. A million seasons raced round within the see-through boundaries, until, rolling off his snout, they smashed against the ledge and shattered.

He lowed in a tone more of creature than man, and that sound flew out toward the horizon. Upon losing speed, it dropped with a splash into the deep ocean and sank, frightening lamprey, scattering herds of sea horses, to eventually settle on the sandy bottom. As Belius wiped his eyes clear, the egg of a bubble his voice had made cracked open, giving birth to the exact sound that had formed it. The sad moan vibrated in every atom of green water for miles around.

Pezimote, the tortoise, was awakened by the racket from his slumber beneath the mud. He struggled up out of sleep, out of the warm ooze, and started slowly swimming toward shore. His shell was orange and black, and he snapped his beak peevishly, because his anatomy did not allow for grumbling. "I am coming, Belius," he thought, and Belius knew instantly that he was coming.

Shuffling and tapping from human foot to hoof, across the cobblestones of the turret, the minotaur reached the side that gave a view of the woods. He rested wearily on the ledge for a moment, but when the frustration that gripped his heart became too much to stand, he struck his horns against the facade, drawing sparks from the cold stone. Another cry went out, this one splitting the sky above the distant trees. Only Vashti, the owl, knew what the strange call meant. She lighted from her branch with graceful wing thrusts that roiled the leaves. "I am coming, Belius," she screeched. Once above the trees, she used her lantern eyes to pinpoint the minotaur's lonely figure on the tower.

After summoning his friends, he took the winding stairway down inside the tall structure. He dressed in formal attire; swallow tail jacket and striped pants. In the kitchen, he brewed cinnamon tea and prepared finger sandwiches with his hooves. He put his books away, rolled up his charts and maps and shooed his pet cat from the study. The niceties he performed for his guests' arrival were all done rather out of habit than conscience. Since the first pang of his malady, nothing made sense; no task seemed worth the effort.

Pezimote sat on the divan because the chairs would not accommodate his giant shell. Having no articulated digits, for every finger sandwich he ate, it was necessary to utilize both of his stumpy appendages. Vashti, perched on the marble bust of Belius, swooped down every now and then and snatched a dainty off the silver platter. Cinnamon tea was not to her liking, so instead Belius had broken into his private liquor cabinet and poured her a glass of dandelion wine. He then stuffed his pipe with the dried petals of the digitalis and lit it. A sweet blue cloud grew around the company. He coughed with vigor and passed the smoldering drug to his companion from the sea. The owl could not take the blue smoke directly. The first and only time she'd tried it, she went stiff as a stone and dropped to the floor. It was enough for her just to breathe their exhalations.

When the group "tuned down," as they had grown to call the state of intoxication the flower gave them, Belius uncrossed his legs and sat forward.

"I'm poisoned," he told them, waiting for their reactions.

Their silence was a lure to draw him out.

"My heart is a snowball, my mind a cracked peach pit," said the minotaur, leaning further forward, his heavy head sinking down as if in exhaustion.

"I see," said Pezimote. "And to what do you attribute this malady?"

"I'm poisoned. I feel as if I am soon going to . . ."

"To what?" asked Vashti, who was now perched on the huge globe of the wider world.

"To perish, of course," Belius cried, losing his patience. At the utterance of these words, three large volumes jumped off the book shelf across the room and fell to the floor.

"Now, now," said Vashti, her feathers ruffled by the physical implications of his anger.

"Who, may I ask, has poisoned you?" said the tortoise, reaching for a deviled ostrich egg the size of a cantaloupe.

Belius shook his head.

"Perhaps you suspect one of us?" said Vashti.

"No, no. You're my closest friends."

"Who then?" asked Pezimote.

"Maybe," said Belius, "it's someone who doesn't want me to complete my Cosmology."

"You've been working on that book, Belius, for years and years. Why now? Most creatures have little interest in reading books and less faith in their messages." The tortoise feared this revelation might wound his friend's pride, so he leaned across the coffee table and stumped him lightly on the knee.

"Look to yourself," said Vashti. "You've poisoned yourself somehow."

"What?" said Belius, straightening up in his chair with a look that as much as said, Absurd! "I'm no weeping willow, Vashti. If I don't mind saying, this tower we sit in was built by these two hooves alone. Each block of coral, I cut myself from the barrier reef and placed with an exactitude that nearly made this chaotic universe reel."

"Yourself," said Vashti, "look to yourself."

"I must agree, Belius," said Pezimote, finishing off the last morsel of egg and eyeing up another. "Your condition reminds me of my wife Chelonia's, unfounded lamentations when the children don't visit for a time."

"Chelonia has other reasons for lamenting, Pezimote," said Vashti, turning her head 180 degrees to face away from the tortoise.

"A cruel cut," said Pezimote, feigning astonishment in the face of the subtle charge.

"So you agree," said Belius. He hoisted himself out of his chair and crossed the room to where a full-length mirror was mounted on the wall. Staring into it, he searched for clues to his own undoing. All looked as it ever had, except for the heavy rings beneath his eyes. His color was good; a creamy, speckled blue that showed no blush of fever nor pallor of weakness. His horns were sharp. His snout was firm; his teeth, white and strong. Sticking out his tongue, he inspected every foot of it with great care. He then turned profile to the glass and peered from the corner of his left eye. "Nothing but handsome," he thought.

"I see nothing wrong," said the Minotaur. But then his eye looked deeply into itself and something toppled his confidence. "And then again . . ." he said and drew closer to the reflection. All was silent but for the sound of Pezimote munching. "And then again . . ." In the dark iris at the center of his left eye there was a minute but conspicuous absence. The light of the lamps did not produce a gleam there as they should have. There was a tiny mote of darker darkness that seemed to consume the light instead of offering it back to the world.

"Wait," said Belius, "I see a black spot within me."

Vashti flew off the globe and came to rest on the minotaur's shoulder. Pezimote rose from the divan and sidled up next to his friend, draping an arm around his wide back. Together they looked into the mirror, into the eye, into the dot of definite nothing.

For the hundredth time that day, the tears came from Belius; big and round as soap bubbles. A moan escaped from somewhere in his third stomach and the sharp self-pity of the sound cracked the glass suddenly as if it had been hit by a rock. The three jumped back. A rough wind entered the room and swirled the smoke of the digitalis into a visible cyclone. Papers were caught up in the storm. Furniture was tilted over. The tray of food flipped onto the floor. The three companions huddled together as books and knick-knacks, fossils and tea cups, flew through the air. The tighter the group held onto each other, the weaker became the power of the gale. When at last they had each other in a knot of strangle holds, the danger dissipated into a light breeze. They broke apart, and Belius stumbled backward against the wall, clutching his head with both hooves.

"Time to be going," said Pezimote, bringing his head slowly out from within his shell. He spoke as he moved toward the door, his voice, as well as his leathery skin, quivering with fear. "I suggest that tomorrow, bright and early, we pay a visit to the ape. Your condition is serious . . . not to mention dangerous."

"Agreed," said Vashti.

Belius nodded, unable to speak for the throbbing behind his eyes.

"Get some sleep," said his visitors in unison. Then Vashti flew through the open window and Pezimote ambled out the door and down the winding steps.

As soon as he was alone, Belius reached for the bottle of dandelion wine. With one mythic gulp, he drained it. His headache lay stunned, barely able to breathe. Packing his pipe with a bolus dose of petals, he lit it. The digitalis was a stake through the heart of his pain. Its frustrated life eased away as he sat back in his chair puffing, too tired to think of sleep. From where he sat, he could see his whole figure in the cracked mirror. He smoked and stared, studying the queer mosaic.

Phantom thoughts skittered through the Minotaur's mind, conjuring no real images or memories and leaving only the vaguest of impressions that he had been thinking at all. From the time his friends had left at dusk, he had remained in his half-stupor, staring straight on and breathing deeply to keep the anguish to a dull ache.

In the meantime, night had come to that hemisphere of the Wider World. As the first waves of darkness rolled across the forest, Siftus the mole put on his snakeskin vest and took up his walking stick. He nosed his way up out of the burrow, which had been his home from birth, and sniffed with delight the rising tide of shadows. He set forth that evening to dine on grubs and the dewdrop liqueur of honey suckle.

The raccoon brothers stole, as they always did, into Belius' garden, but when he was not there to toss rocks at them, they lost their appetites and made off, each with only one ear of corn. After dipping their heist in the ocean for seasoning, and gnawing through a few rows of kernels, they agreed that the ears' mealy taste meant something was wrong with the minotaur.

The ants that lived among the stones of the tower bedded down with atoms of breadcrust and pinprick dreams. The moths flapped out of the bushes and went to work on the cloth of Belius' old coat, which, for the past few months, had been the new personality of the garden scarecrow. Creepers sang a magnificat in a round of ten thousand voices, while bats flew toward fruit they could hear ripening. The fox, the lynx, the weasel, each came awake, as all of the creatures of daylight drew toward sleep.

Belius' cat, Bonita, slipped away from her master's feet, taking the spiral staircase to the wine cellar, where it was a certainty that some rodent would have been dabbling in the stream of a leaky cask and would be too drunk to run. And way off, in the middle of the forest, perched on the uppermost branch of the tallest, most ancient tree, sat Vashti. "Who?" she asked, and as always there was no reply. She flapped her wings and a breeze rolled outward to rustle leaves, bend flowers and push a firefly through the open window of Belius' study.

The insect perched on the tip of the minotaur's snout and worked its electro-chemical trick because it didn't know how not to. Belius was dragged out of his daze by the tiny flash, believing it to be the lost gleam returning to fill the void in his iris. Soon enough, he saw his mistake and brushed the impostor into flight. He rose from his chair with great effort and looked around at the mess his manifest bad feeling had caused. He would have groaned had he not been so weary. Instead, he sighed heavily, causing a hairline fracture in the last unbroken tea cup of the service. Waving his hooves at the shambles, he decided to straighten up in the morning. With hoof-tap and foot-slap, he made his way up the spiral staircase to his bedroom.

He sloughed the swallow tail jacket and striped pants, letting them drop to the floor where he stood. He chose from his armoire the green silk pajamas. All of his sleeping apparel had a good size rock sewn into the collar, which kept him off his back while he slept. Without the rock there, he would roll over, flat out, and begin snoring so ferociously that even the solid structure of his tower was in danger of caving in.

He passed up the book that lay at the foot of his bed, a treatise written by the Sphinx entitled "Riddling Men for Glory and Sport." The fact that he had paid out three casks of his oldest dandelion wine for it meant nothing to him now. He pulled back the quilt of his bed; a massive four-poster, its headboard scarred from the violence of his horns due to recent nightmares. He blew out the candle and then lay down on his side. Trying to corral his thoughts so they would not wander wastefully as they had all day, he concentrated on the bright sliver of moon that hung outside his window. Sleep, he knew, would not come, so he snagged his memory on that hook of a satellite and thought back and back to his earliest days in the lesser world, searching for some insignificant incident that might have planted the seed which had latently germinated and blossomed into the evil flower of his present discontent.

🐾 🐾 🐾

When Belius was born, his father didn't know whether to send him to the barn or swaddle him in blankets and put him in the crib that had been built for his arrival. His mother demanded that he stay in the house. After a lengthy spell of weeping and arguing, his father finally relented, but made one demand, and that, to fill the crib with straw instead of comforters.

The doctor present at the blessed event told his patient that he had seen stranger anomalies of birth in his years as physician to the surrounding farm community. "Once, I saw a little girl born with feathers and wings. She was a darling," he said and rubbed the new mother's back, hoping his anecdote had been a comfort. Later, after he had done all he could, and the mother and child were resting peacefully, he whispered to the father that these types of mixed-up births never survived for more than a few days.

"How could it have happened?" asked Belius' father, his head filled with wild accusations toward his wife.

"Your wife told me that six months ago she was out in the field, over by the swimming pond, picking daisies for the supper table, when she was chased by your prize bull. Do you recall the incident?"

"Yeah, the bull broke from its pen and had wandered out there. She was real upset. It chased her down to the house, almost got her too."

"Not being a university scientist, and not having one within a hundred miles to consult, I would say that the fright of that incident stayed in her mind, imprinting the image of a bull, so that when the child was forming, part of its growth was arrested in the evolutionary state of bovinity and did not make it all the way to becoming human."

Belius' father looked skeptically at the old man. The doctor raised his hands and shrugged his shoulders.

"You could say it was god's work if you like," he said, and then prescribed a good sized dose of alcohol for the younger man and a larger one for himself.

The child was to have been named as his father's junior, but when it came from the womb with the promise of horns and hooves, a different name was promptly chosen. "Belius" had been an ancestor on the mother's side; a personage of antiquity whom no member of the family had any recollection of nor memorable stories to tell about. It was the oldest name recorded in the family Bible, a progenitor to that race of farmers that had taken to tilling the soil of the valley.

Once given a name, the little beast began to take on a definite personality. It did not die as the learned doctor had promised, but thrived under the care of a mother who had waited many years to have a child. She'd had to watch with mixed emotions of jealousy and regret as her sisters of the community grew heavy with joy time and again.

When Belius was born, she hardly noticed his strangeness. She saw past his robin's egg complexion, his blunt snout, to his essence, which was child, and hers at that. She lavished affection on him, treating him as if he were the rarest gem of humanity. His exceptions became the rules by which she judged other children. Her neighbors' little ones were sadly lacking a tail and could not keep the flies off themselves in summer.

Before long, Belius' father almost came around to feeling true affection for the creature that was his son, not exactly loving it, but instead loving his wife's love for it. The three of them made a family and that was what satisfied him most. It gave him a greater reason to work hard and that pleasure took him a long way.

In order to clear things with the community, so that when the time came to take Belius out in public, he would not cause an uproar, his mother, a short time after giving birth, asked permission to speak in front of the congregation after the Sunday service one week. She told about the birth, explained her love for the child and asked that her neighbors accept him as they would any new baby. The members of the parish took the news stoically, with only a modicum of murmuring. There was one extremely old woman who fainted, unable to believe that something could happen that she had never heard of happening before. The reason for the reverent silence of the event was not due to the parishioners being charitable at heart but more to the confinement of the church, for many wore their charity to mass each week the way they wore a Sunday hat. Later, in their homes, a majority of them laughed, others felt threatened, and some confused scorn for pity.

At first, the new mother believed that her son could enjoy a normal life, but the barely audible whispering and the fear that glazed people's eyes on the few occasions she was to bring Belius to town brought her around to a realistic view of the situation. Finally, she was forced to admit his difference to herself. From that time on, she decided that he would spend his young life away from that spirit of ignorance. The young minotaur grew up believing that there was no other existence than that of the fields and surrounding woods, and that there were no other inhabitants of the universe but himself and his parents.

From the time he could first walk, he was lord and master of the farm, allowed to run wild, most anywhere he pleased. The only place that was forbidden to him was the stable in which the bull and two cows were kept. He was strictly told by both mother and father, never to enter that building. On more than one occasion, he would ask what was in there. Then his father would grab him by the horns, spin him around until they were both dizzy and let the boy fly off to land in the dirt.

"That's what's in there," the rough old farmer would say.

Because Belius did not continue to ask did not mean that discovering the secret was not always on his mind. He made many a daring attempt to get inside, but was always caught just as he was pulling back the big red doors, revealing the huge darkness and foul aroma. Each time he was apprehended the punishment was a stiff whipping with a leather belt, the smell of which disturbed him more than the sting.

The cows and bull were sent out to graze at night so that Belius had no chance of coming across them in the fields during his daily adventures. His mother and father lived in fear that he would somehow discover the brutish aspect of his affliction and be shocked out of his learned human traits. The first time he recognized himself in a mirror, it took them hours of lying to make him think that his features were a developmental stage that every child went through. To further this whole charade, his mother gave up eating beef, and, although he could not bring himself to make that sacrifice, his father did vow to take these "cannibalistic" meals in the kitchen, away from his wife and son.

The only time his parents regretted not having told the truth from the beginning was the night on which little Belius first heard the sound of the cows lowing in the field.

"Father, what's that noise?" he asked, running from his bedroom.

His mother and father looked at each other. Being caught unprepared, his father, not a man of quick wit, said, "It's a ghost—spirits of the dead, complaining."

"No it isn't, dear," said his mother. She thought for a short time before she came up with, "It's simply the wind. Your father is trying to frighten you."

"It's no more the wind than a wind from my ass. It's ghosts!" he repeated.

"The wind," she said.

Belius left them to quarrel. Back in his room, he noticed that not a leaf of the tree outside his window so much as stirred. From then on, when he heard the strange noise, he would crawl under his bed and cry with fear, his sobs almost identical to the sounds that sent him into hiding.

When Belius grew old enough to do more than just charge through the corn rows or ram, with his horns, the old door his father had set up for him against the weeping willow, his mother started him working for a few hours each morning in her garden. This early experience led to him always keeping a garden for himself. He turned out to have a special affinity for understanding the needs of vegetables and flowers. She had no idea that he would benefit her small crop so much. In fact, she thought his ungraceful movements and unbounded energy would leave the neat rows in chaos.

By initiating this work period, she hoped to bring Belius around to the point where he could help his father with the daily chores of the farm. She knew that her husband had always wanted a son who could share with him the summer's hard work and the satisfaction at harvest time. He never thought that Belius might be capable of more than just frolicking in the fields. She had told him to try the boy at some small tasks, that it would make him feel good to be more useful now that he was older. To this, her husband replied by shaking his head in reproach as if she were making a cruel joke.

By way of the perfect order and prodigious output of the garden, the farmer realized that the genetic mishap had not stolen his son's ability to work. In a solemn voice, he told his wife, "I think it's time Belius learned to farm."

Belius did as well in the fields as he had in the garden. After a relatively short time, he gradually grew less talkative and more thoughtful. He ignored the old door that leaned against the willow, and, when he entered the corn field, he went about with reserve, not charging blindly, but instead keeping his eyes trained on the stalks for signs of blight or pests. All of the thousands of questions he had been in the habit of asking were now no longer spoken. Instead of haranguing his father for answers, he watched for them in silence. The earth, sky, rain and wind gave the most satisfying replies. He grew stronger with the heavy work, his muscles taking on real definition. His parents knew it was not possible, but to both it seemed that he had grown a whole foot taller in just the first month of farming.

When he and his father would spot each other on the opposite boundaries of a two-acre expanse of alfalfa and wave hello, that is when both felt most content at being partners. As long as there was a fair distance between them they were the greatest of friends. It was only when they were forced into close quarters, forced to speak, that the father panicked as if he were trapped in a broom closet with an actual bull.

At noon, when they took their lunch break behind the barn, they would sit on bales of hay, facing each other. The old man would lean forward with his elbows resting on his knees, a sprig of hay jutting from the corner of his mouth, and drawl forth a strange mixture of simple wisdom and complex ignorance. Belius hardly ever uttered a sound during these sessions, except when his father told one of his obtuse jokes concerning the stupidity of people who lived in towns. Only then would the son force a laugh because he did not want to disappoint his mentor. His father would stay silent for some time out of a sense of false modesty but eventually would join in and react to his own joke. For only a moment, he would feel a closeness to Belius that was even stronger than the one they shared from each side of a wide field. Then he would forget and look up so they were face to face. To see that snout raised toward the sun, to see the large gleaming eyes filled with intelligence and hear the deep animal laugh was more than he could bear. His laughter would stop abruptly, and, whether it was two minutes or twenty into the break, he would return to work.

Belius had begun to be treated more like an adult by his parents. At night, though, he was still forced to stay inside as the cows and bulls were let out and led to pasture. When he heard their eerie moans now, he discounted his previous belief in ghosts and decided it must be the wind. What forced this change in thinking was not so much that he had lost all his childish fear, but more that he had grown so large that he no longer fit under his bed.

One morning in autumn when the leaves in the woods were at the meridian of color between bright yellow and that final blaze of red, Belius' father screamed for him. At the moment the minotaur first heard the voice, he was sitting on the ground beneath the weeping willow, his horns aching, his head spinning from having just taken a charge at the old door. The result was that nothing remained of the target. He had run at it this time with his new strength and weight, and his points went through the solid oak as if it were paper. When his thick skull made contact, the entire barrier seemed to disintegrate like a dream meeting daylight. At first, he thought that his father's wild yell was the audible groaning of the willow, since he had deeply scarred its trunk. When the call came again, though, his head was clearer and he understood. He got off the ground and ran through the stubbled corn field, picking splinters from his arms and chest.

Belius had no idea where his father was calling him from until, rounding the side of the barn, he heard echoing within, a sudden riot of thuds and screams. From the opposite side of the field, he had not recognized the thick vein of agony pulsing through the cry. As he made his way to the entrance, all of the commotion inside grew still and his father's voice fell silent.

The usually secured doors were thrown open wide. From where he stood, bathed in the brightness of the morning sun, he could only make out the vaguest of shadows. Past rebukes from his parents leaped up in his memory and repelled him with a force equal to that of the attraction. He might have stood there for a very long time if his father hadn't again called in a weak gurgle, "Belius, help."

"Father, you want me to enter?"

There was no reply.

Like a traveler trying to make headway against a storm, he leaned forward and took his first step. He continued past the dividing line between day and night and plunged into the shadow. As he waited for his eyes to adjust to the new surroundings, he noticed an unusual aroma permeating the atmosphere. It was an earthy smell, a ripe vegetal smell, but closed in and made stale by the confinement of the wooden walls. It was as if a mound of earth had risen up and taken on the properties of life. He thought it similar to the odor of the plough horse, but it was not as gentle. When he took it into his lungs, it made his facial hair bristle and drew planting rows of bumps from the human flesh of his chest and stomach.

"Belius," his father whispered from somewhere at the back of the barn, "be careful."

"I'm here," Belius called out. He was about to travel down the dark aisle when he heard the unmistakable sounds of the night ghosts. Again, he was unable to move. "They're in the barn," he thought. The distance that he had always felt separating him from his father suddenly disappeared. He put his head down and charged up the aisle between the stalls.

It happened so quickly, as if a mirror had magically appeared in front of him. The bone and horns of Belius' head made contact with what seemed to be a double of themselves. There was a jarring impact. He was lifted off his feet and thrown onto his back. His vision was blurred, but he could, for the first time, make out the enormous figure of what he took to be one of the ghosts. It backed away from him, recoiling for another confrontation. Belius pulled himself up using the stall next to him for support. The monster bellowed, kicked holes in the planks at its feet, and lowered its head, preparing to charge.

This time Belius didn't bring his head down for protection.

He was so dizzy from the first encounter that he knew if he leaned forward, he would continue on to the floor. He stood upright, making himself an easy target. The monster smashed a hole in the back wall of the barn and daylight rushed in around it. As if the sunlight hitting its flank were fire, it lunged forward. Belius waited until the moment when the long, sharp horns of his opponent were only inches from his chest. With all the speed and strength of an animal, and not a single thought in his head, he raised his right arm and brought it down like a sledge hammer on the crown of the enemy's brow, directly between the horns. There was the fleeting sound of a great egg cracking open, and the monster stopped dead in its tracks. It reared onto its hind legs and then fell to the floor with such force that the vibration knocked Belius to his knees.

Blood seeped out of its ears and snout and gushed from the crater in its head. Its eyes were wild. Belius could feel the fear in them. Its jaw moved and it filled the barn with deep raspy squeals—death sounds that rose and fell in a strange rhythm. With each interval, they went through a transformation that brought them closer to speech. Belius listened as if to some piece of music his mother might play on the upright piano in the parlor. Slowly, the sounds evolved into words. "I wanted to see the sun," the monster said to Belius. For the first time, the minotaur realized that the head of his victim was much like his own and that the hooves that carried its massive weight were identical to his and that, whereas neither his mother nor his father had horns, this thing did.

"Speak to me again," Belius pleaded, but the bull was dead.

In the farthest left hand stall, across from the one that held two more creatures similar to the one he had just killed, Belius found his father's body. The horns had passed directly through the stomach and chest. He lifted the limp form in his arms. As he stepped back over the bull on the way out, its two hornless sisters cried, "Murderer, murderer."

Belius took his father into the house and laid him in his bed. Then he sat down in the chair next to the headboard. Until his mother returned from town later that afternoon, he did not move or speak but for the entire time felt the dizziness he would experience when, as a child, the farmer would answer by grabbing his horns and spinning him round.

🐾 🐾 🐾

He sat next to the corpse in the parlor, watching a parade of strange faces pass by the open coffin. His father's old friends and their families spent more time staring at him than they did at the dead man. After the first hour, their whispers had consumed every aspect of reverence the ceremony had originally held.

One man came forward to where Belius was sitting, patted him on the head and fed him a sugar cube. The rest kept their distance but eyed his horns suspiciously after seeing the condition of their neighbor's body. He heard their words, but they did not think he was capable of understanding.

Two hours before the wake was to be over, he motioned to his mother who was in the back of the room, speaking to a distant cousin. His mother came up close to him and leaned over, putting her ear to his snout as if the sound of his voice might frighten the mourners.

"Get rid of them, mother. I've had enough," he said.

"A few more hours, Belius."

With this, he reached up and ripped off his tie, flinging it to the floor.

"Please be calm," she said.

He settled down when he saw the look of embarrassment in his mother's eyes. "I'm sorry," he said, sitting back in his seat. It was too late, though. They'd heard him speak and seen that he was angry. Women and children were ushered out with great haste. The men looked over their shoulders with contempt but could barely restrain themselves from running.

The night of the wake, after hammering the lid on the coffin and carrying it into the living room, Belius left his mother sitting at the kitchen table and went outside to the barn. He opened the big doors and stepped inside. Although the neighbors had dragged away the carcass and buried it, the smell of the dead bull still hung in the air. It sent a shiver through his human flank and raised the hackles behind his ears. He walked slowly down the center aisle, reliving in his mind the battle that seemed as if it had taken place only minutes before. The fit of dizziness finally passed, and he opened the stalls that held the two cows. They pushed back against the wall in fear.

"Out with you both," he bellowed, thinking that it was necessary to scream when dealing with animals. When they would not budge, he lifted his hoof in the air and reenacted the crushing blow he had dealt the bull. This signal was all that was needed to spur them to action. They left their cubicles and brushed quickly by him, mooing messages of fright to each other. Once out beneath the moon, they calmed down, slowing from a trot to a lazy amble. They led Belius to their usual grazing area between the corn field and the boundary of the woods. The night was unusually warm for autumn. A pleasant breeze blew dead leaves out of the nearby stands of trees and into the pasture. The stars were everywhere in the sky, leaving so little to darkness. After wandering around the field for a little while, the cows found a previously undiscovered thatch of clover and settled down to munching. Belius took off his jacket and sat, crossing human over beastly leg.

"First," he told himself, "I must find out whatever else has been kept secret from me. Then, as soon as father is buried, I must begin preparing the farm for winter. When the chores are caught up on, I will then show myself in town, take the abuse that is coming to me for being different and make them so used to the sight of me that I can come and go as I need to get groceries and supplies. I must be a friend to my mother and not punish her for trying to shelter me from my own horrible self. Last, I will learn how to read and write and cipher so that because I resemble an animal, no man or woman can say that I'm stupid."

"But face it, you're a freak," said a voice, drawing Belius' attention from his plans. He looked up in astonishment to see that the cows had sidled up closer to him. Instantly, he remembered the words of the dying bull. Before speaking, he shot a glance over his shoulder, making sure there was no one else there.

"Did you speak to me?" he asked.

"Do you see any other freaks around?" said the cow, standing directly in front of him. "Plension here is all cow, as am I. You are the only halfling present."

"How is it possible?" said Belius.

"Just listen to yourself," said the cow. "Say your name and listen."

"Belius," said the minotaur, but heard nothing strange in the pronunciation.

"Again," said the cow.

"Belius, Belius, Belius . . ." He said his own name twenty times, listening with horror as the sound of it melted from human language into a prolonged animal bleating. Though he could hear the change in it, he still understood the word to be his name.

"You see, you're a monster for sure. There is enough human in you to murder and still enough bull in you to understand the language of your victim. I don't think I've ever heard of such a thing. Have you, Plension?"

"Most certainly not," answered the other cow. "I wouldn't hear of it."

"What do you mean by monster?" asked Belius.

"Calm yourself, I'm only trying to help you. You're partially one of us, remember?"

"No I'm not," he said weakly.

"I won't even answer to that foolishness while I'm standing here conversing with you," said the cow.

"How do you think you're helping me?" he asked.

"I want you to understand a very important thing that your parents failed to mention to you. Perhaps you're already beginning to see it for yourself?"

"You mean that I won't be accepted by people?"

"Precisely."

"I may be part something else, but I'm also part human, and I have devised a plan for myself."

"Did you hear that, Plension? He has a plan."

For the first time ever, Belius heard a cow laugh.

"Do you remember the bull you killed?"

Belius nodded.

"He also had a plan. He was going to escape, because he

couldn't stand living in the shadows anymore. It's alright to live in the dark if you have never seen the sunlight, but, without sunlight, after a while, the eyes dim, the coat loses its sheen, the muscles ache for warmth and the mind goes mushy. We don't like the dark either, but we've learned to adjust a little better. Now if you were to make us go out into the sunlight, we'd probably go crazy. Is that true, Plension?"

"Stark raving mad," said the other cow.

"The bull I killed was trying to get back to the light. That's what it said before it died."

"Yes, you smashed our husband's head pretty handily and that was the end of all his plans. Take it as a lesson."

"It was my fault the bull was kept in the barn all day," said Belius. "It was my fault that he had to try to escape, that he killed my father."

"One could say," lowed Plension, taking the initiative for the first time.

"Do you hate me?" Belius asked.

"We hate the world that men have made. There's no obvious good in the species. Wouldn't you know they'd be the ones to run things."

Belius shook his head, realizing that perhaps the cow was right. The society that would be from that day forward his "yes" and "no" was comprised of frightened, dangerous creatures. "What's the use?" he asked.

"Just like a two-legger," said Plension, moving closer. Her spots, like her sister's, seemed continents of black in a milky ocean. Her face was more gentle but her disposition more severe. "Everything has to be either one way or the other. If things don't go well, then one might as well give up. There's a way, Belius. There's a place you could go to and not be lost as you are here."

"Shhh!" cautioned the other cow.

"Now, Austina, we might as well tell him."

"Tell me. What place is this?"

Plension pounded the earth with her right front hoof, deciding how best to explain. She looked to Austina for help. Austina dipped her massive head and said, "Pay attention, Belius. I'm only going to tell you about this once. You're a halfling, so it isn't exactly treason, but if the pond toads find out we told, or the field mice catch wind of this, we'll never hear the end of it. There's a place that can be gotten to, where, unlike here in the lesser world of men, every creature accepts every other creature. The fox converses with the quail, the condor with the spider, the whale with the wild dog. Language is used there to communicate. It's the Wider World. I can tell you how to get there. It's right next door to here, right over there, right under this field, just at the top of that tree. If I were you, I'd pack up and go. Don't look back." When she finished, both cows looked around to see if anything were crawling or creeping or flying close by.

"I've never heard of such a place," said Belius.

Both cows laughed.

"If it's so wonderful, then why haven't you two gone there?" he asked.

"We're old now and set in our ways," said Austina. "We haven't the strength."

"What about my mother?" asked Belius. "She's sitting right now in the kitchen, crying. I can't leave her. Who'll run the farm?"

"Do as you like, Belius, but when you've been beaten and ridiculed to the point where you'd gladly trade places with your father, don't say we didn't try to help you. That's all the talking that Plension and I will do for tonight. There's still some healthy thistle that the frost hasn't yet bitten." Austina turned her huge body and, with a swish of her tail, walked off to another part of the field.

"Where's this place?" Belius asked Plension. "How do I get to the Wider World?"

The cow slowly closed her eyes, shook her head and made the eerie noise that in years gone by would have made Belius duck for cover.

"Tell me," he demanded, but she moved off to join her sister. The confusion caused by what they'd told him created an unbearable pressure inside Belius' skull. He knew that it demanded release or that his head would pop like a bubble on the surface of the pond. Having cried on and off for the past forty-eight hours, his tear ducts were barren, so instead the building spirit of destruction escaped in a bellowing laugh.

"The Wider World," he managed to say amidst fits of hysteria. The jostling his ribs took made them ache. Clasping his arms tightly around his middle, he rolled from the sitting position onto his side, drawing his legs up toward his chest and his snout down toward his knees.

After his madness had diminished to giggles and then to silence, he lay there in the field, listening to pine cones dropping to the ground in the nearby woods. In the distance, he heard the storm door of the kitchen open. His mother's voice came drifting out over the pasture.

"Belius, Belius," she called.

"Yes, mother," he shouted from his place on the ground.

"What was that terrible noise? It sounded as if one of the cows was dying. Is everything alright?"

"Yes," he called back. The sound of the storm door closing came to him where he lay, and then the darkness moved in around him. In sleep, his plans came back to him disguised in the mask of perfection. That night he began the habit of snoring and the sonic force that rolled from his snout uprooted the willow tree and made the neighbors a mile off think a storm was on the way.

Belius woke suddenly, a few hours before daybreak. Seeing as he hadn't moved his position through the entire night, straightening his body out to its full length was a grim task. When finally he had loosened his knees with continued rubbing from his forearms, he crunched them a few times as a test and then stood up. He looked around to see if the cows were still nearby, but they'd returned to the warmth of their stalls.

On his way back to the house, he noticed that the willow tree had been knocked over during the night. At first the sight saddened and puzzled him, but when he remembered that his father was to be buried that day and that he was responsible for digging the grave, he saw the gaping hole as an omen of good fortune.

He found his mother still sitting in the kitchen, asleep, her head resting upon the table. With one burly arm, he lifted her bodily and carried her to the couch in the parlor, where he threw a blanket over her and tucked the edges in around her chin and shoulders. He sat next to her for a time, remembering his conversation with the two cows. Nothing he had ever learned while working the fields or wandering in the woods had prepared him for the events of the past few days.

Without thinking, he lifted his father's pipe from where it sat on the end table next to his chair. He stoked the bowl from the open tin that lay next to it. Lifting the matches, he struggled to light one. His first draw made him light headed. His second made him sick. Before he could worry about the nausea, though, his eyes fixed on the serpentine trail of smoke as it grew like a vine toward the ceiling. The shifting patterns that it drew in the half-light of dawn set his imagination in gear, and he began to think about what the Wider World must be like.

Dr. Grey, the physician who had delivered Belius, was the only person who attended the burial. He was a man who liked to see all projects through to their completion. Since he had delivered Belius' father many years before, in the time when his face was smooth and his hands trembled from uncertainty rather than alcohol, he felt it his duty to be present at the ceremony. In his gruff voice, he read a passage from the Bible—the first three or so pages of Genesis. The reading had no closure, it just sort of trailed off and ended when he felt as if he had given God his due.

Belius' mother leaned against the minotaur's sturdy side, weeping into the rumpled cloth of his only suit. The day was cold and clear in a show of arrogance toward their grief. Then the doctor cleared his throat, signaling that it was time to lower the coffin. Belius tilted his mother to a standing position and stepped forward. He wrapped his arms around the coffin, his hooves meeting beneath it with a distinct click. With no more than a sigh, he lifted the box, walked over to the pit and cautiously lowered it down. He leaned as far forward as he could without falling in, but it was still four feet from the bottom. "Good-bye," he said to the wooden lid that pressed against his snout and then opened his arms and let the weight drop with a thud. Dr. Grey led his mother back to the house.

Instead of simply filling the grave in with dirt, he propped the willow, which lay nearby, back to an upright posture and filled in around it with dirt.

By the time Belius had returned to the house, the doctor had given his mother a sedative and put her to bed. With flask in hand, the old man sat on the steps of the front porch, indulging in a quiet cry of his own.

"Thank you for coming," Belius said from a distance, not to let Grey think he was spying.

"It's my job," said the doctor.

"How's my mother?"

"She'll be alright in a couple of days. I haven't seen much of her in the past few years. Both her and your father shied away from us neighbors after she had you, but if she's anything like her old self, I believe she'll have the gumption to press on."

"Yes, sir."

"You know it won't be easy. You're old enough to understand that."

"I have plans."

"Good man. You have the farm to take care of now. Remember, be tolerant of others. I have never seen intolerance work as a successful cure for itself."

"I am going to start learning things. My father didn't think I was capable of learning from books, just like he never thought I would be capable of farming. That doesn't matter now, as I see it."

"You'll do well if you can keep that attitude," said the doctor, capping his flask and standing. "I've got to get on my way. There's a girl that lives over the hill there who broke her arm last week. I have to pay a visit and see how it's mending. Why don't you walk me to my carriage, I've got something in there that might help you out."

The uneven pair strolled out to the road where the horse and rig stood tied to a fence post. Dr. Grey assessed Belius' development out of the corner of his eye. He could hardly believe how strong and healthy such an aberration of nature had grown. The way the boy thrived was as much a miracle to the shriveled healer as was the peculiar birth.

As they drew up next to the rig, the doctor turned to Belius and said, "I owe you something. I swore when you were born, you wouldn't live as long as a week. But here you are, bigger than life. Now I must pay up." He reached into the carriage and retrieved something from off the seat. "Here," he said, handing Belius a book. "I picked this out for you from my library this morning. I want you to have it. Have your mother help you with it. It'll keep you out of trouble for a good long time."

"Thank you," said Belius, accepting the gift.

"Tell me what you think of it when you learn to read," Grey said and hoisted himself up into the seat of the carriage.

"What's the name of this book?" Belius asked.

"Inferno," said the doctor. Then lifting his whip, he lashed viciously at the horse's rump and was on his way.

ᛗ ᛗ ᛗ

Pezimote thought he was hurrying, but any creature that measures its life in centuries knows only a lumbering imitation of haste. The gnat that is born, lives out all its years and dies in a matter of forty-eight hours would never perceive the old reptile as having life, but would have passed him in a blur, noting only a large, oddly colored boulder.

"Your gait is kin to a yawn, Pezimote," Belius would tease on their walks along the violet beach.

"I'll make it up to you," the tortoise would hiss in reply. "I'll hurry to your funeral the day they bury you."

Pezimote had been sluggishly creeping about for more than two hundred years. Because of his marvelous age, he was considered by many to be a reliable historian. In reality, his memory was as riddled with holes as a dried honeycomb. This deficiency never prevented him from fabricating past events to please his friends and rankle his foes.

He paddled slowly through the water, heading up the coast toward the spit of land that held Belius' tower. The blue sun was rising out of the sea to the west and, just as Nosthemus, the sperm whale, had prophesied for him on the way home the previous night, it was going to be a clear, yellow day with crisscrossing channels of warm air and plenty of fizz.

"Poor Belius," he muttered as he went, taking a beak full of saltwater for his sympathy. "Such an inquisitive fellow—always wanting to know the 'why' of things and always returning, sadly, to himself." He hoped that their trip to the ape would result in a cure for his friend's suffering. His pity was truly felt, but before he had paddled over the next two waves, he let the minotaur slip from his thoughts. The warm water, the vanishing constellations, brought to mind instead the young female tortoise he had been sneaking around with lately in the early hours of the morning. Unlike Chelonia's, her shell was free of barnacles, her skin almost smooth. She had wondrous orange eyes and flashy markings of red and gold. Counting the diamond shaped quadrants on her underside while swimming with her in the lagoon, he discovered that she was a hundred and fifty years his junior. Contrary to what the prowling night creatures of sea and forest were gossiping, though, he had not yet made love to her. The union was coming soon, he was certain, because he often dreamed of it during the day while catching up on his sleep. They had met one night in the mango grove, not far from the stand of palm trees that he and Chelonia called home. He had been restless in his sleep for the past decade and had gotten into the practice of waking a few hours before sunrise and wandering out in search of a snack. His vast experience had lulled his innocence, leaving him an insomniac. He was not one to moan and fret like Belius. Usually an abalone or a dozen oysters would quell his empty feeling and send him back home tired enough to sleep until dawn.

His wandering in the dark eventually took on the aspects of a ritual. He would wake suddenly from a nightmare involving sharks to the sound of Chelonia's heavy breathing. After making an attempt to get back to sleep, he would try to initiate a round of love making which would invariably be met by hissing and beak snapping. When this sedative was not forthcoming, he would pat his wife lightly on the shell to send her back to sleep and then strike out in search of food.

No more than a month ago, he had awoken as usual and decided seafood would not do, but that something sweet was needed. Scuttling inland past the stand of lime trees, beneath the flitting of the fruit bats, he arrived at the mango grove. He gathered together a half dozen of the twisted trees' prize droppings and began eating away at his restlessness. Just as he was digging into the third piece of fruit, he heard the shrill cry of a young tortoise. "Wolves," he immediately thought, and only hesitating long enough to impale one of the mangos on his beak, he turned around with every intention of stumping back home as fast as possible.

Whereas others might have rushed to the aid of their brethren, Pezimote was no hero. He had not lived so long in the crazy world to end as a delicacy for four legged heathens. Of course, he felt a prick of remorse for what had sounded to be the scream of a young female of the species and also a smaller measure of the same emotion for his own cowardice.

So he charged away at the dazzling rate of a yard a minute. The cries of pain lasted not much longer than the time it took for him to make up his mind to flee. "Soon they'll be done with the hapless child and come sniffing for more," he told himself, but his retreat ended as abruptly as it had begun when he heard a rummaging in the stand of bushes that bounded the sandy path to his right.

"No, they're upon me!" he thought. He stood still, his fear paralyzing any will to escape. Snapping jaws and sharp teeth, claws and stinking fur was the beast that swirled in his imagination. "This can't be," he cried in the storm of his thoughts as the noise in the bushes drew dangerously close. The mango still impaled on his beak, he shivered in the moonlight, waiting for death.

He would later be grateful that the mosquitoes that swarmed on her body had not missed her eyelids. When she crashed through the underbrush and onto the path, she was completely blind. She could, however, tell by way of scent that a male tortoise was standing close enough to hear her.

"Help me, they're draining my blood," she whimpered.

Pezimote dropped his mango and thanked fate for having materialized a tortoise instead of a predator. He was so relieved; he didn't now hesitate to come to her rescue.

"I heard you call out," he said to her writhing form. "My first thought was that you were being attacked by tortoise eaters. Of course, I was rushing to your aid." In this instance, his wide experience did prove an asset. Scuttling to a nearby aloe plant, he broke off a large stem with his beak. "Hold still now," he said when he was again at her side. Placing the plant between his two front stumps, he squeezed its clear sap out onto her head. With gentle strokes, he rubbed the puddle in widening circles over her face and neck, then on each of her legs. The mosquitoes, drunk from the sweetness of her blood, flew slowly away.

Pezimote gazed down upon the young female. Her red and gold markings stood out in contrast to the overall darkness of the rest of her shell, whose lack of barnacles made its surface shine in the light of circling fireflies. He caught a shadowy reflection of his face in the sheen, and, in that moment, he knew that he would eventually have to ride the ocean swells upon her back . . .

Pezimote looked up from his paddling to see Belius' tower looming in the distance. To calm the boiling of his usually cold blood, he brought to mind the vicious sharks that were forever invading his dreams. A hungry hammerhead swam now from ear to ear, circling in his skull. He did such a good job of conjuring the image that not only did it shrink his desire, but he actually began looking back over his shoulder in fear. This specter forced him to increase his speed, and, in record time, he landed on the beach not far from the tower, heaving and wheezing like a hippo trying to climb a palm tree.

As the tortoise crawled up the violet beach toward the path, Belius had just then, in his recollections, reached the point where he was sitting at his father's wake.

Pezimote dallied for a quarter of an hour in the garden, nibbling strawberries off the vine and gorging himself on squash. He entered into a discussion about the weather with Siftus, who was passing by on his way home from the limestone cliffs, having spent much of the night searching for choice hunks of rock to chisel into art. Finally remembering the reason he had traveled to his friend's home, Pezimote rushed off in mid-sentence, leaving the mole bewildered.

As always, when entering the tower, he was compelled to rise up on his back legs and walk the way Belius did. He usually kept the strange posture until he was out of sight of his friend. He told himself that he did it out of respect for the minotaur, but it had more to do with envy. Stumbling up the winding stairway to the study, he found only Bonita there, sitting amidst the mess of the day before. The cat was paging through an old volume brought by her master from the lesser world. Shaking her head, she perused the nonsense of humans and giggled quietly to herself. Pezimote took to the stairs again, climbing up to Belius' bedroom. As the tortoise stumped on the solid wooden door and called, "Belius, are you awake?" Belius was reliving the instant in which Dr. Grey told him, "Inferno." The doctor then lashed his horse's rump and the cracking of the whip brought Belius to his senses.

"Belius, are we going to see the ape?" Pezimote called from the landing.

"Yes, yes, a moment," he answered. He tried to roll his massive body out of bed but found that searching through the past had caused him slowly, over the course of the night, to drive his horns right through the headboard and into the stone wall behind it.

"Come in, Pezimote. I need your help. I'm trapped."

Together they worked out an escape for the minotaur which involved the tortoise pulling at his legs and Belius using his hooves to push out of the predicament. It ended, after a prolonged bout of grunting and cursing, with the horns sliding free and Pezimote stumbling backward against the opposite wall.

"Have you eaten yet?" asked Belius, helping his companion off the floor.

"Not a morsel, I'm famished," said Pezimote.

They ate a light breakfast of clover soufflé and barley broth, smoked a quick bowl of the petals and then left the tower, taking the path through the woods that led to Shebeb's cave.

Shebeb the wise, the merciful, the healer—all of these appellations had been bestowed upon the ape who lived in a cave amidst the thicket of blabbering trees. There wasn't a creature within miles that didn't, itself, or a member of its immediate family, owe its health, and in many cases its life, to the primate's potions, poultices or scalpel. To all, he was an enemy of pain, a friend to life. Sometimes, merely a rough touch of his hairy fingers could mend a broken wing or draw the fever from a victim of disease. He knew how the ants breathed and why the bees had to dance or die of starvation. With his pink ear against a patient's arm, he could hear the rush of blood. Only because of his monthly treatments of herbal compresses could Siftus' failing eyes still distinguish between sunlight and shadow.

Mosier, the patriarch of the crane clan, after being attacked by an alligator, could be seen in the shallows, resting blithely on a prosthesis Shebeb had whittled from an elm branch. He set bones, removed thorns, counseled the mad, and, when death was inevitable, would administer his secret potion that hastened the end but eliminated the fear and pain. For all his services, he asked nothing in return. Some said that he did it because it offered a steady string of subjects to observe and study. Others believed that his empathy was so great, he could feel the distress of each victim and was unable to rest himself until things were set right. Whatever the reason, no one was ever sure because he spoke very little and never left his cave unless he had to.

In stature, he was almost as tall as Belius, but his shoulders were much wider. His stomach hung out in front of him like a destination the rest of his body was traveling to. Long grey hair covered almost every inch of him, save his palms and soles and ears. His gaze was placid, as was his demeanor. The only time he ever showed emotion was when, during a difficult operation, he would be momentarily uncertain of an incision and put his scalpel down to think. Then he would step outside the cave, leap up and grab a low hanging branch of one of the blabbering trees and swing and screech and pound his chest with his free hand until the answer came to him. Although he looked suspiciously like a man to many of the creatures who had seen them, he didn't wear any article of clothing, with the exception of a golden tasseled fez that Belius had given him for once having dislodged a mouse bone from Bonita's throat.

For one as quiet and contemplative as the ape was, it was a mystery to all why he chose to live amidst the clamor of the blabbering trees. Distant cousins to the cypress of the lesser world, these trees were notorious for their twaddle. They murmured and whispered and mumbled all day long, never making any sense. What his neighbors did not realize was that he used strands of the long stringy moss that was indigenous to them for his sutures when sewing up patients after an operation.

All of his instruments and medicines were adapted from nature. His scalpels were razor thin slivers of onyx he hammered from off the wall in a far flung passage of his cave. To check temperatures, he utilized an unopened bud of the telmis bush. If a warm blooded animal's temperature exceeded the danger point, the heat from their body, as they clenched the stem between their teeth, would cut the bud's gestation period to only a few minutes, resulting in a beautiful pink bloom of a warning.

The medicinal herbs he administered were grown by Belius in the garden near the tower. Other useful items (toadstools, snake venom, etc.) were gathered from the wild during a journey that he took early each spring. The cadavers he studied with exquisite patience were donated by their former owners, who, having once been treated by the ape, appreciated his work and hoped that their mortal coils would benefit his future efforts.

When Belius and Pezimote entered the cave, they found the ape sitting at his huge granite desk on a tree stump chair, gazing at a mess of shrew brains laid out before him on a palm leaf. With one hand he held a half-eaten banana, and, with the other, he scratched his head beneath the brim of his fez.

Belius hated to interrupt the physician at his studies, knowing the aggravation he, himself, felt when friends would drop in just as he was penning a crucial passage of The Cosmology.

The minotaur cleared his throat as a gentle attempt to draw the ape's attention.

Shebeb slowly tore his gaze from the labyrinth of convolutions sitting before him and looked over his shoulder. "Please come in," he muttered.

"How are you, Shebeb?" asked Belius.

"I'm well."

Pezimote nodded but gave no greeting. He was wary of the ape ever since Shebeb had asked him if he would consider donating his carcass to the medical cause when he died. "I refuse to die," were Pezimote's last words to him four years earlier.

"What is it, Belius?" asked the ape.

"I'm sick."

"Explain."

"Well, there's a darkness inside of me I can't get rid of. It's as if my worst enemy were sharing my body with me. I can't concentrate. I sit for hours and stare. I sleep too much."

"Headaches?" asked the healer, rising from his chair and shuffling up to grasp Belius' wrist.

Pezimote backed away from the two, taking a seat in the waiting area near the entrance.

"Headaches, eyeaches, heartaches," said Belius.

"Bowel movements?" asked the ape.

"Scanty and hard as diamonds."

"Have you been eating?"

"Light meals."

"Are you still smoking the digitalis everyday?"

"I've cut down considerably," said the minotaur.

Pezimote drew his head inside his shell, but the laugh escaped and echoed throughout the cave.

"I see," said Shebeb with a frown. He took his hand off Belius' wrist and laid it across his forehead between the horns. "Nausea, vomiting, dizziness?"

"No . . . but my anger—I'm angry a lot lately—my anger and my sadness manifest themselves sometimes in physical ways."

"So you feel frustrated. Am I right?" asked the ape, nodding as if he already knew the answer.

"Yes."

"I see, I see. Not surprising. Do you have the day free?"

"Yes."

"Good. I'm going to have to do exploratory surgery. Take off your jacket and roll up your sleeve. Wait over there, I'll be with you in a few minutes."

"What's the verdict?" Pezimote asked. He could see from Belius' heavy breathing that the minotaur was shaken.

"He's going to cut me," Belius answered, sitting down next to his friend.

"Does he have to remove something?"

"No, exploratory surgery."

"Sounds serious," said Pezimote.

"Where's Vashti? I thought she'd be here," said Belius, leaning his head back and nervously tapping his horns against the wall behind him.

"I haven't seen her today. But for Vashti not to keep an appointment, it must be something terribly important."

"Yes, yes," Belius grumbled.

Shebeb was busy moving around the cave, cleaning his instruments and lighting extra torches to make the work area brighter. After a considerable time of preparation, he called Belius over next to the flat slab of marble that was his operating table. Although he hated the sight of any creature's blood, especially that of his friends, Pezimote followed in order to offer moral support. Now he also wished Vashti were there, she being much better at such things, knowing just what to say to instill courage.

The ape left them standing near the table and went to a more distant part of the cave. When he returned a few minutes later, he was carrying, in the palm of one hand, a small wooden replica of a castle. The tiny building was no more than four inches high and three wide. He set it down on the marble slab. Belius and Pezimote leaned over it, marveling at the minute detail of lattice and turret and cupola.

"I want you to meet my assistant," said Shebeb to Belius. Reaching up, he pulled a hair out of his head. With the end of the stout grey strand, he tapped on the gates of the diminutive structure. "Thip, come out," he called in a rough whisper. "We have work."

Almost instantly, the gate came down on microscopic strands, like a drawbridge opening. An insignificant speck of black hopped out of the palace and into view.

"Thip, the flea," said Shebeb as an introduction and waved his hand in the direction of the dark atom.

"What's he do?" asked Belius.

"He's an explorer," answered the ape. "He has made more than two dozen voyages in the name of medicine. I make a cut in your arm and insert him and his raft into your system. He will travel the rivers and channels of your bloodstream, taking notes in an attempt to give me an idea as to what's wrong with you."

"One cut?" asked Belius.

"That's all. One cut and you won't feel a thing. I'll administer the hepbane and nightshade mist before I begin."

"That doesn't sound too bad," said Belius, looking over his shoulder to Pezimote for encouragement. Pezimote could only shrug.

"It must be done, Belius," said the ape. "Your problem is an internal one, I'm sure."

"Well, if it must be done. How long will it take?" asked the minotaur.

"No more than two hours. When the operation is done, though, you must donate ten drops of your blood to him. That's his price. Do you agree?"

"A small price if it will lead to a cure," said Belius.

Shebeb slid Thip's home out of the way. "Get up on the table now and lie on your back," he said.

At his work area, Shebeb measured out the right amount of leaves of each of the plants that would combine to form the anesthetic. He then crumbled them into the bottom portion of a halved, hollowed out coconut shell and set them on fire with a piece of kindling he lit off of the torch burning directly above him. An orange mist began to swirl up from the burning concoction. So as not to imbibe any of it himself, he quickly fit the top section of the coconut over the bottom. He set this down on a tray along with a scalpel, a monocle made from the cornea of an eagle's eye and a pair of delicate tweezers that were a cat's whisker bent in half. "Please, you must now retire to the waiting area," Shebeb told Pezimote.

The tortoise stumped Belius on the shoulder and then dragged himself away, wishing he had packed a lunch with which to pass the time.

Belius looked up from where he lay to see that almost his entire field of vision was eclipsed by the ape's huge head. He hoped for at least one confident smile from the jutting jaw but none was forthcoming.

"Belius, when I open this coconut in your face, I want you to breathe in as deeply as possible. Ready?"

Belius nodded, too nervous to speak.

Shebeb lifted the coconut off the tray and opened it just a sliver beneath Belius' snout. "Breathe in and hold it as long as you can." The orange vapor seeped out of what looked like the laughing mouth of a coconut head. Belius inhaled deeply, taking the full dose in one breath. He held it in like a diver with a hundred fathoms left to ascend.

"Don't let it out yet," ordered Shebeb. "I have one more thing to tell you. When you release the smoke, you will pass out. But, while you are under its influence, your spirit will have the ability to roam around outside your body for the next two hours. You can do whatever you like. Don't worry, nothing can harm you. When the drug wears off, you will be instantly called back to yourself. Do you understand?"

Belius shook his head "no," but it was too late. He felt the hot mist surging up from his lungs. Only as it escaped did he taste its sweetness. There was no tingling or rapid increase in drowsiness; the change came all at once. The last thing he was able to focus on was the voluminous folds of skin beneath Shebeb's sagging chest.

The ape worked quickly now, setting down the coconut and taking up his scalpel. On the underside of Belius' forearm, two inches above the hoof, he made a quarter inch incision. He knew that because the cut was clean, it would not begin to bleed for a few seconds. In this time, he fitted the eagle cornea into his own eye and carefully lifted the delicate tweezers.

Through the magnification of the powerful monocle, he could see that Thip was ready and waiting. The flea stood on his raft, The Sanguinaire. The sail of the vessel was sewn from a scrap of moth wing. There was a rudder at the back and a small cabin bolted to mid-deck. The explorer was dressed in a long shaggy coat woven from a single dog hair, and, on his head, he wore a helmet tooled from the armor plating of a beetle's back. To either side of his stout middle thorax hung one of a pair of infant bee stingers that he could easily reach with any one of his four hands. A master at the art of dueling, he used these weapons on more than one voyage when surrounded by marauding phagocytes.

He was handsome as fleas go, with an aquiline frontal notch and unexaggerated antenna grooves. The males of his species respected him for his unusual extra set of maxillae: the broad sword mouthparts that puncture flesh. The females grew light-headed in his presence for that swaggering gleam that shone from every one of a thousand optical facets on either side of his robust head.

When not journeying for his benefactor through the organs of some alien body, he lived a quiet life with his family in the castle he had paid handsomely for some artisan termites to chew to specifications from a block of mahogany. His wife and three daughters thought the world of him and were always saddened and frightened when he was summoned by the big voice to set sail again. In the peace of his study, he'd spent many hours composing sonnets on the subject of his secret desire to be as gigantic in stature as the patients he explored. This daydream filled most of his time when he was landlocked. While taking the pet tapeworms for a stroll around the grounds, he would let his mind wander, picturing himself an equal in height and girth to Shebeb, straddling his hairy legs across an insect empire. Only a good long voyage could ease these notions and allow him to think clearly for a time. There was nothing he loved more than to be making twenty knots up a wide aorta, heading for the echoing caverns of the heart.

"Thip, pay attention now, we haven't much time," said Shebeb. "You'll proceed north through the vein of the left arm of the minotaur, around the cape of his shoulder and then in a southerly direction as far as the scrotum, making stops at all the major organs along the way to investigate for signs of possible infection, disease, or spiritual distress. After circumnavigating the inner-globes of both right and left testicles, you will sail again in a northerly direction through the duodenum, each of the three stomachs and solar plexus, directly to his heart, where, it is my supposition, the problem lies. After thoroughly investigating the condition of each of the chambers of this muscle, the last leg of the journey will take you to the extreme northern pole, to the brain, to check for the healthy lightning of synapse gaps and to roam through as much of the vast sea of memory as possible, keeping a sharp eye out for aberrations. Finally, when this course has been completed, you are to exit the system through the snout by causing a sneeze. Do you understand?"

The flea nodded emphatically, although only having half listened to the instructions. Instead, he had been visualizing himself carving his name in the smooth, white calcium of a rib as he was wont to do on all voyages through creatures that possessed them. It was his calling card. He liked to think that perhaps some day a young flea, rooting around in the sand on some distant shore, might happen upon the decaying corpse of a creature, and while dipping stupidly into a remaining bit of bloodless grizzle, the youngster would see his name, "Thip," scratched into the curving bone and marvel at the sight of it.

Shebeb had the greatest confidence in his microscopic assistant, knowing he did not have to repeat the procedure. Using the fine tweezer, he lifted Thip and his craft. There was a quick trip through space in which the flea held on tight, his legs and arms wrapped around the rudder. Then the craft set down in the widening pool of blood on Belius' forearm. The flea took the tiller and set a course for the open wound that lay dead ahead, like a tunnel through the heart of a mountain. The light from the torches of Shebeb's cave receded in the distance as The Sanguinaire sailed out of sight into the hidden universe.

Belius yawned, opened his eyes and sat up. "Is it over?" he asked Shebeb, who was once again sitting at his granite table hunched over the palm leaf full of brains. The ape didn't turn around but continued poking playfully at the medulla with his pinky.

"Shebeb, can I get up?"

Again there was no response.

Belius lifted himself off the table and walked over to where the healer was sitting.

"Excuse me, Shebeb, I . . ." Belius could not finish his sentence. The hoof he had meant to tap the hairy shoulder with, instead, passed right through it. He jumped backward. He spun around quickly and gave a tight scream. Lying on the marble slab a few feet away, he saw himself. He rushed over to his sleeping form, wanting to crawl back inside. "Your spirit will leave your body and wander," Shebeb had warned him. Although he found the experience more than a little disturbing, he also now recalled the fact that "no harm could come to him," and his anxiety slowly subsided. He stood quietly for a few minutes, studying himself in detail. The silence of the cave and only the barest burbling of the blabbering trees sifting in from outside gave the whole event a strange aura.

"You poor thing," he said, thinking back on his last few days of torment.

Dragging himself along, weighed down by an unusually strong fatigue, he passed by Pezimote, who was slumped over in the chair, sleeping off his dalliance of the night before.

"A more concerned friend, no minotaur could ask for," he whispered, still as yet not fully aware that he could scream like a peacock and go unheard.

The sunlight, swooping birds, dandelion fuzz on the breeze and the invective of the thicket shot through his transparent being as he trod heavily down the path toward home. "Actually, being nothing is not much different for me than being something these days," he thought to himself. "The world passes through me and I clutch at it with all my might, but I can't retain the merest particle."

🐾 🐾 🐾

Though there were a million places he could have gone and seen anew from an invisible perspective, he had decided the second he left the cave to go home and catch up on his work. For two days he had been unable to write a word. The Cosmology, as if it were a child that could do nothing for itself, cried out to him.

Belius sat at his desk in the corner of the tower study. Before him lay the weight of The Cosmology of the Wider World, a stack of parchment that rose up like a paper mountain. The high plateau of the forbidding manuscript rested a little below eye level. He leaned forward and looked down on the title page. From the day he had begun work on the project, he had never gone back to read over what he had written.

With the patience of a glacier, the fortitude of a bubble rising in honey, he had added sheet after sheet to the edifice. Usually at night, when the louder creatures had gone to sleep, he would sit at the desk and, through his pen, drain the reservoir behind his eyes. Daily, that cranial basin would fill with observations and studies, and, by the hour when the blue sun would descend below the eastern horizon, the backup of ideas would threaten to overflow. So he had gone on and on with the book, like Time, with nowhere to go but forward. Only now, in his incorporeal state, with nothing about him for gravity to draw on, did he consider looking over what he had done. For once, memory could not frighten him. He was on equal, invisible terms with it.

Without thinking, he lifted his left hoof and made to turn over the title page. For all the effect he had on the top sheet of parchment, he might just as well have tried to budge the Wider World itself. After numerous attempts to get to page one, each motion of the hoof yielding another goad to his frustration, he tried to blow the page off the stack. He huffed and blew, inhaling and exhaling in a rage of spittle and silent groans, but the manuscript remained intact, fast as a tombstone in frozen earth.

"Locked out of my own damn book," he finally screamed and that spark of annoyance ignited his ability to manifest his emotions in physical force. The page flew straight up off the stack and brushed against the ceiling. Before it had floated down to land on the arm of the divan across the room, he had begun reading. He went through it slowly, mulling over each word he could not remember his original intent for having used, aware that when he reached the last line on the page, he would again have to work himself into a rage to continue. Halfway through the second paragraph of the preface, he lifted his phantom snout and muttered, "What a pile of shit."

PREFACE

I am not of this world I call my home. I am a refugee from a place where I was no more than a refugee. The future blows cold against me from my own North Sea. My memory pursues me with the persistence with which tomorrow will chase today into the past. My years are all blizzard gale and blindness, all shouting in a deaf ear. Buried to the neck in sand, I can not keep from drifting, wandering, searching for the millionth part of a moment's rest. Half man, half bull. Where the one begins and the other ends is still a mystery after hours of tracing the dividing lines between flesh and hide. The man sneers at the bull and the bull has no respect for the man. I wear the finest clothes and when wearing them gore tree trunks with my horns. I sip tea from china cups and exchange discourse with tortoises and owls and moles.

I have read the wisdom of the wisest men and found it to be so much foolishness. There is more sense in a dog eating its own vomit. Although I scorn these other writers, I realize that they project such confidence only because they are trying to convince themselves that they too are not refugees. With words and ideas they build around themselves a place to call home. Lighting torches on the lightning of certainty, they warm themselves. Chairs and beds of sturdy self-assurance give comfort. They grow fat on feasts of delusions and drink heavily of dreams. "Who are you?" they are often asked, as I often ask myself. The difference is that they can hand you a book that is the place they have built and say, "This is me." The asker reads, and if the writer has known in the building the full power of his original uncertainty then the reader will be drawn into orbit and become another point to fix a position on.

I see no other way to find a place. You can not know who you are if you don't know where you are. I want to know, so I begin this work. Go ahead, tell me it's false, it's not reality, while you are whirled and blown ragged in your own unknowing. Out of pity for you, I will include a moral that agrees with your position, and then I will laugh as I sit in the warmth of my study, sipping tea from china cups, watching out the window as you circle in the storm, whimpering.

CREATION

In the beginning there was everything and just a small bit of nothing. The everything was full of itself; a jigsaw puzzle of interlocking entities composed of all the possible forms that matter ever could or would take. The everything was almost everywhere, spreading out and out to and filling the very limits of the universe, filling even the dreams of the dreaming minds trapped in the tight jumble.

The nothing, being of itself, singular, was considered by the everything to be the center of existence. It was no bigger than an eyeball; almost round and almost transparent. The everything wrapped around it like the fruit around its seed. Although the everything had great potential to exist, it could not because it had nowhere to go. It had been frozen fast for that inconceivable duration that was before time.

There would not have been a problem if the everything was not aware of the nothing, but it was, and that which was closest to the pearl of what it was not felt great envy. The current of this emotion traveled fast through the connected pieces of the puzzle, eventually reaching the limits and awakening the outer things with a spark of jealousy that brought with it consciousness. Each of the individual components of the everything agreed that the barrier that separated them from the nothing should be smashed so that what was not would seep out and there would be room for them to become what they were, apart from each other.

The barrier that came between the everything and the nothing was something though, and, try as they might to exert their unified weight, they could not crack it. All they could do was stare through the misty glass and hope that the things inside the jewel might eventually make a mistake, crack the barrier, and let the universe begin.

Inside the jewel there lived a male and a female. They lived contentedly together, sharing everything they had. They had freedom to roam through the forests and deserts and think and feel whatever they wanted. Each had experienced eons of life and neither of them was bored after having seen and done all that they did. What kept them always interested was the discussions they had. In these dialogues they would each tell what they thought or felt about a particular thing or subject. They hardly ever agreed or saw things in the same exact way, but instead of this causing a problem it fired their respective interests. The next time they saw or did something they had discussed, it would always be colored anew by the opinion of the other. Their lives were perfection; ever changing and vital. It was the strength of their need for each other that made the boundary between the nothing and the everything impenetrable. Every time the everything would look in and see them conversing, it would feel like shouting, but it could not because there was no room for the shout to be born.

Whereas the everything could not penetrate the jewel of nothing with the pressure of its ultimate mass, its jealousy was another matter. After the voltage of that frustrated emotion had traveled out to the limits of the universe, it slammed against the steel walls of the boundary and made its way back toward the center. It did not deflect off the shell of the nothing but passed through at all points as easily as sunlight slips through clear water. The unknown emotion now had free rein where it had never been before and eventually infected both the male and the female.

The effects of the disease made a radical change in both their dispositions. It started slowly with each of them hoarding little items that they admired. Soon it grew to the point where each wanted every object the other was using. Eventually what they wanted more than anything was the other's thoughts and feelings. "Give me yourself," they each screamed and then ran together to take what they wanted. A great battle ensued that lasted longer than the blue sun will burn or the sky will fizz. After clawing and battering, they put their arms around each other and squeezed with all their strength. They strangled each other's bodies with such force that life had to leave them. Together, at the same instant, they fell dead, each having become, from the pressure, part of the other. Time's wind blew dirt over them. The forests dropped their leaves and the waters froze. Snow fell heavily.

Eventually, spring came and a plant grew up from the spot where the two had fallen dead. The plant, having had their bodies to feed on all winter and spring and summer, grew strong and straight. At the end of the summer, an enormous bud formed at the top of the stem. The bud swelled from within with a living weight and finally it broke from the stem and fell to the earth. When it hit the ground it cracked open and a bird flew out. It was an ugly little bird without eyes or feathers. There was no color to it and it made no sound. It flew up into the air and kept flying night and day until it reached the shell. With one tiny tap of its beak it pecked a hole through into the everything and the universe was begun.

🐾 🐾 🐾

Siftus rolled over on his stone bed and opened his eyes as wide as possible.

"Who's there?" he called, straining to make out some presence in the weak light that seeped in at the opening to his burrow. He sniffed once and the matrix of aromas precipitated out into afternoon, clear weather, low tide, the death of a sparrow, the sprouting of foxglove, and the last few remaining atoms of a song sung by the Raccoon brothers the previous night. All of this took but an instant to discern, after which he clawed that stale air away from him, pushing it aside with his long curving nails as if it were a pile of dirt blocking his passage through the underground. He drew in a fresh breath to see who had come to visit. Of course, many of the same ingredients were inherent in this new conglomeration, but this time there was an element that, when analyzed out, totally astounded him.

"It isn't you, is it?" he asked. "How absurd, a bird below ground."

"I'm afraid it's me," said Vashti.

Whereas most other creatures would have moved out into the light to hold their conversation, the owl and the mole stayed right where they were. Vashti had the ability to see field mice move through tall grass from the top of a tree on a moonless night. The lighting conditions underground did not disturb her. What bothered her was the closeness of the place. For one accustomed to flight, an overwhelming aroma of dirt can be paralyzing.

"Come, let's move into the expanse," said Siftus, hastily dressing in his snakeskin vest for decency's sake. He reached for his walking stick and then led the way from the side of his bed, past his kitchen and living rooms, down a long passageway. Vashti followed close behind the mole, jumping every now and then, trying to spread her wings for flight each time a pebble or clod of earth would dislodge itself from the ceiling of the tunnel and fall on her.

"Cave in," she screamed once without thinking and Siftus, usually the most understanding of individuals, laughed sardonically at her. Birds usually did not have a kind word for those of the burrowing persuasion: the badger, the possum, the mole. They were both literally and figuratively looked down upon by the feathered race. "Dirt eaters" was the term applied.

The "expanse," as he called it, was the huge underground studio where he sculpted his smaller works—busts, statues and figurines. It had taken him a solid year of working every night to clear enough dirt out of the area to create the underground cavern.

Once inside the large vault, Vashti's rapid breathing decreased to a normal rate. There was enough room there, even with the crowd of stone animals that crouched and perched in all phases of completion. She surmised that the expanse had another entrance, one large enough to accommodate the considerable blocks of granite and limestone that Siftus cut from the cliffs and dragged beneath the earth to work on.

"What can I do for you, Vashti?" asked the mole, taking a tobacco leaf from his vest pocket. With one quick motion of his left paw, he somehow rolled the tawny leaf into a cigarette.

She looked around her at the silent, staring forms and thought it better to whisper. "Belius is sick."

Siftus reached into his pocket for a flint. Striking the end of the jagged rock against the side of one of his creations, a spark jumped to life. With the agility of a frog's tongue seizing a circling fly, he sniffed out the trajectory of the spark and lunged forward, catching it neatly on the tip of the cigarette. He drew in, deeply inhaling the smoke. As he exhaled, all of his playful antagonism toward the owl left him and he was filled with concern for his friend and patron. "Is it bad?" he asked.

"Pezimote has gone with him to Shebeb's cave today."

"Is there hope?"

"There is if you are willing to help me."

"What then?"

She flapped her wings to clear the smoke from around her

and blinked her wide eyes to punctuate the importance of what she was to say. "Shebeb, granted, is a great healer. I'd go to him if I had a broken wing or a dislocated talon, but for what is wrong with Belius, the ape has no potion or remedy that can cure it. When Shebeb has thoroughly examined Belius, he will tell him he's perfectly healthy, perhaps a little depressed from working too hard on The Cosmology without getting the proper exercise. He will blame much of our friend's problem on the digitalis and after giving him an herb to take that will turn his stools to pudding for a week, that will be it. Shebeb is too practical to see the problem. Belius is lonely."

"Well then, let's plan a party for him," said Siftus, finishing his cigarette and throwing it to the floor. With the tip of his cane he buried it beneath the soft earth.

"When I say lonely, I'm not talking about the loneliness of sitting by yourself on a rainy day when friends can't get out to visit. This is a profound loneliness that he suffers from. He needs someone to love; a mate. We other creatures don't have this problem. There are no other minotaurs in the Wider World, and from what I gather, they are even rare in the lesser world, one being born only as a freak, every thousand years or so. Do you see the problem?"

"I never considered this when thinking of Belius," Siftus said. "Since I've known him, he's always seemed content to live by himself in the tower and work on his book."

"Yes, but all that studying and writing is only an excuse to pass the time. The book doesn't share secrets with him. He may be able to take it to bed, but it can not love him. It will not bear him children. He needs a wife; another minotaur to understand his halfling nature. If there were another, he would not see himself as such an outcast."

The mole was nodding in agreement now. He leaned back against the base of the sculpture he had struck his flint against, a scaled down representation of Nosthemus, breaking the ocean surface. "You say that there are no other minotaurs, so what is there for us to do?"

"That's why I came to you. You're a remarkable artist, and I am said to have a certain wisdom when it comes to affairs of the heart. Yes, there are no other minotaurs, but what I've come to suggest to you is that we create one."

🐾 🐾 🐾

The focused frustration that had lifted the first pages of The Cosmology still performed that task, but the further he delved into the manuscript the accumulated idiocy of what he had spent so many nights penning made this once useful anger now rage out of control and the discarded pages flew wildly about the study like a blizzard in a paperweight. They flew through his ghostly form as he continued reading, cutting him again and again with their inadequacy as his sight passed over fresh embarrassments on each newly revealed page.

"How could it be so bad?" he asked, without the power to stop himself from devouring yet more of it. "One would think that in this many words, by the law of averages, with no conscious mind behind the moving pen, there should still be, at least, one moderately successful line. It's a work of negative genius—drivel purer than a flawless diamond."

He read from the work aloud now, his phantom ear listening to the sounds of his silent voice. "The planet that is the Wider World, suspended in space, is a sentient being, an organism with a mind that contemplates the stars but sees them wrongly because of the interfering void of the yellow atmosphere. In that it knows more than we creatures who live like parasites on its generous crust, because it is larger and can imagine greater things, its seeing wrongly as a result of the distortion of the atmosphere is in direct ratio to our own wrong seeing caused by the veiling atmosphere of each individual creature's desire for immortality. Hence, though it sees more, it is more greatly mistaken in what it sees, and is, therefore, in all its grandeur, no more wise than the most insignificant ladybug, living on the leaf of a giant spruce—one of its nose hairs."

With the suggestion of nose hairs, Belius' own transparent snout began to itch from within. For the first time since sitting down to read, his thoughts were now distracted. His eyes began to water spiritually as the unseen irritation of his nasal passage drew his full attention. Although he left off his reading, the confusion of discarded pages still swirled and flapped in the room. The itch built to an unbearable crescendo, and just as he was frantically trying to lift his corporeal quill off the desk to insert the feathered end up his incorporeal snout, he let go a sneeze so full of manifest disgust that it lifted the remainder of the manuscript to the ceiling and dumped it on his head. He screamed with the fear of being buried alive and then awoke on the operating table in Shebeb's cave.

The roar unleashed by Belius as he rejoined his body, yanked Pezimote from a lascivious daydream and sent him sprawling off the edge of his seat in the waiting area. Shebeb put his arm around Belius' shoulders and, like a mother trying to calm a frightened child, said into his ear, "Shhh, it's over. You're fine. You're fine. It's over."

"Is he cured?" asked Pezimote, who had drawn closer, forgetting that he wasn't on speaking terms with the ape.

"This was to be merely a diagnosis," said Shebeb.

"How long until we know what's wrong with me?" asked Belius, now breathing more easily, sitting with his legs dangling off the side of the table.

"No time," said Shebeb. "As soon as Thip jumps up into my ear and begins telling me what he encountered, I'll relate to you the condition of your inner being. Only then can I prescribe a treatment. You see him there?" he asked and pointed to what looked like a speck of dust on the marble surface next to Belius. "When you sneezed, he landed on your leg."

The tiny black dot moved in one great leap to the edge of the table. From there, it jumped down onto the top of Pezimote's head and then vaulted up to rest on the facial hair beneath Shebeb's left eye. The tortoise and the minotaur both leaned a little in the direction of the ape to watch the flea blaze a trail toward the left ear. They lost the progress of his path for a moment and then found him on the ear lobe a split second before he crawled over the hill of cartilage at the entrance to the auditory canal and disappeared inside.

"We are ready now," said Shebeb. "Thip will speak a sentence to me and pause as I relate the same information to you."

The ape closed his droopy lids. His lips parted to show yellow teeth fiercely clenched. His left ear wiggled slightly with concentration. Shebeb took a deep breath and then began. The words, when they came, rushed quickly from his mouth, screeching as they passed through his clamped teeth. The silences in between seemed measured and, in conjunction with the sounds, gave the recounting of the flea's journey the eerie aspect of a lone, thin-throated toad chanting for rain.

"Greetings to you, minotaur. I commend and envy you for the greatness of your frame, the dazzling rush of blood through your arteries and veins, the enormous weight of brain matter resting between your ears, the ball lightning of impulse traveling your spine. In The Sanguinaire, I journeyed the length and breadth of you, finding much to marvel at and very little to call to the good physician's attention. It's a shame now that I must concentrate on speaking to you only of the problems I encountered, because the delights far outweighed them.

"The circulatory system is rapid moving and rife with protecting, although vicious to me, white corpuscles to ward off invaders. Your major organs, with the exclusion of your heart, seem to be performing each like a virtuoso. Your small and large intestines are clear of blockage and debris and offer the traveler a unique enchantment with their million twists and turns like some elastic network of catacombs. Your ribs, one of which holds my signature, are hard as rock and sharp as bird beaks. For that matter, your entire skeletal system, including your backbone, is a wonderment of architecture. To have one's structure inside the body is a grace I will never know. Your stomachs are intact. Your colon, clean as a whistle.

"Now, I'm afraid, we come to the problems. I encountered a minor problem in your lungs. A few of the small alveoli on the outskirts of those windy chambers are mucked up quite beyond hope by some sticky blue substance. When I passed these diseased sacs, I experienced light-headedness and a sensation of euphoria.

"Next, we must travel south to your testicles, wherein, while circumnavigating them, I noticed a dangerous overcrowding by the indigenous race. It seems that to keep order there among such a runaway population, the more powerful of the society have turned both globes into prisons, enforcing a penal system that offers no escape and has its inmates constantly swimming in circles in order for them to have something to do. I'm not a physician, but I suggest that this problem be taken in hand as soon as possible.

"The third, and last of your problems, the greatest problem you have, is centered in your heart. I have never seen anything like the queer conditions existing in each of the chambers of this vital organ. When I began traversing these quadrants, I was full of vigor, but as I passed from one to the other, a general atmosphere of despair wore me down to the point that, when I exited to head for your brain, I wept for the length of your neck.

"One chamber held within it a desert: hot sand and no drop of water. Another was racked by a great storm: typhoons within tornados within hurricanes. I barely escaped with my life, so buffeted was I by the ill winds. The next was a polar region of snow and ice. Even the air in this winterscape was so cold, I had to push it aside with my arms to make any progress. I remember that as I stood in the center of it, listening to the overall booming of the great muscle, the chill brought premonitions of death, and, for a second, I believed I had actually died. Gladly leaving this frozen chamber behind, I entered the last, which was as empty of warmth and spirit as the previous three. A cavern of black, so dark that not the tiniest particle of the light of your life shone there. I only walked in a few paces, tying myself by a rope to the mast of The Sanguinaire, for fear that I would lose myself in the wicked pitch and never find the entrance again.

"That's all I have to report. By the way, I lost one of my swords in a skirmish with a dormant virus hiding in the osseous labyrinth of your right ear as I exited that side of your brain, so my payment will be increased to eleven drops of blood. Forgive the extra cost, but this type of work has its hazards. Now I'm quite done. May the Wider World preserve us both."

"What did you encounter in the regions of the memory?" Shebeb asked, inhaling the words as he spoke them so that they would hit against the back of his throat and be heard by the flea.

There was a considerable pause, and then the answer came,

the ape speaking it to his patient, "Nothing unusual."

With the eagle cornea inserted in his eye, Shebeb found The Sanguinaire in the breast pocket of Belius' shirt and returned the raft, along with its owner, to the mahogany castle and the welcoming party of Thip's wife, daughters and faithful tapeworms. Belius pricked himself with a splinter of wood and made his offering for the services rendered, adding a twelfth drop for his admiration of the insect's courage. With these particulars out of the way, Shebeb made his diagnosis and suggested a treatment.

"There is an emptiness in your heart, Belius. You must get out of your study more and get daily exercise. All of that reading is turning you upon yourself. I would also suggest, for the third time this year, that you quit the digitalis. To fight off your feelings of sluggishness, I will give you a mixture of herbs to be liberally sprinkled on your dinner every night. In conjunction with all of these things, you must get plenty of sleep and try very hard to see that life is a beautiful thing."

Belius nodded to everything said and accepted the mixture of herbs with a promise that he would use them, but when he and Pezimote left the healer's cave and were passing through the thicket of blabbering trees, he confided to the tortoise that he felt, if anything, somewhat worse.

Pezimote took the bag of herbs from Belius' hand and threw them in the stream. The minotaur made a weak protest, but he couldn't argue with his friend's reasoning. "All this stuff will do is make you crap your pants. I say you have to figure your own way out of this funk."

"Do you think I should quit the digitalis?" asked Belius.

"Don't be a fool. If you do, you'll be as dull as one of these inane trees. Shebeb means well, but he's missing the point of the whole thing. Just stop taking yourself so damn seriously. You could drop over tomorrow, but this universe you consider to be yours will keep right on doing the same nothing it has always done."

Belius and Pezimote walked in silence the rest of the way to the tower. They didn't even speak when they parted but simply waved. As soon as the minotaur was inside and climbing the spiral staircase to his study, Pezimote gave up his erect posture and returned to the normal all fours of his kind. He moved tortuously to the edge of the green ocean and, as he slipped into the cool waters, thought about his friend's problems and muttered, "Such pretensions," shook his head and swam down the coast toward home.

🐾 🐾 🐾

The study was just as Belius' spirit had left it—The Cosmology scattered everywhere, covering everything like the fallout of ash from some volcanic book. Still out of breath from climbing the stairs, he moved lethargically around the room, gathering the sheets of manuscript, paying no attention to the page numbers. When he had every sheet of it again piled on his desk, he picked it up whole and walked to the fireplace. Leaning over, he placed the pages down on the charred remains of the last fire from early spring. Then he plodded to the small end table next to the divan and, lifting his pipe, filled it from his stash of digitalis which lay heaped in a hollowed out chunk of pumice. With the primitive stone and flint lighter of his own invention, he lit a piece of kindling and set to puffing the petals into smoke. He did not, as usual, flick his hoof back and forth to put out the kindling, but walked over to the fireplace with it upright to keep the twig burning.

The top page of The Cosmology, in its disorder, was the title page of the chapter dealing with the inherent attraction of all physical objects, "Satellites of Love." He bent over and set the edge of this page on fire. The manuscript went up as if its original purpose was to someday burn. He moved back away from the heat and positioned his chair so he could sit and watch the flames devour the work of all his nights in the Wider World.

The black smoke of the fire climbed up the chimney and out into the sky above the facade of the tower. It did not disperse in the late afternoon breeze blowing in off the ocean, but hovered there, turning in a great ball until every page in the fireplace was consumed. Then it gathered itself up into a two-legged creature of considerable size. When its form had completely cohered, it floated down to the ground and, with a smooth but frightened stride, made its way through the garden toward the woods.

That night the rain drove in hard from off the ocean, turning the ground to mud and swamping the byways. Lightning sizzled down the sky with long fingers of instantaneous day, striking without conscience at trees and the peaks of high rocky places. The thunder did not roll in the distance, but ripped everywhere, as if the Wider World itself had gone mad and were tearing out great clumps of its own hair. Much to the delight of the younger ants and to the annoyance of the older ones, the armies moved everyone, for their own safety, into the farthest nesting areas of the tunnels that ran throughout the masonry of the tower. The downpour washed away scent, and the moonless sky threw a second cloak of darkness over the landscape, making it a perfect night for predators.

Deep below ground, in the protective quiet of the expanse, Siftus was lost to his work. As unaware of the storm as of the hour, he drew, with one of his long claws, sketches for Belius' mate in the dirt of the cavern floor. As soon as he was finished with one, he would sniff at it, and, upon finding a disproportion, would brush the whole image away and begin again. Out in the ocean, Nosthemus, the whale, dove to the very depths of the sea, where phosphorescent creatures ignorant of sunlight presented a scene of bright stars in a clear black sky. He swam lazily through this cosmos, making believe that he was flying to the moon. He hummed as he went, the songs of his super brain. From beneath wind-bent saplings, scaly things slithered out of hiding to play in the newly formed pools. Up the coast, in the familiar stand of palms, Chelonia snored and Pezimote opened his beak to the fresh rainwater dripping down from the broad leaves that were his roof. He wondered to himself where butterflies slept on stormy nights.

The raccoon brothers, Obadai and Mez, upon sensing the approaching rain had decided to stay in their hollow tree for the night, not bothering to raid the garden. They spent the first few hours of the storm drinking the intoxicating sap of rotting fruit and trading insults. Eventually they sufficiently infuriated each other and began wrestling. When the match was over, and Obadai, the bigger of the two, had his brother's snout pressed down into the dirt, the thought of a nice ripe tomato came to each of them at the same instant.

"What do you think?" asked Mez. "Should we chance it?"

"Why not?" his brother answered and kicked him once in the back of the head before letting him up.

They left the hollow tree and went out into the rain. Giddy from the fruit wine and the fear of being attacked, they laughed as they ran blindly through the woods, bumping into each other and stumbling in ruts. Having made the same raid every night for as long as they could remember, light was not needed to find the tomato patch. Once there, they made their way in amidst the plants and sniffed closely for the largest, unblighted fruit they could find.

"Here it is," cried Mez to his brother who was working another row, "a genius of a tomato. You've got to see it. If I weren't going to eat it, I'd marry it." His sinewy black fingers could barely fit around the prize. Just as he was about to yank it from the stem, he heard his brother right next to him.

"Wait, don't do it. There's something going on here," said Obadai.

"Something going on, like you want to steal my dinner," his brother answered.

"No, no, come here, I'm serious."

Mez could sense his brother's fright and became frightened himself. Moving up close, they made their way cautiously through the garden toward the tower. As they broke into the clearing of the path that ran down the center of the planted rows, Obadai grabbed his brother by the scruff of the neck and pointed his head toward where the scarecrow had stood. In the light issuing from the open door of the tower, they saw that Belius' coat was missing, leaving the figure just a wooden cross, devoid of personality.

"This is bad," said Mez. "Something's wrong."

"Let's get out of here."

Now the wind blew cold against them and they felt its sting. The rain beating on the earth made all manner of odd sounds, causing them constantly to start and turn around in expectation of an attack. They didn't run, but inched their way back toward the hollow tree. Just inside the cover of the woods, they heard a noise that no amount of falling rain could have produced. It was a prolonged moaning, both high and low, and the suffering that was at the heart of it they imagined to have teeth. The weird sound entered them through their ears and worked as an instant antidote to the fruit wine. Without speaking, they moved forward an inch at a time, so close to one another they seemed to be one creature. The sound grew louder as if they were walking into it.

Creeping up behind an oak tree, they peered around its trunk into the clearing their place sat on the other side of. It was too dark to see what it was, but they could hear that the thing was only a few feet from them. Lightning walked the sky and, in that bright spark, they saw Belius, kneeling down on all fours, naked, ripping a clump of grass out of the muddy ground with his teeth. Just before the dark turned on again, he lifted his head, his maw chewing away at dirt and grass and stones, and they saw his eyes, each as huge and deeply hollow as their home.

"Get Vashti," said Mez to his brother. "Belius has lost his mind."

Not worrying any longer about the darkness or the storm, Obadai took off for the center of the woods, for the giant ashe where the owl nested.

Instead of staying on the ground, easy prey to whatever night demon happened along, Mez climbed the tree in front of him and nestled down upon a thick, low branch right next to the trunk. He wrapped his full tail around himself to offer some protection against the high wind and rain.

Each time the lightning would strike and give a clear view of Belius below, swaying and madly chewing, Mez would cover the black mask of his face so as not to see the ugly condition of his friend. He waited for an hour for Obadai to return with help, but, when none was forthcoming, he decided to take matters into his own hands. "This can't go on all night," he said to himself. Gathering a handful of acorns, he inched his way along the limb which jutted out over the clearing until he was directly above Belius. His plan was to pop him between the horns with the tiny seed-nuts and wake him from his unnatural trance.

Grasping the limb with both feet and one hand, he leaned

down and waited for the lightning. With the next flash of white, he aimed quickly and fired. There was no way of his seeing if he had hit the mark because the dark returned within a second. The instant the light went out, he heard a roar from below, and, the next thing he knew, something jarred the trunk of the tree he was in. He wrapped his arms tightly around the branch as the oak trembled again and again with what he saw, in subsequent bursts of light, to be Belius ramming its base with his horns.

When he had sufficiently battered the tree that Mez was in, he moved on to the next one that helped to define the clearing and gave it a dozen whacks with his hard points. From there, he traveled the circle of the clearing, blindly goring the base of each tree and recoiling to strike the next. The rain did not come quickly enough to wash away the froth forming on his mouth. Jets of steam poured from his nostrils, and water glistened on the scratches that the rough bark had cut on his human chest and leg.

By the time Obadai returned with help, the storm had moved on, leaving the sky perfectly clear and the air fresh and cool. Dawn was showing a light yellow in the clearing. Belius lay flat out on his back, unconscious, having knocked himself out, and, although his mind knew nothing, his mouth still chewed mechanically at the cud he had ripped from the earth. Shebeb, dressed in his fez for protection against the rain, stood over the minotaur's body, shaking his big head. Vashti had flown down to perch on Belius' right horn, and the raccoon brothers stood with one arm around the others' shoulders, staring on in disbelief and waiting for the two wiser creatures to make a decision.

"Let's get him to the tower," said Vashti.

"Yes," said the ape, who leaned over and, with great effort, picked Belius up in his arms. "I guarantee he did not follow my advice," Shebeb added as they headed for the tower.

"He's not himself," said Vashti, flying low overhead. "Or should I say, he's too much himself. In either case, it's not your fault, Shebeb, you did your best. Don't worry though, I, myself, have a plan to cure him and the medicine I prescribe doesn't grow on bushes."

As the entourage made its way to the edge of the woods, the yellow day increasingly gathered in the sky. The atmosphere began to fizz and the storm was all but forgotten save for the wet grass and dripping leaves. The raccoon brothers brought up the rear. Even though a pall of seriousness weighed heavily on account of Belius' condition, they tried to trip each other as they went. Watching the whole procession through a distant thicket of sticker bushes was a misty figure, like a human storm cloud, wrapped in a tattered overcoat.

After Belius' friends dressed him in his green silk pajamas with the rock sewn in behind the neck and put him to bed, he remained in a deep sleep for two full days. During this time he had a nightmare in which his father was teaching him how to tie a special kind of knot. Although the farmer's hands moved slowly, Belius could not follow the sequence. The tying of it consisted of a thousand loop-de-loops, a hundred hitches, and one part of it resembled a noose.

"I can't get it, father," said Belius, poking ineffectually at it with his hooves.

His father grabbed it from him and, with one quick pull of a loop, had the entire mess undone and again in the form of a length of cord. For what seemed like the tenth time, the minotaur watched as the farmer's crooked fingers flew to their task and were done almost before they started.

"Look Belius," his father said, "you don't have to be able to tie it. All you have to be able to do is undo it. It's a cinch. If you can figure it out, your hooves will turn into human hands."

Again the farmer tossed him the tangle of cord. Belius worked at it with such intensity that he could feel the veins popping out from his neck and sweat running down his back. "I can't," he finally shouted in frustration. "Tell me the secret." He looked up from the stubborn knot and saw that his father had vanished.

Days later, when he came out of sleep and opened his eyes, he was standing two feet from the bed with his head lowered, his horns readied for the attack. That morning he began a habit of dissolution and despondency. The only efforts he made were to take the stairs into the basement for fresh bottles of dandelion wine and to stoke the bowl of his pipe. He sat in his chair in the study, doing nothing but tipping a wine bottle to his lips and smoking himself into fits of hallucination. During this time, he didn't even put himself to bed at night but stayed in the study, unaware of the hour. His chair became his entire universe, and he was loath to leave it for trips to the bathroom or cellar. Dust collected on the volumes of his library. The garden was overrun with weeds.

Once he tried to lift his writing quill off the desk, but the nearer his hoof moved to it, the more the range of his sight diminished into a black tunnel, so that he believed if he were to touch it, he would go blind. He grew very weak and thin and his mind was filled to brimming with a noisome clamor of nothing. Occasionally, he tried to concentrate on this battle of ghosts in his head, but concentration became something that he could never remember having had the ability for. For the entire duration of his breakdown, whether he be dozing off or just staring, his mouth continued to chew on a nonexistent cud.

His friends came to visit him, but he gave no response to their questions. Vashti made an attempt to feed him some broth, but he would not hold it in his mouth. When she inserted the spoon, he would chew on it and the weak soup would dribble down his chin and chest and stain his pajama top. The other creatures agreed that there should be someone there to sit with him most of the time for fear that he might try to do harm to himself.

Pezimote was chosen to watch over the invalid minotaur, being the one who knew him best and the most likely to get him speaking again. The tortoise's disposition was not well suited for the job. He had never been much for fetching food for anyone except himself. He swam to the tower every morning to wait on Belius. For the first few days he was very attentive. He sat across from his patient and spoke to him for hours about anything that came into his head until he thought he would go mad himself. He made enormous breakfasts and lunches, brunches, dinners, snacks, suppers, but usually ended up eating both his own and Belius' share as well.

Days passed and there was no change in the minotaur. His hours were all chewing with a few feeble moos mixed in. When he wasn't cooking, Pezimote played gin rummy with Bonita. If the cat won, the tortoise would have to scratch her back with

Belius' sharp letter opener. There was never a question as to what the tortoise would get if he took the hand because he never did.

The days of card playing lasted no longer than the first few of conscientious care. Near the end of the second week, Pezimote would start the day with a bottle of dandelion wine and then move on to successive bowls of digitalis. He would sit across from Belius and interchangeably pass the bottle and then the pipe.

It was on the fourteenth day of his vigil that he caught himself, after having consumed the better part of three quarts of wine, making a chewing motion with his beak. "That does it," he said in a rage, throwing the half empty bottle out the window. "This is insane. I am wasting my days here, watching you crawl deeper and deeper into yourself. I can't go to meet my nubile at night, because now I sleep like a log, so tired from all my chores and the drinking and smoking. Chelonia is complaining that I'm never home. Look, Belius, the world is passing us by out there." He pointed to the window. "Last night there was a meteor shower and you missed it. Think of how it would have looked through your telescope. And just yesterday, Nosthemus predicted that in our own lifetimes, a creature would come from the lesser world and cause a great ruckus, but you weren't there to write down his words. Now we'll all forget, and, when it happens, no one who is born after today will believe, when it happens, that the whale really did predict it."

Belius kept chewing, and Pezimote walked up to where he was sitting to look into the dark pupil of his right eye. "Wake up, damn you," he yelled. Belius stared straight through the tortoise. "Enough!" said Pezimote. He wheeled halfway round and then came back, smacking the minotaur as hard as he could on the snout with his thick stump. Belius' head jerked back and hit the chair. He stopped chewing. Pezimote saw a glimmer of recognition in his friend's eye and hit him again. "Where? What? Where?" Belius mumbled. When the tortoise heard him speak, he did not assess the situation but proceeded without a thought. With a nasty snap of his beak, he bit down on the minotaur's human, left nipple, choosing that site because it looked like it would hurt more than any other.

Belius' scream flew out the window with the velocity of an

arrow shot from a bow. It traveled the wind that swept over the tree tops of the woods, then dove down through a thicket of elms and slipped into the opening to Siftus' burrow. It passed his stone bed and the peg on which he hung his snake skin vest and continued down the series of tunnels, ricocheting back and forth off the close walls, to the expanse, where it smashed into the mole's elbow, jarring his paw which held his drawing stick, causing him to, in one fluid motion, add a pair of human female breasts to his dirt drawing when all the time he had been planning to depict an udder on the lower abdomen.

Being the artist he was, he scrutinized the mistake to see if it was something worthwhile, as he had found slips of the stick or chisel to sometimes be in the past. He backed away from the finished picture, the hundredth he had done that day, possibly the millionth he had done since beginning the project, and sniffed the lines to judge their symmetry, their feeling of "rightness." The aroma of the new drawing appealed to him greatly. He rolled a cigarette and smoked, every now and then taking another whiff of his creation. Although he had never seen or smelled a pair of human female breasts before in his life, he thought the configuration of the drawing to be ingenious.

"Why not?" he said, feeling a little crazy himself with all the sleepless hours of toil on the design of the creature. "This will be my signature," he thought. He stood and smoked, leaning against one of his sculptures, basking in the feeling of accomplishment. "I will call her . . . Soffea . . . yes," he said to the darkness, the name coming to him suddenly. He repeated it many times until his cigarette burned down and singed his paw.

That evening, just after sunset, all of Belius' friends made their way through the woods toward Vashti's ashe tree. Two dozen sparrows had combed the land at the owl's behest, carrying invitations to a council that had as its only purpose to gather resources with which to effect the cure of the minotaur.

Vashti sat on the lowest branch of her enormous home, watching the gathering grow beneath her. What was yet more incredible than a bird below ground was that Siftus, a dirt eater, sat next to her on the branch. He tried to hide his fear of heights so that it would seem only natural that a member of his race should be at home in the sky, but, when he rolled a cigarette while already having one lit in his mouth, Vashti could not help but pay him back for his leading her deep below the earth the day she went to see him.

"Cave-in," she said in a whisper.

"Touché," answered Siftus, now with two cigarettes in his mouth, his body in a subtle but constant motion to find the position of ultimate safety on the never-thick-enough branch.

Below them the clearing filled with every manner of creature that slithered or crawled or flew or swung through the tree tops on vines. Inconvenienced by a mere million years of evolution which had robbed him of legs, Nosthemus the whale sent word with Pezimote that he would be psychically present and would transfer the proceedings to other interested members of the sea. The raccoon brothers arrived early, passing the time before things got started by chewing on big wads of tree gum and then throwing them on the ground for others to step in. Shebeb had shown, although he had earlier told Vashti that Belius' problems should be handled by a trained physician. Chelonia came with her husband.

The ants from the tower sent a contingent atop the backs of dragon flies. Bats hung upside down from surrounding trees like wet leather gloves set out to dry. The beaver clan was there in force, from Weeber, the elder, to his great grandson.

The Sphinx, hearing through the unbroken web of living things that there was to be a meeting to help her friend and fellow writer, sent, from half a world away, her swiftest emissary, a giant golden condor, to represent her. The powerful wings of this creature carried him across the ocean in no time. He gladly recounted stories from the exotic West and made a big hit with those present when, at Vashti's request, he lifted Siftus into the tree.

When it seemed as if the crowd could grow no larger, Vashti screeched above the racket of squeaks and barks and chirps and glugs in order to bring everyone to attention. "Here, here," she called out, and, slowly, the gathering quieted down. Of course, once it was perfectly silent, Mez had to fake a monstrous sneeze, which made Hilry, the old anaconda, literally jump out of her skin. The owl turned her piercing yellow eyes on the raccoon brothers, and they immediately took seats on the ground. "Now, thank you for leaving off your hunting or sleeping tonight to come to this meeting. I would not have called you here had it not been a matter of the gravest importance. Our good friend, Belius, is sick. Not a creature here would deny that he would try to help us if we were in the same condition."

"What's the problem?" asked the porcupine.

"It's simple. He needs a mate."

The company nodded its collective head and "ahhed" with affirmation, never having thought of Belius before in terms of needing anything.

"A need of the greatest kind," Chelonia said.

"The utmost, my dear," the tortoise said to his wife and caressed her shell.

Vashti continued, "I have discussed the problem with Siftus, and we see that it would be easy to solve it, but there are no other minotaurs in the Wider World. So, not giving in to failure, especially when our friend's very life might be at stake, we've decided to create a female minotaur."

The silence below broke into a confusion of murmuring and shouts. Some didn't think they'd heard correctly and were questioning those next to them. Others heard perfectly well and were now raising all kinds of questions to the pair in the tree. Both Pezimote and Shebeb shook their heads, each for different reasons.

"Shhhh!" hissed Vashti. "Let me explain. We've worked the project out to its most minute detail, and the work has already begun."

The creatures quelled their objections and questions and let her continue, having faith in her capacity to reason.

"Luckily enough, we have Siftus to help us. He has already done a drawing from which we will build her. If I may say, even though it is not one of his great monuments cut from limestone or granite and is no more than a scratching in the dirt, it probably is his greatest creation to date. It's ingenious. It's beautiful."

The mole, normally a modest creature, was infected by the height of his present position and took a bow. In this motion, though, he lost his balance and toppled forward. The crowd gasped, but Vashti, in one swift lunge, caught him by the collar of his vest with her nearest talon and dragged him back onto the branch.

"Listen carefully, now. Here's the plan," the owl said, continuing her speech with Siftus still in her grasp. "Think to yourselves if there is anything you can do to help. Think if there is any way we can make it better. The form of the body will be molded from river clay, slapped into shape by Weeber and his family. The body will have, running through it, a network of green saplings so that it can move its limbs pliantly. When the form of it is near completion, Siftus will carve the finishing touches onto it—the expression, the beauty marks, and enough wrinkles to make it seem real. The horns will be fashioned from teak branches. The teeth will be pearls from fresh water oysters. The hair on its flanks and neck and whatever other creaturely parts will be donated by whomever can spare a tuft or two. Her tongue will be a single leaf from the blabbering trees, so that she might converse with her mate. The hooves will be cylindrical cuts of branch from my own ashe tree, tapped into the appropriate shapes by woodpeckers.

"Our friend from the West, the Condor, has already promised me that the Sphinx can donate a human foot; one of the body parts she brought with her from her days in the lesser world. He says that it will come with the toenails painted, as is the custom among humans. The breasts will be fish bladders filled with liquid to give them the correct give and will be set high on the chest in the manner they appeared to Siftus in a fit of inspiration. To animate this lovely there will be a dried gourd of bees inserted into the chest cavity, and in their commotion they will initiate locomotion. As for the brain, a mosquito will be trapped in the dried clay behind the eyes and between the ears, filling our sister's head with the sweet buzz of consciousness."

The ants applauded loudly to see the insect community so well represented, when usually they were unknowingly trod underfoot. All the other creatures joined in, considering the planning behind the project nothing less than marvelous. No one could see any reason why it wouldn't work.

"The only thing that we have not decided on is what to make

the eyes from. Given their importance as the organ of communication in the language of love, just anything will not do. Rack
your brains, help us to find a solution while we prepare the rest
of this female."

"Excuse me," said a quiet voice amidst the celebration.
Shebeb stood up and faced the branch on which the owl and
mole were perched. The creatures all around him fell silent, waiting for him to speak his mind. "Vashti, I can appreciate the
reason behind your plan, but I've studied the inner workings of
creatures for years and it's not a handful of bees that gives them
life. Not one of you has a mosquito in your head. Our tongues are
not leaves, our teeth, not pearls. What you propose is beyond our
capacity to produce. I hold that what Belius needs is exercise,
fresh air and abstinence from the digitalis. Only these things will
clear his mind so that he can think through his problems on his
own. You know that I would not try to dissuade you if there was
the slightest possibility of success . . ."

Before the crowd could consider the ape's opinion, Siftus
opened his snout and interrupted. "Wait, Shebeb, you mustn't
work against this plan. Belius is our friend. We love him as we do
ourselves. You, as a physician, are more apt than we are to give
in to what's natural, because you know more than we ever will
the obstacles we will face. But I don't hold with what is, with what
must be. I don't care how many times my heart beats a minute or
why my eyes are failing me. I live through my imagination and
intuition. Don't tell me that what I see so clearly in my dreams I
can't create. If I believed you, I would jump from this tree right
now and kill myself. If I agreed, then it would mean I was already
dead and what would be the loss? I'm very much alive, though,
and so is my vision of the creature I will call Soffea."

The vehemence with which the mole spoke his mind startled
nearly everyone. He had always been an enigma to the other
creatures in that he so ardently pursued a path called sculpture
which had no natural place in the Wider World. Belius had originally interested him in the art and, through trial and error and
years of laborious work, he had created some pieces that were so
beautiful even the unfeeling sharks would swim up close to shore
and beach themselves trying to get closer to them.

Another round of cheers went up, drowning out Shebeb's protests. The ape turned and shuffled back toward his cave, shaking his head the way he might over the corpse of a centipede who had not responded to his treatments. That left only one dissenter amidst the throng of different species, and he was not one to open his mouth to make any statements that would challenge the foolishness of others—he had lived too long.

Away in the tower study, Belius heard the distant clamor of the meeting beneath the ash, but put it off to a delusion caused by his weakened state. His jaw had given up chewing the nonexistent cud, and he had bathed and had some dinner. He dressed himself and performed a few incidental chores that evening to reacquaint himself with those mundanities of life he had left behind for the two weeks he was in shock.

Now he sat at his desk, reading from his copy of Dante's Inferno that had been given to him so many years before by Dr. Grey. His first impulse after dinner was to pick up his quill and begin writing, but he knew that if he wanted to keep his sanity, even at its tenuous status quo, he had better find something more relaxing to do. His reading had gone along quite well, keeping thoughts of the destroyed Cosmology in abeyance. He was almost even enjoying himself, the book bringing back many memories of his childhood from when he had taught himself how to read. Then he reached a certain section of the epic that made him feel uneasy and he went for his pipe. The part that upset him involved the scene when Virgil and the pilgrim meet the minotaur in hell. His reading of the depiction of the mindless, snorting monster came in conjunction with the final round of applause given to Siftus' speech. The muffled shouts seemed to him to be the cries of those tortured by the beast in the seventh bowl of damnation.

As he puffed the digitalis, he stared out the window of the study and surveyed, by way of the moonlight, the ravages of his garden. "I think I'll go out into the rows and work all day tomorrow—work till I sweat, till my muscles ache. If I can just get my crops back in order, perhaps that will set me more at ease. At least I will sleep more soundly for the toil." These thoughts pleased him as those of the Inferno had not. The drug began to work on him, and he felt light headed and tingle bodied.

"Definitely a walk with Pezimote along the beach at lunch," he decided and felt the heat of the sun and practiced with his heightened imagination the dialogue with which he would amuse his friend. The scenario seemed so real that now he even heard what he believed to be his friend, calling his name, probably to signal him to slacken his speed and wait up.

From the scene on the beach, Belius' imagination moved on to contemplate just how pleasant the future could be without his having to sit down every night and write. He began to move away from the window, noticing at the last moment that his coat was missing from the cross that had been the backbone and arms of the garden scarecrow. As he sat down, wondering what had become of it, he heard the tiny voice, calling his name again. "Must have blown off in the storm that night," he thought.

"Belius, Belius," he heard again, but now realized that the sound was centered in his left ear only.

"Who's calling me?" he cried out and spun around in the chair to look over his shoulder, no longer convinced the voice was a remnant from his day dream of well being.

"It's me, Belius, I'm sitting in your ear. It's Thip, the flea. Excuse me for calling so late at night, but I wanted to get you while you were alone."

"Ahh, Thip, I remember you, Shebeb's assistant. What can I do for you?" he asked, cocking his head to its left side as if he were putting his ear closer to a speaker his own size.

"Belius, I'm enamored of your blood. It's so rich in all good things and has had a marvelous effect on me. Shebeb has said, it is the unfamiliar human part that makes it so special."

"Thank you," said Belius.

"Yes, it's made me grow a considerable amount. I can no longer fit in my old armor. None of my pants fit me and my swords that had always felt of adequate size in my grasp now seem no more than toys."

"So, you're growing bigger from it? I hope this will not ruin your ability to go on journeys."

"I don't care if it does. What I want is more. What I want is to grow."

"What are you saying, Thip?" asked Belius, setting his smoldering pipe down on the table next to his chair.

"I'm saying that I want your blood, as much of it as I can get."

Belius heard a change of tone in the small voice. "Well, I'd like to help you out, but I need every drop of blood I've got."

"Minotaur, you will give me your blood. I'll come every day at noon, and you'll let me suck your blood for five minutes."

"Impossible," said Belius. "I think you'd best get back to your castle. I'm not in a good mood these days."

"You'll give it when you hear what I have to tell you."

"I doubt that very much."

"If you don't, I'll tell all of your friends about your past."

"What are you talking about?"

"When I was sailing through the ocean of your memory, I happened to be looking over the side into the clear water, as I do, to see what types of reminiscences are swimming about in the patient's head, things that might have some bearing on the subject's illness. In the reflection, I saw you kill, with your horns, a two legged creature, I suspect to be a man."

Belius instantly straightened up in his seat. "That was no memory; that was a dream."

"I can already tell you are lying by the way your pulse just quickened. Let's not have any of this denial now. If you don't comply, I'll surely tell and you'll be an outcast. You know the law concerning murder. I'm sure you didn't kill that human for food."

All of the air left Belius at once, and he slumped in his chair. "No," he admitted, "I didn't. I killed out of anger, out of revenge. I . . ."

"Personally, I couldn't care less what your reasons were. I just know it happened, and I'm glad it did. With your blood, I'll become a giant. Now, should I tell them?"

"No, don't tell," Belius shouted. "I'll give you what you want."

"I knew that you would. Lay your arm out on the arm of the chair, exposing its underside. I will bite you where the bicep and forearm meet. Come now, do as I say."

Belius used his right hoof to push the sleeve of his shirt up well above his elbow. He laid down his arm on the arm of the chair as he had been instructed.

"Very good of you," he heard in his ear and then felt the insect on the move. The feel of Thip crawling through his facial hair at other times might have gone unnoticed, but now it itched to the point of burning. The flea leaped from the minotaur's lower jaw, landed on his left knee and jumped again, coming to rest in the crook of his elbow. Belius looked down in horror to see Thip, much bigger now than when he had first met him, waving three of his miniscule arms. The insignificant figure bent over, grabbed onto the flesh of the arm, and with a thrust of his disproportionate head, sunk his maxillae into the closest artery. A whimper escaped from Belius' snout. The itch the insect had caused by traipsing across his face was a mere tickle in comparison to that which now tortured his inner arm.

🐜 🐜 🐜

Pezimote could tell by the sound of the breakers that high tide was quickly approaching. He gently tapped Chelonia's back with his beak to see if she was awake. There was no reply from inside the shell, to where she had withdrawn her head and legs earlier when they bedded down beneath the palms. The excitement of the council for Belius had worn her out. He had not seen her so animated in recent years as she had been, making plans and discussing the situation with the other creatures. It made his usual twinge of guilt more pronounced as he made his way toward the shore, away from her sleeping form.

The night was warmed by a tropical breeze; much like the heat that billowed at times from the fireplace in Belius' tower. Above, the constellation of the magpie was resplendent, each of its thirty jewel-like stars sharp as pin pricks with the night bird's eye as red as blood. The minotaur had explained once, on a walk along the shore, that the reason for its color was that it was actually a giant red star, a thousand times larger than the globe of the Wider World. Pezimote put this fact out of his mind as he slipped into the surf, not wanting to concentrate on anything but love. He'd had to put off his rendezvous for two weeks while tending to his ailing friend. "I'll not think of Belius once tonight," he told himself.

He swam quickly in the direction of the barrier reef, where he was to meet his young mistress. In the commotion of the gathering earlier that evening he had whispered a message in his mind to Nosthemus. Pezimote knew that he could count on the leviathan to get word to her that she was to meet him at the barrier reef. In the waters beneath the coral outcropping was a huge facsimile of a shark fin. "I wouldn't," the whale said to him in his mind.

It had become nearly impossible for him to meet Mala anywhere on land. Chelonia had too many friends among the night creatures. They had not come right out and told her yet, but they were hinting as gossips love to do for a while before displaying their fools' gold. At dinner not but three nights before, over one of her special man o' war pies, she said to him, "So, I hear you've been rummaging late at night, dear."

"Who's brought you this stupendous news?" he asked.

"I forget," she said.

"You know my restlessness at night. I go out to have a snack of mangos or what not. It helps me get back to sleep."

"I hear that you were seen with one of our people on different occasions. A young tortoise."

"Oh . . . she's just a child. Sometimes I chat with her on my way to and from the grove, that's all. She's young enough to be my granddaughter. Don't tell me you're jealous."

"No, I'm not jealous. But if you ever go beyond chatting with her, I'll know. I've been with you for a hundred and fifty years now. If you betray me with someone else, I'll know instantly by the look in your eye the next time you face me."

"What do you mean exactly by 'betray'?" he asked.

She said nothing.

Pezimote tried to laugh at her, but it came out a choking sound. "Do be serious," he said.

"I am serious. That's all, now eat your pie." She had cut him a huge slice as was the custom, but for the first time in his entire life, he had lost his appetite. Each piece of it stuck in his throat for a minute before it went down. It was the most bitter man o' war pie he had ever had.

As he spotted the shark fin marker, he heard the familiar

sounds of Nosthemus and his chorus of dolphins welling up from beneath the water. He paddled to within a few yards of the reef and was now deep in the shadow of the fin. Almost immediately, Mala surfaced from beneath the water. Droplets rolled off her smooth shell as she swam toward him. He noticed that she had a triangular piece of mother-of- pearl pressed into the soft flesh of her forehead. She called his name as she approached, but that was all he heard before the chorus began; the overwhelming sound of the opening note drowned out the rest of what she said. She swam right up to him and bit him playfully on the neck. Pezimote's mind went blank with the nip, all his thoughts moving through his body. They didn't bother to speak but set about instantly rubbing stumps and softly pounding each other's shells. The old tortoise trembled with excitement, and the young female with both that and fear. The warm breeze that blew down along the surface of the water grew warmer as did the sea around them, attracting a school of minnows. A frenzy of tiny fish stirred up the plankton, causing it to glow phosphorescent against the night.

The next morning, even before sunrise, work was begun on the body of Soffea. Down by the riverbank, the raccoon brothers and a troop of possums and badgers excavated the special blue clay that would be the substance of the figure, while the lode that had already been mined was being slapped into shape by the wide flat tails of Weeber and his family. Siftus stood close by the beavers, instructing them on each curve of the leg they were presently working on. He now had his drawing well memorized, and he would stoop over the appendage from time to time in order to sniff the progress of its creation. Lemurs had gathered thin green branches from the surrounding trees and stripped the bark off them. Before the mole would put the finishing touches on the leg, these saplings were to be inserted through the length of it.

Off in the woods, other creatures gathered necessary items; the teak branches from which the horns would be cut, the most blathering of leaves from the blabbering trees, tufts of hair from passing creatures who were interested in supporting the project but who had no ready skill. The ants of the tower sent out their famous warrior, Duc-Sin, riding a darning needle, from which he was to lasso as big a mosquito as possible to ignite Soffea's mind. The bees of the honey tree, held a lottery, to see which of their hive would receive the honor of filling the heart. An otter cracked fresh water oysters against a rock, searching for the most beautiful pearls. As all this commotion went on below, Vashti flew to and fro, giving orders, rejecting or accepting parts for the new minotaur and generally rallying the morale of her work force.

Belius rose early that morning. After a light breakfast, he went down into the cellar and gathered his gardening tools. With rake and hoe and shovel over his shoulder, he went out into the rows. He worked like a maniac, weeding and harvesting. The sweat poured off of his back, and, before ten o'clock, he had to remove his white shirt. Not once did he rest for fear that if he had a moment to himself with nothing to do he would again begin to relive the horrible events that the flea had accused him of. By eleven, he was looking over his shoulder every now and then to see if Pezimote was coming. The tortoise never showed up, which was unusual. Then it struck him that none of his friends had come to visit. He began to wonder if Thip had already told on him.

When the sundial cast a shadow at five before noon, he put down his rake and went back into the tower. He climbed the stairs to his study, sat down in his chair and put out his arm. As if out of nowhere, Thip appeared on the table in front of him. The flea was almost three times as large as the night before. Belius could make out his blackmailer's face now and could discern a silk hat and cape. The flea spent no time on amenities but jumped right onto the arm and sunk his spikes into the welt he had made the night before. The grown maxillae were now as big as dull pins, and, when they entered the scar, it was pain on top of pain. Thip drank deeply for five minutes. When finished, he stood up, wiped the blood from his mouth, tipped his hat and leaped to the window sill.

"Till tomorrow," he cried and because of his prodigious growth, Belius could hear him. Then he jumped out the window, the cape flying up behind him, and was gone.

Late that afternoon Belius went down to the sea to look for Pezimote but could not find him anywhere. He sat down on the sand and watched the sun sink into the water. "If I could just talk to my friend, I would tell him what I'd done. I know he wouldn't forsake me. He would have some plan as to how I could clear myself and make everything right." When darkness had nearly taken over, though, he knew the tortoise would not be coming that day, and he stood up and headed home.

On his way along the beach, he happened to glance at the tree line of the woods which came nearly to the ocean's edge. Just at that second, something moved from behind one tree to a position behind another, making a flapping sound like a bird frightened into flight. He stopped and stared now into the darkening woods. For a long time he waited, and then it moved again. What he saw made him clear his eyes with the backs of his wrists. Standing a few yards off, trying to hide behind a tree that was too small for that purpose, was his old overcoat. It appeared as if it were being worn, but he couldn't make out a face or pair of legs.

"I see you spying on me," he yelled. The coat turned and ran. Belius stood in quiet puzzlement for a minute before fear broke out all over him like a rash, and he hurried back to the tower. That night, once again, sleep was sacrificed to memory.

🐾 🐾 🐾

On this particular morning near the end of the winter season, Belius finally traveled the ninth and last horrendous circle of Hell, making his way up and then down the hairy length of Satan to emerge beneath the stars. With the last word read, he gave a great sigh and closed the book as not to further torment the already pitiful souls trapped between its covers.

He stood up and stretched his arms. Through the parlor window, he could see that a light snow was falling. Moving over to that window, he stood and stared blankly for a time, considering how much he had learned in so few months. In the beginning it seemed that he would never even memorize the alphabet, but his mother's patience and encouragement gave him the confidence to conquer his initial fear. On the day that he read and understood his first paragraph by himself, he knew that there was nothing to stop him from completing the Inferno by winter's end.

The Dictionary that had been his Bible for those cold weeks, now lay on the table next to the leather-bound epic, its pages hoof worn, torn and scribbled and separated from the binding. Instead of being stymied by each new word he had never before known existed, he would take it as a challenge and dive headlong into that kingdom of words. Every meaning, like a compound of matter, he found to be made up of smaller atoms of meaning that each in their turn had to be looked up. He adopted his mother's patience and laboriously searched out the smaller definitions and then gathered them together in his mind to create the conglomerate that was the word he had originally sought. In a notebook with the design of a black swan stitched into the cover, he would copy down all of his discoveries.

From the very start, Belius was enchanted by the story that Dante told. Although he was most interested in following the action of the tale, merely trying to see it in his mind's eye and recreate the various torments of Hell as best he could, he knew, through an anxiety located between his heart and his head, that the poor lost poet had much in common with himself. It was as if he were reading about his own future or more his present situation, but seen by a Belius that stood somewhere outside the Belius that was himself.

He read on with intense concentration, struggling to catch up with the words that slowed as he gained, but which refused to relinquish the lead. The exotic Italian place names and surnames that had not been translated were like ruts that twisted the ankle of his concentration and tore him from the dream that their more familiar, domestic counterparts had created.

"I think you would do better to go on by yourself now," his mother had told him after they finished wading through the first few cantos. "I don't think I have ever heard of or seen someone learn to read quite as fast as you have. There's a special gift in that big head of yours."

Her praise elated him, and for a few days, he did not read a word, but took walks through the snowy woods, convincing himself that he was a "genius"—a word he had discovered in the Dictionary not but four days earlier. Plension and Austina happened to overhear him mumbling to himself about his brilliance one evening while he was puttering around the barn, and it was their combined hooting and ridicule that brought him back to his senses.

When he returned to the poem later that week, he saw that the next chapter contained a description of the mindless minotaur of rage that guards the river of boiling blood, and he understood then why his mother, who was in the habit of reading on ahead, had sent him off on his own.

The snow began to fall harder now, sticking to the ground and leaving a thin layer of white on the roof of the barn. The sky was a uniform grey except for one small spot of brighter dimness behind which the sun was hiding. He turned away from the window and went in search of his mother to give her the news that he had finished. As he left the parlor, he knew instantly by the deep brown smell of coffee that she was in the kitchen preparing breakfast.

"Guess what?" he asked as he stepped into the kitchen.

She turned around from the stove where she was frying eggs. Taking one look at what someone unused to her son might take to be a grimace, she smiled and said, "You've finished."

He nodded and a none-too-human grunt came from low in his throat.

"And how was it?" she asked.

"Both beautiful and horrible," he answered with a laugh. By the way she instantly looked back to the eggs on the stove, he knew she was thinking about the scene with the minotaur.

"You've done very well, Belius," was all she said as she set their plates down.

When his mother would look down at her plate, Belius would look up, studying her face. She was old now. He imagined how her looks must have changed drastically when he was born to her. It was a certainty that when his father died, her posture changed as if overnight; the weight of her loss drawing her toward the ground. All of her tears had left erosion lines of wrinkles behind when they had dried, and her eyes, themselves, had sunk back into her head, closer to the memories of her husband. The minotaur wondered, in between glances, if his mother, having passed the greater part of her years considered her life to have been a happy one.

Belius shook his head to rid himself of this knot of thoughts and rose from his seat to get another cup of coffee. As he passed by his mother, he touched her on the shoulder. She looked up to him and smiled, placing her hand for a brief second on his hoof. He stood at the counter pouring his second cup and shuddered. When he'd touched her, it was as if she were made from paper. When her hand covered his hoof, it was as light as a page from the book. He took a sip from his cup to steady himself, but the Inferno flared up in his mind and the hot coffee burned his tongue.

Before he put on his coat and boot and went out to fetch hay for the cows, he knew that he would have to stop in the parlor where his mother sat sewing and break the silence that had been served with breakfast. As he moved down the hallway, though, he heard a knock at the front door. "Diversion," he thought. He stopped where he was and waited for his mother to answer the door. The door opened and then he heard talking. When the door closed and the talking continued, he knew they must have a visitor. Very quietly, shuffling his foot along the wooden floor and tapping lightly with his hoof, he snuck down the hall and peeked around the corner into the living room. There was Dr. Grey, looking yet more wizened than on their last meeting at his father's funeral. The old man had his hat in one hand and with the other he brushed snow from the shoulders and sides of an overcoat that was three sizes too large.

Belius burst into the room but stopped short when he saw that his sudden appearance made the doctor back up a step.

"I finished the book today," he said.

"Well, Belius," the doctor said and moved forward to shake his left hoof. "So you've read the entire thing. Quite an accomplishment for such a short time. I knew you could do it."

"Did you come for it?" Belius asked. "I can tell you what I think of it."

"I'd like that, son, but not today. I'm here on another matter."

"What is it?" Belius' mother asked, seeming to sense some trouble in the way the doctor played with his hat, twirling it by the brim.

"I need your son's help, mam," he said.

"For what?" she asked.

"There's been a pack of wild dogs ranging through the valley, killing livestock. I intend to help track them down and shoot them."

"I'm sorry, doctor," she said. "Belius won't be going. Besides, he can't use a gun, he hasn't any fingers."

"I see," he said and put on his hat. "Let me put it this way, I'd go by myself, but I'm too old to go alone. It's too dangerous. I need someone like Belius, who's young and strong, to help."

"Let the other farmers take care of it," she said curtly.

"I'd very much like to do that, but last night I sat at the bedside of a young girl who was attacked. They ripped her throat almost right off of her neck. She died this morning. This is everybody's problem now. It's your son's duty to help. We're the only two available to cover this area. The boy should go."

"And what do these other people care for my boy?" she asked.

"Makes no difference," he said.

"I'm going," Belius said. He left the room to put on his boot and get his coat.

His mother ran behind him. "You're not going, Belius. I won't have it."

In his bedroom he slipped his human foot into the boot without laces and took his coat from the closet. When he turned to make his way back to the living room, he saw his mother standing with her arms out, blocking the doorway. "I won't have you killed by animals like your father," she screamed. He walked up to her and leaned over so that his head was level with hers. Looking into the depths of her sunken eyes, he made a tremendous mooing noise that rattled every pane of glass in the house. "We're all animals," he said.

They went by foot over the snow-covered fields toward the woods. The doctor had given Belius a large sack to carry.

"What's in it?" the minotaur asked.

"Bait for our friends," the doctor answered.

"What kind of bait?"

"Just some meat," said the doctor and then took a flask from his back pocket and drank so the conversation could not continue.

The wind blew miserably and the storm came harder. The

woods were wrapped in a white silence. Occasionally there was the sound of a branch cracking with the cold and the doctor would reach down and rest his hand on the pistol that sat in a holster slung around his waist. Belius saw how the old man grew more fatigued and winded with every hundred yards they traveled, so he didn't bother to ask any questions. He was pleased just to be there, walking beside Grey, who seemed determined and unafraid.

"If I could only live my life like that," Belius thought to himself. "There'd be no swerving onto lost paths."

Then he realized that he was out on the hunt in his father's stead, and it came to him that he must act as a man would and not a child. The novelty of the adventure gave way to a sense of business and he began peering through the stands of trees in hopes he might catch sight of one of the killers. He decided he would not talk unless spoken to. Never before had he felt so completely human.

When they'd walked for a solid two hours into a part of the woods that Belius had never visited before, the doctor held up his hand and said, "That's far enough for me. If we keep going, we'll be in the next county."

A few yards off to their left they found a clearing. Grey instructed Belius to open the bag he had been carrying over his shoulder and empty its contents on the ground. When the draw string at the top of the bag had been loosened, a powerful smell wafted up. The minotaur's head jerked back as if the old physician had passed a vial of smelling salts under his snout. Belius turned the bag over and a mass of bloody meat spilled onto the snow, dying it a deep red. A cloud of steam swirled into the air. He gagged, turning away from the bait. When he looked back, he saw Grey calmly drinking from the flask and studying his reaction.

"No offense, Belius," he said, nodding toward the mound of carnage. "It's what they go for."

Belius shook his head to let the old man know he understood.

"I couldn't very well have cut up a human now could I?" said the doctor with a crooked smile.

The minotaur mustered a nervous laugh.

They left the clearing and took up a position in a natural blind of saplings and bushes not far off. Belius found a dead log and dragged it behind the cover for them to sit on while they waited. The doctor flipped the bottom of his huge coat over the log and sat down. The minotaur did the same with his tail and also sat.

"I heard you went to town a few months back," Grey said, staring straight ahead into the clearing at the pile of raw meat.

"I did," said Belius.

"How'd it go?"

"Not so good."

"So I heard," said the doctor with a laugh. "Give 'em time. They'll learn."

"I didn't mind the children so much, following me and moo-ing," said Belius. "It was the older people. I tried to introduce myself to them, get into a conversation, but they either ran away or taunted me. The staring eyes were the worst of it."

"Why?"

"I think it's that there are people out there hating you that you don't even know exist. Not even people, just eyes without faces."

"Did you get what you went for?" asked the doctor, turning to look at him.

"The man at the grocery was too frightened not to fill my order. After what happened on the street, I figured if I was going to get what my mother had sent me for, I'd have to be sterner. I didn't try to talk about the weather with him, I just gave him the list, told him to gather the items on it and then I paid him and left. If he only knew I was as frightened as he was. At least I saw how my strangeness could work for me."

"Did you have to knock that boy over in the street before you left?" Grey asked.

"I suppose I didn't. But a bunch of them were all around me and somebody threw a rock that hit me on the side of the head. I figured that if my being mean had worked with the grocer, it might be my only chance to gain respect. He was the closest one. He yelled something about my mother and I couldn't help it. I clipped him on the shoulder. It wasn't much of a swing. When he fell over, the others backed up and I walked to my wagon. I wanted to run, but I walked slowly."

"It may not have seemed like much of a swing to somebody your size, Belius," said Grey, "but I had to treat that boy for a dislocated shoulder that afternoon. His father was all for getting a posse together and hunting you down. Of course, I dissuaded them, but it won't take as much next time to get them thoroughly riled."

"Thanks," Belius said. The word came as cold as the day.

"I understand your frustration. You'll learn as well as they will," he said and reached up and gave Belius' closest horn a tug. "Next time you have to go to town, I'll go with you."

The afternoon wore on without incident or further conversation. Belius was sorely tempted to discuss the Inferno with the doctor, but he knew it wasn't the time or place for it. For the most part they just sat and stared at the mound of beef in the clearing. Every now and then the doctor would take a swig from his seemingly bottomless flask. They took turns getting up and going for short walks to keep the cold out of their bones. As the sun began to set, the snow let up and the wind died down, no longer whistling as it cut through the trees. During their vigil some squirrels had come to inspect the bait, tasted it and went away uninterested. A deer had passed through the clearing, stopped in the middle and getting a whiff of the slaughter took off as if the lifeless mess was a hungry wolf. There was no sign of the dogs though; not even the distant sound of barking. Belius tried to picture the pack. He wondered what it was that had made them mad.

After the old man had returned from his tenth trip behind a leafless oak to urinate, he said, "We'll give it one more hour. After that it will be too dark for us to do any good. I don't fancy getting lost in the dark."

"Where do you think the dogs are?" Belius asked.

"What they usually do is stick to the woods by day, hunting for wild animals, but in the evening, as it starts to get dark they go down to the farms and look for livestock; calves or young goats that can't protect themselves."

"And the girl that was killed?"

"She was just a young thing. Probably thought they were

somebody's pets and went up to them. When you get that many of them together, though, and they're crazy with their freedom and hungry as winter itself, they'll attack just about anything."

"How many?" Belius asked.

"Well, Phil Miller, who owns a farm a few miles from here, shot one of them. He said there were about twenty or so. And the woman whose daughter was killed said there must have been thirty. So, knowing how people like to exaggerate about things that scare them, I'd say there are probably no more than ten."

They waited out the final hour but nothing came for the meat. By the time they decided to head back for the house both Belius and the doctor were shivering. The sun was now only a few minutes over the horizon and still covered by clouds so that night would come quicker than usual. In the gathering darkness the woods took on an eerie aspect with all the bare branches, now black for lack of light, jutting up and out at all angles. A snow owl hooted somewhere over their heads. The surrounding scene reminded Belius of the time he had lain out in the fields all night. Without thinking, he raised his snout toward the tree tops and a mournful lowing sound crept out of his throat. He stopped walking and just stood and listened as if for an answer. An odd tingling sensation traveled slowly up from the tip of his tail to the back of his neck, raising hairs to attention as it went. The doctor had also stopped walking when Belius moaned.

"What is it?" Grey whispered. He reached quickly for his flask and took a drink. "Belius, are you alright?"

Belius meant to answer in words, "There's something nearby," but his response came in a series of grunts and squeals.

The doctor threw the flask on the ground and drew his gun. He turned quickly to look behind himself, the hem of his long coat spinning with the sudden movement. As Belius watched the bottom of the coat, rippling like wind through a field of wheat, an explosion of red went off in his mind. Without thinking, he turned just in time, lowering his head to impale the leaping dog on his right horn. With a wild jerk of his neck, he threw the whimpering creature to the ground and caught it in the throat with the hoof at the end of his leg. There were three gun shots then and the yelp of another dog.

From behind the trees, Belius heard them saying, "Leave the man, he has a gun. Bring down the bull." The message was passed around among the pack. "Bring down the bull." The voices were low and rough. The only thought that traveled the human corridors of Belius' mind was the doctor's previous words, "Hungry as winter itself." He heard another leap and turned back around again to break the ribs of a huge shepherd that had been aiming for his jugular. It fell clear of him but didn't give up. It struck out again as soon as it hit the ground, clamping its teeth around his human leg. With another blow to the skull, blood seeped from behind the dog's eyes and it let go with a gurgling cough.

Belius sensed he was out of danger for the moment and looked up to locate the doctor. Darkness surrounded him now as if night had pounced out of the sky. The doctor was nowhere near and all that could be heard was the vicious growling of the pack.

He stood his ground, knowing there was no sense in running. His ears were erect and listening. He waited for the next leap, the next lunging set of jaws and sharp teeth. From somewhere, not too far off, there came the sound of three more gun shots, followed by a scream.

"Doctor," he yelled into the night, but, again, his language became the language of animals. He was breathing heavily, and his heart pounded with the force of a mallet. Cautiously, he began moving in the direction of the scream. After he had covered no more than five yards, the night materialized two mongrels that charged at him simultaneously through a whirl of snow. As he crouched to meet their attack with his horns, a searing pain shot up through his body from behind. There was a crunching sound, like a tree being cracked in half by a great wind and then the tearing of flesh. Agony ripped through his entire body. He bellowed with such force that the charging dogs were knocked off their feet. The blood poured out from the stump that was left of his tail, and the smell of it sent the pack into a frenzy. All sensation left him and he dropped to his knees.

Four of them circled around him now, waiting for him to fall. Their eyes were bright yellow in the night. Their mouths were wide open, displaying froth and fangs. He knew they were taunting him, but he could no longer hear them. They went around and around his slumping form, and on every third orbit one would jump in and bite him on the arm or the leg. He tried to raise his hooves for protection, but they were heavy as stone.

The dogs whirled faster and faster around him, and his mind adopted their motion until they became a blur. His fear of death was a twister that sucked consciousness into its funnel. Before long he was in the center of the cyclone and it was still and blue. His father handed him the knot. Without thinking, he took one of the loops of the tangled cord and pulled on it. It came apart as if by its own volition, and he fell forward into the snow.

᪣ ᪣ ᪣

Belius woke with his snout buried in two inches of snow and found a fiery pain waiting for him on this side of consciousness. He lifted his head to take a deep breath of the cold night air. The freshness of it stung his snout, and, when he exhaled, the steam came forth mixed with a moan. He rolled over on his left side. Finding that his arms once again worked, but like rusty machines, he lifted the back of one to his eyes and wiped the frost and melted snow from them.

Listening intently over the action of the wind, he heard no growling but instead a wild flapping noise and wondered if it was the owl he had seen earlier in the tree tops. In the time he had been unconscious, the clouds had cleared. Above the swaying branches that clacked together in the wind, the stars and moon shone with frigid clarity. He knew he must get up and try to get away, but there was a ringing in his ears and a weariness in his legs that increased the power of gravity. The ragged stump of tail that was left to him pulsed exquisite pain throughout his spine and flanks as the numerous bites on his arms and legs began to make themselves known, each, in turn, blossoming into a new chord of suffering.

"I'm going to die out here," he thought. The realization made him wild, and fighting his heaviness, he pushed himself up onto his knees. With his arms out in front of him, he managed to crawl a few feet. Every other second, the blackness that he knew he would not awaken from a second time, flitted through his head.

He had dragged himself no more than twenty feet, stopping five times in the process, when he again heard the flapping noise. It seemed to be drawing close to him. He lifted his head and squinted to try to see what it was. In the new moonlight, he could make out a shadow rushing toward him. It seemed to have wings at its sides, and it flew just above the ground. In an instant, it was upon him. Though his mind was completely blank, in his heart he thought, "This is death." He meant his final statement to the world to be a roar, but his bodily weakness diminished the sound to a squeal more fit for a pig.

The doctor took the opportunity of the minotaur's open mouth to pour the remaining whiskey from his flask into it. The liquor brought summer to Belius' insides. The ringing in his ears was drowned out by near instant inebriation. The pain wilted in the heat, and the blackness that had flitted through his mind lay down and slept.

"You've got to get up, Belius," the doctor said.

"The dogs," Belius whispered harshly.

"I think I got the last of them. I'm out of bullets though. We've got to get going now."

"Give me a second, just a second."

"No time," said the doctor, slipping his spindled arms beneath the minotaur's. With a strength that could only have come from somewhere outside his thin frame, Grey hoisted Belius to a standing position.

"I'm going to let go of you for just a second. I've got to get my coat around you."

"Keep your coat, you'll freeze," Belius said without conviction.

The doctor let go of him and the minotaur's huge body swayed in standing circles like a top running down. The coat was quickly sloughed and draped over the wide shoulders that were big enough to actually fill it out. Belius draped one arm around the old man's shoulders, their height difference making Grey's thin body appear a crooked crutch. The two started inching their way back to the farm.

The walk seemed to Belius to take years and years. Grey never stopped talking the whole trip, explaining how he had to run for cover and reload after his first volley. He had made it back to Belius just in time, as the pack was getting ready to move in for the kill. He hit all six of his shots, one right after the other and in the process killed two more of them. The other two took off through the woods, seeing the damage the doctor's gun could do. This was the only information that Belius could cull from the incessant monologue. The rest was just a string of words that at times sounded as if the old man were praying or practicing an incantation.

The doctor let go of Belius and moved toward the kitchen door, calling to the old woman to come help with her son. A strong wind came and toppled the minotaur. Then his eyes no longer worked, and he suddenly realized that he had forgotten to remember.

🐾 🐾 🐾

With a scream, he awoke and found himself in a strange bedroom. The windows had been shattered. Knick-knacks lay broken on the floor. A rocking chair was twisted into a knot. There was a large fissure in the plaster of one wall. Wherever he was, he knew he'd been snoring.

The bed he was in was big enough to accommodate his full size, unlike the one at home where his foot and hoof stuck out over the end almost touching the floor. Blankets and comforters were piled five thick on top of him to keep him from freezing in the cold air that blew freely in through the broken windows. The pillows beneath his head had been tattered by his horns.

He peered out over the edge of the impressive mattress at the decimation his snoring had caused and felt like a castaway adrift on a sea of fragments. Through the broken windows, bright morning light poured in and glimmered against pieces of ceramic and glass. With great difficulty caused by the stiffness of his limbs and the pains that tattooed his whole being, he made it to the edge of the bed, threw back the layers of blankets and sat up.

This simple action caused his head to swim, and from some-where just in front of him, he hallucinated a mad dog, jumping for his throat. He threw his hooves up to protect his face from the attack. With the movement of his arms, the illusion dissipated into nothing.

"I've returned from the dead," he said to himself and laughed softly so as not to jar any of his wounds. This joy filled him and in it he found the energy to lift himself to a standing position. Slowly, he hobbled to the door of the room, trampling even more fully those objects he had sonically destroyed in his sleep. He opened the door and walked out into a long, wide hallway, the new warmth of which made him feel as if he were home in the parlor of his mother's house.

As he wandered through the halls, passing rooms and alcoves, taking a flight of stairs down to another hall, he had every intention of finding Dr. Grey, whose place he surmised he was in. His condition was jittery though, and, when he passed a room, the door of which was opened slightly, and saw a big red leather chair, he decided to enter and sit down for a rest before continuing. When he opened the door to enter, the pain seemed to flee his body.

"My god," he said under his breath, "a library." And then in a voice that was much surer, "Yes, of course I know how to read." He was dizzy with the prospect of such a gold mine of ideas and images, remembering the magical effects of just the one book he had read. He ran his hooves along the spines of the leather bind-ings. Twice, he went around the entire room, tottering and leaning against the shelves as he made his way. His eyes passed over so many wonderful titles that they seemed to make a story in and of themselves. Finally he came to his senses and chose one volume, reaching with his arm extended to the very top shelf to bring it down. He nudged it out of its place with his hoof and then let it fall the rest of the way into his arms. It was a thick book of more than eight hundred pages entitled The Collected Writings of Scarfinati. He didn't bother to sit down in the chair that had at first attracted him, but stood where he was, swaying unsteadily like a buoy in rough water. He opened the book and began reading the first page. Most of what he read made no sense to him, but he continued, lost in a daze that had everything to do with dreaming.

Somewhere in the middle of the twentieth page of the essay, "Evidence of the Almighty's Schizophrenia in the Natural Existence of Living Organisms," he was drawn back from the attraction of the printed words by a noise behind him. He spun around ungracefully, slamming the book closed in case the doctor did not want him hoofing through an expensive volume. Instead of meeting the glance of the old physician, he encountered a young woman. He was as startled as she. Meaning to say something polite as a greeting, his words turned on him and he remained silent. She moved her glance down his figure to stop at a point below his waist. Then putting her hand softly to her cheek, she turned her head away and ran from the room.

"Wait," Belius called. It was not until he had set the book down on the chair and passed out of the door into the hallway that he realized he was naked.

Back in the room he had awoken in, Belius discovered the camel's hair overcoat the doctor had sacrificed to him the night in the woods. He slipped it on and buttoned it up the front. Prepared now against any further meetings, he earnestly went in search of the old man. This time, he again passed the library with the red leather chair, but did not enter. Instead, he simply stuck his snout in for a second and took a whiff of the aging paper and leather bindings the way a child might linger in the doorway of a bakery. The only way he could describe the aroma he took deep into his lungs was rich.

He resumed his journey, and in the course of it discovered the enormity of Grey's house. He knew that perhaps it seemed bigger than it actually was because he had backtracked and gotten lost a few times, but, from his most rational summation, he could say for certain that it had two upper floors and a main floor. The upper floors were defined each by four hallways that formed a square around some central courtyard. These upper passages were lined by rooms as in a hotel. The only difference though was that these rooms were not designed for economy, but for spacious living. A quick look in each of them showed that they were for the most part empty and unused. Every fourth or fifth one would have its walls lined with bookshelves and contain a library as impressive as the first that Belius had discovered.

On the second floor of the house, Belius was rounding one of the four corners of the network of halls, moving quietly like a ghost without a reason to go haunting, when he heard up ahead a female voice singing. Immediately, he knew, from the slight rasp of the voice that it must be the young woman who had seen him naked earlier. To save himself embarrassment, he quickly turned and headed in the opposite direction. Considering his bulk and the clumsiness his wounds imposed on him, he had to move slowly in order not to make a sound. So when he heard the voice approaching from behind him, he ducked into what he thought to be one of the empty rooms and found instead a staircase. With great haste, he hobbled down the steps and out through another door at the bottom of them. This entrance led directly into the kitchen on the first floor.

Sitting at the kitchen table, drinking from a coffee cup and reading the newspaper, was the doctor. Slung around his neck was a stethoscope. Across the front of his partially unbuttoned white shirt was a splotch of dried blood. By the way he lifted the cup with trembling hands and the way he placed it down with placid grace after a long gulp, Belius knew it wasn't filled with coffee.

The old man looked up and saw the minotaur standing in the doorway to his right. His eyes widened with delight. "I'm glad you're finally up and about. Another night of your infernal snoring, and I think the rafters would have splintered," he said. With his foot, he pushed one of the chairs out from its place under the table and nodded, inviting Belius to sit down.

"You've been out for a few days, boy. Lost a lot of blood. How do you feel?"

"Very weak," said Belius, easing himself into the chair and leaning his elbows on the table, "but, if I remember everything that happened, also lucky to be alive."

"Those dogs did you pretty good. I hate to admit to this, but, for a second time since delivering you, I thought for sure you were going to die. My biggest fear was rabies, but fortunately you escaped that horror."

"What am I doing here, doctor?"

"I had to bring you here where I could keep a constant eye on you. Your mother and I actually lifted you into the back of my wagon that night."

"How is my mother?"

"She's angry with me and worried about you. I've been sending somebody by to check on her every day to see if she needs anything. When I told the people in the town what happened, how you risked your life for them, I had more volunteers to help out than was needed. You can go back home in three days but not before. I want to make sure you don't get an infection in one of those bites and that your tail is beginning to heal."

"My tail?" asked Belius. He reached behind him under the coat and groped around with his hoof. A look of fear came over his face. "My tail!" he cried and stood up.

"I had to remove what was left of it. They chewed it almost completely through," said the doctor in a voice that was meant to calm the minotaur.

"But, but . . ." Belius threw the coat off and tried to look over his shoulder behind him, but he couldn't. For the first time, he noticed that the usual tug of its weight at the end of his spinal column was missing. Now he felt the loss of its constant gyration and swish. He concentrated and made believe there was a fly on his left shoulder blade. Tensing the muscles that had always turned the tail into a whip, he didn't feel the bushy end of it brush the spot.

"No tail," he said and his eyes glazed over. The sudden realization of its loss threw his body off balance, and he fell forward to the floor as if now there was no longer enough of him behind to balance things out.

"Nonsense," said Grey, who got out of his seat and came over to help Belius off the floor. "You don't need a tail to stand up. You're overreacting. It's a vestigial appendage, a useless throwback."

Belius was so upset that he took to moving his arms at his

sides in a swimming motion. Instead of interfering, Grey just stood back and watched the minotaur traverse the channel of his loss. After doing three laps around the kitchen floor, he finally came to his senses. He quietly stood up, walked over and picked up the overcoat and put it on. After the two were again seated at the kitchen table, a conversation ensued.

Grey told Belius that the enormous house they now sat in was given to him by the town as a lure to bring a physician to the area since the community was growing so fast, and, what with the nature of the local work, all its hazards of spooked plough horses and errant machinery. Grey had been born in the country and done his apprenticeship with a country doctor. Although he had attended medical school in a big city, he never cottoned to the frantic pace of urban life. He missed getting to know his patients and having long conversations that didn't necessarily have to go anywhere or be concerned with business or the pursuit of status. To him, his practice in the city had been just a long string of complaints with no personalities behind them.

The boarding house had once been owned by an old man of great learning, who would take in people and use the money he gained to buy books. Evidently, at one time, this previous owner had been a scientist in a country across the ocean. Many strange stories were told about him. He didn't set up the boarding house until he was well into his nineties. Still, he supposedly had great vitality for one so ancient. He didn't die, but one day just disappeared, leaving behind all of the books he had collected in the seven years he had lived there. His name was Scarfinati and the libraries upstairs held more than twenty-five works that he had personally authored.

When Grey began discussing the libraries in relation to the previous owner of the house, Belius moved the conversation around to asking Grey if he would mind him looking through the books in the next few days.

"By all means. Someone may as well use them. I find little interest anymore in books. I used to go through them avidly, but not so now," he said shaking his head.

"I hope you don't mind, but I was in one of them today," said Belius.

The doctor waved his hand as if brushing away the thought. "Even when you're well again, I want you to come any time and take what you want. There's just about everything up there. There are ten libraries in all, spaced out in different rooms of the house. If you'll notice, each room contains works on a different subject. By the way, did you happen to see the one with the mummy in it?"

Belius shook his head. He had not seen the mummy, but he had seen the girl and wanted to ask the doctor who she was. He held his questioning, though, knowing that if he mentioned her, he would also have to mention that he had been wandering the hallways naked and was seen by her in that condition. So he let the conversation move on, and they filled each other in on what they had done that winter between the time of Belius' father's death and when Grey had come to call.

When Grey had drained his third coffee cup of whiskey and they had thoroughly discussed everything from the Inferno to the weather, the old man rose from his chair and announced that he was going upstairs to lie down until dinner. "Feel free to roam around, Belius," he said with slurred speech. "I'll see you at seven for dinner right here. By then my niece will be back from town with some clothes for you. You scared the daylights out of her today, walking around the place. She can't quite make out what the hell you are. She didn't mind taking care of you while you were out cold, but, now that you're up and about, I think she thinks you're the devil come to call." Grey laughed as he teetered toward the door through which Belius had entered. There came the sound of him stumbling up the stairs and then perfect country quiet.

Belius remained at the kitchen table. He closed his eyes and rested his head down on the blue and white checkered cloth. The annoyance of his wounds came back to him all at once like a shift of workers returning to their jobs. Mixed in with the ache was a wisp of sleep that grew desperately fast into a thick cloud bank that blotted out even the moaning of his phantom tail. Later that evening, after finishing a dinner of broccoli and potatoes, the Minotaur excused himself from the table and asked the doctor if it would be all right to go up to the libraries to read.

"Certainly," said Grey. "Nona will make up another room for you since your snoring has devastated the one you were in."

"No need," said Belius, waving his hooves to dispel the thought. "I like it very cool when I sleep. Tomorrow I'll repair the windows and clean up the room. I'm afraid, though, that some of the knick-knacks are beyond repair."

"They were junk," said the doctor, leaning back in his chair. "Isn't that right, Nona?"

"Junk," she said softly, the first word she'd spoken in Belius' presence. She smiled at the minotaur, but it was a weak smile that seemed more a plea for him not to devour her.

"Before I go to sleep tonight I'll step outside and pick up a rock. When I have something hard and sharp in the collar of my nightshirt, I don't sleep on my back. I don't snore then. It was my mother's invention."

"I bought some clothes for you today. There's a pair of pajamas with them. I'll bring them to you after I clean up down here," said the girl.

"Thanks," said Belius and bowed toward her. Seeing his horns come down level with her head made her push back her chair a few inches.

Up in the library that held the red leather chair, Belius found a book by Scarfinati, the previous owner of the house. It was entitled Cosmology and was thicker than the unabridged dictionary that sat next to it on the shelf. Instead of taking to the chair to read, he remained in a standing position since the nub of his tail had been agitated by all his hours of sitting.

The house was as calm and quiet as he often imagined the bottom of the pond to be when the thick ice of mid-winter covered it. He paused before opening the book, knowing that once he entered through its black leather door, the voice of the author would begin speaking to him behind his eyes. He concentrated for a moment on Nona. Although the girl had said but few words to him and it was obvious that she was frightened by his strangeness, he knew that his interest in her was something more than plain curiosity. She had not yet given him a genuine smile, but he could tell that if she were to, it would be extraordinary. Nona's eyes were a light hazel and looked as if they might be luminescent in the night. Beyond her initial distrust for him, he thought he saw a personality whose first inclination would be a move toward friendship. As he sat next to her at dinner her closeness had inspired a sense of calm, and once, as she passed him the salt, the edge of his hoof had lightly grazed her thumb.

For the next two hours, Belius knew nothing but what the words on the page in front of him commanded. The introduction to the massive book was over three hundred pages, and, of this, he only finished a little over a third before the weight of ideas and that of the tome made him slam it shut and place it back on the shelf. All of the ideas he had gathered from his reading began to run through his being like a powerful drug. He was not used to such a great dose of concentration all at once, and the effects of it made him stumble to the red leather chair and sit down. There he sat for yet another hour in a stupor, his big head lying to the side, propped on the tips of one hoof, as he let the wise old man's theories percolate behind his eyes.

If the minotaur was correct in his reading, he garnered a few basic ideas from the book. The first was that Cosmology was the study of man's perceptions of the creation, perpetuation and destruction of all that lay outside himself. From here, Scarfinati had gone on to explain that each different epoch in the intellectual history of the human race had its own peculiar view of how the universe operated, and that each of these different views was a reflection of that stage of civilization's perceptions of itself. For instance, during the height of an age where mechanical science is in its greatest stages of discovery and development, the world and surrounding heavens are seen to operate like a mechanism.

None of these epochal Cosmologies, he stated, is any more "correct" than the next. Each is merely a reflection of the face of culture, and each, in its turn, fully captures culture's imagination like Narcissus hypnotized by his own reflection. All of the implications and outcomes of that ancient myth adhere to each given group of people who stare into the pool of creation. In other words, each civilization's Cosmology is an intense love affair with itself that nurtures it and allows it to grow but, in the end, is its undoing.

These thoughts spun about like planets thrown from their

orbits. The one central idea, though, that shone more brightly than a sun was Scarfinati's conviction that Cosmology was of the utmost importance in the formation of civilizations. "It gives to men and women a basic something in common, an illusion of certainty in which they can assuage the fear caused by the fact that they are utterly alone unto themselves."

"Beyond the needs of civilization," Scarfinati wrote, "each individual must have his or her own Cosmology, a personal set of myths by which to live. For to live only in the greater Cosmology of the civilization, is truly to be a ghost that sees everywhere action and creation, but can participate in neither."

It was at this point that Belius stopped reading and closed the book. In his excitement, he believed that what he had read was everything, although some thousand or more pages were still left to read. He didn't even skip to the last page and read Scarfinati's final paragraph. A vague, shimmering reflection of himself was beginning to form before his eyes as he sat in the chair. Now he believed it was entirely up to him to sharpen the focus of this image; to write a Cosmology for himself and also for the civilization of Minotaurs he dreamed he would father.

At the end of his hour of meditation, he rose and stretched. Although the fire of the new ideas was still with him, he was physically exhausted. As he came back to his waking self, he had a distinct urge to gore something; to smash his horns into a tree or the side of a barn. He thought then about the old door his father had propped against the willow for him and what had happened the day on which he rammed it into oblivion. Shaking his head, he tried to disrupt the "unnatural" desire. What he needed at the moment, he knew, was to talk to the doctor. There were a thousand questions to ask about Cosmology.

He left the library and made his way quietly down to the lower level of the spacious house. He came first to the kitchen but did not find Grey there. Instead, he found three cold potatoes, left over from dinner, in the refrigerator. He swallowed them like pills.

From there, he wandered out into the corridors that were different from upstairs in that they opened into large rooms and were not lined with doors. These rooms were mostly unlit, and, from the light of the hallway he could make out the ghostly figures of furniture draped in bed sheets. Occasionally, he would come across one that appeared to have been in use, but it was easy to see by the layer of dust on the mantles and chandeliers that the doctor rarely, if ever, did any entertaining.

For the entire day he'd worn the old overcoat, buttoned to the neck and strapped tightly at the waist in case of any meetings with Nona. He was finally becoming used to the feel of its unsettling lamb's wool lining. He made his way quietly along, sneaking like a burglar from place to place, sweating beneath the weight of the wrap.

Passing three corridors of these larger rooms, Belius entered a fourth that had but one door in the middle of it on the left hand side. A dim light seeped out from around the slightly opened door. The hall was darkened and seemed a place he should not go, but, from within the one concealed room, he heard muffled sounds that escaped with the weak light. He crept up to the door and took a position outside of it. Turning his head so that he could spy through the crack with one eye, he held his breath as to make the least amount of noise and squinted to see into the murky room.

Although lit only by a single fluttering gas lamp, he immediately could tell from the sight of instruments and an examination table that it must be the doctor's office. Below the lamp was a big oak desk, highly polished, behind which was a wall of what he assumed to be medical texts. Grey sat at the desk, slumped forward, his arms laying flat out in front of him on the smooth surface. In the strange light he looked, with his thousand wrinkles, as if he were made from beaten leather. His body shook in intermittent spasms, and, after each of these, he made a choking noise as if he were trying to swallow something made of metal. At first Belius thought he was dying, but then he saw the bottle of whiskey at his elbow and the glass tumbler an inch from his hand, and he realized the physician was simply crying.

Sitting also on the desk top was a huge glass jar. The light from the lamp made the almost clear liquid inside the jar glow like a frosted window catching the sunset. Floating inside was a tiny human form. Its arms were out at its sides and its legs were bent slightly at the knees. The head was thrown back as if in the act of screaming. It did not float near the top or bottom but was suspended directly in the middle.

Back at his room, Belius surprised Nona in the act of laying out the new clothes on his bed. He was still very upset with what he had seen in the doctor's office, and the effects of it cancelled out all of the decorum he had adopted when in her presence. Before she could flee through the open door, he put his hoof out and touched her shoulder.

"Why does your uncle sit in his office and drink and cry?" he asked her.

"He's a man of great feeling," she said.

Belius nodded, hoping she would continue.

A few more moments passed, and then she looked into his eyes. "He sees all of the suffering around him in the world. He tells me that life is only suffering. He has great pity for others. All the time, he seems to be laughing when he is with people, but when he is alone he lets his true feelings out. He doesn't want to let on to them what he knows about the hardships they'll face. He told me once that he wished he could cure everyone's pain, but that he knows the only cure is death. He drinks to forget his feelings."

"Can't he just accept things the way other people do?"

"I suppose not, after having seen so many people suffer in his life. I remember, from when I was very young, my mother telling my father that his wife had died. It was when he lived in the city. He had tried very hard to cure her, but in the end there was nothing he could do. Perhaps that was where his sorrow began."

"Do you believe these things he told you?" Belius asked.

"What's to believe?" she asked and reached into the pocket of her dress. "Will this do?" She pulled out her hand and in it was a rock she could just about get her fingers around. She handed it to him and left the room. He knew, from the way she had spoken, that she no longer had any fear of him.

As he lay in the dark, shivering and blowing silver clouds of steam, listening to the sound of the wind slipping through the shattered windows, he thought about the word "pity." He recognized it as being that enemy of his which had caused his parents to lie to him in his childhood. He saw that it was simply a ghost of a feeling that, if left to grow unchecked, would finally give birth to depression and deceit. In a moment, he was sleeping.

He dreamed he was outside in the cold, standing in a pasture covered with deep snow. In the moonlight, he was able to discern, at the opposite end of the wide field, a barren tree that was so tall that its branches went up into the night to a point he could not see. The trunk of it was thicker than a house and much of the bark had fallen off. He began running toward it with his head bent for impact. The further he ran, the colder the night became. He continued on though, hugging himself with his arms and trying to bury his snout down into the front of the overcoat. He ran toward it for an hour, and during that time the cold had snuck into his body and formed a thin layer of ice on his face and horns and even on the camel's hair of the coat. His joints began to seize and, as he drew close to his target, he moved increasingly slowly. Just as his horns made contact with the smooth white wood, he froze solid. Ice covered him. He tried to yell out for help, but his voice was frozen too. In the depths of the shell of ice, after struggling for a long time to make a sound, he found another dream that carried him away in its current.

Three days later, Belius left the doctor's house. He was wearing one of the new outfits he had just gotten—a white shirt, black pants and a coat with a red and black plaid design. Both he and Grey were sitting in the doctor's wagon, ready to pull out onto the road. Just as the doctor was lifting the whip to spur the horse into action, the front door of the boarding house opened and Nona came running out to them. In her arms, she carried the overcoat. When she reached the side of the wagon, she called up, "You almost forgot this." Belius reached down and took it from her. He smiled and, to his surprise, Nona returned the true smile he had been looking for. The doctor laughed, but Belius noticed that the old man's mirth was louder and lasted longer than ever before.

🐾 🐾 🐾

A week passed and, whereas Pezimote still had not come to call, Thip came every day like clockwork. With each feeding he grew bigger until now he stood a full three inches off the table. The wound on Belius' arm was a festering sore. When the flea dipped into it, his enormous head was capable of draining a quarter of a pint of blood. The lurid transfusions were having a marked effect on both donor and recipient. Though Thip was fat and sluggish, his new height and girth could not be equaled by his dot of a brain which remained its original size.

He ranted and raved in spontaneous verse, the topic of which was always his conquest of the Wider World. He told Belius how his beautiful castle had become too small for him, how he had accidentally killed his devoted wife by trying to have sex with her, how he had eaten his pet tapeworms and been fired by Shebeb. His daughters had fled from the castle and refused to see him. Although he lamented the destruction of his previous life, he could not keep himself from Belius' arm. It had become the reason for his waking in the morning.

The minotaur, on the other hand, grew weak and giddy from the loss of blood. The lack of oxygen to his system was starving his reason. He laughed at everything and couldn't concentrate. All day, he would rush from one task to the next, accomplishing nothing. One minute he would be out in the garden, and, the next, he would be at his telescope, looking through the wrong end into the cracked mirror of his study. Whatever he did he found hilarious, but when the fits of fatigue would seize him and make him sit still, he would realize he was dying and that he was alone. Not one of his friends had come to him for days. It was at these times that he wished he hadn't burned The Cosmology. "At least it would be something to hold," he would say to himself before passing out.

The work on Soffea had gone exceptionally well. Her nearly completed form lay next to the riverbank waiting for the life force that would be supplied by a mosquito and a handful of bees. The golden condor had brought the human foot with toe nails painted as had been promised. The teak wood hooves had been secured in place, the open mouth shone with the iridescent splendor of pearls, and the leaf tongue from the blabbering trees was already at work mumbling and jumbling almost words. Even that part of Siftus that always sought after perfection was satisfied with the results of his own labor.

The one thing that troubled the mole was the fact that to this point nothing had been found to fill the empty eye sockets. Many of the creatures had brought reasonable facsimiles for his approval—pairs of small round jelly-fish, bird eggs with pupils painted on, and, probably the worst of all, two circular globs of amber with trilobites trapped in them. Upon sniffing these offerings for "rightness," the mole could tell immediately that they wouldn't convey emotion or take in and hold another's glance. Vashti was getting fed up with his insistence that nothing would do. He knew in a way that she was right in thinking that something had to be settled on before Belius fell deeper into depression, but he also knew she didn't look on the creation in the same way he did. To her it was a means to an end. To him it was an end in itself. "I don't even care if she's blind," he told the owl, "as long as the eyes are everything that eyes should be."

"Let's just settle on one of the suggestions that's been made. What about the globs of amber? You must admit they have a disarming quality, a certain charm about their strange color."

"You mean disarming in the sense of losing an arm?" he asked.

"You're impossible. Either come up with an alternative, or we're going to have to use what we have. Soffea will walk tomorrow. You have till then, otherwise, her eyes will be amber."

"All right, all right," he said and stormed away along the riverbank, swinging his cane at low hanging branches. He had not slept in days so it was a great effort for him to try to organize his thoughts. "Eyes," he said to himself, but his mind kept returning to an image of his stone bed. He cursed and quibbled with himself for a half mile before, in his near-blindness, he walked into the trunk of a tree and fell onto his back. The snout-first collision jarred everything in his head, allowing an obvious solution to his dilemma to rise to the fore. "That's it," he said and drew the new idea from his mind into his mouth where it was mixed with a wad of spittle. He shot this morsel onto the ground and put his still aching snout to it. The second he smelled its makeup, he knew it was the only answer. He clawed the air once in victory and then, losing no time, set off for Shebeb's cave.

It was a rare few minutes in Shebeb's life when he had no

patients to administer to. When Siftus came upon him, he was in the grove of blabbering trees, collecting the long stringy moss from their branches. The trees were high-strung that day, and their usual palaver sounded more like a song of whippoorwills than speech.

"Shebeb," said the mole, "how are you?"

The ape nodded and continued his gathering.

"The female minotaur is almost ready to walk," said Siftus.

"Almost," said Shebeb with a grunt.

"I could tell from your speech the other night that you don't believe it will even be able to twitch an ear."

"That pile of mud will not move of its own volition for a million years. Of that, I'm positive."

"You're wrong," said the mole, taking out a cigarette. He propped his cane against the tree and lit up.

The ape shook his head and then covered his mouth for just a moment with the palm of his hand.

"Would you care to bet?"

"I don't bet," said Shebeb, "there's nothing I want to win."

"There's got to be something," said Siftus.

"Nothing," said the ape.

"Let's say we have a bet and I lose, I will donate my body to you after I'm dead. What about that? Wouldn't you like to get your hairy fingers on a mole corpse?"

"It would be helpful in my studies," said the ape.

He stopped gathering moss now and looked down as if to size up Siftus' carcass.

The mole blew a cloud of smoke upward to obscure the look on Shebeb's face. "Let's make a bet then. You have sole possession of my body, after I'm dead, of course, if Soffea doesn't walk by herself."

Shebeb scratched thoughtfully at his backside for a moment and then agreed to the deal with one quick nod.

"Don't you want to know what I want if I win?" asked Siftus.

"No."

"You're that sure of yourself?"

"I think that what you want to do, help Belius, is a good thing, but the way you're going about it is all wrong. You're deluding yourself and, in the process, leading everyone to a grave disappointment. Life can't be created by slapping together whatever is at hand. You'll see tomorrow when your statue lays there, a mound of wet clay with things stuck to it."

"All I hope," said the mole, "is that you'll honor your word when the time comes."

Shebeb turned away and headed for his cave.

Taking a long drag of his cigarette, Siftus considered the possibility that he might have been all wrong. If he was, it meant that when he died his body would not be buried deep in the beautiful, loving earth, but, instead, would be scattered about the ape's cave and slowly, over a period of years, picked away to nothing by sharp instruments. He shuddered at the thought of his poor snout forever forced to smell the wicked odors of Shebeb's elixirs. His doubt lasted only a few seconds. Right where he'd stood conversing with the physician, he bent over and quickly dug his way below the surface of the earth. In the past few days he'd spent too much time in the open air, beneath the oppressive yellow sky. Halfway back to his burrow, he stopped to rest and just breathe in the smells of the underground. "Ah, dirt!" he said aloud, frightening an earthworm. He went no further for the time being but closed his eyes and slept.

While Siftus lay asleep underground, the raccoon brothers, although hoping for the best for Belius' sake, offered odds of acorns and measures of honey, ten to one, that the contrived form would remain on the ground until the rains finally washed it away. They found many a willing bettor, especially among those creatures who had forsaken snatches of fur from their own hides in order that the female minotaur might have a luxuriant mane.

The ants of the tower did not take bets, but, being the communal group that they were, initiated a joint meditation of all their brethren, melding together their combined psychic powers in the attempt to produce a modest spark of good faith. A feather fell from Vashti's left wing and floated down from where she perched on a tree near the riverbank, overlooking the unknowing form. It twirled in the air and finally came to rest on the sculpted navel of Soffea. As she watched it land, covering the bodily center of the being yet to be, she saw instantly that if everything worked out and she were to introduce the creation to Belius the next day, it had better have some clothes. She was thankful that she now had a project with which to take up the dreadful time of waiting. She left the believers to the non-believers and went in search of Bonita to see what the cat could come up with by way of material in the storage room of Belius' tower.

Nothing of importance, be it on land or sea, ever escaped the notice of Nosthemus. In one small closet of the vast mansion that was his brain he registered the suspense that had been generated by the possible birth of Soffea and saw it as a prime opportunity to make a prophecy. He swam out from the bay of the coral reef into deep water. Two miles off shore, he sucked in enough oxygen for a bull elephant to breathe recklessly for a lifetime and dove down and down beyond where the sun light shone, beyond the realm of eatable fish, into the shivering darkness at the bottom of the Wider World. As he thrust himself toward his destination with powerful strokes of his tail, he anticipated the impact a correct prophecy of such importance would have on the creatures of the surface. For one, he knew it would add to his own grand status as the baffling mystic. He would have only five minutes to expend on questioning the giant worm that lived in the light and heat of the molten fissure. It was from this ancient first-of-creatures that he got all his prophecies, though no living thing for miles above was aware of it.

The fiery gorge that was like the sun to Floridusk ran for miles across the basin of the ocean: a canyon river that meandered among the enormous mountain range that lay three hundred fathoms down and was like a gaping crack in the skull of the Wider World. The molten lava that bubbled up from the very center of things contained the essence of the planet's dreams and thoughts. It was from the light thrown off by this liquid blaze that Floridusk assumed the knowledge of what was to happen. The giant worm was a creature, but, in its creation, was blessed with the property of photosynthesis. Its special chlorophyll produced oxygen for it to breathe in its cells the way a plant on the surface would. It drew nutrients from the rich volcanic muck it wallowed in. Once, the worm had told Nosthemus that it believed it had been born from a nightmare the Wider World had once dreamt.

After an hour of swimming through pitch dark, Nosthemus could barely make out a thin line of orange unraveling below him. The closer he drew to it, the more the molten light illuminated the barren landscape. Finally, exhausted, the whale could clearly see the peaks of the undersea mountains looming in the distance. Flying in amongst these crags, he continued to descend. The freezing cold diminished, and the heavy water pressing against his slippery skin began to glow with warmth. He spotted the huge round head of Floridusk and swam up close to announce himself.

"Worm!" he shouted at the full moon of a face that could have incorporated within its circumference a hundred of him.

The pale body of the behemoth quit its digestive undulation and rumbling. Thick, mile long lips parted to show teeth and give the effect of a condescending sneer. Floridusk opened one lid to reveal a jelly eye with lavender cornea and iris the color of old snow. The other eye remained closed. This ancient of the depths had the ability to be both asleep and awake at the same time. Earlier that week the sunken corpse of a great white shark had gotten tangled in the sparse hairs of the worm's beard. To scratch the itch that the decaying flotsam caused, he pivoted his head to rub his chin against the bottom of the ocean. This movement created a strong current, making it difficult for Nosthemus to remain in the same spot. "Be still, parasite," Floridusk bellowed in a great release of bubbles, "it's difficult enough to focus on you when you aren't squirming around."

"My apologies," said Nosthemus.

"What is it this time?"

"Just one thing. Will she be born tomorrow?" The whale did not have to elaborate, knowing that Floridusk must already know why he was there.

"Tell me one thing, my swimming insignificance, do you think it really matters whether she walks or talks or cures your friend? Do you think that if this were to happen, you would not still die and float down here to the bottom and rot and turn to muck and be assimilated by me? Do you think the Wider World would shed a tear for such a niggling tragedy or lose a moment of night?"

Nosthemus was used to being belittled by the worm. He had quickly learned to simply go along with the pomposity, groveling as much as possible without whining. "No," he answered, "I suppose it wouldn't matter one way or the other in the larger scheme of things."

"Not matter? Well, you're wrong. Everything matters to this celestial head. I have taken in the light of this matter from the molten glow. I know what will happen. The dream of it bubbled up from the gorge years and years past."

"And what was the outcome? What did the Wider World dream about this?" Nosthemus grew anxious, feeling the tightening up of his innards that always came as his oxygen was running low.

"I'm afraid the dream was explicit in that I was not to tell you when you came to ask. This is a gift for you and your friends from the planet. The thought is that the suspense of having to wait will make all of your lives more rewarding."

The whale knew there was no sense in arguing. "Thank you for recognizing me, worm. I will return."

"That's a prophecy you can take heed of," said Floridusk.

Mustering all his strength, Nosthemus whipped his tail and sent himself shooting up through the incredible pressure of the depths. He hurried, knowing he had stayed down too long. The journey to the surface would take hours. The fiery river receded below him and with it the light. He shot past the tallest peak of the mountain range and entered the zone of complete black. It was in this most lonely part of the return trip that Nosthemus felt himself being chased upward by a giant presence. He swam as hard as he could, but it was inevitable that whatever it was would overtake him.

"What unknown monster of the lightless realm can this be?" he thought as he pushed himself along, using up vital oxygen in his haste. Fear overwhelmed him just as his pursuer did, and he screamed, releasing all his air in a cascade of bubbles. The thing enveloped him, and he thought, at first, that he was being swallowed whole. Then, to his surprise, he found that he could breathe. He took in a great supply of oxygen. As the precious gas eased the incredible aching of his lungs, he heard the earthquake voice of Floridusk echo in his mind. "I knew you wouldn't make it to the surface if I didn't help you with this bubble. I let it frighten you for your charade as a soothsayer in the upper regions. But I admire your foolishness. For this, I will tell you something that will come as prescient news to your friends. The autumn wind will blow tonight and shake the blossoms from the trees."

᭬ ᭬ ᭬

The newborn night was still as a cliff face, and, because the blue sun was only minutes below the horizon, a rich lime shadow submerged the forest. Belius wanted to be quiet, but the laughter forced its way in fitful bursts up from his throat and out his nostrils. "What's so funny?" he asked himself and then spun around quickly as if expecting an answer from someone behind him. There was nothing there. The oak trees stood tall and quiet, supporting the sky. Grass, and dead leaves, chips of fallen bark and deep deposits of brittle pine needles gave off their scents. A lone cricket pulsed out a code that when deciphered told the story of a certain star it had witnessed the extinction of one night in its youth. Belius stopped his sneaking about and listened to the message. Although he was not quick enough to translate the song word for word, its overall effect gave him the mood and as easily as the snorts of laughter came, so did his tears. Slowly, he picked up the rhythm and began to dance in small circles, his arms raised in the air. He sang along and wept. Eventually the cricket became annoyed with what it took to be a mockery of its story and hopped away. The silence returned and with it the minotaur's purpose. He had come down from the tower to hunt the invisible creature that had stolen his overcoat.

So little red blood now ran through Belius' mind and body that his synapses had no energy with which to fire and all his thoughts were a result of the fermentation of his brain. The digitalis he had smoked before leaving his study gave a veneer of assurance to his dementia. He stumbled gracefully amongst the trees with a liquid certainty that his mission was of the utmost importance. "I'll have my coat," he cursed in a rough whisper to a tree stump he momentarily mistook for Shebeb.

A week earlier, when he had first seen the overcoat slipping through darkness of its own accord, he was terrified of it, but, as Thip sucked away at his reason and will, to have the coat again on his back became everything he had ever wanted to accomplish in his life. As his senses dwindled his courage had grown. He swam through the green twilight practicing a left jab as occasional sparks of colored light exploded in his field of vision. Then a cold wind was all around him, blowing down from the north with a force that shook the limbs of the trees the way a child shakes the dead to wake them. White, pink, yellow blossoms tasted ice in the sudden gale and, fearing they had miscalculated the onset of autumn, let go their hold on summer.

Belius turned the collar of his shirt up against the weather as if it were the collar of his old overcoat. Protecting his eyes with a forearm raised to his brow, he peered through the blizzard of airborne petals and dandelion skeletons and moved into the storm. He no longer laughed or mumbled because the shock of the frigid air stole his wind. All around him, he heard the voices of the dog pack that had attacked him in his youth. He forged forward, deeper into the forest, toward the river.

After the minotaur had forgotten why he was trudging through the forest, and when the flight of blossoms was at its heaviest, he saw something move a few yards in front of him. The camel hair color of it caught what little moonlight slipped through the storm of petals and told him immediately what it was. A trace of the lamb's wool lining flew directly up his nostrils. He lowered his horns and snorted. As weak as he was, his muscled arms pumped up and down to the beat of his lunacy. His leg hoof dug into the ground. His human foot took the first step and then he was charging. "I wanted to see the light," the coat seemed to scream as he chased it through the storm, over fallen tree trunks, through webs of vine and sticker shoots, beneath low branches that required him to bend down to the height of four feet. The hunt traced a serpentine path through the trees, doubling back, overlapping previously trampled ground. Never once did Belius lift his head or slow his pace. His target was the wide piece of material between the shoulders at the back of the coat. His horns somehow directed his pursuit.

The smoke-being reached the river bank only seconds ahead of the charging minotaur. With incredible speed, it worked its arms out of the overcoat. The coat fell into the slowly moving waters and was carried away as the spirit of The Cosmology leaped into the air in a high arc, flipped over on its back during the descent, and floated down to mix its atoms with what it took to be the oddly shaped trunk of a fallen tree somehow made of clay. As Belius charged into the clearing by the riverbank, the manifestation of his book closed its eyes within the darkness of its hiding place and passed out.

After spotting the overcoat on the surface of the water, Belius lost all his rage. He walked along the bank, following its progress as it moved toward the mouth of the river. His wild chase had diminished the hallucinatory hold of the digitalis, and a few drops of blood made their way to his brain. A great fatigue came over him, and, for the first time in days, he could think clearly. His first healthy thoughts were of Pezimote, Vashti and Siftus. The realization of his loneliness made him sober for his walk to the sea. He considered wading out into the waters to retrieve his prize, but the autumn wind made the air too cold. The old swatch of camel's hair no longer mattered to him. Before long, he reached the mouth of the river. He watched as the coat met its first wave and sank beneath the foam.

Belius opened the front door of the tower and ascended the winding stairway. He didn't stop at the landing that held his bedroom but continued to the turret. There, he moved across the cobblestones to take up a position leaning against the facade. He stared out to sea, watching as the last few flying blossoms lost the wind and fell. Out past the coral reef, there was an eruption of water. Nosthemus broke the surface gaping for air. The giant whale, who now, by the light of the moon, looked so distant and puny to Belius released a spout of water from his blow hole. With this spray came a psychic message, a prophecy to all the creatures of the Wider World. The minotaur heard it in his head as clearly as he heard the tortured rhythm of his own heart, "The autumn wind will blow tonight and the blossoms will fly." From out of the forest came a chorus of laughter, and then the creatures resumed sleeping or hunting. Belius shook his head as he slipped down to lie on the floor of the roof of his tower. He sank into sleep as his overcoat sank down past the regions of moonlight and eatable fish.

As the blue sun showed itself in the west, both day and night creatures gathered at the riverbank. Obadai and Mez were the first to arrive, hoping they could still take a few more bets before the event got underway. The crowd grew thick and Vashti, who was perched in the branch of a tree situated directly over Soffea, had to keep shouting for the throng not to press in too close on the object of their wonder. The ants from the tower gathered around their hero, Duc-Sin, who held back the brain's intended consciousness with a looped and knotted stem from a honey-suckle bush. The mosquito was five times the size of the fierce warrior.

Siftus winced as he tapped the two globs of amber into his sculpture's eye sockets. When he was finished, he looked over his shoulder up to Vashti and shook his head. He could not actually see her, but it gave him some solace when he sniffed a whiff of agreement from her about the inadequacy of the orbs. Shebeb stood on the fringes of the crowd, arms folded, patiently awaiting failure. He had already assured himself that he would take no pleasure in the embarrassment of the mole and owl, and had even secretly vowed to let Siftus back out of their deal of the day before.

Vashti flew down from her perch, and, as she lighted upon the stomach of Soffea, those petals that had covered the body and fallen around it were blown to a distance by the action of her wings. The pieces of blossom flew up in the faces of the crowd and everyone took a step backward. Only Siftus remained standing next to her. He leaned over and whispered to the owl, "The eyes are terrible, aren't they?" "It's time for her to walk," was all Vashti could think to answer. Then she motioned with her wing, and two woodpeckers hopped out from the circle of creatures. One took up a position on the brow of Soffea, between her horns, and the other mounted the chest above where the cavity of the heart had been sunk into clay. With a nod from the owl, the two red headed birds went to work with their beaks and in no time had drilled the holes through which 'life' would enter the form.

Duc-Sin strode forth and climbed up onto the brow of the sleeping mud form. He began reeling in the incredible mosquito he'd caught in the mango grove. When there was no more stem left, he grabbed the buzzing insect by the throat and, in one swift action, thrust it down into the dark vault that was Soffea's skull. Siftus was right there to smooth the clay before the mosquito could find its way out. With a smooth flip of his paw, he covered over the hole that had been drilled as if it had never existed. The ant contingent applauded their hero, and the other creatures joined in. Siftus then moved down to the chest of his creation and waited for the bees to do their last barrel roll and enter one by one to become the energy of heart and soul. He gave a word of thanks to them before again smoothing over the clay.

Just as the owl and mole stepped back to join the circle, the blue sun peered over the rim of the forest. Its light engaged the leaf-tongue from the blabbering tree and Soffea began to mumble. Siftus initiated the chant, "Rise, rise," and the crowd picked up his rhythm and joined in. The noise of the creatures awakened the sleeping spirit of The Cosmology, which had been hiding, inside the form of Soffea since Belius had chased it through the night.

The clay legs twitched. The chest heaved. The eyelids blinked. The whole sculpture went through a series of convulsions that seemed to emanate from within as if life were percolating and trying to sort itself out. Shebeb unthinkingly pushed aside smaller creatures in order to get closer to the scene. "Impossible," he shouted.

"Possible," Siftus countered and stepped forth to take the fair minotaur's hoof and help her to her feet. She rose off the ground in slow stages, each bit of progress applauded by the crowd. All the time, the tongue blathered on and on as if picking up in the middle of a conversation interrupted from a previous life. As Soffea reached her feet, Vashti flew into the air, screeching and hooting.

The minotaur wobbled on her legs, the disparate parts of her anatomy jostling but staying fairly intact. Her left horn did fall off onto the ground, but it didn't seem to cause her any distress. Her head continued to jerk around, her arms to swing slightly with the cadence of her innocuous monologue. She discovered how to smile and practiced it a few times, baring her pearl teeth in an unknowing show of good will. With a halting syncopation, she took her first steps. The crowd made way for her, and she tottered head on into a tree, bounced off it, turned and stood still as if waiting for something to do.

Vashti called Bonita from the crowd. The cat came forth with a balled-up piece of blue material that had once served as a tablecloth in the tower's kitchen. During the night, she and Vashti had fashioned the cloth into a crude toga. The owl took the simple dress and flew into the air with it, letting it unfurl to its full length as she ascended. Then flying over Soffea, she aimed with her beacon eyes and let the thing fall. It slipped neatly over the minotaur's figure, filling out at the chest and laying neatly down two good inches above the knees.

The owl resumed her perch upon the branch. "Silence," she shouted. The crowd looked up to her and quieted down, all except Soffea. "Look what we've accomplished," she said. "Everyone here has added to the creation of this beautiful creature. Those who didn't have the skill to work on the form or have something to give gave their faith. I'm certain that today when we present Belius with his bride, he'll break out of the cocoon of his depression and also be born anew. Now it's time Siftus and I took her to the tower."

The mole, who had climbed up the tree next to the minotaur in order to replace her errant horn, cried out, "No, it's not quite time. She's lovely, I admit, but . . . her eyes . . ." He backed down the tree trunk and waddled through the crowd to where Shebeb was standing, his long hairless fingers covering his mouth. "Ape," said the mole, "go to your cave and bring back your instruments; the ones that cut. It is time for me to collect." At the utterance of the word 'collect,' Obadai and Mez slipped away from the crowd.

"Rise, rise, rise . . ." This chant reached Belius where he lay on the cobblestones at the top of the tower. The suggestion passed in through the openings of his ears and snout and presented itself to his sleeping consciousness. He took the advice and pulled himself up to his full height before completely awakening. Once his head was clear of the shadow cast by the facade, the sun hit his eyes and forced them to open. As his vision cleared, the world built itself around him. The green feather of nausea blew through his intestines as if, during the night, he had polished off a keg of dandelion wine. His whole body shook violently with fatigue, making his bones crack and his muscles stretch almost to ripping. "Shit," he said, took a step and fell down. As he dragged himself again to his hoof and foot, he wondered how late it was in the day, how long it would be before Thip was back to exact payment. He knew there would not be many days left before he died from lack of blood. "Better off dead," he thought as he moved toward the trapdoor that led to the spiral staircase. He took each step with great caution, inching his way down past the bedroom landing, past the laboratory and bathroom to his study. It was all he could do to make it to his chair and fall into it. The only thing on his mind was, of course, the digitalis, but before he leaned over the little table to his left to prepare the pipe, he needed to rest for a few moments.

Staring into the cracked mirror across the room, the minotaur could not make out any detail but could see from the shattered reflection that his color had lost almost every trace of blue. His hide had paled to the color of the moon on winter nights and his flesh to the sickening shade of a toad's belly. Turning his gaze from the mirror, he looked down to the hooves at the ends of his arms. Each was webbed with networks of cracks and fissures. They would have bled had there been any blood that close to the surface. He feared now, when not under the influence of the digitalis, that if he were even just to tap his horns against something they would break off from his head without so much as a "crack."

He knew that he should have been horrified by the condition of his health, but he felt no emotion. There were no tears, nor was there crazy laughter hiding just the other side of his larynx. There was nothing. He leaned over and, with shaking hoof, tried to fill the bowl of the pipe. The precious leaves of the dried foxglove scattered on table and floor. After three tries the bowl of the pipe was stuffed. He lifted it to his lips and drew on the stem. Five minutes later he realized he had not lit the petals. More fumbling and finally flame. The smoke began to rise. He sucked it in as deeply as his weakened condition would allow, hoping that its high would make him care again, make him think of some way to save himself. When the bowl was spent, the minotaur leaned back in his chair and closed his eyes. The smoke showed him no colors behind his eyelids this time. All was as black as that chamber of his heart Thip had explored. He snorted and moaned, trying to work up a memory. Even a bad memory, the most horrible one, would do for him now but nothing came. Because of the physical exertion, he had to finally give up. He opened his eyes to look at the objects in his study, feeling them more friendly than the "nothing" that was inside him. Across the coffee table from him, sitting on the divan was Pezimote.

"The door was open downstairs," said the tortoise.

Excitement flared up inside Belius, but he couldn't jump out of his seat as he wanted to. "My friend," he said, the words spoken in a weak drawl. "I went every day to the sea to look for you. Why haven't you come?"

"I've been busy ruining my life."

"Chelonia?" Belius asked, somehow guessing the problem from the look in his friend's eyes.

The tortoise nodded. "She's left me. Gone off into the ocean somewhere far away. I don't know where."

"Why?"

"A young female tortoise. I rode the waves on her back and Chelonia saw it in my eyes."

"Couldn't you have made amends?" asked Belius, filling a pipe for his companion.

"I didn't try. I told her to go. I told her she was tiresome . . . but now I miss her terribly. I've never felt such pain in all my long years. I suppose I've never felt anything before. The young tortoise, she's a fool. She talks more foolishness than Shebeb. She's always talking. After Chelonia had gone, it was only a day before I began to weary of the nubile's physical charms."

"Speak of fools," said Belius, handing Pezimote the pipe and his homemade lighter.

"Yes, yes, yes," said the tortoise and leaned over to take the implements. He lit the bowl and drew deeply on the stem. With the release of the blue smoke, he coughed and said, "The things we do to make ourselves seem great."

"She'll come back to you," said Belius.

"No," the tortoise replied and shook his head. "I'm going to find her. I may be gone for a very long time, that's why I stopped to see you."

"See me now old friend, because I will most likely not be alive when you return."

"And what is with you, you look older than I feel."

Belius sat forward in his chair, hesitated for a moment by closing his eyes, and, deciding nothing mattered, told Pezimote the events of the past few weeks. He spoke of Thip's blackmail and the incident from his past that had brought him down. The tortoise sat on the divan as still as the yellow day outside the window. He listened carefully to the tale, as a vision of the total immensity of the oceans of the Wider World filled his head. When Belius was through and silence had swept down between the friends, Pezimote stretched his scrawny neck as far out of his shell as possible and screeched like a magpie. The minotaur knew that the pitiful cry was all that his friend could now offer him. He let it enter his head and, once there, kept it alive, bouncing off the boundary between his horns, echoing through the pitch.

"Good-bye, Belius," said Pezimote and leaned over to set the pipe and lighter on the coffee table. Once these things were set down, he reached even further and stumped his friend on the knee as he had done so many times in the past. Then he rose and walked toward the door. Before leaving, he turned and asked Belius, "And exactly what time is it now?"

The minotaur looked over at the water clock in the corner of the study. "A little before noon," he said and immediately put his hoof to the festering wound at the crook of his opposite arm. Tears came to his eyes. He wiped them away as he listened to Pezimote descend the spiral staircase.

With a great effort he hoisted himself out of the chair and went to the study window. It was a perfect day with no hint that the first wind of autumn had blown only the night before. He looked down from the tower and saw Pezimote standing by the front door. The tortoise stood there for five minutes, and Belius hoped that he was changing his mind. He was about to call out to his friend to come back when he saw Thip strolling down the center path of the garden, now a half a foot in height, dressed in his too small top hat and cape. The flea was drooling and reciting and every few steps would lose control of himself, spin around in a complete circle and then continue toward the tower. As the flea neared the tower door, he took off his hat and bowed to Pezimote. "Good day, Mr. Tortoise," he said.

Pezimote eyed the oversized insect up and down and then spat on the ground to his side. "Good day, Mr. Flea," said the tortoise, and, with one fluid motion, punctuated at its completion by a snap of the beak, he swallowed Thip whole.

Belius lost his breath and leaned over on the window sill. "Pezimote!" he cried in admonishment.

The tortoise looked over his shoulder. "Not quite a man o' war pie," he called to the minotaur and then resumed the unaffected stance of all fours.

Belius watched as his friend moved slowly down the path to the beach. As the waters of the ocean lapped over Pezimote's shell, a shrill squeal rose up from the forest. The mole's horrific cry jarred something in Belius' diminishing brain, and the memory of his last days in the lesser world swept across his darkened mind. Although he had just related the story to Pezimote, the impetus for the telling came only from his tongue. Now, each detail returned to him with frozen clarity.

🐾 🐾 🐾

When Austina caught a whiff of the perfume that Belius had dowsed himself with, she farted to try to clear the air. She called out from her stall in the barn, "Halfling, what's that rancid aroma?"

Belius tried to ignore her as he coaxed the plough horse out into the center aisle.

"Who died?" asked Plension, taking in the minotaur's dress: a black, double-breasted suit, forest green shirt, maroon ascot. He wore a shiny black wingtip shoe on his human foot and had colored with black polish the cuticle of his hoof to match the shoe.

"No one died," Belius muttered, knowing better than to try to explain his new clothes to them.

"I think he's in love," said Austina to her sister over the wooden boundary separating them.

"Is it the human we saw him with in the field last week?" asked Plension.

Austina mooed.

"I'm just going visiting," Belius said to them.

"To the doctor's again," the old plough horse said to the cows.

"That's right. He has a very fine library in his house, and he lets me borrow his books. I have to go there. He's helping me study."

"We totally understand," said Austina. "It's important that you make these concessions in your dress and aroma for the old man."

"It's civilized," said Belius, "to dress properly."

"We just thought you were out to impress the female," said Plension. "See how ignorant we creatures can be?"

The horse and the cows laughed and Belius grabbed the horse's bridle, giving it a rough tug. He led the old plough puller toward the door of the barn, wishing he'd laughed along with them from the beginning.

"How is she on all fours?" Austina mooed after him as he stepped out into the light of the winter day.

He slammed the barn door. The horse was no longer laughing, but Belius could see from the glint in the animal's eye that he was working hard not to.

"You know, I don't have to give you any carrots on this trip," Belius said to him sharply. Then in the same instant he drew a carrot from his pocket. As the horse munched the treat, Belius rigged him to the wagon.

He climbed into the seat of the wagon and took up the reins. "O.K.," he said to the horse. The old animal gave three lethargic pulls against the weight of the wagon and finally got it rolling.

The afternoon was clear and cold, but off in the west dark clouds were gathering. The clean, sharp scent of snow was so prevalent in the air that it even drilled through the lavender-fruit smell of Belius' cologne. He had not worn the overcoat, the suit jacket being enough for him as long as the sun shone. He wanted anyone who passed him on the road to note how well dressed he was. The camel's hair wrap was rolled up and stored in the back of the wagon with the books he was returning to the doctor.

As the wagon moved slowly along the road, passing barren fields dotted with patches of unmelted snow from the last winter storm, Belius tried to think of the concepts he intended to discuss with Grey. He'd been making notes for a Cosmology, reading the great philosophers and scientists and poets, trying to boil down the workings of the universe so they might be presented in the form of metaphor—a scientific/philosophic/epic that would encompass all thought and emotion, that when read would center the spirit of Belius in the souls and minds of his readers. Even while he worked on the farm, planets and stars, great black distances peopled with characters called Gravity and Entropy filled his head. His musings excited him and filled him with the joy of discovery. Youth blanked out any idea of failure, and, as much knowledge as he gained, he was still able to stay ignorant enough to think that he was capable of his task. The only other thoughts that he gave any time to at all dealt with Nona.

Through a slow process that began on his first stay at the doctor's house the previous winter, he had been able to prove to her that he was not the beast he appeared. At first, his only intention was to be friends with her. The sense of calm she inspired in him was like a drug that he knew he must have in increasing doses. On his early visits to Grey, in the weeks following his recovery, he would always make a point of chatting with her about incidentals, making sure not to push her into any weighty conversation that assumed any kind of bond between them. He found it difficult sometimes to know she was right there in the same house with him while he spent the entire day in the doctor's library.

Then one day, late in the afternoon, he was sitting in the red leather chair of the first library he had entered on his original visit, reading an interesting little monograph by Scarfinati, dealing with the mathematical concept of the golden section. He was lost to the ideas of the book, having settled down after a few hours of nothing but staring at the crowded shelves and day-dreaming conversations with Nona. The huge house was silent, which sunk him even deeper into the morass of print. The doctor was out on a house call, delivering Phil and Terri Miller's new child. It was a blustery spring day, and a light rain splashed softly against the outside of the one stained-glass window that interrupted the walls of books. For no reason, he broke off his reading in the middle of an engaging concept and looked up to see her standing in front of him with a tray holding two tea cups and a kettle.

"Am I bothering you?" she asked quietly.

He straightened up in the big chair and uncrossed his legs. At first he was dumb with surprise, but he soon regained his composure and was able to say, "Not at all. I was just going to take a break."

She stood there staring at him. Then he realized that there was no other seat in the library and jumped to his feet. What he had not realized was that his human leg had fallen asleep while he was reading. As he motioned for her to sit down and said, "Please," his unconscious leg buckled beneath him and he lunged forward. She made a graceful movement to the side as if the tray were a red cape and she a matador, turning to foil a charge. "Leg asleep," he yelled to let her know he was up to nothing untoward as he stumbled forward and fell, his horns goring, respectively, the bindings of Aristotle's Poetics and the Letters of Abelard and Heloise. The weight of his embarrassment prevented him from standing, so after he had disengaged himself from the classics, he merely crawled closer to the chair and took up a sitting position. His own stupidity had so dumbfounded him, he just stared at her, hoping she would not run away.

"Are you alright?" she asked as she leaned over and set the tray on the floor between them.

He meant to say yes, but instead he gave a short moo before his words could form.

Her eyes widened at his animal indiscretion, but, all the same, she sat down in the red leather chair and smoothed out the front of her skirt. As she leaned down to pour him a cup of tea, the top of her blouse opened and he couldn't help seeing her breasts. In moving to give him a spoonful of sugar and some cream, the view increased. He quickly turned his head to stare at the stained glass. "Rain," he said quickly, uncertain as to whether she had caught him peeking. "Yes," she said and handed him the cup and saucer.

For the following hour, the conversation came in fits and starts, well padded with many layers of thick silence. They spoke in simple sentences about the weather, Belius' farm, the doctor's most recent cases, how to prepare turnips and a few other things equally as interesting. For Belius though, her descriptions of how to pare a turnip seemed to carry the same philosophical import and excitement as the closing chapter of Scarfinati's autobiography. Only once did the conversation take a crucial turn. Belius happened to mention how helpful the doctor had been to him by letting him use the libraries.

"He likes it when you're here," Nona said. "He finds you very interesting. We both do. Perhaps in different ways."

Belius took a sip of tea, trying to think of a way to ask her to explain without seeming to make too much of her statement. Luckily it wasn't necessary for him to be shrewd. After a slight pause she continued.

"I'm amazed at how much time you can spend reading. You must have a marvelous mind, full of all kinds of wonderful ideas."

He snorted, the sound a little too close to the barnyard he thought and waved his hoof in the air as if to thank her. "Everyone has the same amount of ideas," he tried to explain. "It's just that they're different. One set of ideas is no better or worse than the other . . . as long as they are good ideas, of course. I mean as long as they are ideas about things that are good and are not too evil or uncaring or . . ." He could see in her eyes that he wasn't making much sense, so to cover his foolishness he laughed. "There's a few empty ideas for you."

She smiled but didn't laugh, and it was evident to him for the first time that, given her personality, it would not be right if she had. In that moment, it came to him that she was so very different from him. Life itself seemed to be enough for her, she didn't need a Cosmology or the thoughts of long dead thinkers creeping through her brain or to know the why of everything. When she looked at a tea cup, the picture was not distorted by the concepts of physics or the fact that the matter that formed it might have originated millennia past in the white hot turmoil of an exploding star. She was willing to drift without a center and accept the uncertainty without fear. As she gathered the cups and saucers onto the tray and stood up to leave, he couldn't take his eyes off her.

After that spring day in the library their friendship escalated through different stages, bringing them closer. Near the end of summer, she was making trips to see him during the day. At first it was under the pretense of bringing him some books that the doctor thought he might find interesting. She would stand out in the field with him as he worked, and they would talk. His mother was beside herself whenever Nona would stop in for lunch. The old woman never dreamed that anything even close to romance would ever be part of her son's life. What Belius' mother saw so clearly, Dr. Grey either ignored or was totally unaware of. When he talked to the minotaur, he never spoke of his niece. She was never invited by him to join in their conversations. Belius didn't insist on it, feeling in some ways relieved that the old man took no notice. In the presence of Grey, he sometimes felt guilty about his growing love.

Belius was shivering so hard by the time the old plough horse brought the wagon to a stop in the yard of the doctor's mansion that the hoof at the end of his beastly leg was doing an involuntary tap dance against the foot board. He had not passed one person on the road and was feeling somewhat disappointed, the long ride having taken some of the newness out of his suit. The pants were wrinkled and the left lapel of the jacket had been kept standing so long in the same position by the wind that it now refused to lie down as it was supposed to. As he unhitched the horse and put him in the barn, he tried unsuccessfully to keep one hoof over the lapel. Finally, he gave up on it.

He stood on the porch of the old boarding house, and the wind whipped by with a noise that sounded too much like the bickering of Austina and Plension. Grey answered the door after the second knock and ushered the minotaur in with a handshake and a pat on the back. The old man seemed in fine spirits, and it was obvious that he hadn't yet begun to drink for that day. Belius was pleased with this, not that it ever really bothered him if the doctor was a little under. Sometimes the alcohol would make the old man lose his train of thought right in the middle of a complicated conversation and send him off on an incomprehensible monologue. Being the dutiful student that Belius was, he could never interrupt. He would simply sit there for the duration of the dementia and nod as if he understood everything that was being said.

"What is that smell?" asked the doctor as he led Belius down the hallway to his office.

"Cologne," said Belius.

The old man turned around and reached up to tug on the minotaur's right horn. As Grey entered his office, Belius paused for a second and looked down the hallway over his shoulder to see if he could catch a glimpse of the physician's niece. She was nowhere to be seen. His spirits sank a little when he thought that he might come and go that day without her ever getting a look at him in his new clothes.

In the office, the doctor took a seat behind his desk and Belius pulled up a seat facing him. Whenever they had their discussions in the office, Belius could see that the doctor, when sitting in that chair, couldn't help but treat him somewhat like a patient. Belius would describe what it was he was presently reading and Grey would ask questions as if he were trying to diagnose some malady.

Always present at these discussions, like a third party who had as yet never had anything to add was the homunculus in the huge glass jar at the corner of the desk. Only when the doctor fell into one of his alcoholic rants, did Belius actually recognize how strange an ornament it was. Sometimes the minotaur would just happen to glance at it, and he could swear that he saw it move one of its delicate little fingers or blink an eyelid. Occasionally, when waking in the morning, he would have a vague sense that he had dreamed about the tiny being, but it was as if the dream was always too upsetting for his mind to allow him to take it with him into the waking day.

The topic of conversation that afternoon was an idea that

Belius had dreamed up concerning the natural force of gravity. He was trying to establish some relationship between the attraction of objects in the solar system and the attraction of love between people. Grey admitted he couldn't quite see the analogy. Belius tried to be more specific. The doctor stepped up his side of the argument and, in no time, they were off, soaring into the stratosphere of half-baked ideas. As they sat in the office, lost to the perturbations of a metaphorical cosmos, the blue sky outside the house turned dark with clouds and snow swept down across the valley.

Hours later, there was a knock at the door and Nona's voice called out, "Uncle, it's a blizzard outside." Only now did they hear the wind moaning and the patter of snow against the side of the house.

"Oh, my," said Grey, getting up and moving to the window. "There must be a few feet already."

Belius' mind was on other things than the weather. He straightened up in his chair and pressed down his errant lapel, hoping that Nona would come through the door. She didn't enter, though, and eventually he heard her footsteps moving away down the hall.

"You'd better stay the night, Belius," said the doctor. "I'll have Nona make up a room for you."

"Is it that bad?" asked the minotaur.

"If you go out in this, we won't find you till the spring thaw," said Grey. "Relax, stay the night and leave first thing in the morning when it's over." He moved back to his desk and took a seat. Bending down, he heaved a great sigh and reached into a bottom draw of the desk for his bottle and glass. As he set them up on the desk, he said, "That's enough talk for today. I'm afraid I'm talked out. Why don't you go and have something to eat and then go upstairs and read."

Belius watched as the doctor poured a whiskey and took his first sip. The leathery skin of his cheeks puckered and his eyes shut tight. The gulp of liquor moved down the old man's scrawny throat as if it were a hard-boiled egg. Then, with an audible smacking of the lips, his face unclenched. When the lids of the eyes lifted, Belius could immediately discern the sadness in them.

Grey shook his head and shrugged his shoulders.

"Goodnight," Belius said. "I'll see you in the morning before I leave."

The doctor nodded his head and poured another. "Don't forget to put that rock in your collar tonight. We don't want to wake up with the snow in our faces tomorrow morning," he said as if at the end of a consultation he were prescribing treatment. "The physical attraction of heavenly bodies seen as love," he said as Belius moved toward the door. "You're a hopeless Romantic." He gave a curt laugh and then turned his attention to the glass of amber.

While munching on a celery stalk in the kitchen, the minotaur mulled over the doctor's diagnosis of his aesthetic. In the light of his conviction toward what he was trying to accomplish with his Cosmology, he could not see the epitaph as anything other than a compliment. He continued eating, putting down cold ears of corn left over from some previous dinner, apples and a half a loaf of bread, and decided that he would not worry about Nona that night, seeing as she had not gone out of her way to talk with him. He made plans to find some immense epic poem full of heroes and battles and settle down in the red leather chair to read until his eyes played their usual trick of fatigue—a column of smoke rising out of the yet unturned pages of his book.

Hours died and were carted away into the past while Belius followed the shipmates of the Argo on their search for the Golden Fleece. Wrapped in the solitude of this distant dream, he only thought of her once. As Jason wrestled with the soldiers sprung from dragon's teeth, the minotaur changed his position in the chair and looked up, wishing that he would see Nona there. She wasn't, and he focused for a second on the two books he had gored on that spring day when she had brought him tea. Another fifty pages later, he closed the book and left the study.

What it was that had awakened him, he had no idea, but suddenly he found himself wide awake. The room was cold and the snow could still be heard blowing against the window. He sat up in the bed and listened. There was the occasional groaning of old timbers and the pop of floor boards realigning themselves. The wind complained outside and some small creature scampered across the roof. All of these noises instantly became components of a great silence when he heard the tread of footsteps in the hallway. They came stealthily, stopping every now and then. They drew nearer and nearer to his room and then, just outside the door, halted. He listened more intently and could barely discern the sound of breathing. Minutes passed and, when he could no longer stand the tension his muscles were suffering from his rigid expectation, he whispered, "Hello?"

As soon as the word was out of his mouth, the door opened, someone entered and then it was shut quickly; the only sound, the clicking of the latch.

"Doctor?" he whispered.

"Shhhhh," came the reply, and he knew immediately that it was Nona. A surge of warmth emanated from his solar plexus and moved out in all directions through his body. A slight buzzing filled his head, and, for the first time since waking, he wondered if he were not really still asleep. It was only when he felt the weight of her body press down on the mattress next to him and smelled the telltale hint of lemon from her hair that he was certain it was not a phantom.

His mouth was dry but he finally managed to swallow. "Nona?"

"Shhhh," she cautioned and at the same time placed her open palm flat against his chest. His heart slammed as if trying to break through the skin and fill her grasp. With a gentle nudge she pushed him down onto his back. She stood up and pulled back the covers and climbed into the bed. Her body shivered next to his and he knew without touching her that she wore nothing. He enveloped her in his huge arms. As they lay silent and still his warmth was transferred to her, and he adopted the rhythm of her breathing. After some time, she turned to face him and kissed him just below his left eye. Because of the awkward nature of his snout, he couldn't return the kiss, so instead he stuck out his tongue and licked her shoulder. He ran his hoof across her breasts as she scratched the hide of his beastly leg.

When she mounted him, she quietly gasped. He lowed, but with his mouth shut so the sound stayed within his chest. She began to move and then reached up and grabbed his horns for leverage. The bed creaked and the headboard lightly tapped the wall behind it. As their combined motion became more violent, Belius' mouth would slip open and release a particle of his imprisoned voice. "Shhh," she said, and then sounded off louder than he had. In the middle of their love making, she stopped suddenly.

"What is it?" he asked.

"I thought I heard footsteps," she whispered.

They lay locked together, frozen, listening until neither of them could stand it and they had to continue.

After they had finished, and Nona again lay at his side, Belius didn't know what to say, so he said, "Thank you."

"I love you, Belius," she whispered into his pointed ear.

"How can you?" he asked.

"At first, you frightened me, but I've come to see how gentle you really are."

"Is my being gentle enough for you to love me?"

"Yes."

"I'm so ugly, though," he said.

"It's been a long time since I've thought of ugliness as a matter of looks. I've known real ugliness in my life, and many times it's come from the people with the smoothest faces and most beautiful eyes."

There was silence for a time. They both listened to the storm outside. It was Belius who finally interrupted the quiet. "Can I ask you something?" he said.

"You want to know why I live with my uncle?"

"Yes," he murmured. "I want to know everything."

"Well, I know quite a lot about you from talking to your mother, so I suppose it's only fair. When I tell you, though, you've got to promise me one thing."

"Anything."

"You have to promise that you won't feel badly for me."

"I hate pity," said Belius.

"I know," she said. A few moments passed and then she began, her words coming with the same complacency with which she did everything but make love. "When I was younger, I lived with my parents. My mother is the doctor's sister. Like you, I had keen interests in many things. Life was very powerful. A few weeks after my sixteenth birthday, while my mother was away visiting friends, my father forced himself on me. I had no warning. I was frightened and confused, but when I tried to get away from him, he slapped my face with the back of his hand and I lost consciousness. When I woke up, I was lying on the floor, my dress torn, my blood all over me. He was standing over me, tightening his belt. He warned me, 'If you say anything to your mother, I'll kill you both.'

"I never said a word, but a few months later it became obvious that I was pregnant. I tried to hide it as long as I could, but my mother finally noticed. She was hysterical. She asked me who had done it. My father was right there, shaking his head as if he was completely disappointed in me. My mother wanted to throw me out of the house, but my father told her, 'We all make mistakes, dear. Maybe we can send her to your brother for a cure.' She agreed and I came to stay with the doctor.

"On the second day I was here, he performed the operation. He gave me a shot and made me breathe gas to knock me out. I really had no idea what was happening. When I realized what the operation meant, I was furious at first, but he had always been so kind to me that, as hard as I tried, I couldn't hate him for it. It was almost an act of love. The thing I truly despise him for, though, is having kept my child in that jar on the desk in his office. When he drinks too much, he stares at it and uses it to focus all of his sadness on and it makes it easy for him to cry. He wants the world to be perfect. He doesn't want anyone to suffer except himself. It's hard to imagine such selfishness."

Belius wanted to say something to her, but his animal nature told him to be quiet. He concentrated on trying not to cry and was almost successful, but for two large tears that formed, one in each eye. If he moved his arm to brush them away, she would surely know that he was crying. She lay perfectly still as if exhausted from the telling of her tale. Just as he was about to apologize for having broken his promise, he realized that she had fallen asleep.

As she slept next to him, he remained awake, thinking about the story she had told him. Now that he knew her, he felt as if he also knew himself for the first time. He was no longer half man and half bull, he was a minotaur—a separate entity unto himself. These thoughts circled like a whirlpool in his head until their dizzying action, along with the warmth of Nona's body and the hushed violence of the storm, made him tired. He began to doze off to sleep, his head nodding down beneath the weight of his horns. Just before passing into the realm of dreams, where his father was waiting with the knot, he thought he heard footsteps moving down the hall away from his door.

The next morning, at the kitchen table, Belius searched the old man's face for signs that he might actually have been outside the room during the night. The doctor gave no indication, but was full of jokes and word games and closets full of laughter. It was a beautiful day out; the warm sun already at work on the snow. Belius decided to leave the wagon, doubting it could make it back through the high drifts. He promised to return for the horse and rig in a few days.

After they had all finished eating, the doctor got up to adjourn to his office where soon his patients would be showing up. He wished Belius a safe trip home and promised to look after the plough horse for the next few days. Nona walked the minotaur to the front door. When they were certain that Grey was nowhere nearby, they put their arms around each other. She kissed him on the throat and then pushed him toward the door. He stepped out into the beautiful day, shading his eyes against the reflection of the sun off the snow. As he made his way down the road, his wingtip offering little protection against the icy slush, wearing nothing over his shoulders save the double breasted suit jacket, he was warm inside. For the entire journey, he threw himself into the task of learning how to whistle.

It was during the first of the spring thaw that Nona came to his farm with the news. In their meetings between their night together and now, they had slowly been working up the courage to announce that they would marry. They had decided to wait until the first day of spring. The message that Nona brought with her this day, though, immediately displaced the importance of their decision.

She told Belius, in breathless bursts, that the doctor had said he was long aware of their love for each other and that, when he first discovered it, he had written to a famous medical specialist across the ocean, whom, he had read, was doing some marvelous experiments with anomalies of birth. This famous doctor had created a chemical mixture that, when taken only once, would react upon the physical makeup of the patient, causing the distorted body to achieve the human look it might have had had nothing gone wrong while the fetus was forming. For a nominal fee, the specialist had sent Grey a bottle of the potion. It sat in the cabinet of his office, back at the enormous house, awaiting Belius' decision.

Upon his hearing the news, the pitchfork that Belius was holding slipped out of his hooves and fell to the ground. He cocked his head to the side and stared into Nona's eyes to search for a hint that she might be playing some odd joke on him. She knew what he was about and adamantly shook her head to show that she was in earnest.

"I can hardly believe it," said Belius, forcing a laugh.

"Neither can I," she said, reaching out to touch his arm.

"Is it guaranteed to work?" he asked.

She shrugged her shoulders.

"This is impossible," he finally said and turned his back on her to stare out into the fields.

"What is it, Belius? I thought you'd be happy."

He didn't answer for quite a while but lifted his right hoof up and ran it along the horn on that side of his head. Finally, he asked, "Are you sure this was your uncle's message?"

"Yes," she answered.

"I would have hands," he murmured.

"I could kiss your mouth," she said.

He turned around to face her. "Do you think I would be . . . handsome?"

"Belius, I don't care. I'm willing to marry you as you are. I just thought it would be something for you. It's your decision. It might make your life easier, but then you might change in some ways. I don't know."

"It sounds like a fairy tale," he said. "I can't help it, it sounds too easy."

"Well, my uncle said that this specialist is world renowned and that he has helped thousands of people to be . . ."

"To be what?"

"I suppose I was going to say 'normal.'"

"I need time to think," he said.

"I know you do."

"Tomorrow, I'll come to your house. I'll make a decision tonight. I know I should be ecstatic, but I'm scared."

She moved toward him to put her arms around his wide chest, but he warded her off with his hooves. "Please," he said, "please go. I'm thinking already. I promise I'll come tomorrow." Then he turned his back on her again. He could hear her moving toward the barn where her carriage and horse stood waiting.

Some yards away, she stopped and called back, "Remember, think of yourself."

That afternoon, he did a week's worth of work around the farm. He fixed things that he had already decided to throw out, and, once they were fixed, threw them on the junk heap anyway. He ploughed a good portion of a field that was still too frozen to plough and only stopped because the horse finally reprimanded him for his stupidity. He kept himself desperately busy until the sun went down, the whole time making only one minor decision, and that, to not mention the doctor's message to his mother, whom he knew might go crazy at the very thought of the possibility.

He ate little and spoke less at dinner. His mother inquired if he was sick. "No," he told her, "I'm thinking."

"I saw Nona here today. Did you have a quarrel?"

"No."

"Well, don't worry too much about it. Just drive out there tomorrow and see her. It'll all be fine," said the old woman as she piled more potatoes on his plate.

After moving the potatoes around with his fork for a few minutes, he excused himself and went to his room. A book on Norse mythology lay open on his desk. He sat down and tried to read from it. The words refused to register. For two hours, he sat scanning the lines, saying each phrase quietly to himself, but, when the book was finished, he could remember nothing. "Think of yourself," he repeated as he sat there, his huge head supported by his hooves. It came to him that he had done nothing else for his entire life. Only in the past few months had he grown to like the idea of being a minotaur. It had been such hard work getting to that point, and now, with the doctor's offer, all of his struggle was made insignificant.

He left his desk and went to the mirror that hung on the wall near his bed. Looking at it, he tried to imagine his snout disintegrating into a human mouth. "Where will all of it go?" he wondered. Then his pointed ears shrank to two pink half-circles. His eyes lost their roundness and moved closer to each other in the middle of a face that was forming a chin and cheeks of flesh. The bushy crop of fur between his horns stretched into a slick wave of long stranded hair, and, as an afterthought, he dreamed a mustache and sideburns. The only feature of his anatomy that he could not bring the illusion of change to was his horns. They remained two curved and pointed bones, jutting out from just beside the temples.

"No horns," he thought. The pleasant sensation of goring a tree would be gone forever. Plension and Austina would speak to him and he wouldn't understand. The crops and garden vegetables would no longer tell him what they needed. He'd lose half his enormous strength and probably be a foot shorter. There would be no need for the Cosmology. There would be no race of minotaurs. He pulled himself away from the mirror.

It was well past midnight. Belius stood still as a tree stump in the stand of pines out past the corn field and pasture. It was still cool, so he wore the overcoat, but the fresh, green smell of spring was on the breeze. He stared up past the points of the trees, into the night sky. The moon was a sharp crescent and the stars were brilliant. When he breathed out, steam would obscure his view of the heavens. He had been there for an hour, watching the same small patch of sky. Each dot of white fire had burned its image into his memory. There were as many stars as there were reasons for him not to take the doctor's potion. Then, while he was staring, one of the dots of light in the cluster he had been watching, suddenly went out. There was no fiery explosion, not even so much as a hushed pop, no tremor in the earth. It was there and then it wasn't. He cleared his eyes, only to find that what he thought he had seen had really happened. For the first time that day, he stopped thinking of himself and thought, instead, of Nona. He thought of the future—of marriage and children. He thought of the sacrifice his family would have to make for him.

His decision was finalized before he reached the sleeping cornfield. Before going in to bed though, he stopped at the barn, thinking the cows might still be awake. He hoped they would ridicule him in their usual way, and he promised himself that if they did, he would laugh along with them and scratch them behind the ears.

A little after noon, Belius' wagon pulled up in the yard outside the doctor's house. He unhitched the plough horse and decided to let him roam around the property instead of putting him in the barn. "Don't eat anything you shouldn't," Belius warned the horse with a few low grunts.

"Same to you," said the horse. Belius had told him and the cows everything during the night. Plension and Austina advised him to make the change. They told him it was the only "human" thing to do. He said good-bye to them and thanked them, promising always to be kind to them in the future, when he could no longer understand what they were saying. The horse was in total disagreement, saying he had never heard of anything so unnatural in his life. He had been overruled, though, and finally gave in and wished the minotaur a happy, hornless life.

Before he could even knock, Nona was pulling back the door at the front of the old house. "Belius," she said, full of excitement. This time, he let her put her arms around him and he returned the hug. When they separated, she asked, "What have you decided?"

Belius looked past her to where he saw the shadowy figure of Grey, standing just out of the light let in through the open door. The girl didn't know her uncle was there, but when the minotaur spoke, he knew he was answering both of them. "I've decided to try it," he said.

"Are you sure?" she asked, as if she had truly believed the answer would be different.

He nodded and, as she hugged him again, he saw Grey also nodding. He rested his snout on the top of her head for a moment. When he looked up, the doctor was gone. Nona moved away and closed the door.

"I have to tell you, Belius, I spent all night thinking about this. I was almost hoping that your answer would be different," she said.

"I didn't sleep much, myself," he said. "But I thought about us, not just me, and that finally made me decide."

"You're positive?" she asked.

"Don't ask again," he said, forcing a laugh.

The three of them sat around the kitchen table, staring at the brown, cork-stoppered bottle that rested exactly in the middle of the triangle they formed. The doctor wore his stethoscope and his black bag was nearby at his feet in case of, as he said, "Any emergencies."

"What do you mean, emergencies?" asked Nona. "Isn't this safe?"

"It's as safe as any operation or treatment," said the doctor. "Belius," he said, turning to face the minotaur, "you know that nothing is totally foolproof when dealing with the reaction of a living organism to exotic chemicals. You do understand this, don't you?"

"It's too late for me to worry," said Belius. "I've made my decision."

"Well, what could happen?" asked Nona.

"An allergic reaction . . . too great an excitement of the heart . . . a few things. But the chances are slim. I'm not trying to scare you, son," the doctor said and patted Belius on the arm.

Belius shook his head. "Let's get on with it," he said.

"In a moment," said the doctor, who got up and moved over to the counter where his bottle of whiskey and a glass stood waiting. He poured himself a drink. As he brought the glass to his lips, Belius noticed the old man's hand shaking.

"Are you nervous?" Belius asked.

"No, no, just excited for the two of you." He dashed off the drink and poured another.

"What's this made of?" asked Nona.

"Please, my dear," Grey croaked in between gulps, "I'm nothing but a country doctor. I can't know everything. This cure was prepared by a man so much my superior in intelligence, I couldn't begin to guess. It was made to deal specifically with Belius' problem."

"Bring me a glass, doctor," Belius pleaded, "I don't think I can drink too well from this bottle."

"What would happen if someone else were to drink it?" asked Nona. "Would they die?"

"No, I've already told you it's safe," said the doctor, reaching for a glass in the cabinet. "The eminent specialist . . . Dr. Rodondo, theorizes that a healthy person would take on the characteristics of whatever unfortunate the elixir was intended for."

Grey set the glass for Belius down next to his own and poured himself one more drink. It wasn't so much what he said, but more Grey's faltering voice and trembling hands that told the minotaur, in the animal regions of his being, that the old man was lying. At just this time, he happened to look down at the floor and saw, peeking out of the doctor's opened black bag, the handle of the revolver that had killed so many dogs two winters past.

Belius pushed back his seat and stood up. "What's in the bottle, Dr. Grey?" he asked. The old man's eyes widened and his drink fell from his hand. "No!" he cried and lunged forward. Belius caught him with one arm and threw him back against the counter. It was only after this that Belius realized the old man's cry was not as a result of his being found out. The minotaur turned quickly to see Nona finishing the last of the dark liquid. Before she could even set the bottle on the table, a vicious tremor shot through her body. As the bottle dropped from her grasp and rolled along the table, her eyes turned upward, showing white. She coughed as though she were drowning and blood came from her mouth. The bottle tipped off the table and smashed into a hundred brown shards on the floor. Belius shook off his horror and made it to her side as she was clutching with her hands at the lace collar of her dress. He caught her as she slumped toward the floor. Her body erupted in a fit of spasms that lasted but a minute and then passed.

"She's dead," he screamed in a voice somewhere between

creature and human. "Nona, Nona," he yelled and shook her. "She's dead." He let her body slip gently to the floor. When he turned to face Grey, the old man had the revolver in his hand.

"Poison," the doctor said as he backed up against the wall. His voice was distant and his gaze clouded. "I did it for both of you. It could never have worked between you. It was an atrocity. It would only have been suffering for you both. You were never meant to live. Nona would have borne your horrid children. I should never have let you live. It pained me to think that I made you live in this world where you would never belong. I take it back now, Belius. I take back your suffering." His hand wobbled as he pointed the gun at the minotaur's heart.

"You fool," Belius bellowed. Then his words turned into a raspy squeal and Grey couldn't understand that the sounds were telling him to shoot. "Shoot me. Kill me," Belius roared and pounded the flesh of his chest with both hooves. The old man closed his eyes and began to cry. Upon seeing this, an explosion of red filled Belius' mind, blanking out both feeling and vision. He charged and his horns broke through the bone of Grey's chest and out his back to bury themselves in the plaster of the wall behind him. The crockery on the shelves above them crashed down on the old man's head, pushing him further onto the points until his belly was pressed against Belius' snout. Grey's screams seemed to Belius to be coming from somewhere in one of the libraries upstairs. He didn't feel the old man's hands pushing against the base of his horns. He reared back, lifting the frail body off its feet and then pounded into the wall again.

He cleaned the blood from his eyes with the hem of Nona's dress. Working methodically, he loaded into the wagon every-thing he thought might be of use to him in his refuge. As soon as he had sloughed the weight of the doctor's body and let it hit the floor, he quit his snorting and cursing and realized that he would have to run. "I'll be blamed for both of these deaths," he told himself aloud, standing amidst the bodies, broken glass and china that littered the kitchen floor. In this instant, he desperately wished that he was capable of using the gun. He left it, though, and looted only armloads of books from the libraries upstairs, a telescope, a phonograph, some records and a few loaves of bread from the pantry. There was no time to bury Nona. The first patient that came by to see the doctor would discover the bodies and, after seeing the two gaping holes in his chest, know exactly who the assailant had been. He shook and cried uncontrollably as he went about his work.

As he hitched the plough horse to the wagon, he said to him, "I know you aren't used to running. I've never asked you to in the past, but now, to save my life, you've got to." The horse saw the blood and the wild look in Belius' eyes. He asked no questions, but, once the bit was in his mouth, took the weight of the loaded wagon to his shoulders and pulled with everything he had. Just when it looked as if he were not capable of anything more than a stroll, he somehow overcame the tug of gravity and they were flying down the road at a reckless pace. Froth flew from the horse's mouth, clouds of dust were born from his hooves. They took one bend on two wheels and a pile of books, all about the classification of dinosaurs, spilled onto the road.

Whereas Belius had seen no one the day he wore his new set of clothes, this day the careening wagon passed three other rigs, all going in the opposite direction so that their drivers got a good look at the grim figure of the bloody minotaur. Each of the drivers yelled out for Belius to stop, thinking, at first, that he might be hurt. As he passed each of them, he lowed in such a mournful way and with such force that the animals that drew their masters home from market stopped dead in their tracks.

By the time the wagon rolled into the barnyard of his farm, there was no question in his mind that someone was just then turning over the doctor's body and sticking their fingers into the two neat holes. He leaped off of the wagon seat and went directly to the barn, hoping his mother hadn't seen him from the kitchen window. In five minutes he had apprized the two cows of the entire situation. They stamped in their stalls as they listened.

When he finished with the horror that he, himself, had a hard time comprehending, he had only one question. "How do I get to the Wider World?"

There was silence for a moment.

"Tell him, Austina," Plension lowed. "They'll surely kill him if you don't."

"Let me think for a second, damn it. I have to remember myself."

"You said that it was all around," Belius prompted.

"Yes, yes," said the cow. "All right, yes, I remember. You can take the path that leads through the woods out beyond the pastures. As soon as it is dusk, take to that path and start running. You've got to forget about being part human and run only as an animal would. Don't stop. If you stop, you'll never make it. You must start at sundown and run all night, run until you fall asleep running. That's the key, to keep running even when you've fallen asleep. If you can do this and then begin to dream while you are moving, you will make it to the Wider World. It's extremely difficult, but I believe you can do it. Now go, it's only a short time before the sun disappears."

He didn't thank them or say good-bye. As he left the barn, he took with him the wheelbarrow. Once outside, he noticed that the sun had fallen below the level of the treetops. He moved over to the wagon, to which the horse was still hitched, snorting and rasping from his recent effort, and took all of his plunder and put it into the wheelbarrow. After finishing with this he was out of breath but didn't stop to rest. He walked toward the house, bracing himself for his mother's hysterical inquisition.

She wasn't in the kitchen, watching him as he had assumed. He moved quietly down the hallway to his bedroom. In one giant armful, he gathered all of his clothes and those books most important to the completion of his Cosmology. He took his father's pipe, which he had kept in the top drawer of his writing desk, and the three boxes of embossed paper that Nona had given him as a present at the start of winter.

Unable to see where he was going, he stumbled down the hallway, back toward the kitchen. He knew his mother must be napping in the parlor as she was sometimes wont to do before dinner time. There was no way that he could fully explain to her what had happened in the short time before the sun set. He thought about writing her a note, but he didn't feel capable just then of lifting a pen and thinking hard enough to make everything come out clearly. He told himself that she would be better off knowing nothing when they came to look for him.

As he left the house, his arms were so full he couldn't keep the kitchen door from banging shut. He ran to where the wheelbarrow was sitting and dumped his belongings into it. The pile of books and clothes jutted up out of the carrier, looking as if someone were trying to relocate a small mountain. From inside the house, he heard his mother call his name three times. He lifted the handles of the wheelbarrow, the fulcrum effect lightening the load considerably, and started off across the field. The plough horse whinnied a message after him. "Think nothing, Belius. Let your legs be brilliant." The minotaur ran with all his strength toward the forest beyond the pasture and the path that struck a bull's-eye in the face of the setting sun.

🐾 🐾 🐾

When Belius awakened from the daze of his reminiscence, he found himself slightly crouched, his horns deeply imbedded in the coral wall of his study, the screams of Dr. Grey disappearing into the haze that remained from the last bowl he'd smoked. Sweat glistened from every pore of his flesh and hide, carrying with it, as it ran in rivulets down his body, the aroma of the four bottles of dandelion wine he'd quickly consumed after Pezimote's farewell. Satisfied that he was no longer in the past, he pulled back and, creating a sound of swords being drawn slowly across a whetstone, disengaged his horns.

Although his blood count had had a short time to recoup its recent drastic losses, he was still as giddy as a bee on a blue gardenia. Mingling with this hysteria were the effects of the wine and smoke, all of it combining to send him over the brink into insanity. He pirouetted through the study with a drunken grace that prevented him from knocking anything over and finally landed him in his chair.

"Nicely done," he whispered to himself, and, when he realized that there was no one in the room, he repeated the compliment, this time shouting it. "Lovely day, Belius," he said, at a more normal decibel. "A perfect day for a swim to the barrier reef, or a stroll through the mango grove, or to invent something . . . Yes, yes, I'll invent something, something that it is beyond my power to invent. What will it be? What . . . ?" He sat thinking for a second and that was all it took for him to lose track of the idea that had set him thinking.

He stood up and walked in circles around the chair a few times, each circuit containing at least one mishap, during which he would have to contort his body to keep from falling. "The Wider World has increased its rotational speed while I was dozing," he said with a smile to the bust of himself which Siftus had chiseled. He broke the stumbling cycle to walk over and pat the statuette on the head between the horns. Then he lifted the thing very carefully from its place atop the bookshelf, walked over to the window and pitched it out. Upon hearing it shatter against the cobblestone walk below, he heaved a sigh and giggled. "A damn shame! No doubt . . ." he mumbled and then turned back to the room to size up the globe and see if it would also fit through the opening. As his hooves clasped the Wider World at its tropical poles, he heard a familiar voice behind him.

"Belius, what are you doing?" Vashti inquired as she came to perch on the window sill.

The minotaur spun around from his task. "Vashti," he said, matter-of-factly, "glad you could stop in. I'm just tidying up a bit. I've been out of sorts for some time, and, now that I'm better, I thought I'd catch up on some housekeeping."

"It'll have to wait," said the owl. "You've got to go and change your clothes, I'm bringing a very special guest to meet you in a few minutes."

"Who?"

"A very charming female of your species."

"A woman?" he asked, sticking out his tongue to its full length.

"Don't be a fool. I'm speaking about a minotaur."

"A minotaur," he yelled. ". . . Very well."

"Go and get changed and set up a table and two chairs on the turret. Bring up some wine—and make it something other than dandelion. I think this will be a special occasion, if you know what I mean."

"What do you mean?" asked Belius, just then becoming entranced by the tips of his hooves.

"Never mind. I'll meet you on the tower, with your guest, in a few minutes."

"Vashti, wait," Belius cried before the owl could take off.

"Yes?"

"Pezimote is gone. I think he's gone forever."

"He'll be back to see you soon," she said.

"Very good," he said and dashed out of the study and up the spiral stairs to his bedroom.

Soffea only fell twice on her climb to the turret of the tower. The first time was as a result of her clumsiness with the newly acquired condition called "life." The second was because Obadai and Mez, who were supposed to be helping her as a payment to everyone whose debt they were in from betting against her birth, were so tickled by the first fall that they tripped her up. Each time, she got to her hoof and human foot, head bobbing from side to side, eyes wild but no more so than usual, her tongue blah-blahing like a runaway stone rolling down a mountain. After the raccoon brothers had the last of their fun with her, carving their initials with their claws in the soft clay of her backside, they let her toga fall into place and led her the rest of the way to the turret. It was the plan that they should not be seen, so as soon as she stepped out into the daylight, they scampered back down the spiral stairs.

Vashti was waiting on the turret with Belius, who was now pacing nervously, dressed in a candy-striped blazer, flannel shirt and boxer shorts. His mind still wobbled with the spin of a broken gyroscope: crazy thoughts being born and then leaping out his ears to vanish in the breeze. When Soffea stepped into view, though, he stopped his pacing and stood as if in awe. To Vashti, who perched near him on the facade, he whispered, "She's more lovely than you described."

He didn't wait for the owl to introduce him, but rushed over to the clay ingénue and took her hoof in his. "I'm Belius," he said. "And you must be Soffea. That's a lovely name. It reminds me of incense and soft water."

"Blah, blah, blah," Soffea said in greeting.

Because of the state Belius was in, the fact that she spoke no actual words didn't register with him. She moved her mouth and tongue and sound came out and these sounds were transformed in his feverish brain into phrases that he wished, from the instant he had laid eyes upon her, she would say.

"Nonsense," he told her, "Belius is not near as special a name as yours. You really need not flatter me, seeing that we're both minotaurs. We're already fast friends. Don't you agree?"

"Blah."

"Very good then. Won't you come over and have a seat and join me in a glass of wine?" He led her by the hoof to a chair and held the back for her as she missed the mark and sprawled on the cobblestones. Vashti cringed at the sight of the accident, but, when Belius had lifted his date into the chair and taken his own seat, she knew there was no more she could do. Without bidding the couple good-bye, she spread her wings and flew off toward the forest.

"Will you have some wine, Soffea?" Belius asked, already in the act of pouring her a glass. He looked up to see if there was any protest, and, when there was no reply, he interpreted the constant bobbing of her head to be an answer in the affirmative. "This is my best wine, I brew it from corn that I grow in my garden. It fizzes like the yellow sky." He handed her the glass. She took it, miraculously without spilling a drop, and blathered her thanks to him.

"Drink up. A toast to the Wider World . . . no, better yet, a toast to your eyes, which are each a planet of lovely . . . er . . . uh . . . yes." He tossed back the entire glass he had poured himself with enough gusto to crack a diamond.

Soffea watched her host and then attempted the same feat, but since her aim was not what his was, even in his multiple intoxications, she only managed to drench her face with it.

"You're quite the little pagan, aren't you?" he asked with a laugh, while pouring himself another glass and using it to follow her lead. Now that they were both drenched, he filled their glasses and then settled back in his seat, crossing his legs, to begin what he had decided would be a conversation with a philosophical bent. It was his plan to see if her mind was as promising as her figure. "And what do you think of Cosmology?" he asked.

She didn't answer directly, but had noticed him crossing his legs and was trying to mimic the act. In her attempts, which were never to be successful, she managed only to hook her human foot under the table between them and send it over on its side. "Blah, blah, blah, blah, blah," she expounded.

"Quite right, why should we have physical barriers separating us while we communicate," he said, delighted.

She gave him another mouthful.

"And do you think that an exploding star is actually hotter than an active volcano, or do you believe, as I do, that the light of stars is a cool brightness?"

She agreed with him and then went even further to draw an analogy between the light of stars and the smell of a dog's breath.

"Very perceptive," he admitted when she was done.

The afternoon on the turret went well. Conversation flourished and good will abounded between male and female. Belius drank the better portion of the bottle of wine, and Soffea, who was more demure, tippled daintily at her glass, dribbling most of it down the front of her blue toga. As the evening came on, the wine she had spilled had soaked the old tablecloth she wore to the point where Belius could discern the outline of her sculpted breasts. This, along with the overall beauty he had perceived in her and her keen wit and intelligence, made his member stir and grow to where it was barely hidden by the hem of the right leg of his boxer shorts.

When his passion had reached a critical level, he manipulated the conversation around to the point where he could suggest a tour of the inside of the tower. The last stop, if everything went as he planned, would be the bedroom. She hesitated at the suggestion but then coyly accepted.

In the study, he showed her his maps and books and she was so taken in by the obvious extent of his knowledge that she lost her balance and fell into a bookcase, bringing the whole set of shelves and all their contents to the floor with her. In the kitchen, she managed to stab herself in the thigh with a paring knife, which gave Belius the opportunity to lick the wound. When she thanked him profusely with a torrent of burbling, he knew his scheme of sex had a chance. In the wine cellar, while Bonita watched from a dark corner, Belius explained the process of making wine from dandelions as he gently rubbed her back.

The tour through the confines of the tower brought the couple into close contact time and again, firing Belius' eloquence in a direct ratio to the increase of his desire. It also, because of the warmer climate of the indoors, began to dry the clay that held Soffea together. The first thing to fall off of her was the horn that Siftus had had to refit that afternoon. When it dropped off, Belius was aghast, but, when he saw that she took no notice of it and that it didn't seem to give her any pain, he laughed it off by saying, "Why have two horns when one will do as well?" A little later, though, when her hair began to float away from her mane and she spat out a few teeth, he decided that he must get her to the bedroom before she fell apart completely.

"The master bedroom," Belius said as he swept open the door. She hobbled inside, her wooden hoof beginning to come loose. When she turned her back on him to look around, he slyly closed the door and reached over to lower the flame of the gas lamp that burned brightly on the wall. With the light gone, the leaf from the blabbering tree that was her tongue finally went silent. She turned to face him. They stared into each other's eyes. Her constant motion became subdued and the new calmness was erotic to him.

"You're beautiful, Soffea."

She remained silent, staring.

"Your eyes make me think that I have always known you. As a matter of fact . . ." He craned his neck toward her and peered through the soft shadow. A vague sense of recognition rolled through his skittering mind. ". . . Have I ever met your eyes before? I mean, haven't we met before?" The shock of the familiarity of her eyes disintegrated as his attention was drawn back to her breasts and legs and hips.

"What I've been trying to say, is that I love you."

As the words left his mouth, his passion reached a crescendo and the heat emanating from his body wafted over her, drying her already cracking clay even more. The loose hoof gave way and she stumbled backward, landing on the bed with her legs spread wide in the air and her toga thrown back. He needed no verbal invitation. In seconds he had shed his jacket and shirt and shorts. His member pulsed. He lowered his head and charged, giving a great squeal as he leaped into the air. With an aim that could not be blurred by intoxicants or lack of blood, he came down on her with his full weight. She exploded beneath him, body parts flying out the window and rolling under the bed. The dry clay disintegrated into dust and released her life—the smoke-cloud spirit of The Cosmology of the Wider World. As the stream of fluid that carried in it the potential heirs of the race of mino-taurs left his body, its sudden absence created a great vacuum inside of him. He gasped with the power of an enormous whirlpool sucking down oceans. With this intake of air, the cloud that had once been his book, reentered him, filling his heart and his head with peace.

Instantly, he fell into a deep sleep that assured him in every cell of his body that he would once again write and that his gar-den would flourish and that his friends would join him in his study at night, as they always had, to smoke a bowl of the digi-talis and speak of things they knew and things they didn't. In this sleep he had a strange dream of a giant worm, lying miles long near a burning crater beneath the sea, chewing and chewing his overcoat as if it were a cud of grass.